(007)

# Solo

# 007
# Solo

*A James Bond Novel*

# William Boyd

HARPER LUXE

*An Imprint of HarperCollinsPublishers*

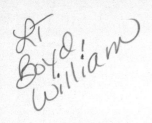

First published in Great Britain in 2013 by Jonathan Cape, a division of Random House.

FIRST HARPERLUXE EDITION

HarperLuxe™ is a trademark of HarperCollins Publishers

Library of Congress Cataloging-in-Publication Data is available upon request.

ISBN: 978-0-06-227854-8

13 14   ID/RRD   10 9 8 7 6 5 4 3 2 1

For Susan

Not for these I raise
The song of thanks and praise;
But for those obstinate questionings
Of sense and outward things,
Fallings from us, vanishings;
Blank misgivings of a Creature
Moving about in worlds not realised . . .

—WILLIAM WORDSWORTH,
*Intimations of Immortality*

# Author's Note

In the writing of this novel I have been governed by the details and chronology of James Bond's life that were published in the 'obituary' in *You Only Live Twice*. The novel was the last to be published in Ian Fleming's lifetime. It is reasonable to assume, therefore, that these were the key facts about Bond and his life that he wanted to be in the public domain – facts that would cancel out various anomalies and illogicalities that had appeared in the earlier novels. Consequently, as far as this novel is concerned, and in line with Ian Fleming's decision, James Bond was born in 1924.

# Author's Note

# Solo

# PART ONE

# Breaking and Entering

# 1

# In Dreams Begin Responsibilities

J ames Bond was dreaming. Curiously, he knew at
  once where and when the dream was taking place –
it was in the war and he was very young and was walking along a sunken country lane in Normandy, a dirt
track between dense blackthorn hedges. In his dream,
Bond turned a corner and saw, in a shallow ditch at the
side of the muddy roadway, the sodden bodies of three
dead British paratroopers, clumped together. In some
shock, he paused instinctively to look at them – they
seemed in their huddled inert mass to be part of the
earth, in a strange way, some vegetable growth germi-
nating there rather than human beings – but an angry
shout from the rear told him to keep moving. Beyond
the ditch a farmer strode behind his team of two toiling
shire horses, busy ploughing his field as if the war were

not taking place and these dead men and this small patrol of commandos walking uneasily and watchfully down his farm lane had nothing at all to do with his life and work—

Bond woke and sat up in bed, troubled and disturbed by the dream and its intense vividness and eerie precision. His heart was beating palpably, as if he were still walking down that muddy track past the dead paratroopers, heading for his objective. He thought about the moment: he could identify it exactly – it had been the late morning of 7 June 1944, a day after the invasion of France – D-Day plus one. Why was he dreaming about the war? Bond rarely ventured into the haunted forest of memory that made up his recollections of that time. He ran his hands through his hair and swallowed, feeling his throat sore, sharp. Too much alcohol last night? He reached over for the glass of water on his bedside table and drank some mouthfuls. He lay back and further considered the events of 7 June 1944.

Bond smiled grimly to himself, slid out of bed and walked naked into the en suite bathroom. The Dorchester had the most powerful showers in London and as Bond stood under the needle jets, feeling his skin respond to the almost painful pressure, he sensed the traumatic memories of that day in 1944 begin to

retreat slowly, washed away. He turned the tap to cold
for the last twenty seconds of his shower and began to
contemplate breakfast. Should he have it in his room
or go downstairs? Downstairs, he thought, everything
will be fresher.

Bond shaved and dressed in a dark blue worsted suit
with a pale blue shirt and a black silk knitted tie. As
he tightened the knot at his throat more details of his
dream began to return to him, unbidden. He had been
nineteen years old, a lieutenant in the Special Branch
of the Royal Naval Volunteer Reserve, attached as an
'observer' to BRODFORCE, part of 30 Assault Unit,
an elite commando charged specifically with the task of
capturing enemy secrets: documents, files and encod-
ing devices – all the legitimate plunder available in
the aftermath of battle. Bond was in fact looking for a
new variation of a *Wehrmacht* cipher machine, hoping
that swift advance would create surprise and pre-empt
destruction.

Various small units of 30 AU were landed on the
Normandy beaches on D-Day and immediately thereafter. BRODFORCE was the smallest of them, just
ten commandos, with an officer, Major Niven Brodie
– and Lieutenant Bond. They had stepped ashore from
their landing craft an hour after dawn at Jig Sector on
'Gold' beach and had been driven inland in an army

lorry towards the country town of Sainte-Sabine, close to the Chateau Malflacon, the SS headquarters of that region of Normandy. They left their lorry with a forward unit of Canadian infantry and advanced on foot, down the deep narrow lanes of the Normandy *bocage*, into the fastness of the countryside. The push inland from 'Gold' had been so speedy that there was no front line, as such. BRODFORCE was leapfrogging the British and Canadian forces and racing with all speed for whatever booty might be waiting for them in the Chateau Malflacon. Then they had seen the dead paratroopers and it had been Major Brodie himself who had shouted to Bond to keep moving . . .

Bond combed his hair, smoothing back the forelock that kept falling forward out of position, as if it had a life of its own. Maybe he should change his hairstyle, he wondered, idly, like that television-presenter fellow – what was his name? – and comb his hair forward in a short fringe, not bother with a parting at all, in the contemporary fashion. No, he thought, *pas mon style*. He swallowed again – his throat *was* sore. He left his room, locking the door behind him, and wandered down the corridor, heading for the lift. He pressed the button to summon it, thinking, yes, scrambled eggs and bacon, many cups of coffee, a cigarette, that would set him on his feet again—

The lift doors opened.

'Good morning,' a woman's voice said from inside.

'Morning,' Bond replied automatically as he stepped into the lift. He recognised the unforgettable scent immediately – the vanilla and iris of Guerlain's 'Shalimar' – unforgettable because it was the perfume his mother used to wear. It was like opening a door to his childhood – so much of his past crowding in on him today, Bond thought, looking over to meet the eyes of the woman leaning in the corner. She smiled at him, quizzically, an eyebrow raised.

'Happy birthday?' she asked.

'How do you know it's my birthday?' Bond just managed to keep the surprise from his voice, he thought.

'Just a good guess,' she said. 'I could tell you were celebrating something last night. So was I – you sense these things. We celebrants, celebrating.'

Bond touched the knot of his tie and cleared his throat, recalling. The woman had been sitting in the dining room last night, a few tables away from him.

'Yes,' Bond said, somewhat ruefully. 'It is indeed my birthday . . .' He was buying a few seconds' time, his mind beginning to work. He was definitely off colour this morning. The lift hummed down to the lobby.

'So – what were *you* celebrating?' he asked. He remembered now – they had both been drinking champagne and had simultaneously raised their glasses across the room to each other.

'The fourth anniversary of my divorce,' she said, drily. 'It's a tradition I keep. I treat myself to cocktails, dinner, vintage champagne and a night in a suite in the Dorchester – and then I send him the bill.'

She was a tall rangy woman in her mid-thirties, Bond estimated, with a strong handsome face and thick honey-blonde hair brushed back from her forehead and falling in an outward curve to her shoulders. Blue eyes. Scandinavian? She was wearing a jersey all-in-one navy catsuit with an ostentatious gold zip that ran from just above her groin to her neck. The tightness of the close-fitting material revealed the full swell of her breasts. Bond allowed the nature of his carnal appraisal to register in his eyes for a split second and saw her own eyes flash back: message received.

The lift doors slid open with a muffled 'ping' at the ground floor.

'Enjoy the rest of your day,' she said with a quick smile and strode out into the wide lobby.

**In the** dining room, Bond ordered four eggs, scrambled, and half a dozen rashers of unsmoked back bacon, well done, on the side. He drank a long draught of strong black coffee and lit his first cigarette of the day as he waited for his breakfast to arrive.

He had been given the same table that he'd occupied at dinner the night before. The woman had been sitting to his left, three tables away, and at an angle of the room so that if Bond turned his head slightly they had a good view of each other. Earlier in the evening, Bond had drunk two dry martinis in Fielding's, the private casino where he'd managed to lose almost £100 at chemin de fer in about twenty minutes, but he wasn't going to let that spoil his night. He had ordered a bottle of Taittinger Rosé 1960 to go with his first course of pan-fried Scottish scallops with a beurre blanc sauce and, as he had raised the glass to himself – silently wishing himself a happy forty-fifth birthday – he had spotted the woman lifting her glass of champagne in an identical self-reflecting gestural toast. Their eyes had met – Bond had shrugged, smiled and toasted her, amused. She toasted him back and he had not thought about it further. She had left as he was preoccupied with assessing the bottle of Chateau Batailley 1959 that he had ordered for his main course – fillet of beef, rare, with pommes dauphinoises – and consequently hadn't really taken her in as she swept briskly past his table, registering only that she was tall, blonde, wearing a cream dress and that her shoes had small chunky gold heels that flashed in the glow of the table lights as she walked out of the dining room.

He sprinkled some pepper on his scrambled eggs. A good breakfast was the first essential component to set any day off to a proper start. He had told his secretary he wouldn't be coming in – part of his present to himself. It would be as impossible to face his forty-fifth birthday with the routine prospect of work as it would without a decent breakfast. He ordered another pot of coffee – the hot liquid was easing his throat. Strange that the woman should be in the lift like that, he thought, and stranger still for her to guess it had been his birthday . . . Funny coincidence. He recalled one of the first rules of his profession: if it looks like a coincidence then it probably isn't. Still – life *was* full of genuine coincidences, he reasoned, you couldn't deny that. Very attractive woman, also. He liked the way she wore her hair. Groomed yet natural-looking—

The maître d' offered Bond a copy of *The Times* to read. Bond glanced at the headline – 'Viet Cong Offensive Checked With Many Casualties' – and waved it away. Not today, thank you. That zip on the front of her outfit – her catsuit – was like a provocation, a challenge, crying out to be pulled down. Bond smiled to himself as he imagined doing precisely that and drank more coffee – there was life in the old dog yet.

---

**Bond returned** to his room and packed up his dinner suit, shirt and underwear from the night before. He threw his toilet bag into his grip and checked that he'd left nothing behind. He needed a couple of aspirin for his throat, he thought: the coffee had soothed it momentarily but now it was feeling thick and lumpy, swallowing was uncomfortable. Flu? A cold, probably – he had no temperature, thank God. However, the day was his to do with as he pleased – he had a few necessary chores, but there were plenty of birthday treats that he had promised himself along the way.

At the checkout desk it seemed that a group of a dozen Japanese tourists were collectively querying their bill. Bond took out his cigarette case and, as he selected a cigarette and put it in his mouth, noted with mild concern that he must have smoked over thirty cigarettes the previous night. He'd filled the case before he'd gone to the casino. But this was not the day to entertain thoughts of discipline and cutting down, he told himself, no, no – today was a day for judicious self-indulgence – then, as he fished in his pocket for his lighter, he smelled Guerlain's 'Shalimar' once more and heard the woman's voice again.

'May I trouble you for a light?'

As Bond lit her cigarette she steadied his hand with two fingers on his knuckles. She had a small cream-leather travelling bag at her feet. She was checking out also – coincidence . . . ? Bond lit his cigarette and looked squarely at her. She plumed smoke sideways and returned his gaze, unperturbed.

'Are you following me, or am I following you?' she said.

'We are seeing rather a lot of each other, you're right,' Bond said. He offered his hand. 'My name's Bond, James Bond.'

'Bryce Fitzjohn,' she said. They shook hands. Bond noticed her fingernails were cut short, unvarnished – he liked that – and her grip was firm. 'Do you always celebrate your birthday alone?' she asked.

'Not always,' Bond said. 'I just didn't feel like company this year.'

She glanced up as the phalanx of tourists began to move away.

'At bloody last,' she said. There was the hint of an accent, Bond thought. Bryce Fitzjohn – Irish?

'After you,' Bond said.

She opened her handbag and took out a card, offering it to him.

'I end my divorce celebrations with a cocktail party. It's at my house, this evening. A few amusing and interesting people. You're most welcome to come. We start at six o'clock and see how it rolls along from there.'

Bond took the card – a small alarm bell ringing in his head, now. The invitation was overt; the blue eyes were candid. I'd like to see you again, was the message – and there might be some sexual fun to be had, was the subtext.

Bond smiled, apologetically, pocketing the card anyway. 'I'm afraid my day is spoken for,' he said. 'Alas.'

'Never mind,' she said, breezily. 'Maybe I'll see you here next year. Goodbye, Mr Bond.'

She sauntered to the checkout desk, Bond noting the lean perfection of her figure, rear view. It had been the correct thing to do, in terms of proper procedure, but all the same he wondered if perhaps he'd been a bit hasty saying no quite so unequivocally . . .

**Bond took** a taxi back to his flat in Chelsea. As it swung into Sloane Square he felt his spirits lift. Sloane Square and Albert Bridge were the two London landmarks that gladdened his heart whenever he saw them, day or night, all seasons – signals that he was coming home. He liked living in Chelsea – 'that leafy tranquil cultivated *spielraum* . . . where I worked and wandered'. Who had said that . . . ? Anyway, he thought, telling the taxi to stop just before tree-filled Wellington Square, whoever it was, he agreed with the sentiment. He strolled into the square and made for his front door. He was searching his pockets for his keys when the door opened and his housekeeper, Donalda, stood there.

'Ah, glad you're back, sir,' she said. 'There's a wee bit of a crisis – the painters have found some damp in the drawing room.'

Bond followed Donalda into his flat, dropping his grip in the hall. She had been with him for six months now – she was the niece of May, his trusted house-keeper of many years, who had finally, reluctantly, retired, creeping arthritis encouraging the decision. It had been May who suggested Donalda. 'Best to keep it in the family, Mr James,' she'd said. 'We're very close.' Donalda was a slim, severe-looking young woman in her late twenties with a rare and diffident smile. She never wore make-up and her hair was cut in a short bob with a fringe – a nun's hairstyle, Bond thought. He supposed with a little effort she might have made herself less plain and more attractive but the hando-ver of May's housekeeping responsibilities had been achieved so seamlessly that he had no desire to see that quiet efficiency alter in any way. One morning it had been May, as ever, then the next day Donalda had been introduced. There was an apprentice period of two weeks when both May and Donalda had run his household life, then May had gone and Donalda took over. Absolutely nothing in his domestic routine had been altered: his coffee was brewed to the same strength, his scrambled eggs had the same consistency, his shirts were ironed identically, the shopping was done, the place kept unimprovably clean. Donalda slipped into his life as if she'd been in training for the job since childhood.

Bond stepped into his drawing room. The rugs were rolled up, the tall bookshelves empty of his books – all boxed and in store – the floorboards were bare and the furniture was grouped in the centre of the room under dust sheets. His nose tingled with the astringent smell of fresh paint. Tom Doig, the decorator, pointed out the patch of damp in the room's western corner, revealed when a bureau had been moved. Bond reluctantly authorised him to investigate further and wrote a cheque for £125 to cover the next period of work. He had been promising himself for years to redecorate his flat. He liked his home – its scale and situation – and had no intention of moving. Besides, his lease still had forty-four years left to run. Bond calculated – I'll be eighty-nine if I last that long, he thought. Which would be extremely unlikely, he reasoned, given his line of work – then he grew angry with himself. What was he doing thinking about the future? It was the here and now that intrigued and fulfilled him and, as if to prove the truth of this adage to himself, he spent an hour going over all the work in the flat that Doig had completed, deliberately finding fault everywhere.

When he'd thoroughly irritated and discomfited Doig and his team he told Donalda not to bother preparing a cold supper for him (she went home at six) and he left the decorators to swear and curse at him behind his back.

There was a hazy afternoon sun and the day was agreeably mild and balmy. He wandered pleasurably west along the King's Road towards the Café Picasso pondering a late lunch of some kind. The King's Road was busy but Bond found his mind wasn't concentrating on the passing parade – the throng of shoppers, the poseurs, the curious, the gilded, carefree young, dressed as if for a fabulous harlequinade somewhere; a noise, a random image, had triggered memories of his dream that morning and he was back in northern France in 1944 walking through an ancient oak wood towards an isolated chateau . . .

To Bond's eyes, it looked as if the Chateau Malflacon had been the victim of a rocket attack by a Hawker Typhoon on D-Day. The classic stone facade was cratered with the shallow impact-bursts of the Typhoon's RP-3 rockets and the left-hand wing of the building had been burnt out, the exposed, charred roof timbers still smouldering in the weak sunshine. Bizarrely, there was a dead Shetland pony lying on the oval patch of lawn surrounded by the gravelled sweep of the driveway. There were no vehicles in sight and everything seemed quiet and deserted. The men of BRODFORCE crouched down amongst the trees of the wooded parkland around the chateau waiting while Major Brodie scanned the building with his binoculars. Birds were singing loudly, Bond remembered. The faint breeze blowing was cool and fresh.

Then Major Brodie suggested that Corporal Dave Tozer and Mr Bond might circle round the back of the chateau and see if there was any sign of activity there. He would give them ten minutes before the rest of the men stormed through the front door, took occupancy and began their search.

It was the same kind of hazy, weak sunshine, Bond recalled, as he neared the Café Picasso – that was what had started him thinking, again – the same sort of day as that 7 June – soft, lemony, peaceful. He and Dave Tozer had cut through the woodland and darted past an empty stable block before finding themselves in a size-able orchard, unkempt and brambly, with some sixty or seventy trees – apple, quince and pear in the main but with some cherries here and there, already showing clumps of heavy maroon fruit. 'Look at this, Mr Bond,' Tozer had said with a grin. 'Let's snaffle this lot before the others come.' Bond had raised his hand in caution – he had caught a scent of woodsmoke and thought he heard voices coming from the other side of the orchard. But Tozer had already stepped forward to seize the glossy cherries. His left foot sank into a rabbit hole and his ankle snapped with a crisp, distinctly audible sound, like dry kindling caught by a flame.

Tozer grunted with pain but managed not to cry out. He also heard the voices now. He waved Bond to him and whispered, 'Take my Sten.' Bond was armed: he had a Webley .38 revolver in a holster at his waist and he handed it to Tozer, with some reluctance, picking up Tozer's Sten gun and creeping cautiously forward through the orchard towards the sound of men's voices . . .

Bond sat down at a pavement table outside the Café Picasso, his mind active and distracted. He looked at the menu and forced himself to concentrate and ordered a portion of lasagne and a glass of Valpolicella from the waitress. Calm down, he said to himself, this all happened a quarter of a century ago – in another life. But the images he was summoning up were as fresh as if they had taken place last week. The fat glossy cherries, Dave Tozer's grimacing face, the drifting scent of woodsmoke and the sound of conversing German voices – all coming back to him with the clarity of total recall.

He forced himself to look around, glad of the diversion afforded by the Café Picasso's eccentric clientele – the dark-eyed girls in their tiny short dresses; the long-haired young men in their crushed velvet and their shaggy Afghan coats. He ate his impromptu late lunch and kept his gaze on the move, easily distracted by the comings and goings. He ordered another glass of wine and an espresso and admired the small-nippled breasts of the girl on the next table, clearly visible through the transparent gauze of her blouse. There was something to be said for modern fashion after all, Bond considered, cheered by the unselfconscious sexuality of the scene. The girl with the see-through blouse was now kissing her boyfriend with patent enthusiasm, his hand resting easily on her upper thigh.

Bond lit a cigarette and found his thoughts turning to the woman in the Dorchester – Bryce Fitzjohn – and their series of encounters over the last twelve hours or so. Was there anything to be suspicious about? He played with various explanations and found the improbabilities too compelling. How could she have known he was staying at the Dorchester? How could she have contrived to be in the lift when he decided to go to the dining room for breakfast? Impossible. Well, not impossible but highly unlikely. True, she could have waited in the lobby for him to check out, he supposed . . . But it didn't add up. He took her card out of his pocket. She lived in Richmond, he saw. A cocktail party at six o'clock with some 'amusing and interesting' friends . . .

Bond stubbed out his cigarette and called for his bill. He found he was thinking about her and her rangy, alluring body. He felt a little animalistic quiver of desire low in his gut and his loins. Lust, more like. The prehistoric instinct – *this is the one for me.* He hadn't felt this sensation in a long time, he had to acknowledge. She was a very attractive woman, he told himself, and, more to the point, she clearly found him attractive also. Perhaps he should check her out further – it would be correct procedure after all – and perhaps the gods of luck were conspiring to send him a birthday present. He threw down a pound note and some coins to cover his bill and a tip, stepped out into the King's Road and hailed a taxi.

# 2
# The Jensen FF

'Back again, Mr Bond, nice to see you,' the salesman said with a wide sincere smile as Bond circled the chocolate-brown Jensen Interceptor I. It was parked on the forecourt of a showroom just off Park Lane, in Mayfair. Bond had visited it three times already, checking out the Interceptor, hence the salesman's welcoming smile. What was his name? Brian, that was it, Brian Richards. Bond's Bentley was out of action, having its gearbox replaced. The old car, much loved, and lovingly customised over the years, was showing signs of its age and its rambunctious history and was beginning to cost him serious money just to keep it roadworthy. It was like an old thoroughbred racehorse – its time had come to be put out to grass. But what to replace the Bentley with? He wasn't particularly enamoured of modern cars – he'd test-driven an E-type Jaguar and an MGB GT but they didn't trigger any pulse of pleasure in him, didn't make his heart beat. But the Interceptor was different – big and beautiful – and this was what kept bringing him back to Park Lane.

Brian, the salesman, sidled up and lowered his voice.

'I'll have the Interceptor II in a few weeks, Mr Bond, after the Motor Show. And I can do you a very fair price – so buying the One wouldn't be that clever, what with the Two coming out, know what I mean? But . . .' He looked around as if he was about to divulge a dark secret. 'In the meantime, come through the back and have a look at this.' Bond followed Brian across the showroom and through a door to a small mews courtyard at the rear. Here were the workshops and extra space for cars to be waxed and polished before they went to the forecourt on display. Brian gestured to what looked like another Interceptor, painted a dull gunmetal silver. Bond walked around it. An Interceptor but somehow longer, he thought, and with two air vents set behind the front wheels.

'The Jensen FF,' Brian said softly in veneration, almost with a catch in his voice. 'Four-wheel drive.' He opened the door. 'Step in, Mr Bond. Try her for size.'

Bond slipped into the driving seat and rested his hands on the wooden rim of the steering wheel, his eyes taking in the grouped dials on the fascia, his nostrils filled with the smell of new leather. It worked on him like an aphrodisiac.

'Take her out for a spin,' Brian suggested.

'I just might,' he said.

'Be my guest, Mr Bond. Take her out on the motorway, give her some gas. You'll be amazed. Take all the time you need, sir.'

Bond was thinking. 'Right. When do you close? I may be a couple of hours.'

'I'm working late tonight. I'll be here till ten. Just bring her round the back and ring the bell on the gate.'

'Perfect,' Bond said and switched on the engine.

**Bond felt** he was in a low-flying plane rather than an automobile as he accelerated the Jensen down the A316 towards Twickenham. The wide curved sweep of the windscreen filled the car with light and the powerful rumble of the engine sounded like the roar of jet propulsion. The four-wheel drive meant the tightest corner could be negotiated with hardly any diminution of speed. When he stopped at traffic lights pedestrians openly gaped at the car as it idled throatily, heads turning, fingers pointing. If you needed a car to boost your ego, Bond thought, then the Jensen FF would do the job admirably. Not that he needed an ego boost, Bond reminded himself as he accelerated away, the speed forcing him back in the seat, cutting up and leaving a Series V Sunbeam Alpine for dead, its driver gesticulating in frustration.

Bond turned left before Richmond Bridge. He went into a post office to ask directions to Chapel Close, where Bryce Fitzjohn lived. He motored down Petersham Road, along the river's edge, found the narrow lane, turned the corner and parked. It was just before six o'clock and he rather liked the idea of being the first to arrive at her little party. A few minutes alone would negate or confirm any lingering doubts he had about her.

Bryce Fitzjohn's home turned out to be a pretty Georgian 'cottage' with a walled garden, the grand houses of Richmond Hill rising behind and beyond. Bond surveyed the driveway and the house's facade from across the lane. Worn, patinated red stock-brick, a slate roof, a moulded half-shell pediment over the front door, three big sash windows on the ground floor and three above – a restrained and elegant design. They weren't cheap, these refined houses on the river – so she wasn't short of money. However bitter her divorce had been, perhaps it had proved lucrative, Bond wondered as he crossed the road, noting that there were no cars parked outside. He was the first to arrive – excellent. He rang the doorbell.

There was no response. Bond listened, then rang again. And again. Now new intimations of alarm began to cluster. What kind of invitation was this? Bond was unarmed and felt suddenly vulnerable, wondering if he was being watched from some vantage point. He looked around him and stepped back out on to the road. A mother pushing her pram. A boy walking his dog. Nothing out of the ordinary. He returned to the house and slipped through the ornate iron gate at the side that led to the walled garden. Bond saw well-tended herbaceous borders edging a neatly mown lawn with a large stone birdbath set on a carved plinth in the centre. At the bottom of the garden, under a gnarled and ancient fig tree, was a wrought-iron bench and table. All very ordered and civilised. Bond followed paving stones set in the turf round to a conservatory at the rear. Beside it was a door that led into the kitchen.

Bond peered through the window. Here, laid out on a scrubbed pine kitchen table were trays of canapés, ranked glasses of various sorts and bowls of nuts, cheese balls and olives. So, there *was* going to be a party . . . But where was the hostess? Bond thought about returning home to Chelsea, but his curiosity was piqued and he felt it was his professional duty to find out if there was anything more clandestine going on here. He just had to gain access to this house. Needs must, he thought to himself, and reached down and removed one of his loafers. He twisted off the heel, revealing the two-inch, dirk-like stabbing blade that projected from it, sheathed by the specially constructed sole. He slipped the blade into the gap by the Yale lock, probed, eased and then turned it, feeling the tongue of the lock spring back and the door yield. He pushed it open. It was all too easy, this breaking and entering.

Bond replaced the heel and slipped his shoe back on. He allowed himself a couple of seconds' reflection – he could close the door and return home, no one would be the wiser – but he felt that having achieved ingress, as it were, it would be wrong not to explore further. Who knew what he might discover? So he stepped in and wandered around the kitchen, listening intently, and, hearing no sound of anyone stirring, he helped himself to a chicken vol-au-vent and then a triangle of smoked salmon. Delicious. There was a drinks trolley with an impressive display of alcohol set upon it. Bond contemplated the array of bottles (some serious drinkers were expected, clearly) and was tempted to have a dram of the Scotch on offer as it was Dimple Haig, one of his favourites – but decided this wasn't the moment. Then he decided it was, so he poured three fingers into a tumbler and left the kitchen to investigate the house.

The rooms were high-ceilinged and generously sized on the ground floor: there was a dining room and a drawing room with fine cornicing and French windows that gave on to the lawn. To the other side of the entrance hall was a cloakroom-bathroom and a small study. He spent some time in the study, one wall of which was lined with bookshelves – mainly biographies and non-fiction, he saw, with a distinct showbiz slant. He opened the bottom drawer of the small partners' desk that sat in a corner (always start with the bottom drawer) and was surprised to find a cache of large glossy professional photographs of Bryce Fitzjohn nearly and provocatively naked. In some she was wearing a tiny leather bikini; in others she was topless, her arm held demurely across her breasts; and there were others of her in full make-up, hair blown awry by a wind machine, her cleavage plungingly on display. There was one set of her sitting up in a rumpled bed, naked, her back to the camera, the cleft of her buttocks visible, her hair tousled, her eyes half closed and invitingly come-hither. The name at the foot of each photograph was 'Astrid Ostergard'. So, Bryce Fitzjohn was Astrid Ostergard in another life. The name seemed familiar to Bond – where had he seen it before? He leafed through the photos – an actress, a dancer, a model? A high-class prostitute? Bond was tempted to take a photo as a souvenir.

He quickly went through the other drawers of the desk and found nothing out of the ordinary. Her passport confirmed her name was indeed Bryce Connor Fitzjohn (aged thirty-seven) born in Kilkenny, Ireland. It was time to go upstairs. Bond drained his glass of Haig and left it on the desk.

On the first floor there were two bedrooms, one with a bathroom en suite and clearly Bryce's. Bond opened cupboards and drawers and the medicine cabinet in the bathroom – he noticed there seemed no trace of a male presence anywhere. In the guest bedroom the bottom drawer of the bedside table revealed an ancient, desiccated half-pack of Gauloises cigarettes and a well-thumbed copy of Frank Harris's *My Life and Loves*. Scant evidence of a man in her life. No, there was really nothing to go on apart from the pseudonymous photographs—

The sound of a motor – diesel – and a tyre-scatter of gravel made Bond freeze for a second before he strode to the window, peering out cautiously. A breakdown van towing a Triumph Herald 13/60 convertible pulled up outside. Bryce Fitzjohn stepped out of the cab of the van and, from the other door, an overalled mechanic emerged, who unhitched the Herald. Bond watched Bryce write a cheque for the driver and see him and his van off with a cursory wave, and then Bond drew back as she unlocked the front door to her house.

Bond moved quickly to the top of the stairs, the better to overhear the series of calls she proceeded to make from the telephone on the small table in the hallway. 'Yes,' he heard her say, 'me again. Nightmare . . . After the breakdown in Kingston . . . It got worse – completely dead . . .', 'Hello, darling, *so* sorry . . . No we'll do it another time . . .', 'I might have been in Siberia, nobody offered to help . . . Took me three hours after I called you to find a garage . . .', 'And then the man said the car was fixed but it still wouldn't fucking start . . . Exactly, so I had to find another garage . . . Day from hell . . . Yes, I'm going to have a hot bath and an enormous gin and tonic . . .', 'Bye, my dear . . . Yes, it is a shame . . . everything was ready . . . No, we'll do it again. Promise . . .' and so on for another few minutes as she rang around apologising to the friends who were meant to have come to her party, Bond assumed.

As he stood there listening he began to wonder what his best course of action would be. Reveal himself? Or try to slip out unnoticed? He heard her go into the kitchen and then a minute later head back across the hall for the stairs. He ducked into the spare bedroom.

He heard her kick off her shoes on the landing and the chime of ice in a glass, then, moments after, the sound of water tumbling into a bath. Bond peered out, carefully. She had left the door to her bedroom open and he was able to watch her undress, partially, in a kind of jump-cut striptease, as she crossed and recrossed her room, shedding clothes. He moved cautiously out into the corridor and saw her reflected in the mirror of her dressing table. She was wearing a red brassiere and red panties, and her skin was very white. He noted the furrow of her spine deepen as she arched her arms back to unclip the fastener of her brassiere. And then she slipped out of vision.

Bond stepped back into the spare bedroom – he was both excited and, at the same time, made vaguely uneasy by this unsought-for act of voyeurism. Everything seemed unexceptionable and explicable: there had indeed been a party planned – that was then cancelled when her car broke down in Kingston on the way back from London. No honey trap after all; sheer coincidence being the explanation behind everything – yet again. Still, he thought, better to be secure in this knowledge than worry that some sort of elaborate scheme of entrapment had been set in motion.

He eased past the door of the spare room, pulling it closed behind him, and paused for a moment on the landing. It was quiet. She seemed to have gone into the bathroom, no doubt luxuriating in a deep bath. For a crazy second he contemplated walking in on her – no, madness, slip out unnoticed while you have the chance. He stepped over her discarded high-heeled shoes and swiftly went down the stairs and into her study. On a piece of her writing paper he wrote 'Thanks for the cocktail. James' and weighted it with his empty whisky glass in the centre of her desk. What would she make of that? he wondered, pleased with his mischief, not bothering to question the professional wisdom of the gesture. To hell with it – it was his day off. He let himself out of the front door, closed it silently behind him and strolled, hands in pockets, nonchalantly back to where he'd parked the Jensen.

**Bond drove** steadily back to Chelsea, not testing the powerful car at all, so caught up was he with the images crowding his brain. Images of Bryce undressing – the red of her brassiere offset by the alabaster whiteness of her skin; the way she'd used a finger to hook and tug the caught hem of her panties back over the swell of her buttock. What was it about this woman, this virtual stranger, that so nagged at him? Maybe it was the fact that he had broken into her home and had spied on her, that his illicit presence in her house made his glimpses of her more . . . what? More charged, more erotic, more perversely exciting? At the back of his mind was the thought that, come what may, he had to contrive a way of seeing her again. It wasn't over.

He wound down the window to allow some cool air into the car. His face was hot, he wiped his lips with the back of his hand, and as he crossed over Chiswick Bridge he drove through the drifting smoke of some early evening bonfire. Instantly, the trigger-effect of the association worked on him and he was back once again in the world of his wartime dream, back in the orchard of the Chateau Malflacon, flitting from tree to tree, Corporal Tozer's Sten gun heavy in his hand, listening to the sound of German voices – chatting, unconcerned – growing louder as he approached.

Bond pulled up at a traffic light. Somebody, seeing the Jensen, shouted, 'Nice motor, mate!' Bond didn't even look round – he was in another place, twenty-five years ago. The woodsmoke, he thought, recalling it as if he was actually there in that Normandy orchard, moving cautiously from tree to tree. As he had reached the edge of the orchard he had seen the actual bonfire, heaped high with concertina files and flung boxes of documents, smouldering weakly, wisps of smoke seeping from the mass of paper but no sign of flames catching. Three young German soldiers – his age, teenagers

– were emptying the last boxes of documents on to the bonfire, laughing and bantering. One of them, his jacket off, exposing his woollen vest and his olive-green braces, was using a long-handled French gardening fork to spear and heave the tied bundles of paper on to the mound. Filing clerks, stenographers, radio operators, Bond supposed, the last to leave the chateau, instructed to burn everything, unaware that Major Brodie and the rest of BRODFORCE were about to thunder in the front door.

The boy threw down his fork and began to empty a jerrycan of petrol over the pile of papers, sloshing the fuel on the bonfire. He dumped his jerrycan on the grass and searched his pockets for some matches. One of the others tossed him a box.

Bond stepped out from the trees, the Sten gun levelled.

'*Weg vom Feuer,*' he said, ordering them to move away from the fire.

They froze – completely shocked to see a British soldier, and then to realise he was speaking fluent German. Two of the clerks turned immediately and raced away, panicked, for the woods beyond. Bond let them go. The boy in the braces fumbled with his matches, trying to be a hero. There was something wrong with them, they wouldn't light.

'*Lass das*,' Bond warned him, cocking the Sten. '*Sonst schiess ich.*'

The boy in the braces managed to light a match and immediately dropped it on the grass. He scrabbled for another. Was he insane, Bond thought?

'Don't be a fool,' he said, in German. He raised the Sten and fired it into the air.

Nothing. The redundant click of the trigger. The gun had jammed. Jamming – the curse of the Sten gun. Carbon build-up in the breech, or a feed malfunction in the magazine. The operating instructions when this occurred were to remove the magazine, tap against knee and reinsert. Bond didn't think he was going to do this.

The boy in the braces looked at Bond and seemed to smile. With deliberate care he took out another match and struck it. It caught and flared.

'Now you are fool,' the boy said, in English. He dropped the match on the bonfire and small flames flickered.

Bond slapped the Sten's magazine and worked the cocking bolt.

Bond pulled the trigger again and again. Nothing. Click-click-click. The boy stooped and picked up the long-handled fork. It had three tines, Bond saw, curved, ten inches long.

Bond worked the bolt again. He aimed the Sten at the boy.

'*Forke weg*,' Bond said. '*Sonst bring ich dich um.*'

The boy quickly stepped towards him and thrust the fork upward. The sharp, curved gleaming tines were suddenly two inches from Bond's chest and throat. Bond imagined them entering his body, effortlessly, puncturing the material of his uniform and then his skin, plunging deep inside him. He couldn't turn and run – he'd be speared in the back. He still had the useless Sten in his hands; he thought in the mad scrambling seconds left to him he could fling himself sideways and smash the gun against the boy's head. Somewhere in the back of his mind rose up the absolute determination that he was not going to die here, in this Normandy orchard.

The boy smiled thinly and pressed the tines of the fork closer, so that they actually touched the serge of Bond's jacket, ready for the fatal thrust.

'*Dummkopf Englander*,' he said.

Tozer's first shot hit the boy full in the throat, the second in the chest and flung him backwards.

Bond glanced round. Tozer was leaning against an apple tree. He lowered Bond's Webley, smoke drifting from its barrel.

'Sorry about that, Mr Bond,' he said. 'Bloody useless Sten, always has been.' He limped forward, raising the revolver to cover the German lying on the ground. 'I think I got him fair and square,' Tozer said, with a satisfied smile.

Bond realised he was shuddering, as if suddenly very cold. He took a few steps towards the boy and looked down at him. His woollen vest was drenched in his blood. The round that had caught him in the throat had torn it wide open. Big thick pink bubbles formed and burst, popping quietly as his lungs emptied.

Bond sank to his knees. He laid the Sten carefully on the ground and vomited.

**The traffic** light changed to green. Bond put the Jensen in gear and accelerated cleanly away. Now he knew why the dream had so haunted him, summoned up from his unconscious mind like a minatory symbol. Why had he remembered it? What had provoked this recollection in every detail and texture? His birthday? The fact that he was aware he was growing older? Whatever it was, the memorable part of that particular day, he realised, 7 June 1944, was that he had been confronted with the possibility that his life was about to end, there and then – it marked the first time he had stared death full in the face. He could have had no idea that this was to be the pattern of the life ahead of him.

# PART TWO
# How to Stop a War

# 1

# Elements of Risk

'Happy birthday, James,' Miss Moneypenny said, as Bond stepped into her office. 'Rather, happy birthday in arrears. Did you have an enjoyable day off, last week?'

'I'd rather hoped you'd forgotten it was my birthday,' Bond said, his voice thick and raspy. He could hardly swallow.

'No, no. It's my business to know these things,' she said, standing and going to a filing cabinet. 'All the mundane little facts of your life.'

Sometimes, Bond thought, Moneypenny's banter could verge on the annoyingly self-satisfied. He was vaguely irritated that she must know how old he was.

'You don't happen to have a couple of aspirin, do you?' he asked.

'You've obviously been celebrating far too enthusi-astically,' she said, returning to her desk and handing him a file. Bond took it, unreflectingly.

'I've got a sore throat,' he said. 'Touch of flu, I think. I've been in bed by eight the last two nights.'

'Your secret's safe with me,' she said in the same dry tone, somehow producing a glass of water and then two aspirins from a drawer in her desk. Bond took them, thankfully, swallowing the pills down.

The light above M's office door changed from red to green.

'Off you go, James,' Moneypenny said and turned to her typewriter.

M was standing at one of the three windows of his office that looked out over Regent's Park. His head seemed hunched down on his shoulders as if his back were tense and knotted. He seemed deeply thoughtful, not registering Bond's entrance in any way. His pipe, Bond noticed, lay on his desk blotter, empty of tobacco, and Bond wondered if he'd have to sit through the usual interminable, tantalising, pipe-filling, pipe-lighting routine before he found out why he'd been summoned. Bond cleared his throat and winced.

'You wanted to see me, sir,' Bond said, going to stand in front of the wide desk, placing Moneypenny's file to one side.

M turned – his face looked tanned, weather-beaten. Working in his garden, Bond thought. He looked fit, full of vigour for an elderly man. What age would M be, Bond found himself wondering? He must be at least—

'What's wrong with your voice?' M asked, suspiciously.

'Bit of a sore throat. Shaking off a cold,' Bond said. 'Moneypenny's given me some medication.'

'Smoking too much, more like,' M said, sitting down and picking up and flourishing his pipe. 'You want to take up one of these. Haven't had a sore throat since I was at school.'

'Interesting idea, sir,' Bond said, diplomatically. He would rather give up smoking than smoke a pipe.

'Sit down, 007, and do light up if you want to.'

Bond sat down and took out a cigarette as M rummaged in a drawer of his desk and drew out an atlas. He opened it, turned it and pushed it across the desk towards Bond.

'Tell me what you know about this place,' M said.

Bond looked at the open page. An African country. A small West African country called Zanzarim.

'Zanzarim,' Bond said, thinking. 'There's a war going on there. A civil war. Civilians starving to death by the thousand.'

'By the tens of thousand, some would have it,' M said, leaning back in his chair. 'Anything else?'

'Used to be a British colony, didn't it?' Bond said. 'Before they changed the name.'

'League of Nations mandated territory to be precise. Upper Zanza State. Got independence five years ago. Old German colony established in 1906. We and the French liberated it in 1914 – split it in two. There was a plebiscite in 1953 and the Zanzaris voted for us.'

'Unusual.'

'You forget how dominant and impressive the British Empire was, even in those days, 007. It was the sensible, obvious thing to do.'

'Oh, yes. Moneypenny gave me this file.' Bond handed it over.

'No, no. It's for you. Open it.'

Bond did so and saw a mass of newspaper clippings and documents entitled 'Agence Presse Libre' – then something fell on the floor and Bond picked it up. It was a plastic identity card and his photograph was on it. 'James Bond. Journalist. Agence Presse Libre' it stated.

'Right . . .' Bond said slowly. 'So I'm to be a journalist for this French press agency.'

M smiled, knowingly. Bond knew he was enjoying himself, drip-feeding the information about his mission this way, toying with him.

'Small, left-of-centre press agency. Good reputation. International reach,' M said. 'Your old friend René Mathis from the Deuxième Bureau arranged it all, cleared everything.'

'And where am I going to be doing my journalism?' Bond asked dutifully, playing along, knowing the answer.

'Zanzarim.'

'And what am I meant to do once I get there?'

M smiled, again, more broadly. 'Stop the war, of course.'

**Bond told** his new secretary, Araminta Beauchamp (pronounced Beecham) that he was not to be disturbed and sat down at his desk to read through all the material on Zanzarim contained in the file that Moneypenny had handed him.

Bond leafed through the newspaper cuttings. The civil war in Zanzarim had become an international crisis because of the mass malnutrition of civilians. There were many shocking and heart-rending images of starving children – stick figures with macrocephalic heads, protruding bellies and glaucous, staring, uncomprehending eyes. Bond selected a Foreign Office briefing document entitled 'The Origins of the Zanzarim Civil War' and began to read.

———

**Zanzarim had** been a small stable West African country when it gained independence in 1964. The name of the country was changed and so was the name of the capital city – to Sinsikrou (it had been Gustavberg, Victoireville and Shackleton in its short colonial history). Zanzarim had a creditable balance of trade surplus, its main exports being cocoa beans, bananas, copper and timber. Then oil had been discovered in the Zanza River Delta – a vast, apparently limitless, subterranean ocean of oil. This benediction soon began to turn sour. The problem was that Zanzarim's capital and seat of government, Sinsikrou, was in the north. The government, moreover, was dominated by the Lowele tribe, the largest in a country of some two dozen tribes. In the south, in the river delta, the paramount tribe was the Fakassa. All the oil deposits had been discovered squarely in the middle of the Fakassa's tribal lands. Not surprisingly, the Fakassa viewed the prospect of an endless flow of petro-dollars as a blessing conferred primarily on them. The Zanzarim government, and the Lowele tribe, disagreed: the oil was for the benefit of the whole country and all Zanzaris regardless of their tribal affiliation. Internecine bickering ensued between Fakassa and Lowele representatives and became more aggressive as it seemed no compromise could be reached. There was a form of uneasy stalemate until 1967 when the first proper assessments of the potential reserves and the scale of their potential revenues were made known.

In Port Dunbar, the central town in the river delta, 200,000 Fakassa took to the streets in protest against this Lowele 'theft' of their patrimony. There were anti-Fakassa riots in Sinsikrou and over 300 Fakassa were massacred by a rampaging Lowele mob. In the south a revanchist anti-Lowele pogrom took place – shops were burnt, traders expelled and their assets seized. Eight Lowele policemen, attempting to flee, were caught and lynched. As the trouble increased and more indiscriminate slaughter ensued, attempts to broker a peace by British and UN diplomats failed and tensions rose inexorably on both sides as massacre and counter-massacre occurred in a deadly and inhuman tit-for-tat. A rush of Fakassa refugees from elsewhere in Zanzarim fled into the tribal heartlands around Port Dunbar. Towards the end of 1967 the south of the country – effectively the Fakassa tribal lands – formally seceded from Zanzarim and a new independent state was created: the Democratic Republic of Dahum. Two brigades of the Zanzarim army invaded Dahum and were repulsed. The Zanzarim civil war had begun.

Bond put the briefing document down. It was like that old Chinese curse: 'May you live in interesting times' – reconfigured as 'May vast reserves of oil be discovered in your country.' He shuffled through the newspaper clippings and selected one written by a defence expert whose name he recognised. In the two years since the war had begun the overwhelmingly superior Zanzarim forces had managed to drive the Dahumians back from their ostensible frontiers to a small hinterland in the river delta concentrated around the town of Port Dunbar. The Democratic Republic of Dahum now consisted of Port Dunbar, an airstrip near a place called Janjaville and a few hundred square miles of dense forest, river creeks and mangrove swamps. Dahum was surrounded and a blockade commenced. The desperate population of Fakassa began to starve and die.

Her Majesty's Government supported Zanzarim (as well as providing military materiel for the Zanzarim army) and urged Dahum to sue for peace and return to the 'status quo ante'. To all observers it seemed that unless this occurred there would be a human catastrophe. It had seemed inconceivable that Dahum could hold out for more than a week or two.

Bond recalled what M had recounted.

'However, it simply hasn't happened,' he had said, shrugging his shoulders. 'It seems heroic – this small, makeshift Dahum army holding out against hugely superior and well-equipped forces. To be sure, there's a clandestine air-bridge flying in supplies at night to this airstrip at Janjaville. But somehow they've completely stopped the Zanzari advance. Every time there's a push from the Zanzarim army it ends in humiliating disaster. It seems the Dahumian army is being brilliantly led by some kind of tactical genius producing victory after victory. The war could drag on forever at this rate.'

Bond picked up a clipping from *Time* magazine that showed an African soldier, a brigadier, with a black beret and a scarlet cockade standing on top of a burnt-out Zanzari armoured car. The caption beneath read: 'Brigadier Solomon "The Scorpion" Adeka – the African Napoleon'. So, this was the soldier who was the architect of Dahum's astonishing resilience – a military prodigy who was somehow contriving to inflict defeat upon defeat on an army ten times the size of his.

'Brigadier Adeka is the key,' M had said, simply. 'He's the man who's single-handedly keeping this war going, by all accounts. He's the target – the object of your mission. I want you to go to Zanzarim, infiltrate yourself into Dahum and get close to this man.'

'And what am I meant to do then, sir?' Bond had asked, knowing the answer but keeping his face impassive, giving nothing away.

'I'd like you to find a way of making him a less efficient soldier,' M had said with a vague smile.

**There was** a knock on his door and Bond looked up,
irritated, and Araminta Beauchamp stepped in. She
was a pretty girl with a fringe of dark hair that almost
covered her eyes. She kept flicking it away with a toss
of her head.

Bond sighed. 'Minty, I said absolutely no interrup-
tions. Don't you understand plain English?'

'Sorry, sir. Q Branch has just called to say that they
can see you any time that's convenient to you.'

'I know that. I've just been speaking to M.'

'I thought it was important . . .' Her chin quivered
and she dragged her fringe away with a finger to reveal
eyes about to weep tears of penitence.

'Thank you,' Bond said, gently. 'You're right. It
probably is. And please don't cry, Minty.'

Bond rode the lift down to Q Branch's domain in
the basement and announced himself. He was met by
a young bespectacled man who introduced himself as
Quentin Dale. He looked about twenty-five years old
and had the eager proselytising manner of a doorstep
missionary.

'I don't think we've met before, Commander,'
Dale said, cheerfully. 'I've only been here a couple of

months.' He led Bond down a corridor to his small office, showed him to a seat and sat down opposite, removing a file from his desk and pushing his spectacles back on his nose.

'You'll need some inoculations if you're going to West Africa,' he said. 'Shall we arrange them or would you prefer your own doctor?'

'I'll deal with that,' Bond said.

'Yellow fever, smallpox, polio – and you'll need a supply of antimalarials. They say Daraprim is very good.'

'Fine,' Bond said, thinking that the only problem with Q Branch was that they treated everyone as a naive, innocent, not to say ignorant, fool.

'We don't think you should go to Zanzarim armed,' Dale said, consulting the notes in his file. 'Because of the war the airport searches at Sinsikrou can be very thorough. And you're working for a French press agency . . .' Dale smiled, sympathetically, as if he was about to break bad news. 'And the French aren't very popular with the Zanzaris.'

'Why's that?'

'They've given a kind of de facto recognition of the Dahum state. The French embassy here in London is where the Dahum diplomatic mission is based.' He screwed up his face.

'I suppose it was their colony for a while.'

'True,' Dale said.

'But I'll be pretty popular in Dahum itself.'

'Exactly – that's the logic.' Dale smiled again, this time approvingly, as if the most backward boy in the class had answered a difficult question. He reached into another drawer and took out a zipped pigskin toilet bag, opening it and showing Bond its contents. Bond saw that it was a luxury shaving kit: safety razor, Old Spice shaving stick and badger-bristle brush, after-shave, talcum powder, a deodorant roll-on, all tucked in their respective pockets and slings.

'We can't give you a gun, but we can give you some potency,' Dale said. He held up the aftershave. 'A tablespoonful of this will knock a man out for twelve hours. Add a teaspoon of this' – he showed Bond the talcum powder – 'and he'll go into a coma for two to three days. It's completely tasteless, by the way. You can put it in any drink or food, no one will notice.'

'What if I add two teaspoons?' Bond asked.

'You'll probably kill him. Best to make it three teaspoons to be on the safe side, if you want to bring about death. Coma, then a massive heart attack,' he smiled and pushed his spectacles back on his nose again. 'Should give you plenty of time to make your escape.'

He took an envelope from his file and handed it over.

603/301

SOLO · 51

'This contains all the information you need. And your plane ticket to Zanzarim. BOAC on Friday evening. One way.'

'So I'm not coming back,' Bond said, drily.

'Our station head in Sinsikrou will arrange your journey home. It's not clear how long you'll be in the country, anyway – or even if you'll be leaving from it.'

'I suppose not. Who's our station head?'

'Ah . . .' he looked at his file. 'One E. B. Ogilvy-Grant. It's been very recently set up. A business card with the address and phone number is in the envelope and confirmation of your reservation at the Excelsior Gateway Hotel. It's near the airport. Ogilvy-Grant will make contact with you after you've landed.'

Bond took the business card from the envelope. It read: 'E. B. Ogilvy-Grant MA (Cantab). Palm Oil Export and Agricultural Services.' There was a telephone number in the corner.

'Anything else, Commander?'

Bond zipped up the toilet bag.

'What about communications? Connecting with base, here?'

'Ogilvy-Grant will take care of all that.'

Bond stood up, slowly. Something was bothering him. It all seemed a bit vague, a bit wing-and-a-prayer, a bit improvised. But maybe this was what a mission to

ORLAND PARK PUBLIC LIBRARY

a civil-war-torn West African country involved. Once he was actually in Zanzarim and had met Ogilvy-Grant the picture would be clearer, surely. He had a few days before his plane left, in any event, so it might be a good idea to do some extra homework himself.

'Good luck,' Dale said, flashing him his boyish smile. He didn't offer Bond his hand to shake.

# 2

# Homework

B ond strolled down the street in Bayswater for the
second time and joined the back of a long queue
at a bus stop and took in his surroundings at leisure.
Across the street was a small shabby parade of shops – an
ironmonger, a newsagent, a grocery store and a seemingly empty premises with a hand-painted sign above
the grimy plate glass window that said 'AfricaKIN'.
Sellotaped to the glass was a poster of a starving child
with rheumy eyes and a distended belly holding out a
claw-like begging hand. The caption was: 'Genocide in
Dahum. Please give generously.'

Bond crossed the road and rang the bell.

He heard a clatter of footsteps descending some
stairs and sensed a presence behind the door scrutinising him through the peephole.

'Who are you? What do you want?' an educated English voice said.

'My name's James Bond. I'm a journalist,' Bond explained, adding, 'I'm going to Zanzarim on Friday.'

The door was opened after a key had turned in a lock and two bolts were drawn. A slim African man stood there, in his forties, smart in a pinstriped suit with his head completely shaven and a neat goatee beard. His gaze was watchful and unwelcoming.

Bond showed his Agence Presse Libre card. The man smiled and visibly relaxed.

'I'm looking for Gabriel Adeka,' Bond said.

'You've found him. Come on in.'

Bond knew from his further researches that Gabriel Adeka was Brigadier Solomon Adeka's older brother. A successful barrister, educated at Rugby School and Merton College, Oxford, he had given up his lucrative legal career to found AfricaKIN, a charity dedicated to alleviating the suffering in Dahum. Bond saw, as he entered, that the linoleum-covered ground floor contained a fifth-hand photocopier and, to one side on a decorator's trestle table, a light box and a typewriter. It must be quite a contrast to his chambers in Lincoln's Inn, Bond thought, as he followed Adeka up the creaking carpetless stairs to his small office on the floor above.

Adeka's office was papered with his various distress-
ing posters and was occupied by a table and chair surrounded by yellowing piles of flyers, news-sheets and
booklets about AfricaKIN and the plight of Dahum.
He shifted some cardboard boxes and found a stool
behind them, placing it in front of his desk for Bond to
sit on.

'May I offer you a cup of tea?' Adeka said, gesturing
towards an electric kettle and some mugs on a tray on
the floor.

'No, thank you . . . I don't drink tea,' Bond added in
explanation.

'And you call yourself an Englishman?' Adeka
smiled.

'Actually, I'm not English,' Bond said, then changed
the subject. 'You seem to be very much on your own
here. One-man band.'

'I've a ready supply of volunteers when the need
arises,' Adeka said, with a weary smile. 'But most of
my funds have gone. I gave up my practice two years
ago and as we all know, money – alas – doesn't grow on
trees. Also, we find ourselves very harassed by the state.
Inexplicable electricity failures, visits by aggressive
bailiffs claiming we haven't paid our bills, break-ins,
vandalism. All this costs me. AfricaKIN isn't welcome
– Her Majesty's Government has made that very clear.'

'Maybe you should move to Paris,' Bond said.

'I've thought about it, believe me. Without our French friends . . .' He stopped. 'I wouldn't be talking to you, Mr Bond, if you didn't work for a French press agency.'

'I'm very grateful.'

'So, what takes you to our benighted country?'

'I'm flying in to Sinsikrou, yes – but then I plan to make my way south, to Dahum. I want to interview your brother – which is why I'm here.'

The kettle had boiled and Adeka made himself a cup of tea – no milk, no sugar. He sat behind his desk and looked at Bond, candidly, silently for a second or two, as if weighing him up, analysing him. Bond sat there, happy to be scrutinised – for some reason he liked Gabriel Adeka and admired his futile ambitions, his sacrifice, his crazy integrity.

'Why do you think I might be able to help you?'

'Well, you are his brother.'

'True. But I haven't spoken to my "little brother" since Dahum seceded in '67,' he said with heavy cynicism. 'Solomon can be very persuasive. He told me what he was planning to do – to secede, to establish a "new" country, keep the potential oil revenues for the Fakassa people. He had very, very big dreams. I begged him not to do it, told him it would be a disaster

for the Fakassa, a kind of race-suicide.' His face taut-
ened. 'I derive no satisfaction from being proved
right.'

'So why didn't he listen to you?'

'You wouldn't understand, Mr Bond. You have to
be a Fakassa to have that depth of feeling, that close-
ness . . .' The words seemed to fail him. 'We've lived in
the Zanza River Delta for hundreds, perhaps thousands
of years. It's our homeland – our heartland – in every
passionate, instinctive sense of the words.' He smiled,
emptily. 'I don't expect you to know what I'm talking
about. You're not African.'

'No, I can understand,' Bond said. 'You make sense.
There's no need to patronise me.'

'I apologise. Do you own a house?'

'I have a flat.'

'Do you like living there?'

'Very much.'

'What would you say if your neighbours came in one
day and took away your carpets and your furniture,
your treasured possessions?'

Bond shrugged. 'It doesn't relate. The Zanza River
Delta is part of Zanzarim.'

Adeka looked a little contemptuous. 'Zanzarim, and
before that, Upper Zanza State, and before that Neu
Zanza Staat was a construct of European colonialists.

They only arrived a few decades ago, at the end of the last century. They drew the country's boundaries on a whim one afternoon when they had nothing better to do.' He grew more serious. 'To the Fakassa people the Zanza River Delta, our tribal homeland, is our birth-right. It has no connection with twentieth-century neocolonial politics or the venal ambitions of European adventurers. Can you understand that?'

'Yes, I think so.'

Adeka yielded a little. 'All the same, my brother, Solomon, should never have tried to create an indepen-dent state. It was madness. I told him so. We fought, spoke very harsh words to each other and we haven't seen each other since.'

'Your arguments didn't impress.'

'He couldn't see sense. Wouldn't. Not surprisingly.'

'What do you mean?'

'Have you any idea how much oil lies beneath the Zanza River Delta, Mr Bond?'

'No.'

'Well, I suggest you try to find out – and then calcu-late roughly how many hundreds of millions of dollars will go to whoever owns it.'

He stood up. 'I can't help you, I'm afraid. You'll have to find someone else who can introduce you to my brother. All I ask is, if and when you reach Dahum, you tell the world exactly and honestly what you see there.'

Bond rose to his feet. 'You can count on that,' he said. 'We're not in the propaganda business.'

Adeka led him back downstairs and at the door handed him his business card.

'I'd be most grateful if you'd send me your articles.'

He extended his hand and Bond shook it, firmly, not thinking about the reality that lay behind his journey to Zanzarim.

'I'll give your salutations to your brother,' Bond said.

'Save your breath,' Adeka said evenly, with no bitterness. 'Solomon looks on me as the worst kind of traitor – he thinks I've betrayed my people.'

They made their farewells and Bond stepped out of the small shop on to the street and heard the bolts on the door slide shut behind him.

Bond wandered up the street, thinking, heading for the Bayswater Road. He glanced around him, remembering Adeka's words about continual harassment, wondering if the AfricaKIN office was under surveillance and, if it were, whether his visit would have been noted and logged. Something was making him uneasy, a prickling between his shoulder blades, an uncomfortableness. He always responded to these instinctive promptings – whenever he'd ignored them he had usually regretted it – so, looking for an opportunity to check his back, he turned into a convenient cinema and bought a ticket for the show but, instead of going into the auditorium, lingered in the foyer, to see who might be following him in. After five minutes he began to relax. No one else arriving at the kiosk to buy a ticket could have been any threat at all.

An usherette approached him asking if she could be of any help, reminding him that the film was due to start in 'four and a half minutes'. Bond reassured her he was aware of that fact and moved outside beneath the cinema's awning, glancing up and down the street. Nothing. Then his eye was caught by the poster. *The Curse of Dracula's Daughter* starring Astrid Ostergard. Bond smiled. There was Astrid/Bryce, naked in a bed, a tattered blood-boltered sheet just about covering her impossibly ripe body, a dark looming shadow of some vengeful monster cast over her. It wasn't a bad likeness, Bond reflected, remembering the glimpses he'd been afforded a few days ago. So this was where he'd seen her name before – B-movie horror-shockers. At least that much was clear now. Yet here was Bryce Fitzjohn/ Astrid Ostergard again. Was there any significance in this curious recurrence? Anything he'd missed . . . ? Stepping into a random cinema foyer couldn't be construed as anything malign or manipulated – this was a harmless coincidence pure and simple. He had another look at the poster and smiled to himself, thinking he really had to make contact with her again once this whole Zanzarim business was over, and turned on to the street and strode confidently on towards the Bayswater Road, looking for a passing taxi he could hail.

# 3

# Welcome to Zanzarim

The BOAC VC10 levelled into its cruising altitude and the 'fasten seat belts' sign was extinguished. Bond ordered a double brandy and soda from the stewardess and as he sipped his drink thought about what lay ahead of him and what unforeseen perils he might have to face. It was always like this as he departed on a mission – and while the unknown generated a certain alarm and pre-emptive caution, Bond also recognised the frisson of excitement that ran through him. This was what he had been trained and honed to do, he re-emphasised to himself; sometimes he wondered if it was what he was born to do. He glanced over his shoulder, checking the cabin – the plane was only half full and Bond had two empty seats beside him. Not many people going to Zanzarim these days, he reflected, even though this flight was routed on to Banjul and Accra. Bond ordered another drink, running over the events of the last few days in his mind. He couldn't remember M sending him on such a vague assignment before: to find a way of infiltrating himself into Dahum and, one way or another, to 'immobilise' the brigadier . . . Perhaps, as far as M thought, his instructions were perfectly explicit, however concise. But, from Bond's point of view there was a lot of room being left for his initiative. Conceivably Ogilvy-Grant would be able to put some flesh on these bare bones.

The plane flew south into the darkening evening sky. Bond switched on his reading light and took out his book – Graham Greene's *The Heart of the Matter*. Bond had been to West Africa only once before, years ago – to shoot down a helicopter, as it happened – but he had not lingered; it had been an in-and-out visit. Greene had served in Sierra Leone during the war – as a spy, moreover – and Bond was hoping that his West African novel might furnish some shrewder insight to the place.

**Eight hours** later the VC10 touched down at Sinsikrou International Airport. As the plane taxied towards the terminal buildings Bond gazed out of the window at Africa, lit by the early morning sun. They passed gangs of crouching workers cutting the runway verges with long thin knives like sabres. Beyond the perimeter fence was undulating dry scrubland dotted with trees – orchard bush, as it was known – that sprawled away in the heat-haze. A row of olive-green MiG-15 'Fagot' fighters and a couple of sun-bleached, oil-stained Bell UH-1 helicopters were drawn up on a separate apron. The Zanzarim air force, Bond assumed. A few soldiers squatted listlessly in the shade cast by the planes' wings.

The VC10 came to a halt and the passengers bound for Sinsikrou headed for the door. All men, Bond noted, and none of them looking particularly salubrious. As he passed through the door on to the aircraft steps the humid warmth hit him with almost palpable force and, as he crossed the parched, piebald asphalt towards the airport buildings, he sensed his body breaking out in sweat beneath his clothes. Soldiers, wearing an assortment of camouflage uniforms and carrying various weapons, looked on lazily as the passengers filed into customs and immigration. Bond glanced around quickly. Parked by the fuel depot was a shiny new six-wheeled Saracen armoured car – recently imported from Britain, Bond supposed, the first patent indication of whose side we were on in this war.

As if to give credence to this analysis Bond's British passport was barely examined. It was stamped, the immigration officer said 'Welcome to Zanzarim,' and waved him through to the customs hall, which was surprisingly busy with a traffic of people who apparently had nothing to do with customs. As he waited for his suitcase to arrive, Bond declined to have his shoes polished, rejected the invitation to be driven in a 'luxury' Mercedes-Benz private car to his hotel and politely refused a small boy's whispered offer of sex with his 'very beautiful' big sister.

A surly customs officer asked him to open his case, rummaged through his clothes and even unzipped his pigskin toilet bag and – finding no contraband – scratched a hieroglyph on the suitcase's lid with a piece of blue chalk and moved on to the next piece of baggage in the queue.

Bond again refused the offer of help with his case as a young man physically tried to prise it from his grasp, and walked out of the building to find a taxi rank. He climbed into the back of a racing-green Morris Minor and happily agreed to pay extra in order not to share the car with others. He instructed the driver to take him to the Excelsior Gateway Hotel.

Even though the Excelsior was barely a mile from the airport the journey there was not straightforward.

Almost as soon as they left the airport perimeter they were waved to a halt at an army roadblock and Bond was asked to step out of the car and show the customs mark on his suitcase. Despite the clear evidence of the chalk scribble he was asked to open the suitcase again. The soldiers at the roadblock were bored and this was a diversion to enliven their long and weary day, Bond realised. Other taxis were halted behind them and soon voices were being raised in angry protest. Bond wondered if he should give the soldier who was listlessly picking through his case some money – a 'dash', as he now knew it was called, thanks to his reading of *The Heart of the Matter* – but before he could do so an officer appeared, shouting in furious rage at his men and waved everyone on.

A further 500 yards down the road they were halted at another so-called roadblock consisting of two oil drums with a plank across them. This looked less official and the demeanour of the soldiers manning it was more lackadaisical, the men contenting themselves with peering curiously through the open windows into the back of the taxi.

'Good morning,' Bond said. 'How are you today?'

'American cigarette?' one soldier said, grinning. He was wearing a tin helmet, a red T-shirt and camouflage trousers.

'English,' Bond said and gave him the Morlands that remained in his cigarette case.

When they eventually reached the hotel entrance Bond paid his fare and pushed through the crowd of hawkers that surrounded him – offering thorn carvings, painted calabashes, beaded necklaces – and finally gained the cool lobby of the Excelsior Gateway, formerly the Prince Clarence Hotel, as an old painted sign on the wall informed him. Ceiling fans turned above his head and Bond gave his suitcase to a bellhop in a scarlet waistcoat with a scarlet fez on his head. He crossed the glossy teak floorboards towards the reception desk where he was checked in. There, an envelope was handed to him that contained a slip of paper with Ogilvy-Grant's address and new contact telephone number at an industrial park. Bond folded the note up and tucked it in his pocket, looking around him as the receptionist busied himself writing down Bond's details from his passport. Potted palms swayed in the breeze produced by the ceiling fans. Through glass doors Bond looked into a long dark bar where a barman in a white jacket was polishing glasses. On the other side of the lobby was the entrance to the dining room, where a sign requested 'Gentlemen, please no shorts'. Another receptionist wearing a crisp white tunic with gold buttons arrived on duty and wished him a smiling 'Good morning, Mr Bond.' For a moment Bond savoured the illusion of time travel, when the Excelsior Gateway had been the Prince Clarence Hotel and Zanzarim had been Upper Zanza State and civil war, mass starvation and illimitable oil revenues were all in an unimaginable future.

# 4

# Christmas

The bellhop in the scarlet fez took Bond to his small chalet in the hotel grounds at the rear of the main building. There were a dozen of these mini-bungalows linked to the hotel buildings by weed-badged concrete pathways, a remnant of the Excelsior Gateway's colonial past. After independence an Olympic-sized swimming pool had been constructed, flanked by two five-storey modern annexes – 'executive rooms with pool-view balconies'. Bond was glad to be in his shabby bungalow. He tipped the bellhop.

'Water he close at noon, sar,' the boy said. 'But we have electric light twenty-four hours.' He smiled. 'We have gen'rator.'

Bond took his advice and had a cold shower while the water pressure was still there. He changed into a cotton khaki-drill suit, a white short-sleeved Aertex shirt and a navy-blue knitted tie. He slipped his feet into soft brown moccasins, thought about removing his socks but decided against it. He reloaded his cigarette case with some of the Morlands he'd brought with him in a 200-cigarette carton and, ready for action, headed out to the hotel entrance.

The doorman shooed away the hawkers and Bond gave him $10.

'I need a taxi with a good driver for several hours,' Bond said. 'Twenty US dollars for the day – and if he's good, I'll give you another ten.'

'Five seconds, sar,' the doorman said and raced off.

Two minutes later a mustard yellow Toyota Corona lurched to a halt opposite Bond. A skinny young man, smart in a white shirt and white shorts, stepped out and saluted.

'Hello, sar. I am your driver, Christmas.'

Bond shook Christmas's hand and eased himself into the back of the Corona.

'Where to, sar?'

'Do you know where the military headquarters are?'

'Zanza Force HQ. I know him. Ridgeway Barracks.'

'Good. Let's go.'

Ridgeway Barracks was a large four-storey pre-war building of faded cream stucco set in a park of mature casuarina pines. Christmas dropped him at the main entrance and Bond showed his press card to the soldier at the gate and was told to follow a sign that said 'Press Liaison'. In an office at the end of a corridor a young captain with an American accent looked over his documentation.

'Agence Presse Libre? This is French. Are you French?'

'No. I'm from the London office. I file all copy in English. It's an international press agency, founded in 1923. Global. Like Reuters.'

The captain thought about it for a moment then stamped and signed a new accredited press card. He smiled, insincerely – Bond suspected that he didn't like journalists or his job – and handed it over.

'The daily briefing is in twenty minutes,' he said. 'Let me take you to your colleagues.'

The captain led Bond out through the back of the building where, at the edge of a beaten earth parade ground, a large canvas tent had been pitched.

'Take a seat – we'll be there shortly.'

Bond slipped in the back and sat down, looking around him. The filtered sunlight coming through the canvas was aqueous and shadowless. It was hot. Sitting randomly on rows of folding chairs were about two dozen journalists – almost all white – facing an empty dais beneath a huge map of Zanzarim. On this map, at the foot, a small bashed circle that was now the diminishing heartland of the Democratic Republic of Dahum was outlined in red chalk. Clusters of sticky-backed arrows threatening the circle indicated offensives by the federal Zanzarim forces, Bond supposed. He wandered down an aisle between rows of empty chairs to get a closer look.

The scale of the map revealed in great detail the massive and complex network of creeks and watercourses that made up the Zanza River Delta. Port Dunbar was at the southern extremity, the notional capital of the secessionist state. Above it, written on a card and stuck on the map, was the name Janjaville, where the vital airstrip was to be found. It was immediately apparent to Bond that bringing an end to Dahum would be no easy task. One main highway crossing many bridges and causeways led south into Port Dunbar and it was here, judging from the clustered arrows, that the main federal thrust into the heartland was taking place. All other roadways were symbolised by dotted red lines, meandering around the obstacles posed by the creeks, swamps and lakes, crossing hundreds of makeshift bridges, Bond imagined. You didn't need to be a military genius to defend this small patch of territory, it seemed to him.

Bond wandered back to his seat – his close look at the map had also allowed him to calculate the distance from Sinsikrou to Port Dunbar – some 300 miles, he reckoned. He began to wonder how Ogilvy-Grant planned to 'infiltrate' him – it didn't seem that straightforward . . .

Suddenly there was a jaded tremor of interest amongst the waiting journalists as a bemedalled colonel in crisp, brutally starched camouflage fatigues pushed through a flap at the rear of the tent and took up his position on the dais, followed by the captain with the American accent, who was carrying a thin six-foot rod, like a billiard cue.

'Good day to you, gentlemen,' the colonel said. 'Welcome to the briefing. We have interesting news for you today.' The colonel took the pointing-stick from the captain and, indicating with it on the map, began to enumerate various federal victories and advances into the rebel heartland. Under his instructions the captain rubbed out a portion of the Dahum circle and redrew it with the red chalk so that a pronounced salient appeared on the main highway south. Bond sensed the minimal credulity in the room diminish, suddenly, like a balloon deflating.

'With the capture yesterday of the village of Ikot-Dussa the Zanzari forces are now forty-two kilometres from Port Dunbar,' the colonel said, triumphantly, turned and left the tent.

A journalist raised his hand.

'Yes, Geoffrey,' the captain said.

'According to my notes,' Geoffrey said, his voice flat, 'the village of Ikot-Dussa was liberated ten days ago.'

'That was Ikot-Darema,' the captain said without a pause. 'Maybe our Zanzari names are confusing you.'

'Yes, that's probably it – my mistake. Apologies.' There was a subdued ripple of badly suppressed chuckles amongst the journalists and many knowing glances were exchanged.

Another journalist's hand was raised.

'You were predicting the unconditional surrender of rebel forces five weeks ago. What's happened?'

The captain leaned the stick against the wall.

'You may have noticed, John,' the captain said, not quite managing to disguise his weariness, 'now you've been in the country for so long, that it's been raining rather heavily these last couple of months. And now it's stopped raining and the dry season has begun – therefore military operations are resuming at full strength.'

And so the briefing continued for another listless twenty minutes as each loaded question was either batted away or rebuffed with confident fabrication.

Bond found he rather admired the captain's tireless ability to lie so fluently and with manifest conviction. He was good at his job but no one was fooled. This war had ground to a semi-permanent halt, no doubt about it. Bond stood up and slipped out of the tent. He had learned a surprising amount on his first day as an accredited journalist for APL. It was time, he felt, to make contact with the British Secret Service's head of station in Zanzarim.

# 5

# E. B. Ogilvy-Grant
# MA (Cantab)

OG Palm Oil Export and Agricultural Services Ltd was to be found in a light-industrial estate halfway between Sinsikrou city and the airport. Bond had telephoned from Ridgeway Barracks, but there had been no reply, so he decided to pay a personal visit. Christmas drove Bond into the complex and stopped in the shade of a Bata Shoe warehouse. Opposite was a small row of premises with storage space below and offices above. OG Palm Oil Export and Agricultural Services was at the end.

'I won't be long,' Bond said, opening the door.

'I stay here, sar.'

Bond crossed the road to the OG section of the building. Sun-blistered metal blinds were padlocked down and the electric bell-push dangled from its flex by the door that accessed the stairwell. Bond rang the bell but it seemed dead to him. He pushed at the door and it swayed open. All very impressive, he thought: as 'cover' went, this might work – a tenth-rate palm-oil exporter on its uppers. He closed the door behind him and walked up the stairs to the offices. He knocked on the door but there was no reply, he tried the handle and the door opened – so, no locked doors at OG Palm Oil Export and Agricultural Services Ltd. Bond stepped into the office and raised his voice – 'Hello? Anybody in?' Silence. Bond looked around: a metal desk with a typewriter and an empty in tray, a wooden filing cabinet, a fan on a tea chest, last year's calendar on the wall, a display table with various dusty sample tins of palm oil set out on it and – touchingly, Bond thought – hanging by the door, a faded reproduction of Annigoni's 1956 portrait of the Queen, a small symbol of the covert business being done here.

Someone's throat was cleared loudly behind him.

Bond turned round slowly. 'Hello,' he said.

A young African woman stood there – a pale-skinned Zanzari, Bond thought, slim, petite, pretty, her hair knotted in tight neat rows, flat against her skull, which had the curious effect of making her brown eyes seem wider and more alert. She was wearing a 'Ban the Bomb' T-shirt, pale denim jeans cut off raggedly at the knee and around her neck hung a string of heavy amber beads. Ogilvy-Grant's secretary, Bond assumed. Well, he could certainly pick them – she was a beautiful young woman.

'My name's Bond, James Bond,' he said. 'I want to buy some palm oil. I'd like to arrange a meeting with Ogilvy-Grant.'

'Your wish is granted,' she said. 'I'm Ogilvy-Grant.'

Bond managed to suppress his sudden smile of incredulity.

'Listen, I don't think you understand—'

'I'm Efua Blessing Ogilvy-Grant,' the young woman said, then added with overt cynicism, 'oh, yes, I'm E. B. Ogilvy-Grant, managing director.' She had a clipped English accent, rather posh, Bond thought, rather like Araminta Beauchamp's.

'Nice to meet you, Mr Bond,' she said and they shook hands. 'My friends all call me Blessing.'

'A Blessing in disguise,' Bond said without thinking.

'Funny – I've never heard that one before,' she said, clearly unamused.

'I apologise,' Bond said, feeling vaguely shamefaced that he'd uttered it.

'I was waiting for you at the airport this morning,' she said. 'Didn't London tell you I'd be there?'

'They didn't, actually . . .' Bond watched her take her seat behind the desk.

'We were meant to meet by the Independence Monument.'

'No one told me.'

'Standard London cock-up.'

She opened a drawer and took out a pack of cigarettes, offering it to Bond.

'They're our local brand,' she said. 'Tuskers – strong and oddly addictive.'

Bond took one, fished out his Ronson and lit her cigarette, then his.

'So – you're our head of station in Zanzarim.'

'Go to the top of the class. That's me.'

Her accent sat oddly with the radical-chic, love-in outfit, Bond thought.

'When were you appointed, if you don't mind my asking?' he went on.

'I don't mind at all. Just over two months ago. Weirdly, we had no one here. Everything was run through the embassy.' She smiled, relaxing a bit. 'My mother is a Lowele. All her family's here in Sinsikrou – my family. I speak Lowele. And my father was a Scottish engineer, Fraser Ogilvy-Grant, who helped build the big dam in the north at Mogasso just before the war. My mother worked as his interpreter – and they fell in love.'

'A Scottish engineer?' Bond said. 'So was my father, funnily enough. And my mother was Swiss,' he added, as if the fact that they were both of mixed nationalities would form an affinity between them.

In fact the information did seem to make her relax even more, Bond thought. That old Celtic blood tie established, the homeland noted – however fragile the connection, however meaningless – worked its temporary magic.

'You don't sound Scottish,' he said.

'Neither do you.' She smiled. 'I was educated in England. Cheltenham Ladies' College, then Cambridge, then Harvard. I hardly know Scotland, to be honest.'

Bond stubbed out his Tusker in the ashtray on her desk, his throat raw.

'Did they recruit you at Cambridge?'

'Yes. Then they arranged for me to go to Harvard. I think they had plans for me in America. But, because of my family connections, this was the perfect first assignment.'

Bond was trying to calculate her age – Cambridge then Harvard, born in the war, maybe twenty-six, or twenty-seven. She was remarkably assured for one so young; but he suspected this job was going to prove harder than he had ever imagined.

'I'm staying at the Excelsior,' he said.

'Yes, I do know that,' she said with elaborate patience. 'And Christmas is your driver.'

'Ah, so you must have arranged—'

'I'm here to help, Commander Bond.' She stood up. 'I must say it's a great privilege to be working with you. Your reputation precedes you, even out here in the sticks.'

'Please call me James, Blessing.'

'I'm here to help, James,' she repeated. 'Shall we have dinner tonight? There's a good Lebanese restaurant in town. We can talk through everything then.' She walked him to the door. 'Make our plans. I'll pick you up at the Excelsior at seven.'

# 6

# Syrian Burgundy-Type

Bond had ordered malfouf – stuffed cabbage rolls – followed by shish tawook – a simple chicken kebab with salty pickles. The food was good. Bond had spent three weeks on a tedious job in Beirut in 1960 and in his endless spare time had developed a taste for Lebanese cuisine. The wine list, however, was a joke, given that he had drunk excellent Lebanese wines in Beirut – all that was on offer here was Blue Nun Riesling and a red described as 'Syrian Burgundy-type' – so Bond played safe and ordered the local beer, Green Star. It was something of a first for him to drink beer with dinner, but the lager was light and very cold and complemented the strong flavours of the garlic and the pickles. Blessing had a cold lentil soup and a dried-mint omelette.

'You're not a vegetarian, are you?' Bond asked, suspiciously.

'No,' she said. 'Just not very hungry. Would it matter if I was?'

'It might,' Bond said, with a smile. 'I've never met a vegetarian I liked, curiously. You might have been the exception, of course.'

'Ha-ha,' she remarked, drily. 'By their food shall ye judge them.'

'You'd be surprised, it's not a bad touchstone,' Bond said, and called for another Green Star. 'Or so I've found in my experience.'

Since he had left her office she had had her hair redone. The plaited rows had gone and it was now oiled flat back against her head almost as if it was painted on. She had a shiny transparent gloss on her lips and was wearing a black silk Nehru jacket over wide flared white cotton trousers, and had some sort of crudely beaten pewter disc hanging round her neck on a leather thong. She looked very futuristic, Bond thought, with her perfect caramel skin, the colour of milky coffee, as if she were an extra from a science-fiction film.

The restaurant was in downtown Sinsikrou, near to the law courts and the barracks. It had a deliberately modest facade with a flickering neon sign that bluntly read 'El Kebab – Best Lebanon', but the first-floor dining room was air-conditioned and there were white linen cloths on the tables and waiters in velvet waistcoats and tasselled tarbooshes. Bond had spotted several high-ranking soldiers and also some of the journalists who'd been at the briefing earlier that day. El Kebab was obviously the only place in town.

They chatted idly as they ate, keeping off the subject of their business with each other – the tables were close and it would be easy to overhear or eavesdrop. Blessing told him more about the civil war and its origins from her perspective. Being half-Lowele, she explained, she thought that the Fakassa junta that had provoked and engineered secession were crazy. What did they think the rest of the country was going to do? Sit on their collective hands? Allow themselves to become impoverished? At least the British government had acted quickly, she said. If they hadn't come down on the side of Zanzarim immediately and refused point-blank to recognise the new republic, perhaps Dahum's de facto existence might have become a foregone conclusion. Alacrity was not normally a virtue of Her Majesty's governments, Bond thought – there would be more at stake here than preserving the rule of international law.

'Do you want a pudding?' Bond asked, lighting a cigarette.

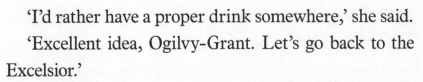

'I'd rather have a proper drink somewhere,' she said.

'Excellent idea, Ogilvy-Grant. Let's go back to the Excelsior.'

Blessing drove them to the hotel, Bond looking out of the window at the garish cinema of the night-time city that was Sinsikrou. Blaring high-life music seemed to come from almost every house, and multicoloured neon tubes appeared to be the illumination of choice. Dogs, goats and hens searched the storm drains for tit-bits; naked children stood in doorways staring at the passing cars, entranced; off-duty soldiers swaggered through the roadside crowds, Kalashnikovs and SLR rifles slung over their shoulders. And every time they stopped at a traffic light or when the gridlock of cars slowed them to walking pace, street-hawkers would appear at their windows trying to sell them combs and biros, dusters and cheap watches.

The bar at the Excelsior was surprisingly busy.

'It's a very popular place,' Blessing said, spotting an unoccupied table at the back of the room. 'Especially since the war began.' They sat down and Bond ordered himself a large whisky and soda and a gin and tonic for Blessing.

The air conditioning was on and working and the chill was welcome after the humid, loud night outside. Not that it was any quieter in here, Bond thought, looking round the room. A lot of white men, some in assorted uniforms, not many Zanzaris.

'Who are they?' Bond asked Blessing, indicating the men in uniform.

'The pilots – they fly the MiGs. East Germans, Poles, a few Egyptians. They're on a thousand dollars a day – cash. Very popular with the ladies.'

Bond had noticed the prostitutes. They sat at the bar or sauntered suggestively among the crowded tables. Beautiful black women with bouffant wigs – modelled on American pop stars, Bond thought, as one of them caught his eye and beckoned him over with a flap of her glossy taloned fingers.

The chatter of conversation was loud and already raucous – everyone drinking heavily. The air smelt of booze, sweat and cheap perfume – redolent of sex and danger. There was a kind of frontier recklessness about the atmosphere, Bond thought, and recognised its allure. These pilots had been out dropping bombs and napalm on Dahum. The temptations offered in the bar at the Excelsior would be hard to resist.

He looked at the men. Ex-Eastern bloc air-force pilots, all on the older side – retired, superannuated, cashiered – earning good money as mercenaries fighting in a nasty little African war . . . $1,000 a day – after three months you could quit, take a couple

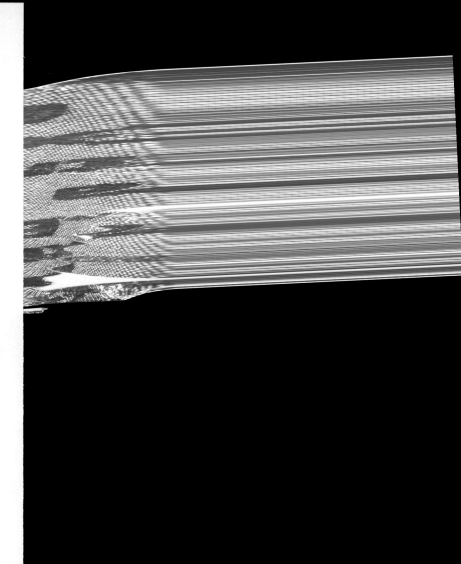

of years off, build a house back home, ◌
foreign car.

He ordered another round of drinks from a ◌
waiter, leaned closer to Blessing and lowered his v◌

'I reckon we can safely talk in this din,' he sai◌
'What's your plan?'

'I did a quick recce last week when I knew you were
coming,' she said. 'The only way into Dahum is by
road, or, rather, by road and water. The main highway's impossible – jammed with non-stop military
traffic.' She sipped at her drink. 'I think you have to
be driven as far south into the delta as possible. Then
a local fisherman – I've made contact with one man –
will take you through the swamps and the creeks by
boat.'

'Is that realistic?' Bond wondered.

'There's no front line as such,' she said. 'And there's
constant smuggling of food and supplies into the heartland. It's a labyrinth, a huge network of waterways and
streams and creeks. That's one reason why the war's
gone on so long.'

'Who'll drive me south? Christmas?'

She looked at him and smiled. 'I thought I would,'
she said. 'I speak Lowele. You'd need a translator,
anyway. It'll all look very plausible if we're stopped and
questioned.'

'Sounds good to me,' Bond said, feeling oddly relieved. 'How long will it take to reach the delta?'

'We'll have to travel on back roads – meander south. I reckon two or three days' driving. Two nights.'

Bond turned the ice cubes in his whisky with a finger, enjoying the sensation of being in Blessing's capable hands as she outlined the plan further. They would stay in local rest-houses, then contact would be made with the fisherman, who would be well paid on Bond's safe delivery into Dahum. Blessing would head back to Sinsikrou and wait until she heard from him.

'Or not,' Bond said. 'I may not come back this way.'

'Of course. As operational necessities dictate.'

'When should we head off?'

'Whenever you want,' she said. 'It's your decision.'

'Let's not wait around,' Bond said. 'How about tomorrow?'

'No problem. I'll have everything ready first thing in the morning. Come over to the office and we'll hit the road. One thing,' she added. 'I would travel light. Just one small bag or a rucksack or something. You may have to hike a bit once you get into Dahum.'

Bond had been thinking about that, feeling the heart-thump of excitement that gripped him whenever a mission was imminent and all the cosy securities of everyday life were about to be cast aside. He took out his cigarette case – empty. Blessing saw this and reached into her handbag for her pack of Tuskers.

'You'll have to go local,' she said, offering the pack. Bond took a cigarette.

'You're Bond, aren't you?' a slurred male English voice said.

Bond turned. A drunk white man swayed there gently. He was wearing a crumpled pale blue drill suit with darker blue sweat patches forming at the armpits. His jowly face was flushed and sweating. Bond recognised him from the press briefing at the barracks: a fellow journalist – one who'd asked a question.

'That's right,' Bond said, flatly. He wanted this encounter to end. Now.

'Geoffrey Letham, *Daily Mail*,' the man said. 'You're with APL, aren't you? Saw you were a new boy today so I checked the accreditation list.' He leaned forward and Bond smelled the sour reek of beer. 'D'you know old Thierry? Thierry Duhamel?'

'I'm working out of London,' Bond said, improvising. 'Not Paris.'

'No, Thierry's in Geneva. Head office. Everybody at APL knows Thierry. He's a bloody legend.'

'I've only just started. I've been in Australia the last couple of years. Reuters,' he added, hoping this would shut the man up. Blessing leaned forward with her lighter and clicked it on, as if to signal that the conversation was over. Bond turned away from Letham and bent his head to light his cigarette. He sat back and exhaled. But Letham was still there, staring at Blessing as though in a trance of lust.

'Hello, hello, *hello*,' he said, with a caricature leer, and then turned to Bond. 'Pretty little thing. After you with her, old chap.'

Bond saw the offence register on Blessing's face and felt a hot surge of anger flow through him.

'Send her round to room 203 when you're done with her,' Letham said, out of the side of his mouth. 'They can go all night, these Zanzari bints.'

Before Blessing could say anything Bond stood up.

'Actually, could I have a discreet word, outside?' Bond said, laying his cigarette in the ashtray and, taking Letham's arm by the elbow, steered him firmly through the crowded bar. 'Man to man, you know,' Bond said, confidentially, in his ear.

'Got you, old fellow,' Letham said. 'Forewarned is forearmed in the young-lady department.'

They stepped out of a side door into the warm darkness of the night, loud with crickets. Bond looked around and saw the back entrance to the bar – dustbins and stacked empty crates – and led Letham towards them.

'She's not expensive, is she?' Letham said. 'I refuse to pay these Zanzari hookers more than ten US.'

Bond turned and punched Letham as hard as he could in the stomach. He went down with a thump on his arse, mouth open like a landed fish, gaping. Then he vomited copiously into his lap and fell back against the wall making breathy whimpering noises.

'Mind your manners,' Bond said, though Letham wasn't listening. 'Don't speak to respectable young women like that again.'

Bond strode round to the front of the hotel and into the lobby, where he found a porter.

'There's a drunk Englishman been sick – at the back behind the bar,' Bond said, indicating. 'I think you should chuck a couple of buckets of water over him.' He slipped a note into the porter's hand.

The porter smiled, eagerly. 'We shall do it, sar,' he said and hurried off.

Bond returned to the noisy bar and joined Blessing at their table, ordering another whisky on the way.

'Sorry about that,' he said. 'He won't bother us further – he's not feeling very well.'

'My knight in shining armour,' Blessing said. 'Did you administer retribution?'

'Powerful retribution,' Bond said, draining his whisky. 'I despise those types – pond life. They need to be taught a sharp lesson from time to time. Shall we go? Busy day tomorrow.'

Bond silently walked Blessing to her car. He felt the tremors of adrenalin slowly leave him and smiled, imagining Letham being gleefully doused by buckets of water. A cooler breeze had got up and a fat yellow moon had risen above the poolside apartment blocks.

Bond gestured at the moon, wanting to break the silence between them.

'Doesn't quite seem the same,' he said, 'now that we've been up there. Lost something of its allure.'

'I don't agree,' she said. 'It seems to belong to us more, now – not some distant symbol.'

'*La lune ne garde aucune rancune,*' Bond said.

'Who's that?' Blessing said.

'Can't remember. Something I learned at school as a boy.'

'You've a very good accent,' she said.

'I spent a lot of my childhood in Switzerland.'

'Classified information, Commander Bond.'

They had reached her car.

'You didn't need to do that, you know,' Blessing said, opening her car door and turning to him. 'Creeps like that don't bother me. I know how to deal with them.' She shrugged. 'But thank you all the same. I appreciate it.'

'I'm sure you do know how to deal with them – but he was getting on my nerves.'

They looked at each other.

'Goodnight, James,' she said and slipped into the driving seat.

'See you tomorrow at the office,' Bond said, closing the door for her. 'Nine o'clock.'

# 7

# On the Road

After his breakfast – a pint of freshly squeezed orange juice, scrambled eggs, bacon and fried plantain – Bond wandered out to the front portico of the hotel and, after some requisite haggling, bought a bag. It was a grip of black leather with the Zanzarim g – a banded quincolour of red, white, yellow, black and green – appliquéd to the side. It was unlined and smelled strongly of recently cured leather. The handles were long enough to be slipped over his shoulder if required.

Back in his room, Bond packed with some thought, deciding to wear an olive-green safari jacket over khaki trousers with suede desert boots on his feet. Into the Zanzarim grip went three dark blue short-sleeved Aertex shirts, three pairs of underpants and socks, a rolled up panama hat in a cardboard tube, his anti-malaria pills and his pigskin toilet bag. It was odd and a little unsettling not to have a gun on him: he felt strangely undressed, almost wilfully vulnerable. He decided to leave all his other clothes in his suitcase – and he'd deposit that in Blessing's office for her to ship home at some stage. He who travels lightest, travels furthest, Bond supposed, and that included weaponry. Into a war zone with a can of talcum powder and some aftershave. He walked down to reception with his suitcase and his new grip, ready to check out and settle his bill. Having done that he had an idea and went into the bar and bought a bottle of Johnnie Walker whisky. For medicinal use – you never knew when it might be needed.

**Christmas dropped** Bond off at the OG offices where he found Blessing standing on the roof of a cream-coloured Austin 1100 with a pot of black paint in her hand. She was painting the word 'PRESS' on the roof in two-foot-high letters and Bond saw, as he circled the car, that the passenger side of the windscreen and the rear window had been similarly inscribed in letters of white sticky tape.

'Couldn't we get a better car?' Bond asked, thinking that this was the sort of vehicle a mother might use to pick up her kids from school or collect the groceries.

'It's perfect,' Blessing said, stepping down. 'We don't want anything showy – we don't want to attract too much attention. We'll just trundle off and no one will notice us.'

Bond helped her load two jerrycans of petrol, two spare tyres and a fifty-litre plastic container of water into the boot. They said goodbye to Christmas, who was going to man the office phone in their absence, and without more ado they climbed into the 1100 and set off, Blessing at the wheel for the first leg of the journey.

She handed Bond a map of Zanzarim with their meandering route south picked out. Bond saw that they would be moving haphazardly from village to provincial town to village again, always a good distance from the main transnational highway. When they set out and had quit the outskirts of Sinsikrou they immediately turned off into the countryside. Bond stared out of the window at the dusty bush, the unfaltering savannah scrub with its occasional trees. However, as they drove on, the vegetation grew steadily thicker until the view from the window was obscured by forest. The roads they travelled on were all tarmac but badly eroded with dangerous, deep potholes. They passed through hamlets and villages of mud huts roofed with grass thatch or rusty corrugated iron, each village with its little cluster of rickety roadside stalls selling bananas, peppers, cassava and various fruits. Seeing Bond's white face at the window of the car as it flashed by provoked shouts and cries of excitement or derision from the villagers – or perhaps they were just pleas to stop and buy something. Bond couldn't tell. He felt the real Africa engulf him, realising that Sinsikrou had nothing to do with the Zanzarim that they were now motoring through. On the roads the only other traffic they encountered was ancient lorries and buses, the occasional cyclist and mule-drawn cart.

They made good progress and at lunchtime they stopped in a more sizeable town, Oguado, and found a roadside bar where they could enjoy a cold drink. Bond ordered a Green Star and Blessing a Fanta and they ate some kind of peppery, doughy cake known as dago-dago, so Blessing told him. It didn't look much, Bond thought, like a beige doughnut with no hole, but it was surprisingly spicy and tasty.

He took over the driving and they headed on through constant scrubby forest, then, at one stage, they passed through a vast plantation of cocoa trees that took them half an hour to traverse. It was hot and the sky hazed over to a milky white. They saw no military vehicles and encountered no roadblocks. Bond remarked on this: you'd hardly believe this was a country in the grip of a two-year civil war, he said, that just a couple of hundred miles to the south half a million people were starving to death.

'It's Africa,' Blessing said with a shrug. She gestured at the village they were passing through. 'These people may have a transistor radio or a bicycle but their lives haven't really changed in a thousand years. They probably don't even know their capital is called Sinsikrou.'

Bond swerved on to the laterite verge to avoid a six-foot pothole. The road ahead was completely straight and the view so unendingly monotonous he wondered if he was in danger of falling asleep. He pulled on to the verge again and said he needed to relieve himself. As he stepped, carefully, a few yards into the forest he soon lost sight of the car. The air was filled with noises – frogs, bird, insects – and he suddenly felt a sense of immense solitariness overwhelm him, yet everywhere he looked there were signs of non-human life: columns of ants at his feet, a trio of magenta butterflies exploring a sunbeam, some angry screeching bird on a high branch, a lizard doing press-ups on a boulder. This specimen of *Homo sapiens* emptying its bladder was just another organism in the teeming primeval forest. He was glad to walk back to the road and the car – feeble symbols of his species' purported domination of the planet – and to smoke one of Blessing's potent Tuskers before she offered to take over the driving for the final stage of the day's journey to their first destination, the Good Companion rest-house on the outskirts of a small town called Kolo-Ade.

These rest-houses were another just-surviving relic of Zanzarim's colonial past. The Good Companion had been built in the 1930s – a solid large airy brick house with a wide veranda and sitting room, dining room and kitchen on the ground floor and eight bedrooms on the floor above – created for the travelling administrators and functionaries who ran the colony in days gone by. The place was showing clear signs of its age – the paint was flaking and the concrete floors needed rewaxing – but it was clean and simple in its efficiency. Bond's room had a bed with a mosquito net suspended above it and a wooden stand with an enamel jug and ewer. There was a WC at the end of the corridor.

He and Blessing sat on the veranda – they were the only guests – watching the bats swoop and swerve in the brief African gloaming as the sun set in its sudden blood-orange termination. They drank whisky and water and smoked steadily to keep the mosquitoes at bay. Blessing showed him on the map how far they had travelled – they had covered some 200 miles on these back roads, she reckoned. The next day's drive would see them enter the fringes of the Zanza River Delta, where they could expect roadblocks and inevitable delays. The soldiers often kept cars waiting for hours in order to up the fee for being allowed to motor on.

Bond savoured this moment on the veranda as they sat and chatted. He had a powerful sundowner in his hand and the heat was leaving the atmosphere as the cool of the tropical night advanced. He felt at ease – and he was also enjoying the company of a beautiful young woman, he realised. Blessing had changed into an embroidered, tie-dyed dress of many hues of vermilion and rose that had the effect of making her look more exotic and African – or was that just the result of their journey into the interior of Zanzarim, Bond wondered, recalling her cool sci-fi beauty of the previous evening. He could tell, moreover, that she wore no brassiere under the dress – he could see her pert breasts shiver as she flicked her hand to shoo away a fluttering moth. He found himself imagining her naked, wondering what her youthful firm body might be like beneath the— Stop right there, Bond! – he issued the stern instruction to himself. Don't go down that road.

A white-haired toothless old man, the manager of the Good Companion, called them in for their evening meal: fruit salad, followed by a tough steak with fried cassava. Bond decided to forego the sago pudding with raspberry jam offered as dessert and called for another whisky. They had been driving for a good eight hours today, Bond realised, and he was feeling tired.

So was Blessing, Bond saw, as she yawned widely, and they both agreed it was time to turn in. They climbed the stairs to their bedrooms and parted on the landing.

'I think we should start at dawn tomorrow,' Blessing said. 'I'll knock on your door.'

'Fine,' Bond said and resisted the urge to kiss her goodnight. 'See you in the morning.'

He lay in his bed under the gauze tent of his mosquito net listening to the night noises beyond the shuttered windows – the tireless crickets, the whooping owls, burping toads and pie-dogs yapping in Kolo-Ade's outskirts. One more day's driving, Bond thought, another night in a rest-house and the infiltration into the shrinking heartland of Dahum. He felt the prickle of the adrenalin rush but also a rare sense of foreboding. The drive through the lonely interior of Zanzarim had reminded him of the problems, not to say the enormity, of the task that faced him. As his surroundings had grown more primitive and elemental so, it seemed, whatever strength, capability and powers he possessed appeared more insubstantial and weak. What was it about Africa that unmanned you so? he wondered, turning over and punching the hard kapok pillow into a more amenable shape for his head – why did the continent so effortlessly remind you of your human frailties?

**When Blessing** knocked on his door it was still dark. Breakfast was a mug of Camp coffee and some toast and marmalade and when they set off the light was growing pearly and the air was wonderfully cool. They made good progress in the morning but, just as they were contemplating their lunch break, they met their first roadblock. There was a queue of around two dozen cars on either side of an armoured personnel carrier that had parked itself across the road. Half a dozen soldiers, in the now familiar patchwork uniforms, lazily scrutinised identity cards and searched the belongings of resigned and unprotesting motorists.

A young officer ambled down the line of cars towards them, attracted by the 1100's self-described press status. He looked smarter than the other soldiers and was wearing a lozenge-camouflaged blouson and trousers and had a moss-green beret on his head.

'Stay there,' Blessing said, and stepped out of the car. Bond watched her talking to the officer in Lowele. From time to time she pointed back at Bond, clearly the topic of their conversation. Then they both returned to the car. The officer looked in the window at Bond, smiling. Bond smiled back.

'Morning, Captain,' Bond said, elevating his rank by two pips.

'Pleased to assist you, sir,' he said and snapped a salute.

Blessing climbed into the car, started the engine, did a three-point turn, then drove back the way they had just come.

'We'd have been there all day,' she said. 'I told him you were late for an interview with Major General Basanjo – he's the commander-in-chief of Zanza Force. The officer said we were heading in the wrong direction.' She glanced over at him and grinned. 'Plan B?'

'Over to you,' Bond said, quietly impressed with Blessing's powers of improvisation. He tried to ignore the little spasms of sexual interest he was suddenly feeling for her, watching her muscles tauten and flex in her slim brown arms as she turned the wheel of the car, seeing the glow of perspiration on her throat, noting the contour-hugging tightness of the T-shirt she was wearing. Keep your mind on the job, he told himself.

They turned off the road at the next junction and headed east for the transnational highway. They made slow progress for an hour or so once they reached the highway as they were constantly waved off the road to give military vehicles right of way. During one of their enforced pauses Bond counted a convoy of over forty army lorries, packed with troops. At another stage, further down the road, they passed five tank-transporters with what looked like brand-new Centurion tanks sitting on them. A low-level flight of MiGs, heavy with napalm canisters, screeched past, ripping through the air with a sound like tearing linen. Everything Bond saw said 'major offensive looming': it was as if Zanza Force was preparing for the final thrust into the rebel heartland. He said as much to Blessing but she was more sceptical.

'They've got all the arms and men, sure,' she said. 'But these new troops are conscripts – badly trained and nervy. They only advance if given free beer and cigarettes. And those tanks are useless in the delta. They don't like the terrain and all the key bridges are blown.'

Then, as if someone had been overhearing them, they passed a line of parked flatbed trucks loaded with the cantilevered sections of Bailey bridges. As they drove by Bond saw white soldiers in what he thought were British Army fatigues.

'Slow down,' Bond said, craning his head round to catch a final glimpse. 'Could they be British? Royal Engineers?'

'There are some "military advisers" out here,' Blessing said. 'I met three of them at the airport the week before you arrived.'

Bond sat back, thinking. If he was right about those soldiers being British then this urgency, this hands-on military aid, also had an oblique bearing on his mission. The British government was clearly keen for this war to end as soon as possible. Why? Bond wondered. Conceivably, he thought, British 'military advisers' could also be manning those tanks . . .

Bond took over at the wheel after a snatched lunch at a roadside food-shack – more beer and dago-dago. He became aware of the landscape changing as they drove south into the river delta – small lakes and stagnant pools of water began to appear on either side of the highway, great expanses of reed beds and more palm trees and mangroves.

Blessing told him to turn off the highway and follow the signs for a small town called Lokomeji on whose outskirts their next rest-house, Cinnamon Lodge, was situated. It was late afternoon by the time they arrived. Blessing dropped him at the portico-ed entrance and drove on into Lokomeji to rendezvous with the local fisherman who would guide Bond into Dahum.

Cinnamon Lodge was virtually identical in structure and layout to Good Companion and belonged to the same colonial era. Standing on his bedroom balcony Bond could look across the dense low-lying forest that made up the Zanza River Delta. From his vantage point he could see the late afternoon sun glinting silver on the creeks and channels that wove their way sinuously through the vegetation. They were perched right on the edge of the huge delta, Bond could see from the map. Port Dunbar was only forty miles away – as the crow flies – but it might as well have been 400 such was the impenetrability of the marshy forest with its maze of watercourses lying in between. The air felt heavy and moist and, in the far distance, he could see a thin column of smoke rising, hanging in the air, dense as a rag, as if reluctant to disperse into the atmosphere. Another flight of MiGs ripped by, heading north this time, wing racks empty. Mission completed, and no doubt their pilots were looking forward to another evening in the bar of the Excelsior Gateway, Bond thought. It seemed like another world.

He was sitting on a cane chair on the veranda with his second whisky on the go when he saw the headlights of the 1100 sweep into the gated compound. Blessing seemed pleased. The fisherman – named Kojo – would meet Bond tomorrow evening at 6 p.m. by the wharves at Lokomeji and take him out, ostensibly for a spot of night fishing – looking for Zanza carp. Lokomeji sat on the edge of a small inland lagoon that merged into the tracery of creeks and inlets that wormed their way through the forest. Kojo was familiar with every twisting inch of the waterways, Blessing said; he'd been fishing at Lokomeji, man and boy, and knew exactly where to put Bond safely ashore in Dahum.

'Good,' Bond said. 'So what'll we do tomorrow? Maybe we could go back to the highway – I wouldn't mind checking out those British soldiers.' He smiled. 'I am a journalist, after all – might make a good story.'

Blessing advised caution. 'We should stay put,' she said. 'The whole of Lokomeji knows there's an Englishman staying at Cinnamon Lodge. You're a rare bird here. Talk of the steamie.'

Bond was amused by the Scottish expression, no doubt picked up from her father, but she was right of course. He thought of the whole empty day ahead of them tomorrow, confined to Cinnamon Lodge, and rather wished he'd brought his unfinished Graham Greene with him. Still, he considered, another twenty-four hours in Blessing's company was hardly purgatorial.

They were alone in the dining room once again, Cinnamon Lodge's only guests, and were served a surprisingly tasty, peppery fish stew with dago-dago dumplings. Bond even ate the pudding – baked bananas with a rum and butter sauce. After supper they drank more whisky on the veranda from Bond's bottle of Johnnie Walker.

'You'll make me tipsy,' Blessing said. 'I'm not used to whisky.'

'Best drink for the tropics,' Bond said. 'It doesn't need to be chilled. You're meant to drink it without ice, anyway. Tastes the same in Africa as it would in Scotland.'

They went upstairs together. Something had changed in the mood between them, Bond sensed – perhaps the evening wasn't quite over yet. He decided to kiss her on the cheek as they said goodnight.

'I know you're the head of station,' he said, 'and I probably shouldn't have done that, but you did well at that roadblock today. Quick thinking.'

'Thank you, kind sir,' she said, a little sardonically. 'I have my uses.'

Bond lay in bed thinking about the plans for the following night – the crossing of the lagoon and trusting this man, Kojo, to deliver him safely. And what then? He supposed he would make his way to Port Dunbar and introduce himself as a friendly journalist, provide himself with new accreditation, and say he was keen to report the war from the Dahumian side – show the world the rebels' perspective on events. Again, it all seemed very improvised and ad hoc. He wasn't used to such—

Blessing knocked on his door.

'James, I'm really sorry to disturb you, but only you can help me with this.'

'Just coming.'

Bond pulled on his shirt and trousers and opened the door. Blessing stood there in a long white T-shirt that fell to her thighs and was looking at him a little sheepishly.

'There's a lizard in my room,' she said. 'And I can't sleep knowing that it's there.'

Bond followed her down the corridor to her room. To his vague surprise it was larger and better furnished than his and it had a ceiling fan that was turning energetically, causing the gauze of her mosquito net to billow and flap gently. Blessing pointed: high up on the wall by the ceiling was a six-inch, pale, freckled gecko – motionless, waiting for a moth or a fly to come its way.

'It's just a gecko,' Bond said. 'They eat mosquitoes. Think of it as a pet.'

'I know it's a gecko,' she said. 'But it's also a lizard and I have a bit of a phobia about lizards, I'm afraid.'

Bond took a wooden coat-hanger out of the cupboard and a towel that was hanging from a hook by her jug and ewer stand. With the end of the hanger he flipped the gecko off the wall, catching it in the towel and balling the material gently around it. He stepped out on to the balcony and let the gecko scuttle off into the night.

'A lizard-free zone,' Bond said, closing the balcony doors behind him. Blessing stood by her bed, the angle of the bedside light and the shadows it cast revealing the shape of her small uptilted breasts under her T-shirt. Bond knew what was going to happen next and everything about Blessing's expression confirmed that she did, also.

He crossed the room to her.

'Thank you, James Bond,' she said. 'Licensed to catch lizards.'

Bond took her in his arms and kissed her gently, feeling her tongue flicker into his mouth.

'As station head in Zanzarim it's important I get to know visiting agents,' she said and slipped her T-shirt off. She let Bond take in her nakedness for an instant and then lifted the mosquito net and slid into bed. Bond shucked off his shirt and trousers and climbed in beside her. He pulled her body against his and kissed her neck and breasts. She was tiny and lithe in his arms, her dark nipples perfectly round, like coins.

He looked into her eyes.

'Ah, the old lizard trick,' he said.

'A girl can only work with the materials at hand.'

'I'm going to miss you in Dahum, Blessing Ogilvy-Grant,' he said, as he rolled on top of her and felt her knees part and lift to accommodate him. 'Expect to see me back in Sinsikrou before you know it.'

'I can't wait.'

**After they** had made love – with an urgency and physicality that surprised them both – Bond fetched his bottle of whisky from his room. They lay naked on the top of the bed, drinking and smoking, talking softly and reaching out to touch each other until they arrived at a new pitch of arousal and they made love again, this time more deliberately and knowingly, prolonging their climaxes with all the expertise of familiar lovers. Afterwards, Bond lay still while Blessing fell asleep, curled at his side, his arm round her narrow shoulders, her arm thrown across his chest. The regular whirr of the ceiling fan blanked out all other noises and, for a moment, before sleep overtook him, Bond allowed himself to float on a sea of simple sensuality, spent and happy, the warmth of a beautiful young woman beside him, giving no thought at all about what might await him tomorrow.

# 8
# The Man with Two Faces

Bond flinched and woke, thinking Blessing's elbow had moved and was digging into his throat. But whatever was causing the pressure was cold and hard. Bond gagged reflexively and opened his eyes. The man's face that loomed above him in the darkness was zigzagged with olive-green camouflage paint. The gun pressing hard into Bond's windpipe made it impossible to speak.

'Don't try to say anything, big boy.'

Bond sensed other hands reach in beneath the mosquito net and grab Blessing. She managed a half-cry before she was stifled and dragged out of bed. The light went on.

'Get up.' The mosquito net was flipped aside.

Bond sat up slowly, rubbing his throat.

Blessing stood in shock, head bowed, shivering, arm across her breasts, a hand covering her groin. Six soldiers in camouflage uniform in mottled greens and greys and brown stood in the room – they looked like giants facing her, bulked out with their packs and ammunition. Five of them were black. The man with the automatic pistol – a big Colt 1911, Bond noticed – was white.

'Move, sonny,' the white man said. The accent wasn't precisely English – more like East African or South African, Bond thought. Bond stood up and went to Blessing, putting his arm around her and making no attempt to conceal his nakedness.

'Aw, Adam and Eve,' the white man said.

The other soldiers chuckled, enjoying the show, covering Bond with their Kalashnikovs. Bond noticed that sewn on their shoulders were small flags – a rectangle halved horizontally, black and white, and in the upper white band was a red disc. The flag of the Democratic Republic of Dahum.

'Look, I'm a British journalist,' Bond said. 'She's my translator.'

'British special forces, more like,' the white man said. There was something wrong with his face, something glinting in one eye, but Bond couldn't see exactly what it was because of the zigzag paint stripes.

'Get dressed,' the man said to both of them. 'Then pack up your stuff.'

Bond pulled on his shirt and trousers, shielding Blessing as she put her clothes on as quickly as possible. She seemed calmer once she was dressed, and Bond gave her as reassuring a look as he could muster before he was escorted down the corridor to his room by two of the other soldiers. He put on his desert boots and safari jacket and packed away the rest of his things in the Zanzarim bag. Back in Blessing's room he showed the white man his APL identification and his accreditation from Zanza Force.

'Good cover,' the man said, unimpressed. Closer to him, Bond could see that half his face looked different from the other, normal, half. The glinting that Bond had spotted was caused by tears – his left eye didn't blink and tears flowed unchecked from it – tears that he wiped away with a constant motion of his thumb or dried on his cuff. There were two small round scars below his left eye – bullet entry wounds – that looked like a stamped umlaut and the contours of the left-hand side of his face were strangely dished, the cheekbone missing. Some awful trauma to his face had left him in this state, obviously.

Bond and Blessing were ushered downstairs – no sign of the manager or the staff of Cinnamon Lodge – and out into the warm darkness of the night. Bond glanced at his Rolex – it was just after four in the morning. They were led out of the compound and down a pathway to a small creek. Bond feigned a stumble, dropped his bag and as he stooped to pick it up, bumped up against Blessing.

'They're from Dahum,' he whispered.

'That's what I'm worried about.'

Then they arrived at the water's edge where a twelve-foot fibreglass dory was moored. Bond was shoved up to the front and Blessing told to sit in the stern. Bond acknowledged the Dahumian soldiers' discipline and good training. They moved confidently and briskly about their business with very little conversation. He heard one of the men say 'We are ready, Kobus.' So he was called Kobus, Bond noted – Kobus short for Jakobus. The man with half a face or, rather: Kobus, the man with two faces.

Kobus cast off the dory and sat down in the stern beside Blessing. The other men picked up short paddles and swiftly, silently, propelled the dory down the creek and out into the wider expanse of the lagoon. Bond could see a few lights burning in Lokomeji – no rendezvous with Kojo tomorrow – and it began to dawn on him that Kobus and his men must have come specifically to snatch him, thinking he was one of the

British military advisers for Zanza Force. Bond smiled ruefully to himself – it would have been quite a coup if he had been. Blessing had said everyone in Lokomeji knew he was staying in Cinnamon Lodge – word had spread. So Kobus and his men had seized their opportunity and sneaked out of Dahum on a kidnap mission.

Paradoxically, this analysis made Bond feel marginally more relaxed. There was nothing on his person or in his belongings that would identify him as a member of a special-forces team. For once he was hugely relieved that he wasn't armed. Perhaps when the Dahumian authorities realised that he appeared to be what he was claiming to be – a journalist working for a French press agency – they would hand him and Blessing over to civilian authorities in Port Dunbar. It was something to hope for.

They crossed the lagoon surprisingly quickly and entered one of the winding watercourses. Bond heard the dry whisper of the soft night wind in the tall reeds that lined the channel and sensed rather than saw the overarching bulk of the mangroves and other trees. The men paddled on, tirelessly, and soon the sky began to lighten as dawn neared and with it Bond became aware of a mounting nervousness in the soldiers as they glanced around watchfully and muttered to each other. They clearly didn't want to be caught out on the water in daylight. Then Bond heard the rhythmic judder of a helicopter's rotors as it took to the air and the distant sound of diesel engines revving. They must be passing through the Zanza Force lines that surrounded Dahum's diminishing heartland.

Soon they reached a ramshackle cribwork jetty and they disembarked. The dory was hauled ashore and covered with palm leaves. Then the small column moved down a forest path to a clearing where a canvas tarpaulin had been erected as shelter, draped with camouflaged netting. Bond was ordered to sit down beneath it at one end and Blessing at the other. Kobus took both their bags away and their hands were tied behind their backs. One soldier was left to guard them and Bond saw Kobus posting lookouts on the trails that led into the clearing. As the sun began to rise, he heard the sporadic *crump, crump* of heavy artillery being fired.

Kobus came in and squatted by Blessing and began to interrogate her, but he kept his voice low and Bond couldn't hear his questions or her replies. Then Bond saw him stand up, look round and wander over to him.

He had removed the zigzag stripes from his face and Bond was able to see the full damage – the tear-fall from the unblinking eye and the saucer-deep declivity where his cheekbone should have been made Bond think that half his upper jaw had gone as well. He searched Bond roughly, taking his passport, his APL identification and his remaining wad of dollars. He also pocketed Bond's cigarette lighter and his Rolex.

'I'll want them back, one day,' Bond said. 'So look after them.'

Kobus slapped his face.

'Don't be a cheeky bugger,' he said.

'Kenya? Uganda?'

'Rhodesia,' Kobus said, with a knowing smile. He nodded over to Blessing. 'Your girlfriend tells me that you're in the SAS.'

'No, she didn't,' Bond said calmly. 'Look, I'm a journalist. I met her in a bar in Sinsikrou. She's smart, beautiful and speaks fluent Lowele and I needed a translator. I was meant to be interviewing General Basanjo today. I thought she'd be useful and we might have a bit of fun on the way, you know? Then you went and spoiled everything.'

Kobus slapped his face again, harder. Bond tasted salty blood in his mouth.

'I don't like your attitude, man. I'll get you back to Port Dunbar where I can do some serious work on you and find out exactly who you are. One thing's for sure – you're no journalist.' He stood up and left. Bond spat out some bloody saliva and looked over at Blessing. She was lying on the ground, curled up, turned away from him.

The day crawled by in the steaming heat beneath the tarpaulin. They were temporarily unbound and given some water and a plate of cold beans. Bond could hear the irregular detonations of artillery all day and at one stage two MiGs streaked over the clearing at very low level setting up a squawking and a squealing amongst the riverine birds that took a good five minutes to die down, such was the sky-shuddering guttural roar of the jets.

As dusk approached the men began to pack up the camp – the tarp and the netting were taken down and rolled up and any bits of litter were collected and buried. Bond and Blessing were untied and given another drink of water. Kobus swaggered up to them, smoking, and Bond felt a sudden craving for tobacco.

'We're walking out of here, OK?' Kobus said. 'If one of you tries to run I'll shoot you down and then I'll shoot the other. I don't care. Just don't be clever. Clever means death for you two.'

When it was dark they marched into the forest in single file, Kobus leading, followed by Blessing, Bond at the back of the small column with one soldier in the rear behind him. Bond felt grimy and sweat-limned, itches springing up all over his body. He fantasised briefly about a cold shower then ordered his brain to stop and concentrate. The path they were on was well trodden, Bond could see in the moonlight, and the forest around them was full of animal and insect noises that rather conveniently disguised the sound of their passage, the clink of buckles on machine gun, the dull thump of shifting harness, the tramp of boots on the pathway. Bond could see his Zanzarim bag lashed with a webbing belt on to the rucksack of the soldier in front of him. The fact that it hadn't been abandoned or thrown away he found somehow reassuring, as if it betokened a future for him, however short-lived.

They walked for about an hour, Bond guessed, before Kobus halted them. He signalled them to crouch down where they were and wait. Bond turned to the soldier behind him.

'What are we waiting for?'

'Shut you mouth,' he said simply.

Bond peered ahead – there was a lightening in the general gloom that would signal a gap in the trees and by craning his neck Bond could see the moonlight striking on what seemed like a strip of asphalt. Then Kobus waved them forward to the very edge of the treeline and Bond was able to get his bearings.

They had reached a road – a typical two-lane, pot-holed stretch of tarmac with wide laterite verges on each side. This section ran straight with no curves and the light of the moon afforded a good view a couple of hundred yards in each direction. Kobus obviously planned to cross it and pick up their forest path on the far side. However, they sat there in silence another five minutes or so, waiting and listening. Bond calculated that the distance to the other side was no more than thirty yards, maximum, before you reached the dark security of the forest again. It was the middle of the night, for God's sake, Bond said to himself – what could be so problematic about crossing a road?

As if in answer to his question, Kobus stood and ran briskly at a crouch across the road without pausing and disappeared into the vegetation on the other side. They waited another five minutes. Then he heard Kobus shout an order: 'Femi! Dani! Bring the girl, chop-chop!'

Two of the soldiers stood up, one of them took Blessing's arm and began to jog across the road.

The night erupted in gunfire.

Bond saw the tracer looping a split second before he heard the detonations. There was the usual sensory delay – the lazy flow of glowing light-flashes picking up speed – and then the road surface disintegrated under the impact of the heavy-calibre machine-gun bullets. Blessing screamed and fell to the ground. One of the soldiers seemed literally torn apart, shredded by the impact of a dozen rounds, while the other was spun around in a mad pirouette before Bond saw one of his arms flail off and go tumbling into the undergrowth end over end.

On hands and knees Blessing scrabbled back into cover and Bond grabbed her.

'You all right?' he shouted. The yammering noise of gunfire ripped through the night.

'Yes,' she sobbed. 'I'm not hit.'

Kobus was screaming orders at his men, firing back up the road where the machine guns were. The other three soldiers had opened up with their AK-47s. Leaves and bits of branches were falling on them as the machine guns hosed the sides of the road, raking the forest verge.

This was their moment.

Bond took Blessing's hand and drew her slowly back into the darkness. One yard, two, three. The soldiers were too intent taking cover or returning fire. Bond backed them off the path and deeper into the under-growth. Ten seconds, twenty – they were completely hidden, out of sight. He heard Kobus shouting and then the noise of one soldier blundering down the path.

'They gone, Boss!'

Bond drew Blessing still further into the leafy obscurity.

'Where are we going?' she said, panic in her voice.

'Say nothing,' Bond hissed at her.

Then enormous explosions sent shockwaves through the trees – mortar bombs – brief flashes of brilliant, scalding light. There was a scream from one of the soldiers. Bond grabbed Blessing's hand more firmly and turned, moving as fast as he could, forcing a way through the bushes and the branches, running away from the road and the firefight.

Now there was more firing coming from another direction on their flank. A random spraying of the forest as another group of soldiers appeared to be coming up from the rear.

'Lie down,' Bond said, 'they'll never find us.'

He dragged Blessing off her feet and pressed her down into the dry leafy mulch of the forest floor.

'Keep your eyes down, don't look up.'

Someone would have to stand on them to discover them, Bond reasoned, listening to the chaos of the night, the shouts of men, the staccato rattle of machine guns. It was crazed firing, soldiers loosing off at shadows – staying still and prone was the only solution. Shots thunked into tree trunks near them, ripped through foliage overhead, and every now and then there was another brief flash of light washing through the forest as another mortar shell was lobbed in their general direction.

He could hear men thrashing through undergrowth not far from them. Kobus? Or was that the Zanza Force ambush?

Blessing gripped his arm, fiercely.

'James – we've got to get out of here, now!' she whispered harshly at him. 'They're going to find us.'

'No! Don't move – listen, they're moving away.'

He felt her fist pounding on his restraining hand.

'Let me go!'

'Blessing – no – we're safer here—'

She snatched her hand away.

'I'm not going to die here!' she screamed at him. She was uncontrollable, panicked out of her wits. She stood up and ran into the dense gloom of the surrounding trees.

'Blessing!' Bond shouted – and someone, hearing the noise, began to loose off quick bursts of fire in his direction. Bond fell to the ground and crawled away as fast as he could, rolling into a hollow and clawing dead leaves over him. Blessing had first lost her nerve, then lost her head and made a run for it. Fool! Bond thought. Then he heard her scream, shrill and terrified, and a long chatter of gunfire before she screamed again and it was choked off. Bond pressed his forehead into the earth, feeling sick, breathing shallowly and waiting. Slowly the spatter of gunfire diminished and grew more distant. A lot of shouting seemed to be coming from the direction of the road and then he heard a metallic rumble from the tracks of some kind of armoured vehicle approaching.

He lay there motionless, counting the seconds, the minutes. He saw the beam of torchlight through the trees and heard the excited voices of Zanzari soldiers – whoops and shouts. For a brief second he thought about surrendering himself to them but realised that any figure emerging from the trees would be cut down instantly. Best to stay put. Had they taken Kobus? he wondered. Maybe he was dead? He heard the vehicle start up again and move off.

The forest quietened, and then the insects and the animals began their interrupted squeaks and chatterings again. Bond sat up, slowly: he could smell smoke and cordite but there were no sounds of any human presence that he could distinguish. He pushed himself backwards in the darkness until he came up against the bole of a tree. He hugged his knees to him and closed his eyes, trying not to think about what had happened to Blessing. There was nothing more to do but wait for dawn.

# 9

# James Bond's Long Walk

At some stage in the night Bond had fallen asleep in his sitting position against the tree, his forehead resting on his knees, his arms locked around his shins. At first light he woke and, very slowly, stretched his legs out, massaging his thigh muscles back to life and taking his time to rise to his feet. He windmilled his arms and ran on the spot for a minute or two to get his circulation going. Then he pushed cautiously through the undergrowth until he found the pathway and advanced slowly up to the road. There was a crude confetti of shredded leaves everywhere, as if some violent storm had passed, but not a body to be seen, all casualties carted away. The road surface was scarred and torn with bullet strikes and there were two drying pools of blood, humming with flies, where the two soldiers had been hit by the first fusillade.

He cast around half-heartedly up and down the road, not expecting to find Blessing or any trace of her. Brass cartridges glinted everywhere on the ground and he found a bloodstained pack with a few rounds of ammunition in it. Otherwise there was little sign of the firefight and its victims.

He stood in the middle of the road feeling the heat of the rising sun on his face. What to do? Which direction to take? He turned northwards – that was where the Zanza Force fire had come from. If he walked up the road in that direction surely he'd reach the advancing columns of the main army . . . Bond forced himself to think about his options for a while, kicking at bits of the shattered road surface. He could, he supposed, realistically abort his mission, after what he'd been through. M would surely understand. But there was unfinished business and he felt an obscure sense of guilt over what had happened to Blessing. If he'd only held on to her more forcefully, even knocked her out . . . Was she dead? Was she safe in the hands of Zanza Force? Or perhaps Kobus and his men had recaptured her.

Bond looked around him. Kobus's plan had been to cross this road and continue on the forest path they had been walking along. Perhaps that was the option to choose . . . he had no food, no water, no weapon. He could last a couple of days, he reckoned, perhaps longer if he could find something to eat or drink. Bond thought – Kobus knew exactly where this path was heading and that it was the route to follow. Bond made up his mind: he crossed the road and walked into the forest.

He walked for two hours, he calculated, then stopped and rested. It was hot and clammy and he had been bitten by many insects but at least the path was shaded by the tall trees it meandered through. Bond looked up at the high canopy of trees above him, the branches like twisted beams in some giant deformed attic. He set off again. The path remained surprisingly well trodden and occasionally he came across evidence of human passage – a bottle top, a shred of indigo material, a foil wrapper from a chocolate bar. At one stage he found a butt from a hand-rolled cigarette with some shreds of tobacco left – and he cursed the loss of his lighter. There was enough tobacco to provide a good couple of lungfuls of smoke. Bond was about to throw it away when he saw that it wasn't tobacco in the cigarette at all. He sniffed – marijuana or some other kind of potent weed. Was this a hunters' path, he wondered, some traditional route from village to village, from tribal land to tribal land, or, more likely, was it used by Kobus and his men to mount raids and incursions behind Zanzari lines?

He moved on, noting that there were fruits and berries of every hue and size on the plants and bushes that bordered the pathway, but he didn't dare try one and, for such lush and green vegetation, there was no visible water source. He found a smooth round pebble and popped it in his mouth and sucked on it, coaxing some saliva flow to ease his increasingly parched throat.

He rested up again at midday, the sunbeams that penetrated the canopy now shining down directly on the path, and waited until the afternoon shade encroached. He thought he was heading vaguely south, though the path did take many illogical jinks and turns. He came across a gym shoe (left foot) with a flapping sole and a label-less tin with an inch of rainwater in it. He was about to swig it down when he saw that it was hotching with pale yellow larvae.

By dusk he was feeling tired and footsore and uncomfortably thirsty. He found a large ash-grey tree with great buttressing roots and settled down snugly between two of them. Darkness arrived with its usual tropic speed and, to distract himself from his cracked throat and his hollow stomach, he forced his mind to concentrate on matters far from the Zanza River Delta. He debated with himself over the respective merits of the Jensen FF and the Interceptor II, trying to calculate if he had enough ready cash to make the deposit required for an eventual purchase. Then he wondered if Doig and his team had finished redecorating his Chelsea flat. He had instructed Donalda to supervise the work in his absence and issue cheques as required. It would be a bonus to go home to an effectively transformed flat after this job was over, he thought, and he was particularly looking forward to his new shower – then he laughed at himself. He was lost in a tropical rainforest wandering along a path somewhere between two warring armies. The reality sank in and with it came the questions about Blessing and her fate. Blessing whose lithe slim naked body he could see in his mind's eye, their night of intimacy so violently interrupted nearly forty-eight hours ago. He felt bitter and remorseful – but what more could he have done? He had his own survival to focus on now.

He turned up the collar of his safari jacket and thrust his hands in his pockets. He was not the repining kind – he felt absolutely sure tomorrow would prove better than today.

Some fluting bird-call woke him at dawn and he set off again without more ado, his throat swollen and sore, his tongue dry as a leather belt. After about half an hour he noticed the forest was starting to thin. There were clearings of blond grass, the giant trees diminished – lower, scrubbier varieties beginning to dominate. He also lost his shade and felt the sun start to burn. He took off his safari jacket and buttoned it over his head like an Arab kufiyya. Sweat began to drip from his nose and chin.

And then the path simply disappeared. The ground beneath his feet was cracked and arid with tufts of wiry grass – as if the path were a forest creature and this scrubby orchard-bush was not the sort of environment it liked.

Then he saw the pawpaw tree.

It was about ten feet tall and had a solitary ripe fruit on it. He grabbed its rough trunk and gave it a vigorous shake, then butted it with his shoulders, making it whip to and fro and, as the pawpaw was shaken free and fell, he caught it safely in both hands.

He sat in a patch of shade and dug his thumbnail into the yielding skin, breaking off a portion of the fruit. He flicked away the soft, swart seeds and sank his teeth into the warm orange flesh. It was moist and sweet and Bond felt his throat respond and ease as he swallowed avidly. He closed his eyes and suddenly he was transported to the terrace of the Blue Hills Hotel in Kingston, Jamaica, where it was his habit to eat two halves of a chilled pawpaw for breakfast, drizzled with freshly squeezed juice from a quartered lime. He would have happily killed for a cup of Blue Mountain coffee and a cigarette. His impromptu memories of those days and that life brought a thickening to his throat – then, cross with himself for this expression of emotion, he wolfed down the rest of the pawpaw with caveman hunger, eating the seeds as well and scraping the skin free of any lingering shred with his teeth.

It was extraordinary how good he felt having eaten something at last. The morning sun was still clearly in the east so he knew in what direction the south lay. He headed on with fresh purpose. Two hundred yards from the pawpaw tree he came across a rudimentary track for wheeled vehicles. He followed the track and it led him to a dirt road where there was an ancient bleached sign that read 'Forêt de Lokani', some forgotten legacy from the former French colonial days. But where there was a road sign, Bond realised, there must be some kind of traffic. His spirits lifted and he strode down the road with new enthusiasm.

He rounded a bend and saw the thatched conical roofs of a small village half a mile further on. He found a heavy stick to use as a makeshift weapon and advanced cautiously down the road towards the mud huts. There was no smoke rising from cooking fires; the cassava fields were withered and neglected. Bond walked into the village sticking close to the mud walls of the houses. There were about twenty dwellings clustered round a big shade tree. On some of the huts the thatch had been burnt away and one or two had demolished walls, as if hit with some kind of ordnance. As he stepped into the beaten-earth meeting area beneath the tree Bond saw three badly decomposed bodies – a woman and two men – a shifting miasma of flies humming above them. Bond skirted them, moving through the alleyways between the houses looking for water – some well or trough. There must be a stream or a river nearby, he reasoned, from where water could be easily carried – no African village was far from water.

Then in a doorway he saw a small boy sitting, leaning weakly against the door jamb. A small boy as skeletal as an ancient wizened man. Naked, his ribs stretching his slack dusty skin, running sores on his stick legs, his head huge, almost teetering on his thin neck. Flies explored his eyelids and the corners of his mouth. He stared at Bond listlessly, barely interested, it seemed, in this apparition of a white man standing in front of him.

Bond crouched down, disturbed and unsettled.

'Hello,' he said, with a token smile, before realising how stupid he sounded.

Something moved behind the boy and another skull-faced child appeared, staring at him, dully. Bond stood and went to peer into the mud hut but an awful smell made him recoil, rake his throat and spit. It seemed full of the corpses of children. Nothing was moving inside. Starved into this kind of fatal inertia, Bond supposed: crawl away to some shade and wait to die. This was the fate of the weak and forgotten in the shrinking heartland of Dahum.

Bond left the village feeling helpless and depressed. It had been like witnessing some surreal version of hell. What could he do for those two kids? They'd be dead before nightfall, like all the others lying in that infernal room. His powerlessness made him want to weep. Perhaps there was another village further down the road; perhaps help could be sent from—

Then, miraculously, he saw a figure up ahead – a very skinny young man in a tattered pair of shorts. The young man shouted at him and then threw a stone. It kicked up a puff of dust by Bond's feet. The young man shouted at him and threw two more stones.

'Hey!' Bond shouted. 'Come here! Help!'

But the figure turned and sprinted away, disappearing from view behind a copse of thorn trees. Bond gave chase but stopped as he rounded the copse. Here was the water source for the village – a small creek dammed to form a shallow pool. The skinny young man seemed to have vanished into thin air, like some kind of sprite or vision. Bond wondered if he had been hallucinating, but he didn't care any more – he waded out into the centre of the pool and sat down, soaking himself, scooping up mouthfuls of warm cloudy water with his cupped hands. He could press on now, and perhaps see if there was any way of getting some help for those children. He lay back and submerged his head, closing his eyes, feeling weak with relief. When he surfaced a moment later he could hear the distant sound of a car changing gear. His long walk was nearly over.

Bond stood by the side of the dammed creek, his sodden clothes dripping, in a sudden stasis of indecision. No, he couldn't just walk on. He made his way back to the village and found an empty calabash and a large tin that had once contained powdered milk. Returning to the creek he filled them both with water and carried them to the mud hut with the dead children. The little boy had disappeared – crawled back inside, Bond hoped, and he set the two containers down carefully at the threshold. Then he heard a cracked shout from behind him.

A stooped old man stood there at the entry to the meeting square, leaning on a staff. He was incredibly thin, his arms and legs like vanilla pods, wearing a tatter of rags. Bond approached slowly as the old man berated him with hoarse incomprehensible curses. He had a small head with a powdering of grey hair, a collapsed face with white corpse-stubble. He was like something from a myth – or a symbol of death, Bond thought – and his red eyes blazed at Bond with a weary venom.

Bond pointed at the hut with his two water containers placed in front of the door.

'Children – pickin – inside. Help them.'

The old man shook his fist at Bond and continued with his spitting maledictions.

Bond pointed at the doorway again and as he did so saw two tiny claw-hands reach out and drag the powdered-milk tin inside. Now the old man grasped his stave and giddily, powerlessly tried to hit Bond with it. It thwacked painlessly against his leg.

'Help those children!' Bond admonished the old man for a final time and turned and strode out of the village, his head in a swoon of pressure, feeling as if he'd taken part in some atavistic dumb-show – a stranger's encounter with death on the road – all the ingredients of some dreadful folktale or legend. He concentrated. He had heard a car, he would be saved – unless the malign spirits of this place were still tormenting him.

# 10
# Welcome to Dahum

Bond's ears had not been deceiving him. There was indeed a road at the end of the dirt track leading from the village, the usual potholed frayed tarmac ribbon, along which the odd car raced at full speed as if fleeing from some natural disaster or catastrophe. Two flew past him without stopping. Then there was nothing for half an hour and Bond felt his clothes drying in the hot sun. Finally a third car came into view – a Volkswagen Beetle which slowed as Bond flagged it down and the door opened. Like the other cars that had passed, Bond noticed this one had a large red cross painted on the bonnet.

A sweaty grey-haired man was at the wheel. He watched in candid astonishment as Bond slid in beside him.

'Where you go?' he said.

'Port Dunbar,' Bond replied.

'I go drop you at Madougo. I fear too much for the MiGs.'

'Is that why you have red crosses on your car?'

'Yes. Maybe they think we are ambulance.' The man glanced skywards, as if expecting a MiG to appear at any moment. 'If they see one car they come and shoot you. Bam-bam-bam. They don' care.'

Bond told him about the village and the dying children.

'They all die,' the man said.

'No. There are two alive. Maybe more, I couldn't tell.'

'All village are dead,' the man insisted. 'Everybody go to Port Dunbar.'

Bond kept on and extracted a promise from the man that he would report the presence of starving children in the village of Lokani, or whatever name it had. Perhaps something would be done.

Madougo turned out to be another semi-destroyed hamlet of mud huts on the roadside but this time there were signs of life. There was, amazingly, a stall set up on the laterite verge, tended by a toothless old mammy. Bond was dropped here and the VW turned off down a track and sped away. The mammy had a small bunch of unripe bananas, a shrivelled pawpaw and a bottle of Green Star beer. Some stubborn undying commercial instinct made her come to her stall in Madougo and pretend life was going on as normal. And maybe she was right, Bond thought, as, using sign language, he bartered his safari jacket for the bottle of beer. He sat on a wooden stool in the shade cast by her stall and drank it slowly. It was sour, warm and gassy, an ambrosial liquor of the gods.

A few people emerged from the shattered huts, stared at him and went away. The beer had gone to Bond's head and he felt woozy and sleepy, exhausted from his two-day hike through the forest. The occasional car stopped and he was scrutinised but never spoken to. This dirty, unshaven white man lounging in the shade of a roadside stall in Madougo would be the subject of much speculation, Bond reasoned. The bush telegraph would do its business – all he had to do was wait; he would be sought out, he was absolutely sure.

It took longer than he thought but in the heat of mid-afternoon he heard the tooting of a car on the road, heading north. Bond shook himself out of his torpor and stood up to see a dusty black Mercedes-Benz station wagon drive through the village and pull on to the verge by the stall.

The door opened and Kobus stepped out. He was wearing jeans and a blue checked shirt. He took off his sunglasses.

'Mr Bond,' he said, with a brief dead smile. 'Welcome to Dahum.'

**As they** drove south, Bond decided to remain cautiously taciturn, despite Kobus's crude attempts at amiability, as if there were no history between them. After all, this was a man who had thrust a gun in his throat, struck him twice in the face, who had threatened him with death and had stolen all his possessions. Kobus's endeavours at small talk were forced and unnatural, as if he were being paid to be agreeable while everything in his nature rebelled against it. Bond said nothing: he knew Kobus's pleasant formalities and empty smiles counted for nothing.

So they drove on, for the most part in this mutual silence, Kobus interrupting from time to time to ask him to check the sky from Bond's side of the car for sign of any MiGs.

Kobus was obviously aware of the chill between them and, half an hour later, made another semi-reluctant effort to try and break it down. He turned and conjured up another of his awkward smiles. When he smiled he showed both top and bottom rows of teeth – small teeth with gaps that resembled the radiator grille of a cheap car.

'I forgot to say – the name's Jakobus Breed. Call me Kobus, man – everyone does.'

'I'm James Bond. As you know. Call me Mr Bond.'

Kobus took this as a signal that all was now well and began to chatter.

'You walked out of the Lokani forest after two days, Bond. I'm damn impressed, I got to tell you. You're good – for a journalist.' He failed to keep the tone of scepticism out of his compliment. 'Smoke?'

Now this did moderate the chill in their relations, somewhat. Bond gladly accepted one of Kobus's proffered cigarettes. He lit it and inhaled.

'Is this a Tusker?'

'Nah. It's a Boomslang – they make them in Dahum. A boomslang's a snake. It bites but it doesn't kill.' He chuckled and wiped a dripping tear away from his bad eye. 'You get a taste for them – you'll never smoke a Tusker again.'

Bond drew on his Boomslang, feeling the powerful nicotine hit. He remembered Kobus slapping his face.

'No hard feelings,' Kobus said, as if reading his thoughts. 'I had a job to do: snatch the SAS guy, they told me. How was I to know any different?'

'Try using your intelligence,' Bond said.

'Hell, do they love you in Port Dunbar,' Kobus pressed on, ignoring him. 'The government boys jumping up and down: Agence Presse Libre. We haven't had a Frenchie in town for months. When I showed them your ID they crapped all over me. How could you lose him, you stupid douche-bag?' Kobus gave an odd barking laugh, like a seal. 'Then word comes down this lunchtime. An Englishman has just walked out of Lokani forest. I said – that's Bond, that is. Jumped in the car and here we are.' He glanced over again and a tear tracked disconcertingly down from his bad eye. 'Glad you made it. That crazy fucking firefight on the road. Somebody set us up.'

'What happened to the girl?' Bond asked.

'Never saw her, man. I swear. I thought she was with you.'

'She panicked and ran. I heard her scream. Twice. I lost her.'

Kobus grimaced. 'Let's hope she died in the bush. If those Federal boys got her, then . . .' He sniffed. 'She'd be better off dead, believe me. I've seen what they do to women.'

Bond felt that weary heart-sink, that heaviness of loss.

'I looked for her in the morning,' he said. 'But there were no bodies left behind.'

'Pretty girl,' Kobus leered. 'How was she in the sack? A real goer, I'd bet.'

Bond registered this glimpse of the old Kobus, the brutal gun-for-hire, not this purported pseudo-comrade he was being offered, and stubbed his cigarette out in the dashboard ashtray. He didn't want to be friends with Kobus Breed.

They drove on in silence, as if Breed sensed Bond's new sombre mood. There was very little traffic on the road to Port Dunbar. At one stage Breed pulled over to the side in the shelter of a tree convinced he'd heard a MiG. They both sat and listened for a couple of minutes but there was no sound of jet engines, so they motored on.

Eventually, they came to the outskirts of Port Dunbar. They passed through two roadblocks – Breed was waved on – and drove down the main boulevard into the city. Bond looked around him – it appeared to be a typical, bustling provincial capital, even though there were many soldiers on the streets. Otherwise it seemed bizarrely normal; police directed traffic at crossroads, the roadside food stalls were busy with customers, street-hawkers harassed them when they stopped and, as they passed a church, Bond saw that there was a wedding party emerging. Port Dunbar gave no sign of being a beleaguered, besieged city. Bond noticed that on the roofs of the higher buildings – office blocks and department stores – there were batteries of ground-to-air missiles.

'What're they? SAMs?'

'Dead right,' Breed said. 'But they're all dummies. Knocked up by the local carpenters in a couple of hours. No, we got one real S-75 SAM site in the central square and one at Janjaville. Two months ago they shot down a MiG. Now the MiGs don't come near Port Dunbar. Those boys don't want to lose their wages.'

Bond thought of the pilots he'd seen drinking in the bar of the Excelsior.

'So they just shoot up cars on the road,' Breed went on. 'Chalk it up as a kill – military vehicle. Money for old rope, man.'

'How did you get your hands on S-75 missiles?'

'Present from our pet millionaire. He pays for the Janjaville flights as well.'

Pet millionaire, Bond thought, filing away the information for later. Breed was turning off into a compound. He showed his pass to a guard at the gateway and they drove into a courtyard surrounded by neat white two-storey buildings.

'Welcome to the DRD Press Centre, Mr Bond,' Breed said.

It turned out that the Press Centre was a former Methodist primary school converted by the Dahum government after the secession as a comfortable base for foreign journalists and a location where the daily SitRep briefing took place. Forward planning, Bond thought – they knew they needed friendly propaganda. Once again he was impressed by the organisation and efficiency. He signed in at reception where his new accreditation was waiting for him, and Breed showed him upstairs to his room. There was even a private bar that was open from 6 p.m. to midnight. The only problem was, Breed said, that it wasn't like the early days of the war when the place was heaving; now there were hardly any journalists – just three, apart from Bond: an American, a German and another Brit. 'A freelance,' he said, with a sneer.

Breed opened the door to Bond's room. There was a bed, a table fan, a chest of drawers and a desk and a chair. Sitting on the bed was Bond's Zanzarim bag. Breed gave him back his passport, his APL identification and his Ronson lighter and Rolex watch.

'You took a lot of money off me as well,' Bond said.

'I lost that in the firefight, unfortunately,' Breed said, dabbing at his eye with his shirtsleeve cuff. 'Must've fallen out of my pocket. Sorry about that.'

'Yeah, sure.'

'See you,' Breed said, bluntly, moving to the door. Then added, remembering he was meant to be amiable now, 'Oh, yeah. Let me know if I can help with anything.'

He left and Bond unpacked his bag. He checked that everything was there – his shirts, his underwear, his panama hat and his pigskin toilet bag. He unzipped it – everything in its place. He took the panama out of its tube and unrolled it, pulling and tweaking it back into its hat-shape. Then he slipped out the cardboard lining of the tube and unpeeled the twenty new $20 bills that were rolled neatly around it in the interstice. His own idea for a hiding place – Q Branch would be proud of him. He was solvent again.

He gathered up his razor, soap and shaving cream and went down to the shower room at the end of the corridor and cleaned himself up thoroughly – a long shower, a hair wash and a close shave. Then he changed into a clean shirt and began to feel human again. He slipped his Rolex back on his wrist. Ten past six. The bar would be open – time for a drink.

**The journalists'** bar at the Port Dunbar Press Centre served beer, gin, whisky and various soft drinks. Bond changed $20 at reception for 380,000 Dahumian sigmassis and went back to the bar, where, entirely alone, he drank two large whisky and sodas with untypical speed. He also bought a packet of Boomslangs and, with his whisky in front of him on the table and a cigarette lit, felt his mood improve. The mission was full-on, all systems 'go' once more, he realised. He had infiltrated himself into Dahum, his cover was solid and his special equipment was intact. The fact that he had almost died, that Blessing Ogilvy-Grant, Zanzarim head of station, was almost certainly dead, and that he'd spent forty-eight hours lost, walking through virgin forest, seemed almost irrelevant, somehow. He could hear M's voice in his ear: 'Just get on with it, 007.' So he would – phase two was about to commence.

A young man in his late twenties, wearing a crumpled, grubby linen suit, wandered shiftily into the bar. He had a patchy beard and long greasy hair that hung to his collar. He gave a visible start of surprise on seeing Bond and came over, his eyes alive with welcome.

'Hi,' he said. 'I'm Digby Breadalbane – the freelance.' He had a weak handshake and a slightly whiny London accent.

'I'm Bond, James Bond. Agence Presse Libre.'

'Oh, they'll love you here,' Breadalbane said with some bitterness. 'They love anything French, this lot.' He sat down. 'I've been here three months but because I'm freelance they don't rate me.' He leaned closer. 'Thank God you've arrived. There's just a Yank and a

Kraut and me, the Anglo – it's like a bad joke, isn't it? – the foreign press in Port Dunbar.' He rummaged in a pocket for a cigarette but the pack he found was empty. Bond offered him a Boomslang and asked him what he'd like to drink. A beer, Breadalbane said, thanks very much. Bond signalled the barman and a Green Star was brought over. Clearly the beer in Zanzarim didn't distinguish between rebel and federalist.

Breadalbane continued his moaning for a while and Bond dutifully listened. Then the two other journalists appeared, both older men in their fifties. They introduced themselves – Miller Dupree and Odon Haas. Dupree looked fit and had a close-cropped *en brosse* haircut like a marine. Haas was corpulent and his grey hair fell down his back in a ponytail. He also had many strings of beads around his neck and wrists, Bond noticed. Both of them asked him if he knew Thierry Duhamel.

'Ah, Thierry,' Bond said, forewarned by his encounter with Geoffrey Letham. 'He's a legend.' They all agreed on this and that was an end to the matter.

Bond fired questions at them, asking them about the war from the rebels' side and the situation in Port Dunbar. They all confirmed that the city was surprisingly safe – and efficiently run. Postal services worked; public servants were paid; only when you went beyond its precincts did things change – the random danger and meaningless chaos of the civil war reasserted its dominance. No one knew where the front lines were, or where the opposing forces were manoeuvring, or might attack or mysteriously retreat. Bombing and artillery were completely indiscriminate: one village might be razed, another left untouched. Janjaville airstrip was the place to visit, they said. Once you saw what happened there – with the flights arriving after dark – then you could begin to make some sense of this conflict.

Bond was intrigued and, to his vague surprise, found himself enjoying the worldly company of his new 'colleagues'. He bought round after round of drinks with his copious supply of sigmassis and encouraged them to talk. Dupree and Haas were ageing socialists writing for left-wing magazines in their respective countries. Still avid for the cause, they unequivocally supported Dahum's right to secede from Zanzarim. Bond was pleased to note how secure his APL cover was and he began to think that perhaps this mission was not as haphazardly planned as he had once thought. Perhaps this mission was achievable, in spite of everything – all he had to do was find a way of getting close to Brigadier Adeka. Perhaps his new 'friend' Kobus Breed was the man to help him out there.

# 11
# Sunday

B ond had an uneasy sleep, despite all the whisky
 he'd consumed with his new colleagues. His
dream-life was full of the clamour of the firefight in
the forest and Blessing's terrible panic, all merging
with images of the dead children in the hut in Lokani,
stirring, rising, pointing their bony fingers at him in
reproach.

At first light he went and had a cold shower and
forced himself to do half an hour of callisthenics –
star-jumps, press-ups, running on the spot – to clear
his mind and make him feel alert. He strolled down
to the bar – now functioning as a dining room – and
ate the breakfast that was provided: orange juice,
an overcooked omelette and watery coffee. He had
lit his first cigarette of the day when a young man

came into the room and walked over to him, smiling broadly.

'Mr Bond, good morning, sir, I am Sunday. I am your assistant.'

I am your minder, Bond thought. Dupree and Haas had told him about the Ministry of Interior minders that they were provided with. Not for Breadalbane, of course, to his shame and chagrin. These minders also provided transport and accompanied you everywhere.

Sunday was in his early twenties, short and muscle-bound with a cheerful, easy manner and a near-constant smile. His car was a large but bashed-about cerise Peugeot 404. One headlight was missing and there was a neat row of bullet holes punched along the left-hand side.

'The MiGs do this,' Sunday explained. Then laughed. 'But they miss me.'

First stop on their agenda was at the Ministry of the Interior – housed in a former community centre with a chequerboard tile facade, and a lobby filled with empty pinboards. He had a meeting with the Minister of the Interior herself, a handsome, serious-looking woman called Abigail Kross, who had been Zanzarim's first woman judge after independence. Her brother was Minister of Defence in the Dahumian government and, during their conversation, Bond gained a clear impression of the absolute strength of Fakassa tribal loyalties – loyalties and bonds that seemed far stronger than anything equivalent in Western Europe.

Abigail Kross smiled at him.

'I'm counting on you, Mr Bond, to make sure your French readers fully understand our terrible situation here,' she said. 'If the French government could recognise Dahum then everything would change. I know they've been close to this decision – perhaps one more gentle push . . .'

Bond was diplomatic. 'I promise you I'll report what I see – but I have to say I'm very impressed so far.'

'You'll see more today,' she said. 'Our schools, our civil defence, our militia training.' She looked at him shrewdly. 'This is not about stealing oil, Mr Bond, this is a new country trying to shape its own destiny.'

And so Sunday dutifully took him to a school, to the central hospital, to the barracks and a fire station, to underground bunkers and experimental agricultural enterprises. Bond saw workshops where local blacksmiths reconstituted crashed and wrecked cars into hospital beds and office furniture. More intriguingly he saw there was a burgeoning defence industry fabricating their own hand grenades and anti-personnel mines from the most humdrum materials. By the end of the day's touring around, Bond was exhausted. He had deliberately taken notes – acting the journalist – but something about the desperation inherent in all these activities had depressed him. This was a country – barely a country – clinging on to its existence with its fingernails, desperate to survive through its talent for improvisation and inspired gimmickry. But Bond had seen the forces massing against them and knew how doomed and forlorn their efforts were. A hand grenade forged from bits of an old sewing machine and a lawn-mower wasn't going to stop a Centurion tank or a canister of napalm dropped from a low-flying MiG.

'Take me back to base, Sunday,' Bond requested after half an hour of watching smartly uniformed schoolchildren marching to and fro with wooden rifles over their shoulders. 'Oh, yes,' he added. 'I want to go to the Janjaville airstrip tonight. Can you arrange that?'

'We get you special pass,' Sunday said. 'They will issue it at Press Centre.'

They drove back through Port Dunbar's busy but ordered streets. Sunday leapt out of the car and opened the door for him.

'You know what you can do for me, Sunday,' Bond said. 'I need a jacket, a bush jacket, lots of pockets.' He handed over a few thousand sigmassis.

'I get one for you, sir,' Sunday said. 'One fine, fine jacket.'

Bond went to the Press Centre's administration office where a young lieutenant provided him with the special pass that would allow him entry into Janjaville airstrip.

'While we have Janjaville, there is hope,' he said, with evident sincerity.

It sounded like a slogan, Bond thought, something to shout at a rally – but the man's self-belief made him even more curious to see the place and what went on there. He suspected that the placid near-normality of life in Port Dunbar meant that the real target of Zanza Force's efforts would be directed at the airfield. Janjaville seemed the strategic key to the whole war. He reminded himself of the strategic key to his mission.

He smiled at the lieutenant.

'I'd like officially to request, on behalf of the Agence Presse Libre, an interview with Brigadier Adeka.'

'It's impossible, sir,' the lieutenant said. 'The brigadier does not talk to the foreign press.'

'Tell him we're a French press agency. It could be very important for Dahum in France—'

'It makes no difference,' the lieutenant interrupted. 'Since the war began we've had over one hundred requests for interviews. Every newspaper, radio station, TV channel in the world. The brigadier does not give interviews to anyone.'

Bond went back to the bar, perplexed. Perhaps he'd have to try gaining access through Abigail Kross. Breadalbane was sitting in the bar and asked if there was any chance that he could borrow some money, running out of funds and all that. Bond gave him a wad of notes and bought him a cold beer.

# 12

# Janjaville

Sunday's Peugeot bumped over potholes as it approached the perimeter fence of Janjaville airstrip. He had switched off his one headlight as there was a strict blackout imposed. Here and there at the side of the road were little flasks of burning oil providing a dim guiding light – enough to know you were on the right track. Bond looked at his watch. The journey had taken forty minutes, east out of Port Dunbar.

At the gate Bond showed his pass and they were waved through. The perimeter fence was high and heavily barbed-wired, Bond saw, as Sunday parked up behind the airstrip buildings. There was a concrete blockhouse with a towering radio mast and wires looping from it to a mobile radar dish that spun steadily round on its bearings. There was a corrugated-iron hangar, and a few low wooden huts made up the rest of the airstrip's buildings. On the grass by the blockhouse several dozen soldiers sat patiently waiting beside a row of assorted lorries and trucks, all empty.

Bond was wearing the bush jacket Sunday had acquired for him – in fact it was an army-surplus combat jacket with a patched bullet hole in the back and the Dahum flag sewn on its right shoulder – the red sun in its white plane casting its black shadow below. Had it been stripped from a corpse, Bond wondered, cleaned and resold at a profit? He didn't particularly care.

Bond stepped out of Sunday's car and looked around. The runway was closely mown grass but there seemed to be orthodox landing lights, though currently extinguished. In front of the hangar were three Malmö MFI trainers painted in camouflage green and black – single-engined, boxy-looking aircraft with oddly splayed tricycle undercarriages that had the effect of making them look as if they were about to fall back on their tails. Technicians were working on them and Bond saw the spark-shower of oxyacetylene. To his eyes it looked like they were attaching .50-calibre machine guns on to pylons beneath the wings.

'This will be our new air force,' Sunday said with manifest pride. 'Madame Kross, she ask for me to introduce you to Mr Hulbert Linck. Please to follow me, Mr Bond.'

Bond walked with Sunday towards the hangar. As he drew near he saw that there was a very tall European man supervising the work on the Malmös. Sunday approached him, gave a small bow and indicated Bond standing a few paces away. Very tall indeed, Bond realised, as the man turned to look at him. Six foot six, perhaps, like a basketball player, and he had all the lanky awkwardness and ungainliness of the very tall. He was in his fifties and his thinning, fine white-blond hair was blown into a kind of hirsute halo by the evening breeze. He wore faded jeans and canvas boots, his shirt had a tear at the elbow. He looked more like some crazed inventor than a shrewd international businessman and multimillionaire.

Sunday introduced Bond, respectfully. 'Mr Bond from Agence Presse Libre.'

'Hulbert Linck,' the tall man said, in good English with the faintest accent that Bond found impossible to place: Swedish? German? Dutch? He shook Bond's hand vigorously. 'At last, the French are here.'

Bond saw, in the glow from the engineers' lights, the shine of a zealot's near-madness in Linck's eyes. He immediately began talking rapidly.

'When will the French recognise Dahum? Perhaps you can inform me. We've all been awaiting the news from the outside world.' He put his thin hand on Bond's shoulder. 'Everything you write will be vitally important, Mr Bond. Vitally.'

'I'll do my best,' Bond said, changing the subject. 'These are Malmös, aren't they?'

'Bought cheap off the Swedish air force,' Linck said. 'We're converting them for ground attack. When we can strike back from the air the whole context of this war will change. You wait and see.' Linck talked on excitedly, outlining his plans. It was as if the Zanzarim civil war and the survival of Dahum were a personal problem of his own. Dupree and Haas had told Bond of Linck's unswerving support – he had spent millions of dollars of his fortune (his was a pan-European dairy empire, originally: butter, milk and cheese) recruiting and paying white mercenaries, chartering planes, buying illicit military materiel in the shadier locales of the world arms' market, all to keep this fledgling African state alive. There was no rationale, Bond supposed, looking at the man as he spoke and gesticulated, it was a 'cause' pure and simple. It gave him something to live for – it was Hulbert Linck's personal crusade. Bond had asked Haas where Linck was from and had received no precise answer. Nobody seemed to know his early history in any detail. Rumours abounded: that he had made his first fortune smuggling foodstuffs in the black market during the chaos of post-war Europe; that he was the bastard son of an English aristocrat and an Italian courtesan. He had a Swiss passport but was resident in Monte Carlo, Haas had told him; he spoke excellent German and French but no one really knew for sure where he was from – Georgia, someone had said, or one of the Baltic states, perhaps; Haas had even heard rumours about Corsica and Albania. His companies were all based in Liechtenstein, apparently.

Bond looked at him, closely – was the white-blond hair dyed? he wondered suddenly. Another ruse. Were the slightly deranged mannerisms – the wide-eyed enthusiasms, the carelessness about what he wore – more examples of a very clever and duplicitous mask? Everything about him, to Bond's eyes, seemed slightly bogus and worked-up. He realised that for someone like Hulbert Linck the more speculation about his origins, the more wild guesses thrown about, the better the disguise.

Suddenly a bell rang briefly from the blockhouse and Bond sensed a quiver of readiness from those waiting around the Janjaville strip.

'Excuse me, Mr Bond,' Linck said and loped off.

The runway lights were switched on, delineating the grass strip with dotted lines of blue and, seconds later, Bond heard the growing roar of aero engines.

Then out of the darkness he saw landing lights appear and into the blue glow cast from the runway a Lockheed Super Constellation swooped, touching down heavily, bouncing, then great clouds of dust were thrown up as the four propellers went into reverse, slowing its progress so it could turn off and wheel round on to the piste in front of the hangar.

Bond had flown in Super Constellations in the 1950s, when they, along with the Boeing Stratocruiser, were the apogee of airline glamour. They still had a remarkable look about them, Bond thought, watching this one come to rest and the cargo doors in its side open. The three tail fins, the four radial engines, the unusually high undercarriage and the curved slim aerodynamics of the fuselage all gave it a particular degree of beauty for an aeroplane. This one was elderly, its paint finish patched and blistered and there was no airline logo in evidence, no trace of where, or from whom, Linck might have chartered it. Arc lights were switched on and the soldiers and the lorries rushed forward to unload its cargo.

Bond watched, his mind busy, as the plane was unloaded in minutes, the four propellers still turning.

He saw boxes of ammunition, mortars, bazookas, heavy machine guns, food, powdered milk, crates of Scotch whisky and gin, drugs, spare tyres and what looked like household goods – air conditioners, stainless-steel sinks, a couple of coffee tables – all passed down the chain of soldiers' hands from the cargo doors to the waiting lorries and trucks that, once loaded, sped off into the night. Bond looked on, amazed. Then, just as the doors seemed about to close, he saw Kobus Breed run from a building and climb the steps to the plane, handing over a small package to someone inside. The doors were shut, Breed descended and the steps were wheeled away. It wasn't entirely one-way traffic, then, Bond thought to himself. Breed was now talking to Linck – like two familiars, Bond noticed. Linck clapped him on the shoulder and Breed headed off into the darkness.

'The planes come two, three, four times a night,' Sunday said.

'Where from?' Bond asked, turning back to Sunday.

'Dahomey, Ivory Coast, Mali – we don't know for sure.'

Bond looked at the tall figure of Linck, as the Super Constellation revved its engines and turned to taxi back to the runway. It hadn't been on the ground for more than fifteen minutes, Bond thought, watching

Linck waving enthusiastically at the taxiing plane as if he were bidding farewell to parting relatives.

'Mr Linck, he control everything,' Sunday said.

With an accelerating roar of its Wright radial engines the now empty Super Constellation barrelled down the Janjaville runway in a blue-tinged cloud of dust and took off into the night sky. The landing lights were extinguished and all that could be heard was the diminishing drone of the engines as the plane climbed to cruising height. Bond walked back to Sunday's Peugeot, impressed: this rearguard action had real potential, he could see.

# 13

# Ghost Warriors

B ond spent many hours the next day sitting in an anteroom outside Abigail Kross's office hoping for an appointment. When she eventually saw him she seemed distant and preoccupied and her apology was perfunctory. Bond asked if she could use her authority to arrange an interview with Brigadier Adeka. She said that would be impossible. The brigadier had a lifelong distrust of the press and never spoke to journalists. Bond played the French card – 'Agence Presse Libre would see it as an honour to be able to speak to the brigadier exclusively' – but in vain.

'Perhaps you could talk to Jakobus Breed,' Madame Kross then suggested. 'He supervises the foreign military advisers.'

'I'm already familiar with Mr Breed,' Bond said, savouring the euphemism. Then he added, 'I met the brigadier's brother in London,' hoping that this claim would give him a little more credence. 'He wanted to pass on a message to his brother.'

'Gabriel Adeka is no friend of Dahum,' Abigail Kross said, her smile fading permanently. 'His name will open no doors here, Mr Bond. Especially not with his brother.'

Bond left her, thinking hard. Madame Kross was a woman of intelligence and integrity, Bond recognised, but her absolute intransigence seemed almost perverse to him. Why wouldn't the brigadier speak to the foreign press? Propaganda was a highly effective weapon when it was well deployed. Something strange was going on here. Perhaps Hulbert Linck was the man to approach next – maybe he could apply some pressure.

Back at the Press Centre, Bond sent a telex to the fake APL address he had been given and that went straight to Transworld Consortium in Regent's Park. He wrote bland stuff about plucky little Dahum defying the odds, soldiering on gallantly, but Bond knew that the subtext would let M know he was 'in country'. He added a postscript that he was making every effort to interview Brigadier Adeka but 'operational difficulties' made it seem unlikely that it would be granted. He also mentioned that the chief executive of OG Palm Oil Export and Agricultural Services was currently indisposed. Blessing's fate would at least be investigated now.

He spent another bibulous evening with Dupree, Haas and Breadalbane and learned from Haas that anyone could book a seat on an empty outbound flight on the Super Constellation for $100. The actual port of Port Dunbar was completely blockaded and the only way out of the country was by air – or overland, if you were prepared to risk your neck beneath the watchful eye of the MiGs.

Bond climbed upstairs to bed in a bad mood, wondering if he should just pay his $100, quit Dahum and admit failure. It went against his nature, but he couldn't see how there was any way he could get close to Adeka, short of storming his headquarters. And he had a horrible feeling that this military stalemate might leave him stranded in Dahum for weeks or months, like Digby Breadalbane.

He was woken before dawn by an urgent knocking on his door. It was Sunday, in a state of real excitement.

'We have a scoop, Mr Bond. There has been a small battle and we have defeated the enemy. I thought you might like to see it.'

Bond dressed as quickly as possible and Sunday drove him north out of Port Dunbar on increasingly minor roads. As they bumped along through the pearly, misty light Bond wondered if this was a simple propaganda exercise – something staged for him, the gullible newly arrived journalist, who would duly report it as a Dahumian feat of arms. His mood was still sour – he wasn't expecting much.

After an hour's drive, they turned off the metalled road and entered an area of mangrove swamp and winding creeks. The road they drove along was built up above the watercourses on a kind of revetted embankment. Then they began to pass jubilant Dahumian troops returning from the front and in the morning sky they saw smoke curling up above the treeline.

The village they arrived at had been burnt out and destroyed weeks previously: shattered mud huts, charred roof timbers and leafless trees signalled a napalm strike. Bond and Sunday left the Peugeot and walked through exuberant milling Dahumian soldiers towards the giant shade tree at the village's centre. Here they found Breed and half a dozen other white mercenaries standing round eight Zanzari soldiers' corpses laid out in a row. A little way off at another entrance to the village was a still smoking, upended armoured personnel carrier, a hole punched through its side – perhaps, Bond wondered, from a bazooka or an anti-tank gun unloaded from the Super Constellation the night before.

Breed turned to meet him, wiping away a tear. He was wearing a grey T-shirt with 'HALO' printed on the front and his bashed kepi was pushed back on his head at a rakish angle. He was exhibiting his usual shifting cocktail of moods – at once jovial, wired and sinister.

'Yah, we know they were coming so we just waited up here in the village,' Breed said. 'Bang-bang – got these fellas and the others just ran away. We're gonna chase them back to Sinsikrou.'

He shouted orders and some soldiers shinned up into the shade tree with lengths of rope that they secured to the branches and let fall. Then Breed had a man bring him a clinking, heavy sack and from it drew out what looked like giant fish hooks, six inches long, with a large eye. Breed attached the dangling ropes to the hooks and then, to Bond's shock and surprise, he thwacked the sharp end in and under the jaws of the dead soldiers, like a stevedore walloping a bale hook into a sack. He tugged sharply at the hook to make sure its grip was secure under the jawbone.

'Pull away, boys,' he shouted.

The men in the tree hauled on the ropes and the dead bodies were lifted aloft by their jaws. Like so many fishing trophies – like marlin or bluefin, Bond thought – on a dock after a successful fishing expedition.

'Stop!' Breed shouted when the dead men were three feet off the ground. 'Secure them there!'

The ropes were lashed to the branches and the dead men hung there, twirling gently. Bond had seen lynched men before but these bodies looked different, unusually dehumanised by the hooks and the forced jut of their lower jaws and the tearing stretching strain on their necks that were taking the full weight of their bodies. He thought as they hung there that they looked like ghoulish sides of beef in a butcher's chill room, the dangling arms and legs all the more obscene because of the unnatural angle of the head with the giant hook through the jaw.

Breed looked on with an eerie, satisfied smile on his face.

'That's a good haul,' he said. 'The more the merrier. One isn't enough, you need a cluster, like. Once I strung up more than thirty. I tell you it—'

'Why do you do it?' Bond interrupted.

'Because it freaks them out when they see this,' Breed said, cheerfully, lowering his voice as he spoke to Bond. 'I leave them all over the forest, hanging from trees. Scares the shit out of the Zanzaris – bad juju.'

'Where did you learn that little trick?' Bond asked, concealing his disgust.

'Down in Matabeleland in '66,' Breed said. 'I used to string up the ZIPRA terrs we caught like this.' He smiled. 'What do you say in French? *Pour encourager les autres.*'

Bond turned away from the dangling bodies, feeling nauseous, and went to join Sunday, who looked equally distressed.

'Does he do this all the time?' Bond asked Sunday.

'Yes. He like it too too much.'

'I don't like it,' Bond said. 'It's revolting.'

'I go 'gree for you, sar,' Sunday said. 'They are just soldiers, like our own men.'

Bond looked over to see Breed striding around and shouting at the Dahumian troops, forming them into a rough column of about 200 men. They were charged and energised by their victory, armed with an odd variety of weapons – AK-47s, SLRs and ancient World War Two Lee–Enfield rifles. They all had machetes at their waist in leather scabbards or thrust through their belts. Every one of them, Bond noticed, despite their patchwork uniforms, had the red, white and black flag of Dahum sewn on to their right shoulder.

'Bring him on,' Breed shouted and from behind a ruined hut a witch doctor appeared. Bond couldn't think of any other word to describe him. His face was painted white with lurid green circles around his eyes. A great mass of shells and beads was wrapped around his neck and wrists setting up a coarse rattle as he shuffled forward in a half-dance. He was bare-chested and wore a thick dry grass skirt that fell to his ankles and he carried a gourd and a long horsehair fly whisk. He shuffled up and down the column of men – who stood there rapt and rigid – and as he went he drank from the gourd and spat out the liquid through his clenched teeth in a fine spray into their faces and flicked their chests and groins with the fly whisk, chanting all the while in a low monotone. When he had sprayed and touched them all he screamed shrilly, three times, stepped back, made a weird sign of bene-diction over them and shuffled off behind the house again.

'Take 'em away, Dawie,' Breed shouted at one of the other white mercenaries and the men wheeled around and, beginning a chant, started to jog out of the vil-lage in pursuit of the rest of the Zanzari soldiers fleeing back up the road to what they hoped was safety.

Breed whooped encouragement at them. 'I just love that,' he said to Bond, taking out a pack of Boomslangs and offering it to Bond. They both lit up.

'Great show, isn't it?' Breed said. 'That fetish priest is worth a thousand men. They won't fight without his blessing.'

'What does all the mumbo-jumbo mean?' Bond asked.

'He makes them immortal, you see,' Breed said. 'If they die today they come back as spirits and continue the fight. You can't see them but they're fighting beside you.' He chuckled. 'Now they're fearless, those boys. They even want to die – to become a "ghost warrior". Amazing.' He dabbed at his weeping eye. 'If they catch those Zanzaris it'll be quite a picnic, I tell you.' He turned away. 'Let's head back,' he said. 'I just wanted you to see this – good copy for your newspapers, eh?'

Bond was happy to leave the village and its shade tree with its hanging fruit of dangling corpses.

'We'll pull back,' Breed said. 'Mine the embankments. They're attacking us all over the place at the moment – but there'll be no way through here.'

They walked back towards the Peugeot.

'I want to speak to Adeka,' Bond said. 'Can you help?'

'You must be joking,' Breed said. 'Even I can't get to see him.'

'How do you communicate?'

'Most of the time I get these written orders. Reinforce there. Destroy that bridge. Move more men there. Repel this attack. Fall back and regroup. He seems to see the big picture, Adeka. It's uncanny, man.

And he distributes all the ordnance from the Janjaville flights – you get what he gives you. He seems to know what he's doing – for a black brigadier.' He smiled at Bond. 'Fancy a drink?'

He didn't wait for a reply and led Bond over to a US Army jeep with a canvas canopy and a tall whippy aerial. In the back was an impressive-looking, many-dialled radio set and a young man in an over-large tin helmet sat there listening to the traffic. Breed reached into a knapsack and brought out a bottle of schnapps. He fished around some more and came up with two cloudy shot glasses. He set the glasses down on the jeep's bonnet and poured them both a drink. Bond didn't feel like drinking with Breed but perhaps some hard liquor was required after what he'd witnessed in the village.

'*Proost*,' Breed said, and they both knocked back the schnapps in one. Bond felt his throat burn. Strong stuff. Breed topped them up.

'So,' Bond said. 'Matebeleland, 1966 . . . Rhodesian African Rifles?'

'No. Light Infantry. The good old RLI.' Breed pointed at the two scars on his cheek. 'I got shot in the face by a ZANLA terr. Thought he'd killed me. I was six months in a hospital in Salisbury then I was invalided out of the army. Lucky for me Hulbert Linck

came by recruiting. Five thousand US a month in any
bank in the world you choose. Hard to resist. So me
and a few of my RLI mates signed up for Dahum.
They're a good bunch of guys, though, the Dahum
grunts. When the juju man fires them up they'll fight
till they drop.' He grinned. 'That's why, in spite of
everything, we're winning. We've got bigger balls
than the Zanzaris.'

Bond said nothing. Breed poured another schnapps.

'What do you think, Bond?' he suggested. 'There's
a little club in town – nice atmosphere, good music,
European alcohol, very obliging girls. They like us
white boys fighting for their country. Want to meet
there tonight?'

Bond did not want to go out on the town with Kobus
Breed. Not in a thousand years.

'Actually, I'm not sure I can make it. Copy to file.'

Breed's finger tapped the Dahum flag on Bond's
jacket.

'You could pass for one of us.'

There was an audible crackle of static from the radio
in the jeep and Breed turned to see what was going on.
The operator was intent, concentrating, nodding.

'It's for you, Boss.'

Breed strode over and put on the headphones. As he
listened he looked progressively more serious.

'Yah. OK – roger that.' He took off the headphones and wiped his eye.

'What's up?' Bond asked.

'A pretty major shit-storm. All this stuff we did here today was a feint. There's another Zanza Force column moving on the airstrip.' He gestured at the radio, 'That came from Adeka.'

'Himself?'

'No. But relayed from him. I got to move, man. This is serious.'

'Mind if I tag along?' Bond suggested, spontaneously.

Breed looked at him, a little askance. When he spoke his voice was heavy with scepticism.

'You ever been in combat?' Breed asked.

Bond smiled, tiredly. 'You ever heard of World War Two?'

# 14

# The Battle of the Kololo Causeway

B ond stood with Breed on a small bluff and looked through binoculars at the view. A little bit of orientation and a few glances at Breed's map had made everything fairly clear.

The village of Kololo, the main Dahumian strongpoint guarding this eastern approach towards Janjaville, had been lost, abandoned. Some huts in the village were on fire – apparently there had been a MiG airstrike. The troops that had been manning it had fled the village and had retreated across the 200-yard causeway that ran above a great swathe of swampland and had regrouped on the far side, barricading the road with logs and oil drums, ready to repel any new advance out of the village along the causeway.

Bond could see that the village was thick with Zanza Force soldiers and he could spot one Saracen armoured car with a roof turret sheltering by the gable end of a mud hut that was close to the road leading to the causeway. He suspected they were waiting for the MiGs to return before they continued their advance. He remembered Blessing's remarks about their lack of military zeal.

'Well, at least there's only one direction they can attack from,' Bond said. 'But that barricade will last twenty seconds in the face of that Saracen.' He turned to Breed. 'You don't have enough men.'

Breed had explained the problem. Eighty per cent of the Dahumian army faced the Zanza Force advance astride the transnational highway that led to Port Dunbar. That's where the tanks were, and the artillery. It was a stand-off that could be maintained forever, each army waiting for the other one to blink. Consequently most of the action in these later stages of the war consisted of skirmishes as Zanza Force units explored other routes into the rebel heartland. Breed and his flying columns were able to confront and repel any of these secondary thrusts – they were more aggressive in their soldiering and they had the power of the fetish priest and his juju on their side, whereas the Zanzari soldiers could only be persuaded to muster on the promise of

free beer and cigarettes. Bond had seen the consequences with his own eyes that morning. Dahum's hinterland was now so small that sufficient troops could
be rushed here and there to repel any new attempt at
incursion. Except today they had been caught out –
Breed's mercenaries and two heavily armed companies
were chasing fleeing Zanzaris through the forest. And
in the meantime Kololo had fallen.

Breed took the binoculars from Bond.

'I suppose we could try and blow the causeway,' he
said vaguely, peering out over the swamp.

'That's no good. You have to retake Kololo.'

'Oh yeah, good idea. Why didn't I think of that?
That's easy, man.'

'You have to be on the other side of the causeway.
Dug in back in the village.' Bond gestured at the troops
huddling behind their barricade. 'Look at your guys.
Wait until the MiGs get here. They'll blow you away.'

Breed turned and looked at him resentfully.

'So what do you suggest, General?'

Bond shrugged. 'It's not my war – you're the one
getting the big pay cheque. But you're going to be in
real trouble if you let them get established this side of
the causeway.'

Breed swore and spat on the ground. Bond could see
he was worried.

'Have you any second line you could defend back up the road? Another creek, a bridge?'

'No,' Breed said. 'We could fell some trees, I suppose.'

'Then you'd better get your axes out,' Bond said, reclaimed the binoculars and surveyed the panorama in front of him again. There was no way around the swamp that the causeway traversed. On the Dahumian side of the swamp he could see that a deep artificial gully had been dug – probably some old flood-prevention device. An idea was forming in his head. He might be able to apply some useful advantage here, he thought. This situation might just be the opportunity he was waiting for.

'I've got an idea,' Bond said. 'But I need to know what firepower we have.'

He and Breed slithered down from the bluff to the makeshift positions occupied by the soldiers who had fled Kololo. Bond saw at once that any resistance would be purely token. The Saracen alone would brush them aside and then the troops following the armoured car would have a field day.

Bond surveyed the offensive possibilities. There were two 4.1-inch mortars with a couple of boxes of bombs and one heavy .50-calibre machine gun. Then he saw about a dozen galvanised buckets with curious bulbous lids on them.

'What're they?' Bond asked.

Breed sneered. 'They're our Dahumian home-made piss-poor landmines. They call them "Adeka's Answer".'

'Do they work?'

'They go off with a hell of a bang. Huge percussion – burst your eardrums, make your nose bleed, maybe up-end a small vehicle. Saracen'll drive right over it.' Kobus sneered. 'You've got a big charge of cordite. I told them to fill the rest of it with nails and bolts – cut people up – but nobody listens to me.'

'They may just be perfect,' Bond said, thinking, remembering.

'So what do we do, wise guy?' Breed said, with heavy mockery. He was increasingly worried, Bond could see. Any move that threatened Janjaville meant the end of the war. 'Go on, genius. What do we do?'

'If I tell you,' Bond said, 'there's one condition.'

'I don't do "conditions",' Breed said.

'Fine. All the best of luck to you and your men.' He turned and began to walk away.

'All right, all right. What condition?'

Bond stopped and Breed approached.

'If I show you how to get back into Kololo,' Bond said, 'then you have to get me a meeting with Adeka.'

Breed looked at him – Bond could practically hear his mind working.

'You can get us back in that village?' Breed said. 'You guarantee?'

'You can't guarantee anything in a war zone. But I think this will work.'

Breed looked down at the ground and kicked at a stone. Bond could tell he was reluctant to ask for help, as if it signalled some lack of military expertise in himself, showed some fundamental weakness. He spat again.

'If you get us back in that village Adeka will want to marry you.'

'We don't need to go that far,' Bond said. 'A meeting, face to face, will be fine.'

'It won't be a problem,' Breed said. 'I promise you. If you get us back across the causeway you'll be a national hero. But if you fail . . .' He didn't finish.

Bond concealed his pleasure at this concession. 'We won't fail if you do exactly what I say.'

'Where do we start?'

'We retreat,' Bond said. 'In panic. As they say in French: *reculer pour mieux sauter*. Take a step back to jump higher, you know.'

Breed looked at him, darkly. 'You'd better know what you're doing, man.'

'Maybe you have a better idea,' Bond said, amiably.

'No, no. Over to you, Bond. This is your party.'

Bond managed not to smile and began to issue instructions to the non-commissioned officers. He sent teams of men to bury the bucket bombs in the irrigation ditch. He then positioned and precisely sighted the mortars, taking his time, calculating distances as best he could and adjusting the calibration on the sights minutely.

'Don't touch them,' he said to the mortar teams. 'Even after you've fired and you think the range is wrong. Just keep firing, understand?'

Then he had the heavy machine gun taken up to the bluff and set it down where it had a field of fire over the whole causeway. He gave Breed precise instructions and checked on the village again through the binoculars. The troops were gathering. The Saracen had moved away from the protection of its gable-end and was now close to the entrance to the causeway – obviously they weren't going to wait for any air strike.

'We'll let the Saracen through,' Bond said. 'It'll be going hell for leather. Have some men waiting to engage it further up the track. Then, when we "retreat" we'll re-form in the trees and be ready to race across the causeway when I give the word.'

'You seem very confident,' Breed said.

'Well, it worked the last time I tried it,' Bond said.

'When was that?'

'1945. The principle being that, in a battle, confusion can be as important as an extra regiment.'

'Who said that? The Duke of fucking Wellington?'

'I did, actually,' Bond said with a modest smile. 'Now, here's exactly how I expect everything to happen.'

**At midday** the sound of the Saracen's revving and manoeuvring carried across the marsh to the Dahumian positions. It was hot and steamy. Bond was standing by the rudimentary barricade and ducked down as the first fusillade of bullets began to come their way. The Saracen roared on to the causeway, its .30 Browning machine gun firing wildly as the turret traversed left and right, a massed column of troops surging behind it.

'Right,' Bond shouted. 'Everybody run!'

The defending Dahumians took him at his word. With histrionic display they stood up, waved their arms and abandoned their positions with alacrity, pelting down the road away from the causeway, seeking the protection of the forest trees. Leaving the barricade unguarded and undefended.

Bond sprinted back to the mortar crews. Breed was up at the bluff behind the machine gun. Through his binoculars Bond saw the Saracen accelerate, blasting through the log and oil-drum barrier, spraying the forest fringe with its machine gun. Behind it the

Zanza Force troops raced forward over the causeway. It looked like a walkover.

'They are comin', sar,' said the lance corporal who was manning the first of the mortars.

'Wait,' Bond said. He wanted most of the men across the causeway before there was any retaliation.

'OK, fire!' He waved up at Breed.

There was a dull *whump* as the first mortar bomb took off into the air. A split second later the other followed. The bombs exploded some way behind the advancing Zanzaris.

'Keep firing,' Bond said to the baffled mortar crew. 'Don't stop.' He ran off and scrambled up through the undergrowth to where Breed was blasting away with the machine gun.

Bond could see that his ally 'confusion' was already contributing to this firefight. The advancing troops had already slowed, disoriented by this barrage of harmless explosions to their rear. Breed, on Bond's instructions, was also firing at the rear of the troops' advance, raking the causeway with his heavy-calibre bullets, chewing up great gouts of earth and dust. More bombs exploded as the mortars kept up their rate of fire.

'OK. Turn the gun on the rear ranks.'

Breed swivelled the gun and worked the bullet impacts closer to the shifting static mass of Zanzari soldiers. One or two of them were cut down. Others flung themselves in the swamp. There was a collective race to get off the causeway as the troops desperately began to search for cover from this baffling assault from behind.

The irrigation ditch lay there invitingly. The perfect place to keep your head down. Men began to pour and slither into the security its depth provided.

Further up the track Bond could hear firing and explosions as the Saracen was engaged. The irrigation ditch was packed with cowering men as Breed kept up his fire, hosing bullets along the ditch's edge. Now, Bond thought, all we need is 'Adeka's Answer'.

The first of the bucket bombs exploded and Bond felt the shockwave even up on the bluff. That detonation set off a chain reaction and the others exploded in a Chinese firecracker of eruptions along the irrigation ditch.

'Breed – get your boys across the causeway and into the village.'

Bond didn't want to think about what had happened in the ditch. He could hear the screams of wounded men and a great billowing pall of smoke and dust obscured the view.

On Breed's signal – a green flare – the Dahumians in the forest began to stream across the causeway towards

Kololo village. There was some sporadic firing as they advanced but the debacle on the far side of the causeway must have been very visible to whatever troops had remained behind.

Breed was on his feet with the binoculars.

'Yes, they're running away,' he said. 'True to form. Big bunch of girls.'

Bond looked down at the irrigation ditch as the smoke cleared. Stunned and wounded soldiers were staggering and crawling out of it, being rounded up by Breed's men.

'Don't kill them,' Bond said. 'A nice large group of prisoners might be a useful bargaining chip, one day.'

'Whatever you say, Mr Bond,' Breed chuckled, wiping his eye on his cuff, and then looking at him with something that might just have been respect, Bond thought. Score one for the Agence Presse Libre.

'Remember my condition,' Bond said. 'Remember your promise. I got you back into Kololo – so get me to Adeka.'

# 15
# Gold Star

B ond sat in the bar of the Press Centre, drink- ing his second whisky and soda, his mind full of the battle that he'd directed and won. One hundred and eighty-two prisoners had been captured and the Dahum army was back in Kololo, dug in and secure in its fortified bunkers. Breed had been exultant and had promised him a face-to-face meeting with Adeka within twenty-four hours. If that were the outcome then a momentary reverse in the Zanza Force advance would have been well worth it. There was every chance that the larger objective might be achieved. *Reculer pour mieux sauter*, indeed.

To be honest, Bond had to admit that he hadn't thought much about what he was doing once the urgency of the situation was apparent and the beautiful clarity of his plan had seized him. All that had concerned him was how best to execute it. And it had been incredibly exciting: the gratification of seeing mental concepts vindicated so completely in a small but classic wartime encounter between infantry units – one so skilfully turning defence into attack and eventual victory. The Battle of the Kololo Causeway could be usefully taught at military academies, he thought, with a little justified pride.

Digby Breadalbane came diffidently into the bar, saw Bond and strode over and sat down – looking for a free drink.

'How was your day, James?' he asked.

'More intriguing than I expected, Digby,' Bond said, circumspectly, and offered to buy him a beer.

Breadalbane seemed chirpier than usual as he sipped his beer, foregoing his usual litany of moans and complaints.

'How long do you think this war will last?' he asked.

'Who knows?' Bond shrugged.

'I mean, it's not going to end next week.'

'You never can tell.'

'No, it's just that I've decided to stay on, no matter what, and see things out to the bitter end. I expect you and the others will fly out on a Constellation when the

end is nigh. I can't afford the fare, so I thought if I witness the fall of Port Dunbar then that'll be my scoop.
You know – the sole eyewitness.'

'It would make your reputation, Digby,' Bond said,
his face straight. 'You'd be famous.'

'I suppose I would, wouldn't I?' Breadalbane said,
liking the idea.

'And if you could get slightly wounded, even better.'

Bond saw Sunday poke his head around the door
and beckon to him.

Bond stood and dropped a few notes on the table.

'I bet you'd get a salaried job out of it as well,' he
said. 'Have another on me.'

He crossed the room to Sunday leaving Breadalbane
to his dreams of journalistic glory.

'Please to come with me, sir,' Sunday said. 'We have
to leave now.'

'Where are we going?'

'I'm not permitted to say.'

Sunday drove Bond out of Port Dunbar, heading
south towards the harbour. Then they turned off into a
high-walled compound containing three private houses
all linked by covered walkways. As they parked,
Bond noticed that Sunday seemed cowed and oddly
apprehensive.

'I wait here for you, Mr Bond.'

Bond stepped out of the car and, at the door to the main building, was met by a young bespectacled man in a white coat.

'Mr Bond? I am Dr Masind. Please follow me.'

He sounded Indian or Pakistani to Bond, who obediently followed him through the house – that had clearly been converted into some kind of clinic: clean, brightly lit, nurses hurrying to and fro – and out on to a walkway, leading to a separate house, guarded by two armed soldiers and with, Bond noticed, a tall thin radio mast towering above it.

They went upstairs and Bond was asked to wait in a corridor. After about five minutes, a young officer, a colonel, emerged and introduced himself. He was smart, slim and dapper, his dark green fatigues neatly pressed. He had a small pencil moustache, like a matinee idol.

'I'm Colonel Denga,' he said, speaking with the slightest accent. 'I want to thank you for what you did for us today.'

'It was very spur-of-the-moment. As you know I'm just an APL journalist – but the situation did call for fairly drastic action,' Bond said. He was aware that his self-effacingness could be counterproductive and he was conscious of Denga looking at him shrewdly.

'Not every journalist can dictate and control a battle on the spur of the moment . . .'

Bond smiled. 'I didn't say I was inexperienced. I'm older than you, Colonel. I served with British commandos in World War Two. You learn a lot, and fast.'

'Well, wherever your expertise originates – we're very grateful. Please – go in.'

He opened a door and Bond stepped through into a dark room, with only one light burning. A man was lying on a hospital bed with a saline drip attached to his neck. He was terribly gaunt and thin, his hair patchy and grey. He gestured to Bond to come closer and spoke in a weak, semi-whispering voice.

'Mr Bond – I am Brigadier Solomon Adeka. I wanted to thank you personally for what you achieved at the Kololo Causeway.'

Bond stared, astonished, taking in every detail. Adeka was obviously gravely, terminally ill – that fact apparent from his drawn face and his dead eyes. Some kind of aggressive cancer, Bond supposed. Adeka reached out a quivering hand, all bones, and Bond shook it briefly. There was no grip at all.

Adeka signalled to Colonel Denga – who had slipped into the room behind Bond – and the colonel stepped forward, reached into his pocket and drew out a slim leather case.

'You'll probably laugh,' Adeka said, 'but I wanted you to have some symbolic evidence of our gratitude. The Republic of Dahum salutes you.'

Bond took the case from Denga and opened it. Inside, on a bed of moulded black velvet, was an eight-pointed gold star hanging from a red, white and black silk ribbon.

'The Gold Star of Dahum – our highest military honour.'

Bond was both surprised and oddly touched. 'Well . . . I'm very grateful,' he said slowly. 'Very flattered. But I don't feel I'm really—'

But then Adeka began to cough, drily, and Bond saw how his frail body was wracked with the effort as it quivered and shook beneath the blankets.

'We should go,' Denga said, quietly.

'Goodbye, Brigadier,' Bond said, not wanting his farewell to sound final but knowing he would never see the man again – and knowing also that his mission was now effectively over. He turned and left the room.

He sat in silence as Sunday drove him back to Port Dunbar. He felt a human sadness, he had to admit, that Adeka's life was ending so early, and at the same time a gnawing sense of unease that he had been sent here precisely to achieve that object – to make him 'a less efficient soldier'. No need for that now.

'Is everything OK, sir?' Sunday said, cautiously, aware of his sombre mood.

'Yes,' Bond said. 'I've just been given a medal.'

'Congratulations,' Sunday said, cheering up. 'Do you want to go to Janjaville? There are five flights tonight. Two already come and go.'

'No thanks,' Bond said. 'Take me back to the Press Centre. It's been quite a day – I need another drink.'

Bond went straight to the bar and bought a bottle of whisky. He intended to sleep well and soundly tonight and he knew whisky to be an excellent soporific. There was no sign of his colleagues but he didn't mind drinking alone. He sat down and poured himself a generous three fingers of Scotch. Then the door to the bar opened and Geoffrey Letham walked in.

# 16

# A Very Rich Man

All five members of the foreign press corps in
Port Dunbar were invited to Brigadier Solomon
Adeka's state funeral, three days later. The journalists
stood in a loose, uneasy group at the rear of the dusty,
weed-strewn cemetery that adjoined Port Dunbar's
modest cathedral – St Jude's – as a guard of honour
carried Adeka's coffin to the graveside. Through a
crackling PA system Colonel Denga gave a short but
passionate eulogy, outlining Adeka's virtues as a man,
a patriot and a soldier, describing him as the 'first
hero of Dahum' and saying emphatically that the
struggle for freedom would continue – this brought
cheers and applause from the large crowd that had
gathered beyond the cemetery walls – and that the
people of Dahum should draw their inspiration, their

courage, their endurance from the memory of this great man.

A firing party raised their rifles and delivered a ragged six-shot volley into the hazy blue sky as the coffin was lowered.

Bond looked on in an ambivalent state of mind and then became aware that Geoffrey Letham was sidling over in his direction. They had greeted each other curtly the other night, not shaking hands, and Bond had swiftly taken himself off to his room with his bottle of whisky. He had managed to avoid him subsequently, having Sunday fill his days with endless rounds of official sightseeing. However, there was no escaping him now, as Letham appeared at his shoulder, mopping his florid face with a damp ultramarine handkerchief.

'I say, Bond,' he whispered in his ear, 'Breadalbane tells me you met Adeka just before he died. What was all that about?'

'Nothing important.'

'What was he like?'

'Under the weather.'

'Most amusing. Why did he want to meet you? I was told he refused to speak to the press. I'd come to Dahum expressly to interview him. The *Mail* was going to pay him serious money.'

'I've no idea,' Bond said.

'All very curious, I must say.' Letham gave an unpleasant smile. 'In fact, you're a very curious man, Bond. For a journalist of your age and alleged experience, no one seems to have heard of you. You and I must have a little chat about it one day.'

'I don't speak to the press, Letham, hadn't you heard?'

Bond wandered away, wondering if Letham was issuing some kind of covert threat. He had arrived on a Super Constellation flight, having left Sinsikrou after his encounter with Bond and travelled to Abidjan in Ivory Coast. There, he'd paid Hulbert Linck to be flown in, posing as a friend and supporter of 'plucky little Dahum'. Initially Bond was more irritated than perturbed by Letham's surprising presence – he could deal with dross like Letham effortlessly – but what was disturbing him now was that nothing in Dahum had changed with the death of Adeka. It had been announced in a black-bordered edition of the *Daily Graphic* – Dahum's sole newspaper – but the expected collapse of morale in the army and population had not taken place. The junta had simply announced that Colonel Denga was the new commander-in-chief of the Dahumian armed forces. The king was dead – long live the king.

Bond saw Kobus Breed talking with a group of his fellow mercenaries. He wandered over and called his name and Breed turned to greet him.

'Hail the conquering hero,' he said, not smiling.

Bond ignored this and asked him how he and his fellows had taken the news of Adeka's death.

'Well, it was a bit of a kick in the crotch,' Breed said with a shrug. 'But, you know, Denga's as smart as a whip. Learned everything at Adeka's knee. And, hey,' he grinned, 'we've got an air force now. The Malmös are ready for their first mission. Everyone's in good heart – and of course we still have our secret weapon.'

'What's that?'

'Tony Msour.'

'Who is?'

'Our juju man. Our fetish priest. Makes our boys immortal.'

'Oh, yes, of course.'

Bond walked back to the Press Centre from the cemetery, thinking hard, composing in his mind a telex message to M at Transworld Consortium. He could let M know that Adeka had died – though surely that news had broken by now – and point out that Adeka hadn't in fact been the vital key to Dahum's survival as everyone in London had supposed. What more could he do?

he wondered. Perhaps he should book a $100-seat on the next Constellation out.

Bond duly sent his telex and received a swift and brief reply from Agence Presse Libre. 'Suggest you stay in Port Dunbar until hostilities cease. Have you any idea when that might be?'

Bond detected M's hand in the message's ironic terseness. He could read the subtext: his mission was not over, that much was clear.

**Two days** later the foreign press corps was invited to reassemble to witness the first attack by the Dahumian air force on a key Zanzarim army position – a substantial bridge over one of the many tributaries of the Zanza River. Bond happily allowed Breadalbane to travel with him in Sunday's Peugeot. They set off well before dawn and after a two-hour drive along bumpy minor roads they arrived, as the sun was rising, in a village called Lamu-Penu, a half-mile from the targeted bridge. There were no villagers in evidence, just 300 well-armed Dahumian soldiers drawn up in a long column, waiting for the fetish priest. Hulbert Linck was there in a Land Rover equipped with a radio that gave him contact with the Janjaville strip. The fetish priest arrived and proceeded to 'immortalise' the troops, spraying liquid from his magic gourd through his bared teeth at them, and flicking at them with his horsehair whisk. Bond looked over at Letham, who was trying to suppress his hilarity, his shoulders rocking, small snorts coming from his nose and throat.

Then Linck called in the Malmös and ten minutes later they flew low over the village, waggling their wings in salute to great cheers and exultation from the massed troops waiting to follow them in. Seconds later came the sound of their machine guns as they strafed the bridge defences and, with whoops and yells, led by Breed and his men, the soldiers jogged off to do battle.

It was all over in fifteen minutes and the journalists were duly called up to the bridge to bear witness. Clearly Zanza Force's aptitude for swift and sudden retreat had prevailed again, Bond thought. He paced around, thoughtfully, looking at the marginal damage – some burst sandbags, discarded equipment, the odd bloodstain on the tarmac – and ran into an exhilarated Hulbert Linck.

'Look what we can do, Bond, with three little aeroplanes. Wait until the ship arrives.'

'What ship?'

'We're going to run the blockade at Port Dunbar,' Linck said, tapping the side of his nose. 'Don't worry – I'll keep you informed.'

Bond went in search of Breed to see if he could shed more light on this mysterious ship and its cargo. He found him stringing up three Zanzari corpses – the only fatalities of the air strike – busying around them with his ropes and his fish hooks, hauling the bodies up by their jaws into the trees above the road that approached the bridge and the river.

'Linck told me about the ship,' Bond said.

'Did he?' Breed said, impressed. 'It's meant to be a deadly secret. He must think you're one of us – now you've won your medal.'

'So, what's with this ship?'

'Big cargo vessel. Got some serious stuff on board. Going to change everything.' He cuffed away a tear and turned to his men in the trees. 'Take 'em up a bit higher, boys. Up! Up! Heave-ho! We want everyone to have a good view.'

On the drive back to Port Dunbar, Bond began to feel a debilitating sense of impotence. What was he meant to do in this situation, for God's sake? Hulbert Linck was a one-man arms industry coming to the rescue of embattled Dahum – and what was this 'serious stuff' Breed mentioned? Bond wondered if there was any way he could immobilise Linck, somehow take him out of the equation . . . But how to get to him? And then there was still the Dahum army, fighting on efficiently under Colonel Denga—

The sound of a car horn being tooted angrily behind them interrupted his thoughts and Sunday pulled in promptly.

A glossy black Citroën DS swept by, curtains drawn in its rear windows.

'Who the hell's that?' Breadalbane asked.

'That's Tony Msour,' Sunday said. 'Very rich man.'

Bond remembered where he'd heard the name before: Kobus Breed's juju man. Bond watched the Citroën roar down the road, its hydropneumatic suspension coping effortlessly with the potholes. Nice cars. The nudging intimations of an idea were beginning to nag at him.

# 17

# The $50 Peugeot

B ond said he needed a private word with Sunday so
Breadalbane left them in the car and slouched into
the Press Centre alone.

'Have I made mistake?' Sunday asked, full of
apprehension.

'No, no – I just want to ask you a few questions.'
Bond smiled, keen to reassure him. 'For example: how
much would you sell this car for – in US dollars?'

Sunday thought for a moment. 'Twenty dollar – but
for you, Mr Bond, I say fifteen.'

'All right – but I'll give you fifty for it,' Bond said,
enjoying the look of joyful astonishment registering on
Sunday's face. 'But I also need you to get me a few other
things. I want a hat – like the one Mr Breed wears –
and a belt, a webbing belt. Oh yes, and two litres of
drinking water and a small sharp knife.'

'I get them for you, sar.'

Bond counted out $50 and handed the notes over.

'Bring the car tonight, at six-thirty. I won't need it until then.' Bond raised a warning finger. 'Don't tell anybody, Sunday. This is our little secret.'

**At lunch** in the Press Centre Bond pocketed a bottle of ketchup and, in the lavatory later, emptied it and washed it out thoroughly. Back in his room he unzipped his pigskin toilet bag and prepared his solution of talcum powder dissolved in aftershave. He screwed the lid on tightly and shook the bottle until the liquid was clear. He took the lid off again and sniffed – completely odourless.

At six Bond went down to the bar and ordered a whisky and soda while he waited for Sunday to arrive. Dupree and Haas were in a corner playing chess but there was no sign of Breadalbane. Bond drained his drink and was on the point of going outside to wait for Sunday when Letham came into the room and, seeing Bond, made straight for him.

'Can I have a word, Bond?'

'I'm afraid I'm busy.'

'You said you worked in Australia before this job. Reuters.'

'That's right.'

'Funny – none of my Reuters friends in Oz can remember you.'

'I was a bit of a loner – got to go.'

Letham touched his elbow, looked like he was going to grab his arm and then thought better of it.

'Sydney or Melbourne?'

'It's really none of your business, Letham, but the answer is both.'

Bond left, annoyed with himself for being goaded by Letham into answering. He shouldn't have told him anything.

Sunday was parked outside the front door, sitting on the bonnet of the Peugeot. He handed Bond the car keys.

'Not yet – I need you to drive me somewhere, Sunday. Did you get everything?'

He had and, in the car, Bond tucked his trousers into his desert boots, buckled the webbing belt round his combat jacket and put on the soft, peaked kepi that was the headgear of choice for most of the mercenaries.

'How do I look?' he asked Sunday.

'Like soldier, sar.'

'Excellent. Do you know where Tony Msour lives?'

'Everybody know. Big, big house on the road to Janjaville.'

'Right. Take me there.'

---

**It was** completely dark by the time they reached Tony Msour's house, a large concrete villa with a balcony circling the first floor, set behind high breezeblock walls with a sliding metal gate. Bond could see the black Citroën DS squat on its haunches outside the front door. Sunday parked by the gate and Bond said he would take over from here. Sunday gave him the keys and set off walking jauntily on the road back to Port Dunbar.

There was an intercom on the gate and Bond pressed the button.

'Yes?' a crackling voice said after Bond had rung a second time. 'Who there?'

'Kobus Breed,' Bond said. 'It's very urgent.'

The buzzer sounded and Bond slid the gate back and stepped into the compound. A light above the front door came on and a couple of chained dogs barked angrily at him. The door opened and Tony Msour stood there in a string vest and a pair of loose mauve cotton trousers. He was smoking a small stumpy cigar. It was strange seeing him in his civilian persona, Bond thought, minus the white face and the green circles round his eyes. In fact he was a handsome man with fine features and very dark skin – more Nilotic or Nubian than Fakassa. He had two little vertical tribal scars under his eyes. Bond gave a loose salute.

'Where be Breed?' Msour said, a little suspiciously.

'He sent me. They're trying to recapture the bridge at Lamu-Penu.'

'Jesos Chrise.'

'Exactly. Breed's rushing men up. He needs you – fast.'

Msour thought for a second. 'It will be one hundred dollars.'

'Of course. Breed said the money wasn't a problem. There's real trouble up there.'

Msour dashed back into the house and emerged minutes later with a shirt on and a large kitbag – containing his beads, skirt, gourd and whisk, Bond supposed – and followed Bond out to the Peugeot. Msour chucked his kitbag in the back and climbed into the car beside Bond.

'I don't like to doing this at night, you know. That is why I go charge you extra, extra.'

'I quite understand,' Bond said and started the engine, roaring off down the road towards Port Dunbar at high speed. After five minutes they passed through a large plantation of oil palms and Bond slowed, keeping his eyes open for the turning he'd spotted earlier on the way out. He turned off the road on to a dirt track that led into the plantation, the one headlight of Sunday's Peugeot illuminating the serried trunks of the palm trees.

'Where you dey go?' Msour asked.

'Short cut. We're in a hurry,' Bond said and then turned off the track and drove into the plantation itself, bumping along the avenue of palm trees.

'You done go craze, man!' Msour shouted.

'Shit. Wrong turning,' Bond said. 'Sorry.' He stopped the car, put the gear lever into reverse and then punched Msour full in the face, knocking his head back so heavily against the windowpane that it smashed with a tinkle of glass. Msour cried in pain and Bond reached across him, opened the door and kicked him out of the car. Bond leaped out and ran round to find Msour on his hands and knees, shaking his head as if he couldn't believe what had happened to him. Bond stood above him and brought the edge of his hand down full force on to the exposed nape of his neck with a karate chop. Msour was flattened, face in the dirt, poleaxed, out cold.

Bond opened the boot and dragged Msour's limp body over, tipping him into the space. Msour made no sound as Bond rolled him on to his back and forced his mouth open. He unscrewed the cap on his ketchup bottle and filled Msour's gaping mouth with some of the solution. He sat him up and heard the fluid go down with a reflex gurgle then repeated the process. He should be comatose for at least forty-eight hours, according to Quentin Dale of Q Branch. Then Bond added the kitbag and the two litres of water Sunday had provided in a plastic container and slammed the boot shut, locking it. He took the clasp knife Sunday had brought out of his pocket and punctured all four tyres. The Peugeot settled with a hissing wheeze of escaping air. Then with a rock he smashed the windscreen and the remaining windows. Finally he kicked dents in the bodywork and threw handfuls of dirt and leaves over the car.

He looked around. He was in the heart of the plantation far from the road and the dirt track. It was doubtful that anyone would casually come across the Peugeot here – if they did there was little to scavenge; it looked like an old wreck. And even if Msour came round in a day or so and shouted and banged on the lid of the boot it was highly unlikely he'd be heard. Bond was hoping for two or three days, at least. With a little luck Msour might be missing for even more.

He walked back to the track and, turning, saw that the Peugeot was invisible. He set off and after five minutes regained the road to Port Dunbar. He tossed his hat and webbing belt into a deep ditch by the roadside, untucked his trousers from his boots and flagged down the first taxi he saw, asking to be taken to the

Press Centre. A good night's work, he thought – $50 well spent – time for a drink, a bite to eat and then bed. He just wished it could be as easy to deal with Geoffrey Letham. The Letham problem nagged at him – he realised it would be for the best if he could find a solution to that issue as well.

# 18

# One-Way Ticket Out

B ond kept very much to himself the next two days. He stayed in his room writing up an account in encrypted plain-code of everything that had happened to him (the narrative looked like notes for an article set in rural France: he was a woman, Blessing a man, the war a complex property deal). It would mean nothing to any other reader but for him it would function as an important aide-memoire for his eventual report to M, given that absolutely nothing about this mission had really gone to plan.

On the first morning, Sunday reappeared in an ancient woodwormed Morris Traveller that he had bought for $10. They set off in it for a day trip to the blockaded port of Port Dunbar – which, because of the copious silting of the Zanza River Delta, was now some ten miles to the south of the city itself. Bond wandered along its empty quays and wharves, its giant rusty cranes and derricks standing sentinel over empty tracts of water, listening to the far-booming surf beyond the harbour. He knew that out at sea the two ex-Royal Navy frigates that comprised the Zanzarim Marine Force were patrolling the Bight of Benin looking for blockade runners. And further out at sea, waiting for its moment, was Hulbert Linck's cargo vessel full of 'serious stuff' that might just change the course of this war.

Bond stood on the dockside looking out at the horizon feeling himself in a strange kind of limbo, thinking that everything would change – or that nothing might change. He thought of Tony Msour unconscious in the boot of the Peugeot hidden in the midst of an oil-palm plantation – what effect would his mysterious absence have on events? It was an act of audacious inspiration that might have no consequence at all, or else it would materially alter everything. It was all in the balance – he had played his best cards, now he could only wait and see.

As one day dragged into the next he began to feel that time was a curious irrelevance. He had his room in the Press Centre, he was fed, he could buy a drink. Somewhere to the north of the city, on the forest roads and tracks, across creeks and marshy expanses, by collapsed bridges and mined causeways, Zanzarim soldiers confronted Dahumian ones, everybody waiting – waiting to see what might happen next.

Then the first symbol of that possible change arrived in the late afternoon of the second day after the abduction of Tony Msour. Suddenly, the city's air-raid sirens sounded and for the first time Bond sensed something crack in the ordered discipline of the population of Port Dunbar. It wasn't panic but it was fearfulness, anxiety, and the streets became full of people running, frantically looking for shelter. He thought he could hear the distant roar of jet engines and a SAM missile was fired – more in hope than expectation – from the battery in the central square. Then, after twenty minutes the all-clear sounded. Breadalbane said that a MiG had been shot down but no one believed him.

The next morning Kobus Breed came to see him at the Press Centre. Bond was surprised.

'You booked your passage out?' Breed asked.

'Not yet,' Bond said, carefully. 'Why do you ask?'

Breed lowered his voice, as if he might be overheard. 'I might need your expertise,' he said. 'We've got a massive Zanza Force build-up on the main highway. We've seen heavy armour – Centurion tanks. And the artillery shelling has gone up two hundred per cent. Something big's about to happen.'

'Look,' Bond said. 'Kololo was a one-off. You're the brave soldier being paid five thousand dollars a month to fight for Dahum, not me.'

'We could always arrange something.'

'I'm not a military man any more,' Bond said. 'You're on your own.'

'And our bloody fetish priest has disappeared,' Breed said. 'Can you believe it? Picked up by a "white soldier" three days ago.'

'One of your guys?'

'Absolutely no.'

Bond shrugged. 'Can't you get another fetish priest?'

'You must be joking. He's the only one they believe in.'

It was enough of a sign for Bond – equilibrium had gone – or was going fast. That evening he drove out to Janjaville and paid Hulbert Linck $100 to fly out on a Super Constellation the following night.

Linck looked at him shrewdly.

'Do you know something we don't, Mr Bond?'

'I've been summoned home,' Bond said, resignedly. 'Personally, I'd love to stay on. See your famous running of the blockade. See your ship come in. I'm missing the big story.'

'The sooner the better,' Linck said, looking worried. 'There's a big Zanza Force push coming. We've got eight flights due in tonight.'

He turned and looked at the Constellation as it was being unloaded. As a truck backed away the wash of its headlights momentarily illuminated the nose of the plane. Bond peered closer – and was astonished to see, stencilled just below the cockpit, a sign that he had last observed in Bayswater, London: AfricaKIN.

He glanced at Linck but he was giving nothing away. What was this all about, Bond asked himself? And then thought – perhaps it was a former AfricaKIN charter; someone had simply forgotten to remove the logo. But it was another coincidence – and here in Dahum Bond was very suspicious of coincidences. What connection could Gabriel Adeka have with Linck and his blockade-running? Some sort of subterfuge? Were they using AfricaKIN funds? Exploiting its good name . . . ?

'Well, good luck to you,' Bond said, his mind still turning with the implications. 'See you tomorrow night.'

Bond slept badly. He kept hearing, in his half-sleep, urgent knocking on his door. Convinced it was Blessing he went to open it twice. Of course it was all in his troubled imagination. At dawn he woke to hear the distant sound of explosions and again the air-raid siren went off. This time a solitary MiG streaked low over the city, just above the rooftops, shattering the morning peace – too low and too fast to loose off a SAM.

Another indication, Bond thought, as he packed up his few belongings and emptied the remains of his coma-inducing drugs down the toilet. He had lunch with Breadalbane who told him that Dupree, Haas and Letham had gone up to the front to see if this news of a Zanza Force thrust was genuine or not.

Bond told him he was booked out on a flight that night and he could see the news disturbed Breadalbane.

'But why?' he asked, uncomprehendingly. 'You're going to miss everything.'

'I just think it's time to go,' Bond said and offered him the loan of $100 if he wanted to leave also.

'Can't do that,' Breadalbane said. 'No, no. I have to stick it out. Have to. Otherwise why have I spent all these months here?' He thought for a while. 'Actually, the loan would be very handy, all the same – if you could spare the cash.'

Dupree and Haas came back in the afternoon in a state of shock. There had been a massive breakthrough on the transnational highway – Centurion tanks crossing rivers on improvised bridges had outflanked Dahumian defences. More worryingly, there was panic and mass desertion by the normally steadfast Dahum troops – all resistance, all morale suddenly gone.

'No juju man,' Haas said. 'Breed is going insane. He shot three of his own men for deserting. Even the mercenaries are talking of leaving now.'

By late afternoon the heavy detonation of artillery shells was audible in central Port Dunbar and columns of black smoke were rising from the northern outskirts. The streets of the city emptied as if in response to some silent order. Sunday drove Bond out to the airport in sombre mood.

'We done lose this war, Mr Bond. It finish. We don't want fight no more.'

They motored out to Janjaville past columns of dishevelled soldiers retreating on the airstrip, where some sort of final defensive ring was being formed. Bond noted the new trenches, barbed wire and gun emplacements but there seemed little sign of martial spirit among the troops. He saw officers striking men with bamboo batons and the soldiers looked frightened and resentful. No one wants to be the doomed rearguard, Bond realised. In the distance the sound of gunfire and explosions grew ever louder as the Zanzarim army advanced into Port Dunbar.

Janjaville airstrip had never been busier. Two DC-3s and a Fokker Friendship were parked in front of the hangar and, as Bond arrived, he saw Linck's Malmös take off and head east, away from the fighting, their mercenary pilots all too aware of what was impending.

Bond said a heartfelt farewell to Sunday and gave him the remains of his dollars. He told Sunday to go to the oil-palm plantation the next morning. 'You'll see the Peugeot there, off the track'. He gave more specific directions. 'There's a man locked in the boot. I want you to let him out. Don't say anything. You were just passing by.'

'I don't know you, sar.'

'Exactly. It'll be our secret.'

They shook hands and Bond wished him good luck.

**Bond confirmed** that his place was secure on the flight, due to leave in an hour. He encountered Hulbert Linck, who was agitated and fretful. 'How could this have happened?' he kept repeating, rhetorically. 'A week ago we were in total control. Total control.' To Bond's eyes Linck seemed untypically distressed, all his old confidence gone, as if there was something more at stake than the fate of Dahum, something that touched him personally.

'That's the fortunes of war for you,' Bond said, conscious of the scant comfort in this lame adage. He said goodbye to Linck and walked over to the Quonset hut that did duty as a departure lounge.

Soon Haas and Dupree joined him, complaining that the price of a seat on the Constellation had now risen to $500, and then the mercenaries began to arrive, awkward in their civilian clothes, their guns and swagger left behind. They looked edgy and uncomfortable, having no desire to be subject to the full-blooded retribution of the Zanzarim army.

Bond stood by the window watching the families and retainers of the Dahumian junta board one of the DC-3s and the Fokker Friendship. And then came the members of the government themselves – he saw Abigail Kross and Colonel Denga amongst them. The die was cast now. He watched both planes take off and realised that the Republic of Dahum was officially rudderless – he wondered if the terrified soldiers manning the perimeter knew that they were now on their own.

Just as he was beginning to worry vaguely that their own departure might not take place he saw the Constellation swoop in, land and taxi round to its usual position in front of the hangar. However, this time the engines were cut. The plane was empty, Bond supposed. And once again he saw the AfricaKIN logo on the nose – and it was a different Constellation from the one he'd seen the night before, traces of an old airline livery marking it out as another aircraft. What had Gabriel Adeka to do with these last perilous flights in and out of the shrinking Dahum heartland? Why this overt connection? Bond turned away from the window, questions yammering in his head. Was it some final gesture of solidarity between the Adeka brothers? A sign that Gabriel had heard of Solomon's death and had stepped in? Or simply some futile, symbolic despatch of aid before the war ended . . . ? He wandered back to rejoin Haas and Dupree, thinking there was no point in further speculation. Once he had safely left Dahum he could investigate further.

The mood in the Quonset hut was increasingly tense. The sound of small arms was now audible – the pop and chatter of machine guns – and from time to time nervous sentries triggered bursts of aimless fire into the darkness of the night. Bond sat apart, taking in the images of almost-chaos of a small country about to forcibly lose its brief identity forever. Its government had fled; its highly paid foreign mercenaries – about to flee – were passing themselves off as civilians; a few hundred frightened and reluctant troops had been ordered – at gunpoint, no doubt – to keep the airstrip open until the last rat had left the sinking ship and they could all throw their guns away and go back home.

He was not pleased to see Letham arrive. He was wearing a white linen suit with a raffish navy bandana at his neck and he actually asked Haas to take a photograph of him standing beside the armed soldier guarding the door. His new picture by-line, Bond assumed. Ace foreign correspondent Geoffrey Letham reporting fearlessly from the world's crisis zones. Bond saw him look over in his direction and was grateful when he didn't approach. He and Letham had nothing more to say to each other – and, with a bit of luck, would never see each other again after tonight. There were minor satisfactions to register about the fall of Dahum, he considered.

A crew member came in from the Constellation and all the mercenaries were invited to board. Bond heard the engines spark and fire up, generating their throaty rumble. The four journalists joined the back of the queue.

Haas looked round, his face was sweaty. 'They seem to be getting closer,' he said.

'Did you see Breadalbane before you left?' Bond asked. 'I lent him some cash – thought he might have changed his mind and decided to join us.'

'I told him,' Dupree said. 'I said that with all the mercenaries gone he'll be the only white man in Port Dunbar. Not a good idea, I said. A most uncomfortable situation. I thought he'd be here.'

Bond was about to reply when three soldiers pushed their way in, all carrying AK-47s, swathed in bandoliers of bullets and somehow looking more capable and alarming than the demoralised men manning the defences. They wore the soft, peaked kepis that the mercenaries favoured. Everyone went quiet.

'Who is James Bond?' one of the soldiers called out.

Bond stepped forward. There was no hiding place here.

'I am,' he said.

'Come with us. The rest of you please to board the plane.'

Bond picked up his grip, feeling his mouth dry, suddenly. What was this – had Msour been found and somehow identified him? He followed the three soldiers out of the Quonset hut, glancing back over his shoulders to see the others striding energetically across the grass towards the Constellation, its four engines now turning in a shimmering blur in the airport lights.

'What's going on?' Bond asked, feigning minor irritation – he was feeling concern mount in him. 'I need to be on that plane.'

'Someone wants to talk with you,' the soldier said.

Perhaps it was Linck, Bond thought, though his worries didn't subside. The last DC3 was still there, its propeller blades now beginning to revolve slowly as the generator fired up the engines, the exhausts coughing out smoke. Perhaps Linck wanted them to fly out together. But.Bond recognised the symptoms – he was trying to put a benign gloss on serious alarm. It never worked – something was wrong here.

Bond was being led towards the concrete blockhouse of the control tower, he saw. A door in the side was opened and he was ordered in. He found himself in a windowless cement cell with a neon tube in the ceiling casting an unkind glaring light.

'Excuse me. What's happening?' he asked, still managing to preserve his tone of mild irritation. 'Can you tell me? Who am I meant to meet?'

One soldier left, to fetch the person who wanted to talk to him, Bond supposed. The other two stood by the closed door, hands resting on the AK-47s slung across their fronts.

Bond paced slowly to and fro, affecting unconcern, but his mind was hyperactive. Something must have gone very wrong – but what? No clever strategy suggested itself.

Two minutes went by, then five. The only thing that reassured Bond was that the idling motors of the Constellation hadn't changed pitch. It must still be in position, waiting for the final passengers to arrive before taking off.

Then Kobus Breed came through the door. He was wearing a light blue seersucker suit and a yellow tie. Bond almost laughed – he looked so different. Bond noticed that he held one hand behind his back.

'Kobus, hello,' he said. 'You look very smart. What's going on?' Breed's thick neck didn't suit a collar and tie, Bond thought. It looked like a bad disguise.

Breed wasn't smiling any more. 'What's going on is that you're a devious bastard, Bond.'

'No more devious than you are,' Bond said. 'We all have our strategies for survival. Look at you.' He gestured at Breed's new clothes. 'Very man-about-town, all of a sudden.'

'Yah. But your strategy's just been discovered. What did you do with Tony Msour?'

'I don't know what you're talking about.'

Breed let the hand that was behind his back swing into view. He was holding one of his big fish hooks.

'I don't have time to piss around with you, Bond. This hook's got your name on it. I'm going to let you swing from the control tower – a special welcome for Zanza Force. But, before I kill you I just want you to know that I know what you did and I know who you are. Your fellow journalist, Letham, was most helpful. Seems nobody in the entire world of journalism has ever heard of you.'

'Letham is scum. I wouldn't believe anything he says.'

Breed stepped up to him and punched him in the face. Bond ducked and Breed's fist slammed into his left temple. He went down. Breed kicked him heavily in the ribs and Bond felt one stave in.

His vision blurred. He heard the noise of the Constellation's engines grow more shrill as the revs were increased. Bond hauled himself to his feet, swaying, a sharp pain in his side.

'Look, Breed, whoever told you I—'

He stopped, completely astonished. It was as if he'd seen a vision.

Blessing Ogilvy-Grant had stepped quietly into the room.

'We've got to go,' she said sharply to Breed.

'I've got unfinished business with Mr Bond, here,' Kobus said. He dropped his hook with a clang and took a small automatic out of his inside pocket.

Bond was experiencing a kind of accelerated revelation, an unwelcome one, a massive and dramatic reorganisation of everything he thought he knew.

'Better not mess around,' Blessing said. She looked at Bond but her eyes were cold, lifeless. 'We've no time.'

'OK, I know,' Breed said. 'Let's take the lover out of lover-boy – before I string him up by his jawbone.'

He aimed his automatic at Bond's groin and pulled the trigger.

In that split second Bond turned and the bullet thunked into his right thigh just below the hip with a splash of blood as it exited. Bond felt the hot tear in the meat of his muscle and went down, heavily, spinning with the impact, feeling more pain in his rib. He sensed his trousers dampening with the blood flow.

Hulbert Linck shouted from outside.

'We leave in ten seconds!'

Blessing snatched Breed's gun from him.

'Stop fooling around!' she snarled and fired.

Bond felt the punch as the bullet hit him in his chest and he fell back.

He heard the door slam shut and sensed his consciousness begin to leave him, encroaching shadows gathering at the edge of his vision. He tried to sit up but his hand slipped in the spreading pool of his own blood and he fell back to the floor again. Best not to move, he told himself as the room went steadily dark, best to stay very still. The last thing he heard was the sound of the Constellation taxiing to the end of the runway and the roar of its engines as it took off, fading, fading, fading . . .

# PART THREE

# Going Solo

# 1
# Care and Attention

James Bond stood a little shakily under the hot shower, both hands gripping the chrome rails on either side of the stall. He closed his eyes, letting the water run over his face, hearing the sharp patter of the spray on the sheets of plastic that were taped over his dressings on his thigh and chest. It was his first shower in almost five weeks. It felt like the first shower of his life, so intense was the pleasure he was taking in it. He managed to wash his hair with one hand – still holding on with the other – and then turned off the water and stepped out. He'd forgotten his towel – left on the end of his bed in his room.

The door opened and Sheila McRae, the nurse he liked best, came in, his towel in her hand.

'Just in time, eh, Commander?'

Bond stood there naked, dripping, as Sheila checked the plastic protection over his dressings. She chattered away.

'It's a wee bit chilly this morning but at least it's no raining. Aye, they're all fine.'

She helped Bond on with his dressing gown after he'd dried himself and Bond reflected on the curious, intimate non-intimacy that existed between nurse and patient. You could be standing there, naked, as your bedpan was emptied or a catheter was inserted in your penis, chatting to the nurse about her package holiday in Tenerife as if you were passing time at a bus stop waiting for your bus to arrive. They had seen everything, these nurses, Bond realised. Words like prudish, embarrassed, shocked, disgusted or ashamed simply weren't in their vocabulary. Perhaps that was why people – why men – found them so attractive.

Sheila was in her late twenties with an animated, fresh prettiness about her. She had thick unruly blonde hair that she found difficult to pin up neatly beneath the little starched white bonnet that topped off the nurses' uniforms here. She had two children and her husband was a welder at the Rosyth dockyards. She had told Bond a great deal about herself over the weeks of his recovery. The covert nature of this wing of the sanatorium meant that all the conversational traffic tended to be one-way.

They walked back slowly along the corridor to Bond's private room, Bond still limping slightly. He had a drain in his thigh wound, a corrugated rubber tube emerging from the muscle with a clamp at the end. When he slipped back into bed it would be connected to a glass Redivac suction jar with two erect antennae that flopped limply when the vacuum was spent. He had developed a perverse dislike for the suction jar but there was still some infection in the thigh wound and the drain still dripped. However, his chest had healed remarkably well, the entry and exit wounds now two puckered rosy coins, new additions to the palimpsest of scars his body carried.

He was in a military sanatorium located in a discreet corner of a large army base to the south of Edinburgh. There were six private rooms in his wing all reserved for soldiers, sailors and airmen with serious health issues requiring twenty-four-hour intensive care. Or, to put it another way, rooms reserved for military personnel who needed to keep their injuries secret – almost all of the patients were from special forces.

'Oh, yes, I forgot to tell you,' Sheila said as they reached his door. 'You've got a visitor.'

Bond stepped into his room and to his astonishment saw M standing there looking out of the window. He turned and smiled. He was wearing a heavy brown tweed three-piece suit. He was so out of context that Bond felt it was like seeing Nelson's Column on a village green.

'James,' he said. 'You're looking extremely well.'

They shook hands.

'It's very good of you to come all this way to visit me, sir,' Bond said, feeling a great upwelling of affection for this elderly man, all of a sudden.

'Oh, I didn't come to see you. I've got a few days' shooting in Perthshire. Thought I'd kill several birds with one stone.' M chuckled, pleased with his joke. 'Got anything to drink?' he asked.

'They give you a bottle of sherry to help with your appetite but I wouldn't recommend it. Wouldn't even cook with it. I haven't touched a drop.'

'Thought as much,' M said and took a half-bottle of Dewar's whisky out of his pocket and placed it on Bond's bedside table.

'I was going to bring grapes and chocolate but I thought you'd prefer this,' M said. 'I do hope you won't get into trouble.'

Bond went into his bathroom and found a tooth-glass. He washed out a teacup and poured a fair-sized dram for them both.

'*Slangevar*,' M said and clinked his glass against Bond's cup. 'Here's to your speedy recovery.'

Bond took a cautious sip of his whisky. It was the first alcohol he'd drunk since Dahum. He felt its wondrous, comforting warmth bloom and fill his throat and chest.

'Perfectly, magnificently therapeutic,' he said and topped them both up.

'When will they let you out?' M asked.

'In a week or two, I think. Getting stronger every day.'

'Well, take a month's leave when they do,' M said. 'Get properly fit again. You deserve it. It's not every day a man can say he ended a war.'

'And I even got a medal,' Bond said, a little sardonically.

'And you've earned the gratitude of Her Majesty's Government.' M fished his pipe out of his pocket. 'Can I smoke in here?'

Bond said he could and lit a cigarette himself.

'I know you'll write a full report, eventually,' M said, 'so there's no need to go through the whole business now. But you may have some questions for me.'

Bond did, indeed. 'How did I get out?' he asked. When he'd regained consciousness he was tied down on a gurney in a Royal Air Force transport plane heading for Edinburgh. None of the various doctors who'd treated him since then could give any explanation of what had happened to him.

'You were found by a journalist called Digby Breadalbane,' M said. 'He was making for the airstrip himself but got held up in the chaos – panicking troops, deserters, total disarray. By the time he arrived the last plane had left. Once the planes had gone no defence was offered and the Zanzari army overran the airstrip in minutes. Still, there were a few bullets flying around so this Breadalbane fellow went to take shelter in the control tower and found you, unconscious, lying in a pool of blood.'

Bond took this in, nodding. Digby Breadalbane, his guardian angel . . .

'Actually there was a rather good article by him in the *Observer* last Sunday. "Death of a Small Country". You should read it – no mention of you, of course.'

So Breadalbane had his scoop after all, Bond thought.

M plumed smoke at the ceiling light. 'Fortunately some of our special forces were with the Zanzarim army.'

'Ah, yes, the "advisers", of course.'

'Yes . . . They patched you up as best they could and put you in a helicopter for Sinsikrou. Twenty-four hours later you were on your way here.'

'I was lucky,' Bond said, feeling a little disturbed at all these contingencies that had randomly conspired to save him.

'Lucky 007,' M said with an unusually warm smile.

Bond thought back to that night at the Janjaville airstrip and the chilling look in Blessing's eyes as she'd levelled the gun at him and pulled the trigger. Lucky, yes . . . Her shot had hit him high on the right side of his chest, in under the collarbone and out at the shoulder. The right lung collapsed but no other internal damage.

'Any news of Ogilvy-Grant?' Bond asked.

'He's very well and living in Sinsikrou and wondering why you never made contact.'

'*He?*'

'Edward Benson Ogilvy-Grant, fifty-one years old, ex-Royal Marine captain, head of station in Zanzarim.'

'The Ogilvy-Grant I dealt with was a young woman.'

M looked shrewdly at him. 'Yes. You were well duped. And you didn't follow procedure.'

'I did follow procedure.' Bond resented the implication. 'Q Branch told me Ogilvy-Grant would make contact after I arrived. And she did.'

'It seems she may have been Ogilvy-Grant's secretary. Her real name is Aleesha Belem.'

'Jesus Christ.' Bond shook his head. 'Which would explain how she knew all about me.' He paused. 'But she was damn good – really good . . . So, who was she working for?'

'We don't know. But a lot of people are interested in Zanzarim.'

Bond thought of Blessing's clever duplicities: the perfect shabby office; Christmas, the driver; her own carefully constructed biography – the Scottish engineer father, her Celtic colloquialisms, Cheltenham Ladies' College, Cambridge, Harvard . . . And the lovemaking, of course. At least M didn't know about that.

'Could she have been working for the Dahum Republic?' Bond asked.

'Could be . . . Did you come across a man called Hulbert Linck?'

'Yes,' Bond said. 'A one-man arms dealer – single-handedly trying to arm, protect and save Dahum. A man of no fixed abode, it seems.'

'Shady character,' M said.

'There was something bogus about him, as if he was acting a part.'

'Be that as it may, he's disappeared. So has she. Perhaps someone killed them.'

Bond topped up his whisky – M declined. 'There was a man called Kobus Breed – a mercenary from Rhodesia,' Bond said. 'A psychopath, but a clever one. She was working with him, I now think. Perhaps he killed her.'

'We can't find Mr Breed, either. But no, it wouldn't have been his show. Somebody else was pulling the strings. Still, they may have got out of Dahum but at least they lost everything.' M smiled. 'Thanks to you. You can't be very popular with that lot – don't expect a Christmas card.'

M stood up and put down his glass, searched his pockets absentmindedly then lifted his hat and coat off the hook on the back of the door.

'Call in when you get back from your holiday,' M said. 'Go somewhere nice and relax. You've had a hell of a time and you're lucky to be alive. Get yourself really fit and well – be self-indulgent.' He patted Bond's shoulder.

Bond stood and they shook hands again as they parted. There was a tiny but palpable current of mutual feeling in the room, Bond thought, of barely discernible emotion. For all Bond knew, M only possessed a superior's affectionate regard for him – the respect due to a trusted and prized operative who'd done a good job and had put his life on the line. But, on his side, Bond wanted to show that he was genuinely grateful for this unexpected, informal visit, all the same – that it marked something out of the ordinary, out of the line of mere duty, somehow – but he couldn't think of anything to say without making a fool of himself or embarrassing M.

'Thanks for the whisky, sir,' was all he could manage in the end.

# 2

# Donalda and May

Three days later the ward sister yanked out the rubber tube draining Bond's thigh. It was one of the most unpleasant sensations he could recall experiencing, as if some sinew or vein had been bodily wrenched from his side. His head reeled as she reapplied the dressing and taped it down again. The sister was a rather wonderful woman who treated Bond with pointed egalitarianism – he could have been a duke or a kitchen skivvy and nothing would change in her manner, he knew.

'There you are, Commander,' she said, with an ironic smile, using his rank for the first time. 'A normal human being once more – no tubes hanging out of you.'

After she'd gone Bond went into his bathroom and looked at himself in the mirror above the sink. He was pale and he'd lost weight and the scar on his face stood out more starkly, he thought. He felt well enough but not particularly strong, not his usual self. Still, he couldn't hang around until his physical status quo returned. There was work to be done. He had been thinking hard since M's visit and the unexpected offer of a month's leave. A whole month – what could be achieved in four weeks? As far as M was concerned he had carried off his mission with flying colours, but from Bond's point of view there was a sour taste of bitter dissatisfaction and incompleteness. Two people had tried to kill him – one had tried to maim him in the most brutal way possible; the other was a woman he had made love to in all openness and generosity of spirit, and she had tried to deliver the *coup de grâce* to a man who was already grievously wounded. He couldn't forget those terrible seconds in the control tower at Janjaville airstrip – he would never forget them. To stare death in the face like that, to feel bullets impact on your own vital body . . . You couldn't, you shouldn't, just write that down to experience, walk away with a shrug and congratulate yourself on your luck. Fate and blind chance had conspired to keep him alive. Many people had tried to kill Bond over his career and, more often than not, he had managed to show them the folly of that ambition. M had told him to relax, get well, cosset himself – but at the forefront of his mind he wanted retribution, he wanted to hunt these people down and confront them. He wanted to be their grim nemesis and revel in that moment. What was the point of a month's holiday when this was your frame of mind? No – this was an opportunity to be seized. His superior officer had gifted him a month of repose and idleness. Bond decided instead, with hardening resolve, that these days were going to be put to exceptionally good use.

He pulled on his dressing gown over his pyjamas, and left the private wing, going down to the ward sister's station at the foot of the stairs. He asked if he could make some telephone calls and was directed to a glassed-in cubicle with a pay telephone inside. Once he'd borrowed some change he made three calls: first to his bank to arrange a transfer of money; then he telephoned Donalda and asked for an address and finally he was put through to his secretary, Minty Beauchamp, and told her he was going on holiday for a month and would be out of contact.

As he lay in bed that night, Bond plotted the nature of his revenge in more detail – revenge on Blessing Ogilvy-Grant (or whatever name she was now going under) and Kobus Breed, the man with two faces. And throw in Hulbert Linck for good measure, he thought, if it turned out he'd been involved in Bond's purported assassination. And as he speculated about what he might do to these people, as and when he caught up with them, he felt peace of mind slowly returning, but he didn't forget that they too, if they were alive, might simultaneously be plotting their revenge on James Bond, the man who had messed up their little war in Africa. Somehow he was sure that they would know he hadn't died in the concrete cell beneath the Janjaville control tower. Any dead Briton found in the aftermath of Dahum's collapse would have made some newspaper or news bulletin, somewhere. No, the absence of comment would be seen as confirmation of his unlikely survival.

In any event, a plan was slowly taking shape in his mind – but it was a plan he had to carry out himself. It could have nothing to do with his role as a Double O operative, M or the Service. It had to be wholly unauthorised – it had to be rogue action. He smiled to himself in the darkness of his room: in a way the fact that it would be unauthorised would make it all the sweeter. He intended to 'go solo', as he phrased it to himself. In the unwritten ethos of the Secret Service he knew that such solo personal initiatives were strictly forbidden. Punishments for going solo were draconian. Bond smiled to himself – he didn't care. He knew absolutely what he wanted to do.

The next day he dressed in a dark navy flannel suit, white shirt and black tie (his clothes had been sent from

Chelsea by Donalda) and went down to administration and informed the duty officer that he was discharging himself. A doctor was summoned who strictly forbade him to leave – he needed at least another week to ten days to recover fully. Bond said he was going to stay with a cousin on his estate in South Uist in the Hebrides and gave a name and address – there was no telephone but he could always be reached by telegram – and took full responsibility for his decision.

Bond sought out Sheila and said goodbye, thanking her warmly and kissing her on the cheek, then a taxi was summoned and he was driven to Edinburgh. In a bank in George Street he withdrew £300 in cash. He next went to an oyster bar off Princes Street where he ordered a bottle of Veuve Clicquot, a dozen oysters and smoked salmon and scrambled egg. At Waverley Station he bought a first-class sleeper ticket to London and boarded the train. He took a sleeping pill and slept all the way through the night as the train thundered southwards. A steward woke him at six in the morning with a cup of strong British Rail tea and two digestive biscuits. Bond ignored the tea – he didn't drink tea – but gladly ate the biscuits.

He booked himself a room in a clean but somewhat decrepit bed and breakfast near King's Cross under the alias of Jakobus Breed and considered his few options.

As far as he was concerned everyone would think he was convalescing in the Hebrides for a month. The address he'd given to the hospital and to Minty was that of Donalda's uncle. The key factor, Bond thought, was that nobody knew he was in London. He had plenty of cash and he had plenty of time – somewhere in the city he would pick up the ghost of a trail that would lead him to his quarry and he had a good idea where to start. But first of all he needed some essential equipment and information that were hidden in his Chelsea flat.

**Bond sat** in a booth at the rear of the Café Picasso on the King's Road, a carafe of Barolo and a plate of spaghetti amatriciana in front of him, his eyes on the door. He'd finished his spaghetti when Donalda entered and he waved her over. She sat down at the table, unable to conceal how pleased she was to see him as they greeted each other.

'The flat's all finished, sir,' Donalda said. 'And they did a grand job. It's a shame you haven't been here to enjoy it.'

'I've been abroad,' Bond said.

'Have you no been very well? You look a bit pale, sir.'

'I got some kind of bug.'

Bond supposed that May had told Donalda the bare minimum about her employer's unusual job. The less she knew and the fewer questions she asked, the better.

'I don't want anyone to know I'm back in London,' Bond said, choosing his words carefully. 'That's why I'm meeting you here – I think someone may be watching the flat.'

'I've seen nobody suspicious in the square,' Donalda said. 'And I've been popping in every two or three days – just to check, like, and gather up the post.'

'Good. So you could pop in again, now, and unlatch the big window that looks on to the back garden.'

'Yes, of course.'

'Then leave, and come back as usual in a couple of days.'

'All right, sir.' She couldn't help a small smile of excitement at all this subterfuge.

'And your uncle knows what to say if anyone comes looking for me.'

'You've gone to Inverness. Fishing trip.'

'Perfect. Thank you, Donalda.' Bond poured himself another glass of Barolo. 'Do you want a glass of wine?'

'I'll just have one of those wee frothy coffees, if you don't mind, sir.' She opened her handbag and took out some envelopes. 'There's a few bills need paying and I ran out of cheques.'

Bond gave her the necessary cash and ordered a cappuccino.

'What do I do if I need to get hold of you?' Donalda asked.

'Call the usual number and leave a message for me. Then I'll call you back.'

'Fine,' Donalda said and smiled brightly. 'Delicious coffee, here.'

After Donalda left to go to the flat Bond waited ten minutes then walked down the King's Road to the street adjacent to Wellington Square. There was a covered passageway off the street that led to a small mews where the former stables and coach houses had been converted into workshops and tiny flats. It was possible to ascend a flight of stairs and shin over the wall and drop into the garden that belonged to Bond's basement neighbour. It was an easy matter to gain access to his rear window – there was a stout trellis and a convenient drainpipe. It was a route that Bond had occasion to use from time to time when he wanted to leave his flat clandestinely. His neighbour – a flautist in a symphony orchestra who was often away on tour – was both incurious and happy with the arrangement. He left his spare set of keys with Bond for safe keeping.

Bond stood on the trellis and pushed up the big sash window then, stepping on to a horizontal length of drainpipe, he climbed easily into his drawing room.

The flat still smelled of paint and builder's putty. He needed to smoke a few cigarettes in the place, he thought, make it his own. He went into his study and lifted the false radiator off the wall by the desk. There was an airbrick behind it that pulled out to reveal a small cavity that contained a spare Walther PPK automatic, extra clips of ammunition, some cash, a set of keys to a bedsit in Maida Vale that he rented as a safe house, and a list of crucial telephone numbers and addresses.

Bond was after some essential contacts and he jotted the telephone numbers down that he might need. He slipped the gun and a clip into his pocket and debated about the Maida Vale bedsit. He decided that the King's Cross bed and breakfast was more anonymous – he didn't want to encounter any other occupants in the house and have to start making up stories about his long absence.

He replaced the brick and rehung the radiator and went to look at his new bathroom. Doig and his team had done a good job. The marble tiling was laid faultlessly, the grouting and the mastic professionally smooth, and the new shower's chrome fittings gleamed invitingly behind its plate-glass door. Bond slid it open and turned on the shower: he heard the pump kick in quietly in its concealed housing beneath the bath. Ordered from America, the pump boosted London's water pressure fourfold. He turned the tap off. There would be plenty of time for domestic pleasures later. Still, he thought, maybe he would make himself a cup of coffee and smoke a cigarette in his new streamlined kitchen. He switched off the lights and padded along the recarpeted corridor and pushed the kitchen door open.

Donalda lay face down on the floor, the hair on the back of her head matted with fresh blood. Bond crouched down beside her and for a ghastly second thought she was dead – then she gave a little moan. Bond gently rolled her on to her side and she opened her eyes – and winced.

'Don't move,' Bond whispered. 'Just lie there.'

He took the Walther from his pocket and quickly searched the flat again, finding no one and no trace of intrusion. But someone must have already been inside when Donalda arrived to unlatch the window. Someone looking to see if James Bond had returned from abroad . . . ?

He returned to the kitchen and carefully sat Donalda up. He found a dishcloth, soaked it in warm water, wrung it out, and dabbed the blood off the back of her head where he could see she had a nasty two-inch cut. She still seemed very dazed.

'I think I'm going to be sick,' she said.

Bond managed to grab a saucepan out of a cupboard before Donalda vomited.

'That's good,' Bond said. 'You're always sick after you've been knocked out. It's a good sign.'

He put the pan in the sink and helped Donalda to her feet, sitting her on a kitchen chair. Then he made her a cup of tea.

'What happened?' he asked. 'Did you see or hear anyone?'

'No. I came in – everything was just as I'd left it. I put the post on the hall table, unlatched the window, came in here and everything went black.'

'Must have been in here behind the door, hoping you wouldn't walk in. Then left.' Bond was thinking: they know where I live. They entered with a key. This was no burglar casually thieving in a Chelsea flat. At least they didn't kill Donalda.

He looked at her as she sat there shivering, both hands cupping her mug of tea, drawing off the warmth. Then she wiped away a tear. The gesture reminded him – Kobus Breed? Could it have been Kobus Breed in his house? As he speculated, Bond felt an unreasoning fury mount in him, not so much at this violation of his personal space but at the fact that Donalda – his Donalda – had been so brutally attacked. Do not prey on my people, Bond said to himself, the consequences for those who do tend to be fatal . . .

He told Donalda he was going to call a taxi to take her to hospital, where her head wound could be examined, cleaned and stitched. She was to say only that she had slipped and fallen – and then to go home and rest in bed for a full twenty-four hours. Then he had a better idea – he called May, who said she would be with them in thirty minutes. Bond relaxed: everything would be taken care of now. While he waited, he packed a few clothes in a suitcase, thinking further. So someone was checking on his movements – was James Bond back in his London flat? Any traces of his presence? If he was truly going solo then he wouldn't be returning here, he felt sure, until this business with Kobus Breed, or whoever else it might be, was fully resolved.

May arrived and took over, telling Bond crossly that he looked 'awfy peely-wally' and that he should take better care of himself, eat three square meals a day and so on. Bond agreed, and promised to do his best. She watched him throw his suitcase into the back garden, say goodbye and climb out of his drawing-room window as if it were the most natural way in the world of leaving your house.

# 3

# AfricaKIN

The AfricaKIN sign had been removed and the poster had been replaced with a 'TO LET – ALL ENQUIRIES' notice in the grimy window, now barred with a sliding iron grille. Bond stood across from the parade of shops in Bayswater feeling frustrated. This had been his key line of investigation; he recalled the shock he'd experienced on seeing the AfricaKIN logo on the nose of the Super Constellation at Janjaville airstrip. He had felt sure that Gabriel Adeka would – unwittingly or not – be the route to Hulbert Linck and then to Breed, or whoever else was behind the whole plot. Bond paced around. With the AfricaKIN door closed maybe Blessing – or Aleesha Belem – was the person to search for, but where would he begin to pick up that trail?

Then the door to the shop opened and a young man came out – a young black man – carrying a typewriter. He chucked the typewriter on the back seat of a Mini parked outside and was about to climb in and drive away, when Bond stopped him with a shout and crossed the road to introduce himself – without giving his name – as a friend of Gabriel Adeka and a long-time donor to AfricaKIN.

The young man – who said his name was Peter Kunle – spoke like an English public schoolboy. He let Bond into the shop so he could have a look around. Everything had gone on the ground floor, even the linoleum, leaving just an empty expanse of noticeably clean concrete amidst the general grime, almost as if it had been freshly laid; and upstairs in Adeka's former office there was only a curling yellowing pile of posters that signalled the place's previous function.

'So did Gabriel close everything down when the civil war ended?' Bond asked Peter Kunle, who had followed him up the stairs.

'Oh, no. AfricaKIN still exists. He's just moved everything to America.'

'America?' Bond was astonished.

'Yes,' Kunle said. 'He's set the whole charity up there – AfricaKIN Inc. He's got major backers, apparently, very big sponsors.'

'When did all this happen?' Bond paced around, picking up a poster and dropping it – a starveling fly-infested child, all too horribly familiar now.

'Maybe a few weeks or so ago,' Kunle said. 'Maybe a bit longer, actually. We all had this round-robin letter explaining what was happening.'

'So everything changed just as the war was ending,' Bond said, trying to get a sense of a narrative.

'Yes. The charity now focuses on the entire continent. Not just Zanzarim – or Dahum, as was. You know, famines, natural disasters, disease, revolutions, anti-apartheid. The whole shebang.'

Bond was thinking hard. 'Where's he gone in America? Do you know?'

'I think it's Washington DC,' Kunle said, adding, 'I didn't know Gabriel that well. I used to help out as a volunteer a little in the early days but there was too much harassment. It was quite frightening sometimes.'

'Yes, he told me,' Bond said.

'He forgot that I'd lent him the office typewriter,' Kunle said. 'That wasn't like Gabriel.'

'What do you mean?'

'He was very scrupulous,' Kunle laughed. 'Self-destructively honest. He even offered to rent the typewriter off me – one pound a week. I said no, of course. So it was odd that he just left it here and didn't tell me. I had to ring up the landlord to get the keys and retrieve it.'

'So, it's now called AfricaKIN Inc.'

'Yes . . . I suppose the offer was too good to refuse. Too much money on the table – a bright shiny future. A shabby rented shop in Bayswater hardly impresses.'

Peter Kunle could tell him little more and apologised as he locked up the place. Bond shook his hand and thanked him for his help.

'Sorry – what was your name again?' Kunle asked as he opened his car door.

'Breed,' Bond said. 'Jakobus Breed. Do tell Gabriel I called round if you ever speak to him.'

They said goodbye and Bond wandered off up the road, pondering his options in the wake of all this new information. So: Gabriel Adeka had upped sticks for the USA and reinvented AfricaKIN in Washington DC as a global philanthropic concern overseeing the entire continent. Perhaps it was all perfectly legitimate and full of charitable integrity. He recalled his meeting with Gabriel Adeka and how impressed he'd been with the force of his quiet zeal and humanity . . . But Bond needed to ask him one pressing question: why was his charity's name on the side of an aeroplane delivering weapons and ammunition to a war zone? What had that to do with his African kinsmen? If he couldn't answer the question he might be able to point Bond in the direction of someone who would.

Bond paused to light a cigarette and noticed he was standing outside the cinema where Bryce Fitzjohn alias Astrid Ostergard's vampire film had been playing the last time he'd been here in Bayswater. What had it been called? Oh, yes: *The Curse of Dracula's Daughter*. It seemed like a year ago, not weeks, Bond thought, smiling to himself as he pictured Bryce's unknowing, innocent striptease for him that night he'd broken into her house. Bryce Fitzjohn – yes, he'd be very happy to see her again, one day.

He wandered on, up towards Hyde Park, still ruminating. There was a trail, thankfully, but it led to America, to Washington DC . . . And thereby lay a major problem. He could buy a plane ticket but could hardly use his own passport to travel. He was meant to be convalescing in South Uist, not taking international flights across the Atlantic. One way or another word would get out and he'd be in trouble.

Bond crossed the Bayswater Road and strolled into Hyde Park. What he needed was a fake passport and he needed it fast – in a day, two days, maximum. This was the major disadvantage about going solo – lack of resources. Normally, he'd call Q Branch and have a perfect used passport – full of stamps and frankings from foreign journeys – with his new name in an hour. He thought about the numbers he'd jotted down from the contact list in his flat. No, there was no one who could do a complete job like that in the short time necessary. Bond sauntered on. Maybe he could steal someone else's? He started glancing at passers-by, looking for men of his age who vaguely resembled him and then realised that most people didn't conveniently carry their passport on them, unless they were foreign visitors. Perhaps he'd need to go to an airport. No, it wouldn't be—

He stopped. It had come to him like a revelation. All you had to do was give your brain enough time to work. A solution always presented itself.

# 4

# Vampiria,
# Queen of Darkness

Amerdon Studios was situated on the banks of the Thames between Windsor and Bray and consisted of a large rambling red-brick Victorian country house with a couple of sound stages built on what had been a parterred garden modelled on Versailles. Around the sound stages there was the usual cluster of wooden shacks and Nissen huts that contained storage rooms for props and equipment and the various technical work-shops that a modern film studio required.

He told the surly man supervising the visitors' car park that he was Astrid Ostergard's agent and was sent to sound stage number two, where *Vampiria, Queen of Darkness* was shooting.

Bond headed over, briskly, a man with purpose, on important business. A couple of phone calls – one to the distributor of Bryce's last film, *The Curse of Dracula's Daughter*, and then to the office of her talent agent, a company called Cosmopolitan Talent International – had elicited the information that Astrid Ostergard was not available to open Bond's new department store in Hemel Hempstead because she was busy filming *Vampiria, Queen of Darkness* at Amerdon Studios. No, absolutely impossible, thank you very much, Mr Bond, nothing you can say will make any difference, goodbye.

As Bond approached sound stage number two he saw groups of extras in dinner suits and evening dress lounging around chatting and drinking tea out of wax-paper cups. One of them left her folding canvas chair and Bond swiftly purloined the script that she'd neglected to take with her. He asked a fat man coiling lengths of electric cable where he could find the production offices and was directed to a long caravan parked beside the sound stage.

Bond knocked on the open door and a harassed-looking woman glanced up crossly from an adding machine into which she'd been ferociously tapping figures.

'Yes?' she said. Tap-tap-tap.

'Randolph Formby,' Bond said in a patrician accent, holding up his script distastefully. 'Equity. I need to see Astrid Ostergard. She's two years behind on her payments.'

Bond had once enjoyed a short affair with an actress who'd told him that every theatrical, televisual and cinematic door opened when the word 'Equity' was pronounced, such was the power and sway of the actors' trade union. Bond was pleased he'd remembered and curious to see if it actually worked.

'Bloody Astrid!' the woman exclaimed. 'So sorry. Typical. Jesus Christ!' She carried on muttering swear words to herself as she walked Bond around sound stage number two to where a row of caravans was parked.

'Third on the right,' she said. Then, adding nervously, 'There's not going to be a problem, is there? With Astrid, I mean. We're already five days behind.'

'I can't guarantee anything,' Bond said with a thin apparatchik's smile. 'She has to pay her dues.'

The woman left, still muttering, and Bond approached the caravan, designated by a scrawled sign stuck to the side with 'Astrid Ostergard/Vampiria' written on it.

Bond knocked on the door and uttered the magic word: 'Equity.'

Seconds later Bryce Fitzjohn flung open her door. She was wearing fishnet stockings and a red satin bustier that pushed her breasts up and together to form an impressive cleavage. She looked at Bond blankly for a moment and then laughed – loudly, delightedly.

'I don't believe it,' she said. 'James bloody Bond.'

'Hello, Vampiria,' Bond said. 'I'm here to apologise.'

'Come into my parlour,' she said.

Bryce pulled on a silk dressing gown and Bond sat on a bench seat opposite a make-up table and mirror. He took out his cigarette case and offered it, Bryce selecting a cigarette and lighting it herself. She stared at him as she blew smoke sideways, eyes narrowing.

'I still don't know how you got into my house.'

Bond lit a cigarette. 'It was wrong of me, I admit. I turned up for your party and there was no one there. I thought you were playing some kind of a game, winding me up. So I left you a note.' Bond smiled. 'You should get a better lock on your kitchen door. It was child's play.'

'So what are you? A professional burglar?'

'I shouldn't have done it,' Bond continued, ignoring the question, 'so I've come to say sorry and invite you to dinner. At the Dorchester,' he added. 'Tonight, if you're free.'

Bryce crossed her long legs and Bond took her in. She was wearing a dense blonde wig with red stripes in it and he found her powerfully alluring. Nothing had changed, he thought, remembering their first encounters.

'Well, it's tempting, but I can't go up to town,' she said. 'I've an early call tomorrow morning.'

There was a knock on the door. 'We need you now, Miss Ostergard,' a voice said.

Bryce stood up. Bond did so as well, and for a moment in the confined space of the caravan they were close. Bond sensed her interest in him, renewed. They were each other's type, he realised, it was as simple as that. The attraction was very mutual, it had been from the beginning, from those first moments in the lift at the Dorchester.

'I've got to go to work,' she said. 'You know where my house is in Richmond, don't you? There's a nice little place nearby we can go to. See you at eight.'

# 5
# Import–Export

B ond slid very quietly out of Bryce's bed and stood there for a moment, looking down on her as she slept deeply, lying on her side, one breast innocently exposed. She was a beautiful mature woman, Bond thought, pulling on his trousers and remembering the last time he'd made love – weeks and weeks ago – and how different in almost every degree his partner had been then. He moved to the door in bare feet and turned the handle slowly, thinking about the rest-house on the edge of the Zanza River Delta with Blessing Ogilvy-Grant in his arms. He smiled with a certain bitterness – that was when all his misfortunes had begun.

He left the bedroom door ajar by an inch and padded downstairs to Bryce's study. He switched on the light and sat at her desk, sliding open the top drawer and taking out her passport. The date of birth pretty much fitted – and he was more than happy to shed a few years. The name was both masculine and feminine. All he needed to do was have the photograph and the gender designation changed – and he had exactly the man in mind who could do that. He would become Bryce Fitzjohn, 'professional actor'. 'Actress' could be easily tampered with. He slipped the passport into the back pocket of his trousers and went through to the sitting room, where he poured himself an inch of brandy into a tumbler and sipped at it, turning his back to the warm embers still glowing in the grate of the fireplace, thinking back agreeably over their evening together.

Bond had arrived on time (in a taxi from Richmond station) and when Bryce opened the door to him she kissed him on the cheek – a good sign, Bond thought – and he smelled the scent of 'Shalimar' on her. She was wearing a black velvet dress to just above the knee with a low scoop neck. Two diamonds glittered at her ears and her thick blonde hair was brushed casually back from her brow. There was a bottle of Taittinger champagne waiting in an ice bucket on a table in the sitting room that she asked Bond to open. They toasted each other as they had done that evening across the dining room in the Dorchester.

'Here's to breaking and entering,' she said.

'Where's this little restaurant of yours?' Bond said. 'We don't want to be late.'

'It's about ten yards away. I thought it'd be nicer to eat at home.'

They both knew exactly what was going to happen later and that knowledge provided a satisfying sensual undercurrent to their conversation as they ate the meal she cooked for him – a rare sirloin steak with a tomato and shallot salad, the wine a light and fruity Chianti, with a thin slice of lemony torta della nonna to follow.

They were both worldly and sophisticated people of a certain age, Bond reasoned, and no doubt her sexual history was as varied and interesting as his. Well, maybe not quite . . . Still, the point was, Bond thought as he looked at her clearing away the plates, that there was no pretence involved here. No artificial wooing or effortful foreplay. They both candidly wanted each other, in the way that men and women know this instinctively, and they were going to bring this state of affairs about with as much fun and seductive expediency as they chose.

They went back through to the sitting room, where Bond lit the fire. They drank a brandy, smoked a cigarette and talked to each other – deliciously postponing the moment they were waiting for. In fact Bond sensed the timbre of her voice change, dropping, growing huskier, as she told him of the disaster of her last marriage – there had been two – to an American film producer with, it turned out, a significant drug problem. He thought it was remembered emotion, but he quickly sensed that the huskiness in her voice was desire: it was a signal, and when Bond stood up and crossed the floor to her and kissed her she responded with an ardency that surprised him.

They made careful love in her wide bed, Bond relishing the smooth ripeness of her body. Afterwards, she sent him down to the kitchen for another bottle of champagne and they lay in bed drinking and talking.

'You say you're a "businessman",' she said, studying his lean form as he lay there beside her. 'Import–export, whatever that means. Yet you've more scars on your body than a gladiator.'

'I had a difficult and dangerous war,' Bond said.

She reached over, her full breasts shifting, and touched the new puckered rosy coin below his right collarbone.

'You're still fighting it, so it seems.'

He kissed her to stop her speculating further.

'I'll tell you all about it one day,' he said. And they began to make love again.

**Bryce's alarm** clock rang at five in the morning and she slipped out of bed, washed and dressed. Bond dressed also and the unit car that came to pick her up for the studio detoured to the station so he could catch an early train back to London.

She stepped out of the car so they could say their goodbyes discreetly.

'What're you doing this weekend?' she asked. 'I'm only free on Sunday. This film has another three weeks to run at the studio and I'm in every scene.'

'I've got to go to America,' Bond said. 'Just for a week or two. When your film's finished I'll come and take you away somewhere very, very special that only I know.'

They kissed goodbye and Bond whispered in her ear, 'Thank you for last night. Unforgettable.'

'For me too,' she said and squeezed his hand. Then they parted and Bond, with a full heart and a smile on his face, joined the jaded commuters on the platform at Richmond station. As he waited for the train he took Bryce's passport from his pocket and felt a twinge of guilt. But if she was working for another three weeks she wouldn't be going anywhere and wouldn't miss it. When he came back he'd replace it in her desk drawer – she'd never know. His conscience was assuaged some-what by the fact that he hadn't made love to her just to steal her passport. He had every intention of seeing his Vampiria, Queen of Darkness, again. He had been stirred and affected by her in a way he had almost forgotten was possible. He'd be back – as soon as he'd administered swift and rough justice to the people who had so nearly killed him. Bryce had no idea how inadvertently important she had been to his plans – he'd find a way to show her his gratitude.

At Waterloo station Bond had his photograph taken in a booth, then he made a telephone call – to one of the numbers he'd retrieved from his flat – and took a taxi to Pimlico, to a shabby street of dirty peeling stucco houses aptly named Turpentine Lane. He rang the door of a basement flat and an elderly man in his sixties, wearing a flat tweed cap and smoking a moist roll-up cigarette, answered the door.

'Mr Bond, sir, always a royal pleasure.'

'Morning, Dennis,' Bond said, stepping past him into the flat to be greeted by a noisome smell of cooking. 'Good God, what's that?'

'Cow-heel stew. Bugger to cook – takes three days – but it tastes something marvellous.'

Dennis Fieldfare was a forger de luxe, occasionally called upon by Q Branch when they felt their own expertise wasn't sufficient. Bond had first met Dennis when he'd needed a post-dated visa to Cuba that would have to pass microscopic inspection. It had raised not the slightest suspicion and had been so good that he'd decided to add Dennis's name to his personal pantheon of experts to be called on, as and when.

Bond showed him Bryce's passport and his photograph.

'Swap the picture, change the sex and tweak "actress" for "actor".'

'That's a bloody insult, Mr Bond. A simple-minded child could do that,' Dennis said, professionally aggrieved.

Bond gave him £50. 'But I need it very fast – this evening – that's why I came to you. Keep the original photo safe – I'll want you to change it back in a couple of weeks. And this is strictly between you and me, Dennis.'

'Doddle, Mr B. And I never seen you,' Dennis said, enjoying the feel of the money in his hand. 'Six o'clock all right?'

At six o'clock that evening Bond had his faultless new passport and was now irrefutably Bryce Connor Fitzjohn, actor, eight years younger than he actually was but he had no complaints there. In fact, he was rather pleased by the coincidence. He had used the name 'Bryce' as a pseudonym before, in the early 1950s as an alias for a long train journey he'd made from New York to St Petersburg, Florida. He'd been John Bryce then and it had worked very well. He hoped Bryce

Fitzjohn would prove equally effective. He had a feeling the new name would bring him good luck.

From Dennis's Pimlico flat he went directly to the BOAC terminal at Victoria and bought himself a first-class return ticket to Washington DC, leaving Heathrow airport at 11.30 the following day. It was perhaps an unnecessary expense to choose first class but Bond, despite being an exceptionally well-travelled man, was not the happiest of fliers. The more pampered and indulged he was on an aeroplane the less uneasy he felt when any turbulence or bad weather was encountered. Anyway, he thought, if you'd decided to 'go solo' you might as well do it in style.

# PART FOUR

# The Land of the Free

# 1
# Bloater

B ond looked out of the oval window as the plane began its descent into Dulles airport, Washington DC. The sky was clear and as the plane banked steadily round he had a fine view of the capital of the United States of America. The city lay far below him – they were still thousands of feet high – but Bond could pick out the familiar buildings and landmarks: the cathedral, Georgetown University, the Capitol, the White House, the mighty obelisk of the Washington Monument, the Tidal Basin, the Library of Congress, the Lincoln Memorial – such was the clarity of the light and the angle of the sun. The umber Potomac wound lazily round the western edge of the District of Columbia, flowing down to Chesapeake Bay and, beyond it, the undulating hills and woods of Virginia stretched out towards the Blue Ridge Mountains. It all looked neat and ordered from this high altitude but Bond felt a tension building in him as he wondered what retribution was going to be meted out by him in those streets, busy with traffic. He would take his time, plan his campaign scrupulously and without emotion. Revenge is a dish best served cold, he reminded himself.

'Welcome to the USA, Mr Fitzjohn,' the immigration officer said, stamping his passport. 'Business or pleasure?'

'Bit of both,' Bond said. 'But it's the pleasure I'm looking forward to.'

He was cleared in customs and picked up his suitcase, moving into the main arrivals concourse. He had changed all his money into dollars in London and felt the comforting flat brick of notes in his breast pocket, snug against his heart. He had left his Walther PPK in London, deciding that it was both safer and more efficient to arm himself in America, and besides, he had no idea what or how much firepower he'd require on this particu-lar mission.

He wandered through the concourse looking for the car-rental agencies. He wasn't particularly enamoured of American cars but decided that he'd—

'Bond?'

Bond heard his name called out but deliberately didn't turn round – he was Fitzjohn, now. But it came again.

'Bond. James Bond, surely—'

The voice was closer and the accent was patrician Scottish and not aggressive or hostile. Bond stopped and turned, feeling angry and frustrated. Barely minutes on American soil and already his elaborate cover seemed blown – somebody had recognised him.

The man who was approaching him – beaming incredulity written on his face – was very stout, mid-forties, Bond estimated, with thinning blond hair above a round pink face, wearing a light-grey flannel suit with an extravagant, oversized Garrick Club bow tie. Bond had no idea who he was. There was something immediately dissolute about his plump features, the bags under his eyes and the unnatural roseate flush to his cheeks. This was a man who lived slightly too well. The stranger stood in front of him, arms spread imploringly.

'Bond – it's me, Bloater.'

Bloater. Bond thought, but nothing came.

'I think you may be confusing me with somebody else,' Bond said, politely.

'I'm Bloater McHarg,' the man said.

And now the name conjured up some dim resonance. Bond had indeed known someone called 'Bloater' McHarg, about thirty years before, at his boarding school in Edinburgh – Fettes College. The fat man's features began to assume the configuration of a familiar. Yes – Bloater McHarg, last seen in 1941, Bond calculated.

Bloater offered his hand and Bond shook it.

'Well, well, well,' he said. 'Bloater McHarg. How extraordinary.'

At the beginning of World War Two fat boys were rare in Scottish public schools. 'Bloater' McHarg, undeniably heavily plump – hence the nickname – had become something of a pariah, routinely mocked for his perceived obesity. Then Bond had persuaded him to try out for the heavyweight class in his newly founded Judo Society, the first ever at Fettes. Bloater learned fast and seemed to have a talent for the sport and the other boys soon stopped teasing him once they were subject to some of his Judo holds and painful clinches. Bond had left Fettes at seventeen and had lied about his age to join the navy. All connections with his school had been cut and he'd never seen a fellow pupil or a teacher since. Until today, he thought, ruefully, here in Dulles airport, Washington DC.

'It is James, isn't it?' McHarg said. 'You know, I was just thinking about you the other day – not that I think about you a lot – but you saved me, Bond. Though you probably don't remember.'

'I do seem to remember you throwing an eighteen-stone man on his back when we won the South of Scotland Judo League.'

'Leith Judo Club. We won seven–six.' Bloater McHarg beamed. 'My finest hour. You showed me how to fight.' He put his hands on his hips and stared at Bond, shaking his head in happy bemusement.

'I recognised you at once,' McHarg said. 'You've hardly changed. Scar on your face – that's new. Always a handsome devil. What're you doing in DC?'

'Bit of business.'

'We have to get together, have a drink. Allow me to show you an exceptionally good time. I'm a second secretary here at the embassy. I know all the places to go.' McHarg searched his pockets for a card and found one. Bond took it. Bloater's first name was Turnbull. Turnbull McHarg.

'I don't think I ever knew your first name, Turnbull.'

McHarg took a pen from his pocket and scribbled a phone number on the back of the card.

'That's my home number,' he said. 'Call me when you're settled and have an hour free – we'll have a few jars et cetera, et cetera.' He winked. 'Do you ever see anything of the old crowd? Bowen major, Cromarty, Simpson, MacGregor-Smith, Martens, Tweedie,

Mostyn, and whatsisname, you know, the earl's son, Lord David White of—'

'No,' Bond interrupted, flatly, keen to stem the flood of forgotten names. 'I haven't seen anybody at all. Not one. Ever.'

'Do call me,' McHarg insisted. 'You can't leave this town without seeing me again. You won't regret it. It's bloody fate.'

It's a bloody nuisance, Bond thought, turning away with a false assurance that he'd call, a grin and a cheery wave. Over my dead body. He left McHarg to whatever errand he was on and continued in search of the car-rental franchises, but hadn't gone more than a few steps when he stopped and cursed himself. You can't hire a car without a driving licence and the only driving licence he had was in the name of James Bond. He considered the options – he had to have a car so perhaps it was worth the risk. Now he was through immigration he reckoned he could play with his two identities as it suited him. In fact it might cover his tracks better – confuse the issue. He went to a desk that said 'DC Car Rental' and asked what cars they had in the high-performance top-of-the-range category. He quickly chose a new model Ford Mustang Mach 1 hardtop. He paid a deposit in cash and was led out to the parking lot.

He liked the Mustang – he'd driven one before
– and there was something no-nonsense about this
hefty new model – two-tone, red over black – with its
big blocky muscled contours and wide alloy wheels.
No elegant European styling here, just unequivocal
300-plus horsepower in a brutish V8 Ramair engine.
He threw his suitcase in the boot – in the trunk – and
slid in behind the wheel, adjusting the seat for the
best driving position. Bloater McHarg, who would
have thought? My God, who could predict when
your past would suddenly blunder into your life? In a
way it was surprising that he'd never met any of the
other boys he'd known at Fettes. Still, not necessarily
something to be wished for. He turned the ignition
and enjoyed the virile baritone roar of the engine. He
pulled out of the parking lot and headed for downtown DC.

He had booked himself a room in a large hotel
called the Fairview near Mount Vernon Square,
between Massachusetts Avenue and G Street. He
wanted a busy hotel with many rooms, to be just one
transient individual amongst hundreds of anonymous
guests. As he headed into the city he began to recognise the odd landmark. He didn't know Washington
well – it was a place he had passed through over the
years, spending the occasional night, mainly in transit

for meetings at the CIA headquarters at Langley. He remembered from his reading somewhere that Charles Dickens had called Washington a 'city of magnificent intentions'. A somewhat loaded phrase – seeming at first glance like a compliment – though it could actually be interpreted as a rebuke: why hadn't those magnificent intentions ever been realised? For all its pre-eminent role and status in the nation's political life, Washington, he thought – outside the pomp and grandeur of its public buildings or the tonier neighbourhoods – appeared a run-down, poor-looking, dangerous place. Every time he told people he was going there he received the familiar warnings about where not to go, what not to do. Consequently, his impressions of the city were coloured by this note of caution and edgy guardedness. For most of the time you were in Washington DC you never really felt fully at ease, Bond thought.

His hotel was ideal. The Fairview was a tall featureless modern block with a middle-distance view of the Capitol's dome on its hill. His room was large and air-conditioned, with a colour TV, and the bathroom was clean and functional. He sat down on his bed and flicked through the telephone directory and then Yellow Pages, finding nothing that led him to AfricaKIN Inc. Then it struck him that Gabriel Adeka had only arrived a few weeks ago. So he called information and was given a number. This second call elicited an address: 1075 Milford Plaza in the Southwest district, south of Independence Avenue. He would check it out in the morning. At least he had found the beginning of his trail.

He unpacked his clothes and toiletries and felt the creeping melancholy of hotel life infect him. The bland room, replicated in thousands of hotels worldwide, made him sense all the drab anomie of the transient, the temporarily homeless – just the number of your room and your name in the register the signal of your ephemeral identity. He thought of Bryce, inevitably, her ripe beauty and their night together and experienced a brief ache of longing for her. Maybe he should never have embarked on this whole business – he should have spent his month's leave in London and come to know her better. It might have been a more therapeutic course of action than revenge . . . He shook himself out of his mood – self-pity was the most rebarbative of human emotions. He had chosen to come here; he had a job to do. He looked at his watch – early evening but midnight for him. Still, he couldn't go to bed.

He went down to the dark loud bar in the lobby – all the other transients drowning their melancholy – and drank two large bourbons and branch water. Then in the half-empty hangar of a dining room he ate as much as he could of a vast tough steak with some French fries. Back in his room he took a sleeping pill: he wanted a full ten hours' unconsciousness before he set about investigating the new configuration of AfricaKIN Inc.

# 2
# The Stake-Out

M ilford Plaza was a new development and had pretensions. Three six-storey glass and concrete office blocks had been positioned round a large granite-paved public space – the 'plaza' – set out with stone benches and a generous planting of assorted saplings. An oval pool with a fountain and a plinth-mounted piece of modern sculpture – three outsized girders painted in primary colours leaning against each other – contributed to its striven-for airs and graces. AfricaKIN Inc. was on the second floor of the central block.

Bond stood in the filtered neutral light of the building's tall marbled lobby – more plants, a giant suspended mobile twirling gently – and pretended to study the gilt-lettered columns of companies that were renting space. He thought about taking the elevator and actually seeing what the AfricaKIN premises were like but he sensed it might be both premature and possibly dangerous. He needed some time – to watch and evaluate, see who came and went, assess the risk factor. There was no hurry, he told himself; he had time on his side; his name was Bryce Fitzjohn.

He strolled outside. The Plaza was let down somewhat by the buildings opposite, across the street – a row of assorted pre-war brownstones showing signs of their age faced the pristine glass and granite. There was a temperance hotel – the Ranchester – a thrift shop, an A&P grocery, a Seventh Day Adventist chapel, a Chinese laundry, a jewellers and assorted eating places and a couple of small convenience stores with boarded-up windows.

Bond lit a cigarette and crossed the street wondering if there was somewhere that he could establish a semi-permanent viewpoint. He could have rented a room in the temperance hotel – it was perfectly positioned – but he refused to humiliate himself by staying in such an establishment. However, a little further along and at an oblique angle to the plaza he saw a building, grandly named the Alcazar, with a faded sign saying 'Office Suites To Let. One, Two, Three Rooms. All Conveniences.' Bond looked up at the five-storey facade. If he could rent somewhere high up at the front he'd have a good view of everyone going in and out of number 1075.

An eager young man in a shiny suit who introduced himself as Abe tried to persuade him to take their deluxe suite at the back of the building, which came with two reserved parking spaces in the lot at the rear. Bond insisted on the front. All that was available was a three-room suite on the fourth floor. Abe showed him around as Bond peered out of the windows checking the sight lines. Perfect. Abe wanted three months' rent in advance but Bond, taking out his fat wad of dollars, offered him just one month in advance – with a private, personal bonus of a hundred for Abe himself, for being so extremely helpful. 'It's a deal,' Abe said, trying to keep his smile of joy under control. Bond duly paid his deposit, slipped Abe his inducement, signed the lease and was given a set of keys. 'Welcome to the Alcazar,' Abe said, and shook his hand.

There were dirty, vertical plastic strip-blinds at the windows, no furniture and stained carpet tiles on the floor. The third and smallest of the rooms gave him the best view. All Bond needed was a seat and a pair of binoculars – then he could survey Milford Plaza to his heart's content. It was time to equip himself.

Bond drove west and crossed the Potomac to a suburb outside DC in Virginia. He cruised the shopping malls and the streets until he found what he was looking for. He parked outside a large, brash-looking store painted canary yellow with, along the facade, huge red letters outlined in neon that said 'SAM M. GOODFORTH. GUNS 'N' AMMO'. Beneath that, in a cursive copperplate, a line read 'Your Firearm Dreams Answered'.

Bond pushed open the door and browsed for a while, checking the place out. All the lethal hardware was contained in locked wire-grilled cabinets behind the long sales counter. The rest of the store was filled with army surplus and hunting and fishing equipment and accessories. Bond chose a folding canvas stool and a soft rubber mattress that could be rolled up. He approached the counter with his purchases.

The thin, muscled man who served him was smoking a cigarette and had his hair shaved almost bald in a severe crew cut with a curious tuft at the forelock. Various crests and emblems were tattooed on his pale arms. Despite his martial air his voice was oddly high-pitched and he had a half-lisp.

Bond also bought a pair of binoculars, ex-US Navy, Zeiss lenses.

'Are you the owner?' he asked.

'I'm his brother, Eugene,' he smiled, showing a black tooth. 'Sam's got an appointment with a lady friend.'

'I need a handgun,' Bond said. 'Have you got a Walther PPK?'

'I got thomething better, thir,' Eugene lisped. 'Thmall but thtrong.'

He opened a drawer and brought out a Beretta M1951. Bond liked Berettas, in fact he sometimes regretted giving up his old Beretta for his Walther. He turned it over in his hand, checking it – it was a 'third series' with the smaller sights – cocking it, squeezing the trigger, ejecting the empty clip – it would take eight rounds of 9 mm Parabellum – and slapping it back in.

'Ain't the first time you had a gun in your hand, I can see that,' Eugene said.

Bond liked the weight of the gun. 'I'll take it,' he said, his eye ranging over the rifles, the M5 carbines, machine guns and shotguns racked behind the grilles. Maybe he needed something for longer ranges . . . And then he suddenly thought that powerful telescopic sight might be a real advantage – a sniper-scope – from his room high up in the Alcazar. Something that could zoom in – better than binoculars.

'I might be doing a bit of hunting,' Bond said. 'I want something with a bit of beef – and that can take a strong scope.'

Eugene Goodforth presented him with a choice of powerful hunting rifles – a CZ-550 with a Mannlicher stock, a Mauser Karabiner and a Springfield 1903 in beautiful condition. Bond was more interested in the sights that he was shown and took the latest model Schmidt & Bender scope to the door to see how it worked at long range.

He looked at passers-by down the street. The zoom magnification was very effective and the little calibrations and illuminated cross-hairs reticle could be changed at the flick of a switch at the side.

He returned to the counter and told Eugene that he needed a rifle that would fit this scope – but one that could be broken up and carried in a bag of some sort.

'Have I got just the baby for you, sir,' Eugene said and went into a room behind the counter emerging with what looked like a black plastic attaché case. He flipped it open and showed Bond the contents.

'Just arrived – a Frankel and Kleist S1962,' Eugene said with reverence in his voice. He took the separate stock, breech and barrel out of their recessed velvet moulds and fitted them together, sliding the scope on top. 'Single shot, bolt action. Point five zero calibre bullet, two-stage trigger set to four pounds.' Bond picked it up and raised it to his shoulder. It was matt black and surprisingly light. Bond fitted his cheek to the cheek rest and drew a bead through the window on a shop sign across the street.

'You turn down the reticle illumination all the way on that scope you can shoot this mother at night, I swear,' Eugene said.

'Perfect,' Bond said. 'You made another sale.'

'What're you after?' Eugene asked with a knowing smile. 'Neighbours?'

Bond laughed. 'Elk,' he said, spontaneously.

'Don't got much elk around these parts,' Eugene said. 'Still, you may get lucky.'

'I'll look hard,' Bond said.

He bought the guns and their relevant ammunition, showed his Bryce Fitzjohn passport, filled in the documentation – giving as his address his hotel, the Fairview – and marvelled, not for the first time in his life, just how easy it was to arm yourself in the land of the free.

# 3

# The Alcazar

The next morning Bond parked his Mustang in an underground garage near the Federal Warehouse and walked the three blocks to the Alcazar, attaché case in one hand, a canvas grip in his other, containing the binoculars, the mattress, three packs of cigarettes and a vacuum flask filled with a weak solution of bourbon and iced water. He could always pop out for a sandwich or a dreaded burger or hot dog if he grew hungry, he reasoned.

Secure in his room, the main door locked, he pulled the little circular chain that turned the blind sideways on to the windows. He set up his folding stool and unrolled his mattress. He sat down and picked up the binoculars. He had an ideal oblique line of sight on to the plaza and anyone entering or leaving number 1075.

The binoculars allowed him an initial identification and the sniper-scope provided a genuine close-up with the aid of the zoom-magnification device. However, with the zoom at maximum the hand-shake distortion was sizeable. He needed a tripod, Bond thought – or, even better, the rifle it was designed for.

He assembled the Frankel and fitted the scope. By resting the barrel on the windowsill he achieved perfect stability. Peering through the sight with the distance calibration and the cross-haired reticle in operation made him feel like an assassin. Just as well the gun wasn't loaded, Bond thought: if he saw Kobus Breed crossing the plaza the temptation might prove too hard to resist.

After a couple of hours' watching, Bond began to feel himself stiffening up. He took off his jacket and did some un-strenuous exercises just to keep the blood flowing. He was feeling stronger every day but didn't want to put any undue strain on his healing tissues. He smoked a cigarette, had a swig of his bourbon and water and sat down again.

Through his binoculars he saw a glossy town car pull up in the indented drop-off spot at the edge of the plaza. A black man in a dark suit stepped out and leaned forward to have a quick word with the driver. Adeka, Bond wondered? He picked up his rifle and zoomed in with the scope.

No – even more interesting, and someone else he'd met before: Colonel Denga, lately commander-in-chief of the Dahumian armed forces. There was the handsome face with the matinee-idol moustache. Bond watched him stroll across the plaza to 1075. He was dapper – the suit jacket was cut long and was waisted and the trousers fashionably flared. Just visiting, or was he now something to do with AfricaKIN Inc?

Bond lunched on a ham and cheese sandwich in a diner, had a badly made dry martini in a bar and, curiosity getting the better of him, once again went into the lobby of 1075 and stood by the elevators wondering whether to chance a visit to the office itself. But if Denga was there, he'd be recognised, and – just so he could gain a sense of the lie of the land – he thought it might be more effective to disguise himself somehow, initially. There are disguises and disguises, Bond knew. He could grow a beard and shave his head and no one would think he was James Bond. But the short-term, provisional disguise had its own particular methodology. The key aim was to focus attention on one or two elements of the disguise so that they obscured the other, more familiar ones. Time for some more shopping, Bond thought.

**The next** morning, Bond strode across Milford Plaza towards number 1075. He was wearing a red and green tartan jacket, heavy black spectacles with clear lenses and a cream pork-pie hat. He rode up in the elevator to the second floor and pushed through the wide, double plate glass doors into the lobby of Africa-KIN Inc.

Everything about the ambience of the long lobby said 'money'. Bond's gaze took in the thick-pile charcoal carpet, the lush plants growing in stainless-steel cubes. At one end there was a seating area composed of curved leather sofas and teak coffee tables. On the linen walls were a couple of large inoffensive abstract paintings. The receptionist – a middle-aged white woman – sat at a mahogany desk with three telephones on it. Behind her on a smoked-glass panel 'AfricaKIN Inc.' was spelt out in large three-dimensional sans-serif aluminium letters. Beyond that Bond could see a wide corridor with offices off it on both sides. It didn't look like a charity, to his eyes, it looked like a successful corporation.

'Welcome to AfricaKIN, sir,' the receptionist said with a smile. 'How may I help you?'

'I'd like to make an appointment to see Gabriel Adeka,' Bond said in a marked Scottish brogue. This is where the provisional disguise should work: if the woman were ever asked to remember him all she could say would be 'Scotsman, spectacles, small hat.' He would guarantee that she'd find it very hard to be any more precise.

'I'm sorry, sir, but that won't be possible. Mr Adeka is extremely busy – on government business.'

'I know him,' Bond said. 'We met in London. I want to make a sizeable donation.' He handed over his card. The receptionist looked at it and handed it back.

'If you care to take a seat, Mr McHarg, I'll see what I can do.' She jotted his name down on a pad. And picked up one of her telephones. Bond wandered off to the seating area and helped himself to some water from the cooler standing there. He saw that there was another corridor, signed with an arrow that said 'Restrooms'. Conceivably there might be a service entrance at the end. Never enter a room without assessing the various ways available to exit it, he reminded himself – Bond had never forgotten his early instructions in procedure. He sat down – he was quite enjoying this – taking care to position himself so that he was screened by a large weeping fig.

He waited. Ten minutes, twenty minutes. Other people joined him until summoned into the office suites for appointments or meetings. Forty minutes passed – the place was busy. Bond sat on, a *National Geographic* magazine open on his knee, his eyes restless – watching, checking, noting. He headed for the restrooms. He was right – there was a door at the end of the corridor that said 'No entry'. He opened it and saw a flight of concrete stairs and a yellow bucket with a mop in it. Bond relieved himself, checked his disguise and returned to his seat.

After he'd been there an hour he began to grow a little worried. Either he could meet Adeka – or he couldn't. He thought of approaching the receptionist again but decided not to – one glimpse of him was all she should have. Then it occurred to him that he was being kept here deliberately, figuring that as long as he was corralled in the lobby anyone could find him. He put the magazine down. Something was now wrong – he was going to abort. He'd been a bit too audacious thinking he'd gain access to Adeka this easily—

Kobus Breed pushed through the glass doors and went straight to the receptionist.

Bond stood up immediately, turned his back and walked unconcernedly down the corridor to the restrooms. He was through the service door in a second and clattered down the stairs. He found himself in a storeroom full of cleaning equipment and rubbish bins. He threw his hat and his glasses into a bin, took off his jacket, turned it inside out and folded it over his arm. He opened another door and emerged at the rear of the elevator banks. Looking straight ahead he made his way through the people waiting for the elevators, strolled easily across the marble lobby with its spinning mobile and walked out into the weak sunshine that was bathing Milford Plaza.

He could still feel the heart-thud of alarm and adrenalin. Breed in Washington DC? Breed summoned to confront this unknown visitor to Gabriel Adeka . . . He had been wearing a dark business suit and a red tie – very smart. Bond remembered that was how he had complimented him in the control tower at Janjaville. Perhaps that suit he'd been wearing that night was the first indication of his new life as an executive of a global charitable foundation.

Bond began to relax, glancing back as he left the plaza – no one was after him and he had learned a lot from his visit. His request to meet Adeka had brought Kobus Breed from wherever he was residing to investigate. AfricaKIN Inc. had nothing to do with the modest grubby shop in Bayswater. Something much bigger was taking place. Something bigger and very wrong.

# 4

# Switchblade

That night Bond went to see a film called *Bob &
Carol & Ted & Alice* but found he couldn't concentrate on it. He left before the end and walked slowly
back to the Fairview, smoking a cigarette, his mind
working, trying to analyse all the permutations that
might make up AfricaKIN Inc. Gabriel Adeka, Colonel
Denga and now Breed . . . What kind of strange alli-
ance was this?

He realised he hadn't been paying attention and had
taken a wrong turn. He could see the top of the lucent
tower that was the Fairview a few blocks away and also
the floodlit dome of the Capitol on the hill. He reset
his bearings and headed off again, aware that he had
wandered into a neighbourhood of near-derelict housing, with many windows boarded up, some of them

seemingly damaged by fire. He passed a burnt-out car with no wheels; half the street lights weren't working; stray cats prowled the alleyways. This could happen so easily in DC. One wrong turning and you found your-self in—

'Hey, man, you got a light?'

Bond looked round slowly. Behind him, on the edge of a yellow semicircle thrown by a lamp above a shut-tered thrift-store doorway, three young men stood – teenagers, Bond thought. They were wearing jeans and T-shirts and were all smoking, so the need for a light was redundant. Two black kids and a white guy, slightly older. Bond glanced behind him – no one – so just these three to deal with, then. All right, come and get me.

They started to walk purposefully towards him flicking away their cigarettes, numbed and heroic with speed, Bond reckoned. The white kid took something out of his pocket and Bond heard the *whish-chunk* of a switchblade being sprung.

'So you need a light,' Bond said taking out his Ronson and clicking it on. He turned the small wheel that governed the gas valve and the flame flared up three inches.

'Hey, funny guy,' one of them said as they fanned out to surround him.

Bond tossed the flaring lighter at the boy with the switchblade. Reflexively, he ducked and swore and in that moment of inattention Bond grabbed his wrist and dislocated it with a brutal jerk. The boy screamed and the knife dropped with a clatter on the sidewalk. Bond turned on the black kid who was rushing him and kicked him heavily in the groin. He fell to the ground, bellowing and writhing in agony – Bond's loafers were fitted with steel caps at the toe. The other black kid began to back off. Bond stooped and picked up the switchblade and held it out.

'You want this?' he said.

The boy turned and ran away into the night.

Bond found his Ronson and pocketed it – then considered his two assailants. The boy with the dislocated wrist was kneeling, holding his wrist with his good hand and sobbing with the pain, his hand hanging limply and at the wrong angle. The other kid was still on the ground clutching his smashed groin and keening in a high-pitched whine of misery, his knees drawn up to his chest.

Bond stamped down hard on his ribcage and kicked the other kneeling boy in the side with his steel toe-caps, knocking him flying, making him scream again. Ribs broken or fractured, he assumed. They would remember him and this night for the next couple of months – every time they coughed or laughed or reached for something.

Bond leaned over them both and swore at them picturesquely, then he added, 'Way past your bedtime, kiddies, run along home.'

He strolled off towards the Fairview, closing the switchblade. It was quite a nice knife, he thought, with a dull ebony handle inlaid with a nacreous pattern of diamonds. He slipped it in his pocket, beginning to feel a little guilty at the unreasonable force of his retaliation. He realised he had vented some of his pent-up rage from Janjaville on these three unfortunates. This was the first 'action' he had seen since he had left the war zone. His blood had come up spontaneously and he had administered swift and efficient retribution. They weren't to know whom they were trying to rob, nor what dark, embittered grudges their potential victim was harbouring: still, he thought, maybe he might have saved them from a life of crime. But he knew he'd taken out his anger on those street punks and punished them for the sins of others. Just their bad luck . . . Tough. He eased his right shoulder as he approached the hotel – no pain – and he massaged the muscle of his wounded thigh. Everything seemed fine after his physical exertions – he was healing fast.

**He spent** a fruitless morning the next day in his office in the Alcazar building, scrutinising Milford Plaza but recognising no familiar faces. He started to wonder if there was a rear entrance for more private comings and goings but he had observed that most people arriving by car were dropped off in the indented parking area off the busy street, so he assumed that was the norm.

Then, just before noon, he saw her. Blessing Ogilvy-Grant came out of the main door of 1075 and began to walk across the plaza. Bond zoomed in with the sniper-scope. She looked different – she was wearing a belted beige trouser suit with wide flared trousers but her hair had changed and was now styled in a short bushy Afro, natural and unoiled – very much the young radical, he thought. She stopped at a hot-dog stand to buy a soda and Bond took his opportunity, racing out of his suite of rooms and down the stairs.

When he emerged from the Alcazar on to the plaza he thought he'd lost her but then he caught sight of her heading up the street towards The Mall. She crossed it on 7th Street and he followed her, being very careful, always staying fifty yards or so behind, sometimes crossing the street and doing a parallel follow, looking back to check that she wasn't being covered in any way, before ducking back behind her again.

He felt the contrasting emotions seethe within him. His heart had lurched spontaneously when her face had grown large in the sniper-scope, as he remembered her beauty and the tenderness she'd shown him. Without thinking, he'd approved of this new look she'd created – very American, very cutting-edge. Then he recalled how casually and coldly she had shot him, taking Kobus's gun and levelling it at his chest without a tremor or any sign of regret. The lover's fond assessment gave way to a bitter, reasoned anger – she had played him exceptionally well, from the moment they had met. She was a highly trained operative, prepared to put her body on the line should it prove necessary, and give herself to her adversary – and also to shoot to kill. He slowed, making sure he kept his distance, assuming that she would routinely verify that she was being followed or not. Bond's expertise had to be at least as good as hers, if not better.

A point worth repeating regularly, Bond told himself, as he watched her turn into a restaurant on E Street called the Baltimore Crab. Bond hovered outside, across the street, watching other lunchers arrive and wondering whom she might be meeting. Perhaps it was just a friend and not sinister business. Even double agents were allowed a personal life from time to time, he told himself.

Bond lit a cigarette and weighed up his options. He had located AfricaKIN. His surveillance was in place and functioning. Nobody knew he was in the US. But there was no point in just watching – some kind of catalyst was needed, and one of his own making; not like Kobus Breed arriving unannounced at the AfricaKIN offices. *Il faut pisser sur les fourmis*, he said to himself with a grin, recalling one of the cruder adages of his old friend René Mathis. Yes, *pisser sur les fourmis* and set the ants scurrying for cover.

Bond crossed the street and pushed open the door of the restaurant. His gaze quickly swept the room. It was bright and airy, decorated in varying shades of blue and embellished with a multitude of nautical motifs on the walls – signal flags, a life belt, a ship's wheel, cork floats and swags of netting. He thought he caught a glimpse of Blessing in the far corner but he looked no further, smilingly approaching the young woman who stood at a lectern at the entrance to the dining room, and asking if he could make a reservation for that evening. The reservation was made, Bond helped himself to a Baltimore Crab business card from the little pile on top of the lectern and left. He was almost one hundred per cent sure that Blessing would have spotted him talking to the woman at the maître d's station. In any event, the next few minutes would prove him right or wrong.

Bond wandered up the street a few yards, hailed a passing cab and climbed in.

'Just wait here for a while,' he told the driver and handed him a $10 note. He hunched down in the rear seat, keeping his eyes on the restaurant door. Sure enough, in about ninety seconds, Blessing hurried out, agitated, looking up and down the street, scanning the faces of passers-by. Bond smiled to himself – the ants were in a real state. Blessing waved down the first cab she saw and got in.

'Follow that cab,' Bond said. 'And there's another twenty in it for you if we're not spotted.'

'Hey, no problem,' the cabbie said. He had a Mexican accent and a droopy, bandit's moustache. 'She your girl?'

'Yes – two-timing bitch.'

'Man, don' get me start on *las chicas*,' the cabbie said and immediately embarked on a long anecdote about his ex-wife in lewd and abusive detail.

Bond let him rant on, keeping his eye on Blessing's cab. He wondered what she would be thinking, what level of shock and astonishment the sight of him would have provoked. To see James Bond saunter into a Washington DC restaurant when she might have assumed he was dead and buried . . . No, Bond thought, the sick jolt of alarm would go quickly and then furious second-guessing would begin. She would intuit almost instantly that this was no coincidence and that he had wanted her to see him. But why? she would ask herself. Then she'd enter the fraught and dangerous labyrinth of pure speculation. This was a man she had shot in the chest in Africa – and yet here he was on her trail in Washington DC. Bond smiled: Blessing's head would be ringing with a hundred alarm bells – she would be well and truly spooked. He sat back – there were many types of satisfaction to be enjoyed in this job.

Blessing's car headed into Georgetown and stopped outside a small, pretty clapboard house on O Street.

'Drive on by,' Bond said to the cabbie, peering out of the rear window to see Blessing run inside, not paying off the driver, keeping her cab waiting, its engine ticking over. They drove on fifty yards and Bond ordered the cabbie to park and wait.

'We go through a lot of zones, mister,' the cabbie said. Bond had forgotten the arcane mysteries of cab-fare calculation in DC.

'Don't worry. I'll pay you well. Get ready to turn around if you have to,' Bond said and fed the man another $20.

'Hey, you can hire me all day, every day, mister,' he turned in the front seat and leered at him. 'I am like to work with you.'

After five minutes Blessing reappeared again, a suitcase in her hand. She locked the front door and hurried into her cab. It pulled away and passed them.

'Don't lose it, whatever you do,' Bond said.

'You got it.'

Blessing's cab headed west out of DC and crossed the Key Bridge over the Potomac. About twenty minutes later it pulled into the forecourt of a large and ugly modern motel called the Blackstone Park Motor Lodge.

'Keep going,' Bond said. They drove on another block or so. 'Stop.'

The cab pulled into the side of the road under a vast billboard advertising Kool cigarettes. Through the rear window Bond could see Blessing paying off her cab and a bellhop picking up her suitcase. So this was where she would be staying. She was smart: she assumed her cover was blown and so she immediately changed address, within minutes. Bond relaxed – he knew where to find her now. She'd check into her room and start making anxious phone calls, warning everyone. The ants' nest would be in swarming disarray.

# 5
# Suite 5K

Bond spent the rest of the afternoon in his Alcazar office watching the comings and goings on Milford Plaza. None of the usual suspects appeared but he wasn't too concerned. As it grew dark he went back to the Fairview, put a pillow and a bottle of bourbon in his suitcase and went out to his car. He drove the Mustang out west across the Potomac to the Blackstone Park Motor Lodge, found a space for his car and went into reception with his suitcase. He had deliberately not checked out of the Fairview – sometimes having rooms in two hotels in a city was better than one.

He was given a large double room in the main block. The Blackstone Park wasn't cheap and nasty, just over-used. The sheets on the bed were crisp cotton but the carpet was threadbare and the paintwork was chipped and scarred. The air conditioner worked but hummed a little too loudly. The lavatory was protected by a sheet of cellophane and the tooth-glass had a little cardboard cap on it, but the shaving mirror was cracked and the shower tray's enamel had been scoured through. Anonymous, large, functional – perfect to hide yourself in.

Bond went down to reception and slipped the bell-hop on duty $10.

'Keep this between ourselves,' Bond said, 'but I think my wife's checked into this motel under a false name.'

'You mean . . . ?'

'Got it in one,' Bond said, putting on an embittered face. 'Yeah – she doesn't know I know.'

The bellhop's name, according to the plastic badge above his breast pocket, was Delmont. His acne had almost gone but had left his skin dimpled like a golf ball. The wispy moustache he was trying to grow was no asset either, but he bought into the male sodality that Bond offered and they talked briefly of the perfidy of beautiful women like two men of the world.

'She's coloured,' Bond said, 'but pale-skinned, you know. Very sexy with a kind of Afro hairstyle.'

'We got two hundred rooms here, sir,' Delmont said. 'But I'll ask around. A babe like that will have been noticed by my colleagues, know what I mean?'

'I just need her room number,' Bond said. 'I'll give you five bucks for it – leave the rest to me,' Bond smiled. 'I'm Mr Fitzjohn, room 325.'

Bond went back to room 325 and poured himself two fingers of bourbon from his bottle and switched on the television while he waited for Delmont. He watched a game of baseball uncomprehendingly – the Senators versus the Royals – thinking that it made cricket seem exciting. Delmont's knock on the door came ten minutes later.

'She's in suite 5K in the new annexe in back by the parking lot,' Delmont said, folding away Bond's $5 into a small pocket in his jacket. 'She paid for two weeks in advance – so it don't look like she's planning on coming home soon.' Delmont commiserated and said if there was anything else he could do then Mr Fitzjohn shouldn't hesitate. Call the front desk and ask for Delmont.

'A thousand thanks,' Bond said, and he meant it. Life was becoming more intriguing by the hour.

**Bond was** up at dawn and drove into DC, stopping at a diner for scrambled eggs and bacon and the hot brown liquid that passed for coffee in this country. He took up his position armed with his binoculars and watched the office workers arrive for the daily round.

Just after nine o'clock, Kobus Breed stepped out of a Chevrolet Impala and strode across the plaza to 1075. Ten minutes later Denga's car arrived and there – Bond swivelled the binoculars – there was Blessing herself, walking fast, her head turning constantly, checking to see if she was being followed. Bond smiled. A council of war? The day was young.

An hour went by, then two. Bond dashed to the rest-rooms at the end of the corridor, cursing the diuretic potency of American coffee, and raced back, hoping he hadn't missed anything or anyone. When he saw Kobus Breed appear twenty minutes later, he relaxed. Kobus was swiftly followed by Blessing.

Bond picked up his rifle and adjusted the zoom on the sniper-scope. There they were – faces close in animated conversation. Bond settled the cross hairs of the sight on Kobus's forehead, watching him dab at his weeping eye with a handkerchief. Then his car arrived and he left. Bond moved the sight to Blessing. Seeing the two of them in ardent discussion had hardened his feelings again, remembering their near-lethal double act in the Janjaville control tower.

He watched Blessing rummage in her bag and take out a pack of cigarettes. She stood there smoking as if in deep thought, pacing to and fro in small circles. Bond moved the cross hairs to her breast. Tempting.

Two inches below the right collarbone, exactly where she'd shot him. Just as well he didn't have a bullet in the chamber—

The click by his ear was unmistakeable. The hammer of a revolver being cocked. He could feel the snub muzzle cold on his jawbone.

'No, Mr Bond. Take your hands off the gun then stand up slowly, arms raised.' There was the hint of a Southern drawl in the voice.

Bond did exactly as he was told, standing slowly, turning and raising his arms above his head.

Two young men stood there covering him with their handguns. They both wore navy blue suits and striped ties. One was blond and one was dark, their hair cut short in military style. CIA, Bond guessed at once. What the hell was going on? How did they know his name?

'The gun isn't loaded,' Bond said. 'You can check. I wasn't going to shoot.'

'Good to know,' the blond man said. 'She's one of us.'

# 6
# CIA

Bond lowered his arms, his brain in some kind of manic overdrive. 'One of us' . . . ? One question at a time, he told himself.

'I'd like to see your ID,' he asked. 'If I may.'

The blond man took out his wallet and showed Bond his plastic card.

'I'm Agent Brigham Leiter,' he said. 'And this is Agent Luke Massinette.'

Bond smiled. 'So you're the famous Brig,' he said. 'How's Uncle Felix?'

'He's well, sir. In fact I know he wants to talk to you urgently.'

'How did you know my name? How did you know I was here?'

Brigham Leiter holstered his gun, as did his partner.

'The lady you were aiming at is called Aleesha Belem. She told us you were in DC – she saw you in a restaurant, by chance, and gave us your name. We traced the hire of a Ford Mustang to one James Bond at Dulles airport then we lost your trail. Luckily we have this whole plaza staked out. We took your photograph. Aleesha identified it. My uncle confirmed it. James Bond, British agent. We found where you'd parked your Mustang. Followed you to these offices. Followed you back to your hotel. It wasn't hard to make the connection to a Mr Bryce Fitzjohn.'

Bond couldn't blame himself for sloppy procedure – it was no lapse on his part, just bad luck. How was he to know that Blessing–Aleesha was a CIA agent? He thought further.

'So this Aleesha Belem is working for you. Since when?'

'Over two years now, I believe.'

'She shot me in the chest. In Africa a few weeks ago. Tried to kill me.'

'I don't know anything about that,' Brig Leiter said. 'She's sound – one of our most reliable people.'

'What's she doing in AfricaKIN?'

'I'm not authorised to disclose that information,' Leiter said.

'I think I'd better talk to your uncle,' Bond said. 'Is he back in the CIA or is he still with Pinkerton's?'

'He "consults" for us from time to time. He's still with Pinkerton's, though.'

Bond thought fondly of Felix Leiter – one of his oldest friends and colleagues. They had endured many a tough assignment together over the years. Felix had been badly injured on one of them, back in Florida in the early 1950s, had even lost an arm and part of a leg. Bond glanced at Felix's nephew, Brig. Felix had often talked about him, a 'chip off the old block'. Bond thought he saw something of Felix in the set of Brig's jaw, the thick blond hair, the grey, candid eyes. He wasn't so keen on the other guy, though. Massinette stood back, surly, watchful.

Still, Bond's head was loud with unanswered questions. If Blessing had been in the CIA for two years how had she managed to . . . ? He stopped himself. There would be time enough to settle these issues later.

'I can hook you up with my uncle,' Brig said. 'He's in Miami.'

Bond broke up and packed away the Frankel and followed Brig and Massinette out of the Alcazar and along the street to the temperance hotel, the Ranchester. They rode the elevator to the fifth floor and Bond walked in on a major CIA surveillance team in a room at the front overlooking the whole of Milford Plaza. There were telescopes, cameras with long lenses mounted on tripods, screens displaying covert CCTV links into the lobby of 1075 and the entrance to the AfricaKIN office itself. Everyone who came in and out of that building could be logged and conceivably identified. Bond wondered if 'Turnbull McHarg' had been spotted – somehow he doubted it.

He was put on the phone to Felix Leiter in Miami.

'Felix, it's James.'

'Welcome to DC, my son. What're you up to? You nearly fouled everything up. Why didn't Transworld Consortium tell us you were on a job?'

'Because I'm not.'

'Uh-oh . . .' Pause. 'Don't tell me – you've gone solo.'

'I'd appreciate it if you didn't inform anyone that I'm here.'

There was more silence as Felix took this in.

'James, do you know what you're doing?'

'Of course.'

'Good. Well from now on we take over, right? Go back to London before anyone finds out. Difficult to keep a lid on this.'

Bond looked around the room at all the hardware, the agents, the money being spent on this job and thought of his own puny individual investment in his act of vengeance.

'Felix, will you tell me what's going on here?'

'No.'

'Come on, Felix, it's me – James.'

'Let's just say we're investigating AfricaKIN Inc. We don't believe all their PR schtick.'

'I might just buy that,' Bond said, 'but you already had an agent in Zanzarim weeks ago. How come she was able to intercept me? How come she tried to kill me?'

'It's a long story, James. Go back to London. I'll tell you all about it as soon as possible.'

They exchanged a few more ribald pleasantries and Bond handed the phone to Brig. He watched as Felix obviously gave him a few explicit instructions. Bond had no confidence in what little Felix had told him: something else was at stake here and his own intervention had been a minor bit of grit in a well-oiled CIA machine.

Brig Leiter put the phone down and turned to Bond.

'We can take you back to your hotel, Mr Bond. The Fairview, right?'

'Yes,' Bond said, a little surge of relief and excitement seizing him. They clearly didn't know about the Blackstone Park Motor Lodge. Maybe he was still one step ahead.

He drove the Mustang back to the hotel, followed by Brig and Massinette in their Buick Skylark. Brig came with him into the lobby and saw him pick up his key.

'Mr Bond,' he said, apologetically, 'believe me, this isn't easy for me. Uncle Felix talks about you all the time. It's a real pleasure to meet you – I just wish I hadn't had to pull a gun on you to say hello.'

'Not a problem at all, Brig,' Bond said with a wide smile. 'I'm out of your hair – now I know the truth about Blessing – about Aleesha. I'll head for home, don't you worry. All's well that ends well.'

'Great. Thank you, sir.' They shook hands and Brig returned to his Buick. Massinette was leaning against it, smoking. They climbed in and drove off.

Bond went into the lobby bar to gather his thoughts and ordered a vodka martini, explaining to the barman the best way to achieve the effect of vermouth without diluting the vodka too much. Ice in the shaker, add a slurp of vermouth, pour out the vermouth, add the vodka, shake well, strain into a chilled glass, add a slice of lemon peel, no pith.

Bond took his drink to a dark corner and lit a cigarette, thinking hard. He had assumed that time was his ally, but now time was his enemy. Any more interference with the CIA operation and Felix would call London and they'd ship him off back home with no compunction. Bond reckoned he had forty-eight hours, at the outside.

# 7

# The Engineer

Bond left his Mustang in the hotel parking lot and picked up a taxi in the street, telling the driver to take him to the Blackstone Park Motor Lodge. When they arrived there he told the cabbie to circle the block twice. Bond looked out of the rear window as they did so – he wasn't being followed. All the same he made sure he was dropped a few hundred yards up the road and walked back, still checking, doubling back, waiting in doorways. There was no one on his tail.

He stayed in his room until it was dark and, every ten minutes or so, would wander out to the parking lot at the rear to see if the lights were on in Suite 5K. On his eighth visit to the parking lot he saw that the room was finally occupied and the curtains were drawn. He caught the silhouette of a figure crossing in front of a window. Blessing . . . ? Bond went back to his room and slipped his Beretta into his jacket pocket – he was taking no chances.

He knocked on the door of suite 5K and called out 'Engineer.' It was always better than 'Room service.'

He heard Blessing come to the door and say 'Please come back tomorrow.'

Bond put on a Mexican accent. 'The man below he say you got a leak comin' from you bathroom. I gotta check it, Mam.'

'OK, OK.'

He heard the lock turn and he took his gun out of his pocket and held it behind his back. Blessing opened the door and gasped. Bond had his gun in her face and was inside in a second, closing the door behind him. He took the gun from her hand – she was taking no chances either, clearly – and tossed it on the sofa, pocketing his own. Blessing had regained her composure, smiling, shaking her head.

'Yep, "Engineer" is good. I'm going to remember that one.'

She was wearing an eau de Nil satin blouse with balloon sleeves and tight, bell-bottom pale blue jeans. Her feet were bare. She watched, amused, as Bond quickly checked the suite.

'I'm alone, don't worry, James.'

Bond glanced in the bedroom. Suite 5K was deluxe and smarter than his room, designed in the Scandinavian style – all curved pale wood, the bed lower than normal, a thick pile navy rug on a slate-grey carpet, a console stereo, black and white photographs of DC's historic buildings on the walls.

'What do I call you?' Bond asked. 'Blessing or Aleesha?'

'What do I call you? James or Bryce?' She smiled. 'Blessing will do fine. It's actually my middle name, James.'

Bond began to relax. They were on the same side, after all.

'We've got a bit of catching up to do,' Bond said. 'Wouldn't you say?'

'What're you drinking?' she asked, going to the phone.

Bond took the receiver out of her hand.

'Let me do it,' he said. 'Bourbon good for you?'

He ordered a bottle of Jim Beam, two glasses, a bucket of ice and a carafe of branch water and told room service to bill his room – Mr Fitzjohn.

'You're staying here?' Blessing said, astonished. 'Does Brig Leiter know?'

'Not yet. I wanted to have some time alone with you.' He smiled. 'I like your hair like that.'

'Thank you, kind sir.'

The bourbon arrived and Bond mixed them both a strong drink. They clinked glasses and Blessing curled up on the sofa with her legs folded under her. Bond sat in an armchair opposite.

'See if this makes any sense,' Bond said. 'Let's start at the beginning. You were never recruited by MI6 at Cambridge. Instead you were recruited by the CIA when you went to Harvard. Maybe they paid for your graduate studies, just so the cover was good.'

'You're getting warm,' Blessing said.

Bond smiled and continued.

'Then, after your training you were sent to Zanzarim and you got a job with Edward Ogilvy-Grant, UK head of station.' Bond took a slug of his bourbon. 'I would have hired you. Who wouldn't, with your qualifications? You're half-Lowele, you speak the language, your family live in Sinsikrou. Perfect. Somehow I doubt your father was a Scottish engineer.'

'Hotter.'

Bond stood up, lit a cigarette and began pacing around the room.

'For some reason,' he went on, 'the CIA wanted to know what the British were up to in Zanzarim and you became their source. Spying on your ally – we all do it, by the way.' He smiled drily. 'Then you told them

I was coming and was to be infiltrated into Dahum. What happened next?'

Blessing reached for her pack of cigarettes, her blouse falling forward for a moment, and Bond saw that she was wearing no brassiere.

'I shouldn't really tell you anything,' she said.

'Then Felix Leiter will tell me when he gets to town. You might as well.'

She sighed and lit her cigarette. 'I miss Tuskers. Lucky Strikes don't do it for me any more.'

'I suppose they ordered you to come with me.'

'Yes. It was a perfect opportunity. They wanted me to get close to Brigadier Adeka – to offer him asylum in the USA. A safe home, money. Everybody could see the war was ending – he had to go somewhere.'

'Why were they so interested in Adeka?'

'I don't know.'

Bond looked sceptical.

'Seriously, I don't – all I had to do was make the offer to him. Make it seem real.'

Bond poured himself another drink. Blessing declined.

'So you set up the fake office and intercepted me.'

'It wasn't difficult. I was Ed Ogilvy-Grant's secretary. I told him you were coming a week later than you actually were. Set up the office, set up Christmas.

Gave you the new address. Phoned in and said I was ill.'

'It fooled me,' Bond said, remembering. 'I think the Annigoni portrait of the Queen was the master touch.' He paused. 'Were you told to seduce me?'

'No. That was my own idea.'

'Did you know that Kobus Breed was going to hit us?'

'No. I was genuinely planning to come in with you by boat through the creeks. Kojo, the fisherman, didn't speak English. You would've needed an interpreter, anyway. Then Breed showed up.' Her face darkened. 'It kind of threw me . . .'

'So when you ran off in the firefight you'd decided to go it alone.'

'Yes – in all that chaos it seemed the right thing to do at the moment.'

'So who screamed – you?'

'I didn't hear any scream. Just gunfire, shouting, explosions. I found a thick clump of undergrowth and crawled in. Soldiers walked right by me. When dawn came it was all quiet. I was lost for a couple of days – couldn't find my way out of the forest. Then I found a dirt track and I walked down it until I came across a half-ruined convent with three nuns left behind. They fed me and watered me and eventually I made it to Port Dunbar, about two days before the war ended.'

Bond smiled ruefully, thinking of his own fraught journey on the bush paths.

'Yes, I had some fun in the forest as well.'

'A letter of introduction had been sent to Adeka. In fact, I was expected,' she said.

'But the brigadier was dead by the time you arrived.'

'Yes,' she said. 'I never met him.'

'I did,' Bond said. 'He gave me a medal.'

'Sure,' Blessing smiled. 'But I did meet Colonel Denga – and Breed again. I made the same offer to them – come to the US. I made it very clear I had the power to bring all this about. My "letter of accreditation" was pretty explicit. When Adeka died I was told that his brother in London, Gabriel, had been contacted and was going to be set up here. They were prepared to spend a lot of money.'

'They?'

'The CIA.' She paused. 'Gabriel Adeka agreed and so the AfricaKIN operation was moved to DC.'

Bond frowned – the whole thing didn't make much sense to him. He sat down again. He was confident that Blessing was telling him what she knew – but what she knew might be very limited.

'Did Breed tell you I was in Port Dunbar?' Bond asked.

'Of course. I told him I wasn't to be mentioned. Anyway, I hardly saw him – everything seemed to be falling apart.' She smiled. 'I'm good – but I don't know how I would have reacted if you and I had met again, there. Best for you to think I was dead.'

Bond considered – there was logic to this. She was on her own mission; he would have been in the way. Too much confusion.

'Why is the CIA so interested in this African charity?' Bond asked, casually. 'Why bring it to America, set them up in those swanky offices?'

Blessing didn't reply immediately. She spread her arms – a gesture of uncertainty. 'To be honest, I don't really know,' she said. 'They only tell me what they think I need. But my feeling is that the person they're really after is Hulbert Linck.'

'What happened to him?'

'He flew out of Janjaville and nobody's seen him since.'

'Didn't he fly out with you on that last Super Constellation?'

'No. There was a DC-3 there as well. I don't know if you saw it.'

'Every detail of that night is burnt in my memory,' Bond said with a cold smile.

'Linck and Kobus Breed left in the DC-3. I flew out on the Constellation with everybody else.'

It still wasn't making much sense to Bond so he changed tack.

'Why did you shoot me?'

Blessing lowered her head, then looked him squarely in the eye. 'Simple. To save you and to save myself. Did you see that hook Breed had with him? He was going to hang you from that, he told me – told me in some detail. Seems it's his special trademark. Also, Breed was very suspicious of me – because I was with you at the beginning. I think he would have killed me that night, in fact.' She smiled, apologetically. 'Killed me and killed you . . . If I hadn't shot you. I shot you exactly where I wanted to, James. We're trained to know what shots will kill and what shots won't. I knew it wouldn't kill you. And Breed was very impressed. He knew I was serious.'

'Does he know you're with the CIA?'

'No. I just represent interested parties with money and influence. He's convinced – even though I wasn't specific.'

But Bond wasn't convinced. Breed may be a psychopath but he wasn't stupid, he thought. He and Denga would be aware that there was a government agency working here, or something similar – too much money, too much power – and recognise it and exploit it. One thing nagged at him: in all their contacts during the final days at Port Dunbar Breed had never told him Blessing had survived the firefight in the forest. He was impressed with Breed's ability to keep that information to himself. It seemed untypical . . .

He lit another cigarette. 'So – the big surveillance at Milford Plaza is to try and nail Linck.'

'Yes.'

'Why? What's so important about Linck for the CIA?'

'I told you – I don't know. Linck must have something we want. Information – some secret. In the end I don't know. Honestly.'

Bond frowned. He had always had his doubts about Linck. 'I never really thought he was just some crazy romantic millionaire who likes lost causes.'

'I think that's what he wants people to think. But there's something more,' Blessing added. 'There's a lot of pressure on me. Too much. It's not normal and it's not fair, to be honest. I'm right in the heart of AfricaKIN. I'm secure. But Brig and the others can't understand why I can't tell them where Hulbert Linck is – or if he's even alive. Sometimes I think that maybe Breed killed him.'

'It's entirely possible,' Bond said.

Blessing stood up. 'Look, I'm going to have a shower. Maybe we can order up some room service, or something.'

'Let's go out and have a proper meal,' Bond said.

Blessing smiled cynically. 'I don't think I should risk being seen dining out with you, James. What if Kobus Breed got to hear about it?'

'Yes – you're right. It's just that I don't fancy the room-service food in this motel.'

She went into the bedroom and soon Bond heard the shower running. He drank another bourbon while he waited, trying to see how the disparate pieces of this puzzle might fit together. And failed. AfricaKIN, Gabriel Adeka, Hulbert Linck, the CIA . . . Kobus Breed had flown out of Janjaville with Linck. More and more Bond felt that Breed was the key to all this.

Blessing came back into the room. She was wearing a boldly printed orange and black cotton dressing gown – short, cut to mid-thigh and belted at the waist. Bond assumed she was naked underneath. Concentrate, he told himself, retrieve as much information as you can.

'Where's Gabriel Adeka?' he asked.

'He runs everything from a big house in Orange County, Virginia, called Rowanoak Hall. It's a kind of clinic – a medical sorting office. A clearing house for the children.'

'What children?'

'The children that the AfricaKIN flights bring in.' She poured herself a tiny bourbon and sipped at it.

'Interestingly, Adeka pays for the big house, not us.'
She said. 'We only pay for the office space at the plaza.'

'Have you been there? To this house in Orange
County?'

'A couple of times for meetings with Denga. It's
almost like a small hospital – state of the art.' She put
her glass down. 'I'm hungry.'

'Is Breed there?'

'He stays there. He and Denga seem to work closely
together.'

'Old military buddies. Where do these flights
arrive?'

'Not in DC. There's a small airport not too far away
– Seminole Field, forty minutes from the house. The
kids arrive on the flights and they're taken to the house
in ambulances and medically assessed and then they're
sent to specialist hospitals in DC, Maryland, Virginia,
depending on their problems. It's quite an operation.'

She sat down on the sofa, being careful not to let the
hem of her dressing gown ride up. Bond tried to stop
himself looking at her slim brown thighs.

'There's a flight tomorrow, in fact,' she said. 'Quite a
big deal. We've got someone from the State Department
meeting it. It's good cover for us – government partici-
pating, approving.'

'Maybe I should check it out.'

'I thought you were going back to London,' she said.

'I am. But there's no tearing hurry. I'm on leave. Convalescing. Somebody shot me in the chest.'

'I feel I owe you an apology,' she said, reaching for her drink and letting the front of her dressing gown gape for an instant before she closed it with a hand.

Bond took a big gulp of his bourbon – remembering her body, that night at Lokomeji in the rest-house.

'I should go,' he said, his voice hoarser than he would have wished.

'Let me say sorry first,' she said and stood up – unbelting her dressing gown, freeing it to fall from her shoulders and crumple on the carpet.

She allowed Bond to study her for a moment then stooped, picked up her dressing gown, slung it over her arm and sauntered into the bedroom, Bond following. She hung the dressing gown on the hook on the back of the door and smiled at him.

'I'm sorry I shot you,' she said and slipped into the bed. 'But I did it to save your life.'

Bond pulled off his tie and began to undo the buttons on his shirt.

# 8
# Chelsea

B ond and Blessing made love, then ordered food and drink – two omelettes and fries and a bottle of champagne – and, after they'd eaten and drunk, they made love again. She was eager and insisting, giving him precise instructions, at one stage rolling him on to his back and sitting astride him, her hands pressing hard on his chest as she rocked to and fro. Bond did as he was told, revelling in her slim brown body, her lissom youthfulness.

Later, when they lay in each other's arms, she told him that she'd been with no one else since that night they'd been captured by Kobus Breed.

'I thought about you a lot,' she said. 'And when I saw you in the restaurant I felt my heart jump, you know . . .' She laughed quietly. 'My first reaction was pleasure – not alarm. What does that tell you?'

'That you've still got a lot to learn,' Bond said.

She punched him gently on his shoulder and kissed him.

'So teach me,' she said.

Bond slipped out of her room in the small hours, having been given all the details about the AfricaKIN flight and the house in Orange County. He had dressed and kissed her goodbye and gave her naked body a final caress as she lay sleepily on the bed amidst the rumpled sheets.

'I suppose we'd better not meet again,' Bond said. 'Until this is all over.'

'I know what,' she said. 'I'll ask to be posted to London.' She sat up and put her arms round his neck. 'That would be fun, wouldn't it, James? You and me in London. Where do you live?'

'You know where I live.'

'No I don't.'

'Chelsea.'

'You and me in Chelsea . . .' She lay back on the pillows, touching herself. 'Think about it, James . . .'

Bond was tempted to tear his clothes off and climb back in the bed.

'There's no harm in thinking,' he said. He kissed her quickly on the lips and left before his resolve collapsed.

As he crossed from the annexe to the main block of the motel Bond paused, some sixth sense making him draw into the shadows of a doorway. He waited, looking about him. The parking lot was almost full, its corralled cars shining dewily in the glow of the arc lights, like some sort of sleeping mechanical herd in its vast paddock. Nobody moving, nobody to be seen. He waited a couple of minutes but there was nothing to worry him. He strode into the rear of the motel, with a wave to the night porter, and rode the elevator up to his room. He requested the motel operator to give him a wake-up call at 5 a.m., slept for a couple of hours then showered and shaved and, as dawn approached, he went down to the lobby and asked the sleepy doorman to hail him a taxi. Thirty minutes later he was breakfasting in the dining room of the Fairview.

**After breakfast** Bond took a taxi to the BOAC offices on Pennsylvania Avenue and confirmed his return flight to London for the evening of the following day. Now he was glad that he'd booked first class – he could rebook without any problem at the very last minute, and even not showing up was unlikely to be penalised as long as notice was given. He left the offices, hailed a cab and paid the driver $10 to take him round the corner and wait. From the shelter of a doorway he saw agent Massinette stroll into the BOAC offices, no doubt to confirm the flight that Bond was leaving on. The CIA would be reassured and Bond assumed that the surveillance of him would be less thorough. Wait and see. Massinette would acquire the necessary information with a flash of his badge and pass it on to Felix Leiter.

Bond climbed back into his taxi and asked to be returned to the Fairview. There was something about Massinette and his demeanour that troubled Bond – some shortfall in the routine CIA professionalism that Brig Leiter embodied. Bond hadn't liked the sullen, aggressive way that Massinette had stared at him that first time they'd encountered each other. Brig Leiter had zeal, an ethic – that was obvious the minute you met him. Massinette was harder to gauge. Bond told himself to forget it. Maybe Massinette had personal troubles of his own that were souring his view of the world – even agents are human beings, after all.

When he arrived at the Fairview Bond went to the parking lot and sat in his Mustang for five minutes. As soon as he was confident no one was watching him he took a leisurely, roundabout route west to Seminole Field airport.

Seminole Field doubled as a commuting hub for small prop planes flying short journeys to Maryland,

Virginia and Philadelphia and was also home to three Air National Guard squadrons of F-100 Super Sabres. Consequently the runway was long enough to service the largest transport planes and commercial jets. Bond parked his car and, taking his binoculars with him, joined the small crowd of plane-spotters on an elevated knoll outside the perimeter fence that gave a good view of the main runway, the apron and the small control tower and arrival and departure buildings. The Air National Guard hangars were on the far side of the airport. He checked his watch: according to Blessing the AfricaKIN flight was due in from Khartoum in an hour. Scanning the piste with his binoculars he could see that an area had been cordoned off with portable railings and there was a small row of bleachers to one side where a few journalists and photographers lounged, chatting and smoking.

After about thirty minutes a small motorcade of town cars arrived and assorted dignitaries emerged and were shown into the airport buildings. Bond spotted Colonel Denga and Blessing. There were men in suits and a few women in dresses and hats – AfricaKIN sponsors and officials from the Department of the Interior, Bond supposed. The welcome committee had arrived but clearly Gabriel Adeka wasn't attending. Then three ambulances with

'AfricaKIN' logos drove on to the apron and parked in a row, waiting for the plane.

On time, a Boeing 707 swooped into the airport and touched down, causing a murmur of excitement among the plane-spotters. As it taxied in Bond saw that the words 'Transglobal Charter' were written on the side but there, stencilled on the nose, was the now-familiar AfricaKIN logo. The plane came to a halt, the dignitaries applauded and stairs were taken to the main doors. Gurneys were rolled in readiness from the ambulances and paramedics stood by.

Then the doors opened and the children appeared. First, those who could walk, some with their heads and limbs bandaged, some with little arm-crutches, then some very young and frail ones carried by male nurses, and finally those who were laid on the gurneys for the photo opportunity.

Bond focused his binoculars as the dignitaries briefly flanked the children and the flashbulbs popped. Denga was standing at one end of the group – immaculate in a beige seersucker suit – with a junior senator; an undersecretary of state at the other with Blessing. Hands were shaken, a short speech was made and there was a polite spatter of applause. Bond noticed that all the children who could walk were in a kind of uniform: peaked baseball caps, pale blue boiler suits and neat little rucksacks on their backs, all displaying the AfricaKIN Inc. logo. Charitable work and decent altruism marching hand in hand with very effective PR, Bond thought.

Within minutes the children were installed in the ambulances, which wheeled away to a gate in the perimeter fence, lights flashing. Bond loped to his car and drove round to the side entrance, where he was in time to see the last in the small convoy of ambulances turning on to the highway heading west into Orange County. Two police outriders led the way. Bond slowed, allowing some cars to overtake him – it was going to be an easy follow.

After twenty minutes the ambulances turned off the highway and the road and the countryside around it became noticeably more rural. They were barely an hour out of DC, Bond calculated, but already it felt very remote. They passed fewer and fewer houses. There were meadows with horses grazing, dense copses of wood – elm, walnut, ash – and a pleasing, gentle undulation to the landscape – valleys and streams, groups of small grassy hills. It was the country – but very civilised.

Eventually, after passing through a small village called Jackson Point, the ambulances swept through a gate between twin lodges that marked the driveway to Rowanoak Hall, the new headquarters of AfricaKIN

Inc – a far cry from a grubby shop in Bayswater, Bond thought. Here in Rowanoak Hall, Blessing had told him, the children were fed, medicated, assessed and then despatched to the various hospitals in DC and surrounding areas that would best treat the children's wounds, diseases or other ailments. Orphaned children, malnourished, suffering children, children wounded by landmines or ethnic violence, removed from harm's way and brought to safety and succour in the United States of America, no expense spared. African kin indeed, Bond considered: nothing appeared better or more slickly organised or more sanctioned by authority. But what was really going on?

He drove slowly along the country lane that followed the ten-foot-high brick walls of the Rowanoak estate. The house was set in a thickly wooded park, carefully planted in the last century with red mulberry, spruce, cottonwood and hickory trees. There was no extra wiring or alarms fitted to the wall that Bond could see. He pulled into a muddy parking space and shinned up a yellow beech tree that would allow him a better view of the house itself.

Bond focused his binoculars and saw a large and rather ugly red-brick nineteenth-century house constructed in somewhat over-the-top Gothic-revival style. There were battlements, towers, buttresses and

clustered crockets, pinnacles and finials and ginger-
bread trim wherever possible. On the wide gravelled
sweep of the driveway in front of the carriage porch of
the house the three ambulances were parked and, as
Bond watched, they were joined by others sent by the
affiliated AfricaKIN hospitals. An hour later, they were
all gone, the children despatched. Bond wondered how
many other staff remained in the house. From time
to time burly men in black windcheaters with walkie-
talkies wandered around the lawns and disappeared
again. They seemed to be the only evidence of extra
security. Bond supposed that they had to be discreet –
AfricaKIN was a charity, after all. Was Gabriel Adeka
inside? he wondered. And Kobus Breed? He imagined
Breed would stay close to Adeka. As far as he could
tell neither Blessing nor Denga had accompanied the
convoy of ambulances.

Bond climbed stiffly down from his vantage point.
Evening was coming on and the sky was darkening
as he drove round to the main entrance and found a
leafy lane where he could park out of sight but with
a view of the gates themselves. As the working day
ended, he watched as a small procession of private
cars came down the drive from the house, some containing uniformed nurses. There was a man living in
one of the lodges who emerged to open the gates and

close them, chatting amiably to some of the staff as they departed.

When no more cars appeared Bond assumed that Rowanoak Hall was now empty, down to its core staff – just Adeka, perhaps, and Breed and their aides and bodyguards. He couldn't know for sure without climbing in and doing a headcount himself. But not tonight, he thought. Once he entered those walled acres he had to be prepared for anything and anyone. Perhaps Blessing could tell him more about the personnel left behind once the gates closed for the night. He started his car and headed back to DC. He was hungry – he hadn't eaten since breakfast.

# 9
# Blessing

Bond asked at the Fairview's reception where the best steak restaurant in Washington was to be found and was told that the Grill on H Street was the place to go. So Bond took a taxi there and asked for a table for one. He knew exactly what he wanted and, while his vodka martini was being mixed at the bar, he consulted the maître d' – slipping him the obligatory $20 – telling him the white lie that it was his birthday, and that he was a fussy eater – all to make sure things were arranged precisely as he desired them.

Ten minutes later Bond was led into the dining room to his corner table. The napery was thick white linen, the silverware heavy and traditional and the glasses gleamed, speck-free. The Grill on H Street replicated the clubby values of a Victorian steakhouse reimagined for America, a hundred years on: dark panelled walls, low-wattage sconces, gilt-framed oil paintings of sporting scenes and frontier battles, the odd stuffed animal trophy on the wall, a chequerboard marble floor and venerable, grey-haired men in long white aprons serving at table.

Bond's preordered bottle of Chateau Lynch-Bages 1953 had already been decanted and, as he sat down, a small lacquered tray was brought to his table that contained all the ingredients necessary to make a vinaigrette to his own secret formula: a little carafe of olive oil and one of red-wine vinegar, a jar of Dijon mustard, a halved clove of garlic, a black-pepper grinder, a ramekin of granulated sugar, a bowl, a teaspoon and a small balloon whisk to mix the ingredients together.[*]

Bond swiftly made his dressing then his filet mignon – *à point* – arrived with a bowl of salad. He had ordered filet mignon because he didn't want a steak that overlapped his plate. It was nicely chargrilled on the outside, pink but not blue on the inside. Bond dressed the salad, seasoned his steak and took his first mouthful of

---

[*] James Bond's Salad Dressing. Mix five parts of red-wine vinegar with one part extra-virgin olive oil. The vinegar overload is essential. Add a halved clove of garlic, half a teaspoon of Dijon mustard, a good grind of black pepper and a teaspoon of white granulated sugar. Mix well, remove the garlic and dress the salad.

claret. As he ate and drank he allowed himself to enjoy the fantasy that life was good and the world was on its proper course – this being the purpose of eating and drinking well, surely? He ended his meal with half of an avocado into which he poured what remained of his dressing. He drank a calvados, smoked a cigarette and called for the check. His culinary hunger assuaged, a new one replaced it. He was hungry for Blessing, for her slim active body. Hungry for her to give him more precise instructions about what she wanted him to do to her.

**Bond sauntered** into the lobby of the Blackstone Park, said hello to Delmont, who was working that night, and went up to his room. He waited until ten o'clock and strolled back down to the lobby, exiting through the rear doors into the parking lot. The lights in Blessing's suite were on. He felt a hot pulse of antici-pation at seeing her.

He knocked on her door. There was no answer. He knocked again and said 'Blessing – it's James.' Still no answer. He repeated himself more loudly. Nothing. He went back to the night porter at the rear entrance and called her room. The telephone rang and rang – no reply. Odd. The night porter had just come on duty and couldn't enlighten him. Maybe Blessing had come in and had to leave in a hurry, forgetting to switch the lights out . . .

Bond went through to the main lobby and sought out Delmont.

'Hey, Mr Fitzjohn, what can I do for you?'

Bond drew him discreetly aside and lowered his voice.

'Delmont, would you do me a favour? Has my wife come back? You know – the lady in suite 5K in the annexe . . .'

'Give me two seconds.'

Delmont scurried off to reception and swiftly returned.

'She's in her room, Mr F,' he said. 'Arrived about an hour and a half ago. She hasn't left or her key would be there.'

'Of course – thanks, Delmont.' Bond smiled reassuringly but he was worried. He walked casually back to the rear entrance and up the stairs to the second-floor suites. He glanced around but the corridor was empty. He unscrewed the heel from his loafer and worked the blade in between the lock and the door frame. He lunged at it with his shoulder and it gave. Bond pushed the door open.

The lights were on. Blessing's handbag was tossed on the sofa. Thus far, so unremarkable. Had she taken a sleeping pill and was fast asleep in her bedroom?

'Blessing? It's me . . .' Bond said, then repeated himself, louder.

Silence.

Maybe his initial assumption was right – she'd rushed out, called away, urgently. But why leave her handbag . . . ?

Bond felt a premonitory nausea – something was making him reluctant to go into the bedroom. He took a few steps then halted.

A thin dark sticky crescent of blood had seeped under the door to the bedroom.

Bond reached for the handle, turned it and tried to push the door open. It was unusually heavy. Bond gave an unconscious, spontaneous moan because he knew what had happened to Blessing and he knew who had done it.

He stood there in an awful balance of inertia, unable to decide whether to turn away and leave or to confront his darkest suspicions. He felt sick at heart – he knew what he had to do.

He leaned his weight against the door and shoved and pushed it open.

One glance was enough. Blessing was dead – naked, hanging by her jawbone from the hook on the back of the door, blood still dripping from her opened throat.

Bond heaved the door to and sank to his knees.

Kobus Breed.

Bond felt the tears smart in his eyes as he hung his head and thought desperately about Blessing and what she must have endured, a conflagration of outrage making him tremble, igniting his seething anger. Then he stood up, his head clearing. He inhaled deeply – the shock was draining from him to be replaced by a new granite-hard resolve. There was nothing so invigorating as clear and absolute purpose. There was only one objective now. James Bond would kill Kobus Breed.

# 10

# One-Man Commando

B ond called Brig Leiter from the Fairview. It was
after midnight.

'Red alert, Brig,' Bond said, his voice heavy. 'Bad
news – your agent has been erased. I'm very sorry.'

'What? Jesus, no. Aleesha? Where is she? In her
house?'

'No, in a motel. It's very nasty. Blackstone Park
Motor Lodge, suite 5K.'

Silence. Bond could almost hear Brig's brain
working.

'How do you know?'

'I saw her.'

'What was she doing in a motel? And how come you
were in her room?'

'She moved. I think she felt safer in a motel.'

'Who killed her?'

'Kobus Breed.'

'My God . . .' there was another pause, then, 'You didn't answer my second question, Mr Bond.'

'I went to her room to ask her something.'

'How did you know she was staying there?'

'I followed her.'

'OK . . . Felix is coming up tonight from Miami.'

'I'm going to miss him,' Bond said. 'I go back to London tonight.' Now Bond paused to let the lie sink in.

'Brig, I don't know what procedures you follow in these circumstances,' Bond said, 'but I think you should get a team round to that motel now and seal the room. I put a "Do not disturb" sign on the door. Lock it down. I wouldn't call the police for twenty-four hours, also. Wait till Felix gets here. He can coordinate with them. You don't want Breed to make a run for it.'

'Yeah, you're right,' Brig said. 'What time's your plane?'

'Nine o'clock this evening.' Let them think for as long as possible that he was going home, he reasoned. They had more important tasks on their hands than worrying about James Bond.

They said goodbye and Bond hung up. He undressed and stood under the pounding shower as if the water would wash away all his bad feelings, his memories of Blessing and her miserable death. Then he tried to sleep but his mind grew busy with the plan that he was forming. He needed to equip himself better if he was going to attack the Rowanoak estate single-handed. He turned his pillow over and rested his cheek on the cooler underside. Why had Breed killed Blessing? There could only be one answer. Breed had followed her to the motel and had seen Blessing with him – Blessing back in contact with James Bond . . . That would have been enough to confer a death sentence on her. Bond recalled that sixth-sense shiver he'd experienced in the parking lot when he left her suite in the annexe – had Kobus Breed been out there watching in the darkness? And Bond knew that the manner of Blessing's death had been a warning directed at him. Breed knew that he could read the signs; Breed was saying to him, I know you're out there – you're next, Bond.

He thought on. Breed hadn't done anything immediately because he wanted to wait until after the flight had arrived and was happy to let Blessing continue with her AfricaKIN duties. So: there must have been something on that flight that came in to Seminole Field that was especially important. Twelve sick children? There had to be something more.

Bond ordered breakfast in his room but only smoked a cigarette and drank a cup of coffee, leaving his eggs untouched. He wasn't hungry. As he left the Fairview he saw Agent Massinette approaching. Bond greeted him amiably enough but Massinette's face remained impassive.

'Brig told me to tell you – we're all locked down at the Blackstone Park. The room's sealed.'

'Good. It should buy you some time.'

'May I ask where you're going, Mr Bond?'

'I'm going to do some shopping – some gifts for friends in London.'

'Yeah? Have a nice day.'

**That evening,** Bond laid out everything he needed on the bed. Weapons: the Frankel and Kleist, fully loaded and with spare rounds of ammunition; his Beretta with two extra clips; the mugger's switchblade with its diamond inlay; a small aerosol canister of OC – oleoresin capsicum pepper spray (concentrate of chilli pepper with the brand name Savage Heat) – and, finally, a sock filled with $10-worth of nickels and dimes, knotted tight to form a cosh. As for his clothing, Bond had bought a black leather blouson jacket with big patch pockets, a black polo-neck jersey, a black knitted three-hole balaclava and a length of nylon rope. He was going to wear his dark charcoal trousers from his suit tucked into his socks with a pair of black sneakers with thick rubber soles.

He smiled grimly to himself. A one-man commando on a one-man commando raid.

He had a final telephone call to make then he would check out of the hotel and head for the airport. He sat down on his bed and took out Turnbull McHarg's business card.

**It was** dark when Bond drove his Mustang up to the Fairview's entry-way and the bellhop placed his luggage in the boot. Bond tipped him and glanced around to see if anyone was paying particular attention to his departure. No sign of Massinette but, Bond reasoned, if he were Brig Leiter running this show he'd have a tail on Bond. Routine. Insurance.

Bond drove out to Dulles airport. He couldn't tell if he was being followed. There was a lot of traffic heading out of town. Not far from the airport he pulled into a gas station and filled the tank, watching to see if cars stopped or slowed. He spotted nothing so climbed back into his car and swung out on to the highway back into town, steadily increasing his speed. At the last minute he turned off at an intersection, changed direction and headed back to the airport again. He began to relax.

He sped past the turn for Dulles and veered off into the quiet streets of Ashburn and drove around for ten minutes or so, stopping and starting, doubling back suddenly and unpredictably. No one was following him; he could safely choose his own route back out to Rowanoak Hall.

**Bond parked** the car down a track not far from the house and changed into his dark clothes. He looked at his watch; ten past eleven. By now Brig and Felix Leiter would know full well that he wasn't on the plane for London. Bond had vanished – one rogue male agent gone solo yet again. It was a calculated risk, this solitary assault on the AfricaKIN Inc. headquarters, and he asked himself if Felix might second-guess what he was planning. He doubted it. Only a fool would attempt such a thing. He wondered if they would try to capture Breed – but again he thought they would hold off. Blessing had said that she thought Hulbert Linck was the key target; the CIA wouldn't want to do anything that would scare him away. All in all, Bond reckoned he had this one night to himself. Whatever happened, there would be no second chance for him – his vengeance had to take place in the next few hours before the CIA tracked him down and pulled him in.

He wound the nylon rope around his body and assembled the Frankel and Kleist. Then he filled the pockets of his jacket with his assorted weaponry. He hoped there weren't dogs – he had seen no sign of them – but he had his OC spray just in case. He had once halted a snarling, slavering Dobermann with a blast of pepper spray – it was infallible.

He drove to the furthest point of the Rowanoak estate and parked the Mustang against the brick perimeter wall. He climbed on to the car roof and shinned over the wall, carefully dropping the rifle (safety catch secured) on to the grass on the other side before he lowered himself down. He pulled on his balaclava and moved off through the wooded park towards the distant lights of the house.

As he drew near the Hall he saw a man standing on the back lawn of the house smoking a cigarette. He appeared to have a walkie-talkie in his hand as he paced about, keeping notional guard. The back lawn was illuminated by a powerful arc light high on the fake battlements. The front sweep of gravel was equally brightly lit – no one could approach the house without stepping into this wide glaring disc of light.

Bond moved easily through the trees and bushes of the park so that he could afford himself a good view of the main facade. Here two big lamps threw a pool of light that extended down the drive to the gatehouses. Bond found his ideal position behind a small sycamore and set the Frankel on a low branch to give him a steady firing platform. Bond clicked the switch on the scope to set it to its night-vision mode. Eugene Goodforth had been right – the dimmed red glow of the reticle did not interfere with the vision beyond. Bond's eye settled to the lens of the sniper-scope and he cleared his aim and waited. Five minutes to midnight. He hoped his diversion would be punctual.

In fact it was ten minutes late, but no matter. At ten past midnight Bond saw the headlights of Turnbull McHarg's car pull up at the lodge gates and heard him toot his horn loudly and peremptorily, as Bond had instructed him. When Bond had telephoned him earlier he'd invited Turnbull to a 'surprise' birthday party that wealthy friends were throwing for him at a big mansion house out of town, Rowanoak Hall. He'd given Turnbull precise directions and instructions. Should be fun. Lots of caviar and champagne. And girls. McHarg had been delighted. I'll be there, James. Look forward to seeing you – lots to catch up on. Thanks a million.

Bond knew they'd never let McHarg past the gates but that was all he wanted. A disturbance – something wrong – and his name pointedly mentioned. He could hear McHarg's voice raised, loudly remonstrating with the intransigent lodge-keeper, demanding entry to the party, insisting he'd been specially invited by the birthday boy himself, James Bond.

Bond drew the Frankel snug against his cheek and settled the cross hairs of the reticle on the first arc light. The sound of the big bulb popping almost drowned the gunshot. He shifted aim and took the second light out. In the sudden darkness Bond heard McHarg's profane exclamation of shock and astonishment, then he raced off into the darkness towards the rear of the house.

Secure in a position facing the back of the house, he quickly shot out the rear arc. Only the lights of the house now glowed and he could hear the consternation inside – shouts, doors slamming. Bond slipped the scope off the mountings on the barrel of the Frankel and slid the rifle under a bush – its job was done. He retreated into the darkness of the park, taking the Beretta out of his pocket and cocking it. As he left he saw three men race out of the rear door, guns and powerful torches in hand, running across the lawn, spreading out until they were swallowed up by the wilderness of the park, only the intermittent beams of their torches giving their positions away. Bond tracked them as best he could with the scope. Three guards, Bond thought, and no dogs – thank God. He stood with his back to a tree scanning the pulsing night around him, waiting for a guard to come close – once he had one, he'd have the others. Always wait for them to come to you, he told himself, don't go searching for your prey. He slowed his breathing as much as he could, standing absolutely still, gun poised, waiting.

It was the crackle of a walkie-talkie that alerted him, rather than a torch beam. Then he saw the torch, playing among the trees. He heard the man's voice.

'Dawie – can't see a thing, man. You sure he's in the park? Over.'

There was the inaudible static of a reply.

Dawie, Bond thought: interesting. Some of Kobus's RLI buddies from Dahum.

The man drew closer but he never heard Bond, who, as he passed, brought down the heel of his Beretta on the back of his head. He dropped at once, inert. Bond quickly lashed his hands behind his back and then tied his wrists to his ankles, using the switchblade to cut lengths of nylon rope. He ripped up a clod of earth and stuffed the man's gaping mouth with turf. Then he fired his gun once into the air. He picked up the walkie-talkie, shouted 'Dawie!' fired again and switched it off.

Bond could hear somebody blundering through the bushes then saw a swaying torch beam sweeping through the trees. The man – it must have been Dawie

– was shouting harshly into his walkie-talkie trying to summon the third guard to join them.

'Henrick – over here, man,' he shouted. 'We're by the west gate.'

Bond aimed slightly above the torch beam and fired twice. He heard a scream and saw the torch spin to the ground. Dawie started bellowing.

'I'm down! I'm down! He's over here!'

Bond crept forward as Dawie continued his shouted instructions, guiding Henrick towards him. Then he saw Henrick's jerky torch beam as he ran through the trees.

Bond took his time, making sure he advanced in total silence. Dawie was moaning in pain and Henrick was crouched over his writhing body, looking for the wound. Bond took his nickel-and-dime cosh out of his pocket and slugged Henrick full on the crown of his head. He went down like a cow hit by a humane killer. He was so still Bond wondered if he'd delivered some kind of fatal blow. He held his fingers to his throat. There was a pulse – a thready one.

'I'm dying. Help me,' Dawie said. Bond turned Dawie's fallen torch on him and saw that he'd been hit low and to the side of his abdomen – not fatal, though he was already pallid from blood loss. Bond said nothing, grabbing his collar and dragging him – groaning – to a tree, where he bound his arms behind it. He checked Henrick again – still breathing but out cold. He roped his wrists together and turned him on his side so that he wouldn't drown if he vomited. He fired both their guns into the air a few times then slung them away into the darkness. He wanted whoever was still in the house to think the guards were engaged in a firefight in the furthest reaches of the park. When it all went quiet they would begin to worry – maybe panic: they had no idea how many potential assailants were out there.

He took one last look at Dawie and picked up his walkie-talkie.

'I got him!' Bond yelled into the microphone. Then switched it off.

'If you shout loud enough someone will come for you,' Bond said to Dawie. He knew it wasn't true – he just wanted a few distant incoherent bellowings to be heard back at the house.

'Don't leave me, man,' Dawie said plaintively, then added with surprising poetry, 'I can feel my life flowing out of me, leaving me. I can feel it.'

Bond said nothing and headed off towards the house.

Some of the ground-floor windows were lit up, others had their curtains drawn, Bond observed as he approached. Through a gap in the curtains of the large oriel window of the main drawing room Bond saw Kobus Breed – his jacket off, his tie loosened at his throat – talking urgently on the phone. From time to time he broke off to shout into the walkie-talkie then hurled it away – obviously the lack of response from Dawie's channel was making him furious.

Bond paused outside – he didn't want to go into the house as he had no idea who else might be in there. Better to try and lure Breed outside into the darkness. Then he decided it might be a more efficient plan to climb and maybe break in on a higher floor and he began hauling himself quickly up one of the heavy lead downpipes that drained the roof gutters. In a few seconds he found himself up on the faux battlements with their Gothic buttresses, polygonal chimney pots and profusion of carved stone finials. Bond's mind was working fast – sensing opportunities, weighing up options, minimising risk. He headed for a dark window and accidently bumped into one of the finials decorating a stumpy brick chimney stack. He felt the masonry slide and grate and the round stone ball on the top almost wobbled free. Bond steadied it. It was about the size of a medicine ball and must have weighed close to fifty pounds. He smiled to himself – he had an idea.

He removed Dawie's walkie-talkie from his pocket and switched it on. He turned the channel frequency selection knob very slightly to one side so that it kept connecting and then cutting out. Through gritted teeth and strangulating his voice he repeated certain phrases into the microphone.

'Come in – over – Bond – I have him – come in, come in – not receiving – Bond, repeat Bond, I have him, over.'

He assumed this garbled message would be picked up by Breed and others listening in. Then he searched his pockets for loose change in vain, before he remembered he was carrying a sock full of nickels and dimes. He unpicked the knot and helped himself to a small handful. He crept round the battlements until he had a good angle on to the drawing room's oriel window. He leaned out and flung the small coins down at the glass and heard them rattle and ping as they hit. Then he threw another handful. He raced back to the finial he had nearly dislodged and, with both arms functioning as a cradle, heaved off the crowning stone ball. It was a dense dead weight, incredibly heavy. He shuffled with it to the edge of the battlements that projected out over the wide door that led from the drawing room to the lawn. Come on, Kobus, he said to himself, muscles straining – you must be curious, Bond is out there, Dawie has him.

The door opened slowly and a wand of light from the drawing room fell across the lawn.

Kobus Breed stepped out cautiously, a gun levelled in his hand.

'Dawie?' he shouted into the blackness. 'Where the hell are you, man? You're not coming through on your radio! You keep breaking up!'

Bond looked down on him, his muscles beginning to ache horribly. Breed's head was a small target from this height – but he wanted to crush it like a ripe cantaloupe melon.

Breed stepped out another yard, his gun sweeping to and fro, expecting the danger to lie in the park beyond, not from above.

'Dawie – show yourself! Have you got him?'

Bond dropped the stone ball and took a step back. He heard the impact – the sound of meaty crunching, bone and flesh compacting – and Breed's bellow of acute, hideous agony and surprise.

He peered down. Breed was on the ground, writhing and moaning, his right arm flapping uncontrollably like some broken wing on a bird. The ball had missed his head but seemed to have landed square on his right shoulder, shattering bone, pulverising it.

Bond slid down the drainpipe and, back on the ground, cautiously approached round the side of the building, slipping his Beretta from his pocket. He should just kill him, he thought, but he wanted Breed to know why he was dying, why his pain and imminent execution were recompense for what he'd done to Blessing. There'd be no point in just blowing him away. Bond wanted to taste sweet revenge.

Bond levelled his gun as he drew near. Breed was face down – the stone ball beside his head – and was clearly in massive, intolerable pain and shock. His whole body was now jerking and twitching spasmodically. The stone ball's impact looked like it had shattered the shoulder blade – and the collarbone. The down-force of the dead weight had also blasted the humerus into pieces. Three inches of thick sheared bone stuck through Breed's shirt at the elbow.

Bond turned Breed over with his foot. Breed screamed as his shattered arm dug into the turf of the lawn. But in the good hand that had been underneath his body he had clung on to his automatic pistol. He fired at Bond and missed – his hand was shaking visibly – and fired again, this time the bullet striking Bond's gun and spinning it off and away in a shower of sparks. Bond threw himself down, knees first, on to Breed's chest and felt ribs crack and his sternum bend. He side-kicked Breed's gun from his hand and rummaged in his jacket pocket for the switchblade. No switchblade but the small aerosol can of Savage Heat pepper spray.

Bond sprayed Breed's un-closable open eye with a thick mist of oleoresin capsicum and heard his scream rip up from deep in his lungs. Breed's right arm was useless so Bond stood on his left and let him writhe in the full torment of his pain, his legs kicking convulsively, the potent reduction of chilli peppers working on his seething eyeball. Breed wailed like a baby and Bond happily enveloped his head in another mist-cloud of Savage Heat.

'This is for Blessing, you filth, you scum,' he said, harshly, bending over him, 'and this is from me,' and sprayed his open eye again from a range of one inch.

Bond reached into his other pocket for the switch-blade. He shot the blade out and tugged Breed brutally over on to his front again, burying the knife deep in the back of his neck, severing the spinal cord. Breed's body jerked and then went slack, his screams dying to a burble of popping saliva in his throat.

Bond stepped back, breathing heavily, a little astonished at his own savagery. He massaged his tingling right hand and reminded himself of what Blessing had gone through – no tender mercies from Kobus Breed. He was angry with himself, however: never again, he thought – execute when the moment presents itself. Emotion – desire for just revenge – had undermined his professionalism, and had almost killed him. If you intend

to kill – kill. Don't hang around wanting to embel-
lish the act in some way. He could hear Corporal Dave
Tozer's harsh voice in his ear: 'DR, you stupid bastard.
Disproportionate Response. Any threat – massive over-
kill. If he spits at you – tear his throat out. If he kicks
you in the shin, take his leg off. Take both legs off.'

Bond began to calm. He looked down at Breed's
body – a mugger's switchblade sticking out of the back
of his neck. He could be carted away later. The fact
that no one had appeared from the house when the
shots were fired was a good sign. Bond roved around
and found his gun. Breed's second round had hit just in
front of the trigger, scarring the metal with a raw weal.
He cocked the gun, shot the clip out, slammed it back
in. It seemed to be working fine.

He took off his balaclava and wiped the smear of
sweat from his face. He pushed through the garden
door into the drawing room and began to move quickly
and watchfully through the public rooms: a library, a
smaller sitting room then down a parqueted corridor
towards the main hall with its wide solid staircase.
Every now and then Bond paused and listened – but
he could hear nothing that suggested there was anyone
else in the house.

A pair of modern swing doors led off the hall behind
the staircase. Bond pushed them open and saw that

here the decor changed completely. Another wide corridor stretched before him, painted pistachio green with white rubberised tiles on the floor. It looked like a hospital and from behind closed doors – inset with panels of glass – came the hum of machinery. Bond peered into one room – incubators, centrifuges, sterilisers, freezers. Another room was fitted out like a ward with four beds and a nurse's station. Other doors were labelled 'X-ray' and 'Dispensary'. There was an office with the name 'Dr Masind' on it – a name that seemed vaguely familiar. This was clearly the state-of-the-art receiving clinic for the children from the AfricaKIN flights.

Bond kept listening and kept hearing nothing that alarmed him. He wondered where Gabriel Adeka was – upstairs? Perhaps he should turn back and explore the upper floors. Then he arrived at the end of the long corridor. To the left was a door and to the right a flight of stone stairs that led down to a basement or cellar area. He pushed open the door to find himself in a kind of schoolroom with two rows of desks facing a blackboard. On the floor in front of the blackboard was a pile of what looked like discarded clothing. Bond switched on the light to see that it wasn't clothing but little rucksacks – the rucksacks the kids had been wearing when they disembarked. Bond picked one up – its bottom had been ripped out. He picked up another similarly torn open. All the rucksacks appeared to have been cut apart.

He turned to switch out the light and saw another rucksack intact on a side table. Beside the rucksack was a Stanley knife. And beside it was a neat stack of what looked like slabs of putty, wrapped in cellophane. Bond picked one up – eight inches long, four wide, one inch thick – about 500 grams, he reckoned. This must have been what Breed was occupied with when Turnbull McHarg had tooted his horn and Bond had shot the arc lights out. Bond picked up the knife and cut away the bottom of the rucksack to reveal in the lining another slab of what he now realised was raw heroin moulded into a flat bar, the size of half a brick. Twelve sick kids, twelve little rucksacks, six kilos of heroin. Who was going to search a malnourished child shivering with fever? Or an eight-year-old amputee? As drug-smuggling went it was heartless, brutal, simple and extremely effective. Each AfricaKIN flight must have its quota of—

Bond heard something – a cough.

He froze, then switched off the light and stepped back into the corridor. He heard the cough again, coming from down the stairs in the basement – lung-racking and feeble. Was there a child down there,

Bond wondered? Some sort of isolation ward for the extremely contagious?

He levelled his gun and began to move carefully down the stairs. There was a night light set in the ceiling that gave off a pale pearly glow revealing a wide landing with two doors off it. The cough came again. No child – an adult, Bond thought. There was a key in the lock of the door behind which the coughing continued. He put his ear to the door and heard the sound of laboured breathing. Bond turned the key and then the handle, and shoved it gently open, his gun pointing into the room. The landing light provided enough illumination for Bond to see that there was a man lying on a mattress in the far corner. He groped for a switch, found it and clicked on the light.

The man was shivering, knees drawn up to his chest, lying on a befouled sheet. An African man, naked except for a pair of filthy underpants. He turned towards Bond and muttered something. His head was shaven and he had a small goatee beard. Gabriel Adeka.

Bond stepped forward, recoiling slightly from the feculent smell. Gabriel Adeka in the grip of terrible cold turkey. His face and shaved head were shiny with sweat and his whole body shook with recurring tremors. On a table across the room was an enamel kidney dish, a Bunsen burner attached to a camping gas canister, a length of rubber tubing, some spoons and several syringes still wrapped in their plastic seals. All the paraphernalia required for shooting up heroin.

Bond was thinking hard – so this was why no one saw Gabriel Adeka any more. Breed had turned him into a junkie and kept him locked in this cellar, no doubt on a regime of drug-injection and then deprivation, turning him into this dehumanised, desperate addict.

Gabriel Adeka reached out a shivering hand to Bond, his big eyes imploring, beseeching. Give me more, I beg you, give me my nirvana in a needle.

Except it wasn't Gabriel Adeka, Bond now saw, and grew rigid at the recognition. The last time he'd seen this man he had been lying in a hospital bed in Port Dunbar. Brigadier Solomon Adeka, military genius, the 'African Napoleon', begging for a syringe full of heroin.

'It's a terrible thing, addiction,' a voice said. 'Put your gun down on the table and turn round very slowly.'

Bond did as he was told and laid his gun down beside the syringes and swivelled round carefully.

Standing in the doorway was the tall lanky figure of Hulbert Linck – except his blond hair was cut short and dyed black and he had a full beard. He was wearing a tan canvas windcheater and jeans and was covering Bond with an automatic pistol. He stepped into the room, glancing at Adeka.

'Forgive the precaution, Mr Bond – I hope you understand. This is all Kobus Breed's doing,' he said. 'Breed has kept me and Adeka here prisoners while he and his men use the charity to smuggle drugs into the USA. He's becoming extremely rich extremely fast.' Linck smiled. 'Funny that it should be you, Bond, who's come to our rescue.' He lowered his gun and put it on the table beside Bond's.

'We are very happy to surrender ourselves to you,' Linck said. 'Very happy.'

The first shot hit Linck just in front of his left ear sending a fine skein of blood spraying from his head and the second smashed into his chest, slamming him heavily against the wall. He slid down it, leaving a thin smeary trail of blood and toppled over. Adeka screamed and gibbered, huddling in the corner.

Agent Massinette irrupted into the room, gun levelled at Adeka. He was followed immediately by Brig Leiter. Bond heard the clatter of other footsteps coming down the corridor overhead.

'You OK, Mr Bond?' Brig Leiter said.

Bond had his eyes on Massinette, who was crouching over Linck's body searching his pockets.

'Why the fuck did you shoot him?' Bond said, his voice heavy with fury.

Massinette turned and stood up.

'He had a gun and was going to kill you.'

'He was putting his gun down. He was surrendering to me.'

'It didn't look like that from the bottom of the stairs,' Brig said. 'We couldn't take any chances.'

Massinette stooped and took something from Linck's pocket. He had another gun in his hand, a little Smith and Wesson .22 revolver, it looked like.

'This was in his pocket, Mr Bond,' Massinette said. 'He was fooling you. He had other plans.'

Bond looked at the two agents.

'I apologise,' he said, though he knew full well that Massinette had just planted the second gun on Linck's body. But why? He stopped himself from trying to answer that question as Felix Leiter came into the room.

'You took your time,' Bond said. 'Still, very pleased to see your ugly face.'

They shook hands warmly. Right hand to left hand.

'The company you keep, James,' Felix said, tut-tutting with a smile. 'Where's Kobus Breed?'

'Out on the back lawn – dead. I'll show you. You'd better get some medical help for Adeka here. He's in a bad way.'

'I'll get on to it,' Brig said, taking a walkie-talkie out of his pocket and calling for an ambulance and medics.

Bond and Felix climbed the stairs and moved through the clinic towards the hallway.

Felix clapped Bond on the back.

'Your friend Mr McHarg called the police with some story about a mansion, gunshots and someone called James Bond. When we'd discovered you weren't on the plane to London we'd put out an APB on you. The police called us and asked if this Bond fellow was part of our operation. Very clever, James.'

'Sometimes you earn your own luck,' Bond said, deciding not to mention his suspicions of Massinette just at this moment. For all he knew Brig Leiter may have been a part in the assassination of Hulbert Linck and he wanted to ensure his facts were right before any accusations were made.

Bond paused in the hallway and looked up the stairs. Linck must have been waiting up there somewhere, he supposed. But why would the CIA want Linck dead . . . ?

'Got a cigarette?' Bond asked.

Felix reached into his pocket with his good hand and shook out a packet of Rothmans. Then with the elaborate titanium device that had replaced his other hand – a small curved hook and two other hinged digits – he took out a book of matches. Bond watched in some amazement as the claw selected, ripped off and lit a match before applying it to the end of Bond's cigarette.

Bond inhaled deeply, relishing the tobacco rush.

'That's quite a gadget you've got there,' he said. 'New model?'

'Yeah,' Felix said with a grin. 'I can pick gnat shit out of pepper with this baby.'

Bond laughed. 'Thank God you're here, Felix. Have I got a tale to tell you. Come on, I'll show you Breed first.'

They went to the main drawing room and Bond pushed through the garden doors and stepped out on to the lawn.

Kobus Breed had disappeared.

# 11

# A Spy on Vacation

'We found two guards,' Leiter said. 'One of them had almost bled to death and the other was trussed up like a Thanksgiving turkey.'

It was dawn and they were standing on the gravelled sweep in front of the house. An ambulance had taken Adeka to hospital while police and forensic teams were searching the building. Forty kilos of heroin had been recovered.

'The third guard was called Henrick,' Bond said, leaning against a police car. 'I slugged him – but he seemed so unconscious I didn't bother to bind his ankles. He must have come round, untied himself somehow, gone back to the house and found Breed's body. Must have carted it away for some reason.'

'You sure you killed Breed?' Felix asked.

'I *was* sure,' Bond said. 'Now I don't know. He was shockingly injured.'

Bond felt sick and angry with himself. Had Henrick simply wanted to deny the authorities a corpse? Or had there been some vital sign of life in Breed's ruined body? Was Breed lying at the bottom of some river nearby weighted with stones? Or was he in some secret surgical theatre being put back together? Bond was troubled – perhaps the *coup de grâce* of the switchblade had just missed.

'Don't worry about Breed,' Felix said. 'We'll pick him up. If you did the damage you say you did he'll have to find a doctor or go to a hospital. Or maybe he'll just die.'

'Possibly,' Bond said, wondering if there was any way Breed could be realistically patched up. His right shoulder and arm had been shattered, pulverised. He wondered what kind of new deformities a living Kobus Breed would display.

'Don't look so serious, James,' Felix said. 'You broke up a giant drug-smuggling operation. We got the bad guys – most of them – and saved Gabriel Adeka. Not bad for a British spy on vacation.'

Bond decided to tell Felix the reality of the situation.

'He's not Gabriel Adeka,' Bond said, flatly.

'You need to go back to your hotel, take a shower, have some breakfast, sleep for a day – and you'll be your old self again.'

'I'm sorry, Felix,' Bond said. 'That man's not Gabriel Adeka – he's Solomon Adeka. Brigadier Solomon Adeka, former C.-in-C. of the Dahum armed forces. He's disguised as Gabriel Adeka – people are meant to think he's Gabriel Adeka. But he isn't.'

'How do you know?' Felix wasn't smiling any more.

'Because I've met him. And I've met his brother. I recognised him. I know them both.'

'Can you prove it?'

'Yes. But . . .'

'But what?'

'It's complicated.'

'Let nothing stand in the way of proof, James.'

'All right,' Bond said, calling Felix's bluff. 'Can you whistle us up an aeroplane?'

# 12

# Zanzarim Revisited

B ond felt very strange being back in Port Dunbar. It was as if the events between his last visit and this one had taken place in a malign parallel universe. Here he was standing in the cemetery that ringed the small cathedral almost exactly in the same location – at the back, the modest spire of the cathedral to his left – as when he had witnessed Brigadier Solomon Adeka's funeral. Except that this time he was alongside Felix Leiter and the guard of honour had been replaced by a magistrate and his clerk, some officials from the interim government of Zanzarim and a small, tracked, orange excavator that was manoeuvring into position in front of Solomon Adeka's grave.

Twenty-four hours after the events at Rowanoak Hall, Felix and Bond had been flown out of Andrews

Field on a USAF Boeing 707 transport. They had been met at Sinsikrou airport by the American ambassador to Zanzarim and then, in a small convoy of embassy cars, they had been driven down the transnational highway to Port Dunbar, where government officials received them at the cathedral and informed them that all relevant permissions and waivers from the ecclesiastical authorities for the disinterment of Solomon Adeka's body had been granted. Bond had been impressed by the level of power and influence such despatch had displayed. It seemed that Felix Leiter just had to snap his fingers and all his demands were met. Why such efficient haste? Bond wondered.Why were they being treated like visiting dignitaries? Once again he felt there were other agendas beside his own that were for the moment invisible to him. He was also aware – because he knew Felix so well – that he was not telling him everything. No matter: he could bide his time because Felix would indeed tell him if he insisted – they were too good and too old a pair of friends to hold anything back if total honesty was demanded. But Bond decided it might be more interesting to watch and wait.

Driving through the city towards the cathedral, Bond could see from the windows of their limousine that Port Dunbar had reclaimed its usual bustle and energy. The journey south had also demonstrated that almost every sign of the civil war was being swiftly erased. There were some temporary Bailey bridges across rivers; here and there a few burnt-out vehicles waited to be carried away for scrap. And there were many more Zanza Force soldiers on the streets – manning checkpoints, directing traffic – than was normal for a peaceful country. All the same, Bond thought, you would hardly believe a bitter civil war had raged here for two years, remembering the time he'd spent in the beleaguered Republic of Dahum as it entered its final days and hours. Once again he thought it was as if he'd existed in a parallel universe or a dream of some kind. A bad dream, Bond corrected himself, because it featured Kobus Breed.

There was a call from the graveside and Bond and Felix made their way towards the small crowd that had gathered now that the key moment was at hand.

The tracks of the digger clattered noisily as it lined itself up and its lobster claw delicately began to scrape away the packed earth in front of the gravestone.

'I remember this funeral well,' Bond said. 'It was all very elaborate and formal. Very cleverly planned – orations, rifle salutes, grieving populace . . . How is Adeka anyway, have you heard?'

'They say he's doing very well,' Felix said. 'Getting the best possible help. Should make a full recovery.'

'Must be strange coming back from the dead.'

'Ha-ha,' Felix said, drily. He was still highly sceptical, but he knew this was the one and only way of proving or disproving Bond's claim.

The lid of the coffin was revealed and six gravediggers stepped forward. After some diligent spadework the whole of the coffin was uncovered and heavy strapping was tied to its brass handles and attached to the digger's boom. Slowly, easily, the coffin was raised, lifted clear of the earth and lowered to the ground. Two of the gravediggers prised open the lid with jemmies.

The gasp of astonishment from those peering in was almost comic. Three sacks of cement were removed and laid beside each other on the parched turf.

Felix looked serious and prodded a sack with his foot as if it might suddenly become corporeal. He looked at Bond.

'Looks like three sacks of cement to me,' Bond said.

'Well, I'll be hog-tied,' Felix said, not amused. 'You were right.'

Bond shrugged modestly.

'So,' Felix said, 'if the man we've got is Solomon Adeka, where's his brother Gabriel?'

Bond lit a cigarette. 'I suspect that if I took you to a small shop in Bayswater and you dug up the concrete floor you'd find his mortal remains.' He paused, thinking. 'It was all very elaborately planned.'

Felix looked shrewdly at Bond.

'Do you know what's going on, James?'

'About eighty per cent, I reckon,' Bond said with a smile. 'I have a feeling you might be able to supply the missing twenty.'

Felix prodded a bag of cement again with his shoe, thinking. Then he looked up.

'Let's go and get a serious drink someplace,' he said.

**The Grand Central Hotel** in Port Dunbar had possessed a variety of names in its short history: the Schloss Gustavberg, the Relais de la Côte d'Or and the Royal Sutherland. Now it was the bland Grand Central, having been requisitioned by the Dahum junta for use as its centre of government bureaucracy during the civil war. It was as if all that history was meant to be effaced by the re-christening. The Grand Central heralded a new and more prosperous future.

There was a bar on the ground floor with a wide veranda that looked over the newly renamed main street – Victory Boulevard. The veranda was crowded so Bond and Felix found a seat in a dark corner underneath a whirring ceiling fan. Bond surveyed the clientele – half a dozen black faces, all the rest white – and all men, men in suits, perspiring over their cold beers.

Bond signalled a waiter over.

'Do you have gin?' he asked.

'Yes, sar. We have everything now. Gordon's or Gilbey's.'

'Good. Bring me a bottle of Gordon's, two glasses, a bucket of ice and some limes. Do you have limes?'

'Plenty, plenty, sar.'

The ingredients were brought to their table. Bond filled the glasses to the brim with ice then poured a liberal few slugs of gin on to the ice and squeezed the juice of half a lime into each glass.

'It's called an African dry martini,' Bond said. 'Cheers, Felix.'

They clinked glasses and drank. The gin was ideally chilled, Bond thought, and the freshness of the lime juice took the edge off the alcohol. They both lit cigarettes, Felix holding his delicately between two of the pincers of his tungsten claw.

'So, Felix,' Bond said, looking at him squarely. 'We know each other too well. Total honesty from us both. Deal?'

'Nothing but,' Felix said.

'Shall I start the inquisition?'

'Fire away, Torquemada.'

Bond paused.

'Why did Massinette kill Linck?' Bond saw Felix's eyes flicker – he wasn't expecting the unravelling of the story to begin there, obviously. He drew on his cigarette, nodded, pursed his lips, buying a few more seconds.

'Because he was going to kill you.'

'Not so. Linck had just "surrendered" to me. He'd put his gun on the table.'

'He had another gun. It was a ruse.'

'Massinette planted that gun,' Bond said. 'I saw him do it.' He paused again. 'Massinette was there to kill Linck, come what may. Linck was going to be killed. Why?'

Felix sighed. 'Total honesty – I don't know. And believe me, Brig doesn't know. Massinette was assigned to the Milford Plaza operation. He's not regular CIA personnel.'

'So what is he? Some kind of CIA contract killer?'

'Like a Double O? Maybe. It doesn't smell good, I have to admit. But Massinette sticks by his story. He killed Linck to stop him killing you.'

'How convenient.'

Felix topped up their glasses from the gin bottle and looked around the room.

'OK. Here's the thing, James. Let's start at the beginning. This is what I know as far as I know.'

Felix lit another cigarette and proceeded to outline the facts. Towards the end of the war in Dahum, when the heartland was shrinking and the military and humanitarian situation was becoming ever more desperate, Brigadier Solomon Adeka was secretly approached by one Hulbert Linck, a philanthropic multimillionaire with an altruistic love of freedom and Africa. Linck offered to supply arms, aircraft, white mercenaries, ammunition, food, essential medical supplies – anything to keep Dahum alive.

'But there was a price to pay,' Bond said. 'Altruism is expensive.'

'Exactly. There always is. There's no money in the free-lunch business,' Felix said and gestured at the crowded bar and the veranda beyond. 'You see all these white men?'

'Yes,' Bond said.

'Who do you think they are?' Felix didn't wait for an answer. 'They're oil company executives.'

'Flies round the Zanzarim honey pot,' Bond said.

'Indeed. The Adeka family have been important chiefs in the Fakassa tribe for hundreds of years. The Zanza River Delta is their tribal homeland. Solomon Adeka is the sovereign chief.'

'No he's not,' Bond said. 'He couldn't be. His older brother is – Gabriel Adeka. I'll explain when you finish.'

'Anyway, the price Hulbert Linck demanded for his military aid was a twenty-five-year lease on the oil rights in the Fakassa tribal homelands. Profits to be split fifty-fifty. Solomon Adeka granted him the lease – anything to save Dahum.'

'So Linck owned the land where the oil was.'

'In fact it's owned by a company in Luxembourg called Zanza Petroleum SA. It's Linck's company. He had all the leases. Signed and sealed.'

Bond was thinking – pieces were fitting together, fast. Signed and sealed – but by the wrong Adeka brother.

'And Linck certainly tried hard,' Bond said. 'I give that to him. For him a free independent Dahum was the best option. I saw what he did, what he spent.'

'But it was never going to work,' Felix said. 'Dahum was never going to win this civil war, was never going to be an independent state. Too many powerful countries had other plans.'

'And Linck was no fool. He could see the writing on the wall, eventually. His leases weren't going to be worth a penny when Zanzarim was reunited. And that's when the conspiracy started,' Bond said. 'Plan B began when they saw that the war was going to be lost.' He sipped at his drink. 'And I suspect another factor was when Linck discovered that the leases weren't Solomon Adeka's to sell. With the war over and the older brother, Gabriel, on the scene Zanza Petroleum would be no more.'

'Go on,' Felix said, leaning forward. 'This is where it gets confusing for me. Remember I thought Gabriel Adeka was alive and well and living in Washington DC.'

'The only way for Linck to keep the integrity of his oil leases going was to have them "authorised" by the older brother – the paramount chief of the Fakassa. How was that to be achieved? Solomon Adeka had to "die" and become Gabriel . . .' Bond felt more clarity arriving as he articulated the plan to Felix. 'I think Linck contacted Gabriel Adeka in London right at the end of the war. Spun him some sort of story about aid to Dahum. That's why the two Constellations I saw suddenly had AfricaKIN painted on them. Even that last night as everyone was fleeing. Linck knew about Gabriel and that he was the older brother – that proves it.' Bond thought further. Gabriel Adeka must have been found and located, agreed to 'partner' Linck in the airlift to Dahum. Perhaps it was just a ruse to gain his confidence. He might even have been dead already when that last Constellation touched down at Janjaville.

'From Linck and Solomon Adeka's point of view the key thing was to have Gabriel Adeka dead,' Bond said, adding – 'not only dead but "disappeared". There would be no body. As far as anyone in London was concerned Gabriel had gone to America to set up the new charity – AfricaKIN Inc.' Bond remembered his encounter with Peter Kunle at the Bayswater offices. How Kunle had been surprised at Gabriel's untypical complacency about his borrowed typewriter, not living up to his usual impeccable behaviour patterns.

'You're saying Adeka and Linck planned all this,' Felix said, frowning. 'To kill Gabriel.'

'Yes, I'm afraid so. The rewards were immense. Fratricide has a long history – starting with Cain and Abel.' Bond added more ice to his glass. 'Solomon Adeka feigned his terminal illness and his death. By the way – you might want to interrogate an Indian doctor called Dr Masind. He was in Rowanoak as well. He must have done the drugging, written the death certificate. It was very effective. Solomon "dies", the war ends and enter the CIA. Gabriel Adeka, meanwhile, has been invited to set up AfricaKIN in Washington DC.' Bond smiled. 'The timing was perfect. Gabriel Adeka apparently leaves London – suddenly he's not there – and another "Gabriel Adeka" arrives in Washington. Meanwhile Solomon Adeka has been buried with full military honours in Port Dunbar.'

Felix shook his head cynically. 'How were we to know? You meet a man who says he's Gabriel Adeka. How could we know that it was the younger brother, Solomon? He had a shaven head and a small goatee, just like Gabriel. Solomon was dead and buried – who's going to be suspicious?' Felix nodded, almost as if he had to convince himself of the elaborate nature of the subterfuge.

'I bet you didn't see much of him,' Bond said.

'No, that's true. There were some initial meetings – "Gabriel" was unwell, we were told – this Colonel Denga was the frontman. Very efficient. Very precise.'

'Part of the team.' Bond lit another cigarette. 'I'm pretty sure this was how it must have happened. Gabriel Adeka was lured into a kind of collaboration with Linck and his aid plans for Dahum. At some meeting an unsuspecting Gabriel would have been killed – probably by one of Kobus Breed's buddies and the body disposed of – buried under fresh concrete in the Bayswater office. Breed is Linck's enforcer – he would have arranged everything. Maybe he's his partner, for all I know. I bet you it was Breed who saw other opportunities for AfricaKIN and its "mercy flights". Maybe Linck was in on it.' He shrugged. 'Clearly he's a man who likes to make a profit, one way or another.' Bond spread his hands. 'But we'll never know now, thanks to Agent Massinette.'

Felix wasn't going to follow this line of speculation, Bond saw. He shook his glass, making the ice cubes spin.

'So, just to be on the safe side, to keep their control, they turned Solomon into a junkie,' Felix added, nodding to himself again.

'Absolutely perfect control,' Bond said, adding more gin to their glasses. They were halfway through the bottle. 'Linck and Breed were running things now. They didn't want their Adeka brother changing his mind in any way.'

'So you reckon Linck wasn't a prisoner at all,' Felix said.

'No. Why would a prisoner dye his hair and grow a beard?' Bond posed the question. 'That little ploy was Linck's escape route, or so he hoped. Kobus Breed was the mastermind. So Linck would have had us believe.'

'Why didn't he just run for it? Why did he surrender to you?'

'You answered that. While he was alive he still – just about – owned Zanza Petroleum. Linck must have known that the whole AfricaKIN cover would be blown. Better to present himself as a victim along with poor Gabriel Adeka. You said the leases were all legal. He might have been able to pick up where he left off. He could have claimed some sort of negotiating position, at least.'

'Except he hadn't reckoned on you – the fact that you knew both brothers.'

'Linck didn't know that. And Massinette blew him away the moment he saw him.' Bond clicked his fingers. 'Just like that. I wonder why . . .'

'I think I may be able to answer that question, now.' Felix nodded. Bond could see clarity was visiting him, also.

'OK,' Felix continued, 'one more thing. I can now understand how the real Gabriel Adeka could be made to disappear in London. And suddenly reappear in Rowanoak Hall. Solomon was "dead" – you'd been to his funeral. How did he get to the US?'

'It was something Blessing told me – Aleesha Belem. She reminded me that there had been another plane that last night at Janjaville – a DC-3. She said Breed and Linck flew out separately on the DC-3 while everyone else was on the Super Constellation. I didn't see that, of course – I was minding my own business bleeding to death.' Bond smiled, wryly. 'I suspect there were a few crates loaded on the DC-3 at the last moment. One of them would have contained Solomon Adeka, drugged and comatose but very much alive and ready to assume his new identity. Gabriel was dead – long live Gabriel. You weren't going to ask any difficult questions – even if you had any – because you were so very pleased to welcome him and AfricaKIN to the US. I wonder why? Sorry to repeat myself . . .'

'Follow me,' Felix said and strolled on to the veranda. Bond joined him. Just below the edge of the veranda was a long row of cars and trucks and utility vehicles. All new and each one with the logo of an oil company on its side. Shell, BP, Texaco, Elf, Agip, Esso, Mobil, Gulf.

'Take a look,' Felix said. 'Every oil company in the world wants to stick its nose in the Zanzarim trough.'

Bond looked at the shiny new vehicles, looked back at the perspiring white men in the bar of the Grand Central Hotel.

'You've got to understand, James,' Felix said, 'the civil war here fouled everything up. Oil had been discovered, sure. But you can't develop oilfields if a war is raging on top of them. It was a disaster for the oil companies. And when the war didn't end in a few weeks and began to drag on and on – one year, two years – and it looked like there was going to be this interminable stalemate—'

Bond interrupted. 'And certain Western governments agreed that if there was some way of stopping the war it would be in everybody's interests.' Bond frowned: not quite everybody's – but he saw how a congruence of different ambitions had merged unknowingly, unwittingly. Britain, the USA, the international oil companies, Hulbert Linck's vicious opportunism, the greed of a younger brother . . .

'Here we are in the heart of the Zanza River Delta,' Felix said. 'We're standing on a gigantic ocean of oil, untapped, barely explored. We don't know how vast these reserves may be. It could be bigger than the Ghawar field in Saudi. These fellows' – he gestured at the bar – 'will figure it out any day now. But it's not just any old oil. It's "light crude". The best oil in the world, so much easier to refine. The world wants it and the world is going to get it.'

Bond smiled cynically. 'And someone like Hulbert Linck couldn't be allowed to stand in the way. Enter Agent Massinette.'

'I don't like to admit it,' Felix said. 'But I can see why it was in everyone's interests if Hulbert Linck was dead – killed by an agent in a shoot-out, for example, during a raid.'

They wandered back to their seats. Felix had a sour expression on his face – a man who had just come face to face with an unpleasant truth about the business he was in, Bond thought. They sat down and Bond added a fresh splash of gin to their glasses. Felix dropped in more ice cubes.

Bond looked at him. 'You say "everyone's interests", Felix, but what you mean is the West.'

'Of course. Figure it out. We don't want to get our oil from the Gulf, if we can help it,' Felix said. 'It's the proverbial powder keg. Islam, Palestine, Israel, Shia and Sunni – it's a goat-fuck. Zanzarim alone could provide up to forty per cent of all US and UK oil needs, I've heard it said. Forty per cent – and not a camel in sight. It changes everything.' He lit a cigarette and spread his arms. 'This is the new Gulf, James. Right here in West Africa. It suits us fine.' He stood up. 'I've got to make a quick phone call. I saw a payphone in reception. Don't finish that gin, I'll be right back.'

He wandered off and Bond sat back in his chair thinking. Sometimes, he reasoned, the stakes – the rewards – can become so high that illegitimacy, malfeasance, even murder seem entirely reasonable, not to say logical, courses of action. All this oil was waiting under the ground in the Zanza River Delta – and one man, Hulbert Linck, knew too much, could cause potential problems, could stand in the way of the new order being established. Wouldn't it just be so much easier if he wasn't there any more? That he didn't have to be factored into any plans? Someone very high up in government circles, someone very important, would make a decision. Don't we have 'people' who can sort these kind of things out for us? Yes, sir. I believe Luke Massinette is the ideal man for the job. And he's available. Fine – so make sure he's an integral part of the search for Hulbert Linck and tell him exactly what to do once we've found him. Don't mess up.

Bond lit a cigarette. 'Dirty tricks' were as old as history. As old as diplomacy. As old as spying. All the same, he had to admit, sometimes the sheer candid ruthlessness of absolute power did shake you up somewhat. He understood why Felix had worn that expression on his face for a second or two.

Felix returned. 'You can telephone the USA from Port Dunbar. That's what I call progress.'

'Realpolitik is not just a German concept,' Bond said. 'Everything can be made to happen.' He smiled. Felix nodded. They both knew the global subtext now, the underlying story.

'What're you going to do with Adeka?' Bond asked, changing the subject.

'I think he likes it in Washington DC. He'll become a wealthy man once the leases are renegotiated with the government of Zanzarim. We can keep an eye on him – and Colonel Denga and this Dr Masind, if necessary. The drug-smuggling issues give us a little leverage. I'm sure they'll behave.'

'Will Adeka be Gabriel or Solomon?' Bond asked.

'I don't think we really give a damn, to be honest. Now everything's sorted out to our satisfaction.'

Felix looked serious and placed his glass down on the table.

'I think we just figured it all out, didn't we?' Felix said.

'Yes,' Bond said. 'How would you express it? We picked the gnat's shit out of the pepper.'

Bond sat back and drained his glass. They looked at each other: two men who knew all too well how the world worked. Bond thought to himself about what had happened – he called it the Thomas à Becket solution. Henry II had understood this in 1170 as clearly as those who had wanted Hulbert Linck eliminated 800 years later. 'Will no one rid me of this turbulent priest?' – so Henry II had asked his leading question. And Thomas à Becket had been duly assassinated. Will no one rid me of Hulbert Linck . . . ? Step forward Agent Massinette. Sometimes the easiest way to solve a problem is to make it go away.

Bond shrugged and smiled. 'At root, most problems are very straightforward. And the solution is usually very straightforward as well. Though sometimes brutal.'

'Except that often it doesn't *seem* straightforward.'

'Ah, but we like that,' Bond said. 'The more smoke and mirrors the better.'

Felix looked at him, closely.

'In the midst of all this smoke, there's just one thing that strikes me, James.'

'What's that?'

'There are very few people in the world who know about Gabriel and Solomon Adeka. Denga must know. Linck did, but he's dead. This Indian doctor, Masind, does. And Kobus Breed – he's probably dead, or out of action anyway. It just strikes me that you – you – are maybe the only person around who's actually ever been face to face with both the brothers.'

'What're you saying, Felix?'

'That you're a man with a very, very privileged piece of information indeed. I would keep it to yourself, James. I certainly won't mention anything of what you told me to any of my people. You know as well as I do that knowledge is power – but owning this kind of knowledge can be as dangerous as owning an unexploded bomb . . . Just be careful, OK?'

'I'll try,' Bond said, and smiled.

# PART FIVE

# Coda in Richmond

# 1
# Un Paysan Écossais

M's office was bluey-grey with hanging strata of pipe smoke and Bond's eyes began stinging within two minutes of their meeting commencing. He must have been smoking all day, Bond thought, and usually that was a sign of trouble.

But M seemed genial – or at least the impenetrable mask he wore was genial. He had sat there without a word, attending to Bond's narrative of events, puffing away on his pipe, with a nod and a smile from time to time, almost like an uncle patiently listening to his nephew recount the details of his school's sports day.

'And there you have it, sir,' Bond said. 'The scramble for Zanzarim's oil is in full enthusiastic swing. I saw it with my own eyes – every oil company in the world wanting a piece of the action.'

'And we're at the head of the queue,' M said, putting his pipe down and smoothing back his thinning hair with the palm of one hand. 'Excellent,' he said thoughtfully to himself, pursing his lips and tugging at an ear lobe. Bond knew the signs, it was not a moment to interject. M would speak in his own good time.

'I should probably discipline you in some way, 007,' M said finally. 'For going solo in such a dramatic and headstrong manner – for vanishing like that. But I've decided that would be perverse.'

'May I ask why, sir?'

'Because – paradoxically, even astonishingly – you achieved everything that was asked of you. The war is over and Zanzarim is reunited. A little corner of Africa is at peace and has a bright, prosperous future. Thanks to your efforts.'

'And we can acquire all the oil we need.'

M's eyes sharpened.

'Cynicism doesn't suit you, 007,' he said. 'Oil has nothing to do with us. We – you and I – are just naval ratings on the ship of state. We were given a task and we carried it out. Or rather you did all the hard work – I only put you forward as the right man for the job.' He allowed himself a half-smile. 'And it turned out I was correct. I know it hasn't been an easy time for you but we'll find a way of recognising that, James, don't you worry.'

Bond noticed the deliberate use of his Christian name. The mood was mellowing again, but he wanted to make his point.

'All's well that ends well,' Bond said. 'For both of us.'

'Us?'

'The British and the Americans. We seem to be sitting pretty.'

'And what could be wrong with that?' M stood up, signalling that the meeting was at an end. Bond rose to his feet also, as M came round from behind his desk. 'Don't go there,' he said, his voice leavened with delicate warning. 'It's not our affair. We're servants of Her Majesty's Government, whatever its political hue. We are part of the Secret Intelligence Service. Civil servants in the pure sense of the term.'

'Of course,' Bond said. 'As you know, sir, *je suis un paysan écossais* – all this multinational, macroeconomic forward-planning is lost on me.'

'He said, disingenuously.'

They both smiled and moved to the door, where M briefly rested his hand on Bond's shoulder.

'You did exceptionally well, 007. Did us proud.'

It was a significant compliment, Bond knew. And suddenly he saw how much had been at stake; how his obscure mission in a small African country had possessed a geopolitical resonance and fallout that he could never have imagined. That he would never have wanted to imagine when he had set out on it, he told himself.

M patted his shoulder again, avuncularly.

'Come in and see me on Monday morning. I think I might have an interesting little job for you.'

No rest for the wicked, Bond thought.

'See you Monday morning, sir.'

'Any plans for the weekend?'

'I have to return some lost property.'

# 2

# Out of the Dark

Bond knocked on Vampiria's door. He had had his hair cut and a massage and was wearing his dark navy-blue worsted suit, a heavy cream silk shirt and a pale blue knitted silk tie. He sensed he was back to normal – feeling as well as he had in months.

Bryce Fitzjohn opened the door to her caravan. She was wearing a ginger gaberdine double-breasted trouser suit with a white cashmere polo neck and her hair was pinned up in a loose bun.

'Too early?' Bond asked.

'No – perfect timing. Vampiria is no more, consumed by hellfire.' She looked him up and down approvingly. 'You seem very fit and well, Mr Bond. Step inside. I don't want to kiss you with half the crew looking on.'

He went inside and they kissed, gently, passionately. Bond felt a kind of release inside him, a rare surge of well-being. Perhaps he could let everything go for twenty-four hours and be himself with this wonderful woman.

'How was your trip to Americay?'

'It was . . . interesting.'

'No new scars?'

'A scar-free sojourn, I'm glad to report.' He smiled, reassuring her, but he made the qualification to himself – at least none visible.

Bond drove her back to Richmond in his Interceptor II.

'Is this a new car?' Bryce asked.

'On approval. I'm not sure I can afford it.'

'Are you all right, James?'

'I am now,' he said with real sincerity. 'I was feeling a bit out of sorts – and then I saw you again.'

'We do our best,' she said, reaching over to touch his cheek with her knuckles. There was an understanding between them, Bond thought. So much of what they communicated was unspoken. She already knew him, it seemed – his necessary reticences, places he couldn't go – and he received in return her covert messages of desire and affection, of real warmth. The hidden currents of their conversation were deep and strong.

Back at her house she told him they were having a repeat meal: champagne, a steak and a tomato salad and a great bottle of red wine. When she went into the kitchen to decant the wine – she'd chosen a Chateau Cantemerle 1955 – Bond slipped into her study and replaced her passport in the top drawer. Dennis Fieldfare had swiftly reconstituted it in its original form – it looked completely identical to the one he'd purloined, though maybe one day Bryce would wonder how she'd acquired those US immigration stamps while she'd been busy filming *Vampiria* in the Thames Valley, but Bond reckoned he'd managed the duplicity without being discovered. She would have no idea how helpful she had been.

They ate, they drank and later they made love like old and practised familiars.

'I'm so glad you're back,' she said, lying in his arms, smoothing the forelock from his brow with a finger. 'I've missed you, absurd though it may sound. And remember you promised me a holiday.'

'I'm going to take you to Jamaica,' he said. 'Ever been there?'

'No, I haven't. How rather wonderful.'

'Stand by for the trip of a lifetime.'

'How can I possibly thank you, Mr Bond?' she said, shifting forward and kissing him, letting her tongue linger in his mouth. 'Maybe I can think of something a little out of the ordinary . . .' She flicked the sheet away from his naked body.

**Bond woke.** He had heard a noise. He heard it again – a sharp patter of fine gravel thrown against the windowpane almost like a rain-shower. He looked at his watch – 4.55 a.m. Bryce was soundly asleep. Bond slipped out of bed and parted the curtains an inch and peered out. The opaque grey expanse of the lawn, lit by the moonlight, was revealed below and beyond it, through a fringe of trees, flowed the silvered river at high tide. Then he thought he saw some shadow move in the darkness and felt himself tense, suddenly. He gathered up his clothes and shoes and quietly left the bedroom, dressing quickly on the landing. He pulled on his socks and shoes and then his jacket, shoving his tie into a pocket. There was somebody out there in the garden, he was sure, and he was going to find out who it was.

He went downstairs, not switching on any lights. It was an old burglar's trick, he was aware – throw some gravel at the bedroom windows and if no lights go on you're pretty much safe to plunder the ground floor. He picked up the poker from beside the fire in the drawing room and crept through to the kitchen and its door on to the garden. Keeping out of sight, he peered through the kitchen windows at the ghostly expanse of the garden within its high walls. Once again he thought he saw something shift in the big herbaceous border by the fig tree. Were his eyes playing tricks with him? But the thrown gravel was no illusion. Perhaps he should just switch the lights on and the interloper would get the message and try to rob another big house in Richmond instead. But Bond had a strange sense about this wake-up call. Thrown gravel. Thrown coins . . . Perhaps somebody wanted to lure him out into the darkness. Well – he was ready for that.

He opened the door and stepped outside. It was cold and his breath condensed, the first intimations of the winter that was approaching. He gripped the poker hard in his fist and walked down a brick path towards the wall and the gate on to the river promenade. He stopped – listening hard. Nothing. A breeze swirled by and leaves rustled. Bond headed for the herbaceous border where he thought he'd seen the movement in the shadows.

He stood at the lawn's edge looking at the plants in the border for any sign of broken stems or leaves. He reached into his pocket for his lighter and clicked it on, crouching and holding the flame close to the ground. Some leaves had fallen, one plant was oddly bent over. He moved the flame so it cast an oblique light – and he saw the footprints. The soil was moist and the freshly moulded imprints were an inch deep, four of them. Someone had been in this garden, hiding. What was odd was that one footprint, the right, seemed unnaturally turned into the other, and the right heel seemed implanted deeper than the left – and there were a series of round holes beside them also, as if a stick or a cane had been used to rest on. This is madness, Bond thought – but another more rational part of his brain was saying this could be someone deformed, someone who cannot walk unaided. A cripple of some kind . . .

Then he heard a noise in the street beyond and ran to the garden gate, turning the key that was in the lock and flinging the door open. He stepped out on to the street. The tide was now fully ebbing in the river, flowing strongly back towards the sea. Bond looked left and right. The river-road here in Richmond was well illuminated by street lights but there was no sign of anyone. He thought he heard a car engine kick into life a street away, and pull off into the night.

He felt a great sinking of heart as he realised what he had to do. There was no other option.

Bond went back into the house and poured himself an inch of brandy in a tumbler, took a gulp and then went into Bryce's study, sat down at her desk and wrote her a brief note on a sheet of her writing paper.

> Darling Bryce,
> I have to go away suddenly, 'on business'. You are too good for me and I could never make you happy. These few wonderful hours I've shared with you have given my life real meaning. I thank you from the depths of my heart and soul. Goodbye.
> With my love, J.

He finished his drink and weighted down the sheet of paper on her desk with his empty glass. She'd find it in the morning when she came down to look for him, calling his name. It was Sunday – they had made plans for Sunday.

**Bond closed** the door softly behind him and slipped into the front seat of the Interceptor. He sat there for a while, running through his various decisions, his mind constantly returning to the horrific images of Blessing, dead at the hand of Kobus Breed. Perhaps what had happened in the garden had been nothing more than a Richmond burglar trying his luck, but Bond knew he couldn't live with the possibility of Bryce becoming a victim – like Blessing – because of her association with him. He couldn't put her in harm's way – particularly if the harm was to be administered by a man like Breed.

He started the engine – its throaty purr was so quiet he doubted Bryce would wake – and drove slowly out of her driveway, the gravel crunching under his wide tyres.

There was a distinct lemony-pewter lightening in the east, heralding the beginning of the new day – a clear sky with no clouds. Bond turned the Interceptor on to the London road and put his foot on the accelerator, concentrating on the pleasures of driving a powerful car like this, trying not to think of Bryce and whatever dangers had been lurking out there in the darkness of her garden.

He drove steadily homewards, his face impassive, his mind made up, an unfamiliar heaviness in his heart.

He pulled into the square off the King's Road and sat for a moment in his car, thinking, already half-regretting his act of spontaneous chivalry – of leaving Bryce unannounced, so suddenly, clandestinely in the night. She'd be shocked and hurt after the time they'd enjoyed together, and the love they'd made – she'd never think such an abandonment was done to keep her safe from the merciless savagery of Kobus Breed. All she knew about James Bond was his name – she didn't have his address or telephone number. She'd never find him, however hard she cared to look. And where would *he* ever find someone like her again? he wondered, with some bitterness. That was the price he paid for the job he did, he supposed. Falling in love with a beautiful woman wasn't recommended.

Bond sighed. It was a calm and beautiful Sunday morning. Tomorrow was Monday and he remembered that M had said he had an 'interesting' little job for him. Life goes on, he thought – it was some consolation . . . He stepped out of his car into a perfumed, sunlit day and as he strolled towards his front door somewhere a spasm of church bells sounded and a gang of pigeons, feeding in the central garden of the square, clapped up into the dazzling blue of an early morning sky in Chelsea – and vanished.

# Ian Fleming

I an Lancaster Fleming was born in London on 28
May 1908 and was educated at Eton College before
spending a formative period studying languages in
Europe. His first job was with Reuters news agency, followed by a brief spell as a stockbroker. On the outbreak
of the Second World War he was appointed assistant to
the Director of Naval Intelligence, Admiral Godfrey,
where he played a key part in British and Allied espionage operations.

After the war he joined Kemsley Newspapers as
Foreign Manager of the *Sunday Times*, running a network of correspondents who were intimately involved
in the Cold War. His first novel, *Casino Royale*, was
published in 1953 and introduced James Bond, Special
Agent 007, to the world. The first print run sold out

within a month. Following this initial success, he published a Bond title every year until his death. Raymond Chandler hailed him as 'the most forceful and driving writer of thrillers in England'. The fifth title, *From Russia with Love*, was particularly well received and sales soared when President Kennedy named it as one of his favourite books. The Bond novels have sold more than sixty million copies and inspired a hugely successful film franchise which began in 1962 with the release of *Dr No*, starring Sean Connery as 007.

The Bond books were written in Jamaica, a country Fleming fell in love with during the war and where he built a house, 'Goldeneye'. He married Anne Rothermere in 1952. His story about a magical car, written in 1961 for their only child, Caspar, went on to become the well-loved novel and film *Chitty Chitty Bang Bang*.

Fleming died of heart failure on 12 August 1964.

## BY IAN FLEMING

James Bond novels
Casino Royale
Live and Let Die
Moonraker
Diamonds are Forever
From Russia with Love
Dr No
Goldfinger
For Your Eyes Only
Thunderball
The Spy Who Loved Me
On Her Majesty's Secret Service
You Only Live Twice
The Man with the Golden Gun
Octopussy and The Living Daylights

Non-fiction
The Diamond Smugglers
Thrilling Cities

For children
Chitty Chitty Bang Bang: The Magical Car

www.ianfleming.com

# HARPER LUXE

## THE NEW LUXURY IN READING

We hope you enjoyed reading
our new, comfortable print size and found it
an experience you would like to repeat.

**Well – you're in luck!**

HarperLuxe offers the finest in fiction and
nonfiction books in this same larger print size and
paperback format. Light and easy to read, HarperLuxe
paperbacks are for book lovers who want to see
what they are reading without the strain.

For a full listing of titles and
new releases to come, please visit our website:

**www.HarperLuxe.com**

Withdra

*For all the students*
*who showed me the way*

. . . . . . . . . . .

# Contents

· · · · · · · · · · ·

## ▣ U n i t **IV**

# What We *Really* Say: Idiomatic Uses   129

## ▣ U n i t **V**

# Making Connections   153

◈ **Unit VI**

## How to Tell One Look-Alike Word From the Other   173

◈ **Unit VII**

## Nuts and Bolts   197

# Preface

. . . . . . . . . . . .

One day at a committee meeting I heard a college administrator debate with an English department chair whether confusion in student papers about where to use *their* and *there* reflected an error in spelling or grammar. The grand irrelevance of this exchange led me to wonder, not for the first time, what such niceties, a momentary diversion for the super-literate, might signify to the basic writer who knows only that any paper submitted will be returned with marks indicating dozens of errors. Most of these marks—*sp, s-v agr, ref,* and the rest—are all too familiar to students, who have, often enough, little comprehension of what they refer to beyond "a run-on is a long sentence," or "a paper must have commas." In reality, little is achieved in terms of improved writing by this intense concentration on error, yet a widely used pedagogy is to *teach* error as a guide to correctness. For a generation, compositionists have emphasized the writing process; this emphasis suggests that we would do better to address the *process* of correctness rather than the *product* of an error-free paper.

It is relatively easy to direct students to whatever section in a handbook provides a grammatical explanation of an error—that is, if we can agree on whether *there/their* and the like fall under the category of spelling or grammar—but it is considerably more difficult to determine what students think they are doing. After all, people seldom make errors deliberately, so there must be a reason for continued mistakes. All of us, basic writers and holders of advanced degrees alike, use and write grammatical forms long before we know what to call them. And we use them no more effectively after we know their names. We have, in short, developed an intuition about how words combine to make sense. Thus, it is not a lack of knowledge of rules that leads students to persist in error. In fact, the rules often get in their way and further their confusion, causing them to overcorrect or misinterpret.

What, then, accounts for their alarming divergence from "correctness"? It may be dialect interference, unfamiliarity with preferred usage, or misinterpretation of instruction, a frequent occurrence. Most often it is because students communicate orally and are unaccustomed to written forms. Hardly ever are their errors attributable to an inability to recite rules of grammar.

*The Longman Writer's Grammar* is based on the belief that writing is essentially a positive act and that concentrating on errors can have only a negative effect, intensifying student problems, problems that must—and can—be dealt with. To this end the lessons in this book are grounded in the way children learn language: in context, prompted by hearing the language used by those around them or by reading the language of standard usage. The lessons follow the pattern of many foreign language texts: a brief excerpt from a published work containing the preferred form the lesson demonstrates, a brief explanation of the form, an opportunity for the student to identify, copy, and use the form. The rationale of this book is that it is more beneficial to lead students to recognize correct forms in the context of real and correct writing rather than to teach them to identify error and to help them distinguish between forms that cause confusion. No incorrect forms are shown in the book. This positive approach takes into account three ways students get into difficulty by trying to follow rules:

1. Students are so paralyzed by fear of error that they overcorrect. For example, many will cross out a correct *looks* or *does* to substitute *look* or *do* not because they don't know singular from plural but because endings in general baffle them.

2. Students misunderstand the rules, sometimes because they interpret helpful hints from teachers as rigid, unchanging strictures. One student persisted in using *in which* as a connective in unlikely places as a result of being told that *because* signals a fragment.

3. Sometimes the rules make little sense. To tell students, especially those whose native language or dialect is not standard English, that subjects and verbs must agree is not only overstating the matter—only third person singular present tense verbs agree with their subjects in English—but opening the way to agreement errors never before dreamed of.

Similarly, we accuse students of run-ons, the usual code for a comma splice, and of fragments, without noting how frequently professional writers employ these constructions. Is it because our students are encountering these forms in their recreational reading that we must work so hard to teach their incorrectness?

*The Longman Writer's Grammar*, therefore, keeps rules and technical terms to a minimum while addressing the actual confusion of words and endings that are found in student papers. The seven units are arranged to some extent in order of frequency of error, but they also take into account the most appropriate order for introducing concepts. Recognizing sentence boundaries is essential to producing even the simplest composition and thus is the subject of Unit 1. Mechanics, however, are left for last, not so much because the topic is a difficult one but because only a student who has produced a certain amount of writing and has some confidence about it can be expected to attend to matters of punctuation and capitalization. The units cover seven areas in which students have difficulty without attempting to address every possible aspect of English grammar; instead only those topics to which the most common student errors are attributable are included.

1. **Sentences:** The sentence is the basic unit of communication—a structure that has an infinite number of forms, all of which must contain a subject and a verb. This is not a difficult concept for students; it underlies all of the instruction in this book. Although a large part of the traditional composition curriculum is spent on teaching students sentence errors, in this book the emphasis from the beginning is on what a sentence is and how to write one. Every exercise requires students to write at least two sentences. One of these is often a sentence-combining exercise that provides valuable practice in methods of relating ideas.

2. **Compound verbs:** Students face two possibilities for confusion when they encounter verbs with auxiliaries: first, they must deal with the inflected forms of the auxiliary, and second, they will find in the participles that complete the compound more unfamiliar forms, particularly of irregular verbs. This book provides practice in recognizing compound verbs and their auxiliaries in context rather than isolated in paradigms unconnected to sentences.

3. **Inflections and suffixes indicating parts of speech:** Students tend to omit or affix indiscriminately when they are unsure of preferred usage. Thus the -*s* indicating third person singular present tense is confused with the plural -*s* of the noun and the -'*s* of the possessive. A similar mix-up occurs with the participle endings and with those for adjectives, nouns, and adverbs. One that crops up frequently is failure to recognize the distinction between "I am excit*ed*" and "I am excit*ing*." Because a word's root is more readily registered than the affix that also carries meaning, the ending is often either confused or omitted.

4. **Common idioms:** Although not often treated as such in handbooks, prepositions are extremely idiomatic, whether used as part of a prepositional phrase or semi-adverbially with two-word verbs. The entry in *Webster's New World Dictionary* for the preposition *for* contains twenty-one separate definitions for its idiomatic use. Articles are even more elusive—witness the difficulty of explaining why we say "to school" but "to *the* hospital" (or why the British say "in hospital"). Only by repeated recognition of these forms in context will students develop the necessary familiarity with their use.

5. **Transitional devices:** Whether conjunctions or adverbials, these are not often used by students in speech, although they are essential in writing to establish relationships. When attempting to make such connections in writing, basic writers often resort to something like the all-purpose *which* or give up and settle for a comma splice. Yet, students are eager to learn these words and phrases, and while their initial efforts produce some awkward sentences, they are quick to master the use of conjunctive devices. This is especially true of writers who have some command of the matter of earlier units and are beginning to be conscious of style.

6. **Homonyms, homophones, and polysemous pairs:** *Their/there* and *to/two/too* are only the tip of this iceberg as student papers demonstrate vividly. Whether the problem is labeled spelling or grammar is far less important than that students begin to see the differences and likenesses in these words in their reading and to develop an intuition about where to use them. And because students need to be made aware of the complications of exceptions, a selection of irregular verbs and of plural nouns is included in Unit 6.

7. **Mechanics:** Many students would like to begin the writing course with instruction on where to put commas, not realizing that these and other marks of punctuation and capitalization can be used only after the process of writing has been understood. There is little reason, with students below the level of freshman composition, to go into every subtlety of sophisticated punctuation; their greatest need is to gain a secure sense of how to mark clause boundaries and when to capitalize.

All of the above topics are treated in traditional handbooks in a variety of unrelated sections on tense, agreement, plurals, verb parts, and kinds of pronouns—abstract grammar rules rather than concrete letters or words, rules that are often interchangeable as students perceive them. *The Longman Writer's Grammar* introduces these matters to students as part of the organic whole that writing is rather than as an unchanging set of laws of usage exemplified by isolated sentences framed to demonstrate the rule. By concentrating on one ending, or group of endings, at a time while preserving the context of a piece of writing of intrinsic interest, this book helps students generalize about the environments in which certain forms occur. It encourages students to operate on several cognitive levels simultaneously which, as writers, they must do: reading comprehension, morpheme perception, writing practice, and composition. The aim here is to provide students with an ease and familiarity regarding the forms that give them most trouble, so that they can engage themselves fully in the writing process uninhibited by fear of the red pencil. The format of *The Longman Writer's Grammar* is simple:

1. A brief reading passage chosen from published fiction or nonfiction dealing with material they may recognize from other courses. The reading selections are connected thematically and provide a continuity to the writing assignment with which the unit ends.
2. A brief exercise asking students to write a sentence commenting on the passage, or to combine sentences to produce a commentary.
3. An introduction to the student explaining the form in question and using terms from the brief glossary included at the end of the book.
4. An exercise asking students to identify the form in the passage—for example, words that end in -*s*—and space to copy those words.
5. An exercise asking students to write a sentence using the form being discussed.

After each lesson, at the teacher's discretion, students may be directed to turn to an appendix of review exercises for further practice. Each unit ends with writing instruction and a suggestion for a writing assignment based on the readings in the lessons. These are phrased to elicit the kind of expository writing in which students most need practice rather than the personal experience or opinion papers they frequently produce.

Initially the writing assignments are restricted to sentences and later expanded to paragraphs. Some students may wish to attempt more ambitious work; they should be reminded that in writing, as in perfecting a tennis game or learning a musical instrument, intensive practice in the basic moves is essential to perfecting performance.

## Acknowledgments

I am grateful to all of those students whose encounters with the written word have taught me much about what goes on during the writing process. I must acknowledge my indebtedness as well to William Kerrigan's *Writing to the Point* and its approach to composition, a method that leads students to value their written work as something more than an exercise in correction for the teacher. My thanks also to all those whose thoughtful reading and perceptive comments helped me revise and strengthen this book: Linda A. Austin of Glendale Community College, Marta O. Dmtrenko-Ahrabian of Wayne State University, Stevina Evuleocha of California State Univeristy at Hayward, Caren Kessler of Blue Ridge Community College, Drema Stringer of Marshall Community and Technical College, Kendra Vaglienti of Brookhaven College, and Jayne L. Williams of Texarkana College. Thanks to Steven Rigolosi for his guidance and encouragement and to Brandi Nelson for tactful suggestions on what works. Not least, a very large and special thank you to Sheila Kovacs and Lita Porter who, with unfailing good cheer, did so much to make it happen.

Patricia Silber

# The Oh-So-Correct Writer

## Introduction to Students: You *Do* Know Grammar

The French playwright Molière wrote about a rather foolish man who, having made a good deal of money, decided to buy for himself all the accomplishments he imagined fashionable people to have. He hired dance teachers to show him the latest steps, topflight designers to make him the trendiest clothes, and writing teachers to help him write love letters. When he demanded of the last to be taught prose, he was astonished to learn that he had been speaking prose all his life.

Many writing students today—especially those who say, "I don't know anything about grammar"—are like that character in Molière's play; they don't realize they have understood grammar all their lives. Think about the sentence "I don't know anything about grammar." It follows a variety of grammatical rules that determine word order, pronoun case, negation of verbs, contraction, idiomatic prepositions, and perhaps a few others. You can look any of them up in a grammar book and find detailed explanations about their usage.

Whether you need these detailed explanations is another question. The point is that you do understand grammar, easily and naturally, without reciting the rules. Some language authorities say that we are programmed to speak our native language before we even learn to speak. Like most of us, you probably began talking somewhere around the age of two. Almost immediately you put your words into the grammatical forms of the language spoken around you. What's more, you produced sentences, even if they came out as "Me catch the ball," or "Mommy taked it away from me." Silly baby talk? Not at all. These two examples follow some of the same rules of grammar mentioned in the previous paragraph: word order, use of pronouns, and prepositions. They also demonstrate that the foundation of any human language is the sentence, a very short story in which someone or something is or does something. Does that happen in our examples? Of course! It is clear that the speaker of the first sentence has made a great catch. . .and that the child knows the following about grammar:

1

1. That it has pronouns—*I, we, she, it, they, ours*—that stand for names like Tanya or Joey, or ball, or coat, or parents. (Don't worry about the child's use of *me* as the subject; she will soon find that *I* is the way most people say it. How many adults do you hear say "Me go to class"?)
2. That a sentence usually begins with a subject, followed by a verb and, often, an object.

The baby who invented the second sentence knows these two things about grammar and more besides, most importantly that verbs have *tenses* that tell us whether an action is taking place now, took place in the past, or will take place in the future. (Again, don't worry about *taked* instead of *took*; Baby will learn the preferred form very soon.) Why did I say "invented" rather than "imitated"? First, it is clear that no one but a very young child would say "Mommy *taked* it away from me." Second, the sentence shows that even a baby knows, without having learned any rules, about tense, and is able to make up a past tense verb.

Now, neither this child we're talking about nor you sat down with a grammar book before producing sentences, hundreds and thousands of them, all of them grammatical, even if they sometimes contain an "incorrect" form. Well, fine, you've been speaking under the influence of grammar for years. Why, then, have teachers been telling you, and—worse—you agreeing with them, that you "don't know anything about grammar"? The answer is related to the *me* and *taked* in our sample baby talk and to the difference between the language we speak and the language we write. Many of the forms that we use in our writing are forms that we neither use nor hear when we speak. "I shoulda talk to im" is what we say. When we write it, it comes out, "I should have talked to him." This difference between the way we talk and the way we write, by the way, is true of everybody, including teachers; listen to yours and see if you don't agree.

There is still another reason beginning writers get into trouble with teachers because of their "grammar": the preferred forms in formal written English often differ from those in informal speech. Think about it. Do you use the same words and expressions when you speak to your parents and to your friends? How about when you're in a job interview? Or when you're introduced to your girlfriend's parents? Of course, your language changes depending on who you're talking to. And the same is true of writing. When we write, we don't have the advantage of seeing the person addressed and observing reactions, or being able to answer questions. We have to make clear what we mean in the words we choose and in the form we put them in. That is why we use standard forms understandable and acceptable to anyone.

Still, it is not necessary to memorize pages of grammar rules in order to find out where spoken forms creep into our writing and to change them to the appropriate written forms; in fact, too much worry about the rules can keep us from concentrating on something much more important: clear writing that makes a point.

To sum up, while everyone knows quite a lot about grammar and follows the rules all the time, many people do not know all the acceptable forms for writing, forms that college students, and graduates, are expected to use routinely. That is the point of this book. We do need to know these forms, but before we can use them easily, we need to see how writers use them.

This book will *show* you these preferred forms, not tell you the rules that govern them, and will show them used by writers whose work is read and enjoyed by millions of people. No one worries much about whether these writers "know grammar"; what they have written gives us too much pleasure. But their writing *does* follow the standard usage we have been talking about, and shows us how we can do the same.

In each unit you will be asked to read excerpts from a published work by an author whose books are read, not because they are "correct" but because their stories are exciting or because they show us another time or place or help us understand our own lives better. In their writing you will have a chance to pick out the ways they use formal written language to get their meaning across and to arouse the reader's emotions. Best of all, you will begin to use the forms these writers use in your own writing.

But before you go on, you should keep in mind a few terms we use when we talk about writing.

**Sentence:** The group of words that tells what something or someone is or does. It must have a subject and a verb.

**Subject:** The something or someone that is or does something in a sentence. Usually it is a noun or pronoun that answers the question "who" or "what."

*Who* drives that old Beetle?

*Millicent* drives the Beetle and *it* burns a lot of gas.

**Verb:** One or more words that answer the question "what's happening?" The car *burns* oil, too.

In most sentences, the verb will consist of more than one word. Together, all of the words that go with the verb are called the *predicate*.

**Tense:** The verb form that tells *when* something happened. Often this is shown by adding an ending to the root word. It stall*ed* on a hill yesterday. Sometimes it is another word. Millicent *will sell* it next week.

**Clause:**      A group of words containing a subject and verb and connected to another sentence. For example: When the *car was* new, *it drove* like a dream. The first clause is *dependent,* the second *independent.* Many sentences consist of more than one clause. The exercises in this book will give you practice in combining short sentences into more meaningful ones.

**Adjective:**    A word that answers the question "what kind?"

The *ugly* Beetle is a clunker.

**Adverb:**     A word that answers the questions "When?" "Where?" "How?" or Why?

It breaks down *often.* [when]

It stalled *here.* [where]

It drives *noisily.* [how]

*Therefore,* it isn't safe to drive. [why]

**Participle:**   A form of a verb that can be used as an adjective or noun. The *present participle* ends in *-ing.*

*Driving* that car is a headache.

The *past participle* either ends in *-ed* or is a different word.

Our trip ended with a *heated* argument.

The *broken* transmission was the last straw.

**Infinitive:**   A form of a verb that is written with *to.* It can be used as a noun, but not as the verb of a sentence.

She had hoped *to drive* it to the junk yard.

**Root Word:**  The part of a word that carries the main meaning.

*girl,* a young female;

girl*s,* more than one young female;

girl*ish,* like a young female.

# UNIT 1

# In the Beginning Is the Sentence

**W**ithout sentences nothing we say or write would ever make any sense. Did you ever think about that? In a sentence someone or something *is* or *does* something. The first someone or something is the subject, and a subject all by itself doesn't have any meaning. "The mouse." Well, what about the mouse? "The *mouse tells* the cursor where to go." *Mouse* is the subject, *tells* is the verb, and without both subject and verb there is no sentence; something is missing.

Most sentences, like the one above, have more than just a one-word subject and a one-word verb, of course. Pick out the subjects and verbs in these sentences:

> The retreat began at seven that night. They made their way back about a quarter mile to a fairly solid floe, and pitched camp. All hands were called early the next morning. Most of the men were sent out to hunt seals.
>
> —Alfred Lansing, *Endurance*

In the first sentence *the retreat* is the subject and *began* is the verb. In the next sentence *they* is the subject of two verbs: *made* and *pitched*. *All hands* is the next subject, with *were called* as its verb. Finally, *most of the men* is the subject of *were sent out*. You probably noticed that both subjects and verbs sometimes consist of more than one word. We'll be talking further about that.

All of this sentence making is something you've been doing without even thinking about it since you were about two years old. Why does it become such a chore when you have to write sentences for your composition assignments? It's certainly not because you can't make up a sentence. Perhaps it is because writing a sentence needs information that you may give with your facial expression or tone of voice when you speak. Imagine the simple sentence "Duane, come here!" Will it sound the same when a mother sees her

5

toddler heading for a busy street and when a teacher addresses a mischievous sixth-grader? Of course not. So we have to add the extra words and the punctuation that make the difference clear.

Different languages have different ways of saying things, but all of them—more than 4,000 of them throughout the world—arrange their words in sentences.

|  | **English** | **Spanish** | **Tagalog** |
| --- | --- | --- | --- |
| **Present** | I go | voy | punta ako |

Notice how different these mini-sentences are, not just in the words they use but in the *way* they use them: English places the subject first, followed by the verb; Tagalog (the main language of the Philippines) places the verb first, then the subject; in Spanish the subject *I* is understood. Some languages, like Swahili and Turkish, put the entire sentence into a single word.

Another notable point about these forms is that all of them change in order to show *when* the action is happening—now, or a week ago, or tomorrow. So we can add to our definition of a sentence that the verb must have *tense*. Notice that sometimes a verb consists of two words, one of them a helper, or auxiliary, usually a form of the verbs *to be, to have,* or *to do*. What's more, the word itself can change, as it does in the English past tense and in the past and future tenses in Spanish.

|  | **English** | **Spanish** | **Tagalog** |
| --- | --- | --- | --- |
| **Past** | I went | fui | puntana ako |
| **Future** | I will go | iré | pupunta ako |

# L E S S O N  1
## Subjects and Verbs

Every sentence must have a subject and a verb (with tense). Most sentences have more than a one-word subject and a one-word verb. Here's an example: *Her blue <u>sweater</u> <u>kept</u> Marina warm in the chilly room. Sweater* is the subject and *kept* is the verb, but *blue, Marina, warm,* and *in the chilly room* tell us more about the subject and the verb.

In the lessons that follow, we'll look at some sentences from real writers. Charles Lindbergh wrote *The Spirit of St. Louis* about his historic flight from New York to Paris in 1927, the first ever to cross the Atlantic Ocean. In it he uses a variety of sentences. Read the following description about what Lindbergh sees as his plane begins the flight.

### On the Way

[1]The great landscaped estates of Long Island pass rapidly below: mansion, hedgerow, and horse-jump giving way to farms and woodlands farther east. [2]I hold my plane just high enough to clear treetops and buildings on the hills. [3]By flying close to the ground, I can see farther through the haze. [4]That finger of water on my left is part of the bay-broken shore line of the Sound. [5]It must be at least five miles away. [6]Then visibility to the north is improving. [7]The clouds look a little higher too.

—Charles Lindbergh, *The Spirit of St. Louis*

- Write a sentence explaining why Lindbergh is flying close to the ground.

_____

- Even though there are additional words and phrases in the story, each sentence has one subject and one verb, sometimes a verb made up of two words. Write the subjects and verbs below. The first one has been done for you.

| | Subject | Verb |
|---|---|---|
| 1. | *estates* | *pass* |
| 2. | | |
| 3. | | |
| 4. | | |
| 5. | | |
| 6. | | |
| 7. | | |

■ If you had a choice, where would you like to fly to? Write a sentence about the place you chose. _____

_____

## LESSON 1a
## More About Subjects and Verbs

· · · · · · · · · ·

No matter how many words a sentence has, it must always have at least one subject and one verb. Both subject and verb will usually consist of more than one word. In the passage below, the subject is *Miss Crawford's entrance hall,* and the verb is *opened,* although the entire predicate is *opened onto a magnificent room with a huge white Christmas tree at the end and many brilliantly wrapped presents.*

### Hollywood Christmas

¹Miss Crawford's entrance hall opened onto a magnificent room with a huge white Christmas tree at the end and many brilliantly wrapped presents. ²Crawford came to the door in person. ³And she was drawing all the limelight of the afternoon to herself, very much lady of the manor in a white satin dressing gown and white mules with pom-poms. ⁴I didn't know why the star was in a dressing gown in the afternoon. ⁵She and her white satin gown were the stuff of dreams. ⁶Well, I already loved Joan Crawford. ⁷And I had, since seeing her as a child in the Tivoli Theater. ⁸Indeed she was larger than life. ⁹Glamorous, cagey, smart, ambitious, ruthless, tough, always acting, pretending to be sick in bed the night she feared they wouldn't give her the Oscar.

—Liz Smith, *Natural Blonde*

■ Combine these sentences:

When she was a child, Liz Smith saw Joan Crawford movies. She loved Joan

Crawford. _____

_____

■ Find the subjects and verbs in *Hollywood Christmas* and list them below. The first one has been done for you.

|  | **Subject** | **Verb** |
|---|---|---|
| 1. | *entrance hall* | *opened* |
| 2. | | |

| Subject | Verb |
|---|---|
| 3. _____ | _____ |
| 4. _____ | _____ |
| 5. _____ | _____ |
| 6. _____ | _____ |
| 7. _____ | _____ |
| 8. _____ | _____ |
| 9. _____ | _____ |

■ Have you ever been close to a celebrity on the street or in a store or other public building? Write a sentence about how it happened. _____

_____

## LESSON 1b
## Another Look at Sentences
• • • • • • • •

Many sentences have more than one subject and verb, but some have only one of each. *The <u>class</u> <u>begins</u> at nine A.M.* is an example. Look at the sentences in the following excerpt.

### A Lonely Airport

¹<u>I</u> <u>sat</u>, once more in the late hours of darkness, in the airport of a foreign city. ²I had missed a plane and had almost a whole night's wait before me. ³I could not sleep. ⁴The long corridor was deserted. ⁵Even the cleaning woman had passed by. ⁶In that white efficient glare I grew ever more depressed and weary. ⁷I was tired of customs officers and police. ⁸I was lonely for home. ⁹My eyes hurt. ¹⁰I had an ocean to cross; the effort seemed unbearable. ¹¹I rested my aching head upon my hand.

—Loren Eiseley, *One Night's Dying*

■ Why is an airport depressing late at night? Write your answer in a sentence.

_____

■ For each subject on the lines below, write the verb that goes with it in *A Lonely Airport*.

|                 Subject                 |          Verb          |
| :-------------------------------------: | :--------------------: |
| 1. _____ I _____                | _____ sat _____ |
| 2. _____ The long corridor _____        | _____ |
| 3. _____ the cleaning woman _____       | _____ |
| 4. _____ the effort _____           | _____ |

■ What is the loneliest place you can think of? Write a sentence about why you find it lonely. _____

_____

For more subject-verb identification, see Review Exercises 1, 3, 4, 6.

# The Sentence Again

Sometimes a sentence will have more than one subject or one verb: *Angela and Lewis found the lost book.* Sometimes a sentence will have more than one verb for one subject: *The angels sang and danced.* And sometimes there will be several subjects and verbs in one sentence. We can see examples in this paragraph.

## Staying Awake

[1]The brilliant light and the strangeness of the sea awaken me. [2]Any change stimulates the senses. [3]Changing altitude, changing thought, even the changing contours of the ice cakes help to stay awake. [4]I can fly high for a while and then fly low. [5]I can fly first with my right hand and then with my left. [6]I can shift my position a little in the seat, sitting stiff and straight, slouching down, twisting sidewise. [7]I can create imaginary emergencies in my mind. I can check and recheck my navigation. [8]All these tricks I must use and think of others.

—Charles Lindbergh, *The Spirit of St. Louis*

■ What does Lindbergh do to keep awake? Write a sentence to explain. _____

_____

■ For all of the verbs listed below, show the subject or subjects from *Staying Awake*. The first has been done as an example. Note that some of these verbs have a helper, *can*, which becomes part of the verb.

| | Subject | Verb |
|---|---|---|
| 1. | light, strangeness | awaken |
| 2. | | stimulates |
| 3. | | help |
| 4. | | can fly |
| 5. | | can shift |
| 6. | | can create |
| 7. | | can check |

■ What people or happenings distract you from concentrating on studying for an exam? Write a sentence naming two things that take your mind off what you should be doing. _____

_____

# LESSON 2a
# Sentences with More Than One Subject and Verb

. . . . . . . . . .

Depending on the complexity of the idea being expressed, a writer can choose to use two or more subjects and verbs in one sentence. *Mrs. Purlman* *handed out* *the papers and then* *wrote* *the questions on the board.* The subject is *Mrs. Purlman* and the two verbs are *handed out* and *wrote.*

### The Slingshot

¹Jody took his slingshot from the porch and walked up toward the brush line to try to kill a bird. ²It was a good slingshot, with store-bought rubbers, but while Jody had often shot at birds, he had never hit one. ³He walked up through the vegetable patch, kicking his bare toes into the dust. ⁴And on the way he found the perfect slingshot stone, round and slightly flattened and heavy enough to carry through the air. ⁵He fitted it into the leather pouch of his weapon and proceeded to the brush line. ⁶In the shade of the sagebrush the little birds were working, scratching in the leaves, flying restlessly a few feet and scratching again. ⁷Jody pulled back the rubbers of the sling and advanced cautiously. ⁸When he was twenty feet away, he carefully raised the sling and aimed. ⁹The stone whizzed; the thrush started up and flew right into it. ¹⁰And down the little bird went with a broken head.

—John Steinbeck, *The Red Pony*

■ Combine these sentences:

Jody had a good slingshot and the perfect stone. The stone hit the thrush. _____

_____

■ Note that some subjects in *The Slingshot* have two verbs. For each of the subjects listed below, write the verbs that go with it.

|   | **Subject** | **Verb or Verbs** |
|---|---|---|
| 1. | Jody | took, walked |
| 2. | He | |
| 3. | Jody | |
| 4. | the thrush | |

■ Have you ever hiked in the woods? Write a sentence about what you might expect to see on such a hike. _____

_____

## LESSON 2b
## Sentences with Two Subjects and One Verb
· · · · · · · · ·

Very often a sentence will have two or more subjects. Note that this will make the subject plural, which means it must be followed by the *plural* form of the verb in the present tense. So, while we write, *Nanci likes to watch basketball,* we change the verb when we write, *Nanci and her friends like to watch basketball.* There is no *-s* on the plural form of *like.* (See Lesson 13 for more about this topic.) Some sentences will have more than one subject, and some will have more than one verb: <u>*Mike*</u> *and* <u>*Joe*</u> <u>*jumped*</u> *in the car and* <u>*drove*</u> *to Seven-Eleven.* *Mike* and *Joe* are subjects and *jumped* and *drove* are verbs.

### Goodbye Before Sailing

[1]By midafternoon the *Andrea Gail* is ready. [2]The food and bait have been stowed away, the fuel and water tanks have been topped off, spare drums of both have been lashed onto the whaleback, the gear's in good order, and the engine's running well. [3]Bobby climbs off the boat without saying anything to Bugsy and walks across the parking lot to Chris's Volvo. [4]They drive back across town to Thea's and trot up her front steps in a soft warm rain. [5]Thea hears their feet on the stoop and invites them in. [6]"I've got some errands to do," she says. [7]"Make yourselves at home." [8]Outside the rain taps on. [9]Chris and Bobby can't see the ocean but they can smell it, a dank taste of salt and seaweed that permeates the entire peninsula and lays claim to it as part of the sea.

—Sebastian Junger, *The Perfect Storm*

■ Why does the rain make this scene seem sad? Write your answer in a sentence. _____

_____

■ Find the subjects and verbs in *Goodbye Before Sailing* and write them below. Be sure to include *all* the subjects when there are more than one. Sentence 2 has examples of more than one subject.

| Subject or Subjects | Verb |
|---|---|
| 1. _____ | _____ |
| 2. _____ food, bait _____ | _____ have been stowed _____ |
| 3. _____ | _____ |
| 4. _____ | _____ |
| 5. _____ | _____ |
| 6. _____ | _____ |
| 7. _____ | _____ |
| 8. _____ | _____ |
| 9. _____ | _____ |

■ Has the weather ever affected your mood? Write a sentence about a time when it made you happy, excited, or sad. _____

For more work on subjects and verbs, see Review Exercises 1, 3, 4, 6.

# L E S S O N 3
## Clauses and Conjunctions:
## Two Sentences in One

Very often a sentence with its subject and verb will be connected with another sentence with its own subject and verb. When this happens, each of the sentences is called a *clause*, and the two must be connected by (1) a *coordinating conjunction*—words like *and, but, for,* (2) a *subordinating conjunction* like *although, because, as,* or (3) a *relative pronoun*—*who, which, that.* The entire sentence is classified as either *compound* or *complex.* For example, two independent clauses like, *It's a rainy day* and *The class canceled the trip to the beach* can be combined with a coordinating conjunction to become a compound sentence: *It's a rainy day, and the class canceled the trip to the beach.* We'll have more about this in Lessons 33 and 34. For now, let's continue to look for subjects and verbs.

### Iceberg Alert

[1]Soon there are icebergs everywhere—white patches on a blackened sea, sentries of the Arctic. [2]The wisps of fog lengthen and increase in number until they merge to form a solid layer on ahead. [3]But, separating as I pass above them, they leave long channels of open water in between—stripes of gray fog and black water across my course. [4]With every minute I fly, these channels narrow. [5]Finally all the ocean is covered with a thin, undulating veil of mist. [6]At first it doesn't hide the denser whiteness of the icebergs, but makes their forms more ghostlike down below. [7]Then the top of the veil slopes upward toward the east—real fog, thick, hiding the ocean, hiding the icebergs, hiding even the lights of ships if there are any there to shine. [8]I ease the stick back slightly, take five miles from my speed, and turn it into a slow and steady climb.

—Charles Lindbergh, *The Spirit of St. Louis*

▪ Combine these two sentences into one that describes how the icebergs look from the air:

The icebergs are ghostlike. Fog covers their tops. _____

_____

▪ Underline the subjects and verbs in *Iceberg Alert*. For each of the subjects listed below, write the verb that belongs with it. If the sentence has more than one clause, write the connecting word as well.

**15**

| | Subject | Verb | Connective | Subject | Verb |
|---|---|---|---|---|---|
| 1. | icebergs | *are* | | | |
| 2. | wisps | | | *they* | |
| 3. | I | | | *they* | |
| 4. | channels | | | | |
| 5. | all | | | | |
| 6. | it | | | | |
| 7. | top | | | *any* | |
| 8. | I | | | | |

■ Write a sentence about some sign of danger from the weather that you have experienced. _____

_____

# LESSON 3a
# Coordinating Conjunctions

· · · · · · · · · ·

The common coordinating conjunctions are *and, but, for, or, nor, so,* and *yet.* They join independent clauses—clauses that can stand alone as sentences. For example: *Mona likes to watch daytime serials. She doesn't like talk shows.* These two sentences can be combined into one: *Mona likes to watch daytime serials, but she doesn't like talk shows.*

| The Seven Coordinating Conjunctions | | | | | | |
|---|---|---|---|---|---|---|
| and | but | for | nor | or | so | yet |

### Gandhi and His People

[1]Mahatma Gandhi loved not mankind in the abstract but men, women, and children, and he hoped to help them as specific individuals and groups of individuals. [2]He belonged to them and they knew it and therefore they belonged to him. [3]By harboring the disloyal, he dispelled their disloyalty. [4]His loyalty begot theirs. [5]In this wise, during the worst years of defeat and depression from 1924 to 1929, he prepared for later triumphs. [6]India now called him "Bapu," Father.

—Louis Fischer, *Gandhi: His Life and Message for the World*

■ Combine these sentences:

Gandhi saw people as individuals. People regarded him as a father. _____

_____

■ Find the subjects and verbs in the excerpt on the previous page. If the sentence has more than one clause, write the conjunction as well.

| Subject/Verb | Conjunction | Subject/Verb |
|---|---|---|
| 1. *Mahatma Gandhi loved* | *and* | *he hoped* |
| 2. _____ | _____ | _____ |
| 3. _____ | _____ | _____ |
| 4. _____ | _____ | _____ |
| 5. _____ | _____ | _____ |
| 6. _____ | _____ | _____ |
| 7. _____ | _____ | _____ |

■ Think of a person who is admired by everyone you know. Write a sentence about that person. _____

_____

## LESSON 3b
## Subordinating Conjunctions, Relative Pronouns

• • • • • • • • •

Subordinating conjunctions are the words used to join clauses. They include *though, while, before, because, if, when, where,* and *although.* Relative pronouns like *which, that,* and *who* also serve to join clauses. *Sasha, who likes fast cars, could only afford an old Chevy.* The two clauses are *Sasha could only afford an old Chevy* and *who likes fast cars.*

| Subordinating Conjunctions | | | |
|---|---|---|---|
| after | although | as | because |
| before | if | though | when |
| where | whereas | while | |

**After the Hurricane**

[1]About two hours after the windows first broke in young Ryan Ochmanski's bedroom in Whispering Pines, the winds start to ease up a little. [2]As dawn breaks and the winds begin to let up, the Ochmanskis find a haven at a nearby house, which has plywood covers over the windows and seems to be in good shape. [3]A neighbor who is a registered nurse treats Tom's cuts and bruises, and the bruises the others have suffered. [4]Miraculously, none of the family is severely injured. [5]Later that morning, as the rain ends and the winds decrease, Tom and some neighbors return to their houses to see what's left of them—in several cases, not much, almost nothing at all. [6]It turns out that the object that has destroyed the front of the Ochmanski house is a very large chunk of a concrete tie beam. [7]It had sailed with part of the roof still attached over the tops of the houses across the street from the Ochmanski home before crashing into their living room wall.

—Dr. Bob Sheets and Jack Williams, *Hurricane Watch*

- Combine these sentences:

The storm destroyed houses. The people were not seriously injured. _____

_____

- For each of the clauses below, indicate whether it is dependent or independent.

| | Clause | Dependent/Independent |
|---|---|---|
| 1. | after the windows first broke | dependent |
| 2. | as dawn breaks | |
| 3. | the Ochmanskis find a haven | |
| 4. | who is a registered nurse | |
| 5. | none of the family is severely injured | |
| 6. | as the rain ends | |
| 7. | It turns out | |
| 8. | the object that has destroyed the front | |
| 9. | It had sailed | |

- Think of a time when a neighborhood got together to help someone in need. Write a sentence about what everyone did to help. _____

_____

For more work on clauses, see Review Exercises 2, 5, 9, 12, 21, 46.

# L E S S O N   4
# Dependent and Independent Clauses

Clauses that can stand by themselves as sentences are called *independent* clauses. *I slept late this morning* is an example. Clauses that *must* be connected to an independent clause to form a sentence are called *dependent* clauses. An example of this is *Because the alarm didn't go off*. Even though it has a subject and verb, to make sense it has to be joined to *I slept late this morning*.

### The Future of Flying

[1]What limitless possibilities aviation holds when planes can fly nonstop between New York and Paris! [2]The year will surely come when passengers and mail fly every day from America to Europe. [3]Of course flying will cost much more than transportation by surface ship, but letters can be written on lightweight paper, and there'll be people with such pressing business that they can afford the higher price of passage. [4]With multiengined flying boats the safety of operation should be high. [5]Weather will be the greatest problem. [6]We'd have to find some way to fly through sleet and land in fog.

—Charles Lindbergh, *The Spirit of St. Louis*

■ How accurate was Lindbergh's prediction about flying? Write a sentence explaining your answer. _____

_____

■ Underline all of the subjects and verbs in the above paragraph. You will see that some of the clauses are independent and some are dependent. For every sentence that has more than one clause, rewrite each of the clauses as a separate sentence as in the example below.

| Clause 1 | Clause 2 |
|---|---|
| 1. *What limitless possibilities aviation holds* | *Planes can fly nonstop between New York and Paris.* |
| 2. _____ | _____ |
| _____ | _____ |
| 3. _____ | _____ |
| _____ | _____ |

■ Write a sentence describing either what you like or do not like about flying.

_____

**19**

## LESSON 4a
## More Clauses

· · · · · · · · · ·

Most writers use a combination of dependent and independent clauses to make clear the relationships between their ideas. For example: *The spaghetti got cold while we played Scrabble.* In this sentence *the spaghetti got cold* is an independent clause, and *while we played Scrabble* is dependent on what happened to the spaghetti. Look for both independent and dependent clauses in the following passage.

### Saved!

¹At that moment the boss noticed that a fly had fallen into his broad inkpot, and was trying feebly but desperately to clamber out again. ²Help! Help! Said those struggling legs. ³But the sides of the inkpot were wet and slippery; it fell back again and began to swim. ⁴The boss took up a pen, picked the fly out of the ink, and shook it on to a piece of blotting-paper. ⁵For a fraction of a second it lay still on the dark patch that oozed round it. ⁶Then the front legs waved, took hold, and, pulling its small sodden body up, it began the immense task of cleaning the ink from its wings. ⁷Over and under, over and under, went a leg along a wing, as the stone goes over and under the scythe. ⁸Then there was a pause, while the fly, seeming to stand on the tips of its toes, tried to expand first one wing and then the other. ⁹It succeeded at last, and sitting down, it began, like a minute cat, to clean its face. ¹⁰Now one could imagine that the little front legs rubbed against each other lightly, joyfully. ¹¹The horrible danger was over; it had escaped; it was ready for life again.

—Katherine Mansfield, *The Fly*

■ Combine these sentences:

The fly was drowning in the ink. It recovered when it was lifted out. _____

_____

■ Identify the clauses in *Saved!* If a clause is *dependent*, change its wording so that it becomes *independent*. The first has been done as an example.

1. *A fly had fallen into his broad inkpot, and it was trying feebly but*

   *desperately to clamber out again.* _____

2. _____

3. _____

4. _____

5. _____

■ Do you remember seeing or reading about an animal being rescued? Write a sentence describing what happened. _____

_____

## LESSON 4b
## Dependent Clauses with
## Relative Pronouns

. . . . . . . . .

One of the most common ways of connecting clauses is with the relative pronoun *which*, but *who* and *that* are also frequently used. For example: *My car, which needs an oil change, stalled on Main Street*. The independent clause is *my car stalled on Main Street*, and the dependent clause is *which needs an oil change*. Note how relative pronouns that connect clauses can sometimes be the subject of the clause, as *that* is in this sentence.

### A Record Tying Pitch

¹On the afternoon of October 2nd, 1968—a warm, sunshiny day in St. Louis—Mickey Stanley, the Detroit Tiger shortstop, singled to center field to lead off the top of the ninth inning of the opening game of the 1968 World Series. ²It was only the fifth hit of the game for the Tigers, who by this time were trailing the National League Champion St. Louis Cardinals by a score of 4–0. ³The next batter, the dangerous Al Kaline, worked the count to two and two and then fanned, swinging away at a fastball, to an accompanying roar from the crowd. ⁴A moment later, there was a second enormous cheer, louder and more sustained than the first. ⁵The Cardinal catcher, Tim McCarver, who had straightened up to throw the ball back to his pitcher, now hesitated. ⁶The pitcher, Bob Gibson, a notoriously swift worker on the mound, motioned to his battery mate to return the ball. ⁷Instead, McCarver pointed with his gloved hand at something behind Gibson's head. ⁸Gibson, staring uncomprehendingly at his catcher, yelled, "C'mon, c'mon, let's *go!*" ⁹Still holding the ball, McCarver pointed again, and Gibson, turning around, read the illuminated message on the centerfield scoreboard, which perhaps only he in the ballpark had not seen until that moment: "Gibson's fifteenth strikeout in one game ties the all-time World Series record held by Sandy Koufax."

—Roger Angell, *Late Innings*

■ Why did Gibson want McCarver to return the ball? Write your answer in a sentence. _____

_____

■ Underline all the relative clauses in *A Record Tying Pitch*. Rewrite them as *independent* clauses, following the example given below.

1. *The Tigers by this time were trailing the National League Champion St. Louis Cardinals by a score of 4–0.*

2. _____

3. _____

■ Write a sentence about an exciting moment in sports that you have experienced. _____

_____

For more work on relative clauses, see Review Exercises 2.21.

## L E S S O N   5
# Infinitives and Participles: Verbs Without Tense

. . . . . . . . .

*Infinitives* are verb forms that do not have tense and cannot serve as the verb of a sentence. They are always combined with *to: to walk, to go, to see.* *Participles* are verb forms that can have tense only when combined with help-ing verbs. The *present participle* ends in *-ing* (see Lessons 20–23): *Maria is writing, Jo is reading.* The *past participle* sometimes ends in *-d,* sometimes in another form (see Lessons 17 and 18): *Evan had studied. Randi has spoken.*

### Fighting Sleep

[1]The *Spirit of St. Louis* is climbing slowly. [2]I push the stick forward—and left to lift the wing, left rudder to stop the turn. [3]I keep my head in the slipstream, breathing deeply. [4]Now I see clearly. [5]Now, my mind and my senses join. [6]The seriousness of the crisis has startled me to awareness. [7]I've finally bro-ken the spell of sleep. [8]I feel as though I were recuperating from a severe ill-ness. [9]When you're suffering from a disease, the time comes when you know the crisis has passed. [10]The fever leaves; a sense of health returns, and you're increasingly able to use your normal mind and body.

—Charles Lindbergh, *The Spirit of St. Louis*

■ Combine these sentences:

Lindbergh was startled awake. The plane did not crash. _____

_____

■ Find the past and present participles, and the infinitives in *Fighting Sleep.* Write them in the columns below, following the examples.

| | Present Participle | Past Participle | Infinitive |
|---|---|---|---|
| 1. | *is climbing* | | |
| 2. | | | *to lift, to stop* |
| 3. | | *has startled* | |
| 4. | | | |
| 5. | | | |
| 6. | | | |
| 7. | | | |

**23**

- Have you ever fallen asleep in class or on some other occasion when you were supposed to be alert? Write a sentence about it. _____

---

For more work on infinitives and participles, see Review Exercises 7, 16, 30, 39.

## LESSON 5a
## More Verbs Without Tense

. . . . . . . . . .

Remember that verbs without tense—infinitives and present and past participles—cannot serve as the verb of a sentence *unless* they are joined with an auxiliary or helping verb. Look for these forms in the next passage:

### The Tribe's Values

¹Chee put down the ledger. ²He was being racist. ³He had been thinking like a racist ever since he'd met Janet Pete and fallen in love with her. ⁴He had been thinking that because her name was Pete, because her father was Navajo, her blood somehow would have taught her the ways of the *Diné* and made her one of them. ⁵But only your culture taught you values, and the culture that had formed Janet was blue-blooded, white, Ivy League, chic, irreligious, old-rich Maryland. ⁶And that made it just about as opposite as it could get from the traditional values of his people, which made wealth a symbol for selfishness, and had caused a friend of his to deliberately stop winning rodeo competitions because he was getting unhealthily famous and therefore out of harmony.

—Tony Hillerman, *The Fallen Man*

- Write a sentence explaining the belief of Chee's people about values.

---

---

- Find the past and present participles and the infinitives in *The Tribe's Values*. Write them in the columns below, including any auxiliary verbs that go with them.

| Infinitive | Present Participle | Past Participle |
|---|---|---|
| 1. _____ | *was being* | _____ |
| 2. _____ | _____ | *had been thinking* |

| | Infinitive | Present Participle | Past Participle |
|---|---|---|---|
| | *to stop* | | |
| 3. | _____ | _____ | _____ |
| 4. | _____ | _____ | _____ |
| 5. | _____ | _____ | _____ |

- Think of a custom or belief that belongs to your family's culture. Write a sentence about it. _____

_____

# LESSON 5b
# Participles and Infinitives

• • • • • • • • •

Although infinitives never serve as the verb of a sentence, both past and present participles can do this if they have the help of an auxiliary or helping verb, a part of the verb *to be* or of the verb *to have*. See Lessons 17–18 and 20–22 for more on this topic.

| Remember that the forms of *to be* and *to have* are irregular. | | | |
|---|---|---|---|
| **The present tense of *to be* is** | | **The present tense of *to have* is** | |
| *I am* | *we are* | *I have* | *we have* |
| *you are* | *you are* | *you have* | *you have* |
| *he, she, it is* | *they are* | *he, she, it has* | *they have* |

### The Story of Hastings

[1]The Battle of Hastings has been fought on paper innumerable times, but strictly military accounts of it have always had to leave some mysteries unsolved. [2]One source of the mysteries is that the early accounts are entirely one-sided. [3]Within the lifetime of the men who fought, nothing was recorded on the English side. [4]So one can only see the English army from the point of view of the men who attacked it: one cannot know what happened inside its ranks. [5]Moreover, the historians on William's side were not writing dry and factual narratives, they were telling exciting stories, each for a receptive audience of his own: Guy for the French, the chaplain for

the Norman admirers of William, and the tapestry designer for the illiterate majority who preferred a strip-cartoon to a written page.

—David Howarth, *1066: The Year of the Conquest*

■ Combine these sentences:

Our knowledge of the Battle of Hastings is one-sided. There are no records from

the English. _____

_____

■ Identify the infinitives and the past and present participles in the above excerpt. Write them below, including the helpers if they are part of the verb.

| Past Participle | Present Participle | Infinitive |
|---|---|---|
| 1. *has been fought* | | |
| 2. | | *to leave* |
| 3. | *were telling* | |
| 4. | | |
| 5. | | |

■ Think of an exciting story that you know from history. Write a sentence

about it. _____

_____

For more work on participles, see Review Exercises 7, 16, 30, 39.

# YOUR WRITING
*Finding a Thesis*

Why does virtually every college and university require one or more composition courses of its students? It is quite simply because no matter what we do in life in whatever profession, occupation, or undertaking, we will be called on to write, and to do it in a clear, concise way that will convey significant information to others. A student once challenged me on this, insisting that she knew of a job—dance teacher—that involved no writing. When I asked her what such a teacher does, she replied, "She writes down the steps of the dance. . . ."

Recording dance steps may seem far removed from the kind of composition you are asked to submit in your writing class, but it does confirm the need for writing in your daily life and work. What we do in a writing class can be compared to what we do when learning to play an instrument or mastering a sport like tennis or swimming: we practice, practice, practice.

No one can play a sonata or hit a line drive without many hours of practice. The same is true of writing; behind a first-rate term paper, an impressive annual report, or a persuasive application letter are thoughtful revisions and rewritings.

Where then do we begin if we want to practice the art of writing?

The sentence is the bottom line! It is the basis of all human language. Animals, as you probably know, have ways of communicating: some birds have a call warning of danger, some monkeys can signal with a sound indicating that food is available. But no matter how sophisticated an animal's means of communication may be, we know of none that can produce sentences. We humans are thus unique in being able to communicate in sentences. And we can go on indefinitely producing sentences that have never been spoken before.

It's no wonder, then, with a tool as powerful as the sentence, that all writing should begin with that familiar combination of subject and verb. Of course, not just any old sentence will do. Sometimes you need a sentence that must express in just a few words the entire contents of a composition you are about to write. How can you do that? You do it by saying that someone or something is or does something, and then going on to write a good deal more about *both* the subject and the predicate. For example: *Internet cafes can bring people together.*

Now, a statement like this may seem at first like a contradiction, since we often hear about people being isolated by spending so much time at their computers. But the student who wrote about this managed to find many things to say about people socializing at cybercafes, from sharing meals to playing games.

The point is that she made a statement about something that then called for a good deal more explanation, and that is what you are being asked to do when you're assigned to write a paper.

Whether we call this statement an assertion or, most often, a thesis sentence, without it our papers run the risk of having no structure; we may find ourselves going off in a dozen different directions and, finally, not making a point. And, after all, isn't the reason for writing anything to make a point? Think about that. If your writing doesn't make a point, isn't all the work you put into it in danger of being a waste of time?

What kind of sentence is a thesis statement? First of all, it must be simple. Its purpose is not to tell a story, paint a picture, or show how to do something. But it must say something that you can demonstrate by writing a great deal more about it. Consider, for example, *The computer simplified writing.* You may think immediately of the ease of correcting your work, of the ways it can be saved, and of how professional-looking the printed-out result is.

Write five sentences that could be the thesis statement for a composition. Some of them could be about an invention that has changed peoples' lives.

1. _____

2. _____

3. _____

4. _____

5. _____

Now choose one of these sentences, the one you think you can write much more about. Is it a simple declarative sentence? Does it make one point? Then it can serve as your thesis when we begin the next lesson.

# UNIT 11

# With a Little Help . . .

**M**any years ago schools didn't teach English to English-speaking students. After all, the teachers figured, students know their own language; why should they have to be taught it? So instead the students were taught Latin! Now, even though many of our words originally came from Latin, the language itself is almost as different from English in other ways as it can get. For example, every noun, pronoun, and adjective has a different ending, depending on how it is used in a sentence, and they all have to agree with one another. And that's not all! Every verb, in every person, every number, and every tense has a different ending, for a total of 135 verb forms.

Compare all of those with the regular verb endings we have in English: *-s* for the third person singular present tense, *-ed* for the past tense and most past participles, and *-ing* for the present participle. Well, does that mean we can't say as many things in English as we can say in Latin? Far from it. It just means that we have *different* ways of saying them. Helping verbs are one way we do this.

Look at the verbs in the following excerpt:

All afternoon the plane **had soared** through the thin mists of the upper atmosphere, far too high to give clear sight of what lay beneath. Sometimes, at longish intervals, the veil **was torn** for a moment, to display the jagged outline of a peak, or the glint of some unknown stream. The direction **could be determined** roughly from the sun; it was still east, with occasional twists to the north; but where it **had led** depended on the speed of travel, which Conway **could not judge** with any accuracy.

—James Hilton, *Lost Horizon*

More than half of them have a helper, or *auxiliary* to give them a shade of meaning they would not otherwise have. Verbs that are combined with such helpers are called *compound verbs*.

**29**

# LESSON 6
## Verbs Combined with *Have*

. . . . . . . . . .

We use the past tense to indicate that something happened in the past: *Joe saw the light.* Another way of showing that something happened in the past but continues to be true is to write *Joe has seen the light.* This is usually called the present perfect tense. Still another way to indicate a past action is to say that something happened once in the past, but is unlikely to happen again under the same circumstances: *Joe had seen the light.* We call this the past perfect tense.

**The present perfect uses these forms of the verb *to have***

| | |
|---|---|
| *I have* | *We have* |
| *You have* | *You have* |
| *She, he, it has* | *They have* |

Remember that only the *she, he, it* form has an *-s* at the end.

**The past perfect uses these forms of to have**

| | |
|---|---|
| *I had* | *we had* |
| *you had* | *you had* |
| *he, she, it had* | *they had* |

### The Inheritance

[1]The High Lama, after waiting awhile, resumed: "You know, perhaps, that the frequency of these talks has been unusual here. [2]I have waited for you, my son, for quite a long time. [3]I have sat in this room and seen the faces of new-comers, I have looked into their eyes and heard their voices, and always in hope that some day I might find you. [4]My colleagues have grown old and wise, but you who are still young in years are as wise already. [5]My friend, it is not an arduous task that I bequeath, for our order knows only silken bonds. [6]To be gentle and patient, to care for the riches of the mind, to preside in wisdom and secrecy while the storm rages without—it will all be very pleasantly simple for you, and you will doubtless find great happiness."

—James Hilton, *Lost Horizon*

■ Combine these sentences:

The High Lama has chosen his successor. The successor is young but wise.

_____

_____

■ Find the present perfect verbs in *The Inheritance*. Write them below followed by the simple past tense form of the verb, as demonstrated in the example below:

| **Present Perfect Tense** | **Simple Past Tense** |
|---|---|
| 1. *has been* | *was* |
| 2. | |
| 3. | |
| 4. | |
| 5. | |

■ Identify a character trait that you think indicates wisdom and write a sentence about it. _____

_____

_____

## LESSON 6a
## Compound Verbs with *Have*

· · · · · · · · ·

Present perfect verbs usually indicate something that happens more than once—a continuing action. *I have gone to the beach every weekend this summer. Jake has become a serious student this semester.*

### Flying into the Storm

¹Headwinds along the leading edge of the rain band are so strong that it feels as if the helicopter has been blown to a stop. ²Ruvola has no idea what he has run into; all he knows is that he can barely control the aircraft. ³Flying has become as much a question of physical strength as of finesse; he grips the collective with one hand, the joystick with the other, and leans forward to peer through the rain rattling off the windscreen. ⁴Flight manuals bounce around the cockpit and his copilot starts throwing up in the seat next to him. ⁵The pilot starts in on the shutdown procedure, and suddenly the left-hand fuel hose retracts; shutting off the engine has disrupted the air

flow around the wing, and the reel-in mechanism has mistaken that for too much slack. [6]The line has been destroyed by forty-five minutes of desperate refueling attempts.

—Sebastian Junger, *The Perfect Storm*

■ What is the most important quality for a helicopter pilot to have when flying in a storm? Write your answer in a sentence. _____

_____

■ For each of the subjects below, write the compound verb that completes it.

| Subject | Compound verb |
|---|---|
| 1. *the helicopter* | *has been blown* |
| 2. *he* | |
| 3. *flying* | |
| 4. *the line* | |

■ What do you consider an extremely hazardous job—flying a helicopter, washing the windows of a skyscraper, doing police work? Write a sentence about someone you have seen working on a dangerous job. _____

_____

# LESSON 6b
# More Compound Verbs with *Have*
· · · · · · · · ·

The present perfect—*have* plus the *past participle*—is a useful way to talk about an activity that continues over some time, like the study of the universe discussed in the following passage. Often writers will place an adverb between the helping verb and the past participle: *Milo had often called Jenna for help with his homework.*

## The Expanding Universe

[1]In the decades that astronomers have debated the fate of the expanding universe—whether it will all end one day in a big crunch, or whether the galaxies will sail apart forever—aficionados of eternal expansion have always been braced by its seemingly endless possibilities for development

and evolution. [2]In the last four years astronomers have reported evidence that the expansion of the universe is not just continuing but is speeding up, under the influence of a mysterious "dark energy," an antigravity that seems to be embedded in space itself. [3]If that is true and the universe goes on accelerating, astronomers say, rather than coasting gently into the night, distant galaxies will eventually be moving apart so quickly that they cannot communicate with one another. [4]In effect, it would be like living in the middle of a black hole that kept getting emptier and colder.

—Dennis Overbye, *The End of Everything*

▪ Combine these sentences:

The expansion of the universe may be speeding up. Galaxies will be moving apart quickly. _____

_____

▪ Underline all the compound verbs with *to have* from the excerpt above and write them below, including any adverbs that may divide the verb and the auxiliary.

| Helping Verb | Adverb | Verb |
|---|---|---|
| 1. _____have_____ | _____always_____ | _____been_____ |
| 2. _____ | _____ | _____ |
| 3. _____ | _____ | _____ |

▪ Write a sentence about a scientific discovery that you find exciting. It might be one that took place centuries ago or one that happened recently. _____

_____

For more about helping verbs, see Review Exercises 8, 10, 16, 44.

## LESSON 7
# Verbs Combined with the Past Tense of *Have*

The past tense of *have*, in all its forms, is *had*. Combined with a verb it becomes the past perfect tense, a tense that shows something happened for the first and only time in the past. For example: *The ship had sailed at dawn.*

### Settling in to Shangri-La

[1]By that time the party had settled themselves into something like a daily routine, and with Chang's assistance the boredom was no more acute than on many a planned holiday. [2]They had all become acclimatized to the atmosphere, finding it quite invigorating so long as heavy exertion was avoided. [3]They had learned that the days were warm and the nights cold, that the lamasery was amost completely sheltered from winds, that avalanches on Karakal were most frequent about midday, that the valley grew a good brand of tobacco, that some foods and drinks were more pleasant than others, and that each one of themselves had personal tastes and peculiarities. [4]They had, in fact, discovered as much about each other as four new pupils of a school from which every one else was mysteriously absent.

—James Hilton, *Lost Horizon*

■ What did the travelers find pleasant about Shangri-La? Write your answer in a sentence. _____

_____

■ Find the verbs in the excerpt above that combine the past participle with a form of the auxiliary *have*. Write them below.

| Auxiliary | Past Participle |
|---|---|
| 1. *had* | *settled* |
| 2. _____ | _____ |
| 3. _____ | _____ |
| 4. _____ | _____ |

■ Think about a time you met a new group of friends—the first day of school or at camp. Write a sentence about the experience. _____

_____

## LESSON 7a
## The Verb *Have* Combined
## with the Past Participle

. . . . . . . . .

When a story—or *anecdote*—is already being told in the past tense, things that happened even earlier can be told by using a compound verb with a form of the verb *to have. The class had a quiz that week. They had had a test every Friday of the semester.*

### Adventures of the Round Table

¹At the feast of Pentecost it was customary for the knights who had been on Table quests to gather again so as to relate their adventures. ²Arthur had found that this made people keener on fighting in the new way of Right, if they had to tell about it afterwards. ³Most of them preferred to bring their prisoners with them, as witnesses of their stories. ⁴Sir Bedivere came and admitted how he had swapped off his adulterous wife's head. ⁵He had brought it with him, and was told to take it to the Pope as a penance. ⁶Gawaine came gruffly and told how he had been rescued from Sir Carados. ⁷Besides these, there were many people from adventures which we have left out—mainly knights who had yielded to Sir Lancelot when he was disguised as Sir Kay. ⁸Kay was inclined to throw his tongue a bit too much, and he had got himself unpopular on account of this. ⁹Lancelot had been compelled during the quest to rescue him from three knights who were pursuing him. ¹⁰All these people gave themselves up.

—T. H. White, *The Once and Future King*

■ Combine these sentences:

King Arthur held a feast at Pentecost. The knights related their adventures.

_____

■ Find the compound verbs formed with a part of *to have* in the passage above and write them below; then write the simple past tense of the verb, as the example shows.

| Compound Verb | Simple Past Tense |
|---|---|
| 1. _____ *had found* _____ | _____ *found* _____ |
| 2. _____ | _____ |
| 3. _____ | _____ |

| Compound Verb | Simple Past Tense |
|---|---|
| 4. _____ | _____ |
| 5. _____ | _____ |

■ What is your favorite kind of adventure story: espionage, or police thriller, or science fiction or something else? Write a sentence explaining why you enjoy this type of writing. _____

_____

# LESSON 7b
# More Verbs with *Have*

· · · · · · · · · ·

A compound verb and its helper are often separated by one or more adverbs, as in this example: *Sonya has definitely decided to major in biology.*

### Fred's Failures

[1]His failure in passing his examination had made his accumulation of college debts the more unpardonable by his father, and there had been an unprecedented storm at home. [2]Mr. Vincy had sworn that if he had anything more of that sort to put up with, Fred should turn out and get his living how he could; and he had never yet quite recovered his good-humoured tone to his son, who had especially enraged him by saying at this stage of things that he did not want to be a clergyman, and would rather not "go on with that." [3]Fred was conscious that he would have been yet more severely dealt with if his family as well as himself had not secretly regarded him as Mr. Featherstone's heir; that old gentleman's pride in him, and apparent fondness for him, serving in the stead of more exemplary conduct.

—George Eliot, *Middlemarch*

■ Combine these sentences:

Fred's failures were not very severely dealt with. His family expected him to be

Mr. Featherstone's heir. _____

_____

▪ Identify the compound verbs with *have* in this excerpt. If there are any adverbs between the auxiliary and the verb, write them in the appropriate space, as shown in the example.

| **Verb** | **Adverb(s)** |
| --- | --- |
| 1. *had recovered* | *never yet quite* |
| 2. | |
| 3. | |
| 4. | |
| 5. | |
| 6. | |

▪ Think of an examination you were particularly worried about passing. Write a sentence explaining why it was so important to you. _____

For more about compound verbs, see Review Exercises 8, 10, 16, 44.

# LESSON 8
# Verb Combinations with *Be* and Its Forms as Helpers

. . . . . . . . .

The verb *to be* is very irregular. In the present tense its forms are as follows

| | |
|---|---|
| *I am* | *we are* |
| *you are* | *you are* |
| *he, she, it is* | *they are* |

In the past tense the forms of *to be* are as follows

| | |
|---|---|
| *I was* | *we were* |
| *you were* | *you were* |
| *she, he, it was* | *they were* |

### The Departure

[1]All the time, though he hardly heard him, Mallinson was chattering about the journey. [2]How strange that their long argument should have ended thus in action, that this secret sanctuary should be forsaken by one who had found in it such happiness! [3]Now, at that moment, it was farewell. [4]Mallinson, whom the steep ascent had kept silent for a time, gasped out: "Good man, we are doing fine—carry on!" [5]Conway smiled, but did not reply; he was already preparing the rope for the knife-edge traverse. [6]Towards dawn they crossed the divide, unchallenged by sentinels, even if there were any; though it occurred to Conway that the route, in the true spirit, might only be moderately well watched. [7]Then all was as Mallinson had foretold; they found the men ready for them, sturdy fellows in furs and sheepskins, crouching under the gale and eager to begin the journey to Tatsien-Fu—eleven hundred miles eastward on the China border.

—James Hilton, *Lost Horizon*

■ Combine these sentences:

The two men must cross the precipice. They want to reach the guides for their

journey. _____

_____

■ Find the verbs in the excerpt above that combine an auxiliary, or helper, part of the verb *to be*, with a present participle and write them below, as shown in the example.

|  | **Auxiliary** | **Verb** |
|---|---|---|
| 1. | *was* | *chattering* |
| 2. | | |
| 3. | | |

■ Write a sentence about a trip you have taken that involved some danger.

_____

## LESSON 8a
## The Present Participle with *Be*

. . . . . . . . .

This is a useful way to show that an action goes on for a period of time rather than just happening and stopping. For example, *Lucia looks out the window* does not provide as much information as *Lucia is looking out the window all day instead of studying.*

### Birds in Flight

¹It was a late hour on a cold, wind-bitten autumn day when I climbed a great hill spined like a dinosaur's back and tried to take my bearings. ²The tumbled waste fell away in waves in all directions. ³Blue air was darkening into purple along the bases of the hills. ⁴I shifted my knapsack, heavy with the petrified bones of long-vanished creatures, and studied my compass. ⁵I wanted to be out of there by nightfall, and already the sun was going sullenly down in the west. ⁶It was then that I saw the flight coming on. ⁷It was moving like a little close-knit body of black specks that danced and darted and closed again. ⁸It was pouring from the north and heading toward me with the undeviating relentlessness of a compass needle. ⁹It streamed through the shadows rising out of

monstrous gorges. [10]It rushed over towering pinnacles in the red light of the sun, or momentarily sank from sight within their shade. [11]Across that desert of eroding clay and wind-worn stone they came with a faint wild twittering that filled all the air about me as those tiny living bullets hurtled past into the night.

—Loren Eiseley, *The Judgment of the Birds*

■ Why does the writer use *bullets* as an analogy for flying birds in this passage? Write your answer in a sentence. _____

_____

■ Write below the compound verbs in this excerpt formed with the auxiliary *to be* and the present participle. Note that not all words ending in *-ing* are verbs in this excerpt. Then write a sentence using the simple past tense of the verb, as shown in the example.

|   | **Verb** | **Sentence** |
|---|---|---|
| 1. | *was darkening* | *The sky darkened in the evening.* |
| 2. | | |
| 3. | | |
| 4. | | |

■ Have you ever watched a flight of birds heading south for the winter? Write a sentence explaining what they reminded you of. _____

_____

# LESSON 8b
# More Verbs with Present Participles

As with past participles, compound verbs with present participles can be divided by an adverb. For example, *Greg was intently studying his Sociology notes.*

### Never Alone

[1]It was a bright cold day in April, and the clocks were striking thirteen. [2]Winston Smith, his chin nuzzled into his breast in an effort to escape the vile wind, slipped quickly through the glass doors of Victory Mansions

though not quickly enough to prevent a swirl of gritty dust from entering along with him. ³Outside, even through the shut windowpane, the world looked cold. ⁴Down in the street little eddies of wind were whirling dust and torn paper into spirals, and though the sun was shining and the sky a harsh blue, there seemed to be no color in anything except the posters that were plastered everywhere. ⁵The black-mustachio'd face gazed down from every commanding corner. ⁶There was one on the house front immediately opposite. ⁷BIG BROTHER IS WATCHING YOU the caption said, while the dark eyes looked deep into Winston's own. ⁸Behind Winston's back the voice from the telescreen was still babbling away about pig iron and the overfulfillment of the Ninth Three-Year Plan.

—George Orwell, *Nineteen Eighty-Four*

■ Combine these sentences:

There was a telescreen in every room. All of a person's movements were watched. _____

_____

■ Underline the compound verbs in the passage above, then write them on the lines below. Be sure to choose only verbs formed with *to be* and *-ing*. For each verb write a sentence using the simple present tense of that verb.

|  | **Verb** | **Sentence** |
|---|---|---|
| 1. | *were striking* | *The clock strikes the hour.* |
| 2. | | |
| 3. | | |
| 4. | | |
| 5. | | |

■ Think about a poster you have seen that surprised or frightened you. Write a sentence explaining why it had this effect. _____

_____

For more about present participles, see Review Exercises 7, 16, 30, 39.

# L E S S O N   9
## Helpers Without Tense

· · · · · · · · ·

A large group of helping verbs, sometimes called *modal auxiliaries*, is used to show that an action may or may not take place. These are words like *can, could, may, might, must, ought, should,* and *would.* Unlike other verbs and helpers, they have no endings for tense or number.

| | | | |
|---|---|---|---|
| *I can* | *We can* | *I might* | *We might* |
| *You can* | *You can* | *You might* | *You might* |
| *He, she, it can* | *They can* | *She, he, it might* | *They might* |

Here's an example of a modal auxiliary used in a sentence: *Juanita may play the oboe.*

### The First View

[1]To Conway, seeing it first, it might have been a vision fluttering out of that solitary rhythm in which lack of oxygen had encompassed all his faculties. [2]A group of colored pavilions clung to the mountainside with none of the grim deliberation of a Rhineland castle, but rather with the chance delicacy of flower-petals impaled upon a crag. [3]Beyond that, in a dazzling pyramid, soared the snow slopes of Karakal. [4]It might well be, Conway thought, the most terrifying mountainscape in the world, and he imagined the immense stress of snow and glacier against which the rock functioned as a gigantic retaining wall. [5]Someday, perhaps, the whole mountain would split, and a half of Karakal's icy splendor come toppling into the valley. [6]He wondered if the slightness of the risk combined with its fearfulness might even be found agreeably stimulating. [7]Hardly less an enticement was the downward prospect, for the mountain wall continued to drop, nearly perpendicularly, into a cleft that could only have been the result of some cataclysm in the far past.

—James Hilton, *Lost Horizon*

■ What is terrifying about Conway's first look at Karakal? Write your answer in a sentence. _____

_____

**43**

■ Several of the compound verbs in this excerpt are formed with modal auxiliaries. Some have more than one helping verb. Find them, then write them on the lines below, as shown in the example.

| Modal Auxiliary | Other Auxiliary (if there is one) | Verb |
|---|---|---|
| 1. _____ might _____ | _____ have _____ | _____ been _____ |
| 2. _____ | _____ | _____ |
| 3. _____ | _____ | _____ |
| 4. _____ | _____ | _____ |
| 5. _____ | _____ | _____ |

■ Think of the most exciting natural wonder view you have ever seen—a mountain, an ocean, or some other scenic place. Write a sentence explaining how you felt when you first saw it. _____

_____

## LESSON 9a
## More Helpers Without Tense

Very often helpers form contractions with their verbs. An interesting example is *would have*, which becomes *would've*. Sometimes this is mistakenly written *would of* because that is what it sounds like. Be careful about this.

### The Umpire's Brush

[1]Probably the most important piece of equipment the umpire has is the whisk brush which he uses to clean home plate. [2]These brushes are not easy to find in stores because they have to be wide, but must have very short handles so they will fit into a back pocket. [3]Brushes last for many years and umpires become very emotional about them. [4]If an umpire can't find his brush before a big game he might go crazy. [5]Gugie had a brush that should be in the Hall of Fame. [6]He must've used it for twenty seasons and by the time I worked with him it only had a few stumpy bristles left on it; because of this it took him a long, long time to clean the plate. [7]He'd be scratching the dirt off home and the batter or catcher would suggest he buy a new brush. [8]To Gugie this was like insulting his best friend.

—Ron Luciano, *The Umpire Strikes Back*

■ Combine these sentences:

Umpires are very attached to their whisk brushes. The right kind is hard to find.

_____

■ In the excerpt above underline the verbs formed with modal helpers and write them below. Be sure to note that some of them are contractions, like *he'd be* for *he would be*.

|  Helper | Verb |
|---------|------|
| 1. _____*must*_____ | _____*have*_____ |
| 2. _____ | _____ |
| 3. _____ | _____ |
| 4. _____ | _____ |
| 5. _____ | _____ |
| 6. _____ | _____ |
| 7. _____ | _____ |

■ Write a sentence about a sporting event you attended at which your favorite team was defeated at the last minute. _____

_____

## LESSON 9b
## Helpers and Their Verbs

• • • • • • • • •

Unlike helping verbs that are combined with past and present participles, those without tense are combined with the infinitive form of the verb, the form without any changing endings. *To go, to look, to walk, to understand, to seek* are just a few examples of the infinitive form. For example, *we want to take the bus to the game.*

### After the Concentration Camp

[1]Even though conditions such as lack of sleep, insufficient food and various mental stresses may suggest that the inmates of concentration camps were bound to react in certain ways, in the final analysis it becomes clear that the

sort of person the prisoner became was the result of an inner decision, and not the result of camp influences alone. ²Fundamentally, therefore, any man can, even under such circumstances, decide what shall become of him—mentally and spiritually. ³He may retain his human dignity even in a concentration camp. ⁴I became acquainted with martyrs whose behavior in camp, whose suffering and death, bore witness to the fact that the last inner freedom cannot be lost. ⁵It is this spiritual freedom—which cannot be taken away—that makes life meaningful and purposeful.

—Viktor E. Frankl, *Man's Search for Meaning*

■ What example does the writer give of inner freedom? Write your answer in a sentence. _____

_____

■ Underline the modal helpers in the passage above. Use them to complete the sentences below.

1. To do well in school one ___*must*___ study.

2. We _____ decide to go to the ball game.

3. Matt _____ take us in his car.

4. _____ we pack a picnic lunch?

■ Think of a proverb or wise saying that you hear people using frequently, like *Early to bed, early to rise.* . . . Write a sentence about the usefulness of that statement. _____

_____

For more about helping verbs, see Review Exercises 8, 10, 16, 44.

## L E S S O N  1 0
# A Special Kind of Helper

• • • • • • • • •

Two very familiar helping verbs, *shall* and *will,* combine with the verb to form the future tense. Unlike many other languages, English has no ending to indicate that a verb is in the future tense. Instead it uses these helpers to show that an action is to take place at a later time: *Sam will arrive on the ten o'clock train.*

### A New Dark Age

[1]"The Dark Ages that are to come will cover the whole world in a single pall; there will be neither escape nor sanctuary, save such as are too secret to be found or too humble to be noticed. [2]And Shangri-La may hope to be both of these. [3]The airman bearing loads of death to the great cities will not pass our way, and if by chance he should he may not consider us worth a bomb. [4]I believe that you will live through the storm. [5]And after, through the long age of desolation, you may still live, growing older and wiser and more patient. [6]You will conserve the fragrance of our history and add to it the touch of your own mind. [7]You will welcome the stranger and teach him the rule of age and wisdom; and one of these strangers, it may well be, will succeed you when you are yourself very old. [8]Beyond that, my vision weakens, but I see, at a great distance, a new world stirring in the ruins, stirring clumsily but in hopefulness, seeking its lost and legendary treasures. [9]And they will all be here, my son, hidden behind the mountains in the valley of Blue Moon."

—James Hilton, *Lost Horizon*

■ Combine these sentences:

The Dark Age will end. The new world will seek the lost treasures. _____

_____

■ The excerpt above is predicting things to happen in the future. Find the future tense verbs and write them below, as shown in the example.

| Auxiliary | Verb |
|---|---|
| 1. _____ *will* _____ | _____ *cover* _____ |
| 2. _____ | _____ |
| 3. _____ | _____ |
| 4. _____ | _____ |

**47**

|            Auxiliary            |              Verb              |
| ------------------------------- | ------------------------------ |
| 5. _____ | _____ |
| 6. _____ | _____ |
| 7. _____ | _____ |
| 8. _____ | _____ |

▪ Write a sentence explaining one of the qualities you would include if you could design an ideal world. _____

_____

## LESSON 10a
## Future Tense Verbs

· · · · · · · · · ·

The future tense is most often expressed by the helping verb *will* and the simple present tense form of the verb: *will see, will talk, will remember, will swim.* For example, *Commencement will take place next Sunday.*

### The Knight's Vigil

[1]What happens when you are made a knight? Only a lot of fuss. [2]You will have to undress him and put him in a bath hung with rich hangings, and then two experienced knights will turn up—probably Sir Ector will get hold of old Grummore and King Pellinore—and they will both sit on the edge of the bath and give him a long lecture about the ideals of chivalry, such as they are. [3]When they have done, they will pour some of the bath water over him and sign him with the cross, and then you will have to conduct him into a clean bed to get dry. [4]Then you dress him up as a hermit and take him off to the chapel, and there he stays awake all night, watching his armour and saying prayers. [5]People say it is lonely and terrible for him in this vigil, but it is not at all lonely really, because the vicar and the man who sees to the candles and an armed guard and probably you as well, as his esquire, will have to sit up with him at the same time.

—T. H. White, *The Sword in the Stone*

▪ Why is it necessary for the knight-to-be to have a lecture about the ideals of chivalry? Write your answer in a sentence. _____

_____

■ Underline the future tense verbs in *The Knight's Vigil* and write them below.

1. _____*will have*_____   4. _____

2. _____   5. _____

3. _____

■ Did you ever have to go through a test or initiation to join a club or other

organization? Write a sentence about what happened. _____

_____

## LESSON 10b
## More Future Tense Verbs
• • • • • • • • •

One of the common contractions of verbs adds *'ll* to the subject, as in
*The class'll start later* or *We'll see you tomorrow.*

### A Friendlier World

[1]If you don't like people, put up with them as well as you can. [2]Don't try to
love them; you can't, you'll only strain yourself. [3]But try to tolerate them. [4]On
the basis of that tolerance a civilized future may be built. [5]For what it will
most need is the negative virtues: not being huffy, touchy, irritable, revenge-
ful. [6]I have lost all faith in positive militant ideals; they can so seldom be carried out without thousands of human beings getting maimed or imprisoned.
[7]Phrases like "I will purge this nation," "I will clean up this city," terrify and disgust me. [8]They might not have mattered when the world was emptier; they
are horrifying now, when one nation is mixed up with another, when one city
cannot be organically separated from its neighbours. [9]Tolerance, I believe,
will be imperative after the establishment of peace. [10]It is wanted in the
street, in the office, at the factory, and it is wanted above all between
classes, races, and nations.

—E. M. Forster, *Tolerance*

■ Combine these sentences:

We don't have to like people to tolerate them. We can live peacefully only with

tolerance. _____

_____

■ For each of the subjects below, write its future tense verb from the passage above.

| Subject | Verb |
|---|---|
| 1. You | *will strain* |
| 2. It | |
| 3. I | |
| 4. Tolerance | |

■ What do you consider the most important quality to ensure that people in a group get along with each other? Write your answer in a sentence. _____

_____

# LESSON 11
## The Many Forms of *Do*

. . . . . . . . .

The verb *to do*, like *to have* and *to be*, can sometimes be a helper. *Does* Joey play hockey? I *do* like ice cream.

*Do* is also used with *not* to turn a verb into a negative. A positive sentence, *We listen to the radio in the car*, becomes negative with the addition of *do not: We do not listen to the radio in the car*.

### Lo-Tsen

[1]There was a fragrance about Lo-Tsen that communicated itself to his own emotions, kindling the embers to a glow that did not burn, but merely warmed. [2]And suddenly then he realized that Shangri-La and Lo-Tsen were quite perfect and that he did not wish for more than to stir a faint and eventual response in all that stillness. [3]For years his passions had been like a nerve that the world jarred on; now at last the aching was soothed, and he could yield himself to love that was neither a torment nor a bore. [4]As he passed by the lotus-pool at night he sometimes pictured her in his arms, but the sense of time washed over the vision, calming him to an infinite and tender reluctance. [6]He did not think he had ever been so happy, even in the years of his life before the great barrier of the War.

—James Hilton, *Lost Horizon*

▪ Combine these sentences:

Passion can cause an ache. His love for Lo-Tsen was soothing. _____

_____

▪ Rewrite each of the sentences below to make it negative, as in the example shown.

1. Alana swims on Tuesdays.    *Alana does not swim on Tuesdays.*

2. Students like to take exams.    _____

3. We lost the map of the campus.    _____

4. Mike travels during the summer.    _____

5. Some flowers bloom in the fall.    _____

■ Think of a romantic novel you have read or movie you have seen. Write a sentence explaining what you like about it. _____

_____

## LESSON 11a
## Negatives with *Do*

· · · · · · · · · ·

Most negatives are formed with *do* as a helper followed by *not* and the infinitive form of the verb. Example: *Jasmine does not enjoy horror movies.*

### A Royal Marriage

[1]A charming lady of twenty-nine may fascinate a youth of eighteen, but after fifteen years their marriage will be severely tested. [2]That was the fate of the marriage between Henry and Eleanor. [3]To begin with they were excellent friends. [4]The evidence suggests that though the royal couple did not meet very often, when they were together they were passionately in love. [5]Even the difficult question of the government of Aquitaine did not make a breach between them. [6]In her private life Eleanor was more discreet as Queen of England than she had been when Queen of France; probably because her lusty second husband satisfied her as the pious Louis could not. [7]Henry's casual infidelities were no more than might be expected from any King; it does not seem that Eleanor minded them, since the unimportant harlots concerned possessed neither social position nor political power. [8]It is significant that in later years Rosamund Clifford was a lady of good family, and that the King lived with her openly. [9]For the first time in her second marriage Queen Eleanor was faced with a genuine rival, instead of a harlot who might be ignored.

—Alfred Duggan, *Devil's Brood: The Angevin Family*

■ Combine these sentences:

The King had mistresses of low rank. The Queen did not mind. _____

_____

■ Identify the negative statements in *A Royal Marriage*. Write them below.

|   | Auxiliary | Negative | Verb |
|---|-----------|----------|------|
| 1. | *did* | *not* | *meet* |
| 2. | | | |
| 3. | | | |

■ Do people today care about social rank as much as they once did? Write a sentence giving the reason for your answer. _____

_____

## LESSON 11b
## More About *Do* as a Helper

. . . . . . . .

*Do* and *not* together form a negative, but *do* can also be combined with the verb to intensify its meaning, as in *Professor Jones does believe in a lot of homework*. It also helps ask a question: *Do you know the teacher's name?* And, of course, it can also be a simple verb: *Antoine does his homework every day.*

### Who's the Boss?

[1]The producer said, "The first thing I always do when I arrive on my set is fire someone." [2]I was stunned. [3]The idea that firing someone could be regarded as either fun or strategic had never occurred to me. [4]Since I don't go to such extreme measures, I wondered, do my crews think I'm a wuss? [5]Absolutely not. [6]Do they know who's boss? [7]Absolutely. [8]Somehow, although I am a short female who does not fire people the first week without cause, my crews *still* know that I am the boss because I make it my business to know what they're doing. [9]And my reputation, for better or for worse, precedes me. [10]This need to scream, berate, fire a lowly employee, demonize, or terrorize is fake power. [11]Most powerful people don't need to coerce; their mere presence is coercive.

—Lynda Obst, *Hello, He Lied and Other Truths from the Hollywood Trenches*

■ Why would a movie producer want to fire someone the first day of filming? Write your answer in a sentence. _____

_____

■ The passage above uses *do* to form a negative or to ask a question, and as a simple verb. Find each of these uses and write them below, indicating which category they are in.

| Verb | Function |
|------|----------|
| 1. *I do* | *simple verb* |
| 2. _____ | _____ |
| 3. _____ | _____ |
| 4. _____ | _____ |
| 5. _____ | _____ |
| 6. _____ | _____ |
| 7. _____ | _____ |

■ Misusing power is also called *bullying*. Write a sentence that illustrates an example of bullying. _____

_____

For more on *do* as a helper, see Review Exercises 13, 35.

# YOUR WRITING
## *Developing the Thesis*

So now you've written your thesis sentence. You've checked to be sure it is a statement that makes a point. You know there is much more to be said about it. What comes next? Why, more sentences, of course.

And here's where the real challenge comes in. You must be sure that these sentences are about, and *only* about, the statement you've made in your thesis. This is when it's easy to get off the track of what you want to say, and once you've lost your way it's not easy to find it again. So let's take an example of sticking to the point by making a statement about preserving natural resources.

Wasting energy threatens our sources of power.

Now, there are three ideas in that sentence that will have to be in *all* the sentences that follow although not necessarily in the same words: (1) *wasting energy*, (2) *sources of power*, and (3) *threat*. Ways in which we waste energy are easy to think of; they can be anything from leaving lights on in empty rooms to driving cars that use a lot of gas. The same is true of sources of power, from coal and oil to nuclear energy. What are some of the sentences we can write as follow-ups to our thesis, the sentences that will become *topic sentences* for the paragraphs that follow?

Leaving lights on in empty rooms can make power plants run out of the fuel they need to produce electricity.

Throwing out plastic containers instead of recycling them means manufacturers will need more of the petroleum products that are their raw materials.

Driving to the movies instead of riding a bike uses up gasoline.

The thing to notice about each of these sentences is that they give an instance of *wasting energy* while posing a *threat* of diminishing our *sources of power*. If your thesis is *Wasting energy threatens our sources of power*, however, you will have little chance of producing a successful paper by following it with, *SUVs use a lot of gas, but the Explorer is an awesome car*. What's wrong with the sentence about the Explorer? First, only a part of the sentence is about saving energy. Next, we're not comparing cars but looking at practices that waste power. The three key ideas—*waste*, *threat*, and *power*—aren't there.

In the spaces below, write a thesis statement followed by five sentences that give specific instances of the thesis. You may be tempted to say at this point, "Why all this endless writing of sentences? I want to write something more substantial than that!" The reason is the same as that for practicing a swimming stroke over and over, or a tennis serve, or a guitar chord: to do anything well requires practice, and practice by its very nature is repetitious.

So, think of this not as producing polished prose but as a step on the way to achieving that aim.

Thesis Statement _____

_____

1. _____

2. _____

3. _____

4. _____

5. _____

# UNIT III

# Endings and Their Meaning

**N**early a thousand years ago the people of England lived in great fear of sea raiders from Scandinavia called Vikings. Some of the Vikings, though, proved to be not so fierce after they invaded the country. They settled down beside the English and became neighbors. In fact, they got along rather easily because the English and Scandinavian, or *Old Norse*, languages were much alike, both coming from an old form of German. So where the English said *brothor* for *brother* and *thrie* for *three*, the Old Norse said *brothir* and *thrir*.

The biggest difference between the two languages is easy to spot: in the endings of the words. Such endings were used at that time not to show what a word meant, but how it was used in a sentence: perhaps as a subject or an object, or to show possession.

Eventually the Vikings and the English compromised, choosing one or another form of word ending to serve for both languages, and sometimes dispensing with endings altogether. Today English has evolved into a language with a fixed set of endings, endings that are essential to our understanding one another clearly.

Many of the old endings fell into disuse and were lost. A few remained in either English or Old Norse: in English the third-person singular present tense ended in -*th*, the Norse in -*s*. Eventually the -*s* prevailed and today we say *she does* instead of *she doth*. So, now we have in English far fewer word endings that have meaning, but failure to use them, especially when we write, can make for a good deal of confusion. There is a big difference between "I am excit*ed*" and "I am excit*ing*."

It certainly comes as no surprise to hear that parts of words have meaning; you may even know that these parts are called *morphemes*. You have probably learned about *prefixes*, letters before the root word, and *suffixes*, letters that come after, and the ways they change meanings. But have you ever thought about how the simple letter -*s* changes the meaning of the word it is added to? It can, in fact, turn an apple into two apples or six hundred apples. It can change a person, *her*, into something belonging to a person, *hers*. What -*s* can do to change a word's meaning will be the matter of our next lesson.

## LESSON 12
# The -s Ending and Its Uses: Singular and Plural Nouns

· · · · · · · · ·

We all know that one person, place, or thing requires a *singular* form and that more than one person, place, or thing requires the *plural*. Most nouns show that they are plural by adding -s, for example, *one shoe/two shoes, one book/many books, one car/a parking lot full of cars*.

Rachel Carson's *The Sea Around Us*, published in 1951, awakened interest in the environment and led to the activism of today. Here are some examples of her writing, which uses endings that have meaning.

### The Sea's Origins

[1]Beginnings are apt to be shadowy, and so it is with the beginnings of that great mother of life, the sea. [2]Many people have debated how and when the earth got its ocean, and it is not surprising that their explanations do not always agree. [3]For the plain and inescapable truth is that no one was there to see, and in the absence of eyewitness accounts there is bound to be a certain amount of disagreement. [4]So if I tell here the story of how the young planet Earth acquired an ocean, it must be a story pieced together from many sources and containing whole chapters the details of which we can only imagine. [5]The story is founded on the testimony of the earth's most ancient rocks, which were young when the earth was young; on other evidence written on the face of the earth's satellite, the moon; and on hints contained in the history of the sun and the whole universe of star-filled space.

—Rachel Carson, *The Sea Around Us*

■ Why do we need the evidence of heavenly bodies to learn about the beginnings of the sea? Write your answer in a sentence. _____

_____

■ Go back and look at all the words in the excerpt above that end in -s; if the -s makes a singular noun plural—*shoe, shoes*—write the word below:

1. _____*Beginnings*_____      6. _____

2. _____      7. _____

3. _____      8. _____

4. _____      9. _____

5. _____

▪ Write a sentence about something we can learn from observing nature.

_____

_____

## LESSON 12a
## More Plural Nouns

• • • • • • • • •

Although most plural nouns end in -s or -es, a few, like *children*, have irregular endings or even no plural ending at all, like *sheep*. You will find more about these in Lesson 41.

### The Dance

¹Reality was also Binetou, who went from night club to night club. ²She would arrive draped in a long, costly garment, a gold belt, a present from Modou on the birth of their first child, shining round her waist. ³Her shoes tapped on the ground, announcing her presence. ⁴The waiters would move aside and bow respectfully in the hope of a royal tip. ⁵The couples held each other or danced apart depending on the music, sometimes slow and coaxing, sometimes vigorous and wild. ⁶When the trumpet blared out, backed by the frenzy of the drums, the young dancers, excited and untiring, would stamp, jump and caper about, shouting their joy. ⁷Modou would try to follow suit. ⁸The harsh lights betrayed him to the unpitying sarcasm of some of them, who called him a "cradle-snatcher." ⁹What did it matter! ¹⁰He had Binetou in his arms. ¹¹He was happy.

—Mariama Bâ, *So Long a Letter*

▪ How is Binetou treated at the night club? Write your answer in a sentence.

_____

_____

▪ Find the plural nouns that end in -s. Write them below, followed by their singular form, as the example shows.

1. _____*shoes/shoe*_____     5. _____

2. _____     6. _____

3. _____     7. _____

4. _____

■ Write a sentence about a party at which you had a wonderful time.

_____

_____

 ## LESSON 12b
## More Plurals with -s
· · · · · · · · ·

Most nouns that end in *-y* change their endings to *-ies* in the plural. *Parties, butterflies,* and *centuries* are examples.

### Gandhi's Travels

[1]For seven months Gandhi toured the countryside in torrid, humid weather, moving in hot, crowded, dirty trains and addressing mass assemblies of a hundred thousand or more, who, in those premicrophone days, could only hope to be reached by his spirit. [2]Clamoring multitudes everywhere demanded a view of the Mahatma; it hallowed them. [3]The inhabitants of one place sent word that if his train did not halt at their tiny station they would lie down on the tracks and be run over by it. [4]The train did stop, and when Gandhi, roused out of a deep sleep, appeared, the crowd, theretofore boisterous, sank to their knees on the railway platform and wept. [5]During those strenuous seven months of travel, all his meals, three a day, were the same and consisted of sixteen ounces of goat's milk, three slices of toast, two oranges, and a score of grapes or raisins. [6]They filled him with energy.

—Louis Fischer, *Gandhi: His Life and Message for the World*

■ Combine these sentences:

Gandhi ate very lightly. His meals filled him with energy. _____

_____

■ Find the plural nouns in the passage above. Choose five of them and write a sentence using the singular form. Then write the plural word from the passage.

| **Sentence** | **Plural Word** |
|---|---|
| 1. _It took me a month to finish Chapter 10 in the textbook._ | _months_ |
| 2. _____ | _____ |

|              Sentence              |           Plural Word           |
| ---------------------------------- | ------------------------------- |
| 3. _____ | _____ |
| 4. _____ | _____ |
| 5. _____ | _____ |
| 6. _____ | _____ |

▪ Think of a meal you had while traveling. Write a sentence explaining what was good or bad about it. _____

For more on plural endings, see Review Exercises 23, 25, 31.

## LESSON 13
# The *-s* Ending and Its Uses:
# The Third-Person Exception

. . . . . . . . .

Unlike many languages, English has only one verb ending that changes in the present tense to agree with the subject, the third person singular. That means the subject can be *she, he,* or *it,* or any noun for which these pronouns can be substituted. For example: *Tonya goes to class. She goes to class.*

### Life in the Sea

[1]Sea life in the tropics, then, is intense, vivid, and infinitely varied. [2]In the cold seas it proceeds at a pace slowed by the icy water in which it exists, but the mineral richness of these waters (largely a result of seasonal overturn and consequent mixing) makes possible the enormous abundance of the forms that inhabit them. [3]For a good many years it has been said categorically that the total productivity of the colder temperate and polar seas is far greater than the tropical. [4]Now it is becoming plain that this is not necessarily true. [5]In many tropical and subtropical waters, there are areas where the sheer abundance of life rivals the Grand Banks or the Barents Sea or any antarctic whaling ground. [6]These are the places, as in the Humboldt Current or the Benguela Current, where upwelling of cold, mineral-laden water from deeper layers of the sea provides the fertilizing elements to sustain the great food chains.

—Rachel Carson, *The Sea Around Us*

- Combine these sentences:

It was once thought that cold seas were more productive. Many tropical waters

have an abundance of life. _____

_____

- Look for the words in the excerpt above that end in *-s.* If they are present tense verbs, decide whether they agree with a third person subject—*he, she, it*—and write them below together with their subjects.

1. _____*it proceeds*_____   3. _____

2. _____   4. _____

5. _____    8. _____

6. _____    9. _____

7. _____    10. _____

▪ Have you visited a body of water—seashore, lakeside, riverbank—where you had a particularly good time? Write a sentence describing what happened.

_____

## LESSON 13a
## Another Look at Person

• • • • • • • •

Grammatically, the *first person* is *I*, the speaker, and the *second person* is *you*, the one spoken to. The *third person* is the one spoken about, that is, any person or thing for whose name *he, she,* or *it* can be substituted. For example, *The marathon runner trains by running. She trains by running every morning.*

### The Crook's Conscience

¹Both Raffles and Bunny, of course, are devoid of religious belief, and they have no real ethical code, merely certain rules of behavior which they observe semi-instinctively. ²Raffles and Bunny, after all, are gentlemen, and such standards as they do have are not to be violated. ³Certain things are "not done," and the idea of doing them hardly arises. ⁴Raffles will not, for example, abuse hospitality. ⁵He will commit a burglary in a house where he is staying as a guest, but the victim must be a fellow-guest and not the host. ⁶He will not commit murder, and he avoids violence wherever possible and prefers to carry out his robberies unarmed. ⁷He regards friendship as sacred, and is chivalrous though not moral in his relations with women. ⁸He will take extra risks in the name of "sportsmanship," and sometimes even for aesthetic reasons. ⁹And, above all, he is intensely patriotic.

—George Orwell, *Raffles and Miss Blandish*

▪ Why does Raffles prefer to carry out his burglaries unarmed? Write your answer in a sentence. _____

_____

■ Find the present tense verbs with third person singular subjects in the excerpt above. Write them below, then write them with a plural noun for the subject, as shown in the example.

1. _____*idea arises*_____    _____*students arise*_____

2. _____    _____

3. _____    _____

4. _____    _____

5. _____    _____

■ Have you ever seen a movie comedy with bumbling burglars? Write a sentence about why they are funny. _____

_____

## LESSON 13b
# The Present Tense—Subjects and Verbs

· · · · · · · · ·

While languages like Spanish and French have different endings for singular and plural verbs and for those in which the subject is *I* or *you,* English changes the verb ending only for singular verbs with *she, he,* or *it* as subject: *the clock* (or *it*) *shows the date and the time.*

### Mountain Climber

[1]As Jeff Mathy hunkers down in base camp on Mount Everest, waiting through the days before his attempt at the summit later this month, he resides in a land full of dreams. [2]Mathy is well on his way to becoming the youngest person to reach the seven summits, the highest mountains on each continent, of which he has climbed five. [3]It is an adventure now financed by an American corporation to the tune of about $150,000. [4]A tea company made sense because that is what mountain climbers drink, believing it keeps them better hydrated than water. [5]Sherpas, the Himalayan natives who live at these extreme altitudes, drink it almost exclusively. [6]But no one knows why. [7]The climb will take two months from start to finish. [8]Camp 4, at 26,000 feet, is the last before the summit, which they should attempt to reach in late May.

—Lynn Zinser, *Mount Everest Is the Highest, But Not the Only One to Climb*

■ What is Jeff Mathy's climbing goal? Write your answer in a sentence.

_____

■ Look for the present tense verbs above with third person singular subjects. Write each of them with a plural subject, as shown in the example below.

1. _____*hunkers*_____     _____*the climbers hunker*_____

2. _____     _____

3. _____     _____

4. _____     _____

5. _____     _____

6. _____     _____

■ What adventure have you undertaken? Write a sentence explaining what made it an adventure. _____

_____

For more about endings in -s, see Review Exercises 23, 25, 31.

# The -s Ending and Its Uses: Possessives

· · · · · · · · ·

A *possessive* is a word used to indicate that something belongs to someone. It is written as -*'s*. Wait. Did you look carefully at that? For the possessive of nouns we put an apostrophe, an upside down comma, before the -*s* that ends the noun. *Cella's* is a possessive noun. There is *no* apostrophe in possessive pronouns like *hers, his,* and *its*. See Lesson 50 for more about this.

## How Climates Change

[1]Pettersson's fertile mind evolved a theory of climatic variation. [2]Marshalling scientific, historic, and literary evidence, he showed that there are alternating periods of mild and severe climates which correspond to the long-period cycles of the oceanic tides. [3]The world's most recent period of maximum tides, and most rigorous climate, occurred about 1433, its effect being felt, however, for several centuries before and after that year. [4]During the latest period of benevolent climate, snow and ice were little known on the coast of Europe and in the seas about Iceland and Greenland. [5]Then the Vikings sailed freely over northern seas, monks went back and forth between Ireland and "Thyle" or Iceland, and there was easy intercourse between Great Britain and the Scandinavian countries. [6]Eric the Red "came from the sea to land at the middle glacier. [7]The first year he wintered on Erik's Island." [8]This was probably in the year 984.

—Rachel Carson, *The Sea Around Us*

■ Why did the Vikings make their voyages in the tenth century? Write your

answer in a sentence. _____

_____

■ Look again at the -*s* endings in the excerpt above. Pick out those nouns and pronouns that are possessives and write them here along with what it is they possess.

1. _____*Pettersson's mind*_____    3. _____

2. _____    4. _____

■ Think of a winter you can remember that was colder than usual. Write a sentence about how it affected you. _____

_____

## LESSON 14a
## Plural Possessives

• • • • • • • • •

When a plural noun ending in *-s* is also a possessive, the apostrophe follows the plural *-s*. *Florida is a three days' journey by car.*

### Naming a Hurricane

[1]*Storm*, a novel published in 1941, surely deserves some of the credit for the practice of giving women's names to storms in the Northern Hemisphere. [2]The novel follows the career of a Pacific storm that eventually affects much of North America; a "Junior Meteorologist" plotting the storm on a weather map gives it the name "Maria" without telling his boss or his colleagues. [3]"Not at any price would the Junior Meteorologist have revealed to the Chief that he was bestowing names—and girls' names at that—upon these great moving low-pressure areas." [4]The first official naming of storms in the Atlantic Basin began in 1950. [5]Six-year lists of only female names continued through 1978. [6]The following year the policy was changed to include both men's and women's names, as it was for typhoons in the Pacific.

—Dr. Bob Sheets and Jack Williams, *Hurricane Watch*

■ Where did the idea of naming storms in the Atlantic Basin originate? Write your answer in a sentence. _____

_____

■ In the spaces below write all of the possessive nouns or pronouns from the excerpt above.

1. _____ *women's* _____     3. _____

2. _____     4. _____

■ Sometimes, watching a storm can be exciting. Write a sentence about a thunderstorm or other violent kind of weather you have seen. _____

_____

## LESSON 14b
## More Possessives

• • • • • • • • •

Don't forget that pronouns as well as nouns can be possessives, but that they don't have apostrophes before the *-s*. *The boy's eyes were on his shoes.* The noun *boy* has an apostrophe before the *-s*, but the pronoun *his* does not.

### Possessive Pronouns

| | |
|---|---|
| *my, mine* | *our, ours* |
| *your, yours* | *your, yours* |
| *his, her, hers, its* | *their, theirs* |

### Meeting the Pony

[1]They crossed a stubble-field to shortcut to the barn. [2]Jody's father unhooked the door and they went in. [3]They had been walking toward the sun on the way down. [4]The barn was black as night in contrast and warm from the hay and from the beasts. [5]Jody's father moved over toward the one box stall. [6]Jody could begin to see things now. [7]He looked into the box stall and then stepped back quickly. [8]A red pony colt was looking at him out of the stall. [9]Its tense ears were forward and a light of disobedience was in its eyes. [10] Its coat was rough and thick as an airedale's fur and its mane was long and tangled. [11]Jody's throat collapsed in on itself and cut his breath short. [12]Jody couldn't bear to look at the pony's eyes anymore. [13]He gazed down at his hands for a moment, and he asked very shyly, "Mine?"

—John Steinbeck, *The Red Pony*

▪ Why is Jody's breath cut short when he sees the pony? Write your answer in a sentence. _____

_____

▪ Find the possessive pronouns and nouns in the excerpt above and write them on the lines below, noting whether the word is a noun or a pronoun.

1. _____ *Jody's [noun]* _____        4. _____

2. _____        5. _____

3. _____        6. _____

▪ Write a sentence about a time when you were surprised to get something you had wanted very much. _____

_____

• • • • • • • • •

The *-s* at the end of a word doesn't always have a special meaning. Sometimes it is just the way the word is spelled, like *stress* or *impress*. *Can you guess whether you will pass the exam?* In *guess* and *pass* the final *-s* is the words' spelling.

### The Power of the Tide

[1]There is no drop of water in the ocean, not even in the deepest parts of the abyss, that does not know and respond to the mysterious forces that create the tide. [2]No other force that affects the sea is so strong. [3]Compared with the tide the wind-created waves are surface movements felt, at most, no more than a hundred fathoms below the surface. [4]So, despite their impressive sweep, are the planetary currents, which seldom involve more than the upper several hundred fathoms. [5]The masses of water affected by the tidal movement are enormous, as will be clear from one example. [6]Into one small bay on the east coast of North America—Passamaquoddy—2 billion tons of water are carried by the tidal currents twice each day, into the whole Bay of Fundy, 100 billion tons.

—Rachel Carson, *The Sea Around Us*

■ Combine these sentences:

Waves are surface movements. Tides are felt in the deepest part of the ocean.

_____

■ Some words, like *glass* and *press*, end in *-s* because of their spelling, not because of any significance of the *-s* ending. Look again at *The Power of the Tide* and find those words that end in *-s* because they are spelled that way. Write them in the spaces below.

1. _____*abyss*_____     3. _____

2. _____     4. _____

■ Write a sentence about a natural phenomenon you have observed. It might be the tide going out or coming in, or a shooting star, or a thunderstorm.

_____

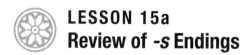

## LESSON 15a
## Review of *-s* Endings

· · · · · · · · ·

We have seen that *-s* at the end of a word can mean

- more than one of something
- a present tense verb with a subject that can be replaced by *she, he,* or *it*
- a word showing possession

Sometimes an *-s* may have no meaning, and just be part of the word's spelling.

### Poverty

[1]Most of Morocco is so desolate that no wild animal bigger than a hare can live on it. [2]Huge areas which were once covered with forest have turned into a treeless waste where the soil is exactly like broken-up brick. [3]Nevertheless a good deal of it is cultivated, with frightful labour. [4]Everything is done by hand. [5]Long lines of women, bent double like inverted capital Ls work their way slowly across the fields, tearing up the prickly weeds with their hands, and the peasant gathering lucerne [alfalfa] for fodder pulls it up stalk by stalk instead of reaping it, thus saving an inch or two on each stalk. [6]The plough is a wretched wooden thing, so frail that one can easily carry it on one's shoulder, and fitted underneath with a rough iron spike which stirs the soil to a depth of about four inches.

—George Orwell, *Marrakesh*

■ Combine these sentences:

The land in Morocco is dry and unproductive. Farming requires enormous work.

_____

■ Find all the words in the excerpt above that end in -s. Write them in the appropriate column below.

| Plural | Present Tense Verb | Possessive | Spelling |
|---|---|---|---|
| 1. *areas* | *is* | *one's* | *treeless* |
| 2. _____ | _____ | _____ | _____ |
| 3. _____ | _____ | _____ | _____ |
| 4. _____ | _____ | _____ | _____ |

|  | Plural | Present Tense Verb | Possessive | Spelling |
|---|---|---|---|---|
| 5. | _____ | _____ | _____ | _____ |
| 6. | _____ | _____ | _____ | _____ |
| 7. | _____ | _____ | _____ | _____ |

■ Write a sentence about an extremely hard job you have done or have watched someone else do. _____

_____

## LESSON 15b
## Another Look at -*s* Endings
. . . . . . . . .

You remember that a word ending in -*s* can be a plural noun, a third person present tense singular verb, or, with an apostrophe, a possessive noun. Sometimes the -*s* is just the spelling of the word.

Here are more words ending in -*s* for you to identify. Find plural nouns, third person singular present tense verbs, possessives, and words whose spelling ends in -*s*.

### The Magic Bottle

[1]By this time Alice had found her way into a tidy little room with a table in the window, and on its top (as she had hoped) a fan and two or three pairs of tiny white kid-gloves: she took up the fan and a pair of the gloves, and was just going to leave the room, when Alice's eye fell upon a little bottle that stood near the looking-glass. [2]There was no label this time with the words "DRINK ME," but nevertheless she uncorked it and put it to her lips. [3]"I know *something* interesting is sure to happen," she said to herself, "whenever I eat or drink anything: so I'll just see what this bottle does. [4]I do hope it'll make me grow large again, for really I'm quite tired of being such a tiny little thing!"

—Lewis Carroll, *Alice in Wonderland*

■ Why does Alice drink the liquid in the bottle? _____

_____

■ Find all the words ending in *-s* in the excerpt above. Write them in the appropriate column below.

| Plural | Present Tense Verb | Possessive | Spelling |
|---|---|---|---|
| 1. _pairs_ | _does_ | _its_ | _looking-glass_ |
| 2. _____ | _____ | _____ | _____ |
| 3. _____ | _____ | _____ | _____ |
| 4. _____ | _____ | _____ | _____ |
| 5. _____ | _____ | _____ | _____ |
| 6. _____ | _____ | _____ | _____ |

■ *Alice in Wonderland* is a favorite story of many children. Write a sentence about your favorite children's story. _____

_____

# YOUR WRITING
*Filling in the Details*

As we have seen, the whole point of your composition should be included in your thesis statement. Does this make you think there is nothing further to be said on the subject? Look at this paragraph from *The Sea Around Us*.

> Neither the Pacific Ocean nor the Indian Ocean has any submerged mountains that compare in length with the Atlantic Ridge, but they have their smaller ranges. The Hawaiian Islands are the peaks of a mountain range that runs across the central Pacific basin for a distance of nearly 2000 miles. The Gilbert and Marshall islands stand on the shoulders of another mid-Pacific mountain chain. In the eastern Pacific, a broad plateau connects the coast of South America and the Tuamotu Islands in the mid-Pacific, and in the Indian Ocean a long ridge runs from India to Antarctica, for most of its length broader and deeper than the Atlantic Ridge.

What is the thesis here? It is that the Pacific and Indian Oceans have smaller mountain ranges than those to be found in the Atlantic. How does the writer go on to illustrate her thesis? She provides examples. And this is one of the ways in which you can continue your composition after you have stated your thesis. Try it on this question:

> What aspect of protecting the environment concerns you most: pollution, natural resources, genetic engineering?

Write a thesis statement explaining why one of these is a particular concern. For example, you might write, *Air pollution contributes to breathing problems in humans.* Next, think about what some of these problems are. *Children may develop asthma. Older people may suffer from shortness of breath. Almost everyone runs the risk of being stricken by a disease of the lungs.* Each of these offers a possibility for a paragraph giving further information about the condition. *What are the symptoms, the treatments, the prospects for recovery? Why is a particular age group especially susceptible? What kind of pollution poses the greatest threat for each?*

You can see how keeping what you write focused on your thesis will bring up questions, the answers to which will provide abundant material for an interesting and informative paper.

Try this: Write a thesis sentence based on one of the ideas above or on one of your own choosing. Then, write five sentences that are about *all* of that thesis statement and that could serve as topic sentences for the paragraphs of your composition.

Thesis _____

_____

1. _____

2. _____

3. _____

4. _____

5. _____

# LESSON 16
# The Meanings of the -*d* Ending

Just as -*s* endings can change the meaning of a word, sometimes -*d* can also signal a change in meaning. For example, we know this ending can often mean that something happened in the past: *we look* (now), *we looked* (last evening). In this case it changes the verb to *past tense.* It can also be used to turn a verb into an adjective, and, of course, it can have no meaning at all when it is simply the way a word is spelled.

Here are some examples of -*d* endings taken from the classic suspense thriller, *Dracula.*

### The Body in the Crypt

¹Then I stopped and looked at the Count. ²There was a mocking smile on the bloated face which seemed to drive me mad. ³A terrible desire came upon me to rid the world of such a monster. ⁴There was no lethal weapon at hand, but I seized a shovel which the workmen had been using to fill the cases, and, lifting it high, struck, with the edge downward, at the hateful face. ⁵But as I did so the head turned, and the eyes fell full upon me, with all their blaze of basilisk [a mythical monster] horror. ⁶The shovel fell from my hand across the box, and hid the horrid thing from my sight.

—Bram Stoker, *Dracula*

■ Write a sentence explaining what the narrator feels about the Count. _____

_____

■ Find all the verbs in the excerpt above that end in -*d*. Which of them is past tense? Write the past tense verbs below followed by their present tense forms.

| Past Tense Verb | Present Tense Verb |
|---|---|
| 1. *stopped* | *stop* |
| 2. | |
| 3. | |
| 4. | |
| 5. | |
| 6. | |

■ Write a sentence about a scene from the scariest movie you have seen or book you have read. _____

_____

# LESSON 16a
## Past Tense Verbs Ending in *-d*

. . . . . . . .

The past tense of *regular* verbs ends in *-ed*. The past tense of the irregular verb *have*, often used as a helping verb, is *had*, which also ends in *-d*. See Lesson 7 for more about this topic.

### A Giant's World

[1]Neither the birds nor the mammals, however, were quite what they seemed. [2]They were waiting for the Age of Flowers. [3]They were waiting for what flowers, and with them the true encased seed, would bring. [4]Fish-eating, gigantic leather-winged reptiles, twenty-eight feet from wing tip to wing tip, hovered over the coasts that one day would be swarming with gulls. [5]Inland the monotonous green of the pine and spruce forests with their primitive wooden cone flowers stretched everywhere. [6]No grass hindered the fall of the naked seeds to earth. [7]Great sequoias towered to the skies. [8]The world of that time has a certain appeal but it is a giant's world, a world moving slowly like the reptiles who stalked magnificently among the boles of its trees.

—Loren Eiseley, *How Flowers Changed the World*

■ Combine these sentences:

Plants and animals were gigantic. The landscape was monotonous. _____

_____

■ Find the past tense verbs that end in *-d* or *-ed* in the excerpt above. Write them below, then use their present tense forms in a sentence.

| Past Tense | Present Tense |
| --- | --- |
| 1. _____ seemed _____ | *Harry seems very happy today.* |
| 2. _____ | _____ |
| 3. _____ | _____ |

|            Past Tense            |          Present Tense          |
|----------------------------------|----------------------------------|
| 4. _____ | _____ |
| 5. _____ | _____ |
| 6. _____ | _____ |

▪ Write a sentence about how trees and other plants make the world a more pleasant place to live in. _____

_____

## LESSON 16b
## More Past Tense Verbs

• • • • • • • • •

While a great many past tense verbs end in *-d, irregular* verbs have other forms like *break/broke, begin/began,* and *choose/chose.* See Lesson 40 for more about this topic.

### The Secrets in the Palm

[1]Wilson began to study Luigi's palm, tracing life lines, heart lines, head lines, and so on, and noting carefully their relations with the cobweb of finer and more delicate marks and lines that enmeshed them on all sides; he felt of the fleshy cushion at the base of the thumb, and noted its shape; he felt of the fleshy side of the hand between the wrist and the base of the little finger, and noted its shape also; he painstakingly examined the fingers, observing their form, proportions, and natural manner of disposing themselves when in repose. [2]All this process was watched by the three spectators with absorbing interest, their heads bent together over Luigi's palm, and nobody disturbing the stillness with a word. [3]Wilson now entered upon a close survey of the palm again, and his revelations began. [4]He mapped out Luigi's character and disposition, and eccentricities in a way which sometimes made Luigi wince and the others laugh, but both twins declared that the chart was artistically drawn and was correct.

—Mark Twain, *Pudd'nhead Wilson*

▪ Combine these sentences:

Wilson examined Luigi's palm. He identified characteristics of Luigi's personality.

_____

■ Identify all of the past tense verbs in the excerpt above, including any that do not end in -*d*.

1. _____*began*_____        8. _____

2. _____        9. _____

3. _____        10. _____

4. _____        11. _____

5. _____        12. _____

6. _____        13. _____

7. _____

■ Examining fingerprints was once a key tool in crime detection. Write a sentence about the new test that has replaced fingerprinting. _____

_____

For more about -*d* endings, see Review Exercises 20, 26.

# The Past Participle

The past participle is formed from a verb, but it can never be a verb by it-self; it must be combined with a *helping* verb like *has* or *had*. Some examples are *he has walked, people have been, Joaquin had spoken.* Look for past partici-ples in the following paragraph.

### Deepening Mystery

[1]During the past two or three days several cases have occurred of young children straying from home or neglecting to return from their playing on the Heath. [2]In all these cases the children were too young to give any properly intelligible account of themselves, but the consensus of their excuses is that they had been with a "bloofer lady." [3]It has always been late in the evening when they have been missed, and on two occasions the children have not been found until early in the following morning. [4]It is generally sup-posed in the neighbourhood that, as the first child missed gave as his rea-son for being away that a "bloofer lady" had asked him to come for a walk, the others had picked up the phrase and used it as occasion served. [5]There is, however, possibly a serious side to the question, for some of the chil-dren, indeed all who have been missed at night, have been slightly torn or wounded in the throat.

—Bram Stoker, *Dracula*

- Combine these sentences:

Children have been missing. They were found with wounds in their throats.

_____

- Underline the past participles that are combined with auxiliaries, or help-ing verbs, to form the main verbs of sentences in the excerpt above. Write them in the spaces below, along with their auxiliaries.

| Auxiliaries | Past Participles |
|---|---|
| 1. _____*have*_____ | _____*occurred*_____ |
| 2. _____ | _____ |
| 3. _____ | _____ |
| 4. _____ | _____ |

|              Auxiliaries              |           Past Participles            |
| ------------------------------------- | ------------------------------------- |
| 5. _____     | _____        |
| 6. _____     | _____        |

■ *Dracula* is a story about a vampire. Write a sentence explaining what a vampire is. _____

_____

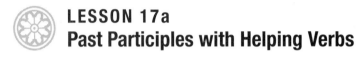

# LESSON 17a
# Past Participles with Helping Verbs

· · · · · · · · · ·

A compound verb is more specific about the time something happened than is a simple past tense verb. For example, *Olga cried when we went to sad movies. She has cried at every movie in which lovers are parted.*

### The Flight of the Century

[1]The idea for the flight came to Lindbergh above the Illinois prairie, on one of his St. Louis–Chicago mail runs in 1926. [2]Raymond Orteig, a French-born hotel owner in New York, had offered a $25,000 prize to the first aviator to cross the Atlantic in an airplane from Paris to New York or vice versa. [3]In 1919, two British pilots had flown across from Newfoundland to Ireland, a difficult 1,900-mile trip, but not nearly as challenging as New York to Paris. [4]The prize had yet to be won. [5]The Spirit of St. Louis was sufficient to its task, where others had failed. [6]A tall 25-year-old aviator known as Slim, Lindbergh had taken off from Roosevelt field, outside New York City on Long Island. [7]Through daylight and dark, fog and sleet and gathering clouds of fatigue, he flew 33 hours 30 minutes and covered 3,610 miles. [8]After dark on May 21, 1927, he landed at LeBourget Field to the wild cheers of the French crowd.

—John Noble Wilford, *The Man and the Aircraft Were One*

■ Combine these sentences:

Lindbergh took off from Roosevelt field. He reached Paris more than 33 hours later. _____

_____

■ Use verbs formed with past participles from the passage above to complete these sentences.

1. The kindly neighbor __*had offered*__ candy to the children on Halloween.

2. The birds _____ north as soon as the weather warmed up.

3. Oriana _____ history that semester.

4. Rory and Joe _____ their sweaters because it was so hot.

■ Lindbergh's flight is said to have made history. Write a sentence about an accomplishment you consider history-making. _____

## LESSON 17b
## Irregular Past Participles

· · · · · · · · ·

A great many past participles end in -*d*, but others end in -*n*, like *broken* and *taken*. Still others, like *brought* or *sung*, have a completely irregular form. See Lesson 40 for more about irregular verb forms.

### Westminster Abbey's Beginning

[1]Thorney Island had been a place of holy reputation since the earliest days of Christendom in England. [2]Several churches had been founded there and dedicated to St. Peter; in the seventh century, the saint was said to have appeared in person to bless the latest building. [3]This was the place the King had chosen for what he considered his life's most important work, the creation of the abbey that came to be known, in distinction from St. Paul's cathedral in the city, as the West Minster. [4]He had planned and supervised the work year after year, and while he lay sick the weather vane was mounted on the cupola of the central tower to symbolize completion of the building. [5]On Wednesday, 28 December, Childermas or Holy Innocents' Day, the great new church was consecrated.

—David Howarth, *1066: The Year of the Conquest*

■ Why was Thorney Island considered a holy place? Write your answer in a sentence. _____

▪ Find the compound verbs in the excerpt above, both those with regular and those with irregular past participles. Write them below, as shown in the example.

|            | **Auxiliary** | **Past Participle** |
|------------|---------------|---------------------|
| 1.         | *had*         | *been*              |
| 2.         |               |                     |
| 3.         |               |                     |
| 4.         |               |                     |
| 5.         |               |                     |

▪ Write a sentence about a building you have seen that impressed you—because it is beautiful or historical or because of the activities that take place there. _____

_____

For more about participles, see Review Exercises 7, 16, 30, 39.

# LESSON 18
# Past Participles as Adjectives

Sometimes the past participle form of the verb acts as if it isn't a verb at all. It can appear in a sentence as an adjective. Examples of this are *the whispered message, a hidden treasure.*

### Vampire's End

[1]She seemed like a nightmare of Lucy as she lay there; the pointed teeth, the bloodstained, voluptuous mouth—which it made one shudder to see—the whole carnal and unspirited appearance, seeming like a devilish mockery of Lucy's sweet purity. [2]Arthur took the stake and the hammer, and when once his mind was set on action his hands never trembled nor even quivered. [3]He placed the point over the heart, and as I looked I could see its dint in the white flesh. [4]Then he struck with all his might. [5]The thing in the coffin writhed; and a hideous, blood-curdling screech came from the opened red lips. [6]The blood from the pierced heart welled and spurted up around the stake. [7]And then the writhing and quivering of the body became less, and the teeth seemed to champ, and the face to quiver. [8]Finally it lay still. [9]The terrible task was over.

—Bram Stoker, *Dracula*

■ From the information in this passage from *Dracula*, explain in one sentence what steps are necessary to do away with a vampire. _____

_____

■ Find all the verbs that end in *-d* in the excerpt above. Some are past participles acting as adjectives, describing nouns. Write these below along with the nouns they describe.

| Past Participle/Adjective | Noun |
|---|---|
| 1. _____*pointed*_____ | _____*teeth*_____ |
| 2. _____ | _____ |
| 3. _____ | _____ |

■ Do you think it takes courage to destroy a vampire? Write a sentence about it. _____

_____

### LESSON 18a
## More Past Participles as Adjectives

• • • • • • • • •

Like all adjectives, the past participle used as an adjective can sometimes follow the noun it describes instead of going before it. *The picture painted by Rembrandt is in the museum.*

### Awakened by the *Titanic*

[1]Overriding everything else, the *Titanic* also marked the end of a general feeling of confidence. [2]Until then men felt they had found the answer to a steady, orderly, civilized life. [3]For 100 years the Western world had been at peace. [4]For 100 years technology had steadily improved. [5]For 100 years the benefits of peace and industry seemed to be filtering satisfactorily through society. [6]Most articulate people felt life was all right. [7]The *Titanic* woke them up. [8]If wealth meant so little on this cold April night, did it mean so much the rest of the year? [9]If it was a lesson, it worked—people have never been sure of anything since. [10]The unending sequence of disillusion-ment that has followed can't be blamed on the *Titanic*, but she was the first jar. [11]That is why, to anybody who lived at the time, the *Titanic* more than any other single event marks the end of the old days, and the beginning of a new, uneasy era.

—Walter Lord, *A Night to Remember*

■ Combine these sentences:

People were satisfied with life. The *Titanic* shocked them out of it. _____

_____

■ Find the past participles in the excerpt above. For each of them, write a sentence using the present tense form of the verb.

| | Verb | Sentence |
|---|---|---|
| 1. | *had found* | *Maria finds biology fascinating.* |
| 2. | _____ | _____ |
| 3. | _____ | _____ |
| 4. | _____ | _____ |

■ *Titanic* is only one of many disaster movies that have been produced. Write a sentence about one you liked—it could be *Titanic*—and why you liked it.

_____

## LESSON 18b
## Past Participle Adjectives After the Verb

• • • • • • • • •

Often, when a past participle is used as an adjective, it will follow a form of the verb *to be*, as in *The letter is* <u>*dated*</u> *May 20th*. *Dated* in this sentence describes the letter.

### A Solemn Ceremony

[1]On Trinity Sunday, the 10th of June 1172, all the candles were alight in the dark thick-walled cathedral of Poitiers. [2]The vaulted nave was a sea of colour. [3]The Bishop and his chapter were almost hidden by clouds of incense, but on the altar steps two handsome figures showed plain. [4]Queen Eleanor was fifty years old, and still the most beautiful queen in Christendom, so beautiful that poets on the far side of the distant Rhine yet sang her praises. [5]Her face was wrinkled by the fierce southern sun; but her regular features were unblemished, and the grey streaks in her hair were hidden by her silk kerchief. [6]Above her kerchief gleamed the gilded coronet of Aquitaine, which was hers by inheritance from her grandfather; but her scarlet mantle of state was worked all over with the ramping golden leopards of Anjou which she bore by right of marriage. [7]While the long psalms were chanted she stood motionless, her face half-turned; so that while her eyes remained fixed on the altar, as was proper in church, the spectators had a clear view of her flawless profile.

—Alfred Duggan, *Devil's Brood: The Angevin Family*

■ Why does Eleanor have her face half-turned? Answer this question in a sentence. _____

_____

■ Find the past participles used as adjectives in the excerpt above. Write them as shown in the examples below, noting whether they occur before the noun or after the verb.

|     | Past Participle | Noun | Verb |
| --- | --- | --- | --- |
| 1. | *hidden* | | *were* |
| 2. | *gilded* | *coronet* | *gleamed* |
| 3. | | | |
| 4. | | | |
| 5. | | | |
| 6. | | | |

■ Write a sentence about a ceremony you have witnessed—anything from a graduation to the inauguration of a public official. _____

_____

# L E S S O N   1 9
# Word Roots Ending in *-d*

The *-d* ending doesn't always have a special meaning. Sometimes it is merely the way the root word is spelled, as in *bread, sound,* and *behold* (not to mention *and*). For example, *The <u>sad child shed</u> tears for the <u>cold redhead</u>.*

### Out of the Trance

[1]"Something is going out; I can feel it pass me like a cold wind. [2]I can hear, far off, confused sounds—as of men talking in strange tongues, fierce-falling water, and the howling of wolves." [3]She stopped and a shudder ran through her, increasing in intensity for a few seconds, till, at the end, she shook as though in a palsy. [4]She said no more, even in answer to the Professor's imperative questioning. [5]When she woke from the trance, she was cold, and exhausted, and languid; but her mind was all alert. [6]She could not remember anything, but asked what she had said; when she was told, she pondered over it deeply for a long time and in silence.

—Bram Stoker, *Dracula*

- Combine these sentences to explain what is happening in the passage:

Mina woke from her trance. She could not remember what she had said. _____

_____

- Find the words in the excerpt above that end in *-d* because that is the spelling of the root. Be careful not to confuse them with past tense verbs or past participles. Write the root words below.

1. _____*cold*_____   4. _____

2. _____   5. _____

3. _____   6. _____

- Did you ever wake up in a strange place, not knowing where you were? Write a sentence about how you felt. _____

_____

## LESSON 19a
## Review of -*d* Endings

Be sure to think twice about a word with a spelling that ends in -*d*. The -*d* can mean it is a past tense verb, like *looked*—which can also be a past participle—or it can be the way a word is spelled, like *blind*.

### A Woman's Work

¹And this is how I came to know my mother: she seemed a large, soft, loving-eyed woman who was rarely impatient in our home. ²Her quick, violent temper was on view only a few times a year, when she battled with the white landlord who had the misfortune to suggest to her that her children did not need to go to school. ³During the "working" day, she labored beside—not behind—my father in the fields. ⁴Her day began before sunup, and did not end until late at night. ⁵There was never a moment for her to sit down, undisturbed, to unravel her own private thoughts; never a time free from interruption—by work or the noisy inquiries of her many children. ⁶And yet, it is to my mother—and all our mothers who were not famous—that I went in search of the secret of what has fed that muzzled and often mutilated, but vibrant, creative spirit that the black woman has inherited, and that pops out in wild and unlikely places to this day.

—Alice Walker, *In Search of Our Mothers' Gardens*

▪ Why does the writer emphasize that her mother worked "beside" her father in the fields? Write your answer in a sentence. _____

_____

▪ There are ten past tense verbs or past participles in the passage above. Choose five of them and write a sentence using the verb in the present tense, as shown in the example.

| Sentence | Verb |
|---|---|
| 1. *Myrna seems happy with her grade.* | *seem* |
| 2. _____ | _____ |
| 3. _____ | _____ |
| 4. _____ | _____ |
| 5. _____ | _____ |
| 6. _____ | _____ |

■ Write a sentence explaining your idea of what "women's work" is. _____

_____

## LESSON 19b
## Spellings That End in *-d*

• • • • • • • • •

If a *-d* ending is not part of the spelling of a word—like the word *word*, for example—it may indicate the past tense, *stepped*, or the past participle, *have talked*.

### Eleanor of Aquitaine

[1]The lady Eleanor was a typical daughter of the south, incompatible in every characteristic with her dour and devout northern husband. [2]Her wit was as famous as her beauty. [3]She could read, as was usual with members of the upper class; and write also, a more rare accomplishment. [4]Her complexion was dark, with black eyes and black hair; her figure curved generously, but even in old age she never grew fat. [5]The story goes that she was one of the founders of the "Courts of Love," where the technique of the love-affair was dissected in public by experts. [6]For romantic love is the great contribution of southern France to civilization, and it was then a new idea.

—Alfred Duggan, *Devil's Brood: The Angevin Family*

■ Combine these sentences:

Eleanor was accomplished. She could read and write, and could speak several

languages. _____

_____

■ Give examples from the excerpt above of two past tense verbs ending in *-d* and of two other words that are not verbs with spelling that ends in *-d*.

1. _____*curved*_____     3. _____*old*_____

2. _____     4. _____

■ Eleanor was a celebrity in her day. Write a sentence about what one of to-day's celebrities is famous for. _____

_____

For more on words ending in *-d*, see Review Exercises 20, 26.

. . . . . . . . . . . . .
.    .  .

# YOUR WRITING
## *Details for Clarity*

We have seen that adding examples is a very useful way to *develop* or add to the thesis of your paper. What other means of strengthening your point are there? One easy and profitable way is to pay attention to details. This means providing more than just the simplest kind of reference to a person or object: *The book was next to Marc's computer.* How much more information about why Marc is not getting his homework done do we find in *A new issue of Dragonball II was lying open next to Marc's closed Toshiba laptop.*

Notice how Bram Stoker uses details in this passage from *Dracula*:

> There, in one of the **great** boxes, on a pile of **newly dug** earth, lay the Count! He was either dead or asleep, I could not say which—for the eyes were **open** and **stony,** but without the **glassiness** of death—and the cheeks had the **warmth** of life through all their **pallor**; the lips were as **red** as ever.

Would that picture of the Count lying in a box of soil in a dark basement be as frightening without the highlighted details?

Try getting those telling details into your writing in response to the following thesis: *Young people enjoy being scared by horror stories and movies.* Here are some sentences—the *topic sentences*—that might begin the paragraphs that follow:

1. They find the suspense exciting.
2. They like the strange characters.
3. They try to guess how it will end.
4. They are dazzled by the special effects.

What kinds of details might you add to these sentences to develop the paragraphs in your composition? Suppose you are writing about *Dracula* and want to use details to develop sentence 1 above. You might refer to the suspense of worrying about which girl, Mina or Lucy, will be turned into a vampire next. Or you could discuss why the madman Renfield wants to eat spiders and how garlic can defeat Dracula. Notice that we bring in the names of the characters, the behavior they show after being attacked by a vampire, and some of the weapons that can be used against vampires. Similarly, in sentence 2 we would want to learn about Dracula's black cape, his blazing eyes and sharp, pointed teeth, and his ability to change appearance to that of a bat. All of these details are what makes your writing real communication.

Write a thesis statement about the kind of entertainment you have observed that young people most enjoy. Follow it with four topic sentences that explain why they enjoy it. For each of the topic sentences, list as many details or examples as you can that will support what your sentence says.

Thesis: _____

_____

Sentence 1: _____

_____

Details: _____      _____      _____

_____      _____      _____

Sentence 2: _____

_____

Details: _____      _____      _____

_____      _____      _____

Sentence 3: _____

_____

Details: _____      _____      _____

_____      _____      _____

Sentence 4: _____

_____

Details: _____      _____      _____

_____      _____      _____

# LESSON 20
## The *-ing* Ending and Its Uses

Like the past participle, the verb part called the *present participle,* ending in *-ing,* cannot be used as the verb of a sentence unless it is combined with an auxiliary like *am, is, are, was, were.* But it can be used as a noun, *the loud talking,* or an adjective, *running water.* And, of course, sometimes the *-ing* simply represents the spelling of a word—*morning.*

You will find examples of all these in the excerpt below from George Orwell's *Animal Farm,* a fable about totalitarian government in which animals play the leading roles.

Don't forget that the present participle is the verb of a sentence when combined with the auxiliaries *am, is, are, was, were.*

### The Battle Begins

¹As the human beings approached the farm buildings, Snowball launched his first attack. ²All the pigeons, to the number of thirty-five, flew to and fro over the men's heads and muted upon them from mid-air, and while the men were dealing with this, the geese, who were hiding behind the hedge, rushed out and pecked viciously at the calves of their legs. ³However, this was only a light skirmishing manoeuvre, intended to create a little disorder, and the men easily drove the geese off with their sticks. ⁴Suddenly, at a squeal from Snowball, which was the signal for retreat, all the animals turned and fled through the gateway into the yard. ⁵The men gave a shout of triumph. ⁶They saw, as they imagined, their enemies in flight. ⁷As soon as they were well inside the yard, the three horses, the three cows, and the rest of the pigs, who were lying in ambush in the cowshed, suddenly emerged in their rear, cutting them off.

—George Orwell, *Animal Farm*

■ How are the animals trying to defeat the humans? Answer in a sentence.

_____

■ Find the present participles used as verbs in the excerpt above. Write them below along with their auxiliaries and subjects.

| Present Participle | Auxiliary | Subject |
|---|---|---|
| 1. *dealing* | *were* | *men* |
| 2. _____ | _____ | _____ |
| 3. _____ | _____ | _____ |

**94**

■ Can you think of an example of an animal behaving with surprising intelligence? Write a sentence about what that animal did. _____

_____

## LESSON 20a
## More Present Participles with Helpers

The present participle, with a part of the verb *to be* as helper, is often called the *present progressive tense* because it indicates that a movement is continuing. For example, *Emily is wearing new earrings to the dance.*

### Shooting in the Rain

[1]By 11:20 P.M. rain was pouring from sprinklers attached to the scissor-lift crane. [2]Tom Hanks was dragging the reluctant dachshund out of the building. [3]Inside, the animal's handler was calling out encouragement. [4]Schwab was talking to a friend who had dropped by the set. [5]DePalma sat in the middle of the downtown lanes of Park Avenue under a giant umbrella. [6]He was watching the monitor, analyzing the composition of the fake rain and the fake lightning and the fake wind. [7]When he felt it worked, he nodded at Chris Soldo, the first assistant director. [8]Soldo yelled, "Save the rain."

—Julie Salamon, *The Devil's Candy*

■ Combine these sentences:

The movie has a scene in the rain. The movie makers are using machinery to

produce fake rain. _____

_____

■ Find the verbs formed with present participles in the excerpt above. Then write each in a sentence of your own.

| Verb | Sentence |
|------|----------|
| 1. _____*pouring*_____ | *Water was pouring from the leaky pipe.* |
| 2. _____ | _____ |
| 3. _____ | _____ |

| Verb | Sentence |
| --- | --- |
| 4. _____ | _____ |
| 5. _____ | _____ |

▪ Write a sentence about a movie scene you found especially effective.

_____

_____

## LESSON 20b
## More Compound Verbs

• • • • • • • • •

The present participle with an auxiliary is often called the *present progressive tense* because it indicates that a movement is continuing, as it is in the excerpt below. As we saw with verbs formed with past participles, the verb and helper can sometimes be divided by an adverb: *He had often spoken to me.* Here's what you might find with the present participle: *Molly is always looking for a new brand of jeans.*

### A Different World

[1]In a movement that was almost instantaneous, geologically speaking, the angiosperms [a class of flowering plants] had taken over the world. [2]Grass was beginning to cover the bare earth until, today, there are over six thousand species. [3]All kinds of vines and bushes squirmed and writhed under new trees with flying seeds. [4]The explosion was having its effect on animal life also. [5]Specialized groups of insects were arising to feed on the new sources of food and, incidentally and unknowingly, to pollinate the plant. [6]The flowers bloomed and bloomed in ever larger and more spectacular varieties. [7]Honey ran, insects multiplied, and even the descendants of that toothed and ancient lizard bird had become strangely altered. [8]Across the planet grasslands were now spreading. [9]A slow continental upthrust which had been a part of the early Age of Flowers had cooled the world's climates.

—Loren Eiseley, *How Flowers Changed the World*

▪ How did the Age of Flowers change the nature of animal life on earth? Write a sentence with your answer. _____

_____

■ Find the compound verbs in the excerpt above formed from present participles. If their subjects are singular, the helper will be *was*; plural subjects will be followed by *were* as a helper. Write the subjects and verbs in the appropriate column below.

|  | **Singular Subjects** | **Plural Subjects** |
|---|---|---|
| 1. | *grass was beginning* | *insects were arising* |
| 2. | | |

■ People use flowers to beautify their surroundings. Write a sentence about a flower garden that impressed you, either as part of a public place or in someone's yard or even as part of a collection of indoor plants. _____

_____

For more about helping verbs, see Review Exercises 8, 10, 16, 44.

# LESSON 21
## The Present Participle as a Noun

Although it is a form of the verb, the present participle is often used as a noun in such forms as *painting* or *serving*. You can tell a present participle is being used as a noun if a determiner—another name for the articles *the*, *a*, and *an*—can be placed before it. Example: *I ordered a serving of fries.*

### Marching Pigs

[1]It was just after the sheep had returned, on a pleasant evening when the animals had finished work and were making their way back to the farm buildings, that the terrified neighing of a horse sounded from the yard. [2]Startled, the animals stopped in their tracks. [3]It was Clover's voice. [4]She neighed again, and all the animals broke into a gallop and rushed into the yard. [5]Then they saw what Clover had seen. [6]It was a pig walking on his hind legs. [7]And a moment later, out from the door of the farmhouse came a long file of pigs, all walking on their hind legs. [8]And finally there was a tremendous baying of dogs and a shrill crowing from the black cockerel, and out came Napoleon himself, majestically upright, casting haughty glances from side to side, and with his dogs gambolling round him.

—George Orwell, *Animal Farm*

- Combine these sentences:

Clover was terrified. A pig was walking on his hind legs. _____

_____

- We can tell that some of the words in the excerpt above that end in *-ing* are used as nouns because they have a determiner. Write these words in the appropriate spaces below.

1. _____ the neighing _____    3. _____

2. _____

- Do you have a pet that does tricks? Or do you know someone who has? Write a sentence about the cleverest trick you have seen. _____

_____

**98**

# LESSON 21a
# The Present Participles as Subject or Object

. . . . . . . . . .

A present participle is used as a noun when it is the subject or object of a sentence or the object of a preposition such as *at, by, for, in, to*. For example, *Speaking* is a way of *communicating*.

### Concentration Camp Life

[1]We could hold endless debates on the sense or nonsense of certain methods of dealing with the small bread ration, which was given out only once daily during the latter part of our confinement. [2]There were two schools of thought. [3]One was in favor of eating up the ration immediately. [4]This had the twofold advantage of satisfying the worst hunger pangs for a very short time at least once a day and of safeguarding against possible theft or loss of the ration. [5]The second group, which held with dividing the ration up, used different arguments. [6]The most ghastly moment of the twenty-four hours of camp life was the awakening, when, at a still nocturnal hour, the three shrill blows of a whistle tore us pitilessly from our exhausted sleep and from the longing in our dreams. [7]We then began the tussle with our wet shoes, into which we could scarcely force our feet, which were sore and swollen with edema. [8]And there were the usual moans and groans about petty troubles, such as the snapping of wires which replaced shoelaces.

—Viktor E. Frankl, *Man's Search for Meaning*

■ Why did some people in the camp choose to eat their ration immediately? Answer this question in a sentence. _____

_____

■ In the spaces below write the present participles that are used as nouns in the excerpt above.

1. _____*[the] dealing*_____    5. _____

2. _____    6. _____

3. _____    7. _____

4. _____    8. _____

■ We have to make decisions, large and small, all the time. Write a sentence about a difficult decision you have made. _____

_____

# LESSON 21b
# Present Participles with Adjectives

• • • • • • • • •

Sometimes, when a present participle is used as a noun, it may be modified by an adjective. For example: *Marti's excellent playing of the clarinet won him a place in the band.* Look for adjectives before the present participles in the following excerpt.

### A Moviemaker's Problem

[1]Though all of De Palma's artistic training had taken place in the theater and in movies, he too found endings to be nearly impossible. [2]It wasn't all that different from life. [3]Beginnings were thrilling, the opening up of all kinds of possibilities. [4]But endings, endings implied some kind of resolution, an epiphany or a summing up—and such moments seemed elusive to him, and false. [5]He could rarely see how to sum up a story without trivializing it. [6]The idea of the Magic Hour made so much more sense, an acknowledgment that it was difficult to pinpoint the exact moment when day ended and night began, that endings and beginnings were linked in some mutable, magical way.

—Julie Salamon, *The Devil's Candy*

■ Why does the director find endings difficult? Answer this question in a sentence. _____

_____

■ In the spaces below write the present participles that are used as nouns. If they follow adjectives, write the adjectives as well.

1. _____*[artistic] training*_____    4. _____

2. _____    5. _____

3. _____

■ Do you find it easier to begin writing a paper than to end it? Write a sentence explaining why or why not. _____

_____

# LESSON 22
## The Present Participle as an Adjective

Used as an adjective, the present participle describes a noun. Remember that it cannot be the verb of a sentence without a helper, or auxiliary. But as an adjective it can provide descriptions—for example, *deafening applause* or *Anya, laughing happily.*

### The End of the Windmill

¹In their spare moments the animals would walk round and round the half-finished mill, admiring the strength and perpendicularity of its walls and marvelling that they should ever have been able to build anything so imposing. ²November came, with raging south-west winds. ³Finally there came a night when the gale was so violent that the farm buildings rocked on their foundations and several tiles were blown off the roof of the barn. ⁴The hens woke up squawking with terror because they had all dreamed simultaneously of a gun going off in the distance. ⁵The animals came out of their stalls to find that the flagstaff had been blown down and an elm tree at the foot of the orchard had been plucked up like a radish. ⁶They had just noticed this when a despairing cry broke from every animal's throat. ⁷The windmill was in ruins.

—George Orwell, *Animal Farm*

▪ Why are the animals so upset to find the windmill in ruins? Write your answer in a sentence. _____

_____

▪ Find the words ending in *-ing* in the excerpt above that are used as adjectives. Write them below along with the nouns they modify.

| Present Participle | Noun |
|---|---|
| 1. _____admiring_____ | _____animals_____ |
| 2. _____ | _____ |
| 3. _____ | _____ |
| 4. _____ | _____ |
| 5. _____ | _____ |
| 6. _____ | _____ |

■ Have you ever had something you prized destroyed by the weather? Write a sentence about what happened. _____

For more about participles, see Review Exercises 7, 16, 30, 39.

## LESSON 22a
## The Present Participle as Adjective Again

Used as an adjective, the present participle is usually found before the noun, but it sometimes follows the noun, as it does in this sentence: *Annie, reading the letter, nearly fainted at the news. Reading* here is an adjective describing Annie.

### Introduction to the Hotel X

[1]The Hotel X was a vast, grandiose place with a classical facade and at one side a little, dark doorway like a rat-hole, which was the service entrance. [2]The assistant manager led me down a winding staircase into a narrow passage, deep underground and so low that I had to stoop in places. [3]There seemed to be miles of dark labyrinthine passages that reminded one queerly of the lower decks of a liner; there were the same heat and cramped space and warm reek of food, and a humming, whirring noise (it came from the kitchen furnaces) just like the whir of engines. [4]We passed doorways which let out sometimes a shouting of oaths, sometimes the red glare of a fire, once a shuddering draught from an ice chamber. [5]The kitchen was like nothing I had ever seen or imagined—a stifling, low-ceilinged inferno of a cellar, red-lit from the fires, and deafening with oaths and the clanging of pots and pans.

—George Orwell, *Down and Out in Paris and London*

■ Combine these sentences:

The front of the hotel is grand and imposing. The kitchen is an inferno. _____

▪ Find the present participles in the excerpt above that are used as adjectives. Write them below next to the nouns they modify.

| Present Participle | Noun |
|---|---|
| 1. _____ *winding* _____ | _____ *staircase* _____ |
| 2. _____ | _____ *noise* _____ |
| 3. _____ | _____ *draught* _____ |
| 4. _____ | _____ *inferno* _____ |

▪ Think of a place you've visited that was either very hot or very cold. Now write your own sentence about the experience. _____

_____

## LESSON 22b
## More Participle-Adjectives

• • • • • • • • •

Sometimes the present participle as an adjective will follow the noun it describes. *The actress, checking her makeup, walked onstage* is an example. Look for more present participles like this in the excerpt below.

### Homework Before Practice

[1]On a typical afternoon at the Williams house, practicing French comes before practicing tennis. [2]Venus Williams and her sister Serena can see their three private practice courts from the bedroom window. [3]But the courts at the family's 10-acre compound will remain empty today. [4]Venus and Serena have homework to do. [5]Most young pros spend grueling days honing their backhands, not their French accents. [6]Missing practice might mean missing out on ranking points, paychecks and endorsement deals. [7]Venus is nonchalant about skipping practice, and tournaments. [8]The traveling circus of the women's tennis tour has encamped at a Hilton Head resort this week without her. [9]While her would-be opponents perform before cheering crowds, she hears cows mooing on the neighbors' property.

—Linda Robertson, *On Planet Venus*

■ What does Venus Williams find more important than practicing her tennis game? Answer this question in a sentence. _____

_____

■ For each of the present participle/adjectives in the excerpt above, find another noun to fit the meaning of the adjective.

| **Present Participle** | **Noun** |
| --- | --- |
| 1. _____ ranking _____ | _____ Points _____ |
| 2. _____ traveling _____ | _____ |
| 3. _____ cheering _____ | _____ |
| 4. _____ mooing _____ | _____ |

■ Did you ever practice especially hard for some event or competition? Write a sentence about it. _____

_____

· · · · · · · · · ·

Sometimes the *-ing* ending has no meaning; it is just the way a word is spelled. Or we might explain its use in another way: the *-ing* means *nothing*.

### The Bitter Winter

¹In January food fell short. ²For days at a time the animals had nothing to eat but chaff and mangels [animal food]. ³One Sunday morning Squealer announced that the hens, who had just come in to lay again, must surrender their eggs. ⁴When the hens heard this, they raised a terrible outcry. ⁵They were just getting their clutches ready for the spring sitting, and they protested that to take the eggs away now was murder. ⁶For the first time since the expulsion of Jones, there was something resembling a rebellion. ⁷Led by three young pullets, the hens made a determined effort to thwart Napoleon's wishes. ⁸Whymper heard nothing of this affair, and the eggs were duly delivered, a grocer's van driving up to the farm once a week to take them away.

—George Orwell, *Animal Farm*

■ Combine these sentences:

The hens were angry. Squealer planned to take their eggs away. _____

_____

■ In the excerpt above, find those words ending in *-ing* that are not a verb form and write them below.

1. _____*nothing*_____     3. _____

2. _____

■ Write a sentence about a time you or someone you know took action to prevent what you saw as injustice. _____

_____

## LESSON 23a
## More Words Spelled with *-ing*

· · · · · · · ·

One of the most common nouns in the language, *thing*, ends in *-ing*. Some other nouns with this ending are *ring* and *swing;* verbs ending in *-ing* include *fling* and *sing*.

### Arthur's Arrival

[1]It was a quiet morning, so still that you could not tell where the mist ended and the surface of the lake began. [2]It seemed a kind of desecration to break the hush and plunge into that virgin water, but the fresh chill of it washed away the clinging strands of the night, and when I came out and was dry again and dressed, I ate my breakfast with pleasure, then settled down with my fishing rod to wait for the morning rise, and hope for a breeze at sun-up to ruffle the glassy water. [3]No ring or ripple broke the glassy water, no sign of a breeze to come. [4]I had just decided that I might as well go, when I heard something coming fast through the forest at my back. [5]I had been wrong in thinking that nothing could come through the forest as fast as a fleeing deer. [6]Arthur's white hound, Cabal, broke from the trees exactly where the stag had broken, and hurled himself into the water. [7]Seconds later Arthur himself, on the stallion Canrith, burst out after it. [8]He shouted something, and came cantering along the shingle.

—Mary Stewart, *The Hollow Hills*

■ Combine these sentences:

The morning was quiet. Arthur's coming shattered the stillness. ___ _____

_____

■ Underline those words from the excerpt above that end in *-ing* because that is part of the spelling. Then for each find another word that expresses nearly the same meaning.

1. ____*a quiet dawn*____    4. _____

2. _____    5. _____

3. _____

■ Write a sentence about eating outdoors, while camping, having a picnic, or cooking a backyard barbecue. _____

_____

# LESSON 23b
# Other Words Ending in *-ing*

Most words ending in *-ing* are present participles, but we find verbs like *sing* and nouns like *anything* where the *-ing* is just the way the word is spelled.

**Chimps Out!**

[1]There was one particular week I'll never forget. [2]It began one morning when someone in the compound shouted "Chimps out!" [3]I ran to the seven-acre handling facilities and saw three chimps walking on top of the wall. [4]Patrick ran around shouting at the chimps and they scrambled back into the enclosure. [5]We searched all around The Wall looking for a hole, then went down to the river to see if they had got out that way, but could find nothing. [6]One of our staff fled down to the river, and Rita must have gone down there after him. [7]I do not know what happened next, but I think the man must have hit Rita with something or at least taken a swing at her, because we suddenly heard that Rita was attacking him. [8]Dave announced that the only way to keep the chimps in was to run another strand of electrical wiring along the top of the wall. [9]The escapes stopped promptly and we all caught a much-needed rest while the chimps took some time to find another way out.

—Sheila Siddle, *In My Family Tree: A Life with Chimpanzees*

- Why would the chimpanzees keep looking for a way out of their enclosure? Write your answer in a sentence. _____

_____

- On the lines below write those words in the excerpt above that end in *-ing* because they are spelled that way.

1. _____*morning*_____    3. _____

2. _____    4. _____

- Have you ever had a problem with a pet that had a mind of its own? Write a sentence about what happened. _____

_____

## YOUR WRITING
*Using Anecdotes*

Sometimes telling a little story or *anecdote* will provide further development to your composition. In George Orwell's *Animal Farm*, Moses the raven does this:

> Moses, who was Mr. Jones's especial pet, was a spy and a tale-bearer, but he was also a clever talker. He claimed to know of the existence of a mysterious country called Sugarcandy Mountain, to which all animals went when they died. In Sugarcandy Mountain it was Sunday seven days a week, clover was in season all the year round, and lump sugar and linseed cake grew on the hedges.

The story Moses tells is meant to make the animals forget their plans for a rebellion with the promise of a glorious future. Some of them even believed the story and lost part of their enthusiasm for the revolt. So, even though it is a story, it adds to the point of Orwell's tale.

Think about a class trip you have taken. Write a thesis sentence that makes a statement about either the educational value of the trip, the entertainment you enjoyed, or the responsibility it required of you. Whichever you choose, write topic sentences for three paragraphs that will follow. Here are some suggestions:

> The trip taught me the value of another country's money.
>
> I had some lessons in getting along with others.
>
> I found out how to use public transportation in a new city.

Once you have written your own sentences, write a brief anecdote for each paragraph. Each anecdote should be no longer than three sentences.

Thesis: _____

_____

Sentence 1: _____

_____

Anecdote: _____

_____

_____

Sentence 2: _____

_____

Anecdote: _____

_____

_____

Sentence 3: _____

_____

Anecdote: _____

_____

_____

# L E S S O N   2 4
## Endings That Form Nouns

. . . . . . . . .

We saw at the beginning of this unit how word endings were lost on many root words long ago when the Vikings and English needed to communicate. But English has continued, like many other languages, to change the *parts of speech* of words by adding *suffixes*, an ending syllable added to a verb, noun or adjective. Think about the adjective *brave* in the following example: *His saving the child was a brave action.* You can change the adjective to a noun meaning the quality of being brave by adding the suffix *-ry* which gives you the word *bravery*: *His bravery saved the child.*

### Endings that produce a noun of quality

| | | |
|---|---|---|
| *-ance* | rely. . . | reliance |
| *-dom* | king. . . | kingdom |
| *-ence* | provide. . . | providence |
| *-ism* | cynic. . . . | cynicism |
| *-ity* | generous. . . | generosity |
| *-ment* | govern. . . | government |
| *-ness* | happy. . . | happiness |
| *-ship* | friend. . . | friendship |
| *-tion* | admire. . . | admiration |

### The *Titanic* Sinks

[1]As the cries died away the night became strangely peaceful. [2]The *Titanic*, the agonizing suspense, was gone. [3]The shock of what had happened, the confusion and excitement ahead, the realization that close friends were lost forever had not yet sunk in. [4]A curiously tranquil feeling came over many of those in the boats. [5]With the feeling of calm came loneliness. [6]Lawrence Beesley wondered why the *Titanic*, even when mortally wounded, gave everyone a feeling of companionship and security that no lifeboat could replace. [7]In No. 3, Elizabeth Shutes watched the shooting stars and thought to herself how insignificant the *Titanic's* rockets must have looked, competing against nature. [8]In Boat 4, Miss Jean Gertrude Hippach also watched the shooting stars—she had never seen so many. [9]She recalled a legend that every time there's a shooting star, somebody dies.

—Walter Lord, *A Night to Remember*

■ Why did people in the boats feel calm after the ship sank? Write your answer in a sentence. _____

_____

■ Several nouns in the excerpt above have been formed by affixing endings on other parts of speech. Write them below along with the word they were formed from.

| Noun | Original Word |
|------|---------------|
| 1. _suspense_ | _suspend_ |
| 2. _____ | _____ |
| 3. _____ | _____ |
| 4. _____ | _____ |
| 5. _____ | _____ |
| 6. _____ | _____ |

■ Think of an exciting event you have been present at—a championship game, a concert, a celebrity's appearance. Write a sentence explaining how you felt then. _____

_____

## LESSON 24a
## Suffixes Forming Nouns

• • • • • • • •

Many of the nouns formed by suffixes are derived from verbs—for example, *talker* from *talk* and *education* from *educate*. A few, however, come from adjectives—for example, *weakness* from *weak* and *loyalty* from *loyal*.

### The Back of the Bus

[1] On December 1, 1955, Rosa Parks propelled the civil rights movement into a new stage of activism when she refused to give up her seat and move to the back of a Montgomery, Alabama, bus, so a white rider could sit down. [2] It

wasn't the first time she'd done so, but it was the first time a bus driver had her arrested for it. [3]Her arrest set off the yearlong boycott in which hundreds of African-Americans walked or carpooled to work rather than ride the buses. [4]Pressure on local authorities to change their policies spawned a lawsuit that ultimately made its way to the U.S. Supreme Court. [5]In November 1956, the court ruled in *Browder v. Gayle* that Alabama's bus segregation laws were unconstitutional.

—Constance Jones, *1001 Things Everyone Should Know About Women's History*

▪ What led to the end of Alabama's bus segregation laws? Write a sentence explaining your answer. _____

_____

▪ Identify those nouns in the excerpt above that are formed from verbs or adjectives. Write them below together with the verb or adjective from which they come, indicating the suffix, as *confine-ment* from the verb *confine*.

| Noun | Verb or Adjective/Suffix |
|------|--------------------------|
| 1. _____ *movement* _____ | _____ *move-ment* _____ |
| 2. _____ | _____ |
| 3. _____ | _____ |
| 4. _____ | _____ |

▪ Have you ever observed a protest? Explain, in a sentence, what form it took.

_____

## LESSON 24b
## More Suffixes Forming Nouns

• • • • • • • •

In addition to verbs and adjectives, some nouns can also form new nouns. One example of this is seen in the suffix *-ship*: the noun *fellow* can become the noun *fellowship*, a group of fellows.

### Baseball Vacation

[1]The last traces of my baseball neutrality disappeared during the month of August, which I passed on vacation in Maine, deep in Red Sox country. [2]Far from any ballpark and without a television set, I went to bed early on most

nights and lay there kept almost awake by the murmurous running thread of Bosox baseball from my bedside radio. [3]I felt very close to the game then—perhaps because I grew up listening to baseball over the radio, or perhaps because the familiar quiet tones and effortless precision of the veteran Red Sox announcers invited me to share with them the profound New England seriousness of Following the Sox. [4]I have spent many summers in this part of the world, but this was the first year I could remember when the Red Sox were in first place all through August—a development that seemed only to deepen the sense of foreboding that always afflicts the Red Sox faithful as the summer wanes.

—Roger Angell, *Late Innings*

■ Combine these sentences:

New Englanders root for the Red Sox. The team is seldom in first place. _____

_____

■ Find the nouns formed from verbs, adjectives, and other nouns and write them below. Be sure to indicate what part of the noun is the suffix and the original word from which the noun is formed.

| Noun | Verb, Adjective, or Noun |
|---|---|
| 1. *neutral—ity* | *neutral, adjective* |
| 2. _____ | _____ |
| 3. _____ | _____ |
| 4. _____ | _____ |
| 5. _____ | _____ |
| 6. _____ | _____ |

■ Often people like to root for the underdog. In a sentence explain why you think this is so. _____

_____

For more about suffixes, see Review Exercises 15, 18, 28, 45.

# LESSON 25
## Endings That Show Who or What Performs an Action

• • • • • • • • •

The heading above includes the verb *performs*; people who perform are called *performers*. An *-er* or *-or* ending can change a verb, an action word, into a noun—a person or thing—that performs the action. For example: *Josh loves to act, so he became an actor.*

### On the March

[1]On Friday morning, October 26, a group of us gather on the outskirts of New Orleans to begin walking the 80 miles to Baton Rouge. [2]Several TV and radio stations and newspaper reporters show up. [3]Reflecting back I realize now, even more than I did then, just how crucial the media are to public education on this issue, and I am struck by how many reporters and journalists become sympathetic to the cause once they become knowledgeable about the issue. [4]We're an interesting assortment: black and white, ex-cons and nuns, secretaries and teachers, housewives, students, a carpenter, a woman whose sister was murdered but who opposes capital punishment, some family members with sons on death row, a Vietnam vet. [5]We arrive in Baton Rouge as the sun is setting. [6]A young man, one of the marchers, touches my arm and points to the bottom of the steps where the counter-demonstrators are and says that the man down there wants to talk to me.

—Helen Prejean, C. S. J., *Dead Man Walking*

■ Combine these sentences:

A group is marching to Baton Rouge. Many different kinds of people are in the

group. _____

_____

■ Find the nouns in the excerpt above that show by their endings the performer of an action. Write them below with the words from which they are formed.

| Performer | Verb |
|---|---|
| 1. _____*reporter*_____ | _____*reports*_____ |
| 2. _____ | _____ |

**114**

|  Performer  |  Verb  |
|-------------|--------|
| 3. _____ | _____ |
| 4. _____ | _____ |

- Think of a long walk you have taken. Write a sentence about why you did it—to prove a point, to reach a place you wanted to be, or just because it was a nice day for walking. _____

_____

# LESSON 25a
## Suffixes That Turn Verbs into Agents

· · · · · · · · ·

The person who performs an action is sometimes called an agent. One who *writes* is a *writer*, one who *orates* is an *orator*. Note that the suffix for these words is sometimes spelled *-er* and sometimes *-or*.

### An Ambitious Doctor

[1]Does it seem incongruous to you that a Middlemarch surgeon should dream of himself as a discoverer? [2]Most of us, indeed, know little of the great originators until they have been lifted up among the constellations and already rule our fates. [3]Lydgate would be a good Middlemarch doctor, and by that very means keep himself in the track of far-reaching investigation. [4]This was an innovation for one who had chosen to adopt the style of general practitioner in a country town, and would be felt as offensive criticism by his professional brethren. [5]But Lydgate meant to innovate in his treatment also, and he was wise enough to see that the best security for his practicing honestly according to his belief was to get rid of systematic temptations to the contrary. [6]Perhaps that was a more cheerful time for observers and theorizers than the present; we are apt to think it the finest era of the world when America was beginning to be discovered, when a bold sailor, even if he were wrecked, might alight on a new kingdom; and about 1829 the dark territories of pathology were a fine America for a spirited young adventurer.

—George Eliot, *Middlemarch*

■ How does Lydgate hope to make his mark on the world? Write your answer in a sentence. _____

_____

■ Find the nouns in the excerpt above in which verbs are turned into agents by the suffixes *-er* or *-or*. For five of them, write a sentence using the verbs from which they are formed, as shown in the first example.

| Noun | Sentence |
|---|---|
| 1. _____ discoverer _____ | *Did you discover the date the paper is due?* |
| 2. _____ | _____ |
| 3. _____ | _____ |
| 4. _____ | _____ |
| 5. _____ | _____ |
| 6. _____ | _____ |

■ Write a sentence about a goal you have achieved. It might be the ability to cook, to run for a touchdown, or to play the guitar. _____

_____

## LESSON 25b
## Changing More Verbs into Nouns

•  •  •  •  •  •  •  •  •

Remember that you can recognize a verb if it has an infinitive form such as *to think, to shout, to row*. Nouns formed from these verbs are *thinker, shouter,* and *rower*.

### Captain Cook's Misjudgment

[1]Cook learned much about Fiji, but evinced no curiosity to visit it and its neighbouring islands. [2]He did not so much as point his prow in Fiji's known direction. [3]Instead he courted disaster to his sloops when sailing carelessly through a channel, was nearly assassinated, caused more distress than happiness among these child-like islanders, showed a new side of his nature to

his concerned officers, lost a large number of his precious livestock, and experienced a lowering in the morale of his sailors. [4]William Bligh was among those who could not understand his commander's inaction. [5]If he had been in command he would soon have sought out these islands. [6]And by a strange chance of fate, Bligh was to do just that. [7]In these same waters, a group of his men led by Fletcher Christian was to rise up against him and cast him and eighteen of his men—that admirable tough gunner William Peckover and the amiable gardener David Nelson among them—into the ship's launch. [8]He then headed for those islands, sailed through them in the most masterly piece of navigation in history, charted them as well as he could from his tiny overloaded vessel, and thus became, instead of Cook, their famed discoverer.

—Richard Hough, *The Last Voyage of Captain James Cook*

■ Combine these sentences:

Cook lost an opportunity. He might have discovered Fiji. _____

_____

■ Find the nouns in the excerpt above indicating performers that are formed from a verb with the suffix *-er* or *-or* and write what they do, as the example shows.

| Noun | Verb |
|------|------|
| 1. _____*a sailor*_____ | _____*sails*_____ |
| 2. _____ | _____ |
| 3. _____ | _____ |
| 4. _____ | _____ |
| 5. _____ | _____ |
| 6. _____ | _____ |

■ Think of someone you admire for making a discovery of a place or thing. Write a sentence explaining why you admire this person. _____

_____

# LESSON 26
## Endings That Form Adjectives

Adjectives, the words that indicate *what kind,* are frequently formed from nouns and verbs by adding endings. For example, *question* can become *questionable, depend* becomes *dependent,* and *zeal* becomes *zealous.*

### Endings That Form Adjectives

| | | |
|---|---|---|
| *-able* | love. . . | lovable |
| *-al* | condition. . . | conditional |
| *-ant* | triumph. . . | triumphant |
| *-ary* | custom. . . | customary |
| *-ent* | depend. . . | dependent |
| *-ful* | peace. . . | peaceful |
| *-ible* | contempt. . . | contemptible |
| *-ic* | photograph. . . | photographic |
| *-ish* | girl. . . | girlish |
| *-ly* | friend. . . | friendly |
| *-less* | friend. . . | friendless |
| *-ous* | harmony. . | harmonious |

### In the Lifeboats

[1]The crew did their best to make the women more comfortable. [2]In No. 5 a sailor took off his stockings and gave them to Mrs. Washington Dodge. [3]When she looked up in startled gratitude, he explained, "I assure you, ma'am, they are perfectly clean. [4]I just put them on this morning." [5]In No. 13, Fireman Beauchamp shivered in his thin jumpers, but he refused to take an extra coat offered him by an elderly lady, insisting it go to a young Irish girl instead. [6]Besides the cold, the number of lady oarsmen dispelled the picnic illusion. [7]In No. 6 the irrepressible Mrs. Brown organized the women, two to an oar. [8]One held the oar in place, while the second did the pulling. [9]In this way Mrs. Brown, Mrs. Meyer, Mrs. Candee and others propelled the boat some three or four miles, in a hopeless effort to overtake the light that twinkled on the horizon most of the night.

—Walter Lord, *A Night to Remember*

- Combine these sentences:

Everyone was cold. Everyone in the boats tried to help the others. _____

_____

■ Find the adjectives in the excerpt above that have been formed from other words. Write them in the column below, then write a sentence for each using the words from which they are formed, as the example shows.

<table>
<tr><td></td><td style="text-align:center">**Adjectives**</td><td style="text-align:center">**Sentence**</td></tr>
<tr><td>1.</td><td style="text-align:center">*comfortable*</td><td style="text-align:center">*The socks were a comfort to*<br>*Mrs. Dodge.*</td></tr>
<tr><td>2.</td><td>_____</td><td>_____</td></tr>
<tr><td>3.</td><td>_____</td><td>_____</td></tr>
<tr><td>4.</td><td>_____</td><td>_____</td></tr>
</table>

■ Write a sentence about a generous action you have seen someone do for another person. _____

_____

## LESSON 26a
## Suffixes That Form Adjectives

• • • • • • • • •

Many adjectives are formed from nouns, such as *sorrowful* from *sorrow* and *marvelous* from *marvel*. Some can be made from verbs, like *different* from *differ*.

### All-Purpose Cells

[1]The human body looks and works like a seamless whole, but it is constructed of individual units too small to be seen, some 100 trillion living cells. [2]Stem cells have recently burst from the obscurity of the research laboratory into the arena of national politics, propelled by assertions that they are either the fruits of murder or the panacea for the degenerative diseases of age. [3]Obtained from the surplus embryos generated in fertility clinics, human embryonic stem cells have not yet been much studied because many biomedical researchers were forbidden to work on them. [4]Embryonic stem cells are of great interest because of their all-purpose nature. [5]But the body's adult stem cells also hold high medical promise. [6]The promise of stem cell research is that it may allow doctors to bend the rules of this harsh game just a little, by using the vast generative power of stem cells to extend life and health.

—Nicholas Wade, *In Tiny Cells, Glimpses of Body's Master Plan*

■ Combine these sentences:

Stem cells have not been studied much. They hold medical promise. _____

_____

■ Match the list of nouns and verbs below with the adjectives that you can find in the excerpt above.

| Nouns and Verbs | Adjectives |
| --- | --- |
| 1. seam | *seamless* |
| 2. nation | |
| 3. degenerate | |
| 4. embryo | |
| 5. medicine | |
| 6. generate | |

■ What recent scientific discovery do you find most exciting? Write a sentence explaining what it is. _____

_____

# LESSON 26b
# Adjectives and Adverbs

· · · · · · · ·

We have seen a number of adjectives formed from nouns. These adjectives, in turn, are often turned into adverbs—words that tell how—by adding -*ly* to an adjective. For example, *natur-al*, an adjective formed from the noun *nature* and the suffix -*al*, can become the adverb *natur-al-ly*, the way in which one acts. Some others are *use-ful-ly, plenti-ful-ly,* and *beauti-ful-ly.*

### A Dictionary Maker

[1]Noah Webster (1758–1843) was by all accounts a severe, correct, humorless, religious, temperate man who was not easy to like, even by other severe, religious, temperate, humorless people. [2]All Webster's work was informed by a passionate patriotism and the belief that American English was at least as good as British English. [3]He worked tirelessly, churning out endless hectoring books and tracts, as well as working on the more or less

constant revisions of his spellers and dictionaries. [4]In between time he wrote impassioned letters to congressmen, dabbled in politics, proffered unwanted advice to presidents, led his church choir, lectured to large audiences, helped found Amherst College, and produced a sanitized version of the Bible. [5]Like Samuel Johnson, he was a better lexicographer than a businessman. [6]Instead of insisting on royalties he sold the rights outright and never gained the sort of wealth that his tireless labors merited.

—Bill Bryson, *The Mother Tongue: English and How It Got That Way*

■ What in this excerpt indicates the reason Webster could be called "not easy to like"? Answer the question in a sentence. _____

_____

■ Find the adjectives in the excerpt above that are formed from nouns or verbs and list them on the lines below. If there are any adverbs formed from adjectives, list them too.

| Adjective | Noun or Verb | Adverb |
|---|---|---|
| 1. *humorless* | *humor* | *humorlessly* |
| 2. _____ | _____ | _____ |
| 3. _____ | _____ | _____ |
| 4. _____ | _____ | _____ |
| 5. _____ | _____ | _____ |
| 6. _____ | _____ | _____ |

■ People who achieve remarkable things are not always pleasant human beings. Can you think of anyone famous who has a reputation for being hard to get along with? Write your answer in a sentence. _____

_____

For more on suffixes, see Review Exercises 15, 18, 28, 45.

# LESSON 27
## Endings That Show More or Most

Adjectives not only indicate the quality of a person or thing; they can also show the *degree* of this quality, as in the familiar *good, better, best.* Thus a glass of lemonade can be *cold,* another glass can be *colder,* and still another glass can be *coldest.* These forms are called the *positive,* the *comparative,* and the *superlative.* We can use these endings on nearly all adjectives to show more or most of the quality. We can also write that some sunsets are *beautiful,* others are *more beautiful,* and that last night's was the *most beautiful* of all. We use this form when the adjective formed by *-er* or *-est* would be more difficult to say or write.

### After the Sinking

[1]In the case of the living, the Register carefully ran the phrase, "Arrived *Titan-Carpath,* April 18, 1912." [2]The hyphen represented history's greatest sea disaster. [3]What troubled people especially was not just the tragedy—or even its needlessness—but the element of fate in it all. [4]If the *Titanic* had heeded any of the six ice messages on Sunday . . . if ice conditions had been normal . . . if the night had been rough or moonlit . . . if she had seen the berg 15 seconds sooner—or 15 seconds later . . . if she had hit the ice any other way . . . if her watertight bulkheads had been one deck higher . . . if she had carried enough boats . . . if the *Californian* had only come. [5]Had any one of these "ifs" turned out right, every life might have been saved. [6]But they all went against her—a classic Greek tragedy.

—Walter Lord, *A Night to Remember*

- Combine these sentences:

People were troubled by the sinking of the *Titanic.* There was an element of fate in what happened. _____

_____

- Underline all the adjectives in the excerpt above that end in *-er* or *-est.* Write them below in their positive, comparative, and superlative forms, as shown in the example.

|  | Positive | Comparative | Superlative |
|---|---|---|---|
| 1. | *great* | *greater* | *greatest* |
| 2. | | | |

122

|  | Positive | Comparative | Superlative |
|---|---|---|---|
| 3. | _____ | _____ | _____ |
| 4. | _____ | _____ | _____ |

- Think of a time when the weather affected your mood. Write a sentence about how much of a change it made in the way you felt. _____

_____

## LESSON 27a
## More Adjectives of Degree

• • • • • • • • •

Although most adjectives add *-er* or *-est* to show degree, note that some must use *more* or *most* to signal such changes.

### Paris in the Spring

[1]I bade adieu to Paris the twenty-fifth of February, just as we had had one fine day. [2]This one fine day brought out the Parisian world in its gayest colors. [3]I never saw anything more animated or prettier, of the kind, than the promenade that day in the *Champs Elysées*. [4]But a French crowd is always gay, full of quick turns and drolleries; most amusing when most petulant, it represents what is so agreeable in the character of the nation. [5]We have now seen it on two good occasions, the festivities of the new year and just after we came was the *mardi gras*. [6]An immense crowd thronged the streets this year to see it, but few figures and little invention followed the emblem of plenty; indeed few among the people could have had the heart for such a sham, knowing how the poorer classes have suffered from hunger this Winter. [7]All signs of this are kept out of sight in Paris.

—Margaret Fuller, *These Sad but Glorious Days: Dispatches from Europe*

- Combine these sentences:

Spring in Paris is beautiful. The poor are kept out of sight. _____

_____

■ Some of the adjectives that appear in the excerpt above can show changes in degree with *-er* or *-est*, while others need *more* or *most*. Choose five adjectives, and show how they can be compared, as shown in the example.

| Adjective | Comparative | Superlative |
|---|---|---|
| 1. _____clear_____ | _____clearer_____ | _____clearest_____ |
| 2. _____ | _____ | _____ |
| 3. _____ | _____ | _____ |
| 4. _____ | _____ | _____ |
| 5. _____ | _____ | _____ |
| 6. _____ | _____ | _____ |

■ Write a sentence about a beautiful spring day that had something sad about it, as thoughts of the poor affect the writer's feeling about the day in Paris. _____

_____

# LESSON 27b
# Adjectives Having Irregular Degree Forms

While many adjectives show comparative and superlative degree by adding *-er* or *-est*, others do this by preceding the adjective with *more* or *most*, and still others are completely irregular, like *bad, worse,* and *worst.*

### The Discovery of Hawaii

[1]At dawn on 18 January Cook could just make out the shape of the first of the Hawaiian islands he was to note in his log and describe in his journal. [2]They were clearly on the brink of making the greatest discovery of this voyage so far. [3]Oahu bore almost due east, its mountains sharply defined in the clear air, but no nearer than before. [4]Kauai was directly ahead, mountainous, too, and already giving evidence of rich fruitfulness. [5]Gore "saw a high hummock of land" at 5:30 p.m., rising straight from the sea at the east end of the island, then gentler slopes along the south side with trees higher up, and along the shore and hinterland villages, plantations

of some root crop, sugar and plantains. <sup>6</sup>The natives were massing in groups on favourable headlands and staring out wonderingly at the strange sight of these great vessels running before the wind half a league off the shore.

—Richard Hough, *The Last Voyage of Captain James Cook*

■ Why does the writer believe that this was to be the greatest discovery of the voyage? _____

_____

■ Underline the adjectives in the excerpt above. Choose three and write them below in all three forms, as shown in the example.

| Adjective | Comparative | Superlative |
|---|---|---|
| 1. *fine* | *finer* | *finest* |
| 2. _____ | _____ | _____ |
| 3. _____ | _____ | _____ |
| 4. _____ | _____ | _____ |

■ Are any voyages of discovery being made today? Write a sentence about one you have read of. _____

_____

# YOUR WRITING
*Being Specific*

*The movie was exciting.* What goes through your mind when you read a sentence like this? Chances are you'll have questions immediately: What was the name of the movie? What was exciting about it? At what theater is it playing? In order to communicate information it is essential to provide details like these. Yet very often sentences, while accurate enough, are not informative enough. What can you do to produce writing that gives a reader a clearer picture of what you want to say? There are several ways, the ones you have been practicing throughout this unit.

- Be as specific as you can. Does Lora have a new top? Make it a fire-engine red sleeveless cotton T-shirt. How about the car Hari's brother is lending him to go to the beach? It's a black Mustang convertible with five speeds, isn't it? Don't be shy about including information; it's almost impossible to have too much.
- Use examples to provide information. Are you telling someone how difficult a science class can be? Don't just say biology or chemistry is tough. Be specific: *The hardest part is memorizing the periodic table of the elements.* Or perhaps *Preparing a slide for the microscope is extremely difficult.*
- Make your examples more interesting with an *anecdote* or brief story. (Be careful here to keep it *brief.*) It could be something like, *For the fourth morning in a row Maybelle didn't hear the alarm clock and walked into her Spanish class just ten minutes before the period ended.*
- Be sure to include plenty of details to provide a clear picture: brand names: not just *toothpaste,* but *Crest Tartar Control Toothpaste;* colors: *magenta, burnt orange;* places: *Sam's Pizzeria, the Fifty-Ninth Street station, Lake of the Woods;* titles: *Bridget Jones's Diary, Of Mice and Men;* flavors: *mint chocolate chip* . . . this list could go on indefinitely.

Notice that the people in the examples above have names, the classes have titles. and the car has a transmission as well as a brand name. These are ways of providing specific information to your reader.

It's time now to write a paragraph.

Sister Helen Prejean's book, *Dead Man Walking,* is written to support a cause in which she believes deeply. If you have ever supported a cause, whether collecting clothing for the homeless or campaigning for better traffic signals, write a topic sentence that explains your reason for supporting it. (If you haven't, write about a cause you've heard about.) Now go on to write a paragraph of at least five sentences.

_____

_____

_____

_____

_____

_____

_____

_____

_____

Read your paragraph again, making as many words as possible more specific and adding as many details as you can think of.

# UNIT IV

# What We *Really* Say: Idiomatic Uses

. . . . . . . . . .

We saw in Unit 3 that English once had many more word endings that changed meanings than it now has. A word's ending signaled whether it was the subject or object of a sentence, for example. Thus the poet of *Beowulf* could write *Tham wife tha word wel licodon*—literally *To the woman the words well pleased.* *Tham wife* indicates by the endings *-m* and *-e* that the meaning is *to the woman,* and *tha word* signifies a plural noun. Endings also carried information that affected word order, which was much less important than it is in today's English, which would say, *The words pleased the woman well.*

But endings affected more than word order; they provided such information as *where, when,* and *whose.* For example, *to the king* was *thaem cyninge* and *belonging to the king* was *thaes cyninges.* What happened after these endings were lost to make clear what was being said? People began to use prepositional phrases like *after the game, across the river,* and *the point of the assignment* (the assignment's point). Read this:

> It was only hours since I had last seen them, but they had changed and I had changed. *In the very front rank*, two men were wounded and staggered along, trailing blood *behind them*. No drummers here, no pipers, and the red coats were covered *with a fine film of dust*. They marched *with bayonets fixed*, and as fixed *on their faces* was anger, fear, and torment.
>
> —Howard Fast, *April Morning*

You probably identified several prepositional phrases in that excerpt. Something else to notice is that while prepositions show time, direction, and possession, the phrases they produce often fall into the category known as *idioms*—expressions in a language that are peculiar to themselves and cannot be reduced to rules. It is the reason we say that some people wait *in line* and

**129**

others wait *on line*, and it accounts for expressions like *to the store* but *to Macy's* and *around town* but *around the block*. Idioms also make use of prepositions to form two-word verbs like *put on, take off, go out, wash up* and many more, as we'll see.

But before we go on (notice the idiomatic two-word verb), let's look at how *determiners* or *articles* are used idiomatically. You know that *the* is used for one or more specific things and that *a* and *an* refer to something that is not specified. *The dog* [my friend Spot] *chased the stick. A dog* [a stranger whose name I don't know] *chased me down the street.*

We'll be looking for examples of these idioms in Howard Fast's *April Morning*, a novel about the beginning of the American Revolution as seen by a teenaged boy.

# LESSON 28
# Prepositions That Indicate
# *Where* and *When*

• • • • • • • • •

Prepositions are usually small words—*to, by, at, of*—but they are words we cannot do without. They show us many things: when and where things happen—*after the game, we went to the picnic*; how they happen—*we watched the movie with excitement*; and who makes them happen—*the class read the story by Stephen King*. In the passage below look for prepositions that give you information about *when* and *where*.

### A Brother's Comfort

¹We sat quietly in the darkness for a few minutes. ²Levi pressed close to me, pushing his face into my jacket. ³He felt small and helpless, and I was filled with guilt for all the times we had quarreled and all the names we had called each other, and I told myself that from now on, I would take care of him just as if I were his own father. ⁴But when Levi slipped out of the smokehouse, I was alone again and afraid again, and had no one to come between myself and my fear and grief.

—Howard Fast, *April Morning*

■ Combine these sentences:

Levi is my younger brother. I reassured him. _____

_____

■ Underline the prepositional phrases in the excerpt above. Decide which ones describe *when* and *where* something is happening. Write them below, as shown in the example.

| Phrase | Where or When |
|---|---|
| 1. _____*in the darkness*_____ | _____*where*_____ |
| 2. _____ | _____ |
| 3. _____ | _____ |
| 4. _____ | _____ |
| 5. _____ | _____ |
| 6. _____ | _____ |

**131**

|                   Phrase                |            Where or When            |
| --------------------------------------- | ----------------------------------- |
| 7. _____ | _____    |
| 8. _____ | _____    |

- Write a sentence about a time when you felt especially close to a friend or a member of your family. _____

_____

### LESSON 28A
### More Prepositional Phrases

. . . . . . . . . .

We depend so much on prepositional phrases to show us directions— *over, under, between*—that we may forget how frequently they occur in our writing. See how many you find in the passage below.

**New Chimp in Town**

¹Milla appeared to be most taken with The Babies in the cage next to her. ²Most were about two years of age and, in addition to the Rwandan chimps, all arrived within an eighteen-month period. ³Milla would some-times lie on the ledge next to their cage and pretend to be asleep, allowing the braver souls like Pan to sneak up and grab or bite any part of her that seemed to stick through the bars—a finger or foot, or even just a toe. ⁴Though Milla was fully awake, she never showed any reaction to this nasty behavior. ⁵In fact, Milla often encouraged Dora to approach and groom her through the bars, sometimes even turning her back, and with a finger indicating to Dora a spot she'd like scratched. ⁶Milla blossomed in the fourteen-acre enclosure.

—Sheila Siddle, *In My Family Tree: A Life with Chimpanzees*

- Combine these sentences:

Milla liked The Babies. She let them tease her. _____

_____

▪ Fill in the blanks below with prepositional phrases that show direction. Your answers need not be in the exact words of the excerpt.

1. The Babies were ___*in the cage*___, _____ Milla. She liked to lie

_____ and let her arm or leg stick _____. She really

enjoyed being _____.

▪ Have you ever watched puppies or kittens or other baby animals? Write a sentence about how they behave. _____

_____

_____

## LESSON 28B
## Prepositional Phrases That Tell *When*

. . . . . . . . .

Many of our common prepositional phrases indicate *when* something happened—or will happen. For example, *I'll meet you after the movie* or *That happened before my time.* Look for some of these phrases in the following paragraph.

### Women Writing Sports

[1]The arrival of the first female reporters in the Yankee clubhouse last September had perfectly predictable results. [2]On the night that Judge Motley's order took effect, the Yankee clubhouse was suddenly crowded with strangers, male and female, who had come to report on the new socio-journalistic phenomenon. [3]After the first night, however, the clubhouse was a much quieter place, and the players, caught up in their excruciating race, talked mostly baseball. [4]On Friday night, the Yankees announced that the clubhouse would be closed to all reporters for forty-five minutes after the game, to permit the players to shower and dress. [5]The reporters were badly upset.

—Roger Angell, *Late Innings*

▪ Combine these sentences:

Reporters interview players after the game. They get the best story in the

clubhouse. _____

_____

▪ Find the prepositions in the excerpt above that indicate *when*. Write them in the spaces below to complete the sentences.

1. The Yankee clubhouse was suddenly crowded _____ *on the night* _____.

2. The clubhouse was a much quieter place _____.

3. The Yankees announced that the clubhouse would be closed _____

    _____.

4. The closing would be _____.

5. It would happen _____.

▪ Do you have a favorite sportswriter? Explain in a sentence what you like about that writer's style. _____

_____

For more on prepositions, see Review Exercises 11, 14.

# LESSON 29
# Prepositions That Indicate
## *How* and *Why*

• • • • • • • • •

Some prepositional phrases, like *by chance* or *for the reward,* tell how or why something happens. *Alice explained her research project with a PowerPoint presentation.* Look for this kind of phrase in the following paragraph.

### Silence

[1]I was awakened by the silence. [2]I guess it was the first silence in six or seven hours, and it was just unbelievable and a little frightening as well. [3]I don't mean that it was a complete and total silence, or anything unnatural or spooky. [4]There were sounds in the distance and in the background, as there always are, but even these sounds were muffled by the tangled pile of trees; and missing were the violent and awful sounds of battle, the crash of firearms and the savage shouting and swearing of men in anger and pain. [5]It was still daylight outside, but under the windfall was a sort of comforting twilight, and being used to gauging time without a pocket watch, I had a feeling that at least an hour had passed.

—Howard Fast, *April Morning*

■ Why would anyone be awakened by silence? Write your answer in a
sentence. _____

_____

■ Find the prepositional phrases in the excerpt above. Write them in the spaces below to answer the following questions.

1. How is the narrator awakened?           _____*by the silence*_____

2. By what are the sounds muffled?         _____

3. What is the crash?                       _____

4. What is the savage shouting and swearing? _____

5. How do the men shout?                    _____

6. How does the writer gauge time?          _____

**135**

■ Now write a sentence about how you felt in a very silent place you have been in. _____

_____

## LESSON 29A
## *Why* and *How* Prepositional Phrases

. . . . . . . . .

Using a prepositional phrase to indicate how something is done or why someone chooses to do it can be a less complicated way of showing these relationships than writing one or more sentences of explanation: *Jonny uses a dictionary for finding synonyms.*

### A Latin Language?

[1]English grammar is so complex and confusing for the one very simple reason that its rules and terminology are based on Latin—a language with which it has precious little in common. [2]In Latin, to take one example, it is not possible to split an infinitive. [3]So in English, the early authorities decided, it should not be possible to split an infinitive either. [4]But there is no reason why we shouldn't any more than we should forsake instant coffee and air travel because they weren't available to the Romans. [5]Making English grammar conform to Latin rules is like asking people to play baseball using the rules of football. [6]It is a patent absurdity. [7]The early authorities not only used Latin grammar as their model, but actually went to the almost farcical length of writing English grammars in that language.

—Bill Bryson, *The Mother Tongue: English and How It Got That Way*

■ Combine these sentences:

Some people try to apply Latin rules to English. English is an entirely different language. _____

_____

■ Identify the prepositional phrases in the excerpt above that help to answer the following:

1. Why English is confusing                *for the one very*    *simple reason* _____

2. To whom was air travel not available?          _____

3. On what did early authorities base English rules _____

4. What Latin grammar was used as _____

5. How some English grammars are written _____

■ What might happen if a language had no rules? Write your own sentence to

answer this question. _____

_____

### LESSON 29B
## More on *How* and *Why*
. . . . . . . . .

We have seen prepositional phrases that answer *when, where, how,* and *why.* In the following passage look for more prepositional phrases that answer these questions.

### Black Comedy

[1]In the postwar years, as the civil rights movement gained force and the pop culture universe expanded, black comedians seized the moment. [2]So just what is black humor and, by extension, its entertainment offshoot, black comedy? [3]Mr. Watkins describes certain characteristics that sound remarkably like those mentioned by the comedians. [4]Foremost among them are realism, a willingness to poke fun at the predicaments of life, and delivery, owing to the more expressive and flamboyant styles of Black America. [5]Generally speaking, the black comedians agreed that the spread of urban culture, and rap music in particular, was helping to bridge the sensibility gap between black and white audiences, further blurring distinctions between black and white comedy.

—Fletcher Roberts, *Explosive, Realistic, but Most of All Funny*

■ How can the development of urban culture benefit our society? Write your

answer in a sentence. _____

_____

■ Find a prepositional phrase in the excerpt above that answers each of the following questions, as shown in the example.

1. When? _____ *In the postwar years* _____

2. How? _____

3. What? _____

4. Where? _____

■ Write a sentence explaining why your favorite comedian makes you laugh.

_____

For more about prepositional phrases, see Review Exercises 24, 27.

# LESSON 30
# Prepositions That Show Possession

Much of the time we indicate that something belongs to someone or something by adding -'s. Another way of doing it is by a prepositional phrase beginning with *of*: *the roof of the house* means the same as *the house's roof*. Here are some examples.

### The Return

[1]When I saw the tower of the meetinghouse, I felt better, and then I saw the Parker barns on the outskirts of town, and I told myself that if they had burned one, they would have burned the other too. [2]You might think we would run in our haste to be there and see what had happened, but you don't hurry for bad news. [3]Also, we were tired, all three of us. [4]So we came up to the town slowly, and bit by bit we realized that it still stood, only the three houses that I spoke of before burned down. [5]It was the ending of a day when I had seen many bodies, bodies of redcoats and bodies of Committeemen.

—Howard Fast, *April Morning*

■ What feeling do you get from this passage? Write a sentence explaining why you feel this way. _____

_____

■ Among the prepositional phrases in the excerpt above are some that show possession. Write them below, followed by the form with an apostrophe, as shown in the example.

1. _the tower of the meetinghouse_     _the meetinghouse's tower_

2. _____     _____

3. _____     _____

4. _____     _____

5. _____     _____

▪ Sometimes we can see that something unusual has happened nearby—a fire engine, a police car's flashing lights, a gathering crowd. Write a sentence about such a scene that you have come upon. _____

_____

## LESSON 30A
## More Possessive Prepositional Phrases

· · · · · · · · · ·

You can determine if a prepositional phrase is a possessive simply by turning it around: *the face of the clock* can be rewritten as *the clock's face.*

### The Stranger in the Water

[1]The side of the ship made a belt of shadow on the glassy shimmer of the sea. [2]But I saw at once something elongated and pale floating very close to the ladder. [3]Before I could form a guess a faint flash of phosphorescent light, which seemed to issue suddenly from the naked body of a man, flickered in the sleeping water with the elusive, silent play of summer lightning in a night sky. [4]With a gasp I saw revealed to my stare a pair of feet, the long legs, a broad livid back immersed right up to the neck in a greenish cadaverous glow. [5]One hand, awash, clutched the bottom rung of the ladder. [6]He was complete but for the head. [7]A headless corpse! [8]At that I suppose he raised up his face, a dimly pale oval in the shadow of the ship's side.

—Joseph Conrad, *The Secret-Sharer*

▪ Combine these sentences:

The narrator thinks he sees a headless corpse. He sees a face. _____

_____

▪ Find the prepositional phrases that serve as possessives in the excerpt above and write them as they would be formed with an apostrophe, as shown in the example.

1. _____*the ship's side*_____    4. _____

2. _____    5. _____

3. _____    6. _____

■ Write a sentence about a scene in a horror movie that made you jump in your seat. _____

_____

### LESSON 30B
## Still More Possessive Prepositional Phrases

· · · · · · · · ·

Sometimes we choose to write a possessive as a prepositional phrase because a simple -'s would sound awkward. For example, in sentence 2 below we would wind up with *the eighteenth-century ruined fortresses' shelter.*

**Laundry and Civilization**

[1]At Acre, the stronghold of the Crusaders on the Mediterranean, west of Galilee, the fortifications stand in golden ruins, piled on the foundations of earlier ruins. [2]Arabs lived in the shelter of the eighteenth-century ruined fortresses, and even now in the years of the establishment of Israel, burning with its mixture of religion, hygiene, and applied sociology, the poor Arabs still hung out their washing on the battlements, so that it fluttered all along the antique sea-front, innocent of the offense it was committing in the eyes of the seekers of beautiful sights and spiritual sensations, who had come all the way from the twentieth century, due west of Acre. [3]Indeed, the washing draped out on the historic walls was a sign of progress, enlightenment, and industry, as it had been from time immemorial; it betokened a settlement and a society with a sense of tomorrow, even if it was only tomorrow's clean shirt, as against the shifty tent-dwelling communities of the wilderness.

—Muriel Spark, *The Mandelbaum Gate*

■ Why does the writer find the washing hung on the city walls a sign of civilization? Write a sentence explaining your answer. _____

_____

■ Find the prepositional phrases in the excerpt above that show what possesses each of the following:

1. the stronghold          *of the Crusaders*

2. foundations          _____

3. shelter          _____

4. establishment        _____

5. eyes                 _____

6. communities          _____

■ What kind of scene represents civilization for you? Write your answer in a sentence. _____

_____

For more on prepositional phrases, see Review Exercises 11, 14, 24, 27.

# Two-Word Verbs

Some prepositions are an integral part of what we call *two-word verbs—put down, take up, make over,* and many more. Each of these two-word verbs has a meaning of its own distinct from the meaning of the verb alone. (Think about the difference between *put down* and *put.*) Prepositions used like this are called *particles.*

### The Night Rider

¹I heard it now, and Levi was right. ²The sound was of a horse being raced through the night, and clearer and clearer came the drumbeat of its hoofs. ³I strained my eyes toward the Menotomy Road, but it was too dark and there were too many trees obstructing my vision for me to make out a rider. ⁴But the rider was nearer now, and the hoofbeats echoed through the whole village; and then he pulled up in front of Buckman's, and I heard him shouting at the top of his lungs, although I couldn't make out his words. ⁵We heard him shouting again. ⁶Mother came in, carrying a candle. ⁷Lights were beginning to flicker in some of the houses. ⁸Middle of the night or not, the village was up and awake, and every man and boy in town was either already at the common or heading for it. ⁹I dashed out of the house and took off for the common.

—Howard Fast, *April Morning*

- Combine these sentences:

A horseman has arrived. The village is excited. _____

_____

- Find the two-word verbs in the excerpt above.

1. _____*make out*_____      3. _____

2. _____      4. _____

- Think of a time you were surprised when an unexpected visitor arrived at

your home or school. Write a sentence about it. _____

_____

## LESSON 31A
## More Two-Word Verbs

One way to recognize a two-word verb is by testing to see if a pronoun can appear between the verb and the preposition. For example, we can *take it off* but we can't *take off it*. Here's another example: *Wally wants to take up snowboarding as a hobby. He would really like to take it up.*

### Danger at Sea

¹Sometimes a storm would hit the Grand Banks and half a dozen ships would go down, a hundred men lost overnight. ²On more than one occasion, Newfoundlanders woke up to find their beaches strewn with bodies. ³The Grand Banks are so dangerous because they happen to sit on one of the worst storm tracks in the world. ⁴In the old days, there wasn't much the boats could do but put out extra anchor cable and try to ride it out. ⁵As dangerous as the Grand Banks were, though, Georges Bank was even worse. ⁶Currents ran in strange vortexes on Georges, and the tide was said to run off so fast that ocean bottom was left exposed for gulls to feed on.

—Sebastian Junger, *The Perfect Storm*

■ Why is Georges Bank more dangerous than the Grand Banks? Write your answer in a sentence. _____

_____

■ Identify the two-word verbs in the excerpt above and write them below.

1. _____*go down*_____     4. _____

2. _____     5. _____

3. _____     6. _____

■ What is the most dangerous place you have ever seen? Write a sentence about that place. _____

_____

# LESSON 31B
## Two-Word Verbs and Prepositional Phrases

· · · · · · · · ·

Another way to recognize two-word verbs is to note whether they are followed by a prepositional phrase, as in *Oscar looked out over the sea. Looked out* is a two-word verb and *over the sea* is a prepositional phrase.

### The First Practice

[1]The coaches stand there looking at us the way a mechanic eyes his socket wrenches, as tools to be picked up, used, and thrown aside. [2]There is only this simple equation: as a ballplayer, I am expected to do as I'm told, lay my body on the line or else get out of the way for somebody who will. [3]Everybody in the room knows and understands this and, when asked, will put himself in harm's way with the dim, deluded hope that he will come out the other end a star. [4]The speech begins, and it's like every other coach's speech. [5]He lays down the rules about how we're here to win and anything less is simply unacceptable.

—Elwood Reid, *My Body, My Weapon, My Shame*

■ Combine these sentences:

A football player must use his body. His only purpose is to win. _____

_____

■ Two-word verbs may be followed by a direct object or by a prepositional phrase. On the lines below write the two-word verbs you find in the passage, along with either the direct object or the prepositional phrase that follows.

| Two-Word Verb | Direct Object or Prepositional Phrase |
|---|---|
| 1. *look at* | *us (direct object)* |
| 2. _____ | _____ |
| 3. _____ | _____ |

| Two-Word Verb | Direct Object or Prepositional Phrase |
| --- | --- |
| 4. _____ | _____ |
| 5. _____ | _____ |

▪ The writer of the excerpt on the previous page puts his body through pain to play football. Write a sentence about some other activity that is painful but rewarding. _____

_____

# Articles

Think about some of the smallest most frequently used words in English—for example, *the, a,* and *an.* These are called *articles,* and they indicate whether a noun is a particular one of its kind, a definite article—*the hat Sandy wore yesterday*—or any of a larger group of things, an indefinite article—*A hat is necessary in cold weather.* Before a vowel *a* becomes *an: Alyce wore an orange skirt.* Articles are also called determiners.

## The Blockade

[1]There was a place our people had in mind where the Menotomy Road dips between two banks of earth, with a great tangle of wild blackberry bushes on one side and a windfall of dead trees on the other. [2]I knew the place well, because the bramble patch made for the best rabbit hunting in the whole neighborhood, and many was the time Father and I hiked down there for an early morning's shooting. [3]Now the plan was to drag enough fallen trees across the road to block it, and then back the trees up with rocks and dirt. [4]With such a breastwork, we felt we could hold the British long enough for a considerable army of Essex men, who were said to be marching in under the leadership of Colonel Pickering, to lead us.

—Howard Fast, *April Morning*

▪ Write a sentence explaining what the people are planning. _____

_____

▪ Underline all of the articles, with their nouns, in the excerpt above. Then, for five of them, write a sentence using the noun with another article, as shown in the example.

1. _____*the Menotomy Road*_____     *Our town has a Menotomy Road.*

2. _____     _____

3. _____     _____

4. _____     _____

5. _____     _____

6. _____     _____

■ Write a sentence about a special place you go to when you want to think things over. _____

_____

# LESSON 32A
# Recognizing Articles

*A, an,* and *the* are sometimes called *determiners* because they provide information, such as number, about their nouns. *An apple* tells us that there is only one piece of fruit, while *the apples* tells us there are two or two dozen pieces.

### You Name It

[1]Whether you call a long cylindrical sandwich a hero, a submarine, a hoagy, a torpedo, a garibaldi, a poor boy, or any of at least half a dozen other names tells us something about where you come from. [2]Whether you call it cottage cheese, Dutch cheese, pot cheese, smearcase, clabber cheese, or curd cheese tells us something more. [3]If you call the playground toy in which a long plank balances on a fulcrum a dandle you almost certainly come from Rhode Island. [4]If you call a soft drink tonic, you come from Boston. [5]If you call a small naturally occurring object a stone rather than a rock you mark yourself as a New Englander. [6]If you have a catch rather than play catch or stand on line rather than in line clearly you are a New Yorker. [7]Whether you call it pop or soda, bucket or pail, baby carriage or baby buggy, scat or gesundheit, the beach or the shore—all these and countless others tell us a little something about where you come from.

—Bill Bryson, *The Mother Tongue: English and How It Got That Way*

■ Combine these sentences:

People use different words and expressions in different places. Your speech can tell others where you are from. _____

_____

■ Pick out five nouns in the passage above and write them, without any adjectives, first with the definite article, *the,* then with the appropriate form of the indefinite article, *a* or *an.* The first one is an example:

| Noun | Definite Article | Indefinite Article |
|------|------------------|--------------------|
| 1. _sandwich_ | _the sandwich_ | _a sandwich_ |
| 2. _____ | _____ | _____ |
| 3. _____ | _____ | _____ |
| 4. _____ | _____ | _____ |
| 5. _____ | _____ | _____ |
| 6. _____ | _____ | _____ |

■ Now write your own sentence about an expression that is used in your family or your neighborhood but not usually by other people. _____

_____

# LESSON 32B
## More Articles

• • • • • • • • •

For students whose native language is not English, it is often difficult to determine when to use *the,* when to use *a* or *an,* and when not to use an article at all. Unfortunately, there are no rules for this; students must listen to native speakers and read to determine when to use articles.

### Sports Overload

[1]We are heading toward sports overload. [2]Screens are melting down. [3]Remotes are imploding. [4]Then comes Saturday. [5]Viewers will face a menu of events that appears to have been conjured by beer sponsors desperate to keep people homebound and unsuspecting of competitive nonsports programming. [6]The viewing commences at 11 a.m., Eastern, with the French Open women's final on NBC. [7]It reaches a late afternoon crescendo on NBC with the Belmont Stakes and will conclude around midnight with the Mike Tyson–Lennox Lewis pay-per-view circus. [8]"I look at Saturday and think

every indication says, 'Buy stock in La-Z-Boy,'" said Robert J. Thompson, a professor of media and popular culture at Syracuse University. [9]"All of a sudden, the lounge chair becomes something you inhabit, not just something you sit in."

—Richard Sandomir, *For Saturday, Buy the Chips and the Visine*

■ Combine these sentences:

There are many sports events on television. People can spend the entire day

watching them. _____

_____

■ Identify the nouns and their determiners in the excerpt above. Following the examples shown, write two nouns that are a particular kind of thing (following *the*), two that are one of a larger group (following *a* or *an*), and two that have no article before them.

| Particular Kind | One of a Group | No Article |
|---|---|---|
| 1. *the viewing* | *a menu* | *viewers* |
| 2. | | |
| 3. | | |

■ Write a sentence about whether it is better to be present at a sporting event

or to watch it on television. _____

_____

# YOUR WRITING
## *Making Connections*

In Lesson 31 you were asked to combine the following sentences:

*A horseman has arrived.*
*The village is excited.*

You may have written, "Because a horseman has arrived, the village is excited" or "Ever since a horseman arrived the village has been excited" or "Now that a horseman has arrived the village is excited." You will notice that each of these well-formed compound sentences conveys a slightly different meaning. In the first, it is the arrival of the horseman that *causes* the village to be excited; in the second, the excitement starts *when* the horseman arrives; in the third, there is a suggestion that the village *has been waiting* for the horseman. Changes in just a word or two have shifted the emphasis of the combined sentences from cause to time to anticipation. Changes like these can clarify your points by making your sentences more informative.

You've had practice combining sentences in many of the exercises in this book. It's time now to test your skills in a paragraph.

Have you ever been part of some dramatic event: winning a big game, taking part in a rally, watching a fierce storm? Write a topic sentence that makes clear why you consider the event important, then go on to complete a paragraph of at least five sentences. In each of these sentences be sure to include as many details as possible. If you decide to write about a game, don't just say what the game is. Name the teams, and at least some of the players and describe the color of their uniforms. How many fans are in the crowd? What is the name of the stadium? What do the banners say?

Topic Sentence: _____

_____

_____

_____

_____

_____

_____

Go through your paragraph, deciding which sentences can be combined and making whatever changes are necessary to produce informative statements that clarify the point, making as many words as possible more specific and adding as many details as you can think of.

# UNIT V

# Making Connections

. . . . . . . . . .

In Unit 1 we saw that a sentence must have at least *one* subject and *one* verb. We also saw that one sentence, or *clause*, can be joined to another to form a longer and more informative sentence. Doing this can clarify your ideas as well as provide more details about your subject. Consider these sentences:

The weather was steaming hot.
Hanna and Lulu were wearing jeans.
They ate delicious burritos at the snack bar.
The pool opened at ten.
They went swimming.
They ran into their friend.
Roberto made a date.
The movie started at seven.

What do we have here? Well, we have a nice list of sentences, each with at least one subject and one verb but without much to do with the other sentences. In fact, the sentences don't seem to have *anything* to do with each other. And what information do we learn from these sentences? Very little when you come right down to it. Something seems to be happening, but it's hard to figure out exactly what. One reason is that we have very few details to fill out the meaning of these sentences. Another is that these sentences are *unconnected*, all by themselves with nothing to pull them into a meaningful whole. Let's see what happens if we add a few words:

Although the weather was steaming hot, Hanna and Lulu were wearing jeans as they ate the delicious burritos at the snack bar while they waited for the pool to open at ten. Later, after they finished swimming, they ran into their friend, Roberto, who made a date to meet them at the movie, which started at seven.

Is the picture getting clearer? Even without the name of the movie or the brand of the jeans, we have the beginnings of a story. Events happen in a certain order. Even more important, the ideas are related to one another so we can see the *how* and *why* of what's happening through the use of just a few small words: *although, as, later, after, which.* Words like these—we know them as conjunctions, relative pronouns, conjunctive adverbs, and sometimes transition words and phrases—pull ideas together and thus create a narrative or a scene rather than a list.

### Conjunctions in Action

Some conjunctions join two or more clauses, either of which could stand alone: *Josie wants to shop, but Leon wants to play basketball.* Each of these is a perfectly good sentence by itself, telling what Josie and Leon want to do, so they are joined by the coordinating conjunction *but.* If we change this to *Josie wants to shop while Leon plays basketball,* we have an independent clause, *Josie wants to shop,* and a dependent or subordinate clause in *while Leon plays basketball.* This second clause tells us *when* Josie wants to shop—*while Leon plays*—and thus needs the independent clause to make sense.

### The Relative Clause

Another kind of dependent clause uses a relative pronoun—*who, which, that*—to be joined to the independent clause: *Anthony slipped on the stairs, which had just been polished.* Notice that in this case the relative pronoun *which* refers to *stairs* and acts as the subject of *had just been.*

Although we use conjunctions and relative pronouns to join clauses, we use transitional words and phrases to introduce ideas and to show how these ideas are connected. For example, we may contrast one assertion with another by writing *on the other hand.* Similarly, to present more facts in our argument, we may write *in addition,* and we might add *finally* to conclude a statement.

The psychologist B. F. Skinner created a utopia for the twentieth century in his *Walden Two.* Here are some examples of words that connect ideas from that book.

# LESSON 33
# Coordinating Conjunctions

. . . . . . . . .

Independent clauses—clauses that can stand as sentences on their own—are connected by the coordinating conjunctions, *and, but, or, no, for, so, yet.* Thus we can have the sentence, *It rained all night,* an independent clause, connected to another independent clause, *We canceled the picnic,* by the conjunction *so: It rained all night so we canceled the picnic.*

## Individuals and Groups

[1]Our interests conflict with the interests of everybody else. [2]That's our original sin, and it can't be helped. [3]Now, "everybody else" we call "society." [4]It's a powerful opponent, and it always wins. [5]Oh, here and there an individual prevails for a while and gets what he wants. [6]Sometimes he storms the culture of a society and changes it slightly to his own advantage. [7]But society wins in the long run, for it has the advantage of numbers and of age. [8]It enslaves one almost before he has tasted freedom. [9]Considering how long society has been at it, you'd expect a better job. [10]The behavior of the individual has been shaped according to revelations of "good conduct," never as the result of experimental study.

—B. F. Skinner, *Walden Two*

- Does Skinner believe that individuals have little chance of changing "society"? Explain your answer in a sentence. _____

_____

- Find the independent clauses in the excerpt above. Underline the subject and verb of each clause and the coordinating conjunction that connects them, then write them below. For example: <u>He was working on faith</u> <u>and it bothered him.</u>

| Subject/Verb | Conjunction | Subject/Verb |
|---|---|---|
| 1. *that is our original sin* | *and* | *it can't be helped* |
| 2. _____ | _____ | _____ |
| 3. _____ | _____ | _____ |
| 4. _____ | _____ | _____ |
| 5. _____ | _____ | _____ |

**155**

■ Write a sentence explaining why you believe—or don't believe—that an individual can make a difference in society. _____

_____

## LESSON 33A
## Independent Clauses

· · · · · · · · · —

Sometimes independent clauses are sentences by themselves; sometimes they are joined to other independent clauses by a coordinating conjunction or a semicolon. For example, *The comedian told a joke, but we didn't laugh.* We use a semicolon when ideas are closely related but cannot easily be joined by a coordinating conjunction. *The temperature was high for January; it made us think of spring.*

### Another Chance

[1]Michelle Kwan didn't even win. [2]But even with a silver medal around her neck, Michelle Kwan couldn't lose. [3]Four years later, she is held to a different standard. [4]But in Salt Lake City she will have the advantage of skating before an American crowd. [5]The crowd can only do so much, however. [6]Although elegant as ever, Kwan has been painfully inconsistent on jumps all season, falling in competition on several occasions. [7]She still hasn't mastered an important triple-triple combination, and it's unlikely she will in time for the Olympic long program.

—Sam Weinman, *Kwan Goes It Alone*

■ What is lessening Michelle Kwan's chance at a gold medal? Write your answer in a sentence. _____

_____

■ Underline the independent clauses in the excerpt above. Write them below, indicating whether they are single sentences or part of a compound sentence joined by a conjunction. You need show only the subject and verb of the independent clause.

|  | **Clause** | **Conjunction, If Any** |
|---|---|---|
| 1. | *Kwan didn't win* | *Single Sentence* |
| 2. | | |

| Clause | Conjunction, If Any |
|--------|---------------------|
| 3. _____ | _____ |
| 4. _____ | _____ |
| 5. _____ | _____ |
| 6. _____ | _____ |
| 7. _____ | _____ |

■ Write a sentence about a time you had a second chance to improve your performance at some sport or other accomplishment. _____

_____

## LESSON 33B
## More Independent Clauses

• • • • • • • •

Remember that an independent clause can be a sentence by itself, it can be connected to another independent clause, or it can be connected to a dependent clause:

Marsha likes peanuts.
Marsha likes peanuts, but Jojo likes potato chips.
Marsha likes peanuts because they are salty.

### Freedom

[1]The body has fewer inhibitions than the mind. [2]It made good use of the new freedom from the first moment on. [3]It began to eat ravenously, for hours and days, even half the night. [4]It is amazing what quantities one can eat. [5]One day, a few days after the liberation, I walked through the country past flowering meadows, for miles and miles, toward the market town near the camp. [6]Larks rose to the sky and I could hear their joyous song. [7]There was no one to be seen for miles around; there was nothing but the wide earth and sky and the larks' jubilation and the freedom of space. [8]I stopped, looked around, and up to the sky—and then I went down on my knees.

—Viktor E. Frankl, *Man's Search for Meaning*

- Combine these sentences:

Freedom affects the body as well as the mind. Former prisoners ate ravenously.

_____

- Choose two pairs of independent clauses in the excerpt above, then combine them as either independent or dependent clauses. The first is done for you.

1. *Because the body has fewer inhibitions than the mind, it made good use*
   *of the new freedom.*

2. _____

3. _____

- Were you ever hungry enough to eat something you don't like? Write a sentence about it. _____

_____

For more about conjunctions, see Review Exercises 21, 34.

# LESSON 34
# Subordinating Conjunctions

A *subordinate* or *dependent clause*, introduced by a subordinating conjunction, does not make sense by itself. It needs an independent clause to complete the idea of the sentence. For example, *while I was taking a nap* doesn't make sense until you join it to *I had a funny dream.* The subordinating conjunctions include *as, if, although, because, since, when, whereas, while, which, that,* and many others.

### Smoking Permitted?

[1]Very few people smoked in Walden Two—Frazier not at all, so far as I could tell, though I remembered him as a heavy pipe-smoker in graduate school. [2]In such company my own consumption of tobacco had fallen off. [3]At first this was because I had felt conspicuous when smoking, and rather guilty, although not the slightest objection was made or implied. [4]Later I found that my interest had weakened. [5]I was surprised to note that I was still on the pack of cigarettes I had slipped into my pocket Wednesday morning. [6]I had smoked only twice since breakfast. [7]I began to wonder whether I might not be able to give it up, after all.

—B. F. Skinner, *Walden Two*

■ Does the writer really want to stop smoking? Write a sentence explaining

your answer. _____

_____

■ Underline the subordinate clauses in the excerpt above. Write five of them below with an independent clause of your own to complete the sentence. The first is an example.

| Subordinate Clause | Independent Clause |
|---|---|
| 1. *Though I remembered him as a heavy pipe-smoker,* | *he did not smoke now.* |
| 2. | |
| 3. | |
| 4. | |
| 5. | |
| 6. | |

■ Write a sentence about a habit you managed to put an end to. _____

## LESSON 34A
## Dependent Clauses

Complex sentences contain at least one independent and one dependent clause, but some may also contain more than one of each, like this one: *When the train was late, I decided to go by bus although I knew that it would take longer.* We have here one independent clause, *I decided to go by bus,* and three dependent clauses: (1) *when the train was late,* (2) *although I knew,* and (3) *that it would take longer.*

### A Strange Population

¹This was a good opportunity to see the country, too, and the more I saw of it, the better I liked it. ²We rolled through many villages and towns, and I soon saw that the parklike beauty of our first-seen city was no exception. ³We stopped for lunch in quite a sizable town, and here, rolling slowly through the streets, we saw more of the population. ⁴They had come out to look at us everywhere, but here were more; and when we went in to eat, in a big garden place with little shaded tables among the trees and flowers, many eyes were upon us. ⁵And everywhere, open country, village, or city— were only women. ⁶Old women and young women and a great majority who seemed neither young nor old, but just women; young girls also, though these, and the children, seeming to be in groups by themselves generally, were less in evidence. ⁷We caught many glimpses of girls and children in what seemed to be schools or in playgrounds, and so far as we could judge there were no boys.

—Charlotte Perkins Gilman, *Herland*

■ Combine these sentences:

Children were in playgrounds. All of them were girls. _____

■ Choose two sentences in the excerpt above that contain dependent clauses. Rewrite them as two separate sentences, making the necessary changes in wording so that they will be independent clauses. The first is an example from sentence 4.

1. _____*We went in to eat.*_____    _____*Many eyes were upon us.*_____

2. _____    _____

3. _____    _____

■ Think of the first time you saw a new place. Write a sentence about your re-action. _____

_____

## LESSON 34B
## More Dependent Clauses
• • • • • • • • • •

A dependent clause must always be attached to an independent clause to form a sentence. *When I was a child.* What about it? Did something happen then? Was there a difference in beliefs, in appearance, in friends? As you can see, this clause is asking for further information to make sense. That information might be *When I was a child, I went barefoot at the beach,* or it might be *I liked ice pops when I was a child.* Be sure that your dependent clauses are attached to independent clauses.

### A Northern Language

[1]The Eskimo language reaches its apogee in describing the land and man's activity in it. [2]Young people in modern Eskimo villages, especially in the eastern Arctic, say that when they are out on the land with their parents, they find it much more difficult to speak Inuktitut, though they speak it at home all the time. [3]It is not so much a lack of vocabulary as a difficulty with constructions, with idioms, a lost fluency that confuses them. [4]It is out on the land, in the hunting camps and traveling over the ice, that the language comes alive. [5]The Eskimo language is seasonal—terms for the many varieties of snow emerge in winter, while those for whaling come into use in the spring.

—Barry Lopez, *The Country of the Mind*

■ What parts of the Eskimo language are used only at certain times? Answer this question in a sentence. _____

_____

■ For each *dependent* clause in this passage write the conjunction that connects it to an *independent* clause as well as the subject and verb.

| Conjunction | Subject | Verb |
|---|---|---|
| 1. _____ *when* _____ | _____ *they* _____ | _____ *are* _____ |
| 2. _____ | _____ | _____ |
| 3. _____ | _____ | _____ |
| 4. _____ | _____ | _____ |
| 5. _____ | _____ | _____ |

■ Do you speak a different language with your friends at school than you do at home? Write a sentence about how it is different. _____

_____

For more about clauses, see Review Exercises 5, 9, 12, 21, 46.

# LESSON 35
# Dependent Clauses with Relative Pronouns

. . . . . . . . .

Very often a dependent clause will be connected to the independent clause by one of the relative pronouns—*which, that,* or *who.* When this happens, the relative pronoun may become the subject of that clause: *Gary finished the paper that is due next Friday. That* functions as a pronoun representing *paper;* it is also the subject of *is.*

### Labor and the Good Life

[1]That's the fatal flaw in labor reform. [2]The program calls for a long, dreary campaign in which the leaders not only keep their men dissatisfied but stir up additional and often spurious grounds for dissatisfaction. [3]No man knows how much heavier the lot of the worker is made by the very people who are trying to make it lighter. [4]Here, there's no battle. [5]We can freely admit that we like to work. [6]Can you believe that we don't need to keep an accurate account of each man's contribution? [7]Or that most of us have stored up enough spare credits to take a long vacation if we liked? [8]We have time for sports, hobbies, arts and crafts, and most important of all, the expression of that interest in the world which is *science* in the deepest sense.

—B. F. Skinner, *Walden Two*

■ Combine these sentences:

Workers are dissatisfied with their jobs. Labor leaders want them to oppose

management. _____

_____

■ Find the clauses in the excerpt above that are connected by relative pronouns. For each relative pronoun, write a sentence with a dependent clause of your own.

| Independent Clause | Relative Pronoun | Dependent Clause |
|---|---|---|
| 1. *We need a quiet room* | *in which* | *we can study our chemistry formulas.* |
| 2. _____ | _____ | _____ |
| 3. _____ | _____ | _____ |
| 4. _____ | _____ | _____ |

**163**

■ Have you had a job you really enjoyed doing? Write a sentence about it.

_____

## LESSON 35A
## Relative Pronouns

· · · · · · · · · ·

When joining a dependent clause to an independent clause, a relative pronoun often becomes the subject of the clause. *Sampson found the keys that opened the locked closet.* The relative pronoun *that* refers to *keys* and also acts as the subject of *opened*.

### Madonna and Evita

¹Unlike Madonna—the daughter of a technician who designed tanks, and who enjoyed a middle-class childhood in a whites-only neighborhood of middle America—Evita was the illegitimate daughter of a servant who grew up in grinding poverty in the Argentinian countryside, coming to Buenos Aires as an impoverished teenager in the hope of finding work. ²She lived as a prostitute and worked as a radio actress before meeting and marrying a rising politician, Juan Perón, who became the nation's president in 1946. ³Together they made a golden couple on the national stage, enhancing Perón's charisma, and thus his power, for which he had an insatiable appetite. ⁴Like other stars who died young, nothing in her life became her like the leaving it. ⁵As hard as Madonna tried to soften Evita's image, the truth is that the two women had essential qualities in common: a driving ambition and a craving for the adoration of the masses.

—Andrew Morton, *Madonna*

■ Although Madonna did not think highly of Evita Perón's background, she was like her in some ways. Describe them in a sentence. _____

_____

■ Find the relative pronouns in the excerpt above that are subjects of dependent clauses. Write them below together with the nouns to which they refer.

| **Dependent Clause** | **Noun** |
| --- | --- |
| 1. _____ *who designed tanks* _____ | _____ *technician* _____ |
| 2. _____ | _____ |

| Dependent Clause | Noun |
|---|---|
| 3. _____ | _____ |
| 4. _____ | _____ |
| 5. _____ | _____ |
| 6. _____ | _____ |

- Think of a celebrity who has been the subject of a movie. Write a sentence about your reaction to the film. _____

_____

## LESSON 35B
## Relative Clauses

Dependent clauses that are joined to the rest of the sentence by a relative pronoun are called *relative clauses. Jana found a history book, which she brought to the lost and found office.* The clause beginning with *which* is a relative clause.

### Behind Football

[1]Football is about hard work, pain, and losing. [2](Messages that the game is all about winning—such as "Just win, baby," which is the Raiders owner Al Davis's hipster re-statement of Vince Lombardi's famous remark "Winning isn't everything, it's the only thing"—are actually less than half the story.) [3]Football is the only common language we have in which to talk about the pitiless, hit-or-be-hit side of America. [4]The game's origins lie in a hazing ritual that was practiced at Ivy League colleges in the 1820s. [5]Freshmen would be summoned to a field to play a rugby-like game during which the upperclassmen would welcome them to school by beating the crap out of them.

—John Seabrook, *Tackling the Competition*

- How do the game's origins tell us that football is about pain? Write your answer in a sentence. _____

_____

■ Underline the relative clauses in the excerpt above. Write the relative pronouns they begin with below, then write another clause using the same relative pronoun.

| Relative Pronoun | Clause |
|---|---|
| 1. _____ which _____ | the third question which was very complicated |
| 2. _____ | _____ |
| 3. _____ | _____ |
| 4. _____ | _____ |
| 5. _____ | _____ |

■ Think of a game, or some other activity, that can be painful. Write a sentence describing the pain. _____

_____

# Transitions That Connect

Among a writer's most useful devices is the transitional word or phrase that shows how one sentence is connected to another. Some of these are adverbs like *before* and *after*, some are prepositional phrases like *at that time*. They indicate additional material, emphasis, contrast, time sequence, location, and conclusion.

## Frequently Used Transitional Words

**To add facts**
*additionally*
*also*
*as well as*
*for example*
*for instance*
*further*
*furthermore*
*moreover*

**To emphasize**
*actually*
*in any case*
*indeed*
*in fact*
*in other words*
*it is true*
*that is to say*
*therefore*

**To show contrast**
*evidently*
*however*
*instead*
*merely*
*nevertheless*
*on the contrary*
*on the other hand*
*otherwise*
*yet*

**To show time**
*after*
*at last*
*before*
*in the meantime*
*later*
*next*
*often*
*subsequently*
*temporarily*
*thereafter*

**To show result or conclusion**
*as a result*
*certainly*
*consequently*
*finally*
*in conclusion*
*in the end*

### Freedom and Control

[1]Control is necessary for the proper functioning of the community. [2]Certainly our elite do not command a disproportionate share of the wealth of the community; on the contrary, they work rather harder, I should say, for what they get. [3]"A Manager's lot is not a happy one." [4]And in the end the Planner or

Manager is demoted to simple citizenship. [5]Temporarily, they have power, in the sense that they run things—but it's limited. [6]They can't compel anyone to obey, for example. [7]A Manager must make a job desirable. [8]He has no slave labor at his command, for our members choose their own work. [9]His power is scarcely worthy of the name. [10]What he has, instead, is a job to be done. [11]Scarcely a privileged class, to my way of thinking.

—B. F. Skinner, *Walden Two*

▪ Combine these sentences:

People at Walden Two choose their own work. Managers have no power. _____

_____

▪ Find the transitional words and phrases in the excerpt above and write them below, indicating whether they add, emphasize, show contrast, time, or result.

| Transitional Word(s) | Function |
|---|---|
| 1. _____*certainly*_____ | _____*result*_____ |
| 2. _____ | _____ |
| 3. _____ | _____ |
| 4. _____ | _____ |

▪ Think of a job you have had with an understanding boss. Write a sentence about why it was easier than another job. _____

_____

## LESSON 36A
## Phrases That Connect

Don't overlook the simple words *and, but,* and *now* as connectives. They are the ones we use most often, as in *The weather was bad, but class was not canceled.*

### Meeting the Producer

[1]What producers do is rarely understood and seldom appreciated. [2]Simpson's stock-in-trade, we had been told, was trying to intimidate writers, and he, in fact, considered himself the coauthor of any script he produced.

³In general, however, we prefer doing business with the bully boys than with the smoothies. ⁴We, in fact, had gone to school with perhaps the all-time top-seeded Hollywood bully boy, Otto Preminger. ⁵As neophyte screenwriters in 1970, we were the fourth of eight writers on Otto's production of *Such Good Friends,* and right off learned that if Otto thought he could beat up on you, then he would beat up on you without mercy. ⁶Although Otto's rage was never far beneath the surface, we always found him rather engaging.

—John Gregory Dunne, *Monster: Living Off the Big Screen*

■ Combine these sentences:

Producers intimidate writers. Writers can do business with them. _____

_____

■ Find the transitional words and phrases that connect the ideas in the excerpt above. Write them below, indicating whether they show time, cause, addition, or emphasis.

| Transition | Function |
|------------|----------|
| 1. _____ *in fact* _____ | _____ *emphasis* _____ |
| 2. _____ | _____ |
| 3. _____ | _____ |
| 4. _____ | _____ |
| 5. _____ | _____ |

■ Have you ever had difficulty dealing with someone who bullied others? Write a sentence about it. _____

_____

## LESSON 36b
## More Phrases That Connect

• • • • • • • •

Note that, with the exception of *and* and *but,* transitional words and phrases do not always occur at the beginning of a sentence. For example, *My mother likes to garden. My father, however, prefers fishing.*

### A Fisherman's Place

[1]Herman Melville wrote his masterpiece, *Moby Dick,* based on his own experience aboard a South Seas whaling ship. [2]It starts with the narrator, Ishmael, stumbling through a snowstorm in New Bedford, Massachusetts, looking for a place to spend the night. [3]Finally he comes to the Spouter Inn. [4]"I thought that here was the very spot for cheap lodging and the best of pea coffee." [5]His instincts were sound, of course; he was given hot food and a bed to share with a South Seas cannibal called Queequeg. [6]Queequeg became his adopted brother and eventually saved his life. [7]Since the beginning of fishing, there have been places that have taken in the Ishmaels of the world—and the Murphs, and the Bugsys, and the Bobbys. [8]Without them, conceivably, fishing wouldn't even be possible.

—Sebastian Junger, *The Perfect Storm*

■ Why wouldn't fishing be possible without a place for fishermen to stay on land? Write your answer in a sentence. _____

_____

■ Listed below are transitional phrases from *A Fisherman's Place.* For each, continue with a sentence of your own, following the example of the first.

1. Finally, _____ *the day of the big game arrived.* _____

2. Of course, _____

3. Eventually, _____

4. Conceivably, _____

■ Write a sentence about a time you stayed away from home—at a friend's house, at camp, at a motel, or in some other place. _____

_____

# YOUR WRITING
## Combining Sentences

When you're writing about your thesis, do you sometimes find that your sentences are more alike than you want them to be? You may have a series of short, declarative sentences something like these:

1. Recycling soda cans helps the environment.
2. There is less to go into the landfill.
3. Riding a bicycle to the beach helps the environment.
4. It means using less gas.
5. Gas is a petroleum product or fossil fuel.
6. Fossil fuels are nonrenewable resources.

Now, if your thesis statement is, *Conserving natural resources contributes to a healthy environment,* these are all perfectly good sentences for expanding your thesis. They may seem, though, like so many odd pieces of wood in a pile with nothing to hold them together until someone with a hammer and nails builds a table out of them.

What serves as hammer and nails to pull your sentences together for a well-shaped paragraph? One of the most effective ways is to combine sentences so that a reader can see how they are related, as we did in Unit 3. For example, *Because recycling soda cans means less refuse goes into the landfill, putting your used can into the bin helps the environment.* Try this kind of combining with sentences 3 to 6 above.

_____

_____

_____

_____

_____

_____

Throughout history people have imagined perfect societies. What one element would you consider essential to a perfect society? Write a thesis statement followed by a topic sentence that begins a paragraph explaining your choice.

_____

_____

_____

_____

Go carefully through the sentences you have just written to see if any will be clarified by combining them or adding connective words. If so, make the changes.

# UNIT VI

## How to Tell One Look-Alike Word From the Other

**C**omplaints about English spelling have been around for a long time. Some say it's not phonetic. . .and often it isn't. Others say it hasn't kept up with changes in the language. That, too, is frequently the case. The playwright George Bernard Shaw once claimed that the word *fish*, if it followed the logic of English spelling rules, should be spelled *ghoti*: the *gh* as in *cough*, the *o* as in *women*, and the *ti* as in *nation*. He was exaggerating, of course, but his example demonstrates how we can be confused by spelling.

### Webster's Word Book

In the nineteenth century Noah Webster proposed to simplify the language by introducing spellings like *thru* instead of *through*. Some of his reforms caught on; as a result today we write *color* and *honor* instead of *colour* and *honour*. He put all of his reforms in the first American dictionary and now his name has become almost synonymous with the word *dictionary*.

Part of the reason for irregular spelling is that long ago, before the invention of printing, no standardized system existed; scribes, who copied long texts by hand, wrote words as they pronounced them—but very often they pronounced them according to where they lived, which was different from the way they were pronounced by other scribes. Printing was invented in the fifteenth century and, along with it, efforts to spell words in a more regulated way.

**173**

Despite all that the reformers have done, much confusion remains in the way English words are spelled. You'll probably agree that the most common difficulty is with what we call *homophones*, words that sound the same but have different spellings and different meanings. Some of the most familiar of these are *to, two, too; there, their, they're;* and *bear, bare.* Another bit of confusion comes from the irregularity of verb forms, and this also goes back to the early days of the English language, hundreds of years ago.

You will find many of these easy-to-mistake words in Toni Morrison's *The Bluest Eye*, a story that shows what tragic results may come from racism.

# L E S S O N  3 7
# Words That Look Alike

. . . . . . . . .

Many words that are spelled the same way can function as different parts of speech. One that we use often is *look*. As a noun, it might appear in a sentence like *Did you take a look at the new TV show?* Notice that as a noun it usually follows *a, an,* or *the.* But, of course, it is also a verb: *I always look at the new shows.* One way of checking whether a word is being used as a verb is to check whether it can be used with the word *to* to form the infinitive: *to look.*

### Living with the Grown-Ups

¹Our house is old, cold, and green. ²At night a kerosene lamp lights one large room. ³The others are braced in darkness, peopled by roaches and mice. ⁴Adults do not talk to us—they give us directions. ⁵They issue orders without providing information. ⁶When we trip and fall down, they glance at us; if we cut or bruise ourselves, they ask us are we crazy. ⁷When we catch colds, they shake their heads in disgust at our lack of consideration. ⁸How, they ask us, do you expect anybody to get anything done if you all are sick? ⁹We cannot answer them. ¹⁰Our illness is treated with contempt, foul Black Draught, and castor oil that blunts our minds.

—Toni Morrison, *The Bluest Eye*

■ Combine these sentences:

Children are bewildered. Adults do not explain things to them. _____

_____

■ Some words in the excerpt above can be either verbs or nouns. Choose five of them; for those used as verbs write a sentence in which the word is used as a noun and for those used as nouns write a sentence in which the word is used as a verb. The first one below is an example.

| Verb or Noun | Sentence |
|---|---|
| | *Our trip [noun] to the beach* |
| 1. *trip [verb]* | *will be on Saturday.* |
| 2. _____ | _____ |
| 3. _____ | _____ |
| 4. _____ | _____ |

| Verb or Noun | Sentence |
|---|---|
| 5. _____ | _____ |
| 6. _____ | _____ |

■ Write a sentence about a time in your childhood when an adult was not able to explain something you asked about. _____

_____

# LESSON 37a
# Verbs That Can Be Nouns

· · · · · · · · ·

Here's a test you can use to distinguish look-alike words that can be verbs or nouns: a verb can take the infinitive form with *to* as in *to risk*, while a noun can be preceded by an article such as *a risk* or *the risk*.

### Fan-tastic

[1]While the game is hugely important to the players and coaches, there is, at the same time, an absence of urgency in the air. [2]I have covered games in Ann Arbor, Columbus, South Bend, and Tallahassee. [3]I have seen the ugliness born of high hopes dashed. [4]I have smiled at the sight of Alabama fans holding a roll of toilet paper and a box of Tide detergent—Roll Tide, get it? [5]I have seen Florida State fans cheer the sight of Miami mascot Sebastian the Ibis being roughed up by Tallahassee police. [6]I have talked to an Arkansas couple who vacationed in Fayetteville every August in order to watch Razorbacks two-a-days. [7]I have thought, but lacked the courage to suggest to these super-fans: *Get a Life!*

—Austin Murphy, *The Sweet Season*

■ In one sentence explain why the writer wants to tell super-fans to get a life.

_____

■ Choose three nouns in the excerpt above that can be changed to verbs. For each, write a sentence using the word as a verb. For example, the noun *time* becomes a verb in *The coach will time the runner's speed around the track.* Then do the same for three verbs that can be nouns.

1. _____ *air [noun]* _____   |   *We air [verb] the winter clothes when they come out of storage*

2. _____     _____

3. _____     _____

4. _____     _____

5. _____     _____

6. _____     _____

7. _____     _____

■ Think of something silly you have seen a fan do at a sports event. Write a sentence about it. _____

_____

## LESSON 37b
# More Words That Can Be Nouns or Verbs

• • • • • • • • •

Sometimes when nouns turn to verbs or verbs to nouns, the meaning becomes entirely different. *To play*, for example, is to take part in a sport or game, while *a play* is usually a performance on a stage. We may *watch* a race while wearing a *watch* to keep time.

### An African Village

[1]Nicoboozu was a clean little town, the huts wide apart, and the chief was old, hospitable and incurious. [2]He dashed us a chicken and a hamper of rice, saw that the hut we were to sleep in was swept, and then retired to his hammock and shade from the midday sun. [3]Nicoboozu was as favourable an example as one would find of a village touched by the Buzie culture. [4]Here the women wore little silver arrows in their hair and twisted silver bracelets, beaten by the blacksmith out of old Napoleon coins brought from French Guinea, and heavy silver anklets; the men wore rings, primitive signet rings with a flattened side, and decorative beaded rings and rings twisted to match the bracelets. [5]The weavers were busy, and every piece of craftsmanship one saw was light and unself-conscious. [6]There was an air of happiness about the place.

—Graham Greene, *Journey Without Maps*

■ Combine these sentences:

The village displayed Buzie culture. The people wore silver jewelry. _____

_____

▪ Write in column 1 the nouns in the excerpt above that can be verbs and in column 2 the verbs that can be nouns. Remember the test of a noun is that it can be preceded by *a* or *the,* and of a verb that it can be an infinitive with *to.*

| Column 1—Nouns | Column 2—Verbs |
|---|---|
| 1. _____ shade _____ | _____ sleep _____ |
| 2. _____ | _____ |
| 3. _____ | _____ |
| 4. _____ | _____ |
| 5. _____ | _____ |

▪ If you could travel to Africa, what souvenir would you like to bring back? Write your answer in a sentence. _____

_____

# LESSON 38
## Look-Alikes That Have Different Meanings

. . . . . . . . .

Some words that are spelled alike, pronounced alike, and are the same part of speech have different meanings depending on the context in which they occur. For example, if we're talking about a boat ride, we may refer to the *river bank*, while a need for more cash will take us to the *savings bank*. *Head, bed, pen,* and *book* are just a few more words of this type.

### The Breedlove House

[1]The plan of the living quarters was as unimaginative as a first-generation Greek landlord could contrive it to be. [2]The large "store" area was partitioned into two rooms by beaverboard planks that did not reach to the ceiling. [3]There was a living room, which the family called the front room, and the bedroom, where all the living was done. [4]In the front room were two sofas, an upright piano, and a tiny artificial Christmas tree which had been there, decorated and dust-laden, for two years. [5]The bedroom had three beds: a narrow iron bed for Sammy, fourteen years old, another for Pecola, eleven years old, and a double bed for Cholly and Mrs. Breedlove. [6]In the center of the bedroom, for the even distribution of heat, stood a coal stove. [7]Trunks, chairs, a small end table, and a cardboard "wardrobe" closet were placed around the walls. [8]The kitchen was in the back of this apartment, a separate room. [9]There were no bath facilities, only a toilet bowl, inaccessible to the eye, if not the ear, of the tenants.

—Toni Morrison, *The Bluest Eye*

■ Explain, in one sentence, what makes the Breedlove home sound unpleasant.

_____

■ In excerpt above some of the words can be used with a different meaning from the ones they have here. Write them in column 1 below, and write their second meaning in column 2.

| Column 1 | Column 2 |
|----------|----------|
| 1. _____*bed for sleeping*_____ | _____*flower bed*_____ |
| 2. _____ | _____ |
| 3. _____ | _____ |

|                 Column 1                 |                 Column 2                 |
| ---------------------------------------- | ---------------------------------------- |
| 4. _____        | _____          |
| 5. _____        | _____          |
| 6. _____        | _____          |

■ Think of a room that makes you feel happy or sad and write a sentence about why it has that effect. _____

_____

## LESSON 38a
## Look-Alike Words with Two Meanings
• • • • • • • • •

What do you think of when you see the word *plant*? You can't be sure whether it means something growing in a pot or a place where computers are manufactured unless the context—the sentence in which it appears—gives you the answer. For example, *The demand for laptop computers was so great that the plant was operating 24/7.* Or it might be, *For my birthday I received a beautiful cactus plant.*

### The Reading Lesson

[1]The male speaker began to read. [2]He was a young man, respectably dressed, and seated at a table, having a book before him. [3]His handsome features glowed with pleasure, and his eyes kept impatiently wandering from the page to a small white hand over his shoulder, which recalled him by a smart slap on the cheek, whenever its owner detected such signs of inattention. [4]Its owner stood behind; her light shining ringlets blending, at intervals, with his brown locks, as she bent to superintend his studies; and her face—it was lucky he could not see her face, or he would never have been so steady.

—Emily Brontë, *Wuthering Heights*

■ Combine these sentences:

His reading earned the pupil a kiss. He gladly returned it. _____

_____

■ Underline the words in the excerpt above that can have two meanings. Write three of these words in the first column, then write the meaning each word has in the passage and the second meaning it can have, as shown in the example.

| | Word | First Meaning | Second Meaning |
|---|---|---|---|
| 1. | table | a piece of furniture | an arrangement of data |
| 2. | | | |
| 3. | | | |
| 4. | | | |

■ Write a sentence about something that distracts you when you are trying to study. _____

_____

## LESSON 38b
## Words with Multi-Meanings: Figures of Speech

• • • • • • • • •

The words that concern us in this lesson like *table* or *bed* have the same part of speech but can be used to mean different things. Often such words are *figures of speech*. A figure of speech is a word or phrase whose primary meaning is extended to a person or thing that has similar qualities. *That baby is an angel* means that the baby's behavior is exceptionally pleasing. For example, similarly, *neck* is used to name a narrow strip of land, or the place where a river flows into the sea is called its *mouth*.

### The City Game

[1]The Hawk, the Goat, the Destroyer, and the Fly are legends of the asphalt city game, epic players in a pastime that is itself legendary, an offshoot of the indoor sport that Dr. James Naismith invented in 1891. [2]It's a fact that the city game is played when and where it was designed not to be played: outdoors, in the sweltering heat, when the gentler games of summer should rule. [3]But the only thing that rules year-round in the canyons of the inner city is the rock-solid stuff beneath your feet. [4]Just now the tiny, fence-enclosed court at West 4th Street in Greenwich Village is rocking. [5]A tournament is under way, one of the dozens of outdoor hoops programs that run all summer long in New York City.

—Rick Telander, *Asphalt Legends*

■ What is wrong with playing city basketball in the summer? Write your answer in a sentence. _____

_____

■ Underline all of the nouns in the excerpt above that can have more than one meaning. For four of them, write a meaning that is different from the one in *The City Game*.

| Noun | Another Meaning |
|------|-----------------|
| 1. _____game_____ | _animals taken in hunting_ |
| 2. _____ | _____ |
| 3. _____ | _____ |
| 4. _____ | _____ |
| 5. _____ | _____ |

■ Most sports have special places in which they are played: football fields, running tracks, baseball diamonds. Write your own sentence about a time you took part in some sport that was played in an unusual place. _____

_____

For more about words with multiple meanings, see Review Exercise 43.

# LESSON 39
# Words That Sound Alike: Homophones

. . . . . . . . .

Many words sound the same although they are spelled differently and have different meanings. They are called *homophones.* Writers can find it troublesome to determine which spelling to choose in sentences like *The dew was still on the grass,* and *Which bill is due this week?* or even *I don't know what to do during the break.* But a reader can be completely confused by a spelling different from the accepted one. (So can your computer's spell checker, since it doesn't know which meaning you intend.)

### Listening to the Grown-Ups

[1]Their conversation is like a gently wicked dance: sound meets sound, curtsies, shimmies and retires. [2]Another sound enters, but is upstaged by still another: the two circle each other and stop. [3]Sometimes their words move in lofty spirals; other times they take strident leaps, and all of it is punctuated with warm-pulsed laughter—like the throb of a heart made of jelly. [4]The edge, the curl, the thrust of their emotions is always clear to Frieda and me. [5]We do not, cannot, know the meanings of all their words, for we are nine and ten years old. [6]So we watch their faces, their hands, their feet, and listen for truth in timbre. [7]So when Mr. Henry arrived on a Saturday night, we smelled him. [8]He smelled wonderful, like trees and lemon vanishing cream, and Nu Nile Hair Oil and flecks of Sen-Sen.

—Toni Morrison, *The Bluest Eye*

■ What clues do Frieda and her sister use to figure out what adults mean?

Write your answer in a sentence. _____

_____

■ Each homophone in the excerpt above has the same sound as another word but is spelled differently. In column 1, write the homophone as it appears above, and in column 2 write a word that sounds the same but is spelled differently and has a different meaning.

| Column 1 | Column 2 |
|---|---|
| 1. *their* | *there, they're* |
| 2. _____ | _____ |
| 3. _____ | _____ |

**183**

|          Column 1          |          Column 2          |
| :------------------------- | :------------------------- |
| 4.                         |                            |
| 5.                         |                            |
| 6.                         |                            |
| 7.                         |                            |
| 8.                         |                            |
| 9.                         |                            |
| 10.                        |                            |

■ Can you remember a grown-up whose appearance impressed you when you were a child? Write a sentence about that person. _____

_____

 ### LESSON 39a
### More Homophone Sound-Alikes
• • • • • • • • •

Because English has so many homophones, you must be especially careful when using your computer's spell checker. *Son* and *sun* are both correct spellings but a spell checker will not always know which one to use in a sentence: *My mother's son is my brother,* but *The sun rose at six this morning.* The computer will not know which meaning you have in mind.

#### The Lady of the Castle

[1]The *châtelaine* [the lord's wife] of a castle more often than not had to manage alone when her husband was occupied elsewhere, as he generally was, for the sun never set on fighting in the 14th century. [2]If not fighting, or attending the King, he was generally being held somewhere for ransom. [3]In such case the wife had to take his place, reach decisions, and assume direction, and there were many besides Jeanne de Monfort who did so. [4]Marcia Ordelaffi, left to defend Cesena while her hot-tempered husband (he who had stabbed his son) held a second city against the papal forces, refused all offers to negotiate despite repeated assaults, mining of walls, bombardment day and night by stones cast from siege engines, and the pleas of her father to surrender.

—Barbara Tuchman, *A Distant Mirror: The Calamitous 14th Century*

■ Combine these sentences:

The husband was often at war. The lady took charge of the castle. _____

_____

■ List five homophones from the excerpt above in column 1. In column 2, write a sentence using its sound-alike with another meaning.

| Column 1 | Column 2 |
|---|---|
| 1. _____ *not* _____ | _____ *The knot was untied.* _____ |
| 2. _____ | _____ |
| 3. _____ | _____ |
| 4. _____ | _____ |
| 5. _____ | _____ |
| 6. _____ | _____ |

■ Think of a time when someone you know had to take over in an emergency, perhaps when a family member was sick or injured. Write a sentence about what happened. _____

_____

## LESSON 39b
## Still More Homophones

. . . . . . . . .

As we have seen, words that sound alike even though they are spelled differently and have different meanings are called *homophones.* Keeping them straight can be confusing. *Will you have two quizzes to study for, too?*

### A Mysterious Noise

[1]And then, because of the strange anxiety at her heart, she stole upstairs to her son's room. [2]Noiselessly she went along the upper corridor. [3]Was there a faint noise? [4]What was it? [5]She stood, with arrested muscles, outside his door, listening. [6]There was a strange, heavy, and yet not loud noise. [7]Her heart stood still. [8]It was a soundless noise, yet rushing and powerful. [9]What in God's name was it? [10]She ought to know. [11]She felt that she knew the

noise. ¹²She knew what it was. ¹³Then suddenly she switched on the light and saw her son, in his green pyjamas, madly surging on the rocking-horse. ¹⁴The blaze of light suddenly lit him up, as he urged the wooden horse, and lit her up, as she stood, in her dress of pale green and crystal, in the doorway.

—D. H. Lawrence, *The Rocking-Horse Winner*

■ Write a sentence explaining what has frightened the woman. _____

_____

■ Underline the homophones in the excerpt above. For three of them, give definitions, first of the word in the excerpt, then of its homophone.

|  | **Homophone 1** | **Homophone 2** |
|---|---|---|
| 1. | *heart: an organ of the body* | *hart: male of the red deer* |
| 2. | | |
| 3. | | |
| 4. | | |

■ Why is a strange sound in a dark house so frightening? Write a sentence explaining your answer. _____

_____

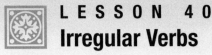

# LESSON 40
## Irregular Verbs

. . . . . . . . .

You remember that all verbs have four principal parts: (1) present tense (the same form as the infinitive), (2) past tense, (3) present participle, and (4) past participle. The verbs we call *regular* look like this:

| | | | |
|---|---|---|---|
| *walk* | *walked* | *walking* | *walked* |

You may say, "That's fine, but what about a verb like *teach, taught, teaching, taught?*" The answer is that *teach* is one of many *irregular* verbs. These too go back to the early days of the English language and we recognize most of them by the vowel change in the past tense and past participle. Let's look at some that we find most frequently. These verbs have a vowel change in the past tense *and* the past participle:

| | | | |
|---|---|---|---|
| *drink* | *drank* | *drinking* | *drunk* |
| *ring* | *rang* | *ringing* | *rung* |
| *sing* | *sang* | *singing* | *sang* |
| *sink* | *sunk* | *sinking* | *sank* |
| *swim* | *swam* | *swimming* | *swum* |

These verbs have a past participle ending in *-en*:

| | | | |
|---|---|---|---|
| *break* | *broke* | *breaking* | *broken* |
| *eat* | *ate* | *eating* | *eaten* |
| *give* | *gave* | *giving* | *given* |
| *know* | *knew* | *knowing* | *known* |
| *see* | *saw* | *seeing* | *seen* |
| *speak* | *spoke* | *speaking* | *spoken* |
| *take* | *took* | *taking* | *taken* |
| *throw* | *threw* | *throwing* | *thrown* |

These verbs do not change in the past tense:

| | | | |
|---|---|---|---|
| *cost* | *cost* | *costing* | *cost* |
| *let* | *let* | *letting* | *let* |
| *put* | *put* | *putting* | *put* |

These verbs have the same past tense and past participle:

| | | | |
|---|---|---|---|
| *bring* | *brought* | *bringing* | *brought* |
| *catch* | *caught* | *catching* | *caught* |
| *teach* | *taught* | *teaching* | *taught* |

These verbs do not fit in any of the above categories:

| | | | |
|---|---|---|---|
| *begin* | *began* | *beginning* | *begun* |
| *go* | *went* | *going* | *gone* |

These verbs (*to be* and *to have*) are extremely irregular:

| | | | |
|---|---|---|---|
| *I am* | *I was* | *I was being* | *I have been* |
| *you are* | *you were* | | |
| *she is* | *he was* | | |
| *they are* | *they were* | | |
| *I have* | *I had* | *I was having* | *I have had* |
| *you have* | | | |
| *he has* | | | |

### Outdoors

[1]Outdoors, we knew, was the real terror of life. [2]The threat of being outdoors surfaced frequently in those days. [3]If somebody ate too much, he could end up outdoors. [4]If somebody used too much coal, he could end up outdoors. [5]People could gamble themselves outdoors, drink themselves outdoors. [6]Sometimes mothers put their sons outdoors, and when that happened, regardless of what the son had done, all sympathy was with him. [7]He was outdoors, and his own flesh had done it. [8]To be put outdoors by a landlord was one thing—unfortunate, but an aspect of life over which you had no control, since you could not control your income. [9]But to be slack enough to put oneself outdoors, or heartless enough to put one's own kin outdoors—that was criminal. [10]There is a difference between being put *out* and put out*doors*. [11]If you are put out, you go somewhere else; if you are outdoors, there is no place to go.

—Toni Morrison, *The Bluest Eye*

■ Explain the difference between *out* and *outdoors* in a sentence. _____

_____

■ Find the irregular verbs in the excerpt above. Write them in the columns shown for each of their principal parts.

| | Present Tense | Past Tense | Present Participle | Past Participle |
|---|---|---|---|---|
| 1. | *know* | *knew* | *knowing* | *known* |
| 2. | _____ | _____ | _____ | _____ |
| 3. | _____ | _____ | _____ | _____ |

| Present<br>Tense | Past<br>Tense | Present<br>Participle | Past<br>Participle |
|---|---|---|---|
| 4. _____ | _____ | _____ | _____ |
| 5. _____ | _____ | _____ | _____ |

■ Toni Morrison explains that to be outdoors is to be in disgrace. Write a sentence about what might be considered being in disgrace among your friends.

_____

 ## LESSON 40a
## More Irregular Verbs

· · · · · · · · ·

Some verbs have completely different forms in the past tense, irregularities that go far back in the history of the language. Think about *go/went buy/bought,* and *take/took.* Because there are no easy rules, we have to memorize all the forms of such verbs.

### Beginning of an Affair

[1]The chapel bell started to ring and Barbara leapt eagerly out of bed. [2]But as she poured the enamel can of hot water into her basin, she began to wonder how she was going to get through the six long hours before it would be half past two. [3]It was a wonder that she managed to do any work at all these days, for even writing essays for Francis had lost some of its attraction. [4]He didn't seem to listen very attentively now and even stopped her sometimes before she had finished reading, and began talking about things that had really nothing to do with tutorials. [5]Barbara believed that Francis liked talking to her, and that she was able to bring into his life something which had been lacking in it before—sympathy, understanding, perhaps even love.

—Barbara Pym, *Crampton Hodnet*

■ Combine these sentences:

Barbara is young. Barbara has little knowledge of love. She thinks she loves

Francis. _____

_____

■ Underline the irregular verbs in the excerpt above, then use one of their principal parts to complete each of the sentences below.

1. The runner was ____*leaping*____ over the hurdles.

2. The class had just _____ the exam.

3. Marsha and Roy _____ to the movies last night.

4. Have you _____ your homework yet?

5. Manya will _____ a party next weekend.

■ Did you ever have a crush on a teacher or some other older person? Write a sentence describing that person. _____

_____

## LESSON 40b
## Irregular Endings

· · · · · · · · ·

The past tense of some verbs, like *sleep* and *leap*, is spelled with *-t* rather than *-ed, slept, leapt*; this is a result of the way we pronounce them. Other verbs, like *find/found* and *seek/sought,* change their vowels in the past tense.

### The New Woman

[1]As an influence on fashion, on manners, on the complex art of civilized living, the vanished lady had been superseded. [2]Her successor, for the American public, was the movie star. [3]The lady's daughter, or granddaughter, was usually being taught some means of earning her livelihood. [4]She was to be found, in increasing numbers, making a career for herself; in the offices of women's magazines, in Hollywood and the theater, among entertainers in nightclubs, among professional models, in fashionable shops; occasionally in the practice of law or medicine, or teaching in a college. [5]Whatever she was doing, it seemed clear that she was seeking that free development irrespective of its bearing on the other sex which announced her final emancipation and declared her refusal to be—as the lady often had been—a ready-made garment, designed to fit the average man.

—Lloyd Morris, *Postscript to Yesterday: American Life and Thought 1896–1946*

■ In a sentence explain what the writer means when he says the lady was "designed to fit the average man." _____

_____

■ Find the irregular verbs in the excerpt above and decide whether the form is past or present. If it is present, write a sentence using the past tense form; if it is past, write a present tense sentence.

| **Verb** | **Sentence** |
|---|---|
| 1. _____ *taught* _____ | _*Mr. Simpson teaches Biology.*_ |
| 2. _____ | _____ |
| 3. _____ | _____ |
| 4. _____ | _____ |
| 5. _____ | _____ |

■ What woman or women have a great influence on American life today: rock stars, politicians, sports figures? Write a sentence explaining your choice. _____

_____

. . . . . . . . . .

To indicate more than one, most nouns add an -*s* or -*es*. A few, however, are irregular, keeping the forms they had in early forms of English. In some the vowel changes in the plural, giving us *mouse/mice*. Others, like *ox/oxen* have plurals in -*en*, and some have no plural marker at all: *one sheep* and *twenty sheep*.

### Women's Life

[1]Everybody in the world was in a position to give them orders. [2]White women said, "Do this." [3]White children said, "Give me that." [4]White men said, "Come here." [5]Black men said, "Lay down." [6]The only people they need not take orders from were black children and each other. [7]But they took all of that and re-created it in their own image. [8]They ran the houses of white people and knew it. [9]When white men beat their men, they cleaned up the blood and went home to receive abuse from the victim. [10]They beat their children with one hand and stole for them with the other.

—Toni Morrison, *The Bluest Eye*

■ Does the author give these details about black women to show how difficult the women's lives were or does she have another reason? Write your answer in a sentence. _____

_____

■ The excerpt above has a number of plural nouns, most of them regular. Find the irregular plural nouns and indicate what type of change it is: in spelling or in form of the word ending.

| Noun | Change |
|------|--------|
| 1. *women* | *spelling* |
| 2. _____ | _____ |
| 3. _____ | _____ |

■ People in some jobs are never recognized for the hard work they do. Write a sentence about someone who does a job without getting the credit he or she deserves. _____

_____

## LESSON 41a
## More Irregular Plurals

As we have seen, some plurals end in -*n* rather than -*s* or -*es*. These include *child/children* and *ox/oxen*. In others we find a vowel change between the singular and the plural: *foot/feet, goose/geese, louse/lice, mouse/mice, tooth/teeth*. Another group of words remains the same in singular and plural: *cattle, deer, fish, sheep*. Some nouns that retain the -*s* ending in the plural change the final consonant of the root, as in *knife/knives, life/lives, wife/wives,* and *wolf/wolves.*

**Country Women**

[1]But there is an eternal quality in the life of farmers' wives which allows one to make a reliable guess at the way they lived in Horstede; even now, there are wives in the remotest parts of Britain, for example the highlands and islands of Scotland, who do all the things the women of Horstede must have done, and do them in much the same way. [2]They carded, spun and dyed and wove the wool and made the clothes, boiled the meat and baked the bread, milked the sheep and goats, perhaps the cow, and made the butter and cheese, loved and scolded the children, fed the hens, worked in the fields at harvest, probably made the pots and brewed the beer, and made love or quarrelled with their husbands, or possibly both. [3]And the children, not burdened by school, herded animals, geese or sheep or goats or pigs according to their size.

—David Howarth, *1066: The Year of the Conquest*

■ Combine these sentences:

Farm wives have always worked hard. Today some do chores the same way they

did centuries ago. _____

_____

■ For each of the nouns with irregular plurals in the excerpt above, write both the singular and plural forms, as shown in the example.

|  | **Singular** | **Plural** |
|---|---|---|
| 1. | *wife* | *wives* |
| 2. |  |  |

|   Singular   |   Plural   |
|---|---|

3. _____   _____

4. _____   _____

■ Have you heard from a grandparent or older neighbor about the way things used to be? Write your own sentence about what you learned. _____

_____

## LESSON 41b
## Plurals That Change Spelling

· · · · · · · · ·

In addition to those plurals that are formed by changing a vowel, like *women* or *feet,* and those without a plural ending, like *fish* or *sheep,* there are some that change spelling in the plural. *Party, parties,* and *knife, knives* are examples of these words.

### A Strange Dream

¹So I drifted, deep in the autumn forest, unheeded as a wraith of the forest mist. ²Straining back now in memory, I see it still. ³Deep aisles of beech, thick with mast, where the wild boar rooted, and the badger dug for food, and the stags clashed and wrestled, roaring, with never a glance at me. ⁴Wolves, too; the way through those high woods is known as the Wolf Road, but though I would have been easy meat, they had had a good summer, and let me be. ⁵Then, with the first real chill of winter, came the hoar glitter of icy mornings, with the reeds standing stiff and black out of curded ice, and the forest deserted, badger in lair and deer down in the valley-bottom, and the wild geese gone and the skies empty. ⁶Then suddenly, one grey dawn, the sound of horses galloping, filling the forest, and the clash of swords and the whirl of bright axes, the yelling and the screams of wounded beasts and men. ⁷Silence then, and the scent of apple trees, and the nightmare sense of grief that comes when a man wakes again to feel a loss he has forgotten in sleep.

—Mary Stewart, *The Last Enchantment*

■ Combine these sentences:

The wolves were not hungry. They had eaten a lot during the summer. They did

not attack. _____

_____

■ In the excerpt above, underline the plural nouns that have irregular spellings, then choose an appropriate singular form to complete each of the sentences below, as shown in the example.

1. The _____*wolf*_____ is often a menace in fairy tales.

2. Bambi is a baby _____ .

3. Some people prefer a _____ for a holiday dinner.

4. The captain was the last _____ to leave the ship.

5. The rain fell from the dark _____ .

■ Think about an unusual dream you have had and write a sentence about it.

_____

## YOUR WRITING
*Putting it Together*

So far you've been writing paragraphs with a strong topic sentence and sentences that stick to the point by keeping their content *only* about what has been asserted in the thesis. Of course, you will be expected to write more than a paragraph for your other classes—and for the kinds of writing you will be doing in your future career. Here are three important things to remember when you write more than one paragraph:

• Be sure to follow the pattern of thesis-plus-topic-sentences-about-the-thesis in every paragraph you write.
• Be sure to use some connecting word or phrase to link one paragraph to the one that goes before.
• Be sure to write a sentence at the end that makes clear that you have made your point. This sentence will *not* repeat the words of your thesis statement but will echo its ideas.

Think of an occupation that requires many different activities. Write three paragraphs explaining why such a job involves many diverse abilities.

¶ _____

_____

_____

_____

_____

¶ _____

_____

_____

_____

_____

¶ _____

_____

_____

_____

_____

# UNIT VII

# Nuts and Bolts

. . . . . . . . . . .

**P**icky, picky, picky. Why does that teacher have to be so fussy about where I put a comma, you may well ask. The best way to answer that is with another question: what does this sentence mean? *Night was falling so suddenly I ran to the boat.* You might reply that I ran to the boat because night was falling so suddenly. Or you might say I ran suddenly to the boat because night was falling. As the sentence stands, both are right. But did the writer have both meanings in mind? This is the kind of ambiguous sentence that is clear when spoken because of where emphasis falls, and the pause occurs. It is not so obvious in writing, however, unless we use a comma to indicate that the pause comes either after *falling* or after *suddenly.*

## Before the Comma

Several hundred years ago, before printing had been invented, when all writing had to be done by hand, there was very little punctuation or capitalization. In fact, even spelling was pretty much left up to the scribe who copied the manuscript; that last word comes from Latin and means simply *written by hand.*

The real reason, then, that teachers are fussy about punctuation is because we need it for meaning. We need it to show where a sentence ends. We need it to show that we are asking a question. Similar reasons explain our need to capitalize some words, to use the accepted spelling, and to follow conventions for abbreviations. These are the *mechanics* of a paper, what we check in our final draft before printing it out to turn in.

Many of our problems with mechanics are made easier by word processing programs that include spelling or grammar checks. Here's a word of warning about these helpers, though. Remember that the spell-check dictionary contains only those words that have been programmed into it. If your composition contains technical words from your subject, or unfamiliar names, the program may mark them incorrect, so it's up to you to do the checking on them. Something else to watch out for is misspellings that would be correct in another context: *ewe no watt eye mien.* Clearly these are not the spellings you intended for *you know what I mean,* but because they are correct spellings of other words, they will not be picked up by your spell checker. The same is true of grammar checks, which can use only the most general rules, rules like ideal sentence length that cannot be applied to all situations. As we've seen, sentences can be two words long or even fifty or more.

There are a few things about sentences that we need to remember before we talk about punctuation:

- A *declarative* sentence is a simple statement—although it can have more than one clause—that usually follows subject-verb-object as word order.
- An *interrogative* sentence is a question. Very often its word order is reversed to object-(*who* or *what*)-verb-subject.
- An *exclamatory* sentence expresses surprise or some other emotion.
- An *imperative* sentence gives a command.

Many examples in this unit are from *All Quiet on the Western Front,* Erich Maria Remarque's novel about World War I and its effect on young lives.

## LESSON 42
# The Period

· · · · · · · · · ·

Most often we signal the end of a sentence by a period, but it is not the only way to signify that we have come to the end; we might use a question mark, —*What time is dinner?* or an exclamation point —*Her answer shocked me!* For now, let's see how a group of short sentences, ending with a period, can be used to show a mood of urgency. For example: *The sky is dark. The woods are silent. My flashlight is lost. I am frightened.*

### Battlefield Gourmet

[1]The sucking pigs are slaughtered. [2]Kat sees to them. [3]We want to make potato-cakes to go with the roast. [4]But we cannot find a grater for the potatoes. [5]However that difficulty is soon got over. [6]With a nail we punch a lot of holes in a pot lid. [7]There we have a grater. [8]Three fellows put on thick gloves to protect their fingers against the grater. [9]Kat takes charge of the sucking pigs, the carrots, the peas, and the cauliflower. [10]I fry the pancakes. [11]The sucking pigs are roasted whole. [12]We all stand round them as before an altar.

—Erich Maria Remarque, *All Quiet on the Western Front*

■ How do you know this dinner is not being prepared in a conventional

kitchen? Write your answer in a sentence. _____

_____

■ For each of the sentences in the excerpt above, list below the simple subject and the simple verb.

| Subject | Verb |
|---------|------|
| 1. *pigs* | *are slaughtered* |
| 2. | |
| 3. | |
| 4. | |
| 5. | |
| 6. | |
| 7. | |
| 8. | |

Copyright © 2004 by Pearson Education, Inc.

|                    Subject                    |                     Verb                      |
| --------------------------------------------- | --------------------------------------------- |
| 9. _____      | _____         |
| 10. _____      | _____         |
| 11. _____      | _____         |
| 12. _____      | _____         |

- Write a sentence about cooking outdoors, perhaps over a campfire or on a barbecue grill. _____

For more about periods, see Review Exercise 11.

## LESSON 42a
## More Periods

· · · · · · · ·

Many sentences contain more than one clause and will eventually end with a period. *While Ben held the door, Jerry carried out the chair.* Read the paragraph below, identifying the clauses and noting that the sentences end with periods.

### The Crowd's Will

[1]But at that moment I glanced round at the crowd that had followed me. [2]It was an immense crowd, two thousand at the least and growing every minute. [3]It blocked the road for a long distance on either side. [4]I looked at the sea of faces above the garish clothes—faces all happy and excited over this bit of fun, all certain that the elephant was going to be shot. [5]They were watching me as they would watch a conjurer about to perform a trick. [6]They did not like me, but with the magical rifle in my hands I was momentarily worth watching. [7]And suddenly I realized that I should have to shoot the elephant after all.

—George Orwell, *Shooting an Elephant*

- Why does the narrator think he must shoot the elephant? _____

■ Underline the subject(s), verb(s), and conjunctions, if there are any, in each of the sentences in the excerpt above. For each sentence with more than one clause, write a sentence of your own in the same pattern. The example shown is based on sentence 1.

|  | **Your Sentence** | **Excerpt Sentence #** |
|---|---|---|
| 1. | *I glanced at the clock that had struck seven.* | _____ |
| 2. | _____ | _____ |
| 3. | _____ | _____ |
| 4. | _____ | _____ |
| 5. | _____ | _____ |

■ Think of a time you did something because the people around you wanted you to do it. Write a sentence about that time. _____

_____

# LESSON 42b
# Another Use for the Period—Abbreviations

Periods are used at the end of abbreviations of titles such as *Mrs.* *Hayes* or *Dr. Burton*, and after initials like *J. D. Salinger*. They are also used at the end of common abbreviations such as *a.m.* and *p.m.* and of days of the week, *Fri.*, and months of the year, *Dec.*

### TV Medicine

[1]There has always been a place for medicine on television. [2]There was NBC's *Medic* in the 1950s, starring Richard Boone; *Dr. Kildare* and *Ben Casey* in the 1960s; *Marcus Welby, M.D.* and *Medical Center* in the 1970s; and *St. Elsewhere* and *Trapper John, M.D.* in the 1980s. [3]*General Hospital* has been one of daytime's most consistent hits for decades. [4]*Marcus Welby, M.D.* was the father of *ER*—claiming the Number 1 slot for doctors 25 years earlier, during the 1970–71 season. [5]If television has always been drawn to the medical profession, it's because medical dramas take place in a controlled setting that's easy to film. [6]*ER*, which hit the hospital floor running on

Thursdays at 10:00 P.M. on NBC, was Welby plus a gaggle of other medicos passed on to the next generation, as doctor shows continued to deal with controversial topics in an uncontroversial manner.

—Steven D. Stark, *Glued to the Set*

■ Why are there so many medical dramas on television? Write your answer in a sentence. _____

_____

■ Find the abbreviations in the excerpt above that match the reasons shown in the first column.

| Reason for Period | Abbreviation |
|---|---|
| 1. _____ Professional title _____ | _____ *Dr.* _____ |
| 2. _____ Academic degree _____ | _____ |
| 3. _____ Religious title _____ | _____ |
| 4. _____ Time of day _____ | _____ |

■ Have you ever met a doctor as dedicated as some of those we see on television? Write a sentence about that person. _____

_____

The question mark, like the period, signals the end of a sentence. We are most likely to see it in dialogue—conversation among characters—enclosed in quotation marks. Notice that the word order of an interrogative sentence is different than that of a statement. *How are you?* is a simple example of the subject *following* the verb in a question. Others may include the verb *do* in framing the question: *Do freshmen go to the class party?* Questions begin with helpers like *do* or modal auxiliaries (see Unit 2) like *can, must,* and *will* rather than either subject or verb. *Must you keep practicing the drum?*

### On Leave

[1]After I have been startled a couple of times in the street by the screaming of the tramcars, which resembles the shriek of a shell coming straight for one, somebody taps me on the shoulder. [2]It is my German-master, and he fastens on me with the usual question: [3]"Well, how are things out there? [4]Yes, it is dreadful, but we must carry on. [5]And after all, you do at least get decent food out there, so I hear. [6]Naturally it's worse here. [7]The best for our soldiers every time. [8]That goes without saying." [9]He drags me along to a table with a lot of others. [10]They welcome me, a head-master shakes hands with me and says: [11]"So you come from the front? [12]What is the spirit like out there?" [13]I explain that no one would be sorry to be back home.

—Erich Maria Remarque, *All Quiet on the Western Front*

- Combine these sentences:

People do not know the devastation of war. They greet the soldier as if he has

been on a pleasure trip. _____

_____

- Find the sentences in the excerpt above that end with a question mark. If their word order is different than it would be in a sentence ending with a period, rewrite it as a declarative sentence.

1. _____*How are things out there?*_____   _____*Things out there are fine.*_____

2. _____   _____

- Write five questions someone might ask you about your college experiences.

1. _____

2. _____

3. _____

4. _____

5. _____

- Do you ever find questions annoying? Write a sentence explaining what bothers you about them. _____

_____

## LESSON 43a
## Rhetorical Questions

While most questions are asked in an attempt to get information, some are meant only to dramatize a writer's point, without any expectation of receiving an answer. These are called *rhetorical questions. The pitcher caught the ball. Can you believe it?*

### Saving Time

[1]The three places Gags spends most of his life—home, office, practice field—form an isosceles triangle no point of which is more than a six-minute walk from the other two. [2]He is not being lazy; he is being time-efficient. [3]You say a six-minute walk, but what about the round trip? [4]That's twelve minutes. [5]Do that five times and you've burned an hour. [6]Who has an hour to burn? [7]What if a man wants to sneak home. . .to do some thinking on his favorite throne? [8]Must that become a twenty-five-minute investment of time? [9]What if John painstakingly makes Jell-O, following the instructions, pouring the mix into the mold, and then puts it in the freezer to harden? [10]This happened a couple weeks ago. [11]Upon learning that the Jell-O goes in the fridge, not the freezer, it was nice for him to be able to speed home and salvage dessert.

—Austin Murphy, *The Sweet Season*

■ Combine these sentences:

John likes to be close to home and work. He doesn't like to waste time. _____

_____

■ Underline the rhetorical questions in the excerpt above. Rewrite them as statements.

1. *A round trip would take twelve minutes.* _____

2. _____ _____

3. _____ _____

4. _____ _____

5. _____ _____

■ Write a sentence about someone you know who is devoted to his or her

job. _____

_____

## LESSON 43b
## Questions as Requests

Sometimes a question is asked not to elicit information but to suggest a course of action. For example, we might say, *Would you like to take a walk?* when we mean, *Let's take a walk.*

### A Proposal

[1]Mr. Latimer looked round the room, as if expecting to receive inspiration from the objects in it. [2]Oh, Canon Tottle, he thought, gazing at a faded sepia photograph, how would you do what I have to do this evening? [3]How would you lead up to it? [4]What words would you use? [5]Looking at the heavy, serious face with its determined expression, Mr. Latimer decided that with Canon Tottle there would be no leading up to it. [6]He would plunge straight in and say what he had to say quickly and definitely. [7]That was obviously the right thing to do if one had the courage. [8]He looked round the room again. [9]The sherry and glasses were still on one of the little tables.

[10]"Oh, Miss Morrow—Janie," he burst out suddenly.

[11]"My name isn't Janie. It's Jessie, if you want to know, or Jessica, really."

[12]"Oh, Jessica," continued Mr. Latimer, feeling a little flat by now, "couldn't we escape out of all this together?"

—Barbara Pym, *Crampton Hodnet*

■ Explain in a sentence why Mr. Latimer is nervous. _____
_____

■ There are several questions in the excerpt above. Write them below and note whether they are rhetorical questions, requests, or questions that seek information.

| Question | Purpose |
|---|---|
| 1. *How would you do what I have to do this evening?* | *Rhetorical* |
| 2. _____ | _____ |
| 3. _____ | _____ |
| 4. _____ | _____ |

■ Did you ever have to prepare for a difficult meeting with someone? Write a sentence about how you felt before it took place. _____
_____

For more about punctuation, see Review Exercises 29, 40, 43, 44.

## LESSON 44
# The Exclamation Point

. . . . . . . . . .

The exclamation point is used to emphasize an important or surprising statement—*What a lovely gift!*—or an interjection—*Holy smoke!* But this mark of punctuation should be used with care; it will lessen the effect the writer wishes to make if it is used too often.

### The Bombardment

¹That moment it breaks out behind us, swells, roars, and thunders. ²We duck down—a cloud of flame shoots up a hundred yards ahead of us. ³The next minute under a second explosion part of the wood rises slowly in the air, three or four trees sail up and then crash to pieces. ⁴The shells begin to hiss like safety valves—heavy fire. ⁵"Take cover!" yells somebody. ⁶When we run out again, although I am very excited, I suddenly think: "Where's Himmelstoss?" ⁷Quickly I jump back into the dug-out and find him with a small scratch lying in a corner pretending to be wounded. ⁸It makes me mad that the young recruits should be out there and he here. ⁹"Get out!" I spit.

—Erich Maria Remarque, *All Quiet on the Western Front*

■ Combine these sentences:

The shelling begins. The soldiers run for cover. _____

_____

■ In the above excerpt, there are two sentences ending with exclamation points; both are commands, a construction frequently used with this punctuation mark. For each of these sentences explain why it is appropriate to use an exclamation point for emphasis.

1. _____

_____

_____

2. _____

_____

_____

■ Write a sentence about an exciting event you were part of. _____

_____

## LESSON 44a
## Exclamations Again

Because exclamations and interjections are used to show excitement and emotion, we ordinarily use only one or two at a time. To use more would have the same effect that a room full of loud talk and laughter would have on your ability to hold a conversation.

### The Christmas Bicycle

[1]That December, with Christmas approaching, she was out at work and Doris was in the kitchen when I barged into her bedroom one afternoon in search of a safety pin. [2]Standing against the wall was a big, black bicycle with balloon tires. [3]I resolved that between now and Christmas I must do nothing, absolutely nothing, to reveal the slightest hint of my terrible knowledge. [4]Nothing must deny her the happiness of seeing me stunned with amazement on Christmas day. [5]In the privacy of my bedroom I began composing and testing exclamations of delight: "Wow!" "A bike with balloon tires!" "I don't believe it!" "I'm the luckiest boy alive!" and so on. [6]They all owed a lot to movies in which boys like Mickey Rooney had seen their wildest dreams come true, and I realized that, with my lack of acting talent, all of them were going to sound false at the critical moment when I wanted to cry out my love spontaneously from the heart.

—Russell Baker, *Growing Up*

■ Combine these sentences:

He accidentally saw the bike. He didn't want to disappoint his mother. _____

_____

■ Although there are four exclamations of delight in the excerpt above, each is enclosed in separate quotation marks. Why didn't the writer put them all together? _____

_____

■ For each of the exclamations listed below, write an expression that conveys the same kind of reaction. For example, instead of *"Wow!"*, you might say, *"Fantastic!"* or *"Cool!"*

1. A bike with balloon tires! _____

2. I don't believe it! _____

3. I'm the luckiest boy alive! _____

■ What's the most exciting gift you ever received for your birthday or some

other special occasion? Write a sentence about how you reacted to seeing it.

_____

# LESSON 44b
# Exclamatory Words and Phrases

. . . . . . . .

Exclamations are often words or phrases rather than sentences, *"Heat!"*, *"What a day!"*, and they are always followed with an exclamation point to indicate that they express strong emotion. We find these most often in dialogue, the written representation of someone's speech. For example, *"Hooray!" said Lorena when she heard that class was canceled.*

### A Day at the Races

[1]He determined to take his nephew with him to the Lincoln races.
[2]"Now, son," he said, "I'm putting twenty on Mirza, and I'll put five for you on any horse you fancy. [3]What's your pick?"
[4]"Daffodil, uncle."
[5]"No, not the fiver on Daffodil!"
[6]"I should if it was my own fiver," said the child.
[7]"Good! Good! Right you are! [8]A fiver for me and a fiver for you on Daffodil."
[8]The child had never been to a race-meeting before, and his eyes were blue fire. [9]He pursed his mouth tight, and watched. [10]A Frenchman just in front had put his money on Lancelot. [11]Wild with excitement, he flayed his arms up and down, yelling *"Lancelot! Lancelot!"* in his French accent.

—D. H. Lawrence, *The Rocking-Horse Winner*

■ In a sentence explain why there is so much excitement at a racetrack. ____

_____

■ For each of the words or phrases with an exclamation point in the excerpt above, rewrite the idea expressed as a complete sentence, as shown in the example.

<table>
<tr><th>Word or Phrase</th><th>Sentence</th></tr>
<tr><td>1. No, not the fiver on Daffodil!</td><td>No, you shouldn't put the fiver on Daffodil.</td></tr>
<tr><td>2. _____</td><td>_____</td></tr>
<tr><td>3. _____</td><td>_____</td></tr>
<tr><td>4. _____</td><td>_____</td></tr>
</table>

■ When you were a child, were you taken to an exciting sporting event? Write a sentence describing your impression of what was happening. _____

_____

. . . . . . . . .

As we all know, every sentence begins with a capital letter. But there was a time, in the eighteenth century, when almost every noun was capitalized. If you look at a historical document such as the Declaration of Independence, notice how many words are capitalized that would not be today. Still, there do remain many places where we begin words with capital letters—for example, names of people, *Lucy*; of places, *Main Street, San Jose*; of teams, *Mets, Yankees*; of buildings, *Baker Hall*; of academic courses, English 101. These are all called *proper nouns*. Words like *people, place, team, building, course*, which do not refer to a particular person or place, are *common nouns*.

### Desperate Times

[1]Our lines are falling back. [2]There are too many fresh English and American regiments over there. [3]We have given up hope that some day an end may come. [4]We never think so far. [5]A man can stop a bullet and be killed; he can get wounded, and then the hospital is his next stop. [6]There, if they do not amputate him, he sooner or later falls into the hand of one of those staff surgeons who, with the War Service Cross in his button-hole, says to him: "What, one leg a bit short? [7]If you have any pluck you don't need to run at the front." [8]Kat tells a story that has travelled the whole length of the front from the Vosges to Flanders of the staff surgeon who, when a man comes before him, without looking up, says "A1. [9]We need soldiers up there."

—Erich Maria Remarque, *All Quiet on the Western Front*

■ Combine these sentences:

The soldiers are bitter. The surgeons have no compassion. _____

_____

■ Below is a list of reasons for capitalizing proper nouns and adjectives. Match each with the proper noun or adjective in the excerpt above that fits the definition.

| Reason | Proper Noun or Adjective |
|---|---|
| 1. Name of a country or nationality | *English* |
| 2. Name of a medal for military service | |

|        Reason         | Proper Noun or Adjective |
| --------------------- | ------------------------ |
| 3. ___ Name of a person ___ | _____ |
| 4. ___ Name of a place ___  | _____ |

■ Write a sentence about an interesting place you visited with a friend—maybe a restaurant, a museum, or an athletic stadium. _____

_____

## LESSON 45a
## Other Uses of Capital Letters

· · · · · · · · · ·

In addition to days of the week and months of the year, names of historical events (*Civil War, American Revolution*) are usually capitalized. So are pronouns as well as nouns referring to deities (*God, Buddha*). We also capitalize titles before names: *Professor Smith, President Lincoln, Senator Roberts.*

### A Milestone in Journalism

[1]Near the end of the First World War, Captain Joseph Medill Patterson of the famous Rainbow Division paid a visit to London. [2]There he talked with Lord Northcliffe, whose tabloid *Daily Mirror* had won a circulation of some eight hundred thousand copies. [3]Would not Americans, likewise, take to the tabloid press? [4]Late in June, 1919, Patterson brought out the first issue of the *Daily News*—"New York's Picture Newspaper." [5]The American tabloid press was born. [6]Eleven years later, the paper was installed in a ten-million-dollar tower; one of the notable masterpieces of modern business architecture. [7]By 1946, when Patterson died, it had the largest circulation of any newspaper in the world.

—Lloyd Morris, *Postscript to Yesterday: American Life and Thought 1896–1946*

■ What made the *Daily News* appealing to a mass audience? Write your answer in a sentence. _____

_____

▪ List below all the capitalized words—except for first words in sentences—in the excerpt above. In the second column, write the reason for the capitalization, as shown in the example.

| Capitalized Words | Reasons |
|---|---|
| 1. *First World War* | *historic event* |
| 2. | |
| 3. | |
| 4. | |
| 5. | |
| 6. | |
| 7. | |
| 8. | |
| 9. | |
| 10. | |
| 11. | |

▪ How do you get the news—from a newspaper, radio, television, or the Internet? Write a sentence explaining your preference. _____

_____

## LESSON 45b
## Capital Letters for Countries and People

• • • • • • • •

We capitalize the names of groups of people whether or not they are part of national groups: *Native Americans, Scandinavians, New Englanders.* The names of religions, such as *Judaism,* and of organizations like *Amnesty International* are also capitalized as are adjectives formed from such names: *English, Islamic, Republican.*

### The Pursuit of Independence

[1]In the early ages of Christianity, Germany was occupied by seven distinct nations, who had no common chief. [2]The Franks, one of the number, having conquered the Gauls, established the kingdom which has taken its name from them. [3]In the ninth century Charlemagne, its warlike monarch, carried his victorious arms in every direction; and Germany became a part of his vast dominions. [4]Charlemagne and his immediate descendants possessed the reality, as well as the ensigns and dignity of imperial power. [5]But the principal vassals, whose fiefs had become hereditary, and who composed the national diets which Charlemagne had not abolished, gradually threw off the yoke and advanced to sovereign jurisdiction and independence.

—James Madison, *The Federalist Papers*

■ Combine these sentences:

The empire could not continue. Individuals sought independence. _____

_____

■ In the excerpt above we have the names of a religion, a country, an emperor, and several peoples. Write them in the appropriate spaces below, as shown in the example.

| Name | Category |
|------|----------|
| 1. _____ *Germany* _____ | _____ *country* _____ |
| 2. _____ | _____ |
| 3. _____ | _____ |
| 4. _____ | _____ |
| 5. _____ | _____ |

■ Write a sentence about someone you met in another state or country that you have visited. _____

_____

For more about capitals, see Review Exercise 22.

# The Semicolon

The semicolon[;] is a useful mark of punctuation. If you have two clauses, closely related in meaning, but cannot connect them with a conjunction, you may put a semicolon between the two. The second clause will *not* begin with a capital letter. For example, *Winter will soon be here; all of the leaves have fallen.*

### Coming Home

[1]There stands the old, square watch-tower, in front of it the great mottled lime tree and behind it the evening. [2]Here we have often sat; we have passed over this bridge and breathed the cool, acid smell of the stagnant water; we have leaned over the still water on this side of the lock, where the green creepers and weeds hang from the piles of the bridge; and on hot days we rejoiced in the spouting foam on the other side of the lock and told tales about our school-teachers. [3]I pass over the bridge, I look right and left; the water is as full of weeds as ever, and it still shoots over in gleaming arches; in the tower-building laundresses still stand with bare arms as they used to over the clean linen, and the heat from the ironing pours out through the open windows.

—Erich Maria Remarque, *All Quiet on the Western Front*

- In this passage the author uses semicolons between many of the clauses. Why do you think he did this instead of using periods or conjunctions? Give examples in your answer. _____

_____

- Where did you hang out after school when you were younger? Write a sentence about your favorite place to meet your classmates. _____

_____

# LESSON 46a
# Another Use for the Semicolon

. . . . . . . . .

When we write a series—a list of people, things, or ideas—the items are always separated by commas [see Lesson 47]. But suppose the items in that series, like a date or an address, have commas already in them: *The meeting may take place on December 4, 2002; December 8, 2002; or January 10, 2003.* As you can see, we avoid confusion in such cases by using the semicolon to separate the items.

### A Feudal Society

[1]By 1066, the system was elaborate and stable. [2]There were many social strata. [3]At the bottom were serfs or slaves; next cottagers or cottars; then villeins, who farmed as much perhaps as fifty acres; then thanes, who drew rents in kind from the villeins; then earls, each ruling one of the six great earldoms that covered the country; and above all, the King. [4]And in parallel to this secular social ladder was the hierarchy of the church, from village priests to archbishops. [5]None of these people could claim the absolute ownership of land. [6]The villeins, to use the old phrase, "held their land of" the thanes, the thanes held it of an earl or the church or the King, and the King held it all of God's grace. [7]And each of them, without exception, owed duties to the others above and below him.

—David Howarth, *1066: The Year of the Conquest*

■ Why could no one in this society claim absolute ownership of land? Write your answer in a sentence. _____

_____

■ The social ranks in sentence 3 above are separated by semicolons. Rewrite each item in the series as a sentence, following the example below.

1. _____*After the serfs came the cottagers.*_____

2. _____

3. _____

4. _____

5. _____

6. _____

■ How is the leader chosen in a group you belong to? Write your answer in a sentence. _____

_____

## LESSON 46b
## More About the Semicolon

The semicolon can pull together ideas that the writer wants to convey in a simple, dramatic way. *The girls wore tankinis, most of the time, at the beach; they wore cut-offs, in the evening, after work; and, most of the time, they wore flip-flops on their feet.*

### Grandmother

[1]My grandmother had a reverence for the sun, a holy regard that now is all but gone out of mankind. [2]There was a wariness in her, and an ancient awe. [3]She was a Christian in her later years, but she had come a long way about, and she never forgot her birthright. [4]As a child she had been to the Sun Dances; she had taken part in those annual rites, and by them she had learned the restoration of her people in the presence of Tai-me. [5]She was about seven when the last Kiowa Sun Dance was held in 1887 on the Washita River above Rainy Mountain Creek. [6]Now that I can have her only in memory, I see my grandmother in the several postures that were peculiar to her: standing at the wood stove on a winter morning and turning meat in a great iron skillet; sitting at the south window, bent above her bead-work, and afterwards, when her vision failed, looking down for a long time into the fold of her hands; going out upon a cane, very slowly as she did when the weight of age came upon her; praying. [7]I remember her most often at prayer.

—N. Scott Momaday, *The Way to Rainy Mountain*

■ Combine these sentences:

Grandmother remembered the old rituals. She had a reverence for the sun.

_____

▪ In the first column, write each word from the excerpt above that is followed by a semicolon. Indicate whether the punctuation connects clauses or a separates the items in a series.

| Words | Connects or Separates |
|---|---|
| 1. _____Sun Dances;_____ | _____Connects two clauses_____ |
| 2. _____ | _____ |
| 3. _____ | _____ |
| 4. _____ | _____ |

▪ Write a sentence naming some things you remember about a grandparent or some other older person. _____

_____

# LESSON 47
## The Comma

The comma is used to *separate*—never connect—words or clauses and to ensure that the sense of a sentence is not lost. As we saw in the introduction to this unit, a sentence can be *ambiguous*—can have two or more possible meanings—when a comma is missing. By the same token, items in a list or series can be confusing if they are not separated by a comma: *for the ski trip I bought boots, hat, and a heavy scarf.* Still another use of the comma is to set off connecting words and phrases like *meanwhile* and *on the other hand* from the rest of the sentence. *Therefore, I stayed home from the party.* When listing several words or phrases, separate them by commas. It is better not to end such a series with *etc.*

### A Waste of Youth

[1]I am young, I am twenty years old; yet I know nothing of life but despair, death, fear, and superficiality cast over an abyss of sorrow. [2]I see how peoples are set against one another, and in silence, unknowingly, foolishly, obediently, innocently slay one another. [3]I see that the keenest brains of the world invent weapons and words to make it yet more refined and enduring. [4]And all men of my age, here and over there, throughout the whole world see these things; all my generation is experiencing these things with me. [5]What would our fathers do if we suddenly stood up and came before them and proffered our account? [6]What do they expect of us if a time ever comes when the war is over? [7]Through the years our business has been killing. [8]Our knowledge of life is limited to death.

—Erich Maria Remarque, *All Quiet on the Western Front*

- Why does the narrator put despair first in his list of the negative emotions

of his life? Write your answer in a sentence. _____

_____

- Underline the series of nouns and adverbs in the excerpt above. For two items, in each of these series, write a sentence showing why the writer feels it is wasting his youth. The first is an example: From the series that begins "despair death, fear . . .".

1. _____ *He has seen the death of other young men on the battlefield.* _____

2. _____

3. _____

4. _____

5. _____

■ Can you think of something your whole generation is concerned about?
Write a sentence explaining what it is. _____

_____

 **LESSON 47a**
**More Commas to Separate**
**Items in a Series**

. . . . . . . . .

As we saw earlier, the semicolon is used to separate the items in a list that
has internal punctuation. For simpler lists, the comma is used. Usually, the
last item will be followed by a comma before *and*. For example, *Apples, oranges, and lemons formed the centerpiece.*

### The Gardens

[1]My mother adorned with flowers whatever shabby house we were forced to
live in. [2]Before she left home for the fields, she watered her flowers, chopped
up the grass, and laid out new beds. [3]When she returned from the fields she
might divide clumps of bulbs, dig a cold pit, uproot and replant roses, or
prune branches from her taller bushes or trees—until night came and it was
too dark to see. [4]Because of her creativity with her flowers, even my memories of poverty are seen through a screen of blooms—sunflowers, petunias,
roses, dahlias, forsythia, spirea, delphiniums, verbena. . .and on and on.
[5]And I remember people coming to my mother's yard to be given cuttings
from her flowers; I hear again the praise showered on her because whatever
rocky soil she landed on, she turned into a garden.

—Alice Walker, *In Search of Our Mothers' Gardens*

■ Combine these sentences:

The family was poor. Mother always had a luxuriant garden. _____

_____

- There are two kinds of series in the excerpt above, one with verb phrases, the other with nouns. For the verb phrases, write the subject, verb, and direct object, if there is one, of each.

1. _____ *she watered her flowers* _____

2. _____

3. _____

4. _____

5. _____

6. _____

7. _____

- Now write the nouns that are separated by commas.

1. _____ *sunflowers* _____    5. _____

2. _____    6. _____

3. _____    7. _____

4. _____    8. _____

- Most people have some kind of hobby—collecting old comic books, fixing broken clocks, or watching romantic movie comedies. Write a sentence about a hobby you have enjoyed. _____

_____

## LESSON 47b
## Still More Series

Note that none of the series we have seen ended with *etc.* It is far better just to decide on the last item and end there. *The class was so boring that students found themselves looking out the window, drawing pictures in their notebooks, and taking naps.*

### A Ship's Supplies Run Out

[1]The expedition had left Sanlúcar with 420 casks of wine. [2]All were drained. [3]One by one the other staples vanished—cheese, dried fish, salt pork, beans, peas, anchovies, cereals, onions, raisins, and lentils—until they were left with kegs of brackish, foul-smelling water and biscuits which, having first crumbled into a gray powder, were now slimy with rat droppings and alive with maggots. [4]These, mixed with sawdust, formed a vile muck men could get down only by holding their noses. [5]Rats, which could be roasted, were so prized that they sold for half a ducat each. [6]The capitán-general had warned them that they might have to eat leather, and it came to that.

—William Manchester, *A World Lit Only by Fire*

■ Why do you think the food supplies ran out on this voyage? Write your answer in a sentence. _____

_____

■ Write three lists in the spaces provided below, showing (1) foods that you might find being served for lunch in the cafeteria; (2) foods that you might have for dinner at home; and (3) foods that you might find in your favorite fast-food restaurant. The first is an example of what you might find in a vegetarian restaurant.

1. *stuffed peppers, asparagus, tomato and onion salad, and sliced kiwis*

2. _____

3. _____

4. _____

■ Write a sentence describing what you like about your favorite food.

_____

# LESSON 48
## Commas That Set Off Subordinate Clauses

. . . . . . . . .

When a subordinate clause begins a sentence or is part of a sentence with several clauses, it is separated from the independent clause by a comma. *Whenever Jake took time for lunch, he was late for class.*

### War's Toll

[1]Just as we turn into animals when we go up to the line, because that is the only thing which brings us through safely, so we turn into wags and loafers when we are resting. [2]We can do nothing else; it is a sheer necessity. [3]We want to live at any price; so we cannot burden ourselves with feelings which, though they might be ornamental enough in peacetime, would be out of place here. [4]And this I know: all these things that now, while we are still in the war, sink down in us like a stone, after the war shall waken again, and then shall begin the disentanglement of life and death. [5]The days, the weeks, the years out here shall come back again, and our dead comrades shall then stand up again and march with us, our heads shall be clear, we shall have a purpose, and so we shall march, our dead comrades beside us, the years at the Front behind us—against whom, against whom?

—Erich Maria Remarque, *All Quiet on the Western Front*

■ Combine these sentences:

Wartime experiences mark the soldier. They will not be forgotten. _____

_____

■ Find four subordinate clauses in the excerpt above that are set off by commas and write them below, as shown in the example.

1. _____ *though they might be ornamental enough in peacetime.* _____

2. _____

3. _____

4. _____

■ Why do we sometimes get more accomplished when we work in a group? Write a sentence explaining your answer. _____

_____

 ## LESSON 48a
## Commas with Subordinate Clauses

A subordinate clause is separated from the independent clause by a comma, especially when it begins a sentence: *Although it was cold, Zelda did not wear a hat.*

### Being a Star

[1]Although she had now achieved the success and adulation she had craved for so long, Madonna the individual struggled to cope with her new life as a modern icon. [2]At first she reveled in her celebrity status. [3]Ever since Madonna had first appeared in a fashion spread in the *Village Voice*, she had saved every press clipping about herself, carefully labeling and dating each one. [4]Each morning she read the New York tabloids and the *New York Times*, scouring them for stories about herself. [5]While publicly she feigned indifference when a critic wrote a withering review or when a reporter made up a negative story about her, she was frequently hurt by such coverage, often losing sleep if a particular remark hit home. [6]It would take several years before Madonna truly began to feel comfortable with her star status.

—Andrew Morton, *Madonna*

■ Why did Madonna save all the press clippings about herself? Write your answer in a sentence. _____

_____

■ Underline each of the subordinate clauses in the excerpt above that begin a sentence. Rewrite each of these sentences as two separate sentences, as shown in the example. *When she went to restaurants, other diners would talk about her or just stare.*

| Subordinate Clause | Sentences |
|---|---|
| *Publicly she feigned indifference.* *She was frequently hurt.* | *While publicly she feigned indifference, she was frequently hurt.* |

1. _____  _____

2. _____  _____

Subordinate Clause                                    Sentences

3. _____            _____

4. _____            _____

■ Have you ever seen a crowd gather when a celebrity appears? Write a sentence explaining why you think this happens. _____

_____

# LESSON 48b
# More Subordinate Clauses

• • • • • • • • •

Remember that a subordinate clause is never a sentence by itself. It must always be joined to an independent clause. When it begins a sentence, it is followed by a comma. The sentence before this one is an example of that. Here is another one: *Because they were late, Gary and Bobby called a taxi.*

### Ambushed by Dogs

[1]When I woke, the sun was low. [2]Looking down from where I lay, I saw a dog sitting on his haunches. [3]His tongue was hanging out of his mouth; he looked as if he were laughing. [4]He was a big dog, with a gray-brown coat, as big as a wolf. [5]I sprang up and shouted at him but he did not move—he just sat there as if he were laughing. [6]I looked about me—not far away there was a great, broken god-road [highway], leading north. [7]I went toward this god-road, keeping to the heights of the ruins, while the dog followed. [8]When I had reached the god-road, I saw that there were others behind him. [9]If I had slept later, they would have come upon me asleep and torn out my throat. [10]As it was, they were sure enough of me; they did not hurry.

—Stephen Vincent Benét, *By the Waters of Babylon*

■ Combine these sentences:

The dogs were menacing. The man looked for a way to escape. _____

_____

■ Find the subordinate clauses that begin sentences in the excerpt above. Write a new sentence beginning with the same clause, as shown in the example.

1. _____ *When I woke, the alarm was ringing.* _____

2. _____

3. _____

4. _____

5. _____

■ Write a sentence about a time you were frightened by an animal. It might be when a bear appeared at your camp or when you heard that a shark was seen near the beach where you were swimming. _____

_____

# LESSON 49
## Commas That Set Off Connecting Words and Phrases

. . . . . . . .

When a connecting word or phrase begins a sentence, it is followed by a comma. If it occurs in the middle of a sentence, it is preceded and followed by a comma. For example, *At last, Greg got the car started. Manya, however, was not ready to go.*

### Katczinsky

[1]We couldn't do without Katczinsky; he has a sixth sense. [2]Katczinsky is the smartest I know. [3]By trade he is a cobbler, I believe, but that hasn't anything to do with it; he understands all the trades. [4]It's a good thing to be friends with him, as Kropp and I are, and Westhus too, more or less. [5]For example, we land at night in some entirely unknown spot, a sorry hole, that has been eaten out to the very walls. [6]We are just dozing off when the door opens and Kat appears. [7]I think I must be dreaming; he has two loaves of bread under his arm and a blood-stained sandbag full of horse-flesh in his hand. [8]Kat gives no explanation. [9]He has the bread; the rest doesn't matter. [10]I'm sure that if he were planted down in the middle of the desert, in half an hour he would have gathered together a supper of roast meat, dates, and wine.

—Erich Maria Remarque, *All Quiet on the Western Front*

▪ Write a sentence explaining why Katczinsky's friendship is so important to

his fellow soldiers. _____

_____

▪ Phrases that are set off by commas can sometimes act as adverbs—for example, *Help arrived quickly, in the nick of time.* Sometimes they are nouns, repeating in other words a noun in the sentence: *My wife, the novelist, has a new book out.* Occasionally, even a very short sentence may set off words with commas: *Larry, my best friend, was there.* These repetitions of a word in the sentence are called *appositives* or *parenthetical phrases* or *clauses*. In the excerpt above, find examples of each of these. Write them below, identifying whether they are acting as nouns, adverbs, or connecting phrases.

| Word or Phrase | Purpose |
|---|---|
| 1. _____ *I believe* _____ | *connecting phrase* |
| 2. _____ | _____ |

**227**

| Word or Phrase | Purpose |
|---|---|
| 3. _____ | _____ |
| 4. _____ | _____ |

- We all know someone who is exceptionally clever at making the best of a trying situation. Write your own sentence about such a person—it might even be you! _____

_____

## LESSON 49a
## More Connectors with Commas

· · · · · · · · ·

Sometimes a phrase that is set off—or separated from the rest of the sentence—by commas signals that the words following will further clarify what has just been written. For example, *My newest friend, Allegra, loves peanut butter.*

### The Spirit of the Kiowas

¹Houses are like sentinels in the plain, old keepers of the weather watch. ²There, in a very little while, wood takes on the appearance of great age. ³All colors wear soon away in the wind and rain; then the wood is burned gray and the grain appears and the nails turn red with rust. ⁴The windowpanes are black and opaque; you imagine there is nothing within, and indeed there are many ghosts, bones given up to the land. ⁵They stand here and there against the sky, and you approach them for a longer time than you expect. ⁶They belong in the distance; it is their domain. ⁷Once there was a lot of sound in my grandmother's house, a lot of coming and going, feasting and talk. ⁸Now there is a funeral silence in the rooms, the endless wake of some final word.

—N. Scott Momaday, *The Way to Rainy Mountain*

- In what way are the plains houses evidence of the weather of that region? Explain your answer in a sentence. _____

_____

- In the excerpt above, there are several parenthetical repetitions of statements. Underline them, then write them below with the nouns they describe more fully. The example below shows what you might do.

1. _____*many ghosts*_____        _____*bones*_____

2. _____        _____

3. _____        _____

4. _____        _____

- Think of a house that holds memories for you. Now write a sentence explaining why those memories are important. _____

_____

# LESSON 49b
# More Parenthetical Phrases

Parenthetical phrases are very useful for providing more information about people—and things—that are part of your composition. They may tell someone's occupation, like *Mrs. Vega, a history teacher*. Or they may identify someone's hometown, *Rosalia, a native of Chicago*.

### The Yacht Race

[1]I was assigned to the crew of the *Barbarian*, a yacht as appropriately named for the sport of ocean racing as any in the fleet. [2]There were eight of us in the crew. [3]There was a professional yachtsman from Australia named Bruce, who'd spent the last year transporting boats about the world and racing for anyone who could afford him. [4]There was Harris, an MIT graduate and a naval architect for Exxon; John, a mechanical engineer for the same company; Herb, an advertising executive; Riley, who has something to do with tax forms, but mainly races; and Donny, the skipper's son. [5]All were young, tan, and athletic.

—Giles Tippette, *Donkey Baseball and Other Sporting Delights*

■ Combine these sentences:

Ocean racing crews come from many occupations. They must be young and

athletic. _____

_____


■ Find five parenthetical expressions in the excerpt above that connect the
writer's ideas and write them below.

1. _____*a yacht as appropriately named*_____

2. _____

3. _____

4. _____

5. _____

6. _____


■ Think of a trip you have made on water—anything from a cruise to a ride

on a ferryboat. Write a sentence about your experience. _____

_____

# LESSON 50
## The Apostrophe

. . . . . . . . .

The apostrophe, the upside down comma ', usually indicates that something is missing. For example, in the contraction *hasn't* the apostrophe stands for the missing letter *o* of *has not*. In *o'clock*, the apostrophe replaces *of the*. The apostrophe in the possessive form of nouns—*Hector's* book, for instance—also stands for the letter *e* that was once part of the ending in Old English. (Remember this from Lesson 14?)

### The Hospital Train

¹Albert is feverish. ²I don't feel too bad. ³I hear from the sister [the nurse] that Albert is to be put off at the next station because of his fever. ⁴On the sister's next round I hold my breath and press it up into my head. ⁵My face swells and turns red. ⁶She stops. ⁷"Are you in pain?" ⁸She gives me a thermometer and goes on. ⁹I would not have been under Kat's tuition if I didn't know what to do now. ¹⁰These army thermometers aren't made for old soldiers. ¹¹All one has to do is to drive the quicksilver up and then it stays without falling again. ¹²I stick the thermometer under my arm at a slant, and flip it steadily with my forefinger. ¹³Then I give it a shake. ¹⁴I send it up to 100.2°. ¹⁵But that isn't enough. ¹⁶A match held cautiously near to it brings it up to 101.6°. ¹⁷Albert and I are put off together.

—Erich Maria Remarque, *All Quiet on the Western Front*

- In one sentence explain the trick the narrator has played on the nursing sister.

_____

- Find the words written with apostrophes in the excerpt above. List them in the appropriate column below.

|  | Possessive | Contraction |
|---|---|---|
| 1. | *sister's* | *don't* |
| 2. | | |
| 3. | | |

▪ Did you ever avoid something you didn't want to do by playing a trick? Write a sentence about it. _____

_____

For more about punctuation, see Review Exercises 29, 40, 43, 44.

## LESSON 50a
## Apostrophes in Contractions

• • • • • • • • •

Many of the words we contract are verbs with *not*—for example, *don't* and *wouldn't*. We also tend to turn *should have* to *should've* and *it is* to *it's*. We do this more often when we speak than when we write. It is important not to confuse the possessive pronoun *its* with the contraction *it's*.

### Tears

[1]That night, for the last time in my life but one—for I was a big boy twelve years old—I cried. [2]I cried, in bed alone, and couldn't stop. [3]I buried my head under the quilts, but my aunt heard me. [4]She woke up and told my uncle I was crying because the Holy Ghost had come into my life, and because I had seen Jesus. [5]But I was really crying because I couldn't bear to tell her that I had lied, that I had deceived everybody in the church, that I hadn't seen Jesus, and that now I didn't believe there was a Jesus any more, since he didn't come to help me.

—Langston Hughes, *Salvation*

▪ Combine these sentences:

The narrator pretended to be saved. The lie made him sad. _____

_____

▪ For each of the contractions in this passage, write in full the verb phrase.

| Contraction | Verb Phrase |
|---|---|
| 1. _____ couldn't _____ | _____ could not _____ |
| 2. _____ | _____ |
| 3. _____ | _____ |

■ Write a sentence about something you did as a child that made you sad because you believed it was wrong. _____

_____

## LESSON 50b
## Apostrophes to Show Possession
• • • • • • • • • •

To show possession for a plural noun ending in *-s* put the apostrophe *after* the *-s* as in *the girls' team won easily.* An important thing to remember about apostrophes is that, when used with nouns, they indicate possession (remember Lesson 14), but they are not used with possessive pronouns.

### Women's Sports

[1]The sport creed's slogans and myths taught me that we control our own fates. [2]If I found myself unable to teach women a sense of free agency, to pursue athletic excellence regardless of parents' or boyfriends' agendas and actions, then the fault must lie in me. [3]What I took away from coaching, besides this haunting sense of my own failure to effect what truly mattered, were only more questions. [4]How, specifically, does muscularity threaten a female's "femininity"? [5]Why would women's pursuit of sporting excellence jeopardize relationships with men? [6]And what, in any case, are issues of women's relationship to men and men's judgment of women's physical appearance doing in *women's* sport?

—Joli Sandoz, *Coming Home*

■ Combine these sentences:

Coaching raised questions for the writer. They had to do with relationships among women, men, and sports. _____

_____

■ Find the possessive nouns in the excerpt above. Put the singular nouns in column 1 and the plural nouns in column 2.

| **Column 1** | **Column 2** |
|---|---|
| 1. _creed's_ | 1. _parents'_ |
| 2. _____ | 2. _____ |
| | 3. _____ |
| | 4. _____ |
| | 5. _____ |

■ Write a sentence about a team you have played on. Was it all men, all women, or both? _____

_____

# LESSON 51
## Quotation Marks

We all know what quotation marks are: those comma-like marks go around anything that a person other than the writer has said or written. For example, *Lori said, "Is it time to go yet?"* As we see in the passage below, quotation marks are used even when the writer is quoting his own thoughts.

### Return from Fear

[1]By afternoon I am calmer. [2]My fear was groundless. [3]The name troubles me no more. [4]The madness passes. [5]"Comrade," I say to the dead man, but I say it calmly, "today you, tomorrow me. [6]But if I come out of it, comrade, I will fight against this, that has struck us both down; from you, taken life—and from me—? Life also. [7]I promise you, comrade. [8]It shall never happen again." [9]The sun strikes low. [10]I am stupefied with exhaustion and hunger. [11]The twilight comes. [12]One hour more. [13]Now suddenly I begin to tremble; something might happen in the interval. [14]Suddenly it occurs to me that my own comrades may fire on me as I creep up; they do not know I am coming. [15]I will call out as soon as I can, so that they will recognize me. [16]I will stay lying in front of the trench until they answer me. The first star. [17]The front remains quiet. [18]I breathe deeply and talk to myself in my excitement: [19]"No foolishness now, Paul—Quiet, Paul, quiet—then you will be saved, Paul." [20]When I use my Christian name it works as though someone else spoke to me, it has more power.

—Erich Maria Remarque, *All Quiet on the Western Front*

- Combine these sentences:

Paul is alone on the battlefield. He tries to calm his fears. _____

_____

- Think of a conversation you had with a friend about an assignment. Write a short paragraph describing what each of you said. Be sure to put quotation marks in the appropriate places.

_____

_____

_____

_____

_____

## LESSON 51a
## Another Use for Quotation Marks

• • • • • • • • •

Quotation marks *must* enclose words that were spoken or written by someone other than the writer. But sometimes we will see these marks around a single word or a brief phrase, when a writer wants to show disagreement or irony. For example, *Jake thought that movie was "great."* We do *not* use quotation marks to emphasize or call attention to a word or phrase. We can do that by underlining or, better yet, by using italics.

### A Man's World

[1]When we say *men, man, manly, manhood,* and all the other masculine derivatives, we have in the background of our minds a huge vague crowded picture of the world and all its activities. [2]To grow up and "be a man," to "act like a man"—the meaning and connotation is wide indeed. [3]That vast background is full of marching columns of men, of changing lines of men, of long processions of men; of men steering their ships into new seas, exploring unknown mountains, breaking horses, herding cattle, ploughing and sowing and reaping, toiling at the forge and furnace, digging in the mine, building roads and bridges and high cathedrals, managing great businesses, teaching in all the colleges, preaching in all the churches; of men everywhere, doing everything—"the world." [4]But when we say *women,* we think *female*—the sex.

—Charlotte Perkins Gilman, *Herland*

■ Combine these sentences:

The men thought all accomplishments were done by men. The women here had

accomplished things themselves. _____

_____

■ Write a short paragraph about the accomplishments of someone you admire—a friend, a member of your family, or a celebrity. Put quotation marks around any words that were written or spoken by someone else.

_____

_____

_____

_____

_____

_____

_____

## LESSON 51b
## Quotations

• • • • • • • • •

In your writing for college courses, you will often be assigned work that requires quotations from books and other sources to prove the points you wish to make about your subject. You must identify these quotations clearly by putting quotation marks around any words that are not your own.

### Swordfish

[1]New Englanders started catching swordfish in the early 1800s by harpooning them from small sailboats and hauling them on board. [2]Since swordfish don't school, the boats would go out with a man up the mast looking for single fins lolling about in the glassy inland waters. [3]If the wind sprang up, the fins were undetectable, and the boats went in. [4]When the lookout spotted a fish, he guided the captain over to it, and the harpooner made his throw. [5]The throw had to take into account the roll of the boat, the darting of the fish, and the refraction of light through water. [6]Giant bluefish tuna are still hunted this way, but fishermen use spotter planes to find their prey and electric harpoons to kill them.

—Sebastian Junger, *The Perfect Storm*

■ Write a paragraph about different kinds of fishing—from boats, in rivers or streams, or any other kind you can think of. Use at least one quotation from the passage on swordfish in your paragraph.

_____

_____

_____

_____

_____

_____

# YOUR WRITING
## *Making a Point*

Throughout the passages you have been reading from *All Quiet on the Western Front,* you have seen some of the psychological as well as physical effects of war on a young man. Now, for the composition you are about to write on the lines below, think of an experience you have lived through that produced lasting feelings and perhaps changed the way you look at the world. As you give details of the events or encounters that led to these feelings, remember all you have learned about producing a paper of three paragraphs that makes a point.

- Stay focused on your purpose: to provide information, *not* to express an opinion or tell a story.
- Begin with a thesis statement that makes clear to your reader what point you are making.
- Be sure *every* sentence that follows, but especially your topic sentences, provides further information about that point.
- Use specific details and examples to make your points clear.
- Combine sentences to show how ideas are related to one another.
- Use connective words and phrases so the reader can follow your thoughts easily.
- Write a concluding sentence that echoes your thesis without repeating it.

_____

_____

_____

_____

_____

_____

_____

_____

_____

_____

_____

# Review Exercises

## Sentences

Remember that every sentence must have a subject, which is often, but not always, a noun or a pronoun: *Joan of Arc. . . .*

Every sentence must also have a verb. Usually the verb is part of a group of words we call the *predicate:* Joan of Arc <u><u>led</u> the French army</u>.

*Led* is the verb and *led the French army* is the predicate. Note that *led* is the past tense of *lead.* The verb in a sentence must have a tense. In the passages below underline the subject of each sentence once, and the verb twice.

### 1

#### Caution: Cellphone in Use

[1]In Japan, where the police have kept track of accidents caused by the use of cellphones, cellphone-related crashes plummeted by 75 percent after 1999 when the country banned the use of hand-held phones when driving. [2]Having a phone in a car is a good idea. [3]It can relieve anxiety in unavoidable delays and be lifesaving in an emergency. [4]But safety-conscious drivers would be wise to avoid using it for casual conversations and should always pull off the road when dialing, talking or answering it.

—Jane E. Brody, "Cellphone: A Convenience, a Hazard or Both?"

▪ For each subject in the excerpt above, write a predicate of your own, following the example below.

| Subject | Predicate |
|---|---|
| 1. _the police_ | _keep the city safe_ |
| 2. _____ | _____ |
| 3. _____ | _____ |
| 4. _____ | _____ |
| 5. _____ | _____ |
| 6. _____ | _____ |

■ Write a sentence about a situation in which you think a cellphone is useful.

---

## 2

### Covering the Palace

[1]Only after many hours of frantic reporting did I have a chance to take a breath and think about Diana's death. [2]I had covered her closely for nearly a year, reporting when she went public about an affair, an eating disorder, her suicide attempts, her unhappiness in her marriage. [3]Just about any woman who is plagued by low self-esteem, who worries about her weight, who has trouble with men, who tries to find herself at the gym or with psychic healers— any woman with everyday problems of the 1990s—found a spokeswoman of sorts in Diana.

—Siobhan Darrow, *Flirting with Danger*

■ Sentence 3 has four relative clauses. Remember, relative clauses cannot stand as sentences on their own but must be connected to an independent clause. Change each of the dependent relative clauses into an independent clause, as the example shows.

| Relative Clause | Independent Clause |
|---|---|
| 1. *Who is plagued by low self-esteem* | *The student with poor grades is plagued by low self-esteem.* |
| 2. _____ | _____ |
| 3. _____ | _____ |
| 4. _____ | _____ |

■ Write a sentence about someone who "has it all" but is still unhappy.

---

## 3

### Promised Land

[1]The Mets entered the promised land on October 16, 1969, after seven years of wandering through the wilderness of baseball. [2]In a tumultuous game before a record crowd of 57,397 in Shea Stadium, they defeated the Baltimore Orioles, 5–3, for their fourth straight victory of the sixty-sixth World Series and captured the championship of a sport that had long ranked them as comical losers. [3]They did it with a full and final dose of the magic that had spiced their unthinkable climb from ninth place in the National League—100-to-1 shots who scraped and scrounged their way to the pinnacle as the waifs of the major leagues.

—Joseph Durso, "The Miracle Mets"

▪ For each verb in the excerpt above, write your own sentence as shown in the example.

<table>
<tr><td align="center">**Verb**</td><td align="center">**Sentence**</td></tr>
<tr><td>1. _____ entered _____</td><td>The class <u>entered</u> the auditorium.</td></tr>
<tr><td>2. _____</td><td>_____</td></tr>
<tr><td>3. _____</td><td>_____</td></tr>
<tr><td>4. _____</td><td>_____</td></tr>
<tr><td>5. _____</td><td>_____</td></tr>
<tr><td>6. _____</td><td>_____</td></tr>
</table>

▪ Write a sentence about a championship—anything from an athletic competition to a spelling bee or a chess match—that you attended or took part in.

_____

### 4
#### One Girl's Life

[1]Maureen Connolly at eighteen was the top woman tennis player in the world and the first in history to hold all four of the world's major crowns. [2]Connolly loved a good time as much as any teenage girl and tried to have as much fun as any player of the top flight. [3]Her hobbies were dancing and music of any and every kind. [4]She liked to eat hamburgers and drink Cokes, go to baseball games and parties. [5]On the court she was all business and had no thoughts for anything but beating her opponent into submission as quickly as she could. [6]But once she was finished, she became a different person, a bubbling eighteen-year-old full of gaiety and friendliness for everyone.

—Allison Danzig, *Little Girl, Big Racquet*

▪ For two of the sentences in the excerpt above, change the subject to you or to someone you know and write a new predicate, as shown in the example.

Sentence 2: _____ Jane loved going to the movies. _____

1. _____

2. _____

▪ Write a sentence explaining why your favorite leisure-time activity is what it is. _____

_____

# 5
## Super

[1]Bryan Bartlett "Bart" Starr, the quarterback for the Green Bay Packers, led his team to a 35–10 victory over the Kansas City Chiefs on January 15, 1967, in the first professional football game between the champions of the National and American Football Leagues. [2]Doubt about the outcome disappeared in the third quarter when Starr's pretty passes made mere Indians out of the AFL Chiefs and Green Bay scored twice. [3]The outcome served to settle the curiosity of the customers, who paid from five to twelve dollars for tickets. [4]The final score was an honest one, meaning it correctly reflected what went on during the game. [5]The great interest had led to naming the event the Super Bowl, but the contest was more ordinary than super.

—William N. Wallace, *The First Super Bowl*

- Find the dependent clauses in the excerpt above and rewrite them to make them independent clauses. The first, from sentence 3, has been done as an example.

| | Dependent Clauses | Independent Clauses |
|---|---|---|
| 1. | *who paid from five to twelve dollars for tickets.* | *The customers paid from five to twelve dollars for tickets.* |
| 2. | | |
| 3. | | |

- Did you ever look forward to a big event that turned out to be unexciting? Write a sentence about it. _____

# 6
## Escaping the War

[1]The Crawfords had half an hour to pack before the last train left the city. [2]Immediately after they had crossed the Seine, Emily heard a terrific explosion. [3]Looking back, she saw that the railway bridge had been blown up. [4]There were many other hazards on the journey, as Emily was to report for several English and American newspapers. [5]After being detained for many days on the line, another train ran into theirs killing eighteen passengers. [6]She and her husband were spared only because, minutes before the crash, they had moved to the rear of the train.

—Anne Sebba, *Battling for News*

■ Look at the subjects from the sentences in the excerpt above. Write the full predicate for each of them.

1. The Crawfords _____ *had half an hour to pack.* _____

2. The last train _____

3. They _____

4. Emily _____

5. She _____

6. The railway bridge _____

7. Other hazards _____

8. Emily _____

9. Another train _____

10. She and her husband _____

11. They _____

■ Write a sentence about a narrow escape you had from some danger. _____

_____

## 7

### A New Life

[1]Rose found herself craving for sugar after the excitement of the day, and significantly enough, made no effort to combat the craving. [2]Freedom and responsibility and an open-air life and a foretaste of success were working wonders on her. [3]Those big breasts of hers, which had begun to sag when she had begun to lapse into spinsterhood, were firm and upstanding now again, and she could look down on them swelling out the bosom of her white drill frock without misgiving. [4]Even in these ten days her body had done much towards replacing fat where fat should be and eliminating it from those areas where it should not. [5]Her face had filled out, and though there were puckers round her eyes caused by the sun, they went well with her healthy tan, and lent piquancy to the ripe femininity of her body.

—C. S. Forester, *The African Queen*

■ You probably noticed that some of the verbs in the excerpt above were made of helpers with a past or present participle. Write both parts of those verbs below and identify the kind of participle that completes it.

| | Verb | Participle |
|---|---|---|
| 1. | *were working* | *present participle* |
| 2. | | |
| 3. | | |
| 4. | | |

■ Write a sentence about an activity you took part in that made you more physically fit. _____

_____

## 8

### Lady on a Ship

[1]As he studied Regina Clausen, he decided that she could use a makeover. [2]She was one of those fortyish women who could have been quite attractive if she only knew how to dress, how to present herself. [3]She was wearing an expensive-looking ice-blue dinner suit that would have been stunning on a blonde, but it did nothing for her very pale complexion, making her look washed out and wan. [4]And her light brown hair, her natural and not unflattering color, was so stiffly set that even from across the wide room it seemed to age her, and even to date her, as though she were a suburban matron from the fifties.

—Mary Higgins Clark, *You Belong to Me*

■ Some of the sentences in the excerpt above have verbs with helpers. Write these verbs below, with a new subject of your own.

| | Verbs | Subjects |
|---|---|---|
| 1. | *could use* | *Mona* |
| 2. | | |
| 3. | | |
| 4. | | |

■ Write a sentence about your favorite color for a special outfit. _____

_____

# 9

## Varieties of English

[1]There are formal and informal dialects, as well as standard and nonstandard ones. [2]Furthermore, standard English is no less of a dialect than any other variety of the language. [3]It is no better and no worse, no more expressive or flexible or beautiful, than any other English dialect. [4]It simply is the variety of English that found itself in the right place at the right time, the dialect that happened to be used by "the right people," those who came to direct the political, economic, and literary affairs of England and eventually, the United States.

—Dennis Baron, *Declining Grammar and Other Essays on the English Vocabulary*

■ Underline all of the subjects and verbs in the excerpt above, then decide which clauses are dependent and which are independent. Write the dependent clauses below, underlining the connecting word that identifies them as dependent, as shown in the example.

1. _____*that* found itself in the right place at the right time._____

2. _____

3. _____

■ Do you speak the same in class as you do with your friends? Write a sentence explaining a difference between the two manners of speech. _____

---

# 10

## The Final Victory

[1]The continent below them was slowly settling beneath the mile-high waves that were attacking its coasts. [2]The last that anyone was ever to see of Earth was a great plain, bathed with the silver light of the abnormally brilliant moon. [3]Across its face the waters were pouring in a glittering flood toward a distant range of mountains. [4]The sea had won its final victory, but its triumph would be short-lived for soon sea and land would be no more. [5]Even as the silent party in the control room watched the destruction below, the infinitely greater catastrophe to which this was only the prelude came swiftly upon them.

—Arthur C. Clarke, *Rescue Party*

■ Helping verbs, or auxiliaries, are used with the present tense form of a verb and with the present and past participles. Find at least one of each of these in the excerpt above and write both helper and verb below, noting which form of the verb is used.

| | Helper | Verb | Form |
|---|---|---|---|
| 1. | *was* | *settling* | *present participle* |
| 2. | _____ | _____ | _____ |
| 3. | _____ | _____ | _____ |
| 4. | _____ | _____ | _____ |
| 5. | _____ | _____ | _____ |

▪ Have you read a story or seen a movie about a disaster? Write a sentence about it. _____

_____

# Prepositions

Most prepositions will be part of prepositional phrases, those groups of words that indicate direction (*under the bridge*) or time (*on the hour*) or means (*by hook or by crook*). Many of these words also form particles—two-word verbs such as *take off, look up,* and *find out.*

## 11

### Finding the Answer

[1]Sherlock Holmes preserved his calm professional manner until our visitor had left us, although it was easy for me, who knew him so well, to see that he was profoundly excited. [2]The moment that Hilton Cubitt's broad back had disappeared through the door my comrade rushed to the table, laid out all the slips of paper containing dancing men in front of him, and threw himself into an intricate and elaborate calculation. [3]For two hours I watched him as he covered sheet after sheet of paper with figures and letters, so completely absorbed in his task that he had evidently forgotten my presence. [4]Finally he sprang from his chair with a cry of satisfaction, and walked up and down the room rubbing his hands together.

—Sir Arthur Conan Doyle, *The Adventure of the Dancing Men*

▪ Underline the prepositional phrases in the excerpt above. For five of them, write another sentence using that phrase, following the example below.

| **Prepositional phrase** | **Sentence** |
|---|---|
| 1. _____*through the door*_____ | _*The teacher walked through the door as the bell rang.*_ |
| 2. _____ | _____ |
| 3. _____ | _____ |
| 4. _____ | _____ |
| 5. _____ | _____ |
| 6. _____ | _____ |

■ Write a sentence about a time you discovered the answer to a difficult question._____

_____

## 12

### Relearning Joy

[1]We came to meadows full of flowers. [2]We saw and realized that they were there, but we had no feelings about them. [3]The first spark of joy came when we saw a rooster with a tail of multicolored feathers. [4]But it remained only a spark; we did not yet belong to this world. [5]In the evening when we all met again in our hut, one said secretly to the other, "Tell me, were you pleased today?" [6]And the other replied, feeling ashamed as he did not know that we all felt similarly, "Truthfully, no!" [7]We had literally lost the ability to feel pleased and had to relearn it slowly.

—Victor Frankl, *Man's Search for Meaning*

■ Some of the sentences in the excerpt above contain more than one clause. Identify these clauses as dependent or independent and underline the word that connects them, as the example shows.

1. _*We saw and realized [ind] that they were there [dep] <u>but</u> we had no feelings about them [ind].*_

2. _____

3. _____

4. _____

5. _____

■ Write a sentence about an event that made you very happy. _____

_____

## 13

### Making It

[1]A lot of movie stars are short. [2]I think it's because you have to have a lot of fight to make it big and short people learn how to fight from the get go, especially men. [3]Tall guys have got it made. [4]Natural selection has already favored them. [5] They're usually good at sports. [6]Other guys don't beat them up as often. [7]They don't have to try so hard to impress women. [8]They don't have to learn to do colorful things like acting in order to get noticed. [9]I am prepared to say that being short culturally prepares the male to develop the character traits that help him become a compelling actor, traits such as vulnerability, courage in the face of adversity and perseverance in the pursuit of goals.

—Marco Perella, *Adventures of a No Name Actor*

■ Some of the sentences in the excerpt above use *do* to form a negative. *Do* is often used to ask a question as well. Following the example, turn four of the sentences into questions using *do*.

1. _____ *Do tall guys have it made?* _____

2. _____

3. _____

4. _____

5. _____

■ Is physical appearance important to a movie star? Write your answer in a sentence. _____

_____

## 14

### Stuck in the Ditch

[1]One morning I backed the car into a ditch while turning it around for my run home. [2]I spun the wheels for a while, then got out and looked things over. [3]I spun the wheels some more, until I was dug in good and deep. [4]Then I gave up and started the trek back to camp. [5]It was nearly three o'clock, and the walk home would take at least four hours. [6]They would find me missing before I got there, the car too. [7]I let off a string of swear words, but they seemed to be coming at me, not from me, and I soon stopped.

—Tobias Wolff, *This Boy's Life*

▪ Underline the prepositional phrases in the excerpt above. Then, following the example, write five more sentences using these phrases.

1. _____ *The dog jumped into a ditch.* _____

2. _____

3. _____

4. _____

5. _____

6. _____

▪ Write a sentence about a time when a car wouldn't start, or a bus broke down, or a train was an hour late. _____

_____

## 15

### Football Fame

[1]Perhaps still the most famous football player ever, Harold (Red) Grange looked in wonderment at the joggers going past his home in Indian Lake, Florida. [2]"I think they're crazy," he said in an interview before Super Bowl XVI in 1982. [3]"If you have a car, why run?" [4]But once he ran like few others. [5]He was fast and strong and so elusive that he seemed to vanish from tacklers. [6]He was a star halfback in the 1920s for the University of Illinois—he once scored four long touchdowns in the first quarter against powerful Michigan—and then went on to play for the Chicago Bears. [7]Grange almost single-handedly popularized professional football.

—Ira Berkow, *A Conversation with the Ghost*

▪ Underline the words in the excerpt above that use suffixes to form nouns or adjectives. Write them in the spaces provided, along with the new word that is formed, as shown in the example. For each indicate the part of speech.

| New Words | Original Word |
|---|---|
| 1. *player [noun]* | *play [verb]* |
| 2. _____ | _____ |
| 3. _____ | _____ |

|        New Words        |        Original Word        |
| ----------------------- | --------------------------- |
| 4. _____ | _____ |
| 5. _____ | _____ |

■ Think of a name that you associate with football or with some other sport. Write a sentence about why this name means that sport for you. _____

---

## 16

### A Call from Movieland

¹When Hollywood entered my life I was sitting in a tiny room in Fort Worth eating meatloaf. ²The phone rang, and I was informed that some people I had never heard of had just bought the movie rights to my first novel. ³Three nights later I was sitting in the best restaurant in Fort Worth, eating a steak so thick that in most parts of Texas it would have been called a roast and discussing title changes with a gentleman from Paramount. ⁴At the time it never crossed my mind to wonder whether the movie would turn out to be better than the book; what I knew for a certainty was that the steak was better than the meatloaf.

—Larry McMurtry, *Film Flam*

■ Underline the verbs in the excerpt above that are formed with a helper and a past or present participle. Write them below, following the example.

1. _____ *was sitting [present participle]* _____
2. _____
3. _____
4. _____
5. _____

■ Think about a movie you have seen that was based on a book. Write a sentence about which version you preferred. _____

---

## 17

### A Profitable Plan

¹Uncle Hal would go to Richmond and set up his company funded with her capital. ²He would make her an officer of the company; her income from the investment would supplement her other earnings until the company

generated enough profit to let her quit working. [3]After the lumber business began to prosper—Easy Street. [4]To start his company Uncle Hal wanted her to put up $100 from her bank account. [5]She wasn't totally credulous about Uncle Hal's ability to put us on Easy Street. [6]If he was asking for $100, she reasoned, he could probably make do with $75. [7]That's what she gave him. [8]The Colonel instantly launched plans to proceed to Richmond and set up business. [9]Before leaving, he sat in the parlor at New Street and wrote her his receipt for $75, "same to be invested by me, Col. B. H. Robinson, in walnut timber, in the name of E. Baker & Co. of Belleville, N. J., which sum she is to receive. . . " [10]It went on and on, finally stating that if he died she was to receive "all proceeds" accruing to the company, "both gross and net."

—Russell Baker, *Growing Up*

▪ Give examples in the excerpt above of periods that mark the end of a declarative sentence or the abbreviation of a name, place, or business. Follow the example shown.

| Period | Reason for Period |
|---|---|
| 1. _her capital._ | _end of a declarative sentence_ |
| 2. _____ | _____ |
| 3. _____ | _____ |
| 4. _____ | _____ |
| 5. _____ | _____ |

▪ Think of your first job, or the first time you earned money. Write a sentence about it. _____

_____

## 18

### Hollywood's Bad Boy

[1]After a long acting drought, Sean Penn's career is undergoing an El Niño-like resurrection. [2]Penn, who makes no bones about how much he dislikes the job he does so well, says this flurry of activity was triggered by the chance to finally film *She's So Lovely*. [3]It's ironic that Penn's return comes in a movie about love, since much of his life has been filled with anger. [4]His temper, his paparazzi punching and his liquor-fueled self-destructiveness are legendary. [5]And for someone who hates the celebrity aspects of show business as passionately as he loves cinema's potential for great artistry, Penn's media-mauled first marriage to Madonna still seems like a willful act of career suicide.

—Bob Strauss, *Q and A with Sean Penn*

■ Underline the nouns and adjectives in the excerpt above that are formed by suffixes. Write them in the spaces provided along with the word from which they are formed. Underline the suffix.

| **New Word** | **Original Word** |
|---|---|
| 1. _resurrection [noun]_ | _resurrect [verb]_ |
| 2. | |
| 3. | |
| 4. | |
| 5. | |
| 6. | |

■ Are people more interested in celebrities who have a reputation for getting in trouble? Write a sentence explaining why or why not. _____

_____

## 19

### Meeting the Star

[1]The next evening we show up at a room in the hotel and Kevin Costner meets us there. [2]We congratulate Kevin on his good fortune in bagging this role and he confides in us that not only does he have the lead in *this* picture, he has a glorious part in something called *The Big Chill*. [3]This work of art will come out soon and the studios are calling and he is, in general, slicing through the butter of life with a very hot knife. [4]Since we are obviously expected to be impressed, Diane and I make soft, reassuring cooing sounds and touch him reverently on his godlike shoulders.

—Marco Perella, *Adventures of a No Name Actor*

■ In the excerpt above, underline the homophones—words that have a different meaning when they are spelled differently. Write both forms of the word below.

| 1. _we_ | _wee_ |
|---|---|
| 2. | |
| 3. | |

4. _____     _____

5. _____     _____

6. _____     _____

7. _____     _____

■ Would you enjoy meeting someone who is considered a celebrity? Write a sentence about your feelings. _____

---

## 20

### Trapped

¹The bed was good, and the pajamas of the softest silk, and he was tired in every fiber of his being, but nevertheless Rainsford could not quiet his brain with the opiate of sleep. ²He lay, eyes wide open. ³Once he thought he heard stealthy steps in the corridor outside his room. ⁴ He sought to throw open the door; it would not open. ⁵He went to the window and looked out. ⁶His room was high up in one of the towers. ⁷The lights of the chateau were out now, and it was dark and silent; but there was a fragment of sallow moon, and by its wan light he could see, dimly, the courtyard. ⁸Rainsford went back to the bed and lay down. ⁹He had achieved a doze when, just as morning began to come, he heard, far off in the jungle, the faint report of a pistol.

—Richard Connell, *The Most Dangerous Game*

■ Words ending in *-d* can be past tense verbs, helper verbs, or past participles, or they may simply be words spelled that way. Find two examples of each and write them below.

1. Spelling: _____ *bed, good* _____

2. Past tense verbs: _____

3. Helper verbs: _____

4. Past participles: _____

■ Rainsford is frightened because he is locked in his room. Write a sentence about something that frightens you. _____

## 21

### The Star Athlete

[1]Bobby had played football for Concrete High. [2]He'd been their quarterback, the smallest and best player on the team, so much better than the others that he seemed alone on the field. [3]His solitary excellence made him beautiful and tragic, because you knew that whatever prodigies he performed would be undone by the rest of the team. [4]He made sly, unseen handoffs to butter-fingered halfbacks, long bull's-eye passes to ends who couldn't catch them. [5]But his true wizardry was broken field running: sprinting and stopping dead, jumping sideways, pirouetting on his toes and wriggling his hips girlishly as he spun away from the furious hulks who pursued him, slipping between them like a trout shooting down a boulder-strewn creek.

—Tobias Wolff, *This Boy's Life*

■ Underline the conjunctions and relative pronouns that connect clauses in the excerpt above. Identify the clauses as dependent or independent, as shown in the example.

| Independent Clause | Connector | Dependent Clause |
|---|---|---|
| *He'd been their quarterback* | *that* | *he seemed alone on the field* |
| 1. | | |
| 2. _____ | _____ | _____ |
| 3. _____ | _____ | _____ |
| 4. _____ | _____ | _____ |
| 5. _____ | _____ | _____ |

■ Write a sentence about a person you know who has accomplished something extraordinary in a sport, on a musical instrument, or in a school subject. (It might be you!) _____

## 22

### The New Russia

[1]Living in Moscow as a CNN correspondent in the 1990s was a completely different experience from life there as the impoverished young wife of a Soviet citizen in the 1980s. [2]I had a BMW so I never rode the metro. [3]I always shopped in the hard-currency stores, spending my dollars on meat imported from Finland instead of lining up for the shoe leather they called meat

in the domestic stores. ⁴My clothes were bought mostly during vacations to Italy. ⁵Instead of trudging through the snow to a laundromat that seemed to eat as many clothes as it cleaned, I had a maid. ⁶Just like the natives, I learned to be a capitalist in the new Russia.

—Siobhan Darrow, *Flirting with Danger*

■ Capital letters are used in several different ways in the excerpt above. In addition to identifying the first word of a sentence, there are abbreviations of company names and names of cities and countries as well. Write the words below, indicating why they are capitalized.

| | Capitalized Word | Reason |
|---|---|---|
| 1. | *CNN* | *company name* |
| 2. | | |
| 3. | | |
| 4. | | |
| 5. | | |
| 6. | | |
| 7. | | |

■ Have you ever lived in a different city or country, even if just for a short time? Write a sentence about the most striking difference you observed in the new area. _____

_____

## 23

### A Lady's Skills

¹Sir Marhalt's lady dazzled him with glowing hair and skin like a rose petal. ²She moved with the slow dignity of music in her gown of blue and gold, and she wore a tall blue cone and a flowing wimple of sheer white satin. ³And when she saw the golden prize her eyes shone so that Sir Marhalt said, "My lady, if fortune and my knighthood can equal my wish, you will wear the prize." ⁴She smiled at him and blushed, and her hands, which could tighten a girth and cook a forest stew, fluttered like pale butterflies, so that Sir Marhalt was aware that being a good lady is as much a skill as being a good knight.

—John Steinbeck, *The Acts of King Arthur and His Noble Knights*

■ The -*s* at the end of some words can indicate a plural, a possessive, or the ending for the third person singular present tense. Sometimes the -*s* has no meaning; it is just the way the word is spelled. Find one word having each type of -*s* ending in the excerpt above and write it in the space provided, as the example shows.

|  | **Word Ending in -*s*** | **Meaning of -*s*** |
|---|---|---|
| 1. | *eyes* | *plural noun* |
| 2. | _____ | _____ |
| 3. | _____ | _____ |
| 4. | _____ | _____ |
| 5. | _____ | _____ |

■ People can have a talent for doing more than one thing. Write a sentence about someone you know who can do two or more things well. _____

_____

## 24

### Knights at Play

[1]When there were no wars or tournaments it was the custom of knights and fighting men to hunt in the great forests which covered so much of England. [2]In the breakneck chase of deer through forest and swamp and over rutted and rock-strewn hills, they tempered their horsemanship, and meeting the savage charge of wild boars, they kept their courage high and their dexterity keen. [3]And also their mild enterprise loaded the turning spits in the kitchens with succulent meat for the long tables of the great hall. [4]On a day when King Arthur and many of his knights quartered the forest in search of quarry, they started a fine stag and gave chase. [5]The proud, high-antlered stag drew them on, and with whip and spur they pushed their foaming horses through tangled undergrowth and treacherous bogs, leaped streams and fallen trees until they overdrove their mounts and the foundered horses fell heaving to the ground, with bloody bits and rowel stripes on their sides.

—John Steinbeck, *The Acts of King Arthur and His Noble Knights*

■ Underline the prepositional phrases in the excerpt above. In the spaces provided, write the phrase that best answers each of the questions, following the pattern shown in the example.

| 1. | *Where* | *in the great forests* |
|---|---|---|
| 2. | *When* | _____ |

3. _____*Whose*_____    _____

4. _____*Why*_____    _____

5. _____*How*_____    _____

- Write a sentence about your favorite recreation after class or after work.

_____

## 25

### The Other Babe

[1]Implausible is the adjective which best befits the Babe. [2]As far as sport is concerned, she had the golden touch of a Midas. [3]When she was only sixteen, she was named to the all-America women's basketball team. [4]She once hit thirteen home runs in a softball doubleheader. [5]Her top bowling score was 237. [6]In the 1932 Olympics she won two events, setting world records in each, and placed second in the third test, although again breaking the world record. [7]At least part of Zaharias's success would be attributed to her powers of concentration and diligence. [8]When she decided to center her attention on golf, she tightened up her game by driving as many as 1,000 golf balls a day and playing until her hands were so sore they had to be taped. [9]She developed an aggressive, dramatic style, hitting down sharply and crisply on her iron shots like a man and averaging 240 yards off the tee with her woods.

—Arthur Daley, *Implausible Is Best*

- Find four different uses of the *-s* ending in the excerpt above. Write them in the spaces provided, identifying the use, as shown in the example.

| Word Ending in *-s* | Reason |
|---|---|
| 1. _____*Midas*_____ | *the way the word is spelled* |
| 2. _____ | _____ |
| 3. _____ | _____ |
| 4. _____ | _____ |
| 5. _____ | _____ |

- Write a sentence about an athlete who excels in two or more sports. ____

_____

# 26

### Crossing the Lake

¹The barge moved silently across the Lake. ²Even now, after years of knowing that it was no magic, but intensive training in silencing the oars, Morgaine was still impressed by the mystical silence through which they moved. ³She turned to call the mists, and was conscious of the young man behind her. ⁴He stood, easily balanced beside his horse, one arm flung across the saddle blanket, shifting his weight easily without motion, so that he did not visibly sway or lose balance as the boat moved and turned. ⁵Morgaine did this herself from long training, but he managed it, it seemed, by his own natural grace.

—Marion Zimmer Bradley, *The Mists of Avalon*

■ A number of words in the excerpt above end in *-d*. This can indicate the past tense, a past participle, or a verb used with a helper or as an adjective, or it may be the way the word is spelled. Find examples of these uses and write them below.

1. _____*moved*_____        _____*past tense*_____

2. _____        ____*past participle as adjective*____

3. _____        ____*past participle with helper*____

4. _____        _____*spelling*_____

■ Think of a skill you have developed in sports or in some other activity and write a sentence about a physical or mental attribute it requires. _____

# 27

### Nim and Nature

¹Nim had just begun to feel comfortable running about by himself. ²During his summer in East Hampton, Nim the Chimpanzee discovered nature. ³While he wandered around outside the house, he often paused to smell and touch flowers. ⁴He also discovered birds. ⁵For many minutes at a time, Nim would gaze up into the branches of a tree as if trying to figure out what produced the bird songs he heard. ⁶If a bird moved away from the tree, Nim would try to catch it while hooting attack cries at the top of his lungs. ⁷He also tried—and failed—to catch rabbits. ⁸Such things occurred almost every time Nim went outside.

—Herbert S. Terrace, *Nim: A Chimpanzee Who Learned Sign Language*

■ Prepositional phrases can answer the questions *when, where, how, whose,* and *why*. Find examples of each in the excerpt above and write them in the spaces provided along with the questions they answer.

| Question | Answering Phrase |
|---|---|
| 1. *where* | *outside the house* |
| 2. _____ | _____ |
| 3. _____ | _____ |
| 4. _____ | _____ |
| 5. _____ | _____ |

■ Most people have a favorite aspect of nature—flowers, the sea, birds. Write a sentence about that part of nature that you especially enjoy. _____

_____

## 28

### Listen and Learn

[1]Studies are showing that spoken language has an astonishing impact on an infant's brain development. [2]In fact, some researchers say the number of words an infant hears each day is the single most important predictor of later intelligence, school success and social competence. [3]There is one catch—the words have to come from an attentive, engaged human being. [4] As far as anyone has been able to determine, radio and television do not work. [5]This relatively new view of infant brain development, supported by many scientists, has obvious political and social implications. [6]It suggests that infants and babies develop most rapidly with caretakers who are not only loving, but also talkative and articulate, and that a more verbal family will increase an infant's chances for success.

—Sandra Blakeslee, *Talking with Infants Shapes Basis of Ability to Think*

■ Many words change their part of speech when a suffix is added: verbs and adjectives become nouns, verbs become adjectives, and adjectives become adverbs. Underline the words formed from such suffixes in the excerpt above and show for five of them the word from which the changed form was derived.

| New Word | Original Word |
|---|---|
| 1. *attent-**ive** [adjective]* | *from attend [verb]* |
| 2. _____ | _____ |

|  New Word | Original Word |
|---|---|
| 3. _____ | _____ |
| 4. _____ | _____ |
| 5. _____ | _____ |
| 6. _____ | _____ |

■ Write a sentence about a word that you like or dislike because you associate it with something else. _____

---

## 29

### Animal Talk

[1]The attempts to communicate with apes have been marked by controversy from the time of the first successful attempt to converse with another animal. [2]The problems are twofold. [3]First of all, the idea that language is what separates man from animal is enormously important to the way we view and act in the world, and is not the type of concept that can be cast aside blithely. [4]Secondly, it is one thing to seem to converse with another animal, but it is quite another to be able to prove that the animal's responses are not simple mimicry or trickery. [5]After all, stories about "talking cats" or "talking dogs" inevitably turn out to be whimsy. [6]Why should anyone take the notion of "talking apes" any more seriously?

—Francine Patterson and Eugene Linden, *The Education of Koko*

■ Several different marks of punctuation can be found in the excerpt above. Name them in the spaces provided, along with the reason for their use.

| Punctuation Mark | Reason For Use |
|---|---|
| 1. _____*period*_____ | _*end of a declarative sentence*_ |
| 2. _____ | _____ |
| 3. _____ | _____ |
| 4. _____ | _____ |
| 5. _____ | _____ |

■ Everyone who has a pet has seen that animal do something remarkable. Write a sentence about an animal whose action impressed you. _____

_____

## 30

### Writing the Unwritten

[1]Jesus Salinas Pedraza, a rural schoolteacher in the Mexican state of Hidalgo, sat down to a word processor a few years back and produced a monumental book, a 250,000-word description of his own Indian culture written in the Nahnu language. [2]Nothing seems to be left out: folktales and traditional religious beliefs, the practical uses of plants and minerals and the daily flow of life in field and village. [3]But it is more than the content that makes the book a remarkable publishing event, for Mr. Salinas is neither a professional anthropologist nor a literary stylist. [4]He is, though, the first person to write a book in Nahnu, the native tongue of several hundred thousand Indians but a previously unwritten language. [5]Such a use of microcomputers and desktop publishing for languages with no literary tradition is now being encouraged by anthropologists for recording ethnographies from an insider's perspective. [6]They see this as a means of preserving cultural diversity and a wealth of human knowledge. [7]With even greater urgency, linguists are promoting the techniques as a way of saving some of the world's languages from imminent extinction.

—John Noble Wilford, *Books in "Unwritten" Languages*

■ The present participle, the form of the verb that ends in *-ing*, can be used, with a helper, as a verb. While it can also be used as a noun or adjective, it should not be confused with words whose spelling ends in *-ing*. In the spaces provided, write each of the *-ing* words in the excerpt above identifying its use, as shown in the example.

| Word Ending in *-ing* | How Used |
|---|---|
| 1. *publishing* | *adjective* |
| 2. | |
| 3. | |
| 4. | |
| 5. | |

■ What would you miss most if we had no written language? Write a sentence about it. _____

_____

## 31

### The Predator

¹Its nose twitching, the small mouse makes its way along the narrow branch. ²The animal's quivering body speaks of caution, yet it remains oblivious to its impending doom. ³The owl is perched on a higher branch, his sharp eyes riveted on the prey. ⁴Silently, motionlessly, the bird calculates the best method of attack. ⁵Suddenly, he swoops down and, with scarcely a pause in his wingbeats, snatches the rodent in his talons. ⁶A few thrusts of his powerful wings and the deadly hunter is safely roosting in another tree, savoring his meal. ⁷Watching the northern spotted owl are three other sets of eyes, the eyes of men. ⁸Two biologists and I have walked to this patch of woods on the northern edge of Washington State's Olympic Peninsula, in pursuit of the most controversial bird in America.

—Keith Ervin, *A Life in Our Hands*

■ An *-s* at the end of a word can mean that the word is plural, that it signifies possession, or that it is a verb in the third person singular present tense. It can also signify nothing more than that is the way the word is spelled. Underline all of the *-s* words in the excerpt above, then write six of them in the spaces provided, identifying how they are used. Be sure to choose at least five different uses.

| Word Ending in -s | Reason |
|---|---|
| 1. _makes_ | third person singular present tense |
| 2. _____ | _____ |
| 3. _____ | _____ |
| 4. _____ | _____ |
| 5. _____ | _____ |
| 6. _____ | _____ |
| 7. _____ | _____ |

■ Write a sentence about an unusual bird you have seen. _____

_____

## 32

### The Family Dog

[1]It used to be that you could tell just about how poor a family was by how many dogs they had. [2]If they had one, they were probably doing all right. [3]It was only American to keep a dog to represent the family's interests in the intrigues of the back alley; not to have a dog at all would be like not acknowledging one's poor relations. [4]Two dogs meant that the couple were dog lovers, with growing children, but still might be members of the middle class. [5]But if a citizen kept three, you could begin to suspect he didn't own much else. [6]Four or five irrefutably marked the household as poor folk, whose yard was also full of broken cars cannibalized for parts. [7]The father worked not much, fancied himself a hunter; the mother's teeth were black.

—Edward Hoagland, *Dogs and the Tug of Life*

- Underline the punctuation marks in the excerpt above. Identify two uses for each of these marks, citing the sentence in which the use appears.

| Punctuation Mark | Sentence | Reason Used |
|---|---|---|
| 1. comma | Sentence 2 | separate dependent from independent clause |
| 2. comma | Sentence 4 | separate phrase in apposition |
| 3. | | |
| 4. | | |
| 5. | | |
| 6. | | |

- Do you know, or have you heard about, someone who has a large number of pets? Write a sentence describing that person. _____

_____

## 33

### The Cowboy Life

[1]Seventy-five years ago, when travel was by buckboard or horseback, cowboys who were temporarily out of work rode the grub line—drifting from ranch to ranch, mending fences or milking cows, and receiving in exchange a bed and meals. [2]Gossip and messages traveled this slow circuit with them, creating an intimacy between ranchers who were three and four weeks' ride apart. [3]One old-time couple I know, whose turn-of-the-century

homestead was used by an outlaw gang as a relay station for stolen horses, recall that if you were traveling, desperado or not, any lighted ranch house was a welcome sign. [4]Even now, for someone who lives in a remote spot, arriving at a ranch or coming to town for supplies is cause for celebration. [5]To emerge from isolation can be disorienting. [6]Everything looks bright, new, vivid. [7]Because ranch work is a physical and, these days, economic strain, being "at home on the range" is a matter of vigor, self-reliance, and common sense.

—Gretel Ehrlich, *The Solace of Open Spaces*

■ Many words look and sound the same but have different meanings. Find five such words in the excerpt above and write them in the spaces provided with two of their meanings and their part of speech.

|   | Word | Meaning 1 | Meaning 2 |
|---|------|-----------|-----------|
| 1. | *travel* | *[noun] a journey* | *[verb] to go on a trip* |
| 2. | | | |
| 3. | | | |
| 4. | | | |
| 5. | | | |
| 6. | | | |

■ Do you prefer to be alone or with other people? Write a sentence explaining your choice._____

---

## 34

### After the Storm

[1]One place where the eraser came down squarely was in the Cathedral Pines, a famous forest of old-growth white pine trees close to the center of town. [2]To enter Cathedral Pines on a hot summer day was like stepping out of the sun into a dim cathedral, the sunlight cooled and sweetened by the trillions of pine needles as it worked its way down to soft, sprung ground that had been unacquainted with blue sky for the better part of two centuries. [3]The storm came through at about five in the evening and it took only a few minutes of wind before pines more than one hundred fifty feet tall and as wide around as missiles lay jackstrawed on the ground like a fistful of pencils dropped from a great height. [4]The wind was so thunderous that people in

houses at the forest's edge did not know trees had fallen until they ventured outside after the storm had passed. [5]The following morning, the sky now clear, was the first in more than a century to bring sunlight crashing down onto this particular patch of earth.

—Michael Pollan, *The Idea of a Garden*

■ Underline all of the connecting words in the excerpt above. Write them in the spaces provided, indicating whether each is a coordinating or a subordinating conjunction or a relative pronoun.

| Sentence Number | Connecting Word | Kind of Connector |
|---|---|---|
| 1.   2 | *that* | *subordinating relative pronoun* |
| 2.   3 | | |
| 3.   3 | | |
| 4.   4 | | |
| 5.   4 | | |
| 6.   5 | | |

■ Some people like storms; others are frightened by them. Write a sentence explaining what your reaction might be to a fierce storm. _____

_____

## 35

### Us Versus Nature

[1]It does seem that we do best in nature when we imitate her—when we learn to think like running water, or a carrot, an aphid, a pine forest, or a compost pile. [2]That's probably because nature, after almost four billion years of trial-and-error experience, has wide knowledge of what works in life. [3]Surely we're better off learning how to draw on her experience than trying to repeat it, if only because we don't have that kind of time. [4]Nature does not teach its creatures to control their appetites except by the harshest of lessons—epidemics, mass death, extinctions. [5]Nothing would be more natural than for humankind to burden the environment to the extent that it was rendered unfit for human life. [6]Nature in that event would not be the loser nor would it disturb her laws in the least—operating as it has always done, natural selection would unceremoniously do us in.

—Michael Pollan, *The Idea of a Garden*

■ The verb *do* is sometimes used as a helper, especially, with *not*, in forming a negative. Sometimes it is added for emphasis. Underline all forms of *do* in the excerpt above and identify how each one is used.

| Form of Do | Use of Do |
|---|---|
| 1. *don't have* | *helper to make have negative* |
| 2. | |
| 3. | |
| 4. | |
| 5. | |
| 6. | |

■ Write a sentence about something in nature that we cannot control. _____

---

## 36

### TV in Our World

[1]Television is the chief way that most of us partake of the larger world, of the information age, and so, though none of us owe our personalities and habits entirely to the tube and the world it shows, none of us completely escape its influence either. [2]Why do we do the things we do? [3]Because of the events of our childhood, and because of class and race and gender, and because of our political and economic system and because of "human nature"—but also because of what we've been told about the world, because of the information we've received. [4]One study after another, not to mention the experience of most of us, indicates that we do in fact often watch television because of our mood or out of habit, instead of tuning in to see something in particular. [5]Even so, we're not staring at test patterns. [6]We also often eat because we're bored or depressed, but the effects are different if we scarf carrot sticks or Doritos.

—Bill McKibben, *Daybreak*

■ Underline each of the punctuation marks in the excerpt above. Give an example of each in the spaces provided, indicating why it is used as it is.

| Punctuation Mark | Why Used |
|---|---|
| 1. *period* | *end of declarative sentence* |
| 2. | |
| 3. | |

| Punctuation Mark | Why Used |
|---|---|
| 4. _____ | _____ |
| 5. _____ | _____ |
| 6. _____ | _____ |

▪ Write a sentence about what you learn about the world from watching television. _____

_____

## 37

### A Shopping Spree

[1]It was exciting to walk through the great markets of Londinium; dirty and smelly as the city was, it seemed like four or five harvest fairs all in one. [2]Yet it was a little frightening to walk through the enormous market square, with a hundred vendors crying their wares. [3]It seemed to her that everything she saw was new and beautiful, something she wished for, but she resolved to see all of the market before she made any purchases; and then she bought spices, and a length of fine woven wool from the islands, far finer than that of the Cornish sheep. [4]And so she also bought for herself small hanks of dyed silks; it would be pleasant to weave on such brilliant colors, restful and fine to her hands after the coarseness of wool and flax. [5]She would teach Morgause, too. [6]And it would be high time, next year, to teach Morgaine to spin. [7]Four years was certainly old enough to start learning to handle a spindle and twist the thread, even though the thread would not be good for much except tying up bundles of yarn for dyeing.

—Marion Zimmer Bradley, *The Mists of Avalon*

▪ Find the irregular verbs in the excerpt above. Write the principal parts of each of them in the spaces provided.

| | Present Tense | Past Tense | Present Participle | Past Participle |
|---|---|---|---|---|
| 1. | see | saw | seeing | seen |
| 2. | _____ | _____ | _____ | _____ |
| 3. | _____ | _____ | _____ | _____ |
| 4. | _____ | _____ | _____ | _____ |
| 5. | _____ | _____ | _____ | _____ |

■ Write a sentence about the best shopping trip you ever had. _____

_____

## 38

### Tire Mountain

[1]The world's largest pile of scrap tires is not visible from Interstate 5, in Stanislaus County, California. [2]But it's close. [3]Below Stockton, in the region of Modesto and Merced, the highway follows the extreme western edge of the flat Great Central Valley, right next to the scarp where the Coast Ranges are territorially expanding as fresh unpopulated hills. [4]The hills conceal the tires from the traffic. If you were to abandon your car three miles from the San Joaquin County line and make your way on foot southwest one mile, you would climb into steeply creased terrain that in winter is jade green and in summer straw brown, and, any time at all, you would come upon a black vista. [5]In some cases they are piled six stories high, compressing themselves, densifying. [6]From the highest elevations of this thick and drifted black mantle, you can look east a hundred miles and see snow on the Sierra. [7]Even before the interstate was there, a tire jockey named Ed Filbin began collecting them.

—John McPhee, *Duty of Care*

■ Circle all of the words beginning with capital letters in the excerpt above. Write five of them below, noting the sentence it is in and indicating why each word is being capitalized. (*Note:* Do not use "first word in a sentence" more than once.)

| Capitalized Word | Reason for Capitalization |
|---|---|
| 1. *Sentence 1: The* | *first word in a sentence* |
| 2. | |
| 3. | |
| 4. | |
| 5. | |
| 6. | |

■ Think about the largest collection of scrap you have ever seen. Write a sentence about it. _____

_____

## 39

### Bird Watching

[1]There was a stirring high up in the peepul tree, and a bubbling noise like pots boiling. [2]A flock of green pigeons were up there, eating the berries. [3]Flory gazed up into the great green dome of the tree, trying to distinguish the birds; they were invisible, they matched the leaves so perfectly, and yet the whole tree was alive with them, shimmering, as though the ghosts of birds were shaking it. [4]Flo rested herself against the roots and growled up at the invisible creatures. [5]Then a single green pigeon fluttered down and perched on a lower branch. [6]It did not know that it was being watched. [7]It was a tender thing, smaller than a tame dove, with jade-green back as smooth as velvet, and neck and breast of iridescent colors. [8]Its legs were like the pink wax that dentists use.

—George Orwell, *Burmese Days*

- The present participle, the *-ing* form of a verb, needs a helper, as in *is laughing*. The present participle can also be an adjective or a noun; some words just end in *-ing*. Write the *-ing* words from the excerpt above in the spaces provided and identify them as verbs, nouns, adjectives, or spelling.

| **Present Participle** | **Reason for Use** |
| --- | --- |
| 1. *bubbling* | *adjective describing noise* |
| 2. _____ | _____ |
| 3. _____ | _____ |
| 4. _____ | _____ |
| 5. _____ | _____ |
| 6. _____ | _____ |
| 7. _____ | _____ |
| 8. _____ | _____ |

- Write a sentence about a wild creature you have watched. _____

_____

## 40

### Tornado

[1]As a boy in Ohio I knew a farm family, the Millers, who not only saw but suffered from three tornadoes. [2]The father, mother, and two sons were pulling into their driveway after church when the first tornado hoisted up their mobile

home, spun it around, and carried it off. [3]With the insurance money, they built a small frame house on the same spot. [4]Several years later, a second tornado peeled off the roof, splintered the garage, and rustled two cows. [5]The Millers rebuilt again, raising a new garage on the old foundation and adding another story to the house. [6]That upper floor was reduced to kindling by a third tornado, which also pulled out half the apple trees and slurped water from the stock pond. [7]Soon after that I left Ohio, snatched away by college as forcefully as by any cyclone. [8]Last thing I heard, the family was preparing to rebuild yet again.

—Scott Russell Sanders, *Settling Down*

■ Some verbs consist of two words, like *take off*, which has a meaning different from *take* alone. Underline the two-word verbs in the excerpt above and write them in the spaces provided with a subject of your choice.

| **Verb** | **Sentence** |
|---|---|
| 1. *Carried off* | *The pirates carried off the treasure.* |
| 2. | |
| 3. | |
| 4. | |
| 5. | |
| 6. | |

■ Write a sentence about damage from fierce weather that you have seen.

---

## 41

### The Topic of the Day

[1]And their talk was of war and rumors of wars. [2]They raged against World War II when it broke out in Europe, blaming it on the politicians. [3]"It's these politicians. [4]They're the ones always starting up all this lot of war. [5]But what they care? [6]It's the poor people got to suffer and mothers with their sons." [7]If it was *their* sons, they swore they would keep them out of the Army by giving them soap to eat each day to make their hearts sound defective. [8]Hitler? He was for them "the devil incarnate." [9]Then there was home. [10]They reminisced often and at length about home. The old country. [11]Barbados—or Bimshire, as they affectionately called it. [12]The little Caribbean island in the sun they loved but had to leave. [13]"Poor—poor but sweet" was the way they remembered it.

—Paule Marshall, *From the Poets in the Kitchen*

■ Circle the punctuation marks in the excerpt above. Identify one of each kind in the spaces provided, along with the reason for its use.

| Sentence Number | Punctuation Mark | Reason for Use |
|---|---|---|
| 1. _Sentence 7_ | _comma_ | _separate dependent and independent clauses_ |
| 2. _____ | _____ | _____ |
| 3. _____ | _____ | _____ |
| 4. _____ | _____ | _____ |
| 5. _____ | _____ | _____ |
| 6. _____ | _____ | _____ |

■ Think of someone you know or have read about who came from another place. Write a sentence about that person. _____

_____

## 42

### This Thing Called Love

[1]Love is still something one hears a great deal about in pop lyrics, but the contemporary version is more hard-headed and down-to-earth than the cosmic, effulgent Love of the 60s. [2]Many of today's songwriters argue that romance isn't as important as material values or sex. [3]"What's love got to do with it?" Tina Turner asked in her recent heavy-breathing hit of the same title. [4]And Madonna, whose come-hither pout and undulating style have made her pop's hottest video star, serves notice in her hit "Material Girl" that she won't worry much about love as long as there's money in the bank. [5]Madonna's carefully calculated image has struck a chord among many of today's more affluent young listeners, though she is perhaps too one-dimensional to be Queen of the Yuppies. [6]And she will never be the darling of the feminists.

—Robert Palmer, *What Pop Lyrics Say to Us Today*

■ Circle the punctuation marks in excerpt above. Write five of them in the spaces provided, along with an explanation of how each one is used.

| Sentence Number | Punctuation Mark | Reason for Use |
|---|---|---|
| 1. _Sentence 1_ | _comma_ | _separates items in a series_ |
| 2. _____ | _____ | _____ |

| Sentence Number | Punctuation Mark | Reason for Use |
|---|---|---|
| 3. _____ | _____ | _____ |
| 4. _____ | _____ | _____ |
| 5. _____ | _____ | _____ |
| 6. _____ | _____ | _____ |

■ Write a sentence explaining what attitude about love is expressed by a pop song you know. _____

_____

## 43

### Women in the Tribes

[1]Through all the centuries of war and death and cultural and psychic destruction have endured the women who raise the children and tend the fires, who pass along the tales and the traditions, who weep and bury the dead, who are the dead, and who never forget. [2]There are always the women, who make pots and weave baskets, who fashion clothes and cheer their children on at pow-wow, who make fry bread and piki bread, and corn soup and chili stew, who dance and sing and remember and hold within their hearts the dream of their ancient peoples—that one day the woman who thinks will speak to us again, and everywhere there will be peace. [3]Meanwhile we tell the stories and write the books and trade tales of anger and woe and stories of fun and scandal and laugh over all manner of things that happen every day. [4]We watch and we wait.

—Paula Gunn Allen, *Where I Come From Is Like This*

■ Underline the words in the excerpt above that can be used as more than one part of speech. Following the example, write five of these words in the spaces provided, indicating the part of speech used here and, in a new sentence, its use as another part of speech.

| Original Word | Sentence |
|---|---|
| 1. _____*pass [verb]*_____ | *I have a pass [noun] to the new movie.* |
| 2. _____ | _____ |
| 3. _____ | _____ |
| 4. _____ | _____ |
| 5. _____ | _____ |
| 6. _____ | _____ |

▪ Think of someone you know who does many things. Write a sentence about some of those things. _____

_____

## 44

### A Woman's Lot

[1]I was slow to understand the deep grievances of women. [2]This was because, as a boy, I had envied them. [3]No doubt, had I looked harder at their lives, I would have envied them less. [4]It was not my fate to become a woman, so it was easier for me to see the graces. [5]Few of them held jobs outside the home, and those who did filled thankless roles as clerks and waitresses. [6]I didn't see, then, what a prison a house could be, since houses seemed to me brighter, handsomer places than any factory. [7]I did not realize—because such things were never spoken of—how often women suffered from men's bullying. [8]I did learn about the wretchedness of abandoned wives, single mothers, widows; but I also learned about the wretchedness of lone men. [9]Even then I could see how exhausting it was for a mother to cater all day to the needs of young children. [10]But if I had been asked, as a boy, to choose between tending a baby and tending a machine, I think I would have chosen the baby. [11](Having now tended both, I know I would choose the baby.)

—Scott Russell Sanders, *The Men We Carry in Our Minds*

▪ Underline all of the verbs in the excerpt above that have a helper. Write five of these verbs with helpers in the spaces provided with a short sentence of your own that uses the verb and helper.

| Verb and Helper | Sentence |
|---|---|
| 1. *had envied* | *The sisters had envied Cinderella.* |
| 2. _____ | _____ |
| 3. _____ | _____ |
| 4. _____ | _____ |
| 5. _____ | _____ |
| 6. _____ | _____ |

▪ What housekeeping job do you find most distasteful? Write a sentence about it. _____

_____

## 45

### A Man's Place

[1]People in the men's movement believe there was once a golden age of masculinity, when strong men hugged, expressed their feelings, honored their elders and served as mentors to younger men. [2]This era is sometimes said to have existed during Arthurian times, when kings, warriors and wise magicians served as role models. [3]These ancient societies offered men clear road maps of how they ought to behave through myths, legends and poetry. [4]There were ceremonies to show respect, and rites to initiate adolescents into adulthood. [5]In modern times, rites and myths no longer exist to set men right, and thus many are deeply confused. [6]A major focus at men's retreats is to enact latter-day rituals to replace the old ones.

—Trip Gabriel, *Call of the Wildmen*

■ Underline the words in the excerpt above that change to another part of speech by adding a suffix. Write five of these in the spaces provided, indicating what the suffix is and what change it has made.

|  | **Word** | **Formed from** |
|---|---|---|
| 1. | *gold-**en** [adjective]* | *gold [noun]* |
| 2. | | |
| 3. | | |
| 4. | | |
| 5. | | |
| 6. | | |

■ Write a sentence about a ceremony that makes a person part of a group.

## 46

### A New Look at the Family

[1]All family sitcoms, of course, teach us that wisecracks and swift put-downs are the preferred modes of affectionate discourse. [2]But Roseanne takes the genre a step further. [3]It is Barr's narrow-eyed cynicism about the family, even more than her class consciousness, that gives *Roseanne* its special frisson. [4]Archie Bunker got our attention by telling us that we (blacks, Jews, "ethnics," WASPs, etc.) don't really like each other. [5]Barr's message is that even within the family we don't much like each other. [6]We love each other (who

else do we have?); but The Family, with its impacted emotions, its lopsided division of labor, and its ancient system of age-graded humiliations, just doesn't work. [7]Or rather, it doesn't work unless the contradictions are smoothed out with irony and the hostilities are periodically blown off as humor. [8]Coming from Mom, rather than from a jaded teenager or a bystander dad, this is scary news indeed.

—Barbara Ehrenrich, *The Wretched of the Hearth*

■ Underline the dependent clauses in the excerpt above, then write them in the spaces provided with a new independent clause of your own.

| New Independent Clause | Dependent Clause |
|---|---|
| | *that we don't really* |
| 1. *I don't believe* | *like each other.* |
| 2. | |
| 3. | |
| 4. | |
| 5. | |

■ Write a sentence about a television show that depends for its humor on wisecracks and put-downs. _____

_____

## 47

### The Job Hunt

[1]Before 1965, the white corporate establishment didn't realize that African Americans even existed. [2]College-trained blacks and middle-class business-people were attached to the separate economy of the ghetto. [3]African Americans who applied for jobs at white-owned companies found that their resumes weren't accepted. [4]Blacks who were hired were placed in low-paying clerical or maintenance positions. [5]With the impact of the civil rights movement, the public demonstrations and boycotts against corporations which Jim Crowed blacks, businesses were forced to change their hiring policies. [6]However, most blacks were placed in minority neighborhoods, having little contact with whites in supervisory roles. [7]They were assigned to mediate black employees' grievances or to direct affirmative action policies, rather than being placed in charge of a major division of the company. [8]Their managerial experiences were limited, and therefore their prospects for upward mobility into senior executive positions were nonexistent.

—Manning Marable, *Racism and Corporate America*

▪ Underline the homophones in the excerpt above, then write them in the spaces provided along with a new sentence using the word that sounds the same but is spelled differently.

|  | Sentence Number | Homophones | New Sentence |
|---|---|---|---|
| 1. | 2 | to | The class meets at two o'clock. |
| 2. | | | |
| 3. | | | |
| 4. | | | |
| 5. | | | |
| 6. | | | |

▪ Write a sentence about an experience you had applying for a job. _____

_____

## 48

### The Welcoming Room

[1]He stopped walking. [2]He moved a bit closer. [3]Green curtains were hanging down on either side of the window. [4]The chrysanthemums looked wonderful beside them. [5]He went right up and peered through the glass into the room, and the first thing he saw was a bright fire burning on the hearth. [6]On the carpet in front of the fire, a pretty little dachshund was curled up asleep, with its nose tucked into its belly. [7]The room itself, as far as he could see in the half darkness, was filled with pleasant furniture. [8]There was a baby-grand piano and a big sofa and several plump armchairs, and in one corner he spotted a large parrot in a cage. [9]Animals were usually a good sign in a place like this, Billy told himself, and all in all, it looked as though it would be a pretty decent house to stay in. [10]Certainly it would be more comfortable than the Bell and Dragon.

—Roald Dahl, *The Landlady*

▪ Underline the irregular verbs in the excerpt above. Write their principal parts. Then write the principal parts of two regular verbs from this passage.

|  |  | Present Tense | Past Tense | Present Participle | Past Participle |
|---|---|---|---|---|---|
| 1. | Irregular | is | was | being | been |
| 2. | Regular | stop | stopped | stopping | stopped |

|  | Present Tense | Past Tense | Present Participle | Past Participle |
|---|---|---|---|---|
| 3. Irregular | _____ | _____ | _____ | _____ |
| 4. Irregular | _____ | _____ | _____ | _____ |
| 5. Irregular | _____ | _____ | _____ | _____ |
| 6. Regular | _____ | _____ | _____ | _____ |
| 7. Regular | _____ | _____ | _____ | _____ |

■ Write a sentence about your favorite room. _____

_____

## 49

### A Missionary's Life

[1]She was hardly ever free from illness and pain, and yet she seemed able to do things which would have been fatal to most Europeans. [2]She never used mosquito-netting, she never wore a hat, she went barefoot despite the prevalence of jiggers and snakes. [3]She never boiled the water, she ate native food, and she kept most irregular hours, for she was often ministering at night and her days were taken up with long 'palavers'. [4]When she died in 1915, in her rough-built hut in Calabar with her native family—Janie, Annie, Maggie, Alice and Whitie—about her, she left the spell of her unconventionality behind her, and the romance of her name drew many others into foreign missions.

—Maria Aitken, *Women Adventures: Travelers, Explorers, and Seekers*

■ Underline the irregular verbs in the excerpt above. Write them in the spaces provided below under the appropriate heading, and add the other principal parts in the remaining columns.

|  | Present Tense | Past Tense | Present Participle | Past Participle |
|---|---|---|---|---|
| 1. | do | did | doing | done |
| 2. | _____ | _____ | _____ | _____ |
| 3. | _____ | _____ | _____ | _____ |
| 4. | _____ | _____ | _____ | _____ |
| 5. | _____ | _____ | _____ | _____ |
| 6. | _____ | _____ | _____ | _____ |

| Present Tense | Past Tense | Present Participle | Past Participle |
|---|---|---|---|
| 7. _____ | _____ | _____ | _____ |
| 8. _____ | _____ | _____ | _____ |

■ Write a sentence about someone who endured hardships in order to do a job properly. _____

_____

## 50
### At Peace with the Animals

[1]There is nothing more disgusting to me than the slaughter of animals for the sake of sport. [2]It is sometimes necessary to kill a gazelle or a zebra for meat. [3]It is occasionally necessary to kill a buffalo or an elephant or a leopard or a lion in order to escape being killed yourself. [4]But on the whole it is safer to live among wild animals than to live in New York. [5]With the exception of the big cats, which are a treacherous lot, few of them will attack unless they are frightened or molested. [6]And I want to live at peace with them.

—Martin Johnson, *Camera Trails in Africa*

■ Underline the words in the excerpt above that are changed in some way by the addition of a suffix. For example, the participle form of a verb can become an adjective, a verb can become a noun, or an adjective can become an adverb. For five of the words you have underlined, explain how they have been changed by a suffix.

| Word | How Changed by Suffix |
|---|---|
| 1. _____ *frightened* _____ | _____ *past participle/adjective* _____ |
| 2. _____ | _____ |
| 3. _____ | _____ |
| 4. _____ | _____ |
| 5. _____ | _____ |
| 6. _____ | _____ |

■ Write a sentence about a time when you made peace as a conflict was about to break out. _____

_____

# Glossary

**Adjective:** A word that describes a noun: *growing girl, purple cow.*

**Adverb:** A word that provides further information about a verb, an adjective, or another adverb: *talked rapidly, narrowly missed, almost home, very often.*

**Apostrophe:** See *Punctuation.*

**Appositive:** A word or phrase that clarifies meaning by naming or describing the same thing: *my car, a red Mustang.*

**Article:** The words *a, an,* and *the,* which are used to indicate a specific noun or any one of a larger number of things. Articles are classified as definite (the dog next door) or indefinite (*a barking dog, **an** unhappy cat*).

**Auxiliary:** Another name for a *helping verb,* a form of *to be, to do, to have* or one of the modals used to form a compound tense. See *Helping Verbs.*

**Clause:** A subject and predicate connected to one or more additional subjects and predicates: *I never saw a purple cow, but I've heard of them.*

> **Dependent Clause:** A clause that must be connected by a conjunction or relative pronoun to form a sentence: *when I was young.* This is also called a *subordinate clause.*
>
> **Independent Clause:** A clause that functions as a sentence by itself: *I liked to play catch.* It can be joined to another independent clause by a *coordinating conjunction: and now I like to play tennis.*
>
> **Relative Clause:** A dependent clause joined to the independent clause by a relative pronoun (*who, whom, whose, which, that*). We watched the boy *who* won the game.

**Comma:** See *Punctuation.*

**Conjunction:** A word that connects clauses by showing the relationship between them: ***When** I was younger, I played tennis.*

**Contraction:** The deletion of a letter or letters for ease of pronunciation. The deletion is replaced by an apostrophe: *can't, don't, didn't.*

**Declarative:** See *Sentence.*

**Helping Verbs:** Also called *auxiliary verbs.* The parts of the verbs to be or to have used with past or present participles: *she **is** going, he **has** gone, they **were** singing.*

> **Modal Auxiliaries:** A helper without tense: *can, could, do, may, might, must, ought, will, would, shall, should. The class **may** go to the museum.* See *Auxiliary.*

**Homophone:** One of a pair of words that sound alike but have different spellings and meanings: *new/knew, ewe/you.*

**Infinitive:** A verb form with *to* that has no tense: *It is fun **to take** a trip.*

**Interjection:** A word or phrase that expresses surprise, shock, or emotion: *How sad! For crying out loud! Holy moley!*

**Mechanics:** Devices such as spelling, punctuation, capitalization that are used to make writing more understandable.

**Negative:** The reversal of a statement: *She has a job. She does not have a job.* Often formed with *do* as a helper and *not*. Sometimes other helpers are used: *can, might, should.*

**Noun:** A person, place, or thing. It may be the subject of a sentence or the object of a sentence or prepositional phrase.

> **Common Noun:** The name of a person, place, or thing that is one of many: *a cat, a city, a telephone, a teacher.*

> **Proper Noun:** The name of a particular person, place, or thing: *James, Washington, Amtrak, McDonald's*

**Number:** The form of a word that indicates how many things, including persons, are referred to.

**Object:** The word or phrase that completes a predicate or a prepositional phrase: *The bat hit **the ball**. He sat down by **the old mill stream**.*

**Participle:** One of the principal parts of a verb. It must be used with a helper. *Jeff is going to the game. Monica has seen that movie.*

> **Past Participle:** A verb form used as part of a verb phrase: *The bird has **flown**.* It can also function as an adjective: *a **finished** product.*

> **Present Participle:** A verb form used with the verb to be: *The children are **running** home.* It can also serve as a noun (*a meeting*) or as an adjective (*shining lights*).

**Particle:** A preposition that combines with a verb to form a two word verb phrase: *She could not make out the form in the dark.* See *Preposition.*

**Person:** The form in verbs, and pronouns that indicates a speaker (first person, *I or we*); the one being spoken to (second person, *you*); and the one spoken of (third person, *she, he, it*).

**Phrase:** A group of grammatically related words. A noun phrase may be the complete subject of a sentence. *The boy named Greg answered the question.* A prepositional phrase may act as an adverb, answering *when, where, why, whose, how.*

> **Parenthetical Phrase:** A phrase that repeats the meaning of one that goes before in different words: *Rick's new car, **his pride and joy**, got a flat tire.*

**Possessive:** A word or mark indicating that something or someone belongs to something or someone else: *the end of the road, the road's end.* Possessive personal pronouns—*his, hers, its*—have no apostrophe.

**Predicate:** The verb phrase that completes a sentence. *The teacher **put the assignment on the board**. Put* is the verb, but the entire phrase is the predicate.

**Prefix:** The syllable added to a word's beginning that changes the meaning of a word: **un**happy, **re**write.

**Preposition:** The part of speech that opens a phrase to answer *where, when, how, why,* or *whose*: ***over** the river and **through** the woods.*

**Pronoun:** A word that substitutes for another: *The assignment was hard. **It** took me three hours.*

> **Personal Pronoun:** A word that substitutes for a person or thing—*I, me, mine, you, your, she, her, he, him, it.*

> **Relative Pronoun:** *Who, which,* or *that.* Introduces a dependent clause identifying the object of the clause it follows: *I finished the assignment, **which** took me three hours.*

**Punctuation:** Devices used in writing to indicate sentence boundaries, to separate words and phrases (never clauses), and to show missing letters or possession.

> **Apostrophe:** An inverted comma that, with - *s*, shows possession or, between letters, as a contraction, indicates that something is missing: *The bird's nest wasn't empty.*

> **Capital Letters:** Also called *uppercase letters*. They are used to begin sentences or proper nouns: *Professor Jones, River City.*

> **Comma:** A mark that is used to separate—a series of items, a word or phrase in apposition, the year in a date: The necklace was made of *rubies, diamonds, and pearls. Jose Nuñez, my old friend,* came to visit. *June 1, 2000* marks the anniversary of our meeting.

> **Exclamation Point:** The mark that follows a word or sentence expressing astonishment: *Good grief!*

> **Period:** The mark that ends a declarative sentence. It is also used with abbreviations: *Jan., Dr., St. Louis.*

> **Question Mark:** The mark that follows a question: *What time is it?*

> **Quotation Marks:** The marks that enclose the words of another, including those in books or other written works. *Maria said, "Let's go to the movies."*

> **Semicolon:** The mark that separates a series of phrases that contain commas. *Green, leafy vegetables are nutritious; rich, dark chocolate is delicious; but a certain amount of protein is necessary to a balanced diet.* It can also be used between closely related independent clauses. *You serve the cookies; I'll make the coffee.*

**Rhetorical Question:** A question that does not require an answer because it is an observation or opinion. *Who knows what tomorrow will bring?*

**Root:** That part of a word that does not change when a prefix or a suffix is added: **move**ment, **go**ing, dis**cover**, in**definite**.

**Sentence:** A group of words in which a subject and a verb, with tense, make a statement, ask a question, or give a command. Often a sentence contains more than one clause.

>   **Compound Sentence:** A sentence with two independent clauses. *I would go for a bike ride, but it is raining.*
>
>   **Complex Sentence:** A sentence with an independent clause and one or more dependent clauses. *The teacher handed out the papers as the class began.*
>
>   **Declarative Sentence:** A sentence that makes a statement: *The author wrote the book.*
>
>   **Exclamatory Sentence:** A sentence that expresses surprise or emotion: *What a frightening experience that was!*
>
>   **Imperative Sentence:** A sentence that gives a command: *Go to the front of the class.*
>
>   **Interrogative Sentence:** A sentence that asks a question: *Did you finish the homework?*

**Singular:** A form indicating one of anything. Singular verbs have as their subjects *I, you, he, she, it,* or a word that can be substituted for one of these: *Richard goes to work on the bus.*

**Subject:** The part of a sentence that performs the action. It can be a noun, a pronoun, an infinitive, or a participial phrase. ***To forgive*** *is divine.* ***Taking a test*** *can be difficult.* ***Olga*** *won first prize.*

**Suffix:** A syllable added to the end of a word that changes its part of speech or the way it functions in a sentence. For example, *teach* [verb] becomes *teacher* [noun]; *look* [present tense verb] becomes *looked* [past tense verb].

**Tense:** The time of an action, taking place in the past, present, or future. It is seen in the form of the verb or of its helper. *I talk, you talked, she will talk.* Irregular verbs may change the forms of their tenses. *I go, you went, she will go.*

**Verb:** The word that indicates the action occurring in a sentence. It is often part of a phrase: *The squirrel climbed the tree.* Verbs have four principal parts: (1) present, (2) past (*-ed*), (3) present participle (*-ing*), and (4) past participle (*-ed*). The forms of these parts change in irregular verbs: *see, saw, seeing, seen.*

# Bibliography

· · · · · · · · · · ·

Allen, Paula Gunn. "Where I Come from Is Like This." *The Sacred Hoop.* New York: Beacon Press, 1986

Angell, Roger. *Late Innings: A Baseball Companion.* New York: Ballantine, 1982.

Bâ, Mariama. *So Long a Letter.* Trans. Modupé Bodé-Thomas. Oxford: Heinemann, 1989.

Baker, Russell. *Growing Up.* New York: Congdon and Weed, 1982.

Baron, Dennis. *Declining Grammar and Other Essays on the English Vocabulary.* Urbana, IL: National Council of Teachers of English, 1989.

Benét, Stephen Vincent. "By the Waters of Babylon." *Thirteen O'clock: Stories of Several Worlds.* Freeport, NY: Books for Libraries Press, 1971.

Brody, Jane E. "Cellphone: A Convenience, a Hazard or Both." *New York Times,* 1 October 2002: 24.

Brontë, Emily. *Wuthering Heights.* London: Zodiac Press, 1955.

Carroll, Lewis. *Alice in Wonderland and Through the Looking Glass.* New York: Macmillan, 1966.

Carson, Rachel. *The Sea Around Us.* New York: Oxford University Press, 1951.

Clark, Mary Higgins. *You Belong to Me.* New York: Simon & Schuster, 1999.

Clarke, Arthur C. "Rescue Party." *Great Tales of Action and Adventure.* Ed. George Bennett. New York: Dell, 1958.

Conan Doyle, Sir Arthur. "The Adventure of the Dancing Men." *Great Tales of Action and Adventure.* Ed. George Bennett. New York: Dell, 1958.

Connell, Richard. "The Most Dangerous Game." *Great Tales of Action and Adventure.* Ed. George Bennett. New York: Dell, 1958.

Conrad, Joseph. *The Secret Sharer.* New York: Bantam, 1981.

Dahl, Roald. "The Landlady." *Kiss Kiss.* New York: Alfred A. Knopf, 1959.

Danzig, Allison. "Little Girl, Big Racquet." *The New York Times Book of Sports Legends.* Ed. Joseph J. Vecchlione. New York: Random House, 1991.

Darrow, Siobhan. *Flirting with Danger: Confessions of a Reluctant War Reporter.* London: Virago Press, 2000.

Duggan Alfred. *Devil's Brood: The Angevin Family.* London: Arrow Books, 1960.

Dunne, John Gregory. *Monster: Living off the Big Screen.* New York: Random House, 1997.

Durso, Joseph. "The Miracle Mets." *The New York Times Book of Sports Legends.* Ed. Joseph J. Vecchlione. New York: Random House, 1991.

Ehrenreich, Barbara. "The Wretched of the Hearth." *New Republic,* 2 April 1990: 28–31.

Ehrlich, Gretel. *The Solace of Open Spaces.* New York: Viking Penguin, 1985.

Eiseley, Loren. "How Flowers Changed the World." *The Star Thrower.* New York: Harvest, 1978.

———. "One Night's Dying." *The Night Country.* New York: Scribner, 1971.

Eliot, George. *Middlemarch.* Stamford, CT: Longmeadow Press, 1994.

Ervin, Keith. "A Life in Our Hands." *Fragile Majesty: The Battle for North America's Latest Great Forest*. Seattle, WA: The Mountaineers, 1989.

Fast, Howard. *April Morning*. New York: Bantam, 1951.

Fischer, Louis. *Gandhi: His Life and Message for the World*. New York: New American Library, 1954.

Forester, C. S. *The African Queen*. New York: Bantam, 1964.

Frankl, Viktor E. *Man's Search for Meaning*. New York: Washington Square Press, 1984.

Fuller, Margaret. *"These Sad but Glorious Days": Dispatches from Europe 1846–1850*. Eds. Larry J. Reynolds and Susan Belasco Smith. New Haven: Yale University Press, 1991.

Gilman, Charlotte Perkins. *Herland*. New York: Pantheon Books, 1979.

Greene, Graham. *Journey Without Maps*. New York: Compass Books, 1961.

Hillerman, Tony. *The Fallen Man*. New York: Harper Collins, 1996.

Hilton, James. *Lost Horizon*. New York: Pocket Books, 1960.

Hoagland, Edward. "Dogs and the Tug of Life." *Red Wolves and Black Bears*. New York: Random House, 1976.

Hough, Richard. *The Last Voyage of Captain James Cook*. New York: William Morrow, 1979.

Howarth, David. *1066, The Year of the Conquest*. New York: Viking, 1977.

Hughes, Langston. "Salvation." *The Big Sea*. New York: Farrar, Straus and Giroux, 1940.

Jones, Constance. *1001 Things Everyone Should Know About Women's History*. New York: Doubleday, 1998.

Junger, Sebastian. *The Perfect Storm*. New York: Harper Paperbacks, 1997.

Lansing, Alfred. *Endurance: Shackleton's Incredible Voyage*. New York: McGraw-Hill, 1959.

Lawrence, D. H. "The Rocking Horse Winner." Mankato, MN: Creative Education, 1982.

Lindbergh, Charles A. *The Spirit of St. Louis*. New York: Scribner's, 1953.

Lopez, Barry. "The Country of the Mind." *Arctic Dreams*. New York: Vintage Books, 1986.

Lord, Walter. *A Night to Remember*. New York: Bantam, 1956.

Luciano, Ron, and David Fisher. *The Umpire Strikes Back*. New York: Bantam, 1983.

Madison, James. *The Federalist Papers*. Ed. Clinton Rossiter. New York: Mentor, 1961.

Manchester, William. *A World Lit Only by Fire*. New York: Little, Brown, 1993.

Mansfield, Katherine. "The Fly." *The Dove's Nest and Other Stories*. New York: Knopf, 1923.

Marable, Manning. "Racism and Corporate America." *The Crisis of Color and Democracy*. Monroe, ME: Common Courage Press, 1991.

Marshall, Paule. "From the Poets in the Kitchen." *Reena and Other Stories*. New York: Feminist Press, 1983.

McKibben, William. *The Age of Missing Information*. New York: Random House, 1992.

McMurtry, Larry. *Film Flam: Essays on Hollywood*. New York: Simon and Schuster, 1987.

Momaday, N. Scott. *The Way to Rainy Mountain*. Albuquerque: University of New Mexico Press, 1969.

Morris, Lloyd. *Postscript to Yesterday: American Life and Thought 1896–1946*. New York: Harper and Row, 1947.

Morrison, Toni. *The Bluest Eye*. New York: Penguin, 1994.

Morton, Andrew. *Madonna*. New York: St. Martin's Press, 2001.

Murphy, Austin. *The Sweet Season: A Sportswriter Rediscovers Football, Family and a Bit of Faith at Minnesota's St. John's University*. New York: HarperCollins, 2001.

Obst, Lynda. *Hello, He Lied and Other Truths from the Hollywood Trenches*. New York: Little, Brown, 1996.

Orwell, George. *Animal Farm*. New York: Harcourt Brace, 1946.

———. *Burmese Days*. New York: Time Inc., 1950.

———. "Marrakesh," "Shooting an Elephant." *The Orwell Reader*. New York: Harcourt Brace Jovanovich, 1956.

Overbye, Dennis. "The End of Everything." *New York Times,* 1 Jan. 2002: F1.

Patterson, Francine, and Eugene Linden. *The Education of Koko*. New York: Holt, Rinehart and Winston, 1981.

Perella, Marco. *Adventures of a No Name Actor*. New York: Bloomsbury, 2001.

Pollan, Michael. *Second Nature: A Gardener's Education*. Grove/Atlantic, 1991.

Prejean, Helen, C.S.J. *Dead Man Walking*. New York: Vintage Books, 1994.

Pym, Barbara. *Crampton Hodnet*. New York: New American Library, 1985.

Reid, Elwood. "My Body, My Weapon, My Shame." *The Best American Sports Writing of 1998*. Ed. Bill Littlefield. New York: Houghton Mifflin, 1998.

Remarque, Erich Maria. *All Quiet on the Western Front*. New York: Ballantine, 1958.

Roberts, Fletcher. "Explosive, Realistic, but Most of All Funny." *New York Times,* 3 Feb. 2002: 13.5.

Robertson, Linda. "On Planet Venus." *The Best American Sportswriting of 1998*. Ed. Bill Littlefield. New York: Houghton Mifflin, 1998.

Salamon, Julie. *The Devil's Candy: The Bonfire of the Vanities Goes to Hollywood*. Boston: Houghton Mifflin, 1991.

Sanders, Scott Russell. "Settling Down." *Staying Put: Making a Home in a Restless World*. Boston: Beacon Press, 1993.

———. "The Men We Carry in Our Minds." Minneapolis: *Milkweed Chronicle, 1984.*

Sandomir, Richard. "For Saturday, Buy the Chips and the Visine." *New York Times,* 4 June 2002: D5.

Sandoz, Joli. "Coming Home." *Whatever It Takes: Women on Women's Sport*. Eds. Joli Sandoz and Joby Winans. New York: Farrar, Straus and Giroux, 1999.

Seabrook, John. "Tackling the Competition." *The Best American Sportswriting of 1998*. Ed. Bill Littlefield. New York: Houghton Mifflin, 1998.

Sebba, Anne. *Battling for News: The Rise of the Woman Reporter*. London: Hodder and Stoughton, 1994.

Sheets, Dr. Bob, and Jack Williams. *Hurricane Watch: Forecasting the Deadliest Storms on Earth*. New York: Knopf, 2001.

Siddle, Sheila, with Doug Cress. *In My Family Tree: A Life with Chimpanzees*. New York: Grove Press, 2002.

Skinner, B. F. *Walden Two*. Englewood Cliffs, NJ: Prentice Hall, 1976.

Smith, Liz. *Natural Blonde*. New York: Hyperion, 2000.

Spark, Muriel. *The Mandelbaum Gate*. New York: Knopf, 1965.

Stark, Steven D. *Glued to the Set: The 60 Television Shows and Events That Made Us Who We Are Today*. New York: Free Press, 1997.

Steinbeck, John. *The Red Pony*. New York: Bantam, 1955.

Stewart, Mary. *The Crystal Cave*. New York: Morrow, 1970.

———. *The Hollow Hills*. New York: Morrow, 1973.

Stoker, Bram. *Dracula*. New York: Dell, 1965.

Strauss, Bob. "So Is Hollywood's Most Notorious Bad Boy Really a Lovely Guy at Heart?" *Eonline* 3 Mar. 2002 <**http://www.eonline.com/Celebs/Qa/Penn**>.

Taub, Eric A. "Cell Yell: Thanks for (Not) Sharing." *New York Times*, 22 Nov. 2001: G1.

Telander, Rick. "Asphalt Legends." *The Best American Sports Writing of 1998*. Ed. Bill Littlefield. New York: Houghton Mifflin, 1998.

Tippette, Giles. *Donkey Baseball and Other Sporting Delights*. Dallas, TX: Taylor Publishing, 1989.

Tuchman, Barbara. *A Distant Mirror*. New York: Knopf, 1978.

Twain, Mark. *Pudd'nhead Wilson*. New York: Bantam, 1959.

Vecchlione, Joseph J., ed. *The New York Times Book of Sports Legends*. New York: Random House, 1991.

Wade, Nicholas. "In Tiny Cells, Glimpses of Body's Master Plan." *New York Times*, 18 Dec. 2001: F1.

Wade, Nicholas, ed. *The Science Times Book of Language and Linguistics*. New York: Lyons Press, 2000.

Walker, Alice. *In Search of Our Mothers' Gardens*. New York: Harcourt Brace Jovanovich, 1983.

Wallace, William N. "The First Super Bowl." *The New York Times Book of Sports Legends*. Ed. Joseph J. Vecchlione. New York: Random House, 1991.

Weinman, Sam. "Kwan Goes It Alone." *Journal News*, 8 Feb. 2002: K1.

White, T. H. *The Once and Future King*. New York: Ace Books, 1987.

Wilford, John Noble. "The Man and the Aircraft Were One." *New York Times*, 21 May 2002: F1.

Wolff, Tobias. *This Boy's Life: A Memoir*. New York: Harper and Row, 1989.

Zinser, Lynn. "Mount Everest Is the Highest, But Not the Only One to Climb." *New York Times*, 5 May 2002: SP11.

# Index

# Answer Key

• • • • • • • • • • •

The exercises in this book were designed to give students ample practice in writing, particularly sentences. As a result, many of the answers will be of the student's own composition and their acceptability will be up to the teacher.

## LESSON 1

■ Lindbergh is flying close to the ground because he can see farther through the haze.

| | Subject | Verb |
|---|---|---|
| 1. | *Estates* | *pass* |
| 2. | I | hold |
| 3. | I | can see |
| 4. | finger | is |
| 5. | it | must be |
| 6. | visibility | is improving |
| 7. | clouds | look |

■ Sentences will vary.

## LESSON 1a

■ When she was a child, Liz Smith, who loved Joan Crawford, saw all her movies.

| | Subject | Verb |
|---|---|---|
| 1. | entrance hall | opened |
| 2. | Crawford | came |
| 3. | she | was drawing |
| 4. | I | didn't know |
| 5. | the star | was |
| 6. | she and her white satin gown | were |
| 7. | I | loved |
| 8. | I | had |
| 9. | she | was |
| 10. | she | feared |
| 11. | they | wouldn't give |

■ Sentences will vary.

## LESSON 1b

■ An airport is depressing late at night because it is deserted.

| | Subject | Verb |
|---|---|---|
| 1. | I | sat |
| 2. | The long corridor | was deserted |
| 3. | The cleaning woman | had passed by |
| 4. | The effort | seemed |

■ Sentences will vary.

## LESSON 2

- An airport is depressing late at night because it is deserted.

| Subject | Verb |
|---|---|
| 1. light, strangeness | awaken |
| 2. any change | stimulates |
| 3. changing contours | help |
| 4. I | can fly |
| 5. I | can shift |
| 6. I | can create |
| 7. I | can check and recheck |

- Sentences will vary.

## LESSON 2a

- Jody had a good slingshot and a perfect stone, which hit the thrush.

| Subject | Verb or Verbs |
|---|---|
| 1. Jody | took, walked |
| 2. He | walked up |
| 3. Jody | had shot |
| 4. the thrush | started up and flew |

- Sentences will vary.

## LESSON 2b

- The rain makes the scene seem sad by making the peninsula part of the sea.

| Subject or Subjects | Verb |
|---|---|
| 1. the Andrea Gail | is |
| 2. food, bait | have been stowed away |
| fuel and water tanks | have been topped off |
| drums | have been lashed |
| gear | is |
| engine | is running |
| 3. Bobby | climbs and walks |
| 4. they | drive and trot |
| 5. Thea | hears and invites |
| 6. I | have got |
| 7. [you] | make |
| 8. rain | taps on |
| 9. Chris and Bobby | can't see |
| they | can smell |
| taste | permeates and lays |

- Sentences will vary.

## LESSON 3

- Because fog covers their tops, the icebergs are ghostlike.

| Subject | Verb | Connective | Subject | Verb |
|---|---|---|---|---|
| 1. icebergs | are | | | |
| 2. wisps | lengthen and increase | until | they | merge |
| 3. | I they | pass | | as leave |
| 4. I | fly | | channels | narrow |
| 5. all | is covered | | | |
| 6. it | doesn't hide | but | makes | |
| 7. top | slopes | if | any | are |
| 8. I | ease, take, turn | | | |

- Sentences will vary.

## LESSON 3a

- Gandhi saw people as individuals, which led them to regard him as a father.

| Subject/Verb | Conjunction | Subject/Verb |
|---|---|---|
| 1. Mahatma Gandhi loved | and | he hoped |
| 2. he belonged | and | they knew |
| | and | they belonged |
| 3. he dispelled | | |
| 4. his loyalty begot | | |
| 5. he prepared | | |
| 6. India called | | |

- Sentences will vary.

## LESSON 3b

- Although the storm destroyed houses, the people were not seriously injured.

| Clause | Dependent/Independent |
|---|---|
| 1. after the windows first broke | dependent |
| 2. as dawn breaks | dependent |
| 3. the Ochmanskis find a haven | ent |
| 4. who is a registered nurse | dependent |
| 5. none of the family is severely injured | independent |
| 6. as the  rain ends | dependent |
| 7. it turns out | independent |
| 8. the object that has destroyed the front | dependent |
| 9. it had sailed | independent |

- Sentences will vary.

## LESSON 4

- Flying is even more common today than Lindbergh predicted.

| **Clause 1** | **Clause 2** |
|---|---|
| 1. What limitless possibilities aviation holds between | Planes can fly nonstop New York and Paris. |
| 2. The year will surely come | Passengers and mail fly every day from America to Europe. |
| 3. Flying will cost much more | Letters can be written. |
| 4. There will be people | they can afford |
| 5. The safety of operation should be high | |
| 6. Weather will be the greatest problem | |
| 7. We would have to find. | |

- Sentences will vary.

## LESSON 4a

- The fly was drowning in the ink, but it recovered when it was lifted out.

1. A fly had fallen into his broad inkpot, and it was trying feebly but desperately to clamber out again.
2. Over and under went a leg along a wing. The stone goes over and under the scythe.
3. There was a pause. The fly tried to expand first one wing and then the other.
4. One could imagine. The little front legs rubbed against each other.

- Sentences will vary.

## LESSON 4b

- Gibson wanted to continue pitching.

1. The Tigers by this time were trailing the National League Champion St. Louis Cardinals by a score of 4-0.
2. Tim McCarver had straightened up to throw the ball back to his pitcher.
3. Only Gibson had not seen it until that moment.

- Sentences will vary.

## LESSON 5

- Lindbergh was startled awake, so the plane did not crash.

| | **Present Participle** | **Past Participle** | **Infinitive** |
|---|---|---|---|
| 1. | is climbing | | |
| 4. | | | to lift, to stop |
| 5. | | has startled | |
| 6. | | have broken | |
| 7. | were recuperating | | |
| 8. | are suffering | has passed | |
| 9. | | | to use |

- Sentences will vary.

## LESSON 5a

▪ Chee's people believed wealth was a symbol for selfishness.

| | Infinitive | Present Participle | Past Participle |
|---|---|---|---|
| 1. | | was being | |
| 2. | | | had been thinking |
| 3. | to stop | | |
| 4. | | | would have taught |
| 5. | | | had formed |
| 6. | | | had caused |
| 7. | | was getting | |

▪ Sentences will vary.

## LESSON 5b

▪ Our knowledge of the Battle of Hastings is one-sided because there are no records from the English.

| | Past Participle | Present Participle | Infinitive |
|---|---|---|---|
| 1. | has been fought, have had | | |
| 2. | | were not writing | |
| 3. | | were telling | |
| 4. | | | to leave |

▪ Sentences will vary.

## LESSON 6

▪ The High Lama has chosen a successor who is young but wise.

| | Present Perfect Tense | Simple Past Tense |
|---|---|---|
| 1. | has been | was |
| 2. | have waited | waited |
| 3. | have sat | sat |
| 4. | have looked | looked |
| 5. | have grown | grew |

▪ Sentences will vary.

## LESSON 6a

▪ A pilot needs physical strength in a storm.

| | Subject | Compound Verb |
|---|---|---|
| 1. | the helicopter | has been blown |
| 2. | he | has run |
| 3. | flying | has become |
| 4. | the line | has been destroyed |

▪ Sentences will vary.

## LESSON 6b

- Because the expansion of the universe may be speeding up, galaxies will be moving apart quickly

| Helping Verb | Adverb | Verb |
|---|---|---|
| 1. have | always | been braced |
| 2. have | | debated |
| 3. have | | reported |

- Sentences will vary.

## LESSON 7

- The travelers found Shangri La's atmosphere invigorating.

| Auxiliary | Past Participle |
|---|---|
| 1. had | settled |
| 2. had | become |
| 3. had | learned |
| 4. had | discovered |

- Sentences will vary.

## LESSON 7a

- King Arthur held a feast at Pentecost at which the knights related their adventures.

| Compound Verb | Simple Past Tense |
|---|---|
| 1. had found | found |
| 2. had swapped off | swapped |
| 3. had brought | brought |
| 4. had yielded | yielded |
| 5. had got | got |

- Sentences will vary.

## LESSON 7b

- Fred's failures were not very severely dealt with because his family expected him to be Mr. Featherstone's heir.

| Verb | Adverb(s) |
|---|---|
| 1. had recovered | never quite yet |
| 2. had made | |
| 3. had been | |
| 4. had sworn | |
| 5. had regarded | not secretly |
| 6. had enraged | |

- Sentences will vary.

## LESSON 8

- The two men must cross the precipice if they want to reach the guides for their journey.

| Auxiliary | Verb |
|---|---|
| 1. was | chattering |
| 2. was | preparing |
| 3. are | doing |

- Sentences will vary.

## LESSON 8a

- The birds were flying as fast as bullets.

| Verb | Sentence |
|---|---|
| was darkening | The sky darkened in the evening |
| was going | The class went on a field trip. |
| was moving | My family moved to a new house. |
| was pouring | The rain poured all night. |

- Sentences will vary.

## LESSON 8b

- Since there was a telescreen in every room, all of a person's movements were watched.

| Verb | Sentence |
|---|---|
| 1. were striking | The clock strikes the hour. |
| 2. were whirling | Dancers whirl across the stage. |
| 3. was shining | The trophy shines on the shelf. |
| 4. is watching | Big Brother watches you. |
| 5. was babbling | The brook babbles as it flows past. |

- Sentences will vary.

## LESSON 9

- Conway is terrified at the thought that the mountain might topple into the valley.

| Modal Auxiliary (if there is one) | Other Auxiliary | Verb |
|---|---|---|
| might | have | been |
| might | | be |
| would | | split |
| might | | be |
| could | have | been |

- Sentences will vary.

## LESSON 9a

- Umpires are very attached to their whisk brushes since the right kind is hard to find.

| Helper | Verb |
|---|---|
| 1. must | have |
| 2. will | fit |
| 3. can't | find |
| 4. might | go |
| 5. should | be |
| 6. must | have used |
| 7. would | be scratching |
| 8. would | suggest |

- Sentences will vary.

## LESSON 9b

- Inner freedom is retaining human dignity even in a concentration camp.

1. To do well in school one must study.
2. We may decide to go to the ball game.
3. Matt will take us in his car.
4. Should we pack a picnic lunch?

- Sentences will vary.

## LESSON 10

- When the Dark Age ends, the new world will seek the lost treasures.

| Auxiliary | Verb |
|---|---|
| 1. will | cover |
| 2. will | be |
| 3. will | pass |
| 4. will | live |
| 5. will | conserve |
| 6. will | welcome |
| 7. will | succeed |
| 8. will | be |

- Sentences will vary.

## LESSON 10a

- A knight must learn about chivalry so he will behave properly.

1. will have
2. will turn up
3. will get
4. will sit
5. will pour

- Sentences will vary.

## LESSON 10b

▪ Though we don't have to like people to tolerate them, we can live peacefully only with tolerance.

| Subject | Verb |
|---|---|
| 1. you | will strain |
| 2. it | will need |
| 3. I | will clean up |
| 4. tolerance | will be |

▪ Sentences will vary.

## LESSON 11

▪ While passion can cause an ache, his love for Lo-Tsen was soothing.

1. Alana does not swim on Tuesdays.
2. Students do not like to take exams.
3. We did not lose the map of the campus.
4. Mike does not travel during the summer.
5. Some flowers do not bloom in the fall.

▪ Sentences will vary.

## LESSON 11a

▪ When the King had mistresses of low rank, the Queen did not mind.

| Auxiliary | Negative | Verb |
|---|---|---|
| 1. did | not | meet |
| 2. did | not | make |
| 3. does | not | seem |

▪ Sentences will vary.

## LESSON 11b

▪ A producer might want to fire someone to show that he is the boss.

| Verb | Function |
|---|---|
| 1. I do | simple verb |
| 2. I don't go | negative |
| 3. do my crews think | question |
| 4. do they know | question |
| 5. who does not fire | negative |
| 6. they are doing | simple verb |
| 7. people don't need | negative |

▪ Sentences will vary.

## LESSON 12

■ We do not have a written record of the beginnings of the sea.

1. Beginnings
2. explanations
3. accounts
4. sources
5. chapters
6. details
7. rocks
8. hints

■ Sentences will vary.

## LESSON 12a

■ Binetou is treated respectfully in the night club.

1. Shoe/shoes
2. waiter/waiters
3. couple/couples
4. drum/drums
5. dancer/dancers
6. light/lights
7. arm/arms

■ Sentences will vary.

## LESSON 12b

■ Although Gandhi ate very lightly, his meals filled him with energy.

| Sentence | Plural Word |
|---|---|
| 1. It took me a month to finish chapter 10 | months |
| 2. The train was late again. | trains |
| 3. On Thursday we have assembly | assemblies |
| 4. Monday is the day for swimming. | days |
| 5. We followed the track of the bear. | Tracks |

■ Sentences will vary.

## LESSON 13

■ While it was once thought that cold seas were more productive, many tropical waters have an abundance of life.

1. It proceeds
2. it exists
3. richness makes
4. abundance rivals
5. upwelling provides
6. life is
7. it has
8. productivity is
9. this is
10. it is

■ Sentences will vary.

## LESSON 13a

■ Raffles avoids violence, so carries out his burglaries unarmed.

1. Idea arises          students arise
2. he avoids            athletes avoid
3. he prefers           many persons prefer
4. he regards           the teachers regard
5. he is                we are

■ Sentences will vary.

## LESSON 13b

■ Jeff Mathy hopes to climb the highest mountain on each continent.

1. hunkers              the climbers hunker
2. resides              freshmen reside
3. keeps                librarians keep books
4. knows                wise people know
5. is                   many are
6. has                  few have

■ Sentences will vary.

## LESSON 14

■ The weather in the tenth century was favorable for Viking voyages.

1. Petterson's mind      3. world's most recent period
2. its effect            4. Erik's Island

■ Sentences will vary.

## LESSON 14a

■ The idea of naming storms came from a novel published in 1941.

1. women's               3. men's
2. girls'                4. women's

■ Sentences will vary.

## LESSON 14b

■ Jody's breath is cut short because he wanted a pony so much.

1. Jody's [noun]         4. pony's [noun]
2. its [pronoun]         5. airedale's [noun]
3. his [pronoun]         6. mine [pronoun]

■ Sentences will vary.

## LESSON 15

■ While waves are surface movements, tides are felt in the deepest part of the ocean.

1. abyss                 3. mysterious
2. enormous              4. as

■ Sentences will vary.

## LESSON 15a

- Because the land in Morocco is dry and unproductive, farming requires enormous work.

| Plural | Present Tense | Verb | Possessive | Spelling |
|---|---|---|---|---|
| 1. areas | is | | one's | treeless |
| 2. lines | pulls | | | nevertheless |
| 3. Ls | stirs | | | across |
| 4. hands | | | thus | |
| 5. weeds | | | | |
| 6. inches | | | | |
| 7. fields | | | | |

- Sentences will vary.

## LESSON 15b

- Alice drinks the liquid because she believes it will make something interesting happen.

| Plural | Present Tense | Verb | Possessive | Spelling |
|---|---|---|---|---|
| 1. pairs | does | | its | looking-glass |
| 2. kid-gloves | | is | Alice's | nevertheless |
| 3. lips | | | this | |
| 4. gloves | as | | | |
| 5. words | | | | |
| 6. words | | | | |

- Sentences will vary.

## LESSON 16

- The narrator thinks the Count is a horror.

| Past Tense | Present Tense |
|---|---|
| 1. stopped | stop |
| 2. looked | look |
| 3. seemed | secm |
| 4. seized | seize |
| 5. had | have |
| 6. did | do |

- Sentences will vary.

## LESSON 16a

- Plants and animals were gigantic, but the landscape was monotonous.

| Past Tense | Present Tense |
|---|---|
| 1. seemed | Harry seems very happy today. |
| 2. hovered | Sentences |
| 3. stretched | will |
| 4. hindered | vary |
| 5. stalked | |
| 6. towered | |

- Sentences will vary.

## LESSON 16b

- As Wilson examined Luigi's palm, he identified characteristics of Luigi's personality.

| | |
|---|---|
| 1. began | 7. entered |
| 2. enmeshed | 8. felt |
| 3. noted | 9. examined |
| 4. was | 10. entered |
| 5. bent | 11. mapped |
| 6. made | 12. declared |

- Sentences will vary.

## LESSON 17

- Children who have been missing were found with wounds in their throats.

| Auxiliaries | Past Participles |
|---|---|
| 1. have | occurred |
| 2. had | been |
| 3. have | been found |
| 4. have | been missed |
| 5. had | asked |
| 6. had | picked |

- Sentences will vary.

## LESSON 17a

- Lindbergh reached Paris more than 33 hours after he took off from Roosevelt Field.

1. had offered
2. had flown
3. had failed
4. had taken off

- Sentences will vary.

## LESSON 17b

- Thorney Island was considered a holy place because St. Peter was said to have appeared there.

| Auxiliaries | Past Participles |
|---|---|
| 1. had | been |
| 2. have | appeared |
| 3. had | chosen |
| 4. had | planned |
| 5. had | supervised |

- Sentences will vary.

## LESSON 18

- To do away with a vampire drive a stake through its heart.

| Past Participle/Adjective | Noun |
|---|---|
| 1. pointed | teeth |
| 2. opened | red lips |
| 3. pierced | heart |

- Sentences will vary.

## LESSON 18a

- People were satisfied with life until the *Titanic* shocked them out of it.

| Verb | Sentence |
|---|---|
| 1. had found | Maria finds biology fascinating. |
| 2. had been | Sentences |
| 3. had improved | will |
| 4. has followed | vary |

- Sentences will vary.

## LESSON 18b

- Eleanor has her face half-turned so that her beautiful profile can be seen.

| Past Participle | Noun | Verb |
|---|---|---|
| 1. hidden | | were |
| 2. gilded | coronet | gleamed |
| 3. wrinkled | | was |
| 4. unblemished | | were |
| 5. worked | | was |
| 6. chanted | | were |

- Sentences will vary.

## LESSON 19

- When Mina woke from her trance, she could not remember what she had said.

| | |
|---|---|
| 1. cold | 4. wind |
| 2. end | 5. languid |
| 3. and | 6. mind |

- Sentences will vary.

## LESSON 19a

- She emphasizes it because her mother is equal to her father and her work is as valuable.

| Sentence | Verb |
|---|---|
| 1. Myrna seems happy with her grade. | seems |
| 2. | battle |
| 3. | labor |
| 4. | begin |
| 5. | feed |
| 6. | muzzle |
| 7. | mutilate |
| 8. | inherit |

- Five sentences above and concluding sentence will vary.

## LESSON 19b

- Eleanor could read and write, and could speak several languages, which made her accomplished.

1. curved
2. dissected
3. old
4. and

- Sentences will vary.

## LESSON 20

- The animals are trying to defeat the humans by creating an ambush.

| Present Participle | Auxiliary | Subject |
|---|---|---|
| 1. dealing | were | men |
| 2. hiding | were | geese |
| 3. lying | were | who [horses etc.] |

- Sentences will vary.

## LESSON 20a

- The movie has a scene in the rain, so movie makers use machinery to produce fake rain.

| Verb | Sentence |
|---|---|
| 1. was pouring | Water was pouring from the leaky pipe. |
| 2. was dragging | |
| 3. was calling out | |
| 4. was talking | |
| 5. was watching | |

- Sentences above and in conclusion will vary.

## LESSON 20b

- The Age of Flowers changed the nature of animal life by providing food for new species.

| **Singular Subjects** | **Plural Subjects** |
|---|---|
| 1. grass was beginning | insects were arising |
| 2. explosion was having | grasslands were spreading |

- Sentences will vary.

## LESSON 21

- Clover was terrified to see a pig walking on his hind legs.

  1. the neighing
  2. a shrill crowing
  3. a tremendous baying

- Sentences will vary.

## LESSON 21a

- Some people ate their ration immediately to satisfy the worst hunger pangs and to safeguard against theft or loss.

  1. [the] dealing
  2. [the] satisfying
  3. [the] dividing
  4. the longing
  5. [the] eating
  6. [the] safeguarding
  7. the awakening
  8. the snapping

- Sentences will vary.

## LESSON 21b

- The director finds endings difficult because summing up seems to him elusive and false.

  1. [artistic] training
  2. beginnings
  3. summing
  4. endings
  5. opening

- Sentences will vary.

## LESSON 22

- The animals were upset because they were proud of being able to build the windmill.

| **Present Participle** | **Noun** |
|---|---|
| 1. admiring | animals |
| 2. marvelling | animals |
| 3. imposing | anything |
| 4. raging | winds |
| 5. squawking | hens |
| 6. despairing | cry |

- Sentences will vary.

## LESSON 22a

- Although the front of the hotel is grand and imposing, the kitchen is an inferno.

| Present Participle | Noun |
|---|---|
| 1. winding | staircase |
| 2. humming | noise |
| 3. shuddering | draught |
| 4. stifling | inferno |

- Sentences will vary.

## LESSON 22b

- Venus Williams finds studying more important than practicing her tennis game.

| Present Participle | Noun |
|---|---|
| 1. ranking | points |
| 2. traveling | circus |
| 3. cheering | crowds |
| 4. mooing | cows |

- Sentences will vary.

## LESSON 23

- The hens were angry because Squealer planned to take their eggs away.

1. nothing
2. morning
3. spring

- Sentences will vary.

## LESSON 23a

- The morning was quiet, but Arthur's coming shattered the stillness.

1. a quiet dawn/morning
2. the morning/daybreak rise
3. no ring/circle
4. I heard something/a disturbance
5. thinking nothing/no creature

- Sentences will vary.

## LESSON 23b

- The chimpanzees wanted to explore outside the wall.

1. morning
2. nothing
3. something
4. swing

- Sentences will vary.

## LESSON 24

- After the *Titanic* sank, people felt calm because the suspense was gone.

| Noun | Original Word |
|------|---------------|
| 1. suspense | suspend |
| 2. confusion | confuse |
| 3. excitement | excite |
| 4. realization | realize |
| 5. loneliness | lonely |
| 6. security | secure |

- Sentences will vary.

## LESSON 24a

- A Supreme Court decision led to the end of Alabama's bus segregation laws.

| Noun | Verb or Adjective/Suffix |
|------|--------------------------|
| 1. movement | move-ment |
| 2. activism | active-ism |
| 3. rider | ride-er |
| 4. segregation | segregate-ion |

- Sentences will vary.

## LESSON 24b

- New Englanders root for the Red Sox even though the team is seldom in first place.

| Noun | Verb, Adjective, or Noun |
|------|--------------------------|
| 1. neutral-ity | neutral, adjective |
| 2. vacat-ion | vacate, verb |
| 3. precis-ion | precise, adjective |
| 4. announc-er | announce, verb |
| 5. serious-ness | serious, adjective |
| 6. develop-ment | develop, verb |

- Sentences will vary.

## LESSON 25

- A group made up of many different kinds of people is marching to Baton Rouge.

| Performer | Verb |
|-----------|------|
| 1. reporter | reports |
| 2. teacher | teaches |
| 3. marcher | marches |
| 4. counter-demonstrator | demonstrates |

- Sentences will vary.

## LESSON 25a

■ Lydgate hoped to make his mark in the world by innovative treatment.

| Noun | Sentence |
|---|---|
| 1. discoverer | Did you discover the date the paper is due? |
| 2. originator | |
| 3. practitioner | |
| 4. observer | |
| 5. theorizer | |
| 6. adventurer | |
| 7. sailor | |

■ Sentences will vary.

## LESSON 25b

■ Cook might have discovered Fiji, but lost the opportunity.

| Noun | Verb |
|---|---|
| 1. a sailor | sails |
| 2. a commander | commands |
| 3. a gunner | guns [shoots a gun] |
| 4. a gardener | gardens |
| 5. a discoverer | discovers |
| 6. an islander | lives on an island |

■ Sentences will vary.

## LESSON 26

■ Everyone in the boats tried to help the others, although all were cold.

| Adjective | Sentence |
|---|---|
| 1. comfortable | The socks were a comfort to Mrs. Dodge. |
| 2. perfectly | Did the inventor perfect his machine? |
| 3. elderly | The tribe's elder was a wise woman. |
| 4. hopeless | In spite of everything, they had hope. |

■ Sentences will vary.

## LESSON 26a

■ While stem cells have not been studied much, they hold medical promise.

| Nouns and Verbs | Adjectives |
|---|---|
| 1. seam | seamless |
| 2. nation | national |
| 3. degenerate | degenerative |
| 4. embryo | embryonic |
| 5. medicine | medical |
| 6. generate | generative |

■ Sentences will vary.

## LESSON 26b

▪ Webster was not easy to like because he was severe and humorless.

| Adjective | Noun or Verb | Adverb |
|---|---|---|
| 1. humorless | humor | humorlessly |
| 2. religious | religion | religiously |
| 3. passionate | passion | passionately |
| 4. tireless | tire | tirelessly |
| 5. endless | end | endlessly |
| 6. sanitized | sanitize | |

▪ Sentences will vary.

## LESSON 27

▪ People were troubled by the sinking of the *Titanic* because there was an element of fate in what happened.

| Positive | Comparative | Superlative |
|---|---|---|
| 1. great | greater | greatest |
| 2. soon | sooner | soonest |
| 3. late | later | latest |
| 4. high | higher | highest |

▪ Sentences will vary.

## LESSON 27a

▪ Although spring in Paris is beautiful, the poor are kept out of sight.

| Adjective | Comparative | Superlative |
|---|---|---|
| 1. clear | clearer | clearest |
| 2. fine | finer | finest |
| 3. pretty | prettier | prettiest |
| 4. petulant | more petulant | most petulant |
| 5. immense | more immense | most immense |
| 6. agreeable | more agreeable | most agreeable |

▪ Sentences will vary.

## LESSON 27b

▪ Finding the Hawaiian islands was the greatest discovery because they would become important in many ways.

| Adjective | Comparative | Superlative |
|---|---|---|
| 1. fine | finer | finest |
| 2. rich | richer | richest |
| 3. high | higher | highest |
| 4. favorable | more favorable | most favorable |

▪ Sentences will vary.

# LESSON 28

▪ Because Levi is my younger brother, I reassured him.

| Phrase | Where or When |
|---|---|
| 1. in the darkness | where |
| 2. for a few minutes | when |
| 3. into my jacket | where |
| 4. from now on | when |
| 5. out of the smokehouse | where |
| 6. between myself and my fear | where |
| 7. for all the times | when |
| 8. to me | where |

▪ Sentences will vary.

# LESSON 28a

▪ Because Milla liked The Babies, she let them tease her.
▪ The Babies were in the cage, next to Milla. She liked to lie on the ledge and let her arm or leg stick through the bars. She really enjoyed being with The Babies.

▪ Sentences will vary.

# LESSON 28b

▪ When reporters interview players after the game, they get the best story in the club-house.

| 1. The Yankee clubhouse was suddenly crowded | on the night |
|---|---|
| 2. The clubhouse was a much quieter place | after the first night |
| 3. The Yankees announced that the clubhouse would be closed | on Friday night |
| 4. The closing would be | for forty-five minutes |
| 5. It would happen | after the game. |

▪ Sentences will vary.

# LESSON 29

▪ Someone who fell asleep hearing a lot of noise would be awakened by silence.

| 1. How is the narrator wakened? | by the silence |
|---|---|
| 2. By what are the sounds muffled? | by the tangled pile of trees |
| 3. What is the crash? | of firearms |
| 4. What is the savage shouting and swearing? | of men |
| 5. How do the men shout? | in anger and pain |
| 6. How does the writer gauge time? | without a pocket watch |

▪ Sentences will vary.

## LESSON 29a

■ Although some people try to apply Latin rules to English, English is an entirely different language.

1. Why English is confusing     for the one very simple reason
2. To whom was air travel not available?     to the Romans
3. On what did early authorities base English rules?     on Latin
4. What Latin grammar was used as     as their model
5. How some English grammars are written     in that language

■ Sentences will vary.

## LESSON 29b

■ The development of urban culture helps bridge the sensibility gap between black and white audiences.

1. When?     in the postwar years
2. How?     by the comedians
3. What?     of life
4. Where?     between black and white comedy

■ Sentences will vary.

## LESSON 30

■ The passage is sad because it tells of a day full of bad news.

1. The tower of the meetinghouse     the meetinghouse's tower
2. the outskirts of town     the town's outskirts
3. ending of a day     a day's ending
4. bodies of Redcoats     Redcoats' bodies
5. bodies of Committeemen     Committeemen's bodies

■ Sentences will vary.

## LESSON 30a

■ The narrator thinks he sees a headless corpse, but he really sees a face.

1. the ship's side     4. man's body
2. sea's shimmer     5. ladder's rung
3. light's flash     6. lightning's play

■ Sentences will vary.

## LESSON 30b

■ The washing hung on the walls is a sign of civilization because it betokens a settlement and a society.

1. the stronghold of the Crusaders
2. foundations of earlier ruins
3. shelter of the ruined fortresses
4. establishment of Israel
5. eyes of the seekers
6. communities of the wilderness

■ Sentences will vary.

## LESSON 31

- Because a horseman has arrived, the village is excited.

1. make out
2. came in
3. pulled up
4. took off (or dashed out)

- Sentences will vary.

## LESSON 31a

- Georges Bank is more dangerous than the Grand Banks because of currents and the tide.

1. go down
2. woke up
3. run off
4. ride out
5. put out
6. feed on

- Sentences will vary.

## LESSON 31b

- A football player must use his body as if his only purpose is to win.

| Two-Word Verb | Direct Object or Prepositional Phrase |
|---|---|
| 1. look at | us (direct object) |
| 2. pick up | neither |
| 3. get out | of the way (phrase) |
| 4. come out | a star (direct object) |
| 5. lay down | the rules (direct object) |

- Sentences will vary

## LESSON 32

- The people are planning a roadblock to stop the British.

| | |
|---|---|
| 1. the Menotomy Road | Our town has a Menotomy Road |
| 2. a great tangle | The tangle of wires was hard to unwind. |
| 3. the place | The seashore is a restful place. |
| 4. the plan | We have a plan for the holiday. |
| 5. the time | The weekend is a good time for study. |
| 6. the neighborhood | The Hill is a neighborhood in our city. |

- Sentences above and concluding sentences will vary.

## LESSON 32a

- Because people use different words and expressions in different places, your speech can tell others where you are from.

| Noun | Definite Article | Indefinite Article |
|---|---|---|
| 1. sandwich | the sandwich | a sandwich |
| 2. toy | the toy | a toy |
| 3. drink | the drink | a drink |
| 4. stone | the stone | a stone |
| 5. object | the object | an object |
| 6. pail | the pail | a pail |

- Sentences will vary.

## LESSON 32b

- There are so many sports events on television that people can spend the entire day watching them.

| Particular Kind | One of a Group | No Article |
|---|---|---|
| 1. the viewing | a menu | viewers |
| 2. the women's final | a crescendo | screens |
| 3. the Belmont Stakes | a professor | remotes |

- Sentences will vary.

## LESSON 33

- Skinner believes that individuals have little chance of changing society because society has the advantage of numbers and age.

| Subject/Verb | Conjunction | Subject/Verb |
|---|---|---|
| 1. that is our original sin | and | it can't be helped |
| 2. it's a powerful opponent | and | it always wins |
| 3. society wins in the long run | for | it has the advantage |
| 4. it enslaves one | before | he has tasted |

- Sentences will vary.

## LESSON 33a

- Kwan is held to a high standard, but has been inconsistent.

| Clause | Conjunction, if Any |
|---|---|
| 1. Kwan didn't win | single sentence |
| 2. Kwan couldn't lose | single sentence |
| 3. she is held to a different standard | single sentence |
| 4. she will have the advantage | single sentence |
| 5. the crowd can only do so much | single sentence |
| 6. Kwan has been painfully inconsistent | single sentence |
| 7. she still hasn't mastered | and it's unlikely she will |

- Sentences will vary.

## LESSON 33b

- Because freedom affects the body as well as the mind, former prisoners ate ravenously.
- Because the body has fewer inhibitions than the mind, it made good use of the new freedom.
- As I walked through the country, larks rose to the sky.
- There was no one to be seen for miles around, so I could hear their joyous song.
- Sentences above and concluding sentence will vary.

## LESSON 34

■ We know the writer really wants to stop smoking because he says his interest had weakened.

| Subordinate Clause | Independent Clause |
|---|---|
| 1. Though I remembered him as a heavy pipe smoker | he did not smoke now |
| 2. because I had felt conspicuous | I did not smoke |
| 3. though not the slightest objection was made | I left the pack in my pocket |
| 4. that my interest had weakened | I found |
| 5. that I was still on the pack | It was surprising |
| 6. whether I might not be able to give it up | I asked myself |

■ Answers above and in concluding sentence will vary.

## LESSON 34a

■ Children were in playgrounds, but all of them were girls.

| | |
|---|---|
| 1. We went in to eat | Many eyes were upon us |
| 2. We rolled through villages | The parklike beauty was no exception |
| 3. We caught glimpses of children | They were in schools or playgrounds |

■ Answers above and in concluding sentence will vary.

## LESSON 34b

■ Terms for snow and for whaling are used only at certain times in the Eskimo language.

| Conjunction | Subject | Verb |
|---|---|---|
| 1. when | they | are |
| 2. though | they | speak |
| 3. that | [fluency] | confuses |
| 4. that | language | comes |
| 5. while | those | come |

■ Sentences will vary.

## LESSON 35

■ Workers are dissatisfied with their jobs because labor leaders want them to oppose management.

| Independent Clause | Relative Pronoun | Dependent Clause |
|---|---|---|
| 1. we need a quiet room | in which | we can study our chemistry |
| 2. we spoke to our friends | who | had taken the course |
| 3. anyone can see | that | it looks like rain |
| 4. we found the book | which | had been lost |

■ Above sentences and concluding sentence will vary.

## LESSON 35a

- Madonna is like Evita Peron in her driving ambition and her craving for the adoration of the masses.

| Dependent Clause | Noun |
|---|---|
| 1. who designed tanks | technician |
| 2. who grew up | daughter |
| 3. who became | Juan Peron |
| 4. who died | stars |
| 5. who enjoyed | daughter |

- Sentences will vary.

## LESSON 35b

- Because the game's origins were in a hazing ritual, we know that football is about pain.

| Relative Pronoun | Clause |
|---|---|
| 1. which | the third question which was very complicated |
| 2. that | the picture that won the prize was a portrait |
| 3. which | a story which told the history of a game |
| 4. that | the sweater that matched my shirt |
| 5. which | a book which I enjoyed |

- Answers above and in concluding sentence will vary.

## LESSON 36

- People at Walden Two choose their own work, so managers have no power.

| Transition | Function |
|---|---|
| 1. certainly | result |
| 2. on the contrary | contrast |
| 3. in the end | result |
| 4. temporarily | time |
| 5. instead | contrast |

- Sentences will vary.

## LESSON 36a

- Even though producers intimidate writers, writers can do business with them.

| Transition | Function |
|---|---|
| 1 in fact | emphasis |
| 2. however | contrast |
| 3. perhaps | add facts |
| 4. right off | time |
| 5. in general | add facts |

- Sentences will vary.

## LESSON 36b

- If fishermen didn't have a place to stay near the sea, they wouldn't be available when boats were ready to sail.
- Finally, the day of the big game arrived.
- Of course, I studied for the Biology test.
- Eventually, we caught up with the fast walkers.
- Conceivably, I can get an A in English.

- Sentences above and the concluding sentence will vary.

## LESSON 37

- Children are bewildered when adults do not explain things to them.

| Verb or Noun | Sentence |
|---|---|
| 1. trip [verb] | Our trip [noun] to the beach will be Saturday. |
| 2. talk [verb] | The senior gave a talk [noun] to the freshman class. |
| 3. lack [noun] | The club lacks [verb] a leader. |
| 4. orders [noun] | The captain orders [verb] the players to practice. |
| 5. answer [verb] | Our answer [noun] was, "Not today." |
| 6. cut [verb] | The boy has a cut [noun] on his knee. |

- Above sentences and concluding sentences will vary.

## LESSON 37a

- The writer believes the super-fans spend too much of their energy and imagination on their favorite teams.

| 1. air [noun] | We air [verb] the winter clothes when they come out of storage. |
|---|---|
| 2. time [noun] | It is important to time [verb] the cake as it bakes. |
| 3. hope [noun] | We hope [verb] tomorrow will be sunny. |
| 4. roll [noun] | The train rolls [verb] into the station. |
| 5. cheer [verb] | The audience gave a cheer [noun] for the speaker. |
| 6. police [noun] | Officers police [verb] the neighborhood. |
| 7. watch [verb] | My old watch [noun] needs a battery. |

- Above sentences and concluding sentences will vary.

## LESSON 37b

- The village displayed Buzie culture by the people's wearing silver jewelry.

| Column 1—Nouns | Column 2—Verbs |
|---|---|
| 1. Shade | sleep |
| 2. Ring | find |
| 3. air | match |
| 4. place | touch |
| 5. culture | saw |

- Sentences will vary.

## LESSON 38

- The Breedlove home was unpleasant because of the left-over, dusty Christmas tree.

| Column 1 | Column 2 |
|---|---|
| 1. bed for sleeping | flower bed |
| 2. room, enclosed space | enough space for activity |
| 3. tree, a woody plant | a chart of family relationships |
| 4. trunk, elephant's appendage | a container, luggage |
| 5. chair, a seat | head of a committee |
| 6. eye, organ of sight | center of a storm |

- Sentences will vary.

## LESSON 38a

- His reading earned the pupil a kiss, which he gladly returned.

| Word | First Meaning | Second Meaning |
|---|---|---|
| 1. table | a piece of furniture | an arrangement of data |
| 2. book | literary or scientific work | purchase tickets |
| 3. page | part of a book | young assistant |
| 4. lock | a ringlet of hair | fastener |

- Sentences will vary.

## LESSON 38b

- Basketball is too strenuous a sport for the summer heat.

| Noun | Another Meaning |
|---|---|
| 1. game | animals taken in hunting |
| 2. sport | a genetic mutation |
| 3. feet | linear measurement |
| 4. court | a monarch's entourage |
| 5. legend | explanation of a map |

- Sentences will vary.

## LESSON 39

- Frieda and her sister can tell what adults mean by their tone and gestures, even when they do not understand the words.

| Column 1 | Column 2 |
|---|---|
| 1. their | there, they're |
| 2. meet | meat |
| 3. by | buy |
| 4. two | to, too |
| 5. heart | hart |
| 6. made | maid |
| 7. do | due, dew |
| 8. not | knot |
| 9. know | no |
| 10. night | knight |

- Sentences will vary.

## LESSON 39a

- The husband was often at war, so the lady took charge of the castle.

| Column 1 | Column 2 |
| --- | --- |
| 1. not | the knot was untied |
| 2. more | moor |
| 3. for | four, fore |
| 4. sun | son |
| 5. so | sew, sow |
| 6. pleas | please |

- Sentences will vary.

## LESSON 39b

- The woman is frightened by the noise of the rocking horse.

| Homophone 1 | Homophone 2 |
| --- | --- |
| 1. heart, an organ of the body | hart, male of the red deer |
| 2. know, to have knowledge | no, negative particle |
| 3. knew, had knowledge | new, not previously used |
| 4. pale, weak color | pail, receptacle |

- Sentences will vary.

## LESSON 40

- One who is out can go somewhere else, while one put outdoors has no place to go.

| Present Tense Participle | Past Tense Participle | Present | Past |
| --- | --- | --- | --- |
| 1. know | knew | knowing | known |
| 2. eat | ate | eating | eaten |
| 3. drink | drank | drinking | drunk |
| 4. do | did | doing | done |
| 5. put | put | putting | put |

- Sentences will vary.

## LESSON 40a

- Because Barbara is young and has little knowledge of love, she thinks she loves Francis.

1. The runner was leaping over the hurdles.
2. The class had just begun the exam.
3. Marsha and Roy went to the movies last night.
4. Have you done your homework yet?
5. Manya will have a party next weekend.

- Sentences will vary.

## LESSON 40b

- The writer means that a lady acted as men thought she should.

| Verb | Sentence |
|------|----------|
| 1. taught | Mr. Simpson teaches Biology. |
| 2. had | We have swimming classes on Saturday. |
| 3. was | Maria is the commencement speaker. |
| 4. found | I find it hard to concentrate when the TV is on. |
| 5. was doing | Ron is doing a project on national elections. |

- Sentences will vary.

## LESSON 41

- The author gives these details about black women to show how strong they were.

| Noun | Change |
|------|--------|
| 1. women | spelling |
| 2. children | ending |
| 3. men | spelling |

- Sentences will vary.

## LESSON 41a

- Farm wives have always worked hard, and today some do chores the same way they did centuries ago.

| Singular | Plural |
|----------|--------|
| 1. wife | wives |
| 2. woman | women |
| 3. sheep | sheep |
| 4. child | children |
| 5. goose | geese |

- Sentences will vary.

## LESSON 41b

- The wolves, who had eaten a lot during the summer, were not hungry and did not attack.

1. The wolf is often a menace in fairy tales.
2. Bambi is a baby deer.
3. Some people prefer a goose for the holiday dinner.
4. The captain was the last man to leave the ship.
5. The rain fell from the dark sky

- Sentences will vary.

## LESSON 42

- We know this dinner is not being prepared in a kitchen because the cook must make a grater from a pot lid.

| Subject | Verb |
|---|---|
| 1. pigs | are slaughtered |
| 2. Kat | sees |
| 3. we | want |
| 4. we | cannot find |
| 5. difficulty | is got over |
| 6. we | punch |
| 7. we | have |
| 8. fellows | put on |
| 9. Kat | takes charge |
| 10. I | fry |
| 11. pigs | are roasted |
| 12. we | stand round |

- Sentences will vary.

## LESSON 42a

- The narrator thinks he must shoot the elephant because so many people are watching him.

| Your Sentence | Excerpt Sentence |
|---|---|
| 1. I glanced at the clock that had struck. | I glanced at the crowd that had followed. |
| 2. I knew that they expected dessert. | I looked at the faces certain that the elephant was going to be shot. |
| 3. Lora was talking as she watched. | They were watching me as they would. |
| 4. They saw the boy but he did not wave. | They did not like me, but I was worth watching. |
| 5. I knew that it was time to go. | I realized that I should have to shoot. |

- Sentences above and concluding sentence will vary.

## LESSON 42b

- There are medical dramas on television because they take place in a controlled setting that's easy to film.

| Reason for Period | Abbreviation |
|---|---|
| 1. Professional Title | Dr. |
| 2. Academic Degree | M. D. |
| 3. Religious Title | St. |
| 4. Time of Day | P. M. |

- Sentences will vary.

## LESSON 43

- People who do not know the devastation of war greet the soldier as if he has been on a pleasure trip.

  1. How are things out there?  Things out there are fine.
  2. What is the spirit like out there?  The spirit out there is hopeful.
- Student questions and concluding sentence will vary.

## LESSON 43a

- John likes to be close to home and work because he doesn't like to waste time.

  1. A round trip would take twelve minutes.
  2. No one has an hour to burn.
  3. Sometimes a man wants to sneak home to do some thinking.
  4. That must not become a twenty-five minute investment of time.
  5. Someone makes Jell-O and puts it in the freezer to harden.
- Sentences will vary.

## LESSON 43b

- Mr. Latimer is nervous because he is going to propose to Jessie.

  | Question | Purpose |
  | --- | --- |
  | 1. How would you do what I have to do? | Rhetorical |
  | 2. How would you lead up to it? | Rhetorical |
  | 3. What words would you use? | Rhetorical |
  | 4. Couldn't we escape out of all this together? | Request |
- Sentences will vary.

## LESSON 44

- As the shelling begins, the soldiers run for cover.

  1. "Take cover" is a command for the soldiers to protect themselves.
  2. "Get out" is a command to the cowardly soldier to act more bravely.
- The above sentences and the concluding sentence will vary.

## LESSON 44a

- He accidentally saw the bike, but he didn't want to disappoint his mother.
- The writer wanted to indicate that the boy was thinking of different things to say on Christmas morning.
- The response sentences and the concluding sentence will vary.

## LESSON 44b

- A racetrack is exciting because the spectators never know which horse will win.

  | Word or Phrase | Sentence |
  | --- | --- |
  | 1. No, not the fiver on Daffodil! | No, you shouldn't put the fiver on Daffodil. |
  | 2. Good! Good! | That is a good idea. |
  | 3. Right you are! | You are right to do that. |
  | 4. He flayed his arms up and down | He called the name, *Lancelot*, excitedly, yelling "*Lancelot! Lancelot!*" |
- Sentences above and concluding sentence will vary.

## LESSON 45

- The soldiers are bitter because the surgeons have no compassion.

| Reason | Proper Noun or Adjective |
|---|---|
| 1. Name of a country or nationality | English |
| 2. Name of a medal for military service | War Service Cross |
| 3. Name of a person | Kat |
| 4. Name of a place | Flanders |

- Sentences will vary.

## LESSON 45a

- The *Daily News* was appealing because it was a picture newspaper.

| Capitalized Words | Reasons |
|---|---|
| 1. First World War | historic event |
| 2. Captain. . .Patterson | title |
| 3. Rainbow Division | proper name |
| 4. London | city |
| 5. Lord Northcliffe | proper name |
| 6. *Daily Mirror* | name of publication |
| 7. Americans | name of country |
| 8. June | month |
| 9. New York's Picture Newspaper | title of paper |
| 10. *Daily News* | name of paper |
| 11. Patterson | proper name |

- Sentences will vary.

## LESSON 45b

- The empire could not continue because individuals sought independence.

| Name | Category |
|---|---|
| 1. Germany | country |
| 2. Christianity | religion |
| 3. Franks | people |
| 4. Gauls | people |
| 5. Charlemagne | emperor |

- Sentences will vary.

## LESSON 46

- The author uses semicolons because the ideas in the clauses are so closely related.
- Sentences will vary.

## LESSON 46a

■ Everyone in this society held the land by grace of his superior.

1. After the serfs came the cottagers.
2. Villeins came after the cottagers.
3. Next in line were the thanes.
4. The earls were above the thanes.
5. Above all was the King.
6. The King held it all of God's grace.

■ The sentences above and the concluding sentence will vary.

## LESSON 46b

■ Grandmother remembered the old rituals, which gave her a reverence for the sun.

| Words | Connects or Separates |
|-------|----------------------|
| 1. Sun Dances | connects two clauses |
| 2. iron skillet | separates |
| 3. hands | separates |
| 4. praying | separates |

■ Sentences will vary.

## LESSON 47

■ The narrator puts despair first because he sees no hope for the future.

1. He has seen the death of other young men on the battlefield.
2. People unknowingly slay one another.
3. He is in despair because he sees no hope.
4. Soldiers kill obediently, without questioning the reason.
5. At twenty years old he knows only the darkest side of life.

■ The sentences above and the concluding sentence will vary.

## LESSON 47a

■ Although the family was poor, Mother always had a luxuriant garden.
   ■ she watered her flowers
   ■ she chopped up the grass
   ■ she laid out new beds
   ■ she might divide clumps
   ■ she might dig a cold pit
   ■ she might uproot and replant roses
   ■ she might prune branches

1. sunflowers
2. petunias
3. roses
4. dahlias
5. forsythia
6. spirea
7. delphiniums
8. verbena

■ Sentences will vary.

## LESSON 47b

- Food supplies ran out because the voyage was longer than anticipated.

1. stuffed peppers, asparagus, tomato and onion salad, and sliced kiwis.
2. chicken noodle soup, pizza, cole slaw, and frozen yogurt
3. meatloaf, mashed potatoes, string beans, and strawberry Jell-O
4. cheeseburger, fries, vanilla shake, and apple pie

- Sentences will vary.

## LESSON 48

- Wartime experiences that will not be forgotten mark the soldier.

1. though they might be ornamental enough in peace time
2. because that is the only thing
3. while we are still in the war
4. when we go up to the line

- Sentences will vary.

## LESSON 48a

- Madonna saved all the press clippings because she had no self confidence.

| Subordinate Clause | Sentences |
|---|---|
| 1. While publicly she feigned indifference | Publicly she feigned indifference<br>She was frequently hurt |
| 2. Although she had now achieved | She had now achieved the success<br>She struggled to cope with her new life |
| 3. Ever since Madonna had first | Madonna had appeared in a spread<br>She had saved every press clipping |
| 4. When a reporter made up a story | A reporter made up a negative story<br>She was hurt by such coverage |

- Sentences will vary.

## LESSON 48b

- The dogs were menacing, so the man looked for a way to escape.

1. When I woke, the alarm was ringing.
2. From where I lay, I could see the stars.
3. When I had reached the station, I bought a ticket.
4. If I had slept later, I'd have missed the train.
5. As it was, I just made it.

- Sentences above and concluding sentences will vary.

## LESSON 49

■ Katczinsky's friendship is important to his fellow soldiers because he is so resourceful.

| Word or Phrase | Purpose |
| --- | --- |
| 1. I believe | connecting phrase |
| 2. as Kropp and I are | adverb |
| 3. for example | connecting phrase |
| 4. a sorry hole | noun |

■ Sentences will vary.

## LESSON 49a

■ The color of the plains houses is worn away by the wind and the rain.

| Parenthetical Statement | Noun |
| --- | --- |
| 1. many ghosts | bones |
| 2. old keepers of the weather watch | houses |
| 3. feasting and talk | a lot of coming and going |
| 4. the endless wake | a funeral silence |

■ Sentences will vary.

## LESSON 49b

■ While racing crews come from many occupations, all of them must be young and athletic.

1. a yacht as appropriately named
2. an MIT graduate and a naval architect
3. a mechanical engineer
4. an advertising executive
5. who has something to do with tax forms
6. the skipper's son

■ Sentences will vary.

## LESSON 50

■ The narrator has driven the thermometer reading up to fool the sister.

| Possessive | Contraction |
| --- | --- |
| 1. sister's | don't |
| 2. Kat's | didn't |
| 3. | aren't |
| 4. | isn't |

■ Sentences will vary.

## LESSON 50a

■ The narrator pretended to be saved, but the lie made him sad.

| Contraction | Verb Phrase |
| --- | --- |
| 1. couldn't | could not |
| 2. hadn't | had not |
| 3. didn't | did not |

■ Sentences will vary.

## LESSON 50b

- Coaching raised questions for the writer about relationships among women, men and sports.

| Column 1 | Column 2 |
| --- | --- |
| 1. creed's | parents' |
| 2. female's | boyfriends' |
| 3. | women's |
| 4. | men's |

- Sentences will vary.

## LESSON 51

- Paul is alone on the battlefield as he tries to calm his fears.
- This LESSON and the next two require students to write their own paragraphs including properly punctuated quotations.

# Review Exercises Answers

The majority of the review exercises call for students to compose sentences of their own since the principal aim of the text is to increase student facility in recognizing and writing sentences. In these exercises, sentences are suggested, but those written by students will vary.

1. The following are typical of the various sentences that will appear:

   The police keep the city safe.

   Cellphone-related crashes occurred every day.

   The country banned smoking in restaurants.

   Safety-conscious drivers keep to the speed limit.

   Having a phone in a car can be convenient.

   It helps people get roadside assistance.

   Drivers should always drive carefully.

2. Who is plagued by low self-esteem   The student with poor grades is plagued by low self-esteem.

   Who worries about her weight   My friend, Ana, worries about her weight.

   Who has trouble with men   The Hollywood star has trouble with men.

   Who tries to find herself at the gym   An overweight woman tries to find herself at the gym.

3. The class entered the auditorium.

   Our team defeated the champions.

   The police captured the thief.

   Martin did an excellent presentation.

   The red pepper had spiced the bowl of chili.

   The archeologist scraped to find an ancient weapon.

4. Marijane loved going to the movies.

   My best friend was named student of the year.

   While studying, she didn't watch TV.

5. DC: who paid from five to twelve dollars for tickets.

   IndC: The customers paid from five to twelve dollars for tickets.

   DC: what went on during the game

   IndC: Fierce competition went on during the game.

   DC: when Starr's pretty passes made mere Indians out of the AFL Chiefs

   IndC: Starr's pretty passes made mere Indians out of the AFL Chiefs.

6.  The Crawfords had half an hour to pack.
    The last train left the city.
    They had crossed the Seine.
    Emily heard a terrific explosion.
    She saw that the railway bridge had been blown up.
    The railway bridge had been blown up.
    Other hazards were on the journey.
    Emily was to report.
    Another train ran into theirs killing eighteen passengers.
    She and her husband were spared.
    They had moved to the rear of the train.

7.  | Verb | Participle |
    | --- | --- |
    | were working | present |
    | had begun | past |
    | had done | past |
    | had filled | past |

8.  | Subject | Verb |
    | --- | --- |
    | Mona | could use |
    | the boy | could have been |
    | my mother | was wearing |
    | the day | would have been |

9.  that happened to be used by "the right people"
    who came to direct the political, economic, and literary affairs

10. | Helper | Verb | Form |
    | --- | --- | --- |
    | was | settling | present participle |
    | were | attacking | present participle |
    | were | pouring | present participle |
    | had | won | past participle |
    | would | be | present tense |

11. | Phrase | Sentence |
    | --- | --- |
    | through the door | The teacher walked through the door as the bell rang. |
    | to the table | We hurried to the table at dinner time. |
    | with figures and letters | The board was filled with figures and letters. |
    | from his chair | Joe could see the beach from his chair. |
    | with a cry | The baby dropped her toy with a cry. |
    | in front of him | The book was propped up in front of him. |

12. We saw and realized [ind] that they were there but we had no feelings about them [ind]

    The first spark of joy came [ind] when we saw a rooster with a tail of multicolored feathers [dep].

<u>When</u> we all met again in our hut [dep], one said secretly to the other [ind]. And the other replied [ind] as he did not know [dep] <u>that</u> we all felt similarly [dep].

13. Do tall guys have it made?

   Does natural selection favor them?

   Do other guys not beat them up as often?

   Do they not have to try so hard to impress women?

   Does being short culturally prepare the male to develop character?

14. The dog jumped into a ditch.

   I put on my tennis shoes for my run home.

   The rain stopped for a while.

   Olga found the way to camp on the map.

   Children do not know the meaning of swear words.

   Spot ran away from me when I called.

15.
| Original Word/Suffix | Part of Speech |
| --- | --- |
| play [verb] -er | noun |
| wonder [verb] -ment | noun |
| jog [verb] -er | noun |
| tackle [verb]-er | noun |
| power [noun] -ful | adjective |
| profession [noun] -al | adjective |

16.
| Verb | Participle |
| --- | --- |
| was sitting | present |
| had heard | past |
| had bought | past |
| was discussing | present |
| was eating | present |

17.
| Period | Use |
| --- | --- |
| her capital. | End of a declarative sentence |
| Col. B. H. Robinson | Abbreviation of a name |
| N.J. | Abbreviation of a place |
| E. Baker & Co. | Abbreviation of a business name |
| That's what she gave him. | End of a declarative sentence |

18.
| Noun/Adjective | Original Word |
| --- | --- |
| resurrection [noun] | resurrect [verb] |
| activity [noun] | active [adjective] |
| destructiveness [noun] | destructive [adjective] |
| destructive [adjective] | destruct [verb] |
| legend [noun] | legendary [adjective] |

**19.**

| | |
|---|---|
| we | wee |
| in | inn |
| meet | meat |
| role | roll |
| not | knot |
| there | their, they're |
| through | threw |
| very | vary |

**20.**

| Past Tense Verb | Helper Verb | Past Participle | Spelling |
|---|---|---|---|
| looked | could | tired | bed |
| heard | would | achieved | good |
| | had | | and |
| | | | courtyard |

**21.** so much better than the others <u>that</u> he seemed alone on the field [dep]

beautiful and tragic <u>because</u> you knew [dep] <u>that</u> whatever prodigies he performed [dep]

ends <u>who</u> couldn't catch them [dep]

wriggling his hips girlishly <u>as</u> he spun away from the furious hulks [dep] <u>who</u> pursued him [dep]

**22.**

| Capitals | Reason |
|---|---|
| CNN | Company name |
| Moscow | City |
| Soviet | Country |
| BMW | Company name |
| Finland | Country |
| Italy | Country |
| Russia | Country |

**23.**

| -s Word | Reason |
|---|---|
| eyes, hands, butterflies | plural noun |
| Sir Marhalt's | possessive |
| is | tense |
| as | spelling |

**24.**

| Question | Phrase |
|---|---|
| Where | in the great forests, over rutted and rock-strewn hills, to the ground, in the kitchens, through undergrowth, on their sides, through forest and swamp |
| When | on a day |
| Whose | of knights and fighting men, of the great hall, of wild boars |
| Why | in search of quarry, for the long tables |
| How | with whip and spur, with bloody bits |

**25.** | **-s Word** | **Reason** |
|---|---|
| Midas | spelling |
| is, befits | tense |
| women's, Zaharias's | possessive |
| runs, Olympics, events, records, powers, balls, hands, shots, woods, shots | plural |
| as, success | spelling |

**26.** | **-d Words** | **Reason** |
|---|---|
| move-d, impress-ed, turn-ed, manage-d, seem-ed [stood, did] | past tense |
| and, behind | spelling |
| balanced | past participle/adjective |

**27.** | **Question** | **Phrase** |
|---|---|
| When | at a time, for many minutes |
| Where | in East Hampton, outside the house, into the branches, from the tree |
| How | by himself, at the top |
| Whose | of a tree, of his lungs |

**28.** | **Word/Part of Speech** | **Original** |
|---|---|
| attent-ive, adjective | attend, verb |
| develop-ment, noun | develop, verb |
| research-er(s), noun | research, verb |
| import-ant, adjective | import, noun |
| predict-or, noun | predict, verb |
| relative-ly, adverb | relative, adjective |
| scien-tist(s), noun | science, noun |
| politic-al, adjective | politics, noun |
| implicat-ion(s), noun | implicate, verb |
| rapid-ly, adverb | rapid, adjective |
| talk-ative, adjective | talk, noun |

**29.** | **Punctuation Mark** | **Reason** |
|---|---|
| Period: The problems are twofold. | End of declarative sentence |
| Comma: First of all, | Separate transitional phrase |
| Apostrophe: the animal's responses | Possessive noun |
| Quotation marks: "talking cats" | To show irony |
| Question mark: seriously? | Rhetorical question |

**30.** | **-ing Ending** | **Reason** |
|---|---|
| nothing | spelling |
| publishing | present participle/adjective |
| publishing(sentence 5), preserving, recording, saving | present participle/noun |
| are promoting, is being | present participle/verb |

**31.** 

| -s Endings | Reason |
|---|---|
| its, animal's, State's, his | possessive |
| makes, speaks, remains, is, calculates, snatches | present tense |
| eyes, wingbeats, talons, thrusts, wings, sets, biologists, woods | plural |
| oblivious | spelling |

**32.**

| Punctuation Mark | Use |
|---|---|
| Comma | #2: separate dependent from independent clause |
| | #4: separate phrase in apposition |
| Apostrophe | #3: possessive noun |
| | #5: contraction |
| Semicolon | #3: join related clauses |
| | #7: separate items in a series |
| Period | #1: end declarative sentence |
| | #6: end compound sentence |

**33.**

| Word | Meaning #1 | Meaning #2 |
|---|---|---|
| travel | noun, journey | verb, make a journey |
| work | verb, labor | noun, achievement, work of art |
| line | noun, horizontal row | verb, cover inner surface |
| station | noun, train stop | verb, assign duty |
| spot | noun, blemish | verb, see |
| sign | noun, token | verb, write one's name |
| can | noun, container | verb, be able |

**34.**

| Conjunction | Function |
|---|---|
| that | subordinating relative pronoun |
| where | subordinating adverb |
| as | subordinating conjunction |
| before | subordinating adverb |
| until | subordinating adverb |
| and | coordinating conjunction |

**35.**

| | |
|---|---|
| don't have | helper to make have negative |
| does seem | emphasis |
| do | present tense verb |
| does not | helper to make teach negative |
| has done | past participle |
| would do | infinitive |

**36.**

| Punctuation Mark | Reason |
|---|---|
| period | #1: end of declarative sentence |
| comma | #1: separate subordinate clause |
| question mark | #2: end of question |
| quotation marks | #3: irony |
| apostrophe | #3: contraction |

37.

| | | | | |
|---|---|---|---|---|
| see | see | saw | seeing | seen |
| make | make | made | making | made |
| buy | buy | bought | buying | bought |
| teach | teach | taught | teaching | taught |
| weave | weave | wove | weaving | woven |

38.

| Capitalized Word | Reason |
|---|---|
| The | first word in a sentence |
| Interstate 5 | name of a road |
| Stanislaus, San Joaquin | names of counties |
| California | name of a state |
| Stockton, Merced, Modesto | names of cities |
| Great Central Valley | name of a place |
| Coast Ranges, Sierras | names of mountains |
| Ed Filbin | name of a person |

39.

| -ing Word | Reason |
|---|---|
| stirring | noun |
| bubbling, boiling, trying, shimmering, eating | adjective |
| were shaking, was being | verb |
| thing | spelling |

40.

| Verb | Sentence |
|---|---|
| carried off | The pirates carried off the treasure. |
| hoisted up | We hoisted up the trunk with a rope. |
| spun around | The baby watched the top spin around. |
| peeled off | Each marcher peeled off in turn. |
| pulled out | The train pulled out of the station. |
| snatched away | The wind snatched my hat away. |

41.

| Punctuation Mark | Reason |
|---|---|
| comma | #7: separate dependent and independent clauses |
| period | #1: end of declarative sentence |
| quotation marks | #3: words of a speaker |
| apostrophe | #3; 4: contraction |
| question mark | #5: end of question |

42.

| Punctuation Mark | Reason |
|---|---|
| Comma: cosmic, effulgent | #1: separates items in a series |
| Comma: pop lyrics, but the | #1: separates independent clauses |
| Apostrophe: today's | #2: possessive |
| Apostrophe: isn't | #2: contraction |
| Quotation marks: "What's love" | #3: song title |
| Question mark: with it? | #3: end of question |
| Period | #1-6: end of declarative sentence |

**43.** Word | Second Meaning
- pass [verb] — I have a pass[noun] to the new movie.
- fire(s) [noun] — The boss will fire [verb] the slow worker.
- fashion [verb] — Maria wears the latest fashion [noun].
- cheer [verb] — The students gave a cheer [noun] at the news.
- bread [noun] — The cook breaded the cutlets.
- dance [verb] — We went to the Senior Dance.
- dream [noun] — I dream [verb] of traveling.

*Other examples are* stew, hold, book, trade, *and* laugh.

**44.** Helper/Verb | Sentence

| Helper/Verb | Sentence |
|---|---|
| had envied | The sisters had envied Cinderella. |
|   had looked, had been asked | |
| would have envied, would have | The winner would choose the prize. |
|   chosen, would choose | |
| did(n't) see, did realize, did learn | Julio did learn how to ski. |
| could be, could see | We could see that it was time for class. |

**45.** Word | | Change

| Word | | Change |
|---|---|---|
| move [verb] | becomes | move-ment [noun] |
| masculine [adjective] | becomes | masculin-ity [noun] |
| Arthur [noun] | becomes | Arthur-ian [adjective] |
| social [adjective] | becomes | soci-ety [noun] |
| deep [adjective] | becomes | deep-ly [adverb] |
| gold [noun] | becomes | gold-en [adjective] |

**46.** Independent Clause | Dependent Clause

I don't believe [ind] that we don't really like each other [dep].

We soon learn [ind] that wisecracks and put-downs are the preferred modes [dep]

It is the jokes [ind] that give *Roseanne* its special frisson [dep].

The show tells us [ind] that even within the family we don't like each other [dep].

It is not a joke [ind] unless the contradictions are smoothed out with irony [dep].

**47.** Homophone | Sentence

| Homophone | Sentence |
|---|---|
| to (too, two) | Class meets at **two** o'clock. |
| for (four, fore) | We had **four** winners. |
| their (there, they're) | **They're** the best on the team. |
| in (inn) | The **inn** has a vacancy |
| or (oar) | We need an **oar** to row the boat. |
| right (write) | Please **write** the letter of thanks. |

**48.**

| | Present | Past | Present Participle | Past Participle |
|---|---|---|---|---|
| Regular: | stop | stopped | stopping | stopped |
| Irregular: | go | went | going | gone |
| | see | saw | seeing | seen |
| | tell | told | telling | told |
| | is [be] | was | being | been |
| Regular: | stay | stayed | staying | stayed |

**49.**

| | | | |
|---|---|---|---|
| do | did | doing | done |
| wear | wore | wearing | worn |
| eat | ate | eating | eaten |
| keep | kept | keeping | kept |
| take | took | taking | taken |
| leave | left | leaving | left |
| draw | drew | drawing | drawn |

**50.**

| Word | Change |
|---|---|
| frightened | past participle/adjective |
| occasion-al-ly | noun > adjective > adverb |
| safe-r | adjective>comparative |
| except-ion | verb > noun |
| treachery-ous | noun >adjective |
| molest-ed | past participle >adjective |